Christabel Burniston, known in the world of education as a pioneering spirit in promoting oral skills, founded the English Speaking Board in 1953 and remains Life President of this international organisation today. Christabel Burniston (née Hyde) grew up in Yorkshire, finally training in Leeds as a teacher of English, speech and drama including dance and movement. At the end of the war her talents spread beyond formal teaching when she became County Drama Organiser for Lancashire and the contiguous counties. As a national adjudicator she served with the British Federation of Festivals, the Guild of Drama Adjudicators and various educational bodies. She wrote several books on oral communication, notably *Speech for Life*. It was through her courses for education authorities, and as founder of the North West School of Speech and Drama, that she realised the need for oral education for teachers. This inspired her to create the English Speaking Board in 1953, which gained her a world-wide reputation. Her achievements were acknowledged with an MBE in 1979 for services to education. Fellow of the College of Teachers – Honoris Causa 1996. A ninetieth birthday celebration given by the ESB was held in the House of Lords in 1999. Her present positions include: A Vice-President of the Society of Women Writers; Founder Member of the Women of the Year Association and Life Member of the British Federation of Festivals, the Guild of Drama Adjudicators, the Society of Teachers of Speech and Drama and FRSA.

By the same author:

Life in a Liberty Bodice

Speech for Life

Creative Oral Assessment

Spoken English in Further Education

Anthology of Spoken Verse and Prose

Speech in Practice

Speaking with a Purpose

Rhymes with Reasons

Into the Life of Things

Direct Speech

Sounding out your Voice and Speech

THE BRASS AND
THE VELVET

Christabel Burniston

The Book Guild Ltd
Sussex, England

First published in Great Britain in 2001 by
The Book Guild Ltd
25 High Street
Lewes, Sussex
BN7 2LU

Cover photograph of the brass and velvet album by Geoffrey Holland

Typesetting in Baskerville by
Keyboard Services, Luton, Bedfordshire

Printed in Great Britain by
Athenaeum Press Ltd, Gateshead

A catalogue record for this book is
available from the British Library

ISBN 1 85776 772 1

*To the memory of my mother, Annie Hyde,
one of the many brave new women
of the 19th century, who faced the 20th
'with hope of freedom in their souls and
light of science in their eyes'.*

FOREWORD

To write a very successful biography on a full and colourful life is one thing. *Life in a Liberty Bodice* brought delight to many, and especially so when later issued as a reading for the blind.

To write a superb work of fiction – and that at the age of 90 – is, however, quite another matter. Perhaps it is only because all those years have allowed Christabel Burniston to file away in both mind and eye her observations of others, that the characters which she has so skilfully created within *The Brass and the Velvet* not only stand out but speak to us, where appropriate, in such keenly observed dialect – or in the Victorian tone and manner of an upper Yorkshire class blessed with plenty of brass and velvet and heaped in prejudice. The fact that Christabel's mother, while raising five children, was a supportive suffragette, only serves to confirm a truly compelling storyline, while the author's ability to create true to life characters adds to a most stimulating read.

Having produced the BBC Sunday Radio 4 serials over many years, I can only wish that, along with *Sons and Lovers, Fame is the Spur, Women in Love, North and South, When We Are Married,* et cetera, *The Brass and the Velvet* had also been written in those times.

This novel is surely a certain winner for television or film. To me it is written in Technicolor.

Trevor Hill
July 2001

ACKNOWLEDGEMENTS

It is impossible to name all the enthusiasts who contributed in so many different ways either in person or through correspondence and telephone. Happy years of exploration strengthened old friendships and created new. As music is the message of love in the novel I called on my musical friends, *Kenneth Roberton, Denise and Maurice King* to reinforce my own favourites.

On one of her frequent visits to Paris, *Vera McKechnie* checked and reinforced necessary details, as they would have been in Paris in the latter years of the 19th century.

My close friends, *Rhona Davis* and *Dr Kirsty Cochrane* and her brother *Professor James Bade*, all New Zealanders, sent first-hand records of sheep farming and the wool trade with Britain and the long sea voyages which this involved.

Staying so near to Bradford I had several sessions with the *Reverend Arthur Wilson*, chaplain of High Royds Hospital. He filled in the picture of a typical Victorian asylum, grandly built but packed with unfortunates.

Ron Sweeney, a distinguished Bradford citizen, knew every building ancient and modern. He took me into a preserved 19th century chemistry laboratory, where I spent a morning handling well-worn apparatus. As a consequence we consulted *JJR Kirkpatrick* of Glasgow to give definitive detail on the medical treatment of a hundred years ago. *David Walls*, at one with the industrial and rural vistas, gave me an expert introduction to the working life of the great canals.

Of course I was consulting libraries all of which contributed in a personal and practical way: Bradford including its Industrial Museum; the National Museum of Photography; Film and Television; Salts' & Listers' Mills provided archive records as did the Keighley Library.

The Bradford *Telegraph & Argus* newspaper supplied their historical supplements covering a hundred years of the great city's evolution. The libraries of Leeds and Liverpool, two cities linked by sea and canal, were a rich source of information as were the York Railway Museum, Edinburgh University and the Royal

Infirmary. The reference librarians in Cheltenham rooting out archive material made every visit a pleasure.

Informal meetings with the following, and others not listed, added to the enrichment of my visits. *Arthur Bantoft, Sally and Martin Bird, Jack Danby, Ian Dewhurst, Colin Dews, Jack Downing, Andrew Edwards* of BBC Radio Leeds, *Joyce Goldsworth, Ena Hinchliffe, John Hyde, The Manager of the Old Swan Harrogate, John Pennington of Pennington Midland Hotel, Christine and Michael Waddington of Farrah's Toffee, Joan Walls* and *Helen Weir* gave me days in the magnificent Yorkshire wolds and dales.

Of the many whose names I never knew, two are vividly memorable. On a train journey from Cheltenham to Edinburgh chatting with a lively ninety-five-year-old led her to disclose her life as a former matron of the Royal Infirmary. Like the Ancient Mariner she 'held me with her glittering eye' recalling every clinical and personal detail of her demanding job. Edinburgh revisited, especially the Royal, now rang with her recall.

Back in Yorkshire I needed to have a grasp of the workings of the Five Rise Locks on the Leeds and Liverpool canal. It was the keeper, intrigued by this part of the story, who physically took me and Ashton in hand to open the top lock gate.

I was fortunate indeed on being able to profit from friends with special skills: *Peter Fabian*, lecturer and broadcaster, for reading each chapter as it was written, and responding so warmly to the script and research behind it.

A professional publisher's reader *Mary Hope*, generously read the manuscript in its entirety. Among her wise critical and constructive comments was the firm directive that severe cuts of detail were crucial. 'These could be swept up by screening, then the themes of *new women*, the romance and various social and religious prejudices "would come triumphantly through" ... a gift for TV with characters who would be very exciting to cast.'

Trevor Hill, a significant personality in the annals of the BBC, editing and producing TV and radio, used his skilled eyes and ears to prune the text with readers, listeners and viewers in mind.

Pauline Lyons, my 'human word processor' prepared the manuscript and she with *Jocelyn Bell* as guide, philosopher and friend patiently dealt with the proofs.

My daughter, *Liz Macfarlane*, a former RSC actress, seized on the novel's film potential, citing names for major parts.

AUTHOR'S INTRODUCTION

The catalyst which set *The Brass and The Velvet* in motion was an opulent Victorian album, bound and crafted for endurance. Back in the 1980s, in an antique shop window, it had caught my eye several times, looking as if it pleaded for an owner. I didn't need the album but I had a gut feeling it needed me.

I was curious about this family, so obviously successful. Not a single name could be found of either the owner or the people, now immortal in sepia.

The photographers had planned this better, their names and towns were in permanent gilt; Bradford, Leeds, Harrogate, Dewsbury, Halifax ... where their clients made their *brass* in the great wool metropolis of the West Riding. It was in this area, within smoke distance from Leeds, that I was born.

In the late 1980s I re-tracked much of the West Riding when writing my childhood autobiography, *Life in a Liberty Bodice*. In the 1990s I returned to the industrial area, with all my senses alerted, deep into the heart and history of the final years of the 19th century and examined mills, past and present; especially Listers and Salts, where fabrics from serge to velvet had been sent all over the world.

With common interests one quickly makes friends. I did not need the sepia photographs any more, but I did need a second home where I could meet real people who trod this ground. I found it, not very far from Ilkley Moor, in Menston where Moyra Platts, a small ninety-year-old woman with a big mind, lived. Her family had been land and mill owners in Yorkshire and created iron works in West Scotland which are still prosperous. Mills and mansions; Methodists and Masons; writers and readers; from finger bowls to fish fingers ... Moyra knew them all.

I also needed a patient driver willing to stand and stare, point out details and reminisce. It was Moyra who provided Ashton Harvey, who became my guide. He knew from experience the grim grind and decline of the wool industry. He is not sentimental about old mills. For example at Salt's Mill, now aglow with

David Hockney's sun-stroked paintings, his eyes were less on the Hockneys than on the floorboards. He made me stop to smell the air and explained that there had been a spinning frame for worsted right across the floor. The threads had to be sprayed with fine oil to ease them on their way. I shut my eyes and breathed deeply. The smell was still potently present. My imagination was back a hundred years. Sounds now silent: the clatter of clogs, the mill hooter, the puffing smoke of steam trains, all resonated in my ears.

In another mill we visited, now an industrial museum of textile machinery, I joined a class of ten-year-olds from a nearby primary school. A monstrous carding machine dwarfed the children, each clutching a creamy ball of unspun wool. The museum guide, a former mill-hand, now a gifted teacher, diverted their eyes to the windows and asked them why the bottom pane was frosted glass. He answered their puzzled silence with: 'So that the children watching the threads could not look through the window.' This exploitation of child labour was one of the many social and educational reforms afoot in Bradford in the 1890s.

In the First World War my mother and eldest sister became closely involved with the work of Margaret McMillan, the great pioneer of nursery schools, who did so much for the children of Bradford.

My story took me on to Edinburgh, the great city of learning, where my friends, Dr David Boyd and his wife Betty, brought both old and new to life in Auld Reekie. They opened many doors, showing me where my two *new women* would have lodged, listened to lectures, observed clinical practice and made music. Dr Boyd also rooted out for me prospectuses, historical references, books on medical practice and hospital procedure relating to a hundred years ago, not least his own book: *Leith's Hospital 1848–1988*. I now have reading for life! Alas, in a cut-down novel an author cannot digress far from the central characters' personal lives. For errors or omissions, therefore, I am entirely responsible, and I hope understood.

Christabel Burniston

PART ONE
AUGUST 1894

1

Felicity Hargreaves had been home from the Harrogate Academy for Ladies for three weeks now – yet it seemed like three months. It was not that she was yearning for school. She was yearning for a life of her own. These endless days seemed like a rehearsal for eternity, a state she had always considered repugnant. According to Society's calendar she was *finished*. The word was as revolting to Felicity as it was final.

She was sneaking up to the attic in order to try and find a bundle of letters, which she hoped would still be in the lid of her trunk. They contained two from aunt Grace, letters that her mother must never see.

Also, she rather liked the idea of retrieving that celebrated school photograph, which had been lampooned in a Yorkshire paper and was among the items her mother had decreed as not suitable for a lady's bedroom. Felicity giggled to herself at the thought of seeing it again, but the giggling stopped when her mother's voice, sharp but wheedling, travelled up the stairs.

'While you are up in the attic, Felicity, pick out those pots and vases we shall need for the harvest festival, then get Hilda to help you bring them down to the conservatory. By the way I've told the harvest ladies about you joining us. It's quite a privilege, you know.'

Exasperation took over. *God, am I never going to be left alone?* The *God* was not an expletive; it was a fervent plea. But *honour thy father and thy mother* had been a commandment from nursery through the Academy. Along with it went the order: *Don't answer back.*

On hearing the voice, Felicity dwindled back into the mother and daughter relationship, a habit of eighteen years. Her reply stemmed from duty not devotion. 'Yes, Mother.'

She climbed the attic stairs with hands tightly clenched, muttering, 'Now I see why silly girls accept the first proposal. Well, I shan't do that, but I *shall* leave home.'

Every step she trod felt the defiant words: Leave ... home, leave ... home, leave ... home.

Felicity had always had the saving grace of being able to escape into a whole world of imagination. She was mercurial in mood and switched from despair to hope in a flash. Now, walking through the old nursery into the lumber room, she could forget the constant irritations and live, for a time, in the past. She remembered how she used to creep out from the nursery into the lumber room whilst Hilda was busy ironing. When her rocking-horse didn't gallop fast enough or the Noah's ark animals didn't smell real, or the taps in the doll's house didn't turn on, she found endless make-believe in the junk that could be made to do anything. She laughed, as she remembered tipping, chucking and flicking her mother's tea chest of goose-down high into the air in order to make her own snowstorm, and inventing new colours with the half-empty cans of paint.

Why harvest festival pots now? It's not for six weeks, she thought.

She heaved a sigh of relief – the letters had not been removed. She took the Academy photograph out of her trunk and over to the dilapidated sofa and unrolled the lengthy scroll.

With both hands she stretched it out until her arms were wide apart. Her eyes swept across the two hundred girls, the head-mistress and staff. She focussed first on the extreme left and then on the extreme right, laughing until the tears washed away all the morning's exasperation.

There on the one photograph were two Belinda Bennetts!

Belinda had timed the panning camera to pass in front of her and then had run, with the speed of a gazelle, behind the row of girls in their serried ranks. Before the camera had caught up, there she was standing tall and still at the other end, looking like a model of deportment.

The laughter had revived Felicity. Now, relaxed on the sofa, she recalled the entire day. It had started with the headmistress addressing the school assembly on the importance of the occasion. Felicity could hear her voice:

'Today we are making scientific history. The Academy will be the first school in Harrogate to be photographed by the Sanderson moving camera. This new invention makes it possible for head-mistress, staff and girls to be in one inclusive photograph. It will require you all to sit, or stand, in absolute stillness. The camera will be centred in front of you all, taking three minutes to move on the wheeled tripod from the one end to the other end.

4

'When you write your letters home on Sunday you will be pleased to inform your parents that they will have the privilege of buying a photograph three feet long on which their daughter is featured.

'Now please each take a chair outside in order that the groundsmen may arrange you in formation.'

Belinda Bennett, who was really too bright for the Academy, had, during this solemn address, already worked out her little scheme.

From the day Felicity saw the photograph displayed in the entrance hall of the Academy she had a schoolgirl crush on Belinda Bennett, who was one year higher in the school.

All that was three years ago and the only laughter in Stonegarth came from that attic. But now to cope with the coffin-size box – a relic from their old wagon – where large vases and pots were packed away. Felicity unclipped the locks, but the lid, near the sloping ceiling, refused to go more than halfway up. There was nothing for it but to pull the hefty box forward. She tugged at the rope handles in turn and jerked the trunk forward. *Crash!*

Two pictures, stacked behind the box, had fallen down. Peering round the box, she saw on the floor under the cracked glass two portraits she'd never seen before. With careful manoeuvring, she managed to pull them out into view.

They were of two young ladies exquisitely photographed and painted. Their hair had been dressed by the same hand; their deep blue velvet gowns were identical, except that one waist was excessively tightened. The bone structure of the two faces suggested that they were hewn from the same rock. Felicity carried the portraits to the sofa, propped them up, and looked at them more intently. The white line of the centre partings of their hair seemed to be continued in the white-boned line of their aquiline noses.

Twins, she thought, but not identical. Different somehow, different in character. She noted the slightly flirtatious look in the eyes of the one and the lips moist and parted in the manner of a courtesan. She picked up the second portrait with the glass cracked from corner to corner.

Felicity was mesmerised by the forlorn beauty of those deep, dark eyes. She detected vulnerability in the thin line of the lips. It was a lonely, sensitive face.

What happened to her? Why have the pictures been hidden away up here? Why have I never seen these before? she wondered.

It was the voice of Hilda, their housemaid, who broke the long

5

silence. 'I didn't mean to frighten you, luv. Your mother sent me to hurry you up and bring them pots down.'

Hilda had been in service with the Hargreaves all Felicity's life.

'Yer look fair dun up, luv. I hope there's nowt wrong?'

'I had to pull the wagon-box out, and these two pictures must have been leaning against the wall behind and they fell down.'

Hilda tried to hide her shock. 'Ee, don't fret yersel' over those old things. No-one knows them two now.'

'But who were they, Hilda?'

'Well now, if yer must know, they were yer mother's twin sisters, Miss Caroline and Miss Amy.'

'But what happened to them?'

'These pictures were took when they come of age. It were about ten years after that when Miss Caroline wed the local reporter, Jack Fieldhead. Ee! Just think, Miss, twins that had never been parted till that time. They went off, after t'trouble – I think it were to New Zealand!'

Hilda saw the look of astonishment on the girl's face.

'Twins don't part, do they? Surely Caroline couldn't leave her twin all alone in this country.'

Hilda had been brought up a strict Methodist on a farm near Beverley in the East Riding. Telling a lie meant getting a tanning. She hesitated. Felicity read her face and gave her no chance to lie.

'So what happened to Aunt Amy, Hilda?' Felicity stared into the cracked glass.

Hilda knew that if she spoke it would be another lie, so she kept quiet. Very quiet. Too quiet for truth. But she saw the pleading eyes as Felicity laid the one portrait on her lap.

'I thought you and I told each other everything. I've always trusted you, Hilda – even before I could talk, I trusted you.'

''Ow *could* I tell you? Yer mother came into t'kitchen and she made us swear, with our hands on t'Bible as we'd never tell a living soul. It were about yer Aunt Amy, the one you're holding. If it had got out it would have brought disgrace on the whole family. Even if it weren't her fault that she went...' Hilda tried to find the right word. Felicity butted in:

'She went? ... Where? Where did she go? Oh, Hilda, *please*...'

'Well, luv, 'ow can I say? She went off 'er 'ead, that's what rough folk round us say, nobbut tenpence ter t'shilling! No that's not right – she were worse than that – she were raving! They certified 'er. An' when they do that, yer know, folk reckon as it's in t'family blood. 'Tis the devil hisself sucking it away!'

6

Felicity sat numb with horror as she gazed once more at the beauty of Amy. Then she turned the picture in Hilda's direction. The housemaid's tone softened in order to comfort the stricken girl:

'Ee, they should nivver 'ave takken 'er away and shut 'er up like that. She were a luvley lady, so she was. An' such delicate hands.'

Felicity returned her gaze to the picture. There they were, demurely crossed on the deep blue velvet of her lap.

'She always wore that gold chain and cross. An' she used to stroke t'cross as if she was asking God fer summat.'

'But where is she now, Hilda? Oh, please tell me!'

Hilda took Felicity's hand as she now sat with her on the sofa. 'You won't let on, will yer, if I tell yer? She's not a long way from here. She's in *Barlockend*.' The very word said anywhere in Yorkshire shocked whoever heard it.

'*Barlockend*, Hilda? But surely that's a paupers' asylum for folk who are destitute – who have no home, no family! The Ackroyds, with that string of pork butchers' shops, had enough money for a private nurse – several nurses!'

'Ee, luv, they couldn't do that. You couldn't 'ave 'er at 'ome. Folks would *know*, wouldn't they? I don't think it was yer mother and father to blame, it was 'er twin.'

'But *why*, Hilda? Why did they put her in an *asylum*?'

'Well, I don't like to say, luv, but, I know it were 1887 when she went in.'

Felicity's imagination was already leaping ahead. Those twins had evidently never been parted even in school or college. There, of course, they would be in single beds, but they would have shared a double bed at home, all their lives.

Hilda had more to tell. 'Folk had used to say neither would ever get married 'cos no man would ever see either of 'em on their own, like...'

'But what did she do that they put her in a mental asylum?'

'Ee, 'ow should I know, luv. But if yer've been goin' ter t'same room and t'same bed for thirty years and then, wun day yer finds a man in t'same spot as you've lain in.'

Neither Felicity nor Hilda knew the details, but Felicity sensed that, after a while, Aunt Caroline and her husband Jack sold the family home in order to escape from the shame of it all. The wicked cruelty was in not treating insanity as an illness. It would therefore remain a blight on a family for generations. Her thoughts needed both comfort and contradiction.

'If it's in the Ackroyd blood, Hilda, then it's also in mine.'

7

'Don't be daft, luv, yer t'spitten image of yer dad. Not much Ackroyd in you!'

Tears magnified Felicity's troubled eyes and her whispering changed to anger:

'Which doctor said she was a lunatic, Hilda? Who put her in? It's a *paupers'* asylum!'

The question remained unanswered for, suddenly, like a cannon shot, Mrs Hargreaves' voice pierced the stairwell.

'What are you two doing up there? Come down at once!'

Within seconds Felicity, grasping one handle of the clanking basket and Hilda the other, had edged their way down the attic stair, flushed, sideways, like two guilty crabs. The galleried landing and the wide double staircase sobered them for their confrontation with Mrs Hargreaves.

Hilda, now that her fixture in the Hargreaves household was secure, knew precisely how to deal with her mistress's narkiness.

'Whatever have you been doing all that time in the attic, young woman?'

Hilda's voice was soothing as she raised her accent to housemaid's level. 'I thought you'd like me and Miss Felicity to take all these pots and wash them in the conservatory and then they'll all be ready for harvest festival.'

'Be off sharp then. You know what they say about idle hands.'

Mrs Gertrude Hargreaves, who used time like a whip, turned back to the open linen press, where she'd been counting sheets, satisfied that four hands which might have been idle were now occupied. But she thought to herself, If that girl had done more housecraft at the Academy instead of stuff like Latin and algebra, she'd make more use of her time...

The conservatory was the perfect bolthole for Hilda and Felicity. Hilda was relieved that after seven years and the breaking of an oath she was at last able to talk about Miss Ackroyd.

'I'll tell yer wot, luv, wen I 'ave mi 'alf-day next Wensdi I'll drop in on Sarah Maggs and 'er mother Lily. They're both daily cleaners at Barlockend. Not in t'main building, because inmates keep all that clean. The Maggses do t'ballroom and visitors' block; well, t'boardroom and such like. They're out o' bounds for lunatics. Wen they've dun they then do t'passages and they lock up and hand in t'keys. They miss nowt, those two. Ee, they do tell sum rum tales, yer can't 'elp but laff.'

8

Hilda thought Miss Felicity needed drawing out of herself so she would try telling her a tale.

'There's a comic young man 'oo wuz put in there for stealing a bicycle when he was a little lad. Clever 'z a bag of monkeys, he is. Bin in six years, I think she said. Pretends 'ee's t'butler, like, and any folks uz cum into t'asylum get a bow.' Hilda tried miming. ' "Come in!" he says. "Welcome to Barlockend! May I relieve you of your parasol, madam? What name shall I say?" '

Hilda realised her act had fallen rather flat:

'But you should 'ear Sarah do it. She's a real comic is Sarah. She can do the la-di-da, proper.'

Felicity's attempt at laughter choked into anger. 'But who put *him* in, Hilda? He was only a boy. You're not insane if you only steal a bicycle!'

'Ee, I don't know, luv, grander folk 'as funny ways. Yer wonder, don't yer, wot they've got where th'r hearts should be. Sarah's mam Lily tells t'other side of it all.' Hilda hesitated before she whispered, 'Lil said that yer auntie 'ad a red star on 'er prison dress.'

Hilda stopped and covered her mouth. 'Sorry, luv, I shouldn't 'ave said, *prison*. When Lil asked your aunt wot she got it fer, she said, "It must have been for good behaviour." Truth is, luv, that any wun wot's tried to kill themselves 'as t'red star sewn on, so Lil sez. It's meant kindly, like, so that t'warden or nurses can keep an eye on 'em. Sarah, 'oo sees funny side, sez, that two men with red stars work in t'butchery, using great big kitchen knives to cut t'meat for all those 'undreds of folk. They could kill 'em, Sarah said, laffing like.'

Hilda paused. 'No – not funny is it, luv?' She sighed as she quietly said, 'I wunder what Miss Amy does all day?'

Felicity was trying to imagine someone of her social class scrubbing floors for their daily bread.

'Hilda, I've been thinking, and no-one but you must know. What about my finding a way of going to see Amy? There must be a chaplain or someone I could talk to.'

'Well, Lil Maggs'll give it you proper, but I think he's called Thompson.'

Hilda had a further thought.

'Why don't yer just write a letter?'

'But someone might see it. Hilda, do understand – *no-one must know.*'

* * *

9

When Elsie Ellis, the postmistress, had got Miss Felicity safe inside the shop she deftly stilled the metal hoop of the shop bell and fixed the door sneck. Although there was only Tabitha, her cat, to eavesdrop, Miss Ellis (for only a few presumed to call her Elsie) lowered her voice to a conspiratorial whisper and shifted a jar of Terry's fruit drops to bring out the hidden letter.

'I've taken this out from the Stonegarth letters, Felicity; it's stamped: *Edinburgh*.' Giving it yet another glance, she said, 'It is from your aunt Grace, isn't it? You did want me to hold all Edinburgh ones, didn't you? And oh, I meant to say yesterday, you don't have to take the rest of the post – it'd look better if Bob did his usual rounds.'

Felicity's gratitude and trust showed in her gaze. She took the letter and hid it in the lining pocket of her cloak:

'Aunt Grace is my best friend and you're the next, Miss Ellis.'

From childhood Elsie Ellis, counting out aniseed balls or filling a poke with dolly mixtures, had been Felicity's closest ally. There was no question of *Miss* Felicity in this relationship; Miss Ellis was her senior and not a servant. Even at a young age Felicity whittled away all social barriers.

'There should be one from Harrogate soon, Miss Ellis. I'd like you to hang on to it. You see, my parents pry into all my post even now I've left school. You'll be able to recognise Miss Butterworth's handwriting; it's beautiful black copperplate on very pale blue writing paper. Different from my schoolfriends – they simply scrawl! She picked up three other letters. Curiosity got the better of her.

'This big packet is a Harrogate one with the school photographs of Speech Day. I mustn't open it to show you, but one of the photographs will be of father and me. We're standing each side of the new lectern he's presented to the school, a very ornate affair. The photographs will be dreadful. I was embarrassed and he was preening! Mother will seize on them for the blue album. She *reads* little but swoons over photographs. They are conversation spurs for her At Homes. Ah, now! This picture postcard from Paris, with the spidery writing is from my brother Henry. He's there with a schoolfriend to "better" him, as they say. Much good that will do him, he'll think nothing of the Eiffel Tower, he'd rather be watching cricket at Headingley. His usual letters from school are boring and begging and put father in a bad temper. Poor Henry is all of fifteen now but a pretty dim one. He's at the Methodist school not far away. They've clever boys there, but my brother's not one of them.'

Miss Elsie asked the inevitable adult question: 'And what is Master Henry going to do, Felicity?'

'He intends to leave and go into the mill as soon as he's sixteen.'

'Well, he's a lucky lad having your father's mill to go to.'

Felicity was quick to add a shrewd comment: 'Well, you know what they say, Elsie, riches to rags in two generations. I really can't see my dear brother Henry working!'

She returned the post to Elsie and picked up a small newspaper:

'So, I'll leave all those for Bob to deliver but I'll take a *Leeds Mercury*, if I may. I must have some reason for being out so early! It should have a report of the Academy Speech Day. Mother reads bits of the *Mercury* and there'll be photographs for her to look at. She keeps all the Aireley Mill and Hargreaves press cuttings. Father brings the Bradford ones home when he's been on the Wool Exchange.'

Miss Ellis moved to the post office door and opened it as discreetly as she'd closed it. Felicity walked back down Spring Lane with pulse and step quickened. With dear aunt Grace's letter within heartbeat, life held promise.

Stonegarth didn't look nearly as forbidding as it had done earlier that morning. Cold sunshine caught the newly-washed stone steps, which Felicity took two at a stride to the front door. The Italian tiles of the vestibule glistened newly-scrubbed; everything seemed lighter and brighter than half an hour before. Hilda had been busy, of course, but it was the letter which made Felicity so fleet of foot. Aunt Grace was her father's sister with an independent life in Edinburgh, the city that had become her home.

Felicity skipped over the Turkish carpet in the hall, dropped the newspaper on to the drum table, swept past the baby grand piano, and took the wide staircase again two steps at a time. The William Morris stained-glass windows on the landing slanted their light towards the privacy of her room.

There she sat at her dressing table, not to look at herself in the triple mirrors but to ensure her own space and quiet for her aunt's letter. Anyone standing behind her, looking into the mirror, would have seen the hereditary Hargreaves feature: the resolute, often stubborn, jaw. Certainly the two profile mirrors made it crystal clear that if she started anything she would see it through. The centre mirror caught the humour in her eyes and the tilt of a generous mouth.

Although her father's eyes were brown and hers were a changeable greyish green, both she and her father sent out the same signals of determination and occasional acts of defiance. Felicity's more cared-for and carefree life, untouched by the mill, gave her face a refinement and relaxation which life had grudged her father. His humour was dry, caustic and ego-building, usually arising from getting the better of a rival. His tales often ended with steely Yorkshire pride: 'Well, 'e won't try *that* trick again.'

Arthur took for granted, in any conversation, that the other chap should be the listener. Felicity took for granted that both she and the listener enjoyed one another.

Her lively talk, impulsive generosity and her gift of mimicry left their mark in a few fine, but characterful lines. When she was a child her mother had warned: 'Don't pull faces, Felicity! You'll grow like that!'

After the white austerity of her dormitory cubicle, Felicity's bedroom had a lot in its favour. Her mother, never having been away to school, thought a daughter of hers should have nothing less than: a double wardrobe, a handsome tester double bed, a smothering feather mattress, a triple-mirrored dressing table, two bedside commodes and a wash-hand stand, all set out precisely down to the last hair-tidy. But aunt Grace's eighteenth birthday present (sent in July to be there when Felicity's school life ended) was not heavy mahogany but rather an elegant Louis Quinze escritoire of rosewood marquetry. Felicity had given it pride of place and put it alongside her dressing table in the five-windowed bay.

Aunt Grace's letter slid into the secret drawer just as Jessie, the parlourmaid, was beating the breakfast gong. In the Hargreaves household, breakfast was a serious affair: the loud gong, the quiet grace and the outsize chafing dishes gave Arthur and Gertrude Hargreaves a settled start to the day.

During careful folding of the *Airedale Post*, her father glanced up.

'*You* were out early, my lass. If I were you I'd let t'streets get aired first.'

In public he lifted his Yorkshire speech to an appropriate level for his Masonic and councillor status, but relaxed it a little at home. In turn Felicity eased her Academy vowel sounds to disarm the Aireley comment of 'putting it on'. It always amused her that her father had spent what he would call 'good money' to make her speech quite different from his own.

'Oh, getting out before breakfast is a habit now, Father. We all had to do the early morning run every day. Do you remember St John's Well on the Stray? We had to run on the path right round and back to school. Out at eight – back at a quarter past. Breakfast at half past.'

'Even in winter?' her mother joined in, rather pinched. 'It's a wonder you didn't get your death!'

'Yes, and cold baths *too*!' Felicity brightened; she'd never known breakfast get off to such a chatty start. Her father and mother always did justice to the three silver chafing dishes loaded with eggs, bacon and black pudding, and time ticked on in silence except for the occasional confounding of the politics of the *Airedale Post* and his critical comments on the food:

'Bacon's underdone again, Mother. How many times have I told you to tell cook I like it frizzled?'

Gertrude looked peeved but she was pleased to be able to get her own back:

'You know I've never *wanted* a cook, Father. You've brought all this on yourself. Bacon was just right when *I* did it.'

This conversation was a repeated text in their limited repertoire of over twenty years as man and wife.

Gertrude Hargreaves, though only approaching forty-one, had managed to keep her face unlined through habitual complacency. Yet the unfurrowed brow, the absence of laughter lines, the puffy cheeks filling out the usual nose-to-mouth valleys – all possible assets – made her look quite fifty-one. Her hair, which had been fair, had faded through the years to an inconspicuous greyish fawn. It promised to remain like that for many years, for, as Gertrude already had a neutral effect on everything and everybody, the fading hairs were hardly noticed. The platitude '*The daily round, the common task, should furnish all we ought to ask*' suited her, for she had not imagination for the *un*common task.

Forty years with Yorkshire pastry at every meal and little physical exercise had increased her circumference and doubled her chin. Looking at her in profile, it was impossible to know where the face ended and the throat began.

Folk in Aireley who knew Gertrude as a girl had described her as 'pretty', which she now kept as a permanent compliment for life. 'Pretty' was her favourite word for nieces whom she held up to Felicity as being lady-like: 'Such sweetly-pretty girls. Always the same!'

Felicity's moderate breakfast was finished:

'May I leave the table, Father?' She still had to go through this childish ritual.

13

'Steady on now, steady on. Sit yourself down and take a look at this.'

Arthur Hargreaves knew precisely when to be pompous. Taking time to crease the newspaper so that the finance sheet was in Felicity's focus, he pointed to the centre column.

As all our readers are aware, worsted suitings manufactured in the West Riding are known to be the best in the world. Of the many cloths of all weights and designs, those manufactured in and around Bradford are second to none.

Our staple industry has recently been suffering from high tariffs and competitive overseas trade. It is, therefore, with pride that we announce that Hargreaves of Aireley have this week received an order from the Belgian Crown to supply high grade worsted cloth to equip the officers of His Majesty's army and those gentlemen in high office in His Majesty's Court...

The newspaper also featured an article on the success of the last half-century and the demands for the variety of fabrics sent world-wide from the mill towns in and around Bradford. It went on to describe how the Leeds to Liverpool canal had carried heavy loads of coal and raw materials to and from the mills for over a hundred years. Now, except for the coal barges, the London and North-Eastern Railway had become the lifeline of the woollen industry.

'Now,' said her father, 'doesn't that make you proud?'

Before Felicity had thought of something to say, her mother, never quite at ease with her daughter and always appeasing her husband, snapped out: 'Well! Say something nice to your father!'

Felicity, quite ignoring her mother's acidity, chose this response for her own exit line. Leaping up to her father's side she gave him a rare kiss of congratulation. The kiss left Arthur strangely disturbed by his daughter's vibrant skin and nubile body: He was also irritated with his wife's lack of sense in knowing how to deal with her. It was many years since he had kissed his tantalising daughter; even more since she had kissed him. Through the tangle of emotions he knew he needed her. Neither Felicity, nor her mother, sensed that the owner of Aireley Mill had been using the newspaper to give him Dutch courage in order to stave off his approaching doubts about trade overseas.

Felicity back in the blissful solitude of her own room, turned the key of her desk, pressed the centre of a marquetry rose, slid aside the secret panel and took out the letter. Instinctively she turned her chair so that she had her back to the door and read:

Moray Place
Edinburgh

August 17th 1894

My dear Felicity,

The few days' delay in my sending this letter has been in a good cause. You will remember that I promised I would get in touch with my friend, to find out about the entry of women into the medical faculty of the university.

Well, as you know, the war has been going on for years, but, at last, there are signs that the university will agree to open its medical school to women. I am sure that now Dr Jex-Blake is being rewarded and not reviled – even though it may eventually mean closing the medical school for women – she must feel that many of her battles have been won.

Although your Oxford Senior qualifications are reasonable, both in number and choice of subjects, you could, during this next academic year, perhaps receive special coaching in botany and chemistry extramurally in Bradford. (Of course he does not know that your parents have no idea of your plan and of my collusion. There are many hurdles to be cleared before you cross the border.)

You asked in your last letter if women graduated 'MD'. No, my dear, women do a four- or five-year course and are cited MBChB. I think even you, with all your zeal, would not want longer time than that. But you would, with the former quali-fication, certainly not have a doctorate but in practice you might receive the courtesy title of Doctor.

Even so, dear Felicity, we are still a far cry from your father's consent and his being willing to pay for the course. Remember that the charges for lectures and clinical surgery observation can still cost more for women than for men. Another reason for my working for votes for women!

A bright thought has occurred to me. Your father has always held doctors (male, of course!) in high esteem. I got the impression when I last stayed with your parents (you were away at school) that Dr Bennett and his family and yours were on socially friendly terms. Might I advise you, Felicity, dearest, to try to have a talk with him? I understand that his daughter was also at the Academy? And – you must forgive my saying so – the Bennett family are much more liberal-minded than ours.

I must close now, my dear, but it was good to hear, after your Easter visit, that you had fallen in love with Edinburgh. Yorkshire in all its infinite variety is still my native and beloved county but Edinburgh has become my home. This glorious city with its giant castle growing from the grey rock, guarding its great learning and kindliness, has always sheltered me.

That your strength and determination will win through is the loving hope of

Your devoted, aunt Grace

Felicity returned the letter, locked the desk and, removing the key, threaded it on to a silver chain, which she measured round her neck to make sure that the key fell well down into the valley between her small breasts.

She moved to the chintz-covered chair of her dressing table, carrying with her, for no purpose, the silver and mother-of-pearl paper knife that had just opened a new world. The face she lent unheedingly to the looking glass was in triplicate, each face with a secret view of the other. Felicity was not in the habit of sitting at her mirror for long, either in warm satisfaction or in cool judgement.

She was there to think.

Generations of Hargreaves with their dogged way of facing up to things had shaped and honed her strong jawline and her stubborn little chin. They were now in consort with her screwed-up eyes, all asking the same question: 'What do I do next?'

Firstly, the appalling news of the asylum. Now, the daunting hope of her university. She must put her own ambitions in the second drawer and concentrate on Barlockend. The more she thought about it the more difficult it became. There were complicated requests to be made. She addressed the envelope to her friends first:

The Misses Olivia & Kate Winkley, Winkley Hall,
Near Richmond, North Riding.

And then she was stuck. How could she write about an asylum to friends with whom she laughed, danced and had fun? They were not snobs, but they were aristocrats. She put her pen down as memories crowded in of the hilarious times they had together and how Olivia and Kate tried to outdo their clever sister Charlotte, whose school, North London Collegiate, shone in the academic firmament.

But there was no time for reminiscing. Felicity got down to the letter – and without giving any explanation for desperately needing an alibi.

Stonegarth
Aireley
West Riding

August 18th 1894

Dear Olivia and Kate,

How are you enjoying this marvellous weather in your delectable Swaledale? I suppose the shooting season has started.

You very kindly gave me an open invitation to join you whenever you came shopping in Harrogate. In holiday time it was usually a Thursday. We agreed that I should let you know if ever I could join you for luncheon. Pray forgive me if what I am about to ask seems uncivil but an urgent situation has arisen with which I must deal, so I am asking you to excuse my absence.

Can you, my dears, be very tactful? My parents think I am coming to Harrogate to meet you, next Thursday, August 23rd. If the subject ever arises, please do not mention my absence but, rather, act as if I had been with you. When we meet and have a chance to talk privately I will take you into my confidence.

Please give my kindest regards to your parents and your clever sister, Charlotte. How I envy her starting at Girton.

With affectionate good wishes I remain

Your good friend,

Felicity

She sealed the letter, praying that they would understand.

She addressed the second envelope: *The Reverend Anthony Thompson, Chaplain to Barlockend Mental Asylum, Airedale, West*

17

Riding. Then, with a little frown, she started to write her accommodation address:

c/o Miss E. Ellis
Aireley Post Office
Airedale
West Riding

August 18th 1894

Dear Sir,

I write in confidence, which I know you will appreciate, and for the following reason.

I am the daughter of Mr and Mrs Arthur Hargreaves, whose surname will be familiar to you from the large brass plate on the gate of the mill in Aireley. It is quite noticeable. You do not know me, but you may have met my father and mother at various public events, in and around Bradford. Therefore, I must say at once that my parents do not know I am writing this letter and must never know anything of its content.

I am sure you will not have connected anyone in the asylum with my family, since none of the relations will ever have visited my aunt. She is Amy Ackroyd. It has only recently come to my knowledge that she was certified insane and has, for at least seven years, been an inmate in Barlockend.

With your help I hope you will make it possible for me to visit her. May I suggest, if this is a convenient day for you, that I come next Thursday afternoon, August 23rd, when my parents think I have an appointment in Harrogate?

You will appreciate that I have not seen my aunt since I was a child. I should, therefore, be most grateful if you (rather than a nurse) introduced me to her and helped me through those first few moments.

You will understand why I have asked you to leave your reply with Miss Ellis at the post office. She is used to my using her shop as poste restante.

I remain,

Yours confidentially,

Felicity Hargreaves

Opening the minute stamp drawer in her new desk gave her a

spurt of pleasure, heightened by the prospect of seeing Miss Elsie for the second time that day, and, possibly, receiving more news from Edinburgh.

Fixing the penny stamp on the chaplain's letter, she felt a quake of apprehension. How would she introduce herself to her aunt? Would the chaplain stay with her? Would she want him to? What could she take her for a present? Would photographs upset her?

As she walked to the post office Felicity never noticed what a sparkling newly-laundered day it was after the night's gentle rain. The pony and trap, driven by the yeast-man, swept past her. She failed to acknowledge the flip of the whip and his smiling good-day.

She was trying to conjure up an unknown human being cast adrift from all that made life bearable.

She didn't need the post office. Her stamped letter could just be dropped in the VR box, but she *did* need Miss Elsie's calming comfort. She was standing outside watching the yeast-man balancing his brass scales but such was the day that balancing was ignored and liberality took over:

'Over four ounces, Miss Ellis, but a penny, just the same, from you. 'Ee, it's a lovely day! Now don't you stay inside baking bread! Just think, if you hadn't this shop to look after, you'd come with me right over Baildon Moor! And that's a fact!'

'Be off with your bother, Frank Wilson, some of us have work to do.'

He took her penny with a grin, skipped up the step of the trap, tugged lightly at the reins and called out: 'Good-day, Miss Hargreaves, and don't be so long away next time!'

So high was the sun, so polished the brass of the harness, that the startling shafts of light turned the dark grey limestone into gold. It was all that was needed to transform grimness into grandeur.

Felicity was thinking how much friendlier Airedale trades-people were than the studiously courteous shop assistants in Harrogate. Miss Elsie took her arm.

'Don't go, Felicity. Come inside. I've something for you.' She pulled a large envelope from under the Farrah's Harrogate toffee tin. 'It's from Edinburgh, but it's not your aunt Grace, it's official-looking.'

Felicity felt a frisson of fear as she read the envelope addressed: *Miss Felicity Laura Hargreaves.* No-one ever used her second name.

Sensing that she must treat the letter with care, she picked up

19

the counter paper knife and gently prised the flap of the envelope, trying not to break the seal.

She drew out an embossed headed letter, a prospectus and a complicated application form. Overawed by the imposing address and coat of arms, she read:

Dear Miss Hargreaves,

The Board has received an application on your behalf from Miss Grace Hargreaves giving a general outline of your education and your aspirations. She also states that she is prepared to provide testimony regarding your suitability as a potential medical student.

We are, however, obliged to point out that your education and qualifications fall short of what is required for entrance to the Faculty of Medicine.

In order that we may file your particulars for possible future reference we should be obliged if you would complete the enclosed form and send it to the above address at your earliest convenience.

May I ask you to read, most carefully, note 4, in which it is stated that all applicants must have studied at least two of the following sciences: chemistry, physics, botany and biology to Matriculation standard.

Should you be following a preparatory course of study in the coming academic year we earnestly recommend that chemistry and biology be given priority in your choice of Matriculation subjects.

We must point out, however, that such a course does not necessarily ensure a place at the University.

I remain, Madam,

Yours faithfully,

Angus McVitie

Secretary to the Board

Felicity flopped down on the little black bentwood chair alongside the counter and inwardly cursed her parents for sending her to such a feminine school. As she put the letter face down, angrily she thought to herself: There *are* schools in England, even in Yorkshire, where girls can tackle men's subjects. Charlotte, whilst at the North London Collegiate, Roberta Butterworth, an old

20

Cheltenham College girl, both did sciences. Of course, their schools were headed by Miss Buss and Miss Beale.

But it was no time to think of those dominant Miss Bs. Her dejected thoughts ran on: And what do I know? How to answer formal invitations. How to address a Bishop. Enough arithmetic to do household accounts. Enough French to regret crossing the Channel. Embroidery every day and not one science!

Miss Elsie leaned over the counter. 'What's all this brooding? Now come on, Felicity, it's not like you to sulk...'

'I'm not *sulking*, Elsie. I've come to my senses and I'm *angry*! No-one's discovered that I want to learn and to earn a living...'

Felicity's jaw was set in the Hargreaves clench. 'It's just the first time in my life that I've ever had to face the truth ... All that money! I might as well have gone to a Board school! It hurts, Elsie, it hurts. Read that letter, then you'd know why I'm angry, not just sulking.'

Elsie clipped her pince-nez on her stubby little nose, turned the key of the shop door, pushed the cat off the other counter chair and sat down as if taking a chair at a meeting. Her knees almost touched Felicity's.

After digesting every single word Elsie returned the documents to the envelope, and put it into Felicity's bag. Leaning forward, she gripped Felicity's shoulders and gave her a firm shake at eye level. It was a Miss Ellis whom Felicity had never met before:

'Where's your mill-stone grit, Felicity Hargreaves? How do you think yer'll become a doctor, going nesh before you've even seen one drop of blood? Get back home! Fill in that application form! And *don't* come back until you *have*!'

2

The kiss of congratulation which Felicity had impulsively given her father touched him more than she would ever know. Underneath Arthur Hargreaves' dominant, self-satisfied exterior were carnal and emotional tremors to which no Yorkshireman would ever admit. The money spent on his daughter's education and well-being had edged her away from its source and he felt snubbed that she showed no interest in the mill. The truth was, now that she had become a spirited and magnetic young woman, he was disturbed by her physical attraction and rather in awe of her social confidence.

Finishing schools, for that was how the Academy was described, expose the subtle social shortcomings of the families from whom they happily extract their money. They flaunt the names of the titled families to attract other families who may or may not have impressive lineage. Felicity would have been up in arms if anyone had even hinted at snobbery but she, when talking to her peers, avoided using the word *mill*, cognisant that it was too near *trade* for social comfort.

Her father, buying much of the social esteem he enjoyed, allowed the rumour of his beneficence to filter through to the inhabitants of Airedale. His hard-earned brass was there for all good causes, provided they were not at odds with his Methodist and Freemason principles!

The gift of a weighty, extravagantly-carved lectern, commemorating his daughter's departure from the Academy had given him the exalted opportunity to deliver his well-worn public speech. The clichés reeled off his starched cuff as predictably as the threads reeled through his looms.

The girls, rigid in their white dresses, had already gone through the tedium of the school song *'Nunquam non paratus'*; and applauded the curtseys of the predictable prize-winners. The Principal's laudatory list of the Academy's winners, whilst deflating those who had failed to contribute to it, inflated those who had.

22

Even the latter were in no mood to respond to a guest speaker, although they usually produced smiles of appreciation when he announced a half-day. Odd that the biggest boon he could give the girls was to release them from being there!

Arthur Hargreaves' aim in public speaking was to be heard at the back of the hall. So four words only at a time were propelled from lectern to the clock on the back wall, well above and beyond the girls' simulated listening.

As he had never won a prize at his fee-paying day school, he assured the girls that it did not matter whether they won or lost but *how they played the game*. He then handed books to, and shook hands with, thirty-nine highly praised prize-winners!

All this took twenty-five minutes, the hall clock telling him that he still had five minutes to go. Now for his impressive conclusion:

'Madam Principal and Ladies,' he pontificated, 'I yield to no-one in my belief that the Harrogate Academy stands high amongst all those who help to make Britain *Great* Britain and who serve Her Majesty's great Imperial Empire on which the sun never sets...'

The speech, with suitable variations, had already been used for the Methodist Sunday school, the Mothers' Union, the Boy Scouts and the Boys' Brigade and was booked to be repeated in the autumn for the White Ribboners. They were the young members of the Band of Hope. So large was his public benevolence, and so small his stock of words, he had only to change the title and gift and the same speech did for all. Moreover, the familiar words echoing in the minds of the simpler members of the Airedale community gave them a feeling of security and a sense of awe that anyone could get up and *spout* like that.

As one of Hargreaves' wagoners was heard to say: 'Yer can allus rely on t'Governor to give uz plenty 'v gab.'

Her father's loud-voiced charity clearly embarrassed Felicity, even more so at the presentation of the lectern, for, across its base, was a long narrow brass plate bearing the words:

The gift of Arthur Hargreaves Esquire and his daughter
Miss Felicity Hargreaves. July 20th 1894.

It was appropriate, but lost on Councillor Hargreaves, that at the ceremony they sang Felicity's favourite hymn: 'Dear Lord and Father of Mankind, Forgive our foolish ways'.

The day after the significant kiss, when midday meal was being cleared, her father put his arm round her shoulder, and, turning her face towards his, said: 'Did you hear me telling yer mother that we've got some new machinery at t'mill? I wondered if you'd like a look at it. What about this week? How about Wednesday?'

'Yes, of course, Father, I'd like to come, but had you forgotten Mother's At Home is on Wednesday? She expects me to be there – so can it be tomorrow?'

He was as pleased as if the High Sheriff had invited himself. 'Right! We'll let them get a good three hours' start. Nine o'clock sharp!'

Affection and pride made him smile, stroke his oiled moustache, and lapse into his native speech: 'Thaz in for a reet surprise, lass, a reet surprise an' all!'

Hargreaves had built his house a short walk uphill from the mill, with a good view of the valley. It was set back from the road with lawns that looked like Lister's green velvet. A high wall and quick-growing hedges and trees round the lawns ensured privacy for him and his family. They did not see the hordes of black-and-grey-shawled women, the flat-capped men, all clogged, trudging to work in the cold grey half-light of those mean mornings.

The workers on Canal Road and Mill Street down below had their sleep shattered at five in the morning by the knocker-up man tapping his long pole on their upstairs windows.

Less than an hour later the mill hooter ordered them to be on their way. They carried enamel tea cans each holding a spoonful of tealeaves for the breakfast break at eight o'clock. There'd be no tea until a penny had been handed over for the can to be filled with hot water.

The workers never thought of the work as drudgery; *early to rise and put your back into it* had been born and bred in their ancestors, long before the Industrial Revolution.

The gaffers, too, had risen and heard, but did not see, the hundreds of clogs clanking their iron soles on the cobbled road. It was a reassuring sound; that and the sight of the heaven-reaching chimney.

If that great stack isn't a prayer of thanks, Hargreaves thought to himself, I don't know what is.

It was about five minutes' walk to the mill and Felicity emerged well on time in a demure, but close-fitting, grey alpaca dress, a grey straw bonnet and grey silk gloves, a fitting outfit, she thought, for a visit to the mill. Her father glared.

'Go and put a wrap over that dress! It's a mill you're going to not a garden fête!'

It was not the soot and grime which concerned her father. His imagination conjured up the sensual spearing eyes of the men and lads.

'But, Father, it's August. I'll be far too hot!'

'Don't argue with me, lass! I'll go ahead. We're expected prompt nine.'

Felicity, irritated by her father's interference, stamped her way back to the house and up to her bedroom again and flung open the wardrobe door. The opulence of her coming-out garments triggered her mercurial mind from annoyance to perverse glee. *I'll show him!*

She lifted out a long hyacinth-blue velvet evening cloak. Sweeping this round her trim body she set off for the mill with a defiant grin, too amused to be conscious that the white ermine collar set off her mischievous face to perfection.

Her father, waiting in his office, tapped impatiently on the leather top of his imperial desk. 'No-one keeps Arthur Hargreaves waiting,' the fingers said. The blood rose from neck to scalp at the sight of her.

'Take that off, you little fool, and don't let any of the women see it! Do you want a wages strike on our 'ands?'

Felicity had to admit to herself that he had won that round. Defiance meant deadlock. His glare made her put the cloak out of sight. The solid dignity of her father's office sobered her. She adjusted her role to that of obedient daughter of the worsted-mill owner and followed him into the yard, suitably reduced to size by the towering chimney stack reaching up towards a summer sky.

As they walked on near the great wrought-iron and brass gate, Felicity saw how large the letters were: **Aireley Worsted Mill 1797**, and how remote the date.

'Nearly a hundred years old! What about a celebration?'

'Aye, in three years' time, lass. Your mother and me were talking about it. She told me it would be your twenty-first birthday. *She* wants a quiet do at home.'

It was then that Arthur Hargreaves face broke into a broad grin. 'But sithee, lass, *I've* set my mind on a real splash for all the folk in Aireley: Aireley Centenary. Now that *is* something to shout about, eh?'

Felicity began to wish she'd never mentioned it. The subject was dropped as they walked through the mill-yard with its pungent smell of steamy lanolin and dyes; past the furnace and the boiler room, and to the down-to-earth single-storey sheds. The grim charm of all this sprawling masonry began to intrigue her. She had only seen the three-storey building that faced the road with its blue and gold clock keeping Aireley families on time.

She was now so near the chimney that she had to tilt her head back on her spine to examine its decorative cornice. It thrust its railed tip heavenward like a blunted cathedral spire.

Her father pointed skywards. 'See that balcony near t'top? I've walked round that. They say yer could drive a carriage and a pair round Listers and Salts! Get it up first, I say to t'dafties!'

But as they walked past the machines in the sorting and scouring sheds, it was difficult to hear much of her father's explanations. When they moved up to the Mule spinning frames and he talked to the foreman and operatives, Felicity realised here was a language she did not know.

For once in Felicity Hargreaves' life she felt small, dwarfed by the governor, his machines and his workforce. The frightening speed and precision of these non-stop relentless machines filled a whole world of which she was totally ignorant, for here, the men and women who kept these intricate masses of steel going were her superiors, giving and receiving vital orders with a kind of mouth and finger signalling as the sweat poured forth.

Already she seemed to have walked miles. Some of the women gave her a bobbed curtsey, some a shy smile; some glanced with envy at her grand clothes. How childish her getting her own back on her father seemed now. She was glad no-one else had seen that velvet and ermine cloak.

They moved on to the carding room, which seemed light, bright and cool after the steamy heat of the dyeing shed. Father stood by her side, not trying to talk above the noise, while Felicity schooled herself to watch more intently. She mimed her appreciation to the man and two women nearest to her. She watched the wool fibres being put into the feeder and the great rollers with wire teeth bite the threads and masticate them into a smooth continuing mass flowing like a river of rich cream. She was mesmerised.

Her father was obviously determined that his daughter should get some idea of what it meant to go through the mill, as he had done as a boy of fourteen – the governor's son – not receiving any wage until he was seventeen.

'It's a job for experts this, my girl. All these men understand fleeces; long 'airs, short 'airs, and the like ... look at that wavy lot, *crimp* we call that... Sithee 'ere, that yarn'll be most expensive of t'lot.' Hargreaves swept his expert eye assessing and valuing.

To Felicity this was a very different man from the one who sat at the head of their dining table. Here, he was not only more important – but far more intelligent.

'Wot yer've seen, 'appens to all wool manufacturing. But worsted's summat different. An tha's going to see it now, lass.'

Felicity, looking at the length of the room, was amazed that any floor could carry the weight of these massive machines.

Her father put his lips to her ear but still shouted: 'An', what do yer think of that?' There was a gleaming machine which had a look all its own. A large chart between the windows spelt out the machine's identity:

The Noble Combing Engine. Keighley 1893

This time he was determined that she got the message:

'Nah, *that's* wot mi brass 'as gone on this year. Best combing machine in t'world. Carding 'll do for wool, but worsted needs summat that's more choosy. 'Ave a good look at all them weels an' cogs; some clockwise, some t'other way, some up, some down...'

Felicity was enraptured by the intricacy of the movement: stretching, pulling, shifting, coiling – by the magic way in which the short hairs and intrusive oddments were thrown out. What brain could invent this incredible monster?

'Nah yer can see why this 'ere engine is called Prince of the Industry.'

When they moved out to the next staircase conversation was easier.

'If trade gets a move-on, there'll be nowt but this type of combing. They've got it in France. Frogs'll have to look out now.' He puffed a little up the stairs and kept his final thought until they reached the top.

Felicity noticed folk she recognised from nodding acquaintance. She had never thought of these anonymous workers as skilled craftsmen, intelligent folk, identified by their working titles: burlers, cutlers, wool sorters, top makers, worsted weavers, spinners, croppers, perchers who had respect for their jobs, their managers, and over-lookers.

She had not prepared herself for the weaving machines: the deafening noise of the looms which were shooting threads finer than her finest sewing cottons, over and under the warp. It was hard to believe that another genius had designed and invented them. Mimicking man's movements of throwing a shuttle between the threads of the warp, they could outwit man in speed and precision.

Impressed as she had been, Felicity was glad when they moved through the various finishing processes and she could watch, in comparative quiet, the finished worsted being pulled slowly between rollers. Skilled observers were watching like eagles for any microscopic flaw. With his bird's-eye view from the bridge above the machine, the percher was examining every fine line of the warp and weft of the material. One faulty thread and the machine was immediately stopped.

'Come on, lass, I think you've had enough, but ah'd like yer ter see t'despatch department. Yer in fer some surprises there!'

As they walked across the yard to a new building, her father was diverted as he caught sight of four bales of wrapped cloth haphazardly lying on the cobbles.

'Who's responsible for this lot?' he yelled to the wagon driver.

'It's fost time I seed 'em, Sir. I think they're cold pigs.'

'Tell Jenkins in the packing room to come to my office at once. We don't have cold pigs here! You go on on your own, Felicity. *Cold pigs* indeed!'

Within three minutes the governor was behind his desk and Jenkins in front of it.

'Take a look at these labels, Jenkins! Look at despatch date! What in Christ's name are they doing stuck here?' (Arthur Hargreaves was a long way from his Masonic Lodge, the Methodist Church and his home).

'Go sharp and fetch Liza Wheeler!'

By the time the two came back, a letter of apology had been drafted addressed to William Sharp & Sons, Wholesale and Bespoke Tailors, Kirkstall Road, Leeds.

'Type that now, girl. An' see it's left mill in ten minutes flat! Nah, Jenkins, there's a train for Leeds in fifteen minutes. You and those bloody bales have to be on that train and delivered to Sharp's before t'twelve o'clock 'ooter goes. I'll telephone City station an' see wagonette's there. Get thee face washed, and off with that letter.'

'Right, sir. I will, sir.'

'And, Jenkins, don't ever tell a single bugger about them cold pigs! Think on, Hargreaves never 'ave 'em!'

Felicity walked on to the despatch department on her own. She could only guess that cold pigs were rejects. As she entered the door she flicked off flakes of soot from her grey dress and thought again of her stupidity and the velvet cloak.

The manager, a jovial chap in a green baize apron, looked cheerful and ready to see her. 'P'raps you'll take a quick look at this lot and see where *they're* going!'

Felicity quickened her pace between the solid bales of cloth covered in hessian and sewn with fine string. *London; Paris; Berlin; Amsterdam; Madrid; Buenos Aires; St Petersburg...*

She had never associated her father with anywhere outside Yorkshire, although he sometimes went abroad on business. He never described the places he had visited, nor the prices – just the size of the orders. She was surprised to see two small parcels labelled in her father's deliberate hand: *Worth of Paris* and *La Maison du Doucet*. She read the addresses aloud, savouring vicariously the dazzling world of *haute couture*. How impressed her Academy friends would have been!

As she put the two small parcels down a voice came over her shoulder. 'Had you forgotten I was here?'

It was the son of their nearest neighbour and friendly rival, Harold Armstrong, who owned one of the biggest spinning mills in Airedale.

'Well, yes Archie, I had forgotten, but why *are* you here? I understood it was your *father's* mill you were working your way through.'

'I did that last year. The idea is that I get to know *both* mills.'

'And then?'

This blunt question and manner took Archie off his guard. His public school speech cracked into a blunt Bradford accent.

'They've only told me what they want me to know. It's some scheme of your father's to co-operate the two mills. If you ask me, worsted'll get the best of the...' He stopped short as Hargreaves returned.

'Tak' her up to the sample room, my lad, and show her some of those suiting designs you've had an 'and in.' Arthur had more than fine suitings on his mind, he hoped they would suit one another and make a good match.

This partially restored Archie's confidence as he led Felicity up two flights of stairs to a well-groomed reception room. Pieces of smooth worsted suitings with subtle checks and lines of innumerable shades of grey, misty blue, dark red and green were put into her hands.

The threads were so fine and the weave so suave that they evoked pictures of London gentlemen in Savile Row and the Carlton Club, or Bradford businessmen walking out of the Connaught Rooms.

Archie's head bent closer as he asked: 'Have you received my invitation to the Masonic Ball? I posted it yesterday.'

Felicity prevaricated, for she had collected a far more important

29

letter this morning. The one that didn't matter had been left at the post office to be delivered later by the postman.

'I think I have, but I haven't opened it yet.'

The slight was not lost on Archie. Felicity seized the moment to change the subject.

'You must be very grateful that you now understand the complexity of Hargreaves worsted after the simplicity of the Armstrong spinning.'

The barbed arrow was shot with such a ravishing smile accompanying it that Archie's wilting confidence revived enough for him to open the door for her exit and to receive a smiling thank-you.

She returned to her father's office. No-one saw the sleight of hand she used in picking up and lightly rolling the rejected cloak.

'That was wonderful, Papa,' she said as she moved to walk home on her own, 'quite the most fascinating hour I've ever spent! Thank you so much! How fortunate Archie is to have you as a mentor and this mill as his college!'

This was the kind of gush one never heard in industrial West Riding and for a moment her father suspected it was Academy patronage. Felicity caught his look of incredulity and with a grin and firm hand-hold she switched on to her comic West Riding, with which she used to entertain her friends at school.

'Ee, but it were grand, lad! It were reet grand an' all!'

It was beginning to dawn on Arthur Hargreaves that his daughter was in no sense run-of-the-mill. In fact she was beyond him. The trouble was, not only had she a flow of language but the faculty to use it for her own ends with charm and humour – not only to speak well, but to speak true. Hargreaves put it more bluntly: 'Aye! She's a proper cough drop, is our Felicity!'

His daughter walked home a different woman from the one who entered her father's mill.

New thoughts filled her mind:

Why had she put up with the superior attitude of the girls who came from the South? Why had she not realised that it was the fabrics woven in provincial England, mostly in Yorkshire, which were made up in the factories and sold in the shops and salons in London and Paris? Was not the wealth of the South created in the North?

How could she persuade her father to drop his social platitudes and clichés and speak true, not only to promote his own industry but for the welfare of the workforce? Working all hours on those

30

miserable wages! Many of them looked ill. How could they afford a doctor? If that mill were hers it would have its own clinic.

Youth burgeons on ideals. Felicity enjoyed airing hers.

The euphoria from seeing the mill in action had subsided suddenly into a guilt feeling as she mounted the imposing marble steps of her home. True, her father had put his weight behind bringing working hours down from twelve to eleven. But, she protested to herself, no-one should live in the clatter of those machines for eleven wicked hours. And hadn't the wily man made it clear that he expected the same output from the shorter time?

Felicity was now in the hall, where a single envelope lay on the silver tray. It was no surprise that this was the expected gilt-edged card. She hardly gave it a glance as it was too sharp a reminder of Archie's predictable sequence of steps on the dance floor and his unpredictable feet on hers. In her volatile mood, it was just as well that she did not know that her parents were planning to marry her to this scion of the Armstrong spinning mill. Such a family liaison would ensure that their son-in-law would not only be a man of property in his own right. He would be an investment for the Hargreaves.

The Hargreaves' matchmaking conversation was taken up again later:

'I gave Archie the hint to invite 'er to the Ball. I know 'is father's paid for the ticket. Has it come yet, Mother?'

'Well, it was still in the hall where I put it. She may have picked it up by now.'

Felicity had simply propped the card on her bedroom mantelpiece and was now concentrating on a letter to Belinda Bennett, the doctor's nineteen-year-old daughter. She and Belinda had never been close friends, for they were separated by an academic year and a separate building at school, besides four inches in height.

Secretly Felicity longed for the attention of this tall, independent, outspoken girl who seemed to be on such enviable terms with her parents. '*They* encourage her to have a mind of her own,' Felicity muttered to her blotter.

The nearest the two girls had ever got at the Academy was sharing a dislike of sewing and embroidery in the after-school communal sessions in the common room. To Belinda and Felicity, feather-stitching and drawn-thread work seemed the height of human folly:

31

'Why draw threads *out* that overworked weavers have slaved to put *in*?' Felicity's shrewd comment caught Belinda's ear. They shared a distant smile across the common room. This trivial incident spurred Felicity on now to write:

Dear Belinda, (or should I say Miss Bennett)

Now that we are both away from the Academy, and not separated by our year and your course, I hope you will permit me to approach you in friendship.

From your conversations in the common room, which I could not help but overhear, I got the impression that you are in sympathy with *new women* who are making their way in the world. Forgive my curiosity, but I could not help but wonder if you have any plans for widening your horizons beyond Airedale. I hope you will understand when I say I should prefer not to talk on these matters in my own home.

I do visit the Aireley post office each day, usually before breakfast, but if on this coming Friday I change my routine to three o'clock, would it be possible for us to meet and, if the weather is agreeable, walk down to the Five Locks?

Miss Ellis, the village postmistress, has become a great friend and confidante so she will quite understand that we have made her shop our rendezvous.

I am putting this letter into the hands of Bob, the postman, so that he can drop it straight into your letter-box without posting.

If you are unable to come, please give a message to Bob or Miss Ellis, who will both respect our confidence.

I am, (or perhaps I should say, hope to be)

Your friend,

Felicity Hargreaves

Meanwhile there was her mother's At Home to contend with: a duty which Felicity accepted, confident that at least for one afternoon a month, she could appear to be charming, kindly, polite and conventional with women who bored her stiff.

Demure! Is that what her mother would like her to be? Oh no, not *demure*, she decided. And there was always the funny side of these At Homes that she would tuck away for Belinda's ears on Friday.

She dressed in a gown of soft coral silk which the Leeds

32

modiste, Dorothy Davison, had created, using a *toile* sent direct from the House of Worth in Paris. The contretemps that morning had been Felicity's absolute refusal to wear a hat. 'Ridiculous wearing a hat inside one's own home!' was proving to her mother that the Academy had different rules of etiquette. However, as her daughter's presence would make a change from the somewhat predictable local gossip, she weakened to Felicity's obstinacy.

'Well, if you want to make a fool of yourself...'

Hats were the most important item in the calling ritual, often looking as if they had really been intended for an epergne of fruit and flowers on some banquet table. So polished were the cherries and grapes, so life-like were the flowers that they asked to be picked. But these were there not to be praised but deftly poised in order to catch every roving eye.

The two long hatpins guaranteeing the hat's immobility crossed one another at the rear belligerently, in the middle of the chignon, emerging east and west. The only daggers drawn in the room.

One after another, between three thirty and five o'clock, the lady visitors arrived, wives leaving three cards on the silver tray in the hall: two for the absent husband and one for herself. Collecting the cards afterwards, Felicity laughed to see that Mrs Banks, the local merry widow, had left five cards, two for each deceased husband and a pale pink one, black-edged, for herself.

As Gertrude Hargreaves always laid on an afternoon tea to outdo the gentry's sole offering of thin bread and butter, the calling time usually extended from the ritual twenty minutes to half an hour. Jessie the parlourmaid in her starched lace-edged pinafore and Felicity in the irksome white gloves were kept busy; Jessie handing the silver salver with the tea, cream and sugar, and Felicity with the loaded three-tier cake stand, almost pirouetting round each straight-laced lady.

Felicity, of course, was the centre of interest:

'You must be glad to be back in Aireley, my dear.' Each guest picked up a cup but there were no stimulating cues to pick up.

'Your mother must be glad to have you home, Felicity.'

And another: 'They'll be pleased to have you back at the Sunday school...'

Felicity smiled outwardly but cringed inwardly. Back, but I don't intend to be bored, Felicity thought to herself. Her lips were saying with simulated persuasion: '*Do* have a curd tartlet, Mrs Cartwright...'

At five fifteen a ring at the front door alerted everyone, for it

33

could hardly be an invited guest at this time. Etiquette demanded that exit should be before five thirty:

'Mrs Bennett, Madam,' Jessie announced in her afternoon-tea voice.

The doctor's wife, simply but attractively dressed, had an air of insouciance not quite appreciated by the Aireley ladies, nor could they quite accept her apology.

'I'm so glad to be here at last, Mrs Hargreaves, I usually help the doctor on Wednesdays, but today Belinda has taken over for me and so here I am!'

Felicity was fascinated. Ah! *This* was why Belinda was so sure of herself and delightfully easygoing with her parents. She quickly adjusted to quite a different menu of tea conversation, for now she and Mrs Bennett at least had Belinda and the Academy in common. They were *en rapport* at once, thought-catching in and out of their spoken words:

'Oh no, it isn't that we think Belinda *should* be at home but we love having her, she's such fun!'

Felicity had never heard any mother talk in this way about a daughter. Admiration and envy mingled in her mind.

'I would have so much liked to know Belinda better, but a year's difference in school is an impossible barrier to friendship. Besides, she was in the other building for the cordon bleu course *and* she was head prefect.'

Mrs Bennett's laugh rippled under her simple, but stylish, hat. 'She must have got that on her height! However did she manage to conform?'

Felicity was aware that conversation between the two remaining ladies had stopped and, having thanked their hostess, they were now slowing down their exits in order to listen in to more lively conversation.

Mrs Bennett had the social ease and instinctive tact to make her visit last precisely the length of half a scone and one cup of tea. She timed her exit to be able to have a word with Felicity at the front door, well distant from Mrs Hargreaves still at her post in the drawing room.

An uncanny knowledge of Felicity's position in this house made Hazel Bennett adjust her voice to conspiracy.

'Belinda asked me to give you this,' and then in a voice which was meant to carry into the drawing room: 'I do hope you will come to tea, Felicity!'

Felicity's eager response coincided with her swift gesture of sliding the envelope into her over-dress.

As she returned to the drawing room, her mother and Jessie were enjoying the post-mortem, the most interesting part of the afternoon. Mrs Hargreaves' voice and speech had relaxed into comfortable Yorkshire: the kind used by the comely middle-aged sales assistants in millinery departments at Mathias Robinson's in Leeds.

'I love summer hats. What creations we had today! Did you notice that bluebird on Mrs Silcoate's panama pecking at the cherry?'

Felicity was just in time to hear: 'Mrs Bennett's hat was rather plain, wasn't it? But then I suppose she'd had to rush from the surgery. I am surprised at Dr Bennett letting his wife do that... Did I hear she has some kind of diploma?'

Little did they know that the *chapeau* had been bought in the Agnes salon just off Les Champs Elysées and that Hazel Bennett's own medical degree had been toughly earned under the great champion of women's rights and medicine Dr Sophia Jex-Blake.

'Help Jessie with the pots, there's a good girl.' Mrs Hargreaves, now the formalities were over, quickly reverted to the role that was more natural to her.

Felicity, who was always welcome in the kitchen, enjoyed escaping from the antimacassars and aspidistras. It also gave her the opportunity to slip upstairs and read Belinda's note.

The sun would soon be setting on the most exciting three days of her life. She tucked the letter into her secret drawer and glowed with the prospect of Friday.

Walking, in Yorkshire, was the common denominator for all ages and every social class, for the field and moorland walks seemed to grow straight out from the mill yards as if they were compensating for the soot, the smoke and the noise.

Every lad with a fishing rod and every hopeful lass with a glad eye found walking partners to go to the river or to the canal. Mothers and fathers trained their children to step out and breathe deeply so they caught the habit of walking early. It never left them.

Carriage folk too would not miss their daily walk. Sunday afternoons in the tangy moorland air were as near to godliness as their Sunday morning prayers.

Felicity preferred the wild virgin moors round her home to the smoothly scythed grass of the Stray in Harrogate and she was grateful to her parents that they rarely questioned that she went alone. But a dog would give her both purpose and companionship, and be her loyal listener. She would choose her time to approach her father. Like all children in Yorkshire she had been brought up never to *ask* for anything. You got what your parents thought you needed; what you wanted was never put into words.

The preliminary part of Felicity's walk to the post office was over in five minutes and she should not have been surprised to find Miss Elsie and Belinda obviously enjoying one another's company. Felicity's slight shyness on meeting Belinda again was dispelled at once by the natural icebreaker:

'What a very good idea to meet here! Elsie and I are old friends, this is our post office too, you know.'

Felicity noticed the omission of *Miss* and indexed it in her personal glossary of subtle distinctions.

'And you two are old friends, I see.' Belinda swept social barriers away with the warmth of a south-west breeze.

Miss Elsie beckoned: 'Come through here. I'll shut the door and you two can stay there just as long as you like. But don't miss the sunshine!'

They moved into her polished little parlour with its black-leaded kitchen range glinting with brass hinges and fire irons. The clothes' rack rods were almost hidden, so thick were the bunches of herbs hanging down to dry. As a result the usual raw wool smell by which anyone recognised Bradford was spirited away.

But this was no time for nostalgia; it was not appropriate for two *new women* planning their independence.

Felicity held the ace card, or so she thought, and planned to play it first.

'Before we talk, you must read this letter!' So many times had the letter been read that the folds flapped open at Belinda's touch.

There was a tense silence while Belinda pored over it; she could hardly believe what she read.

'I'd like to meet your aunt Grace.' And then more slowly, 'Yes, she's a person I'd certainly like to meet.' Her swift smile then carried a look of sheer incredulity. 'And she's in *Edinburgh* too!'

'But Belinda, what have you to do with *Edinburgh?*'

'Because I'm *going* there!'

Belinda, with her innate sense of timing, thought she would spin out the drama in the fresh air. She just enjoyed being a raconteur. Now watching Felicity's face glow as she had never seen it glow before, she had a feeling that she must never let her down.

36

'Come on, let's get right away!' They went into the shop, where Miss Elsie was slapping butter into pats.

'We're doing what you said, Elsie.' And then in a whisper Belinda said, 'Thank you so much for hiding us!'

They crossed the road, climbed over the stile between the black grey walls, then tramped through a scrubby patch of neglected land to where the grey drystone walls and the sheep were only slightly blackened.

In less than five minutes the scene had changed and the canal, long since man-made, had drawn to itself every kind of tree that enjoyed the northern dales. A myriad of tiny flowers lurked in the undergrowth, each one part of nearly two hundred years' history. There was just room for two people on the towpath if they clung close together. Without discussion, Felicity took the inner position of the female and held her friend's strong arm. Belinda took over firmly on the edge of the canal.

'You know my father well, as your doctor; and you met my mother for just a few minutes in your home – oh, and of course, during the odd moment at the Academy. Well, they *are* rather different, aren't they?'

'Different from mine, you mean?'

Belinda evaded answering, but stood there, tall and confident, the result of her parents' intimate union. Felicity, too, was silent. What was Belinda getting at?

How could such parents possibly benefit her? The question was too crude.

'Belinda, it's difficult walking and talking, let's sit on this bench. There are questions I must ask you. Edinburgh? Where does that come in?'

'Father's a graduate of the medical school in Edinburgh. He's been trying to find out how a young woman with a hopelessly feeble education such as mine can get into the medical faculty. Father's friend Dr Medway said in his strong blunt Scots: "Spouting yards of English poetry won't get her into a Scottish medical school!"'

'But we did spout Scott and Burns, didn't we?' Felicity giggled. 'They're Scots enough!'

'No time for persiflage! Wait for the shock! Try selling this to your mamma! I'm now planning to do a course at Bradford Technical College three days a week: a year's course of biology and chemistry. It's a wonderful college. Wasn't your father at the opening twelve years ago when the Prince of Wales came? I know mine was.'

Felicity had heard about the processions, the pomp and cere-mony; all she heard from her father these days was that some of the mill lads went to evening classes at the so-called Tech.

'You can't be serious, Belinda! It's only for working *boys*, isn't it ... and a few women in the evening classes?'

'Well, at first it was only boys. In September they'll be having two hard-working *girls*. *Us!*'

Felicity spluttered the rest of her reply: 'But my mother? ... She'll say people who go there are "common" ... low class ... un-educated! ... Belinda, you daren't suggest that *I* go? ... My par-ents don't even know I'm thinking of getting away... They both insist I'm needed at home.'

Belinda ignored the obstacles. 'And then, Felicity, after the year at Bradford we shall *both* go on to Edinburgh *together*: September 1895!' Then quietly and seriously she added: 'What about your aunt Grace? Won't *she* help? After all, she is your father's sister.'

'You surely don't think they'll take any notice of her?' Although there was no-one in sight Felicity lowered her voice: 'They don't tell me anything but I get the impression that aunt Grace is a bit of a black sheep.'

Belinda's eyes brightened. 'Ah! Now you see why I'd like to meet her!'

Felicity was following her own thoughts. 'Between you and me, I think it's just that father's rather envious of her. The grand-parents, on their mother's side, had invested money for her in a Scottish bridge-building company. It prospered well when Hargreaves' mill was going through a bad time. I think mother's jealous of her because she resents having a sister-in-law who is independent of any man's money. How can I best explain my mother's dependence? Well, last year, for their twentieth wedding anniversary my mother bought my father a pair of silver hairbrushes. No, *chose* not *bought!* She had to ask him first *if* she could buy them, then they both chose them and the bill went on his account.'

'Well, Felicity Hargreaves, now I'll tell you this. You're not going to be like that! You and I are going to be independent! Neither of us knows much about money but I think I know a bit more than you do. Do you have an allowance?'

Felicity blushed. 'You can hardly call five shillings a week an allowance – but then I only buy pins and needles, stamps and gifts and things like that with it ...'

Belinda ignored her friend's discomfort and revelled in her latest triumph. 'On my eighteenth birthday father told me that I was to go with him to Bradford to open a bank account in my own name. A few days later, he introduced me to the manager at Lloyds. It was so thrilling! Father's settled one hundred pounds as capital, not to be touched, and I now receive fifty-two pounds per year, one pound per week, for all my expenses. I feel like a *new woman*. The odd thing is, Felicity, it's made me not want to spend. Funny if I turned into a hoarder!'

Belinda dominated the conversation for the next ten minutes, holding forth on women gaining independence, until Felicity managed to get a word in.

'Belinda, I really don't think you appreciate my own position. You must know from local gossip that my father is not just well off, he's rich. They never grudge me anything. In fact your allowance would not pay for half of what they spend on me. But, you see, to my father money is *power*. He enjoys being the one who doles out, the one who has to be thanked. To him life is governed by purse strings.'

Felicity had never made such a revealing speech in her life. For her part, Belinda thought it would be tactful not to make any comment.

A heron flew down and stood tall in the slowly moving water. The sound flicked their attention to its flight, freedom and poise.

'Look at that!' Belinda put her arm round Felicity. They stood together, letting the heron signal its message. Trust in one another lingered in the ambience of the slow moving water.

'Time to go back. We've a lot to do. Leave it to me for the time being. I'll deal with my father. Everyone says I *wheedle* him. The point is, Felicity, I don't have to! When he's next in Edinburgh I don't think he'll need much persuading to meet your aunt. Remember three times a day at the Academy we had to say *Grace*!'

'Oh, Belinda, you and your excruciating puns! All right – to that I'll just say, *Amen*.'

They separated at the highest of the five locks. Felicity, arriving home in a few minutes, walked between the tall poplars of the drive just as the gong was sounding for the Yorkshire high tea. Belinda arrived home later, just as her father was getting out of the carriage, having brought another little Aireley child into the world.

'Had a good walk?'

'Yes, Felicity Hargreaves came with me.'

'Um! Nice girl. I brought her into the world, you know.'

'And aren't you glad you did?'

Dr Bennett took this to be a rhetorical question and said, with a gesture towards the horse and gig, 'Would you mind putting this lot away, Belinda? It was a difficult case... I'll go back later tonight.'

Deep devotion to her father curbed her impatience to broach the subject of how he could help Felicity. She had the good grace to keep all that back until tomorrow.

She led the horse and gig to the stables and there found Tom, who had a dual role as groom and gardener. He had a tied bundle of onions slung over one arm and rhubarb tucked under the other.

'Leave gig to me, Miss Belinda, that's my job, but I've been gardening today. Yer dad's enough to do with doctoring. If there were more folk like 'im, t'world would be a better place!'

Belinda, giving a smile of agreement, took the onions and rhubarb, putting them in a trug to take to the house.

'I'll tell yer summat yer don't know, Miss Belinda. T'other day wen he'd bin to see my little lad in t'morning, he walked round again at ten o'clock at night to see if t'fever 'ad gone down. Yer won't know either, but I am telling yer now, 'e's niver sent a bill sin' I came to work 'ere. So mind now an' don't let on if yer see me working down in t'kitchen gardin in the evenings. Say nowt. I've told yer muther. She knows all about it!'

As Belinda walked back to the front of the house, the tramping on gravel made her look at the path leading out from the surgery door. It was the girl from the dairy farm near the canal wearing a neat white bandage on her right hand.

'What have you been doing to yourself, Lucy?'

'I caught it on t'churn, Miss.'

She was not the last patient. Her father would be in the surgery for at least another hour.

3

'But why ask us for an alibi?' Olivia Winkley questioned her younger sister, Kate, as they sat in the Swan Hydro in Harrogate.

'It must be someone very special if she prefers him to us.'

'Why presume it's a "him", you silly girl?' Olivia sounded superior.

'Well, who else could it be?' Although two years younger, life was more romantic for Kate.

'Felicity's never shown any interest in young men, except Miss Temple-Smith's nephew. You remember, the handsome naval officer who poured some of his beer into her glass at lunch and she went all muzzy!'

Olivia and Kate were now in their conversational tandem, which they revelled in.

'And that impossible young man, Archie, who came to the end-of-term garden party and fell into an ice-bucket?'

Kate picked up the cue quickly. 'And do you remember how Felicity snubbed him when he offered to shy a coconut for her?'

Olivia was awaiting the chance to imitate Felicity's haughty voice:

'"Yes, Archibald, I will accept a coconut from you if you will crack it with your teeth!"' Even the giggles of the Winkley sisters had charm and style.

At that moment their parents, Sir Hugh and Lady Winkley, arrived, accompanied by their progressive daughter Charlotte. They had hoped she would have a massage for her tennis elbow, but she had refused.

'Please stop this pampering! I'm as tough as old boots.'

She was. Could she more aptly be compared with her own svelte riding boots?

'We're leaving you now, my dears. We'll wish you good health while we're drinking the nauseating waters. One would think that out of thirty-six wells there would be at least *one* that was palatable.'

It was not the least effort for Hugh Winkley to make each of his

41

womenfolk feel cherished. Several generations of silver spoons had eased the way. Unlike most scions of his class he was not neurotic about an heir. Even the third girl, Kate, had been welcomed on April 23rd with a flag of St George hoisted high above the river Swale: a signal for rejoicing throughout this fairest of dales. Any rumbles of dissension against class privilege remained muted where *noblesse oblige* spread hypnotic wings.

'You lucky girls. You're spared all this. Your mother is trying to make me into a young man again and stop my drinking vintage port! I've ordered lemon squash for you. Mamma and I will be back for luncheon. The head waiter will show you our table. But, darlings, don't sit there gossiping all the morning! Charlotte, what about showing them the water gardens...'

The Winkley family felt at home in the Swan Hydro for they used it as their pied-à-terre on all their visits to Harrogate. Sir Hugh having a financial interest in the Hydro's many amenities meant that the commissionaire and waiters held their bows fractionally longer than they did for other people.

The gracious creeper-covered building with its Palladian portico was a hundred years older than the Winkleys' Georgian country house. They enjoyed the Hydro's relaxed comfort with its elegant sofas and chaise-longues. The great bowls of flowers were not ostentatiously exotic, but rather the blooms that Harrogate grew so lavishly in its Valley Gardens and beds on the Stray. Today the bowls were vibrant globes of multi-coloured sweet peas welcoming every visitor.

Less than twenty miles away the Barlockend Mental Asylum awaited its single visitor.

Charlotte, the eldest of the three Winkley girls, had just completed her final term at North London Collegiate and in October would be going to Girton.

Her presence brought the Felicity conversation to a temporary halt. Charlotte had a way of making the most trivial conversation seem important.

'Did you really like the costume I tried on in Louis Copés? It had a Paris label but I did think the braid on the jacket and skirt were rather banal.'

'I think,' Kate chipped in, 'that you're just thinking you could do better in France.'

'I'm bored with clothes.' Olivia diverted the conversation. 'I'm looking forward to this afternoon when Papa is going to buy me a new saddle for Dixey. But, Charlotte, look at this letter from Felicity. Here, read it!'

Charlotte did so, rather intrigued to find that a girl from the Academy had such spirit.

'Well, if I am any judge of character, and I think I am, there is more to this than a young man. When I watched her playing tennis I thought: with a forearm stroke like that, she could hold her own at North London Collegiate!'

Kate and Olivia were used to their Sister Superior demoting the Academy to nursery level; although not academic, they were bright enough to hold their own with Charlotte. Olivia led the way.

'But what about *lessons*, you don't do lessons with your forearm!'

Kate screwed up her face to say: 'Oh, North London again! We do arithmetic; you do mathematics.'

'We speak French with Mademoiselle, you study French literature with Monsieur Dupont,' piped Olivia with a pseudo-French accent.

'You do boring Latin and Greek,' added Kate.

Olivia, almost out of breath, finished with: 'You do science, we do sewing.' The final word was dismissed with a down-turned mouth of distaste.

Kate played her final sentence as if it were checkmate in chess. 'So how could Felicity do all those subjects if she *had* gone to North London?'

Charlotte's reply tumbled out with exasperation: 'Of course she couldn't do them if she'd never done them. So how could she ever know she could do them if she'd never had the *chance* to do them?'

It was a good summing-up of the obvious blanks in Felicity's education.

They all three laughed in unison and then picked up their neglected glasses of lemon squash. Through the sudden silence a voice of army resonance rang out from a group of hydropathic addicts lounging at the other end of the room.

'Well, you ladies stay if you like. I'm going to the Smoking Room for a little peace!'

The girls just hoped that he was not a friend of their father's.

Charlotte rose, reacting to the cue of disapproval: 'Come, let us take a walk in the fresh air! I hear the Valley Gardens are looking quite delicious. There we shall no doubt meet active people of interest, taking their walks before luncheon.'

During breakfast time at the Hargreaves' home that day, Felicity had popped in oddments of conversation about the Winkleys' visit to Harrogate and Sir Hugh and Lady Winkley taking the waters. She sorted out her hypothetical train journey to Harrogate, accepting all her father's advice.

'Yes, Father, I will of course take a cab from the station. Thank you for the extra florin. That will cover everything. I'm meeting Olivia and Kate at Louis Copés. They are trying on autumn costumes and mantles.'

This was a welcome cue for Gertrude. 'Is it all right, Father, if Felicity looks at one or two garments while she's there? Everybody says it is the best place in the north of England for ladieswear. Give my kind regards to Lady Winkley and tell her that my At Home day is always the third Wednesday in the month. Wait a minute, I'll get you one of my visiting cards.'

Jessie came in to clear the table. 'Sorry, Miss, I thought you'd finished. What time is your train? Madam said I could walk down with you if you liked.'

Felicity's heart sank. Her intention was to use Miss Elsie's as a hideaway until she got the early afternoon train to Barlockend. There was no way now of avoiding Leeds.

'Of course Jessie, do come. The train's at ten o'clock. I'll be ready in a few minutes. Meet you in the hall.'

On the train to Leeds Felicity organised her day. She knew that there was a way in from the station to the back of the Queen's Hotel, which led straight to the Ladies' Retiring Room.

She walked quickly through the station glad that she was wearing a shady hat. Mercifully there was no-one else in the room and it was comfortingly dark and cool. She left the newspapers and magazines unopened and allowed the thought of Barlockend to take over. Whatever kind of hope could she offer her poor imprisoned aunt? She hoped the chaplain was not too godly. Another hour thudded away while she tried to imagine her aunt's face after so many years of neglect and isolation.

A knock at the door brought her back to creature comforts. In two minutes she was agreeing to the suggestion of a locally produced pork pie and tomatoes. Felicity was so hungry she would have said yes to anything.

Then it was time to be on her way to Barlockend.

She settled down in the Ladies Only carriage for this part of her journey, enjoying the short ride, quickly leaving factories behind and looking back on the grandeur of the Leeds Town Hall. The speed of the train helped to dismiss the grim back-to-back houses. Soon there was Kirkstall Abbey, an awesome ruin set among green fields.

It was about fifteen minutes' walk from the station to the long drive of the asylum. A bell on the high wrought-iron gates had to be rung, even though the gatekeeper was sitting there waiting. In fact on ringing a second time Felicity realised she had disturbed his sleep. Reluctantly he pulled back two massive iron bars and opened the gates in a miserly way, making just enough space for her to go through.

'Have you got a pass, Miss?'

'No, but I have a letter from the Reverend Anthony Thompson.'

He pointed to the imposing frontage of Barlockend. 'He doesn't spend much time here at the Lodge. You'll find him down there.'

Felicity saw the high tower and spire well ahead with the clock pointing to two twenty-three. As she approached the immaculate front lawns four men were haphazardly raking the grass. Three of them hailed her with their good-days, two of them seemed quite normal, the third held an imaginary cap high in the air and bowed low. The fourth with a fingered gesture towards the asylum yelled: 'There's no-one in, Miss. No-one lives 'ere now. Ther all dead but uz, Miss, all dead.'

There was no mistaking where she was. A frisson of fright ran like fork-lightning through her body. The hand she put forward to pull the bell was trembling. It seemed to be an age before the clattering of the heavy chain, the iron bolt and the massive key were put into action.

'I've come to see Miss Amy Ackroyd (Number 574). But I think the chaplain will be expecting me. I was to be here at two-thirty.'

'It's two twenty-seven, Madam. Wait here and I'll go and see if I can find him.'

The massive door was shut in her face and every bolt, bar and lock was put into action again. Felicity tried to reason, not easy with a beating heart. 'Of course, they must *have* to do this, I suppose, for security...'

Eventually the tower clock struck the half-hour and, almost synchronising with the stroke, the forbidding door was more quickly dealt with. An impressive figure lightened the gloom. The arms opened wide, winging his black cassock; his head, slightly tilted to one side, seemed to give a welcome even before the words were spoken.

'Do come in, Miss Hargreaves. I hope you had a pleasant journey. How do you like our new railway station?'

She had expected to see a rather careworn solemn face above the dog collar but this chaplain (whose face she had never seen before and whose voice she had never heard) convinced her he could listen. Fear changed to nervous apprehension. He led her through the impressive entrance hall with its intricately tiled and polished floor, where no inmates ever trod. High above was a domed ceiling of stained glass. They walked along the panelled corridor to a reception room of cool elegance where the high ceiling and walls were gripped by a wide and intricate plaster cornice all picked out in gold. The silk-covered walls of pale gold seemed to suggest a civic pride strangely incongruous for the function of the building. Felicity had the feeling that the men who were ushered into this room would be handing over their top hats and silver-topped canes before the solemn business of running an asylum. The tall windows and the vast stretch of lawns, gardens, meadows and woods seemed a far cry from the wild man outside who had declared that everyone was dead.

The chaplain offered her an elegant chair.

'I think I must warn you, Miss Hargreaves, that this asylum is a showpiece for Bradford and district *brass*. Your father was at the opening...'

'I've never heard him refer to it,' Felicity said with an almost menacing pianissimo.

'It's the old cliché, isn't it? Out of sight, out of mind.'

The chaplain was wondering just how much he and Miss Hargreaves were going to say. Safer to keep to his role of guide.

'The rest of the place is solidly built and kept as shipshape as we can. But when you feel critical, as you will, Miss Hargreaves, try to remember that there are over eight hundred patients here, ranging from the dangerously disturbed inmates to gentle folk who should never be kept in.'

'Well, my aunt is one of those, surely?'

The chaplain hesitated. 'You don't *stay* sane, my dear, if you are treated as *in*sane. Keepers are neither trained nor educated and they've each got the total responsibility of anything from thirty to fifty inmates.'

'What about the dangerous ones?' she asked, unsure of her ground.

The Reverend Anthony Thompson thought quickly. Knowing there was to be a visitor today, the nurses would have played for safety and those whose outbursts were unpredictable and spasmodic would be out of view. Jim Smiles, who, every now and again, had to wear padded gloves; the red-haired man the inmates called Willie might expose himself to visiting females; Maggie Jones, who, usually normal, could not keep her fingers away from

46

a female visitor's handbag or jewellery... The chaplain, while keeping up polite conversation, was going through a checklist in his mind.

'Perhaps I should explain that Barlockend is almost entirely self-supporting. All these lost souls have jobs which relate, if possible, to whatever they did before they were put away. It is not always easy to get the right occupation. We have a violinist here with fine sensitive fingers – I'll tell you more about him later – and two schoolteachers, your aunt, of course, is one... However, most of them come from manual or mechanical jobs of some kind.'

'But whatever work do they give my aunt to do? I was told by people who knew her better than I that she was very fastidious, well read and did very fine sewing.'

'Indeed, you may see her sewing this afternoon. The approved ones are having their day-room jobs before and after the band. Your aunt will be there now. Let us go and meet her!'

As they moved out of the central block, so the corridor became darker and greyer. The smell of unwilling cleanliness – a battle fought by carbolic and Sunlight soaps – warned Felicity that human beings were not far away. Travelling through the air were some alarming sounds: cries of lost souls; childish whimpering, sudden shrieks.

How much more normal was the general sound of the fifty or so women sitting on benches lining the walls of the day-room. The unholy sounds must have been coming from far away – where? She was glad when the chaplain shut the day-room door. He and she had been sitting long enough in profile in the reception room for her to notice the patrician bone-structure, the cerebral brow, the almost totally grey generous head of hair. What surprised her most was the air of 'mine-host' he conveyed as he stood up in front of this motley crowd. Without unduly raising his voice he over-topped their mutters, moans and the belligerent silences and spoke as if to friends.

'This is Miss Hargreaves, who has come to see you all today and listen to the band. Shall we give her a clap of welcome?'

The nurse and keeper who were in attendance seemed embarrassed and shared a *not us* look. The chaplain instinctively knew that clapping is an easy, relaxing, friendly exercise and that they had so few occasions that merited it. Only one person in the room – the woman who had a stub where her right arm used to be – would not be able to join in. He quietly went over to the silent young girl and, sitting beside her, stretched his right palm across her body to her left palm and clapped with her until she chortled with joy, hardly able to believe she could produce such a sound. A few clapped grotesquely: one with hands under the sheet she was repairing; another with a hand gripping a darning mushroom inside a man's matted sock: a florid woman with bloodshot eyes clapped her hands on to her puffed-out cheeks, exploding them loudly as she did so. Most of the women, from the boisterous to the limp, kept their eyes on Felicity and stopped clapping as they watched her go to the chaplain and whisper: 'Would you like me to walk round and chat to them?'

His grateful smile gave her courage.

In the last hour Felicity had changed from a cosseted young lady to a woman desperately anxious to show the right kind of compassion. Sympathy would not do.

With very few words, perceptive eyes and generous hands she moved from one to the other, commenting on the sewing, knitting, macramé and rag-rugs. One childlike pretty little woman, her eyes fixed on the pointed ends of the thick knitting needles, was lifting each thread with time-taking precision, chanting, 'In, over, through, off! In, over, through, off!' as if it were her total vocabulary and the dish-cloth her only worldly possession.

Felicity moved on to the next woman, whose eyes were wandering in another world. She picked up a thick crochet needle and was handing it to the toothless distraught old lady.

'Is this yours? What are you knitting?'

'It's for my baby... Have you brought her? She's only a little bairn, you know. She needs me... You will bring her, won't you?'

Felicity felt callous in leaving her but what could she do but move on? She was relieved to find a group of four happily winding wool.

On the other side of the room, quite alone, was a frail woman labelled with a red star. Her head was lowered, almost to her knee. It was obvious that she did not wish to be seen by any stranger. As she bent even lower, the rough cotton handkerchief she was hemming fell down on the floor. Felicity bent down, picked it up and tried to make a friendly overture.

'What neat hemming! It must be difficult to do these corners.'

The chaplain, who had been silently following, startled her with a comment, breathed closely into her ear: 'This is your aunt, Miss Hargreaves. When you have gone round the room would you like to take Miss Ackroyd to the reception room and look at her sewing there?' Then bending down to the withdrawn face he said gently: 'Miss Ackroyd, here is your niece, Miss Felicity Hargreaves,

48

who has come to see you. You are her *aunt*! Isn't it a wonderful surprise to see your niece here?'

The lifeless head shot up, the face contorted into anger and, focussing on the chaplain, she shrieked with a cry one could not believe could come from such a frail form. It was high-pitched, sharp-edged, menacing and mad.

'I'm not her aunt. I'm not anybody's aunt. I'm a sister: a twin sister. I don't know you!' she burst out at Felicity. 'I don't want *you*! I want my sister!' And then in a wail dwindling to despair: 'I've forgotten her name ... her name ... my twin...'

Quietly crying into her rough apron she made her final appeal: 'Bring her, bring her! She'll tell me her name, I know she will...'

The chaplain led Felicity out to a bench in the corridor. Sitting down beside her he touched the back of her hand.

'Now, my dear, try to understand what I am going to say to you. Of course you are upset and you feel, as I do, utterly helpless. But you *have* helped her and you'll never know how much.'

'But I haven't *done* anything, I've just made her angry...'

'Don't you realise? She has talked. You've made her *talk*. There are days and weeks when she never speaks at all. She's has that anger and painful need bottled up. You've released it.'

Felicity took time to accept consolation.

'I think I understand. Perhaps we *all* have things we bottle up and don't tell anybody...'

The chaplain tried again. 'I can't show you her medical report; it's not allowed. The doctor writes a brief comment once a month. I have copied out a few examples.' He took a slip of paper from his pocket and read: ' "Remains apprehensive and rarely speaks... Is quiet and orderly. Lacks self-confidence... Sits in the ward doing nothing... Unable to recount recent happenings... Is not interested in other people... Refuses to answer questions..." ' And then he added bitterly: 'It hardly needs a doctor for that sort of report. I think they just take the nurse's word for it. But then if you have eight hundred or so reports to write, what can you expect?'

'But how *can* she talk without a *listener*?' Felicity said, almost to herself.

The two fell silent. Both were relieved by the diversion of music. The chaplain rose.

'Listen, there's the band! Come to the window and watch!'

Felicity felt as if she were moving somebody else's numb body. It was grotesque that the band was playing *Home, Sweet Home*. The irony of the tune seemed lost on the hundred or so men and women who poured out into the high-walled garden like children into a playground. Some had joined hands; some skipped; others dragged their feet; a few, drunk with the freedom and fresh air, sprang into a wild bacchanalia... The remnants of the crowd tried to heave their clamped up bodies just far enough to see the five bandsmen. Unable to walk any further, they crumpled down defeated on to the grass.

'Ah! Miss Hargreaves, can you see the violinist? He used to be a performer and a teacher. When he's playing he's the sanest man in the world, and the happiest, but he hardly ever plays now because there's a maniac trying to smash his violin. So if he plays he has to have a keeper with him – and they haven't the time... He's asked to be locked up with his violin in a padded cell, but that's not allowed. God, what a waste of a talent and a man!'

'But does he *have* to be in an asylum? Could he not be cured?'

This was such an unanswerable question that the chaplain changed the subject.

'I can't see Miss Ackroyd! Can you see her?'

The band was just finishing: *Come landlord fill the flowing bowl...* The refrain of 'For tonight we'll merry, merry be' seemed singularly inappropriate, thought Felicity, but what song *could* tune in with this bizarre world?

'Let us see if your aunt is still in the day-room, shall we?'

She followed the chaplain through the door, returning to the reek the bodies had left. The carbolic had fought a losing battle, leaving only a trace of the early-morning scrub. The solitary figure was still in the same chair rubbing the rough unhemmed handkerchief backwards and forwards across her body. It was difficult at first to sort out the moaned and muttered words but when Felicity and the chaplain stood in front of her the message and the mime stunned them.

'I am rotten, rotten from here down' – she thumped across her waist almost violently. 'The whole world knows I'm rotten.' Her eyes flashed accusation. 'You've been out to tell them all, haven't you? You don't *need* to tell them. They know I'm rotten ... the whole world knows...'

The longest speech Amy Ackroyd had made since she was a teacher in a classroom echoed around the room... The soliloquy silenced both listeners. Without exchanging a look they brought their compassionate hands to hers. Gradually the outburst diminished into whimpering. Stroked hands calmed the haunted mind.

Felicity remembered that she had a small silver-cased flask of eau-de-cologne in her bag and a very special lace-edged Irish linen handkerchief. She sprinkled the water generously and laid the folded handkerchief across her aunt's troubled brow. Everything went quiet. The strains of *My Bonnie lies over the ocean* came lapping into the room like healing waves from a settled sea. Felicity and the chaplain seemed oblivious that they were both humming invisibly, willing their patient to fall asleep.

Nurse Haslam barged in, not with any intention of being cruel, just asserting her rights. 'Why aren't you out with the others, dearie?'

Her one aim was to unify her charges into apathy.

She turned away with a shrug of her shoulders as the chaplain signalled that Amy was asleep. He was someone she could not order around.

'Not the right place, not the right time,' she muttered to herself as she strutted away.

The chaplain pointed to the institution's wall clock, which ticked these senseless lives away.

'Time to go,' he whispered.

Outside the door he said, 'You still have half an hour before you need to leave for the train, so I suggest we go back to the reception room. If I may, I would like to talk to you. Perhaps I can help you to understand a little of this macabre world.'

She and the chaplain sat each side of a chess table. There were no pieces to move.

'Miss Hargreaves, I want you to have a rest and revive a little before you go home. Just close your eyes and concentrate on the good you have done by coming today, while I get some tea.'

The Reverend Anthony Thompson made his way to the kitchen and returned carrying a tray with china tea-cups. Felicity thought of the stained enamel mugs she had seen stacked up on three-tiered trolleys near the roped kitchen lifts.

'Would you like to pour the tea? I always think ladies do it more graciously than men.'

Felicity felt critical that he could switch into this smooth world with such ease. She tried to steady the shaking teapot but she was glad that he did not offer to pour the tea for her.

He took time before he asked the first question.

'Are you glad you came?'

Felicity hedged. 'Well, *glad* is not quite the word, is it?'

'No, I suppose it isn't. Shall we, between us, try to find the right words?'

'I feel shocked.'

'Yes of course.'

He drank his tea to make a much-needed pause.

'Anything you think you could do?'

'Not at the moment. Just now I feel quite helpless and very, very weak.'

'If I suggest something which perhaps you might do, I hope you will not think I am forcing your return.'

'Does it sound very feeble if I ask that you pilot me again? And then of course I will come.'

'It is not always easy. Remember, there are over eight hundred here. Sometimes I have to forget about their souls and help a keeper or a nurse manacle a troubled body.'

She realised how fragile his social composure had been. He was almost impatient to make her face truths.

'Until today there were only two who had ever had a visitor at the asylum. Now I hope there are to be three. I told you that your aunt has days of not speaking at all. Yet only a few months ago I found her reeling out lines of poetry that she knew by heart. It could have been Browning – or Wordsworth – but poetry falls on deaf ears as far as I am concerned. Suddenly she couldn't remember what came next, so she asked me and I didn't know! And she cried. She asked me to bring her the book which her twin had given her... And there was not a single member of her family, no-one in the world I knew, whom I *could* ask; until you wrote to me!'

Felicity caught her breath. 'But I *can* help. It is a strange co-incidence that earlier this week I found books by the Brownings which my aunts sent to one another for their twenty-first birthday presents. I am sure I can smuggle one out of the house. But will she snatch it from me and not give it back? What would happen to it then?'

'That is a risk we shall have to take. They are not allowed any personal possessions. Anything they receive, which they rarely do, is confiscated or goes into the general pool. They do not even have a locker. That beautiful lace handkerchief you left on her forehead will either be appropriated by a nurse or it will go into the communal laundry of pauper clothes and bed linen.'

There was a practical understanding between them which released questions.

'Mr Thompson, may I ask you, would it help if I *prayed* for her?'

The chaplain's eyes mirrored years of hope, doubt, faith, compassion and despair. He almost looked as if he had been caught out.

The answer came slowly: 'My dear Miss Hargreaves, I have

prayed for these poor souls every day for six years and you can see for yourself how little it has done for them. They are herded together to listen to *me*. What time have I to listen to *them*? And what prayer could I say which would be right for each one? You remember this afternoon, when we were listening to the band, seeing that wild red-headed man pick up a chair and rush the legs towards the keeper? Compare him with your aunt and dear gentle Lawrence the violinist. We're not all equal, my dear. We're grossly, unfairly, miserably unequal. I hang on to my faith – and it is not easy – because some day, some day, I hope to meet this great compassionate God whose vision is so very different from mine.'

The face Felicity was looking at now seemed quite different from the one which had greeted her at the front door. The sad folds around the eyes and the shadowed cheeks spoke of an unfulfilled life and spurious authority. She reverted to her unanswered question.

'Would it help if I prayed for my aunt?'

'Do what you feel you can. You may not help your aunt by praying, but it could help *you*. I'm afraid I use prayer as an escape.'

All Felicity wanted, for she was as intellectually and emotionally lonely as her confider, was for him to go on talking, so she asked: 'Tell me, how would it help?'

'We are all very lonely people, my dear, and in those dark stretches of solitude each one of us is hoping for a listener. I think the trouble is that folk use prayer like a begging bowl. Try not to do that! "*Felicity*," as you must know, means happiness. Whether you pray or not, you could bring snatches of happiness to that wronged aunt of yours. And, if I may say so, also to me.'

It was a relief to both of them to relax into this more practical conversation, which triggered a new thought in Felicity's mind.

'That reminds me of something important I have not asked you as yet.'

He interrupted her with a laugh. 'You treat me as omniscient, but my dear, I can only give you simple, and not exactly virtuous, answers. But carry on. I will try.'

'This is just a plain, factual one: Should I tell my parents I've been to see her?'

'It is neither plain nor merely factual, Felicity. It is a very complex problem and involves too many people you would surely disturb. I suppose a minister of the church should not be encouraging anyone to lie, but some lies wear a comfortable wrapping of divine ignorance. And this is surely one!'

He rose and stood tall with his back to the window. He looked down on her, rather savouring the role of preacher. Lowering himself to the window seat he cupped his face in his hands in thought.

'For all these years your parents have donned useful blinkers which have completely blocked out any sight of Barlockend or of your mother's sister. As far as their small, well-ordered, utterly sane world goes, your aunt does not exist. If you were to tell them of your secret visit – and more especially of your future intended visits – you would only bring down the scaffolding which is supporting both their public lives.'

'But how am I to wangle these visits to Barlockend? I've had a good ruse for this visit but it has been extremely contrived.'

'Well, I have thought of one, but it may not appeal to you. Let me explain. Just to keep myself sane and to keep my brain alert I conduct a Latin class at the Lodge where I live. A small group of us meet once a month and *enjoy* Latin by reading fine prose aloud. It isn't a pompous affair. We work out the meaning without too much reference to grammar. The clean logic of Latin pleases my unpoetic mind. You are most welcome to join us. By the way, do you play or sing, Felicity?'

'Only the piano. I tried the violin but I didn't like the sound. Neither did anyone else.' She was able to laugh now at her ineptitude. 'My young brother Henry said it sounded like an alley cat. And he's tone-deaf! But I enjoy playing the piano.'

'You could do that here!'

As Felicity walked out of Aireley station she was finding it hard to believe that it was only this morning that she had left home. In truth it was a whole lifetime. She had now to remind herself that she had really been in Harrogate all that extraordinary day and that her tea-table conversation would need to reflect it.

The Reverend Anthony Thompson had walked away from the departing train thinking how inadequate he had been in not giving Felicity some sort of support about prayer and belief. Scholarly dogma embarrassed him. She had been the first person he had felt he could talk to since he had deliberately left Magdalen to take on this compassionate service. Her visit offered a challenge. He would accept it with all the tangled web of deception it entailed. But what was her future? Surely she must not become just a lady-in-waiting for a moneyed marriage!

54

I'll write to her, I will write c/o Aireley post office to urge her to use her brains and her imagination to do something useful with her life, he thought.

All the negative thoughts now dissolved away. There seemed some purpose in life. Suddenly a wave of elation ran through him.

This girl, so vital and vulnerable – what would she make of her life?

The Hargreaves' high tea had now graduated to be a meal which could hardly be called dinner – it would have been pretentious to do so – but socially could not be called *tea*.

'And did you see anything you liked in Louis Copés, Felicity?'

'No, Mother.' At least Mrs Hargreaves' daughter was speaking the truth!

'Father,' said Mrs Hargreaves, now feeling that it was time she asserted herself. 'You haven't opened that letter that was pushed through the door. It's there beside your plate...'

The small envelope did not need the large carving knife which her husband used to slit it open, but it quickened the operation. The note was quickly read.

'Well, I can't think what Dr Bennett wants to see me about unless he's begging for some charity. There's no-one ill in this house. He suggests tomorrow after his surgery. Get Hilda to take a message to say any time after eight.'

'Just as you say, Father.'

Felicity's mind ran round in circles: the chaplain; the asylum; her aunt; Belinda; Bradford College; aunt Grace; Edinburgh ... and now this letter.

But all she said was: 'May I leave the table, Father?' Whereupon, Felicity Hargreaves took her overburdened head to the peace and quiet of her own room.

4

The front door bell at Stonegarth announcing the arrival of Dr Bennett was a signal to Felicity to be well out of the way for what would prove to be a tricky conversation. As Jessie went through the front hall to open the door, she and Felicity almost collided at the foot of the staircase.

Dr Bennett, following Jessie across the hall to the smoking room, saw a girl with a slim waist and an erect spine nearing the landing. It looked like their daughter. Why rush upstairs? he thought as he crossed the hall.

'Dr Bennett, Sir,' Jessie announced.

'Come in, Doctor. Fair while since we had a sight of you. But as doctoring is yer job it's a pleasure we can do without.' Hargreaves laughed uneasily at his own joke.

Although it was a warm summer evening they settled down each side of the fire-grate in the stuffy little room. The two heavy leather winged armchairs shut out all that remained of the daylight.

The two heads, less than a foot or two apart, exemplified their different occupations; the pipe-filling ritual showed their contrasting personalities. Hargreaves, without waiting for his guest, picked up a handful of shag, rubbed it in his palm, and packed it tight into his trumpet-shaped meerschaum with his thick tobacco stained forefinger.

The doctor waited to fill his lightweight briar straight from the bowl, casually allowing small strands to stray.

The silent ceremony of pipe-filling gave both a welcome delay in opening the conversation.

Hargreaves leaned over the table and lighted Bennett's pipe from the gas lamp with a taper, and then broke the comfortable silence.

'And what brings you here, Doctor?'

'Knowing what a good Mason you are, Hargreaves – though not in my Lodge – I wanted you to be one of the first to know of a scheme the Templars have in mind, and, of course, to get your advice and help...'

56

'Meaning yer wants some brass, I suppose!'

'Well, you can't do anything without it, can you? But this is going to be a joint affair of all the Airedale and Bradford Lodges. It won't come heavily on individuals. You know better than anyone does how good Masons are at stumping up for good causes. It's not lost on me, either, that your Lodge always tops the list.'

'An' all because I've got a foolproof scheme. When list goes out and we sign our names, I put me own at top with a sum that would shame no-one. Can't put half a crown under that, now, can yer? But let's be hearing what it's all about.'

'Just before I explain what we have in mind, might I ask a personal question?'

'Nothing to stop yer.'

'You're a member of *three* Lodges. Why? You must have a good reason.'

'In business yer needs to know 'oo yer competitors are, 'oo to trade with and where to put yer brass. Not like your job, Doctor, where business comes to your doorstep. But it's not just business – I like Masons' ceremonies, dignified like. Something outside t'mill. I think it's right not to get too cracked on a church or chapel. All very right in their place of a Sunday. I'm a Methodist on account of mi' father, grandfather and great-grandfather. Followers of Wesley! All we have to believe in in t'Masons is one God. We can be any religion we like. That puts the Church of England's high and mighty attitude in its place. They can't turn their noses up at Chapel if they're Masons.' Hargreaves paused, eyeing the doctor with the same penetrating look he gave wool samples. 'But, fair's fair! Let's be knowing why *you're* a Mason. They tell me you're a bad attender anyways on.'

Dr Bennett, taken unawares, realising he had never been asked this question before, took his time.

'I suppose I drifted into it. My father introduced me after I qualified – he was a medieval scholar, interested in the Knights Templars, the Crusaders...'

'Ee, I can't be doing with all that claptrap – what about your missis? I've trained mine. She never asks questions. I keep my leather case with the regalia in my dressing room and she's never seen that case open and never will.'

The doctor stiffened. 'My wife believes in us each having our own interests. I don't interfere with her Votes for Women and she doesn't butt in on my Masonry. But we've one thing in common, though – we both believe in women doctors! Women need them!'

The blood rose in Hargreaves' face. 'I'll tell yer this, Doctor, my wife'd *die* before she'd have a woman mess about with her body. I reckon she's right too. 'Tis a man's job.'

From this remark, Bennett knew that his ultimate battle of getting Felicity to Edinburgh was going to be an uphill job. He had not even started the immediate move, and time was being talked away.

He was ready to make his point just as Hargreaves blurted out: 'Well, don't beat about the bush! Let's be hearing what you want from me.'

'Briefly, Hargreaves, the doctors in the Aire Valley would like to have a biology laboratory where they could send specimens to be tested: blood, sputum, urine... As it is we have to send everything to Bradford or Leeds. You see, you and I, and all the rest of us, are way behind Salts, Listers and Fosters. They have their own sanatorium and Listers have their own laboratory...'

Arthur Hargreaves stopped himself from butting in. Jealousy of Salts had run through three generations of Hargreaves. It was the largest mill in the Aire Valley, the reason for the model village of Saltaire, built by Sir Titus Salt forty years ago and named after him. Even the Wesley Chapel, built with Hargreaves' wool money, stood in the shadow of the classical building of the Salt Congregational Church and the Titus Salt Mausoleum!

'But let's leave this discussion until another day, shall we? I don't want to press you on joining. We've one or two in already who have their eye on the chairmanship...'

That very word jerked Hargreaves into action. 'Na don't get me wrong. I *am* interested. It's only sense that I have a bit of time to turn it over. I think you know that I'd like to see the plans and how the brass is going to be used before I put *my* name to it.'

'Of course, Sir, of course. Your name stands high all over the West Riding. And I think I am right in saying that this enterprise will make it stand even higher.' Dr Bennett paused before adding: 'Oh, there's one thing I forgot to mention. We'd like the laboratory to be used by the woollen industry for tests. Everyone in England knows about the anthrax troubles that the spinning mills had last year. You wool-men would save thousands of pounds if samples of all your wools were tested for pests and poisons. Do you know how many sorters died last year handling that dreadful wool infection?'

Arthur Hargreaves, respected member of the Wool Exchange, needed no more time to think it over. But his Yorkshire pride made him deliver his positive answer with negative caution.

'I'll tell yer this, Bennett, if it's going to have my name put into it, then it's got to be, as my lads would say: "Reet up ter t'mark!"'

The doctor's smile included agreement and respect for the man – in spite of his pomposity.

'I think if we present a good case, Bradford College would provide accommodation. What a marvellous place it is! Did you know it's the largest and most up-to-date technical college in the British Isles, outside London?'

Hargreaves showed some enthusiasm, but extravagant words of praise such as *marvellous* were never uttered by a real Yorkshireman.

'Well, I had heard summat o't'sort.'

Dr Bennett drew on his pipe before uttering his next words. 'Have you ever thought that perhaps you and I were not very selective when we chose the Academy for our two girls? My daughter was made head prefect to use up her energy. She's a leader and so could yours be too. She's made up her mind to study subjects the Academy never heard of: So I'm enrolling her for three days a week at the college, for courses in chemistry and biology, starting September 17th!'

Time was getting on and the doctor, conscious that he had only made two or three winning moves, decided to jump a few hurdles.

'They tell me, Hargreaves, that your daughter Felicity is one of the cleverest girls the Academy ever turned out; that she was way ahead of most of the teachers – especially the piano and singing teachers.'

'If she is, then why didn't they put that on her report? All they said was that she had brains but didn't make enough use of 'em. As for piano playing, so she should be able to, what with two pianos in the house!'

The doctor smiled in quick agreement. 'There you are, Sir, you admit she has brains. Don't *you* want her to use them? You've used yours to good purpose!'

Arthur Hargreaves' enjoyment of the compliment speeded his surrender. He smiled into his pipe, remembering, too, the bargain he had made in buying the grand piano cheap at the old rectory sale. He tapped his empty pipe in satisfying rhythm and slowed down, weighing the future.

'Yer've set me thinking, Bennett. I've always thought she was a cut or two above Aireley girls. Now we'll mebbe prove it. But hold hard. Whatever could she do with chemistry and biology?'

The doctor remembered an announcement in the local paper. 'Didn't I read that you'd engaged a new manager with a BSc degree to marshal all the information on new chemicals in dyes and fibre treatment? And what's this I hear about France leaping way ahead in textiles? What about India? All that competition from abroad. But if I know my man, they're not going to get the better of Arthur Hargreaves. You're surely ahead of Salts with this chap with a science degree!'

'That's different. He's a feller.'

Bennett played a further card. 'Your daughter may be clever, but I hear she can be wilful. Belinda says that if *she* gets something Felicity hasn't got, you'll soon know.'

'Yer don't have to tell me she's strong-minded. She can twist her mother round her little finger. But what's all this got to do with biology?'

'Well, it's not going to be a great success having her at home all the time, is it?'

An awkward silence surrounded the smokeless pipes. The next question surprised the doctor, since it seemed to be one step nearer:

'How's your Belinda getting ter t'Tech? Yer not letting her travel on her own are yer?'

'She'd certainly set her heart on taking Felicity along with her. But I said I thought there was not a hope if some parents hold – well, old-fashioned ideas, shall we say?'

'Old-fashioned! Old-fashioned?' Hargreaves exploded. 'Just you come and look at our new carding machine. The most up to date in the country. That'd stop your gab about *old-fashioned*.'

It was time for yet another compliment from the doctor.

'Yes, folks in Aireley got very excited when all those parts came up on the train. They say it's a beauty! I get the impression from my patients who work for you that they've a lot of respect for their gaffer. And people do tell gossip to their doctors!'

The governor came magnificently into his own as he repeated almost the same words he had said to Felicity, but now in a different accent: 'Why don't you come up and see it? You'll get a surprise, Doctor, a big surprise.' He pushed the tobacco bowl towards his admirer. 'Have another fill.' Taking the taper from the hearth, he reached up to the gas jet thus adding yet more light to the doctor's glowing face.

It was a relief for Jeremy Bennett to finally escape from so much hot air and slice through the cool evening air with his bicycle. He had never anticipated whisky with so much pleasure.

As the glass emptied so he congratulated himself on diagnosing and treating Hargreaves' weak spots. They hardly needed the skill of a general practitioner, just patience and common sense, blended with a smattering of homely psychology.

He liked the chap. After all, he *did* keep over two hundred Aireley folk in work!

It was easier to slump in his armchair than get up to bed. His thoughts wandered. Odd family, the Hargreaves. But that was a great girl he'd brought into the world all of eighteen years ago!

All the time Felicity's father had been in deep conversation with Dr Bennett, her mother having been left alone in the drawing room, Felicity was busily reading and writing letters in her own room.

Wanting to keep a special letter intact, she prised the flap of the envelope without breaking the dark blue seal bearing a capital B.

How exciting that Miss Butterworth should write before term had started! And why? She read the letter not as the *new woman* she intended to be but as a schoolgirl, uncertain of her freedom.

My dear Felicity,

No doubt you will be surprised to see a letter from me before the term has started, but an odd coincidence in my holiday urges me to write to you.

You have been much in my thoughts ever since those final days of term when rejoicing and regrets mingled, especially in your special 'set'.

I shall return to the Academy to the same routine, the stilted politics of the staff room, and shall miss you and your group more than you will ever know.

Now that you have left school, I hope you will allow me to say some of the unspoken thoughts that school walls hide. Spinsterhood I am sure is to be my destiny for I have never met a man with whom I could share my innermost thoughts, and I do not suppose I ever shall. Women are so much more sensitive and imaginative; that is why I enjoyed sharing the love sonnets of Shakespeare, Donne and Keats with you. How privileged I was, too, to make you my Elizabeth in *Pride and Prejudice* and my Catherine in Emily Bronte's *Wuthering Heights* in those private elocution sessions. Many we contrived.

My dear Felicity, God has given you more than a brain and

a body, he has given you a mind, a heart and a soul. I pray you not to waste these gifts. May I help?

My own broken-backed education is a source of deep regret. I think I hinted to you that my father lost all his money on the Stock Exchange in the '70s and was declared bankrupt and that this coincided with my having secured a place at Girton to study law. The Academy post was not my choice but a quick necessity. I can tell you now, that as an unqualified, uncertificated teacher, I receive a so-called stipend of £50 per year. However, it has given me the unconvenanted blessing of teaching literature to eager young girls. You will appreciate that, in teaching literature, I could express those 'sweet silent thoughts' vicariously.

I am writing to you from my home in Knaresborough, in my only exeat, in the hope of seeing you again.

My sister, in term time, and I, in the holidays, tend to go to any lecture or event that takes place in Knaresborough since there are so few. This week the lecture with slides was on 'Medical Missionary Schools in South-West Africa', and who do you think were the speakers? None other than our Academy Chaplain and dear Dr Bennett, Belinda's father!

Before the lecture started he asked if I would stay behind when it was over as he had something he wished to tell me about Belinda.

On and off through the flickering slides I did wonder what Belinda was planning; something outrageous I rather hoped! It never occurred to me that it would have anything to do with *you*. (Although your homes are not far away from one another and her father is your family doctor, I realised that, in a school, a year creates a rigid barrier.)

To my great surprise, Dr Bennett told me that you and Belinda had met and that she was including you in all her plans – the immediate one being to enrol you both as day students at the Bradford Technical College. He was most concerned about how your father would react to the idea. I think he said he was seeing him this week. Apparently Dr Bennett has friends on the governing council who also support the Suffragettes! So that augurs well.

May I give one piece of advice? If you are studying scientific subjects I think it is important for you to balance them with literary and humane studies. If there are English literature classes available I do hope you will take advantage of them, otherwise all the glory will be taken out of the language in writing out H_2O etc. and letters saying: 'Yours of the 4th inst.'

One immediate suggestion I would like to make. Would you, if your parents agree, allow me to come over in the Christmas holiday in order that you, Belinda and I have a few reading sessions together? I have just finished reading Thomas Hardy's *Tess of the D'Urbervilles* and should so much like to share it with you.

I do not think I ever told you that my second cousin is the Vicar of Aireley's wife. They often suggest that I come over to stay with them. Previously I have only ever been for lunch or tea.

The spring term starts on January 14th; I shall, therefore, propose myself to Cousin Miranda to arrive on January 9th and stay until the 12th.

Teachers always seem old to their pupils and so I must seem antique to you. May you and I drop the teacher/student relationship and be trusting friends? First you must know that my birthday is today. I shall be but twenty-four, only six years older than you, and only five years older than Belinda. The life I have led makes me *feel* so much older!

You remember Browning: 'Grow old along with me. The best is yet to be!'

I hope I shall always remain,

Your devoted friend,

Roberta (Butterworth)

P.S. I think I am right in assuming that you and Belinda now share confidences. Knowing your impulsive generosity and how articulate you both are, I think it would be simpler if I gave you permission to share this letter.

Felicity was re-reading Roberta Butterworth's letter for the third time when she heard Dr Bennett departing to her father's 'Goodnight!' and her father's surprising addition: 'Thanks for coming!' Her father's mill-keyed voice carried up the staircase; she could not hear Dr Bennett's more cultivated tones. Why should a letter make her pulse race? What could she write in reply?

Were there emotions for which no words had been compounded? She felt as she did when painting or listening to music – not words – but vibrations raced along the veins and in her heart. She tried to imagine how she, Felicity, would feel if *she* were doomed to the life of a resident mistress in a boarding school.

She imagined the depression that would descend on Roberta on the first day of term, singing that meant-to-be bonding hymn:

> Lord behold us with thy blessing
> Once again assembled here.

Felicity sat on her dressing table stool and let her thoughts drift to the young Felicity in the third form with her wild dreams of her loved one. She blushed into the mirror, not knowing whether to laugh or cry at the trivia which created schoolgirl bliss: walking and talking with Miss Butterworth in crocodile; eating and talking with her twice a term at the lunch table; declaiming Juliet's speeches in duologue (with Roberta as an ardent Romeo) in her private diction lessons:

> My bounty is as boundless as the sea
> My love as deep, the more I give to thee!

There was something innocent and pure about these early loves ... or was there?

She decided not to show Belinda the letter. *Pull yourself together. Don't be an idiot. You're nearly eighteen!* She did pull herself together but was uncertain who was *herself*.

Yes, of course Roberta must come in the Christmas holidays. She would concoct a tale tomorrow of the academic generosity of Miss Butterworth; the opportunity to do extra study.

Better if they had the lessons at Belinda's house.

Her thoughts moved swiftly. If her father had agreed with Dr Bennett then there was no time to lose.

When at last she got into bed all she could see and think about were those wretched souls locked up for the night in the paupers' asylum. What part had her mother played in her aunt being locked away? Honour indeed! *Dear God! Am I expected to honour them?*

Where on earth do I belong?

It was unusual for Gertrude to be wide-awake after ten fifteen or so, but tonight she wanted to keep awake to hear what the doctor and her husband had talked about. He strode through the bedroom to his dressing room, then undressed, had a sketchy wash, donned his huge white linen night-gown and sank into the feather bed beside her with a brief 'Goodnight!' There was only one night

64

in the week, Saturday, when this ritual was lengthened. But tonight, curious about the doctor's visit, she ventured to enquire: 'What had Dr Bennett to say for himself?' The flat Yorkshire tone conveyed nothing of her inquisitiveness.

There was not a stir from the body at her side. 'Just a Masonic matter. Nothing to concern you.'

Gertrude, so used to the cold douche, accepted this reply as normal conversation and turning on her side was soon asleep.

Arthur, who took sound sleep for granted, was irritated that Bennett's long discussion was keeping him awake. *Have I been too soft? What have I been let in for?*

He argued with himself until the grandfather clock in the hall struck eleven; then, reacting to his own persuasion, saw himself opening the new medical biology laboratory in the presence of the Lord Mayor. He seldom dreamt, but tonight, bursting with pride, he travelled in time to see his daughter capped and gowned. Reality is absolute in dreams and the gown did not surprise him. It suited the Hargreaves ego. The dream slid away but left a shadow of purple and ermine on his waking mind.

That Saturday was an eventful day for the Hargreaves and the Bennetts. Life was never the same again.

It was the day when Gertrude asserted herself.

For three years now the Hargreaves had had a cook. It was three years ago that Gertrude and Arthur had gone into battle. Not for the first time, Arthur won.

The building of Stonegarth and its occupation by Arthur and Gertrude Hargreaves was an historic event in Airedale, for the family was moving from a simple double-fronted stone house in the industrial town of Shipley to live near the Aireley Worsted Mill, which Hargreaves had taken over. This more opulent house had a treble-fronted facade with a lavish conservatory on one side and on the other a kitchen and billiard room block, topped with a tower flashing a gilt cock-crowned weather vane. Hargreaves, like all the other Bradford wool-men, never doubted their ability to beat the rest of the world in wool dealing. They travelled and hassled for trade abroad, not to escape the cold, damp and dirt for a sunny climate, but in order to keep the furnaces in the mills and the fires in their thick-walled houses bright with Yorkshire coal.

Sometime before the house was finished, Arthur, carrying out discreet social research, learnt that any mill-owner of worth employed, in his large residence, a cook, a parlourmaid and a housemaid. Nothing less would do. *That's what the missis is going to have, like it or not.*

Gertrude had been brought up in a modest house, over the family pork butcher shop, the only servant being a general and a daily char. The kitchen with its great fire and range, the larder with its marble slabs and the pantry, were her mother's stronghold.

Friday was baking day as rigidly as Sunday was chapel day. By four o'clock on a Friday the two big dressers flaunted a display of large loaves, cobs, tea-cakes, fruit pies, egg and bacon pies, pasties, Eccles cakes, spice loaves and the odd Madeira or seed-cake.

Special days were reserved for the raised pork and veal and ham pies made for the shop. The foods celebrating religious festivals – hot-cross buns, simnel cakes, plum puddings and Christmas cakes – were more important than the ceremonies themselves. Gertrude accepted as the highest compliment that she *kept a good table* and was a *good provider*; she failed to realise that the same compliment was given to upper class women who rarely went into their kitchens.

It was three years ago, the first time in their eighteen years of marriage, that Arthur and Gertrude had a stand-up row. Fortunately Felicity and her brother had both gone back to school.

Gertrude's podgy lips were pouting. 'I never wanted a bigger house, you know that.'

'What yer should know is that a mill-owner's expected to make things easy for his wife! Ther's no pleasing yer!'

'It's not easy having a woman taking my place in the kitchen!'

'Stop whining! Your place is in the home, not over the oven.'

'And who do you think's going to make apple pies and custards the way you like them?'

'Don't be daft! Yer think a professional can't make a blooming apple pie!'

And so on ad nauseam. But his voice over-topped hers and in the end she gave in.

The first two years, though not to her liking, she managed by the simple expedient of giving the new cook three half-days off: Friday, Saturday and Sunday, unheard of in Yorkshire or any other county. All the baking and cooking of any consequence for the week was therefore done by Gertrude on those days. The cook, Ellen, with this bonus, could visit her West Riding family near Leeds and boast to everyone of her generous mistress: 'Ee, she's a real good'un an' a reet good cook, too!'

But this year had been a different matter. Ellen, who made good use of the three evenings of her three half-days off, did some strenuous courting with their groom and left to get married.

Ellen and Bob were the sort of amiable folk who carried good luck with them. Bob, the more literate of the two, had spotted an advertisement for a situation, which could have been made for them:

Wanted married couple: groom and cook.
Lodge gatehouse provided plus gas, coal and home produce.
Apply by letter with references. Box No.147.

Fortunately it seemed (but not for Gertrude) the Rector's maid had a sister-in-law, a widow who had been in service in London who wanted to come back to Airedale. Could Gertrude find a place for her?

And then a dangerous verbal recommendation from the Rector's maid herself: 'She doesn't just do home cooking. Proper la-di-da now, dinner parties and such. She says in 'er letters as she made things like horse doovers, and soofleas.'

After grumbling endlessly, Gertrude once again gave in to Arthur and so Winifred was engaged.

As with Ellen, Gertrude still had the satisfaction of doing the baking on cook's half-days off, which pleased both of them, as Winifred sneered at all the farinaceous food consumed by folk in Yorkshire. The final battle had come only this last week when Winifred had refused to serve Yorkshire pudding and gravy as a separate first course.

'Vulgar,' she'd declared.

For once, Arthur came into battle against cook: 'Ignorant bitch.'

This gave Gertrude courage to finish things once and for all. On this fateful Saturday morning, cook came into the morning room, as summoned, at nine o'clock. Gertrude was sitting on the edge of her chair, rubbing her hands nervously and pulling her thick lips in and out as if sending blasphemous words back into her throat.

To her surprise, it was Winifred who opened the conversation with complete confidence and a steady voice: 'Well, Madam, what can I do for you?'

'What you can do, Winifred, is *go!*'

Neither Gertrude nor Winifred ever remembered just how the conversation ended. All that anyone seems to remember was that Arthur, now they had no groom, drove Winifred, with three months' wages in her purse and her smart baggage, down to the early train. Meanwhile, Gertrude cooked the best steak and kidney pie for dinner Arthur had ever had since they came to Stonegarth.

'And tomorrow, Father, we'll have Yorkshire pudding *and* gravy for dinner, before the meat.'

Felicity Hargreaves was determined to make the best use of this Saturday, since Sundays at Stonegarth had to be kept holy.

So far there had been no time when she could talk to her father, although he had taken Saturday morning off, but that was to support her mother in the cook battle and get Winifred out of the way.

Felicity now set off for her three-mile walk to the Bennetts' house, calling at Elsie's on the way.

'Come through, Felicity. There's a letter from Edinburgh from your aunt Grace.'

Felicity was so used now to having the parlour as her reading room that she went through on her own. She read the letter and called out:

'Come in, leave the shop a minute, Elsie! Hear what aunt Grace says!'

The very words: *aunt Grace* were music to her ears.

My dearest Felicity,

I am delighted that you have, as I suggested, made friends with the Bennetts and that the doctor is helping you and his daughter to enrol for a course in chemistry and biology at Bradford College.

Let me know as soon as your father has carried out his part. You will have to move very quickly if you are to be in class on the first day of term!

When I mentioned Bradford College to my friend, he was delighted and referred to some of the professors and tutors there by name as having national reputations.

Do not be put off when I tell you that some of the women medical students here still have to fight for their right for clinical practice and observation at Leith Hospital and Edinburgh Royal Infirmary.

Believe me, my dear, women will have to fight for many years, in many spheres, and when they do get their rights they will still have more roles to play than men. Life will never be easy. But who wants ease?

Keep in touch, my dear, and never forget the support and love you will always have from

Your aunt Grace

It had been fine dry weather for so long that August that Felicity was surprised to be walking all the way to Belinda's home first in drizzle, then in showers and, finally, relentless rain.

Had her mother realised, Felicity doubted whether she would have been allowed to set off. Today would be a test of whether her parasol could do equal service as an umbrella.

It proved not. The sodden silk took all the weight it could and then became a sieve, making her hat, hair and dress sodden, too.

She expected sympathy and help from Belinda not the guffaws of laughter which greeted her as she stood at the Bennetts' front door, her neat body outlined with wet clothes.

'Come up to my room quick! I'll find you some of mine.'

It was not until the chemises, pantaloons and petticoats were put on that Felicity realised that Belinda's extra four inches in height were balanced by four inches more in girth. Belinda caught sight of Felicity in the wardrobe mirror and laughed aloud.

Probably the whole of their future friendship depended on this moment. Could Felicity laugh at herself? Would Belinda have laughed as much had *she* been soaked to the skin? Could they laugh together?

Felicity, now grinning at herself in the mirror, flapped the webbed-like sleeves over her hands. Then lifting the trailing skirt to free her legs, she stretched her mouth wide, goggled her eyes and did a brilliant impersonation of a frog. As she leaped round the room, so Belinda caught hold of the two webbed hands and led the singing and dancing of: 'A frog he would a wooing go...'

They were back in their carefree childhood days, singing uproarious nonsense concluding with the Lobster Quadrille:

Will you? won't you? will you? won't you?
   will you join the dance?
Will you? won't you? will you? won't you?
   won't you join the dance?

They collapsed on the floor on the final repeated lines, ending: '*Won't* you join the dance?'

With shared nonsense and relaxing laughter, friendship was sealed.

69

'Whatever is Belinda up to this time?' Hazel Bennett was in the surgery when the hilarity upstairs started. So used was she to Belinda's larger-than-life outbursts that, as usual, she ignored them. The noise was beginning to subside when she left the measuring glass and the bottles and went up to Belinda's room. Her first impression, on noticing the other figure, was that a child from the orphanage, dressed in an adult's cast-offs, had wandered in. Realising it was Felicity, she laughed with delight, thinking that one of Belinda's dressing up games was in progress. To Felicity's amazement Mrs Bennett pulled them both up from the floor and polkaed them round the room!

Half an hour's hilarity had gone before the girls even mentioned the reason for the morning's meeting. Questions were asked and answered at speed.

'Father's gone to the college. He's enrolling me. Is yours?'

'I don't know. The last I saw of him he was taking our cook, Winifred, to the train.'

'But doesn't he realise that you have to be enrolled *today*.'

'If we have, Father will be there! He'll go straight from the station. He doesn't miss anything!'

If a job needed doing, Arthur Hargreaves liked to be the one who did it – or saw that it was done! He was determined not to be outshone by their family doctor.

If he had not had to take that stupid Winifred to the train he could have got to the college ahead of Bennett and enrolled his own daughter first. In the event, it was the doctor who was chatting to the chemistry professor when Hargreaves arrived. This situation needed firm forward drive.

'Good morning, Doctor!' Then, not waiting for an introduction to the master, he turned and opened the conversation:

'I think we have met at some public function. You know me, I'm Councillor Hargreaves, but I meet so many people I can't remember names. Yes, now you remind me, we did meet at the Methodist rally. Didn't I present your lad with his attendance certificate?'

Love's blind and self-love blinder still. Hargreaves never noticed the wink which Dr Bennett, MD, and Dr Charles Cartwright, DSc, exchanged as the master moved on to his next aspiring entrant.

Why hadn't these two men brought their daughters with them?

70

he wondered in passing. He would have enjoyed introducing them to old Wilkinson, the college's fiery anti-suffragist.

After a morning of seeing round the vast building, examining its impressive equipment, reading notices, collecting prospectuses and timetables, the two fathers arrived at the foot of the main staircase.

The doctor, bending down towards Hargreaves, said quietly into his ear: 'Are you all right walking up these flights of stairs, Hargreaves?'

It was not meant to be insulting but it braced Hargreaves to make the most of his five foot eight inches. Ignoring the question, he put his feet on the first wide stone stair, which brought his eyes level with Bennett's.

'Yes, if it's fer something worth seeing.'

'Wait, Sir, you'll be pleased. Things have been moving.'

There was plenty of room to walk side by side. The doctor's bicycling had given him better breathing but he tactfully slowed down to Hargreaves' pace.

Strange, thought the doctor, that even at the end of the summer vacation we're breathing an odd mixture of sulphur, ether and methylated spirits! They continued up two flights in breathy silence:

'Here we are, Hargreaves! Or hope to be! I've two friends on the governing body and they have discovered that this room is not in use. They've got their eye on it for our medical biology lab!'

From the look he gave that room, Hargreaves could have been standing in a discarded shippen.

'Nay man, yer must be joking! I'll tell yer this for sure: none of my brass is going on this poky little 'ole!'

The rest of Saturday seemed to be swallowed up with each individual's separate concerns.

Gertrude spent Saturday afternoon in the pantry, changing the position of every cooking and baking pot, which Winifred had put in logical juxtaposition. Refined vowels were not needed for this triumphant chore and equally triumphant monologue. Winifred was put in her place with every pot that was moved.

Jam pan should be at t'back. There's wun o' chureen lids cracked. That's a daft place to put butter pats!

71

* * *

Felicity was down in the sitting kitchen asking Hilda if she could borrow one of her green overalls until she was able to buy two or three for herself in Bradford. This started Hilda off on where to buy the best and cheapest.

'*I'll* coom with yer to t'market! Ther'll see *you* coomin' a mile away, an' no mistake!'

Arthur Hargreaves spent the whole afternoon avidly reading the college prospectus. He was also talking to himself.

'So Bennett knew two of the governors, did he? Let's see who I know.' He scanned the list, trying to work out which were Bennett's supporters. 'Two doctors here on t'list. It could be them. Anyways on, there are four governors I know. Three of them are Masons! I'll go to their next Lodge meeting...' Thoughts, plans and order of action came in fast succession.

He had quite forgotten his daughter.

Sitting alone in his smoking room, thinking of the morning's proceedings he said aloud: 'By Gow, I could give 'em a better room in my mill – and give 'em t'gas and heating too!'

He let his inward eye travel through the mill, scanning every possible space. Then he said aloud: 'What about that room on t'second floor where discarded yarn samples are dumped? They're never used. No-one will ever know if I go and have a look tomorrow afternoon on my own.'

It had to be a very serious matter for Hargreaves to break the Sabbath. And it was!

On this same Saturday afternoon, Dr Bennett sat with his wife and daughter in the blue sitting room concentrating on the prospectus and the timetables. They were in total accord.

'It looks as if you need only go Tuesday, Wednesday and Thursday, Belinda,' the doctor said, handing the bleak statement to his wife and daughter.

'Heavens, Father, look at the next bit: *suitable for candidates in the Medical Board of Physicians and Surgeons.*'

Her mother turned the page: 'Here's the chemistry! Every hour is going to be filled. Oh dear! I'd like to see Mrs Hargreaves' face when *she* reads this!'

General Course in Chemistry – First Year

9 TO 10 A.M.	10 TO 11 A.M.	11 TO 12.30 P.M.	2 TO 5 P.M.

CHEMICAL LABORATORY (TERMS 1 & 2)

TUES   CHEMICAL LABORATORY (TERM 3)

INTRODUCTORY ORGANIC LECTURE

11.30 – 12.30

(TERM 3)

WED   CHEMICAL LABORATORY   CHEMICAL LABORATORY

(TERM 1)

THURS.   TUTORIAL CLASS IN CHEMISTRY

CHEMICAL LABORATORY (TERM 1)

Technical Courses of Study
Introductory General Course for Chemistry
Terms 1 and 2, First Year

The course is intended as an introduction to the study of chemistry, and covers the ground for the preliminary examination of the Victoria University and the matriculation of the London University. It is also suitable for candidates for the first examination of the Conjoint Medical Board (Royal College of Physicians and Surgeons) and for pharmaceutical students.

The course will include a consideration of the general properties of matter, chemical combination and decomposition; preparation, classification, and general behaviour of the more commonly occurring elements and their compounds. Outlines of chemical theory.

Jeremy, Hazel and Belinda Bennett overlapped in conversation:
  'I'll lend you the overalls I use in the surgery, darling. Lucky you and I are the same size.'
  'What about Felicity?'

The doctor could not understand why a simple statement caused such laughter, but both Belinda and her mother could see Felicity looking like a demented frog.

Dr Bennett called them to order. 'Now listen, Belinda, and stop giggling, you idiot. On Monday morning get down early to the station and fill in a form for a travel contract from September to the end of July. Use your own chequebook.'

Belinda thought quickly. Was it an advantage to have one's own account? If her father had been paying she was going to suggest a full calendar year! She kept quiet now.

Her mother was racing ahead. 'I think you'd better make it first class and then you and Felicity can find a Ladies Only compartment.'

The last phrase sent Belinda wild. 'Mother, from *you*! We shall be the laughing stock of all the male students. *And* the women who go full time! They'll all think we are standoffish! And they'll be right!'

Her father used his usual quiet reason. 'Let's all think it over quietly and decide tomorrow.'

Her mother continued her thinking, ignoring the other two. 'Have you thought, Belinda, that Mr Hargreaves will never allow a daughter of his to travel *third*.'

Talk went on before and through Saturday night supper. In the middle of that the surgery bell rang.

'Sorry, sir, it's Mrs Podgson. She's coughing blood, sir...'

Saturday night at Stonegarth followed its usual routine.

Felicity went up to her room, happy that aunt Grace's writing desk made an excuse for her private writing of letters. The only demanding one was to Roberta Butterworth. She would begin it now and then hide it away until she had spent two days at the college, when they would have something to report.

She could hardly believe that her father had fallen in with the college scheme. Did he have an ulterior motive? He had paid her fees in advance and was taking her down to the train on Monday morning to book her first-class contract ticket. There had been no trouble in finding overalls in the big wooden-knobbed chest of drawers in the sitting kitchen. Hilda had forgotten that her mistress had a store that she kept for spring-cleaning.

At nine o'clock that Saturday night the master of the house did his punctilious round of winding-up the twenty-four clocks. Starting with the cheap and noisy alarm clocks in the maids' attic rooms, he worked his way down to the six bedrooms with their assortment of carriage, Delft and travelling clocks in leather cases, cuckoo clocks and delicate china ones brought back from Switzerland and France.

He tried to turn the knob of Felicity's door. It was locked!

'Open the door. It's clock-winding!'

'I can wind them. I have the keys!'

'I'll teach you to disobey your father. Open the door!'

'I can't, Father, I'm undressed!'

'Then put your dressing gown on and open this door!'

If this were to be the beginning of a new life, she must be firm. She tried a tactic she had never tried before. In a voice of magnificent hauteur, she said without raising her voice: 'Surely, Father, you know when a woman is obliged to be alone.'

He had no answer. In any case it was getting late. The grandfather, wall and mantelpiece clocks were waiting downstairs. Felicity felt inches taller as she heard his retreat. She looked searchingly into her triple mirror. She could almost see the growth of feminine guile which she had acquired in the last three weeks.

Finding himself locked out of Felicity's bedroom hit Hargreaves as hard as the breakfast kiss had elated him.

Underneath all his pomposity and bluff was a man fractured with insecurity. An underlying fear of failure made him dominate his wife; scare his workforce and patronise his fellow Masons and councillors. It made him sneak moments in the sales office to scrutinise the gilt-edged ledger for warning signals of thinning orders.

Tonight he needed comfort but had lost the art – if ever he had it – of motivating a comforter.

It had never occurred to Gertrude – why should it? – that this husband who projected rigidity needed comforting. And she, in turn, had lost the art – if she had ever had it – of inspiring affection.

The parson who married them should have donned the black cap when he threatened them with the words: 'To have and to hold from this day forward...' Yet so securely were they manacled in marriage that if either had been offered release neither would have wanted it.

Gertrude, too, like a regulated clock, was also waiting. Arthur was too obtuse to know it was without pleasure.

Gertrude knew that on Saturday nights she should be twenty minutes, rather than fifteen minutes, ahead of her husband. If she had ever been vulgar enough to discuss such a subject she would have boasted that her husband had never seen her naked. In their last house, which had no dressing room, there was a large screen behind which Gertrude dressed and undressed, using her voluminous night-gown as a tent for both operations.

In the master bedroom at Stonegarth the cold air and righteous habit made her still wriggle her garments under her night-gown, though her husband was nowhere in sight.

She arranged the discarded garments tidily over the chair and spread a small silk shawl discreetly over them. The embroidered initials G.A. were singularly out of place now unless they stood for *gone away*.

Trained from an early age to kneel and pray before bed, Gertrude had a special prayer for Saturday night. 'Please God make me a dutiful wife.'

'Ready, my dear.' A voice called quietly, totally lacking in seduction, but now urgent in purpose, as Arthur Hargreaves entered.

Gertrude, unobtrusively returning a small jar of ointment to her bedside cupboard, replied in a voice simulating girlhood: 'Yes, dear!'

The large master bedroom was in darkness for Gertrude had already pulled down the chains which extinguished the gas mantles on either side of the bed. Arthur's candle-lit face coming round the dressing room door was contorted into ghoulish shadows and sensual lights. A spray of saliva synchronised with the darkness as he blew out the flame.

From that moment on everything was in his hands. The habitual missionary method and zeal linked her to him. A false frenzy soon drained his puny passion and, snorting completion, he babbled himself to sleep.

5

Breakfast at Stonegarth was never quite the same again now that Felicity was to join the *hoi polloi*.

'Your father has arranged for you and your friend to have your midday meal at his insurance agents' in the Swan Arcade. We don't want you mixing with those rough lads at dinnertime.'

The reference to Belinda as 'your friend' suggested Gertrude's reluctance to raise the drawbridge to her home. Her husband left his newspaper folded on the table to address his daughter.

'Ah'm coming down to the station with you to collect yer first-class contract – and pay fer it. 'Appen Bennett will 'ave done the same for his daughter. She'll get on at Bingley ah reckon, an' be looking out for you.'

Felicity assumed that she and her father would be *walking* the short distance to the station but the carriage was at the front door with the newly engaged groom, Hawkins. He handed a white carnation buttonhole to his employer. It was Exchange day and he knew the form. It was too late to object but Felicity prayed that Hawkins would stop short of the entrance, where a score or more college students would be boarding the train to Bradford.

'While you're waiting, 'Awkins, get me a *Financial Times*. Ah'll nobbut be more than ten minutes.'

The stationmaster, with top hat raised, was coming out of the entrance.

'I've sent Miss Felicity to the office to be signing her contract. Come this way sharp, Sir, the train's on time.'

A large crisp £5 note was handed over and quickly exchanged for a gold sovereign and one white gilt-edged card on which Felicity had already printed her name and address.

As the train chuffed to a standstill the stationmaster opened a Ladies Only first-class compartment door, raised his hat and stretched out his other arm ready to usher his important passenger to her seat.

Belinda, who had made a quick exit from her third-class carriage to get hold of Felicity, was being pushed back by the guard as Felicity was pushed into the first-class compartment by her father. The guard, using his green flag as a prodder, was yelling to the trio, who by now were locked in conflict. While Hargreaves was tussling with Belinda, so Felicity made a quick exit from the first-class compartment towards the third.

'Mak up yer mind, sharp! This train's going off whether you're on it or not!'

'Shut up, both of yer,' Hargreaves' voice drowned the guard's. 'Get in that first-class seat as I've paid fer, or there'll be no college for you!'

Belinda's upper-class Amazonian voice rang out even above Hargreaves' West Riding roar. Her arm matched her voice.

'Felicity, don't be an idiot, you'll be the laughing stock of the college. I've saved a seat in my third-class carriage and that's where we're both going.'

After a quick exchange with the guard and a sleight of hand snatch of the flag, the station-master, taller than Belinda, dragged her to the open door of the first-class carriage and pushed her in behind Felicity, who had been lifted back again by her father. Herbert Dawson was not having any nonsense with Belinda:

'You'll travel first today, Miss, and act as if you're a lady! If the inspector gets in and asks for your ticket, tell him you had to look after a sick young woman.'

He clanged the door shut; restored the flag to the guard and faced his well-heeled customer, whose battered carnation augured badly for a morning on the 'Change.

They watched the train steam out. Hargreaves removed the carnation and threw it on the line.

Dawson checked with his gold Hunter that the train was leaving three minutes late. These brief occupations concluded, they beamed at one another over their initial success and Hargreaves put out his hand.

'She's a reet tartar, Belinda Bennett is! Anyways, Dawson, you gave 'er what for.'

'Well, Sir, You know what they say: *Hell hath no fury like a woman scorned!*'

Hargreaves nodded. 'Ah couldn't 'ave put it better miself, lad.' Raising his hat to the world in general, but including Dawson in the broad gesture of his left hand, he went out of the station to his patient groom.

''Ere's yer paper, Sir. Summat wrong with the train? It were a fair time getting off.'

Hargreaves, ignoring the question, glanced at the warning

headline in the *Financial Times*, folded the newspaper and put it under his arm.

'It'll 'ave to wait,' he said to himself grimly but outwardly he rose to the grandeur of his leather-cushioned carriage and proceeded to acknowledge, on the ride home, those less fortunate folk who used their feet.

Meanwhile the two girls looked at one another, not knowing whether to laugh or cry. They waited for Belinda's wrath to die down before dealing with the next move. As usual Belinda took the lead.

Such was her self-confidence that even after the humiliating thrust by the three men into the first-class carriage she could still address her captive audience as if she were addressing a public meeting:

'Felicity, I want to make it quite clear that this is the first and last time I shall travel first-class to college. If you insist on doing so, then you will travel alone throughout the day, and for the whole year.'

They went through the next station in silence.

'Why don't you answer? Don't say you're afraid of your father?'

On and on they went, now in and out of Frizinghall station. Still only a cold stare from Felicity.

'We're nearing Bradford. I'm not letting you move out of here until I get an answer.'

Belinda put her full height in front of the door. Felicity, adjusting her hat, which was badly in need of it, spoke into the central mirror.

'While you've been bullying me, and you are a bully, Belinda, I've been thinking it out. You get off the train in Aireley with me this afternoon and we'll both go to see Mr Dawson and apologise for this morning's trouble.'

Belinda picked up her own cue and said: 'Um! And with my cheek and your charm, we'll persuade him to change your contract for third-class, and make him swear not to tell your father. And you'll get some change, darling Felicity, and I'll see you keep it!' Then as an afterthought: 'If honesty gets the better of you, why change it? You can still travel *third* with a first-class ticket.'

As they stepped out of the first-class carriage Felicity had second thoughts. Did she need Belinda to fight her cause? She would see Dawson herself tomorrow morning on her own:

'Yes, Belinda, of course you are right, there is no need to ask the stationmaster.'

They walked arm-in-arm out of Forster Square and boarded the steam tram which would take them up to the college.

They were too pleased with the prospects of life ahead to be unnerved by the students' stares, or even to be offended by the overbearing clay pipes the two flat-capped youths were smoking as they muttered to one another: 'Oo do they think they are? Colleges weren't built for the likes o' them.'

'Nah,' agreed the other. 'Oo's going to give 'em jobs any road?'

Two well-turned-out youths, whose Yorkshire speech had been given a veneer of disguise at a minor public school, had far more interesting things to talk about. From what the girls could piece together from their eavesdropping, they gathered that there had been complaints from residents in Carlton Street about the noise that the students made on Ball nights. Carriages and revellers used the side entrance to the ballroom instead of the main one in Great Horton Road. One boastful remark was meant to carry:

'Oh, I got round the constable. My girl's father is the Town Clerk and I told the feller that I'd to get her home to the top of Manningham Lane by half eleven or her pater would play hell...'

Balls? Midnight revelry? Girls?

Belinda seemed to have more acute hearing than Felicity and had taken it all in. She turned to Felicity.

'I wonder now! Has it dawned on you that you and I are going to do far more exciting things than chemistry and biology!'

'Belinda, you're incorrigible! Can you see my parents giving me permission to be out unchaperoned in Bradford at midnight?'

This dampening question had to be left to speculation for they had arrived at the main door of the college and were swept along, in spite of their ankle-length skirts and face-framing bonnets, into a trousered world.

The entrance hall was impressive. The Bradford men of the 1880s, like those before them, had outsize civic pride and neither labour nor money were spared in the erection of public buildings and monuments.

On the right was the commemorative tablet recording June 23rd 1882, the day when the Prince of Wales had opened the college with great ceremony and every street in the woollen empire put out its flags.

Neither of the girls had expected to be walking up a staircase of polished elegance which they were told led to the point of registration and the chemistry laboratory where most of their classes would be held.

On the halfway landing under a stained-glass window, rich with golden symbols, was the registrar, who did not need to be told their names. He seemed to put an inflection of incredulity on the word *Miss* as if these lady students might be fugitives from a nunnery:

'*Miss* Hargreaves? *Miss* Bennett? Sign here please! Here are your locker numbers and keys. Up the stairs and to your right for the laboratory. You'll find the number of the bench you two are sharing. It's on the key.'

They moved on but were immediately called back. He dropped his voice to an intimate level.

'Sithee here, understand this, there's to be no fraternising with the young men. They have serious work to do.'

For once Belinda was speechless. But the answer tore through her mind! There couldn't be anything more serious than a medical career. What impertinence!

Felicity looked up at her, hoping she would assert their serious intentions. It was a bad start to their *new woman* status.

The lab assistant, somewhat ill at ease, showed them to their bench at the back of the room where there were the usual five stools.

'I've put you two on yer own by yerselves. Lads won't want ter mix.'

Feeling embarrassed, he quickly disappeared from the room.

'Oh well, at least we've got three spare stools, a sink, gas tap and burner of our own – one advantage of being outlawed!'

They sat unnerved on the back bench waiting for the rest of the class to come in. No-one came. Hearing voices from the adjoining lecture theatre it dawned on them that *lecture* on their timetables meant just that.

They collected their things and hurried from the room into the tiered auditorium, where the students sat in serried ranks, now in complete silence.

Their entry was as if a sergeant major had commanded: 'Eyes left!' The whole class, including the lecturer, fixed their gaze on Felicity and Belinda.

The master was standing at floor level behind the demonstration bench with a test-tube in his hand.

'Tak yourr seats on yon top bench and nivverr be late agin!'

So this was the Robert Mackintosh, listed as their chemistry tutor.

Every eye in the businesslike theatre watched the girls' ankles as they lifted their skirts to clear the way up the steps. Even Belinda blushed with embarrassment. It seemed an age before the tapping of their heels on the wooden flooring stopped and they were sitting self-consciously above all the rest.

Robert Mackintosh fixed his critical eye on the latecomers but the twinkle suggested that he was going to have a more interesting audience than he had expected. He had a feeling that the ladies would appreciate his showmanship more than these dour Yorkshire lads.

Even standing at floor level he seemed to have direct eye contact with everyone in the class. His massive body and commanding head outlined with wiry, ginger hair and beard suggested that if the old Queen clapped eyes on him she would have him, as a successor to Brown, in Balmoral or Osborne for her final years.

He brought with him from Scotland tenacity, humour, a thirst for knowledge, and thrift. Qualities not unknown in the West Riding.

'Noo, let me tell you frae the starrt that I hae tae account for a' the chemicals used in this department. So we're no' gaun to waste ony. Every practical session weel be carried oot here, by me. I shall do the experriment and ye will write it doon in yer notebooks. See yer pencils arr sharrpened, aye, *and* yerr seeing, yerr hearring and yer wits!'

He stood like a general addressing an army and held up the Bunsen burner fixed to the gas jet in the centre of the bench.

'Can ony of ye tell me whit this is ca'd?'

'A gas-burner, Sir.'

'Aye, but like you, lad, it's got a proper name! It's a Bunsen burner. Bunsen was a Gerrman (an' nae worse for that!) – a chemist – when he was a lad he fooled aboot wi' a burrner while he was carrying out an experiment and lost an eye. Let that be a lesson tae ye! Sae he was detairrmined to mak a burner that was foolproof and he invented this safe burrner. It's safe if ye know how to use it.

'Noo watch! Hae yerr match lit ready. Turn on the gas! Light it wi' your finger on the air hole. See that lang yellow flame? Weel that's what you dinna want! Tak your finger off the air hole and you get a flame that you can see through – a clear blue. Ye see why I want you here and not in the laborratory. I said it was *fool*-proof – I didna say it was *idiot*-proof. Hoo can I guarrantee that?

'With yer finger on the air hole ye could burn the place doon!

'Now here I have some white crystals. Did I hear someone say washing soda? Weel, they're no sic thing. Much mair costly. *Lead Nitrate!* Keep your eyes open while I haud the test-tube ower the Bunsen burner!'

He clipped the glass tube to the holder.

'Watch these crystals! Can you see them turning yellow?'

'No, Sir!'

'Weel come doon to the front!'

Two rows stampeded. The girls remained on the back row.

'Look at the gas above the crystals. What colour is it?

'Brown, Sir. But wot is it, Sir?'

'That, my laddie, is nitrogen peroxide, and dinna fool about with that! It's poisonous! Now, tell me what's *above* the broon gas?'

'Nowt, Sir!' another volunteered.

'Well, if I were speaking your language, my lad, I'd say: "Nowt is summat."'

Laughter from the class at the Scot's linguistic prowess pleased Robert Mackintosh, who almost forgot that he needed to catch the brown gas before it burnt away.

'Now I've lit this splint. Come here, young man, I think you'll find enough energy to blow it oot! Well done! Is nae he a canny chief? Noo, come here you on the front row that said there was *nowt* above the liquid. Put the splinter in the top above the broon gas. Look! The splint's come to light again! So what was there?'

No answer.

'Weel it's OXYGEN! In your foreign language it looks like *nowt* but it is *summat*! Noo turn the Bunsen burner up high and burn aff every bit of broon gas. Watch out! It's poisonous! Can you see the sticky red stuff in the bottom? 'I'm turning the burner off noo. You can all come roond now and watch the stuff cool. (Dinna be stand-offish, young ladies, I mean you, ye ken.)'

Belinda and Felicity joined the throng but they could have seen much better up aloft.

'Look! Can you see it changin'?'

'Aye, Sir. It's going yeller, like. It's tonning inter glass, like – goin' solid liquid.'

'And that,' said Robert Mackintosh – as if he had distilled the finest malt whisky – 'that is LEAD MONOXIDE!'

Belinda had enjoyed his showmanship and he knew it. He had targetted this final line directly to her, hardly expecting a reply. Her imperious tone silenced the whole class.

'And what use, Mr Mackintosh, would lead monoxide be?'

The class was astounded. Pupils usually were seen and not heard. Other teachers in the college lectured, read notes. And here was a *girl* answering back! The bell excused Mr Mackintosh trying to give an answer.

'There's the bell, lassie. Be off with you!'

The words suggested the dismissal of a small child. The look they shared was both amused and canny.

Felicity had moved away, embarrassed by her friend's audacity. But from that moment on the girls were something to be reckoned with. They, in turn, felt a respect for the college. It was all very different from and in many ways superior to the Academy.

Less than a mile down the road, while his daughter and her friend were having their first introduction to chemistry, Arthur Hargreaves walked into the 'Change confident that he would be welcomed. It was a man's world in which he felt at home.

His London agent, Bernard Entwistle, who had taken a hansom cab from the Midland Station, gave him the usual greeting, but with unconvincing warmth. Entwistle's tilt of the head, in the opposite direction from all the wool-men, gave a clear signal that he wanted a word from his chief away from the rest.

They withdrew into the Members' Room and found two arm-chairs sheltered by a screen.

'Sticky going in London, Sir! There's a change in the market.'

Entwistle gave himself a cigar without offering one to his chief and in doing so conveyed that he was addressing a provincial.

Hargreaves bristled. 'Come to the point! Of course there's a change in the market. Ther allus 'as been and ther allus will be...'

'You see, Sir, it's all our Italian customers – in Rome and Florence – no orders from them for six months... It's our continental lot – those that order through London.'

'Well 'ave yer got to know 'oo they are buying from? We need to know our competitors.'

'It's not just our Italian customers, it's Germans and French, Sir.'

'And what are they makking that we can't make better and cheaper?'

'They are buying from the French, Governor. Their looms adapt better to tropical suitings; silks; supple alpacas; fine polished mohairs and lustres...'

'Well, ah'll tell yer this, Entwistle, our looms, an' I mean *our looms* – Hargreaves' looms – don't need adapting, ther right – and allus will be fer proper cloth: men's suitings, covert coatings, and women's cloaks. It may be a small mill, against Listers, Salts and Priestleys, but we can fight, lad, we can fight. An a'll tell yer this, mi boy, them Franks 'ave got another Waterloo coming, mark my words!'

Defeating France, if only in words, seemed to strengthen Hargreaves' armour. In his estimation Entwistle only knew about buying, selling and meeting customers: Hargreaves thought to himself: An' only *middling* at that. I'll larn 'im!

'Now, Entwistle.' He stood up and pointed towards the buzz of buyers and sellers. 'We're not going through there until you an' me 'ave got things straight. An' yer've a lot to learn about wool business before we do that. Get it into yer thick 'ead that t'great days of t'textile trade has gone! But I'll tell yer this! Yorkshire's *not* gone!

'My dad an' grandad worked in boom days. But they did their share of making it boom. Grandad didn't miss a trick in the Franco-German War. When all t'lot were fighting over there, 'Argreaves 'ad three mills going and took a fair lot'v t'French and German business. It was 1870–1873. A reet laff, my dad said it was, keeping all that lot fighting while we took their trade. Rocketing orders! 'igh prices! Good wages! All Airedale was full to busting with cloth. We couldn't get it over t'Channel fast enough. Grandad bought shares in the Leeds to Liverpool canal, Midland Railway, Midland Hotel. He were a corker!'

'We could do with those days now, Sir,' Entwistle slipped in uselessly, which made Hargreaves change to a minor key: and speak confidentially.

'But yer know, Entwistle, folks forget to use their brains wen things are going well; mi grandad left mi dad with a lot o' troubles and debts. One daft thing – they weren't ready for women's whims, thought they were on a good thing when women used yards of flimsy materials on crinolines and great sweeping cloaks. My grandad had put his biggest mill on to silks, flimsy satins and voiles, tiffany and taffeta an' all that finery...'

Entwistle pulled the lines of his face into a pattern of agreement. 'A sensible thing to do, I would have thought. Surely, Governor, that would please London, Paris and the fashion world?'

'Not for long, my lad. Fashion's as fickle as women theirsens: crinolines went out and skimpy skirts, flimsy clinging dress stuffs, low necks and ankles showing came in. Landed my grandad in ruins. My dad paid all 'is life fer that. Ah suppose yer could say I did too.'

Entwistle drew on his cigar and tried to look and sound knowing: 'But according to the records, Listers & Priestleys dealt with slumps and strikes and came through well, Sir, even through that difficult time, didn't they?'

'Yes, but they're big an' can play one thing off against another an' gamble on new ideas and new machinery. An' if you've to lay off two or three hundred it doesn't show much when you've got seven thousand workers clocking in. They went with fashion but they went with all t'other stuff too. An' what I said in 1892 and again in 1893 is this: There's no need for Britain – well, I'd best say England – ever to 'ave depression if we cut uz coat according to uz cloth. Find markets we can trust. An' that's wot Hargreaves are going to do... Nah listen!'

To do Entwistle justice, he was listening, with perhaps more attention being paid to his own future than ancient history. But he contorted his face again into a receptive pattern and a smile which looked to be on a time meter.

Hargreaves got down to brass tacks. 'Yer've spent too much of yer time supposedly in London gallivanting over to Paris, Berlin, Rome and Florence. Yer don't 'ave ter tell me you didn't enjoy it! Fellers 'v your age do. But yer a married man now, an' Hargreaves' mill has not just got to survive, it's got to *prosper*.

'Yer not going back into t'sale-room, yer going to look at these duties and tariffs. I got them down from t'board this morning and from *Yorkshire Post*. Sithee! America; France; Germany; Italy. Don't tell me we've not got a war on – it's reet 'ere! Aireley Mill's going to prove it can do without Frogs, Wogs, Huns and Yanks. We're going to concentrate on home market; best men's suitings and overcoat cloth, fit fer Ascot and Bank of England, country tweed, fine and made to last for t'gentry, suitings and broad cloths, gaberdines and cashmere for ladies. In fact, cloths for everyone 'oo knows wot's wot!

'An this is weer *you* come in, Entwistle, or *don't* as case may be! You've got to concentrate yer efforts on England and Scotland. Do a lot more placing o' t'samples. An if yer find reet chaps for sub-agents in Edinburgh and Glasgow, just you be sendin' 'em ter me!'

He rubbed his hands as if he could deal with them now.

'If that order book isn't full ter busting by t'end o' t'year, yer *out*, Entwistle, yer *OUT!*'

Entwistle, who had for the last twenty minutes been stroking round and round his bowler hat – impatient rather than nervous – eyed Hargreaves and bowled straight.

'I've got three hours before my train to London. Can we leave the Exchange now and go up to the mill? I'd like to spend an hour in the sample room and about another hour with your designers and then you and I will settle my contract.

'But I must warn you, Hargreaves' (the 'sir' and 'governor' had been dropped), 'that I've had an agency offer from Forth and Royd of Huddersfield. And I don't have to tell you they make the finest men's worsted suitings in the world. Ritzy stuff!'

It was rare for Hargreaves not to get the last word. When the day was over he had to admit, but only to himself, that his London agent knew what questions to ask the men in the sample and design rooms. And he had taken away the right stuff with him.

'Aye, an that were a reet good suit he was wearing,' observed Arthur Hargreaves. 'Where did the bugger get it?'

Entwistle was glad to be back on the train. After putting his despatch case of samples and prices on the rack, he settled down in his first-class Pullman car seat, satisfied with his morning's work. He took off and folded his Savile Row lightweight coat of fine French wool and pressed the service bell, acutely aware that Hargreaves had never even offered him a drink.

It was easy for the newly enrolled girls to walk down the hill from the college in the middle of the day in order to have lunch in the insurance office in the elegant Swan Arcade. Mr Forster gave them a warm welcome.

'Well, well, well to think you're both at the college. It seems no time at all, Miss Hargreaves, since I let you have a climb up the Arcade gate.'

'And you let me have a go on your new type-writer too, Mr Forster.'

The office seemed to have shrunk since Felicity had toddled around emptying waste-paper baskets and pulling sheets off calendars. Belinda, Felicity thought, seemed too big for the room, but she needn't have worried, her impressive friend had a genius for fitting in and making friends:

'How peaceful it is here, Mr Forster; one would never think that the Arcade is next to the clatter of Market Street.'

'Yes, it gets worse every year with more and more trams. We're having electric ones next – they've already got them in Leeds. How's your father, Miss Bennett? Did he tell you we met in court last week? Judge congratulated him on his medical evidence.'

Then bustling into domesticity he said: 'We've put you both in my private office. Cottage pie – I hope it's all right for you two ladies. We get it sent in from the steam-pie shop.'

'Of course it's all right, Mr Forster,' Felicity beamed, but the thought of a whole year of cottage pies – even from the famous steam-pie shop – daunted her. She would talk to Belinda.

The crowded day was over and the girls made for a third-class carriage as if they had been doing that all their lives. The keeping of the carriage to themselves caused no problems; the quietly behaved boys felt that intrusion on ladies' privacy was not seemly; the ones who were anything but well behaved, using the train ride for larks, did not want to be cramped by two stuck-up dames.

It was a chance for the girls to catch up on gossip:

'Which lecture did you enjoy the best, Belinda?' And then as if she knew the answer: 'I was rather shocked the way you spoke to Mr Mackintosh.'

'Felicity, don't be a prude! He loved it. He hadn't an answer. Anyhow, what *does* one do with lead monoxide?'

'Kill rats, I should think.' The inconsequential chatter continued until Felicity got out at the station before Belinda.

'Put your head out of the carriage tomorrow morning and I'll be there! My father *won't!* And by the time the train leaves I'll have worked on that nice stationmaster. He's an amateur actor, you know. He will have enjoyed our little drama this morning!'

The Hargreaves' late high tea was more lively than usual. The parents, who had both been against the whole idea of their daughter going to the college, now seemed to be claiming to be the ones who thought of it. Gertrude checked on all the decencies.

'I enjoy trains when they are clean. You did have linen and lace antimacassars and crystal decanter in your carriage, I hope? It's what we've paid for. Do the teachers correct the broad Yorkshire? From what I'm told, some of them don't know any better themselves. But I suppose it's not noticed at the technical college.'

She edged her vowel sounds to her At Home standards and supplied most of the answers herself.

'Did you remember to take a serviette to Mr Forster's? Jessie put one out for you.'

Father changed the subject from the college and addressed his daughter in quite an affectionate mood.

'Ah've bin thinking about that dog yer want, lass, and I've made enquiries. Yer know that the Yorkshire police 'ave Airedales – an' good uns too. Well, I've been talking to our local bobby an' 'e's told me where to go in Skipton to get one with a proper pedigree. What about Saturday afternoon? Yer've no classes on Saturday. We'll go in t'trap – on uz own.' He gave a fleeting glance of exclusion towards Gertrude who was scowling at his lapse into broad Yorkshire.

'Oh, Father, that's wonderful! You've remembered. I'm eighteen tomorrow!'

The beaming smile she gave her father softened away the hard news he had heard on the 'Change.

Gertrude's maternal remembering of the birthday was coated with ice.

'*I've* remembered, Felicity. I've made a birthday cake and I've iced it. And I've asked the Armstrongs for tea at six o'clock.'

Hargreaves' approval was masked in criticism. 'Well, make it high tea then.'

Felicity always found it easier to be optimistic than pessimistic so she pushed the thought of Archie Armstrong's awkward attentions and her mother's dutiful cake into the background. Instead, she visualised the upstanding, quick-witted Airedale dog they were going to buy.

He was to be her upstanding champion and friend. A match for Belinda!

Her walk to the station the following morning, as an onlooker might have noticed, had a firmness of tread, a poise of the head and a tilt of her pert nose, defining a young woman who knew where she was going. Perhaps Belinda had kindled Felicity's assertiveness and in so doing had added a patina of composure to Felicity's youthful charm. Her call at the post office had purpose. She wasted no time in picking up her letters.

'Thank you, Miss Elsie, you're a good friend!'

The little girl whom Elsie had known for seventeen years seemed to have grown in stature in as many weeks. She no longer needed hiding in the post office parlour, nor would she ever again buy aniseed balls. The postmistress resigned herself to the fact that Felicity might be more guarded in the sharing of confidences. Her manner this morning came from a young woman Miss Elsie had not seen before. The feminine reticule had been replaced with an academic leather case, whilst the two letters, which Elsie handed over, were put away without the usual shared inspection of the postmark.

'I must go for my train, Elsie. Goodbye and thank you.'

There was not the least hesitation in the way she approached Herbert Dawson.

'Mr Dawson, I have decided to travel third-class with my friend, Miss Belinda Bennett. This is no loss to the railway company since the cost of the third-class is less than the first. If, of course, you are willing to exchange my white card for the green one, I shall be pleased to accept the difference in the cost. On no account must my father be informed of the transaction. If on the other hand I retain the first-class contract, I trust your confidence in ignoring how it is used.'

Throughout the elegant speech Herbert Dawson was hardly listening since the content was obvious. In fact his imagination was far away from the rail travellers, as he visualised Miss Hargreaves playing Viola in his winter production of *Twelfth Night*. Could it be possible? Would her parents...?

He raised his hat and with a circular sweep held it against his body as he said, 'I shall, in all my best, obey you, madam.'

Felicity, still harbouring ideas of her superior education, wondered if Dawson knew he was quoting from *Hamlet*. Belinda, looking out of the third-class compartment, also received the top-hat treatment. He could see and hear a promising Cesario as he escorted Miss Felicity to the third-class carriage from where Belinda Bennett (oh what a Beatrice!) was waving an authoritative hand. She beamed broadly as he opened the door for Felicity. They settled down on opposite sides of the compartment, sharing a trust in one another which neither had experienced before in any other relationship.

Did trust, Felicity was turning over in her mind, include sharing letters? One of the two in her hand bore a Guiseley stamp, but more significantly she recognised the handwriting of the Reverend Anthony Thompson. Her thoughts took over. Should she open it? Her aunt's banishment to the asylum was Felicity's most closely guarded secret. In fact the *shame* of the family.

Should she confess to Belinda that a very close relative was certified insane? Was Belinda's father, as a medical doctor, attached to the asylum in any way?

The question she put to her friend was an evasive politeness: 'Would you excuse me if I open my letters, Belinda?'

'Carry on. I've brought the *Daily Argus* with me. I want to read about the two McMillan sisters; Miss Rachel and Miss Margaret are coming up here from London to support the Christian Socialist Movement.'

Felicity tossed it off. 'I'm ashamed to say I don't know anything about them.'

'Well, you soon will, Felicity. I shall see that you do! In fact I had thought of going to one of their meetings.'

They both withdrew into their own silent reading.

After the customary polite enquiries neatly set out in Anthony Thompson's small academic writing, Felicity read:

I did receive your note of thanks following your visit but had rather hoped to have had news of your returning to Barlockend to spend some time with your aunt. It is hard to explain why she is more lonely and isolated than the rest of this ill-fated crowd. Can you understand that her education and fastidiousness are almost her enemies in trying to accustom herself to this life? But sadly she does not try.

In confidence I am copying out (for you only – please,) three samples of recent reports from the doctor. I read these dismissive comments with despair.

> *(Confidential notes from the routine medical report. Destroy after reading.)*
>
> *Sep. 1* Very restless and agitated. Keeps asking same question again and again. While in day-room suddenly pushed her hand through a glass panel in the door. She has given no reason for her act. She has an impaired memory.
>
> *Sep. 7* Wanders about in an aimless fashion. Irrational in manner and conversation. Can give little reliable information. Gives no information about her past life.
>
> *Sep 14* Very much reduced in intelligence. Asks foolish questions. Clean in her habits. Keeps demanding again and again to wash her hands. Indecipherable repetition aloud of what seem to be hymns and poems. (Nurse reports finding her laughing as she said her nine times tables, as if she had an audience.)

Did you ever read Macbeth at school? Look up the sleep-walking scene where the doctor and lady-in-waiting are watching Lady Macbeth. It sums up how inadequate doctors are in treating mental troubles.

The doctor says in despair: 'This disease is beyond my practice ... infected minds to their deaf pillows will discharge their secrets; more needs she the divine than the physician. God, God forgive us all!'

We ministers of the church are equally useless.

However, I do beg of you to try and visit your aunt and give her a change from the 'deaf pillow' into which she must often weep the night away.

You have not let me know the outcome of your wish to attend Bradford College, nor whether progress has been made in your rather vague ambition to study medicine. I do realise that it may be these very issues which have made a visit here difficult.

By the way, did you find the copy of Browning that you mentioned on your last visit? If so, please bring it when you come.

Do understand that this is not a letter of complaint, but rather an admission of my own (male) inadequacy to heal the mind of a distraught woman.

With kindest regards,

I remain,

Yours truly,

Anthony Thompson

The letter, much of it re-read, disturbed the whole of the journey. She looked up to find that Belinda had folded up the newspaper and was putting it into her college satchel. Bending over it she said, 'I'm keeping it for you to read, Felicity. It's time you and I found out a few home truths about Bradford.' Looking up, she saw Felicity's worried face. 'Your long letter doesn't seem to have cheered you!'

It was fortunate for Felicity that at that very moment the train came to a standstill. Conversation stopped.

They walked in silence out of the station through Forster Square and into Market Street untouched by the statue of the great man William Edward Forster who, twenty-four years ago, had brought about the greatest act of legislation that Britain had ever known. His Elementary Education Act was to ensure that children of all classes reached a certain standard of literacy and numeracy. As a result, Board schools had been built and were flourishing. But how could children learn who were ill fed and living in a filthy environment?

Belinda found a more topical diversion: 'Look at the news poster! I told you they were important!' She read it out though it was plain to see:

92

McMillan sisters back!

'Our Maggie' tells School Board

Bradford children underfed.

Filthy conditions.

Although the poster shocked, the day's routine pressed and very soon they were walking past the imposing town hall and up the hill past the huge and lavish Alexandra Hotel. Bradford was not short of cash.

Returning home in the train that day, Felicity was able to bring out the other letter. She left the chaplain's in its envelope inside her chemistry glossary, carefully hiding the family secret. She needed to choose the time and place in which to confide such disturbing news to Belinda.

'My letter this morning was from aunt Grace, the other was from the Academy – you will find yours when you get home – the reunion one. Would you like to hear what she has to say? There's a reference to your father!'

Felicity had opened and scanned the letter whilst sorting out her biology notes. It had to look as if it had been read on the train earlier that day. Even between friends there had to be white lies. She read aloud:

My dear Felicity,

A very happy birthday to you. Eighteen is an important milestone: it certainly was for me.

Thank you for your letter which I received a week ago; my delay in answering is due to an unfortunate episode at the church involving the pastor. I hesitate to tell you anything more since it involves people whose confidences I must respect.

The news of your having sent your formal application to the university with details of your course of study at Bradford which you and Belinda are pursuing, fills me with delight. From my past knowledge of Dr Bennett I felt sure that he would be your champion.

My Sunday soirée friends, a few of whom you met last Easter, are all very excited by the news that Alistair Fraser, the young doctor, son of Professor and Mrs Fraser, is returning from his assignment in Rhodesia to take up a Fellowship in the medical faculty of the university. Apparently he has done wonderful work on native women's diseases and their oppression, so he should be a great asset at the women's hospital here.

Just to remind you of the rest of the Fraser family whom you did meet: Graham, studying law, and Margaret, formerly at the Royal College of Music, is now in the Covent Garden Opera Company! Mary is the one still at home and a regular contributor to our music. They all have, in addition to their professional talents, great musicianship, but they are not in the least superior. They enjoy my simple Scots and Yorkshire tea-breads and have even encouraged me to play my harp and fiddle again. They are the only family I know in Edinburgh who free themselves from Presbyterian sabbatarian prejudices and play their instruments and sing on a Sunday!

So, Felicity, my dear, please do not let all that dabbling in smelly chemicals absorb *all* your time! Do keep your lovely baby grand active! Mine is waiting for you here!

I have addressed more stately birthday wishes to your home. How clever of you and Miss Ellis to arrange this simple code of Miss F.L. Hargreaves to by-pass Stonegarth. But it must not be long before you are quite open with your parents about Edinburgh. Dr Bennett will help you with this confrontation.

Though I have not seen Belinda since a chance meeting some years ago on the sands at Filey please give her my warmest good wishes and remembrances.

I remain,

Your loving aunt

Grace

P.S. Separating *Grace* from *aunt* reminds me to suggest that now you are eighteen and *out*, the *aunt* could be dropped to the more friendly *Grace*.

Belinda, hanging on to every word of the letter with warm appreciation, had not forgotten the twenty minutes' solemn letter-reading in the morning train. It would be tactful to ignore it, but surely genuine friendship rose above tact? She decided to speak.

'We are both eighteen now, Felicity. I think your aunt Grace

94

writes wonderful letters, but it couldn't have been that which troubled you this morning.'

It was said with a questioning intonation but with gentleness, which drew Felicity's hand across to hers.

'Belinda ... be patient with me – there has been no-one in my life to whom I could talk ... and now ... I know, there is you...'

'This birthday starts a new life, Felicity.'

As the train pulled into Aireley station, Belinda was left heartened but deeply concerned.

Herbert Dawson was of the self-educated breed which had left school at twelve. In that little railway house, which any schoolboy would envy, were not only the predictable classics: *Pilgrim's Progress, Robinson Crusoe, Gulliver's Travels* ... and the *Bible*. In addition, filling the home-made bookshelves, were all the novels of Scott, Thackeray and Dickens as well as *Tom Jones* and *Barchester Towers*. On his bedside table was a much-thumbed copy of the *Lyrical Ballads of Coleridge and Wordsworth*, most of which were known by heart.

In the cluttered little parlour, room had been found for quite a presentable upright piano that was treated with loving care and never left idle for long.

The job of stationmaster gave him agreeable intervals for letting his imagination go free. Today, while Hargreaves and his kind had been torturing themselves and one another on 'Change, he had been mentally casting those two splendid girls in Shakespeare roles: tall Miss Bennett, with that fine profile and determined walk, as Rosalind – dressed like a man too! Miss Felicity? The roles were endless – Hermia to her friend's Helena; Celia to Rosalind; Viola to Olivia, Hero to Beatrice ... He'd no girls in the dramatic society who could fill the bill...

His Viola stepped from the train almost unaware of his presence. Why the troubled look, he wondered:

'Enjoying college, Miss Hargreaves?'

Like a flash her face responded to his voice. 'Yes, and the train ride! It's fun!'

After that first day there had been no question of first-class travel – Mr Dawson, intrigued by the idea of getting them into the Airedale Dramatic Society, had escorted Miss Hargreaves to Miss Bennett's compartment and raised his top hat to the two distinguished third-class travellers.

With two friends, train journeys can prove to be the most

evocative of shared pleasures, especially in the case of Belinda and Felicity, whose social class and sex had assured their agreeable isolation. Through the daily relaxed chatter, Belinda had absorbed the atmosphere of the Hargreaves' deadly dull home to which she had yet to be invited. Felicity, sitting opposite, had become curious about the Bennetts' open house: the circle of talented friends; the family games; music; the singing and reading which bonded them all. Only the deep and complicated affection for Belinda stopped her from being bile-green with jealousy.

'Felicity, can you come to supper on Sunday evening? We usually have folk in on Sundays.' Belinda asked the question as if the whole liberation of women depended on the answer.

Felicity felt the blood spreading on her face. So far she had only called in on the Bennetts to meet Belinda or check on homework. Even so, she had always been offered a cup of tea or coffee and a home-made bun. It had seemed so easy to slip in and out of the Bennett home, where there was warmth but no fuss.

With an agony of silence on Felicity's part and frustration on Belinda's the question burst out: 'Well, are you coming next Sunday, Fel, or aren't you?'

Although Felicity longed to be drawn into the Bennetts' circle of friends, her mind ran along several different circuits, all uniting in a negative answer.

The tough Yorkshire girl in her, anxious to assert her individuality, knew that if she always fitted in with Belinda's plans she would have no life of her own. Also she must not let Belinda's easy-going attitude towards churches and chapels undermine her own faith. Belinda had loads of faith – but it was in herself.

The train chuffed its way for a whole minute before Felicity replied: 'No, Belinda! I'm sorry. You see, I don't think I've ever missed a harvest festival. My parents would not allow it. Besides, I enjoy the hymns and the fruit and flowers – and the corn dollies and the barley stooks...'

And then, aware that her speech was not making much impact she strengthened her voice.

'Besides, it's the least we can do to thank God for all living things...' She tailed off, ending lamely, conscious how commonplace her words were and how false the 'living things' seemed when one thought of rats and cockroaches.

Belinda picked up the cue mischievously. 'All living things? Wasps, rats, snakes, mosquitoes?

Felicity knew that neither she nor anyone else could answer that one. There was a checkmate smile on Belinda's face.

Out of the pounding silence Felicity played her last card. 'I forgot to mention, I've promised to play the organ and my parents expect...'

Belinda interrupted with casual impatience, 'All right, Fel, there'll be heaps of other times. But we must choose an evening when we've musical people coming in; then you can accompany on the piano... And play something of your *own*, of course.'

Belinda's afterthought showed insensitivity of Felicity's talent. She covered it quickly with a good-humoured jibe:

'Go to your chapel, Fel dearest, and bang out on the organ! That should help to plough the fields and scatter!'

They both laughed. Their eyes flashed friendship but the glance between them just had a shrewd hint that they were weighing up one another's strengths and weaknesses.

More than anything in the world, Felicity wanted to be included in the Bennetts' ménage, where meals might be sketchy but liberal; where sofas and chair seats were worn into friendly human curves; where the piano lid was usually open; where there were great bowls of uninstructed flowers and upstairs on the top landing an outsize hamper full of dressing-up clothes...

The train rumbled and clacked through the girls' silences.

Belinda tried another tack: 'Felicity, I've not heard you play the piano since the last assembly at the Academy. Have you played to anyone at home this holiday?'

Felicity's groping pauses said more than the words. 'I've played – occasionally – but not to anyone. Who would want to listen? My parents expect me to practise – they've paid for it – that's all...'

Belinda thought: That's the only way they'll get their money's worth, I suppose, but went on to say: 'We have fun being what my father calls a "foetus trio": not quite ready to appear in public! He plays the piano, really well, my mother plays the violin affectionately and I play the cello... Well, you know how they pushed me into the limelight at the Academy when I was not ready for it. Gathering dust in Papa's waiting room is a viola which he used to play!'

Felicity's face was a mixture of ecstasy and agony as the train let out its duet of steam and smoke into Bradford station.

Belinda guided her dazed friend out into Forster Square. 'A quartet, that's what we shall have, Felicity! And *you* shall be the pianist!'

Felicity, looking forward to walking home in the comparatively clean air of Aireley, was surprised to see her father outside the station sitting in the family trap holding the reins of her pony, Sally.

'Surprised to see yer dad on a working day? Cum thi' ways in ter t'trap.'

'Whatever are you doing here, Father? I *can* walk, you know!

'Well, mi lass, ah've got another surprise for yer! Guess wot? 'ave yer forgotten wot ah said nobbut a week ago?'

'But that was to be Saturday and it's only Thursday.'

The longer Felicity had been at home the broader his accent had become. He took a sly satisfaction in shaking off the la-di-da of the Academy:

'Summat you asked for?'

'Well, when I do ask for something you and Mother always say, "We'll see."'

'An that's wot ah did say. An ah seed. Ah've seen wun, a reet goo' un. It's got gumption.'

'Oh, father, a dog! An Airedale? Or is it a golden retriever? You've seen one! Really! I can't believe it!'

'Well, th'aal believe it wen tha sees, my lass, there are two to choose from. They're proper corkers!'

It was unusual for her father to be so skittish and with this approach she was not averse to responding to his interest in her. Quite good-looking, she thought, and not as old as he had always seemed.

She could not remember a time in the last ten years when she had positively enjoyed riding next to her father, either in the stylish carriage or the jaunty little trap.

It was one of those days in this working dale when the west wind blew over the Ilkley and Burley Moors, bringing the tang of heather and gorse and whirling the oily wool smell away over to Leeds and Huddersfield. Sally, the pony, sensed that the governor was in a good mood and tossed her head and lifted her hooves to snatch the air and spurn the earth. Her mistress relaxed into the clip-clop rhythm, humming Strauss's *Tritsch-Tratsch Polka* to the pony pizzicatos.

Her father drew on his pipe and slackened the reins as if there were not a mill in sight. If ever there was a perfect day for all three it was this. He took his meerschaum out of his mouth and levelled the stem down across the moor:

'Look back down there! It's Bratfet. That glint is t'town hall and even higher it's cathedral. Look up the hill! There's Manningham Mills lording it over all t'lot of uz. Biggest in Europe, seemingly.

I'll tell you this, mi'girl, Bratfet's best place to get out of in t'country – nobbut yer don't go Leeds way!'

On and on they trotted on the high open road with the dappled drystone walling tracking the way. On the cold side of the wall, long sharply scripted shadows outlined the strength of the sun. On the sunny side the limestone shone silver, patterning miles and miles of wild scrubland patched purple, gold and bronze with heather, gorse and bracken. Sudden flashes of trickling light between the boulders signalled that there were moorland springs gathering force to tumble into waterfalls. And they, in turn, slowed down into the valley to mingle with the becks and rivers in the dale. Had Felicity ever enjoyed an outing as much as this?

She was tugged out of her reverie with the sudden stop of the trap and a too-familiar voice.

'Wake up! We're 'ere! Yer nodded off.'

Suddenly the yelps and barks of the dogs littered the air round the straggly smallholding. Sally stood alert, sensing possible enemies. None came. Just a strong-limbed young woman, handsome in a gypsyish way, striding towards them, fixing her eyes on Felicity before helping her down from the trap.

Hargreaves turned towards the pump.

'Ah'll be getting water for Sally. She must be fair parched.' He strode off to the pump with the parting shot: 'Don't let 'er give 'er orders, Miss. She's a reet one fer getting 'er own way!'

Felicity thought she had better get a word in first. She had been having second thoughts about an Airedale.

'I've been thinking of a golden retriever. They're so beautiful – and gentle. Our headmistress had one. It used to retrieve shuttlecocks and ping-pong balls for us in the games room and never left a mark on any of them.'

'Yes, I agree. They are lovely. I've got a beauty here – first-class pedigree! Too well-bred for her own good – she's nervy and erratic. But your father's set his mind on an Airedale – I've got two here. The Chief Constable's coming from Skipton tomorrow. They get all their police dogs from here. They'll be choosing one, but you could get in first if you like.'

Her father, returning from the pump, caught the last words.

'Yes, she would like. Let's be seeing 'em. Police will choose the toughest for their job, but I want a tough one too.'

Miss Atkinson bridled. 'I understood it was a birthday present for your *daughter*, Mr Hargreaves.'

'Ther's nowt stopping 'er, Miss Atkinson, if you give 'er the reet advice – an' tha knaws wot that is, don't yer?'

They walked into a caged area behind the house where twenty kennels had space and protection. A loose-limbed golden retriever lolloped towards Felicity, its hair silky gold in the sunlight.

'Oh what a beauty! I don't think we need go any further, Miss Atkinson.'

'Frankly, Miss Hargreaves, I don't think your kind of life would suit a retriever. As I said, this one is too well-bred for its own good. It's going to need a great deal of care, but it needs to use its retrieving skills too.'

Felicity felt snubbed but realised that this breeder had knowledge and skills far beyond taking a dog out for a walk. Hargreaves was glad it had been rejected.

'Aye, we don't want a nesh one. Let's be seeing yer Airedales.'

Seeing those two terriers standing tall, ears twitching, tails pounding, Hargreaves turned to Felicity and back again to the dogs, not questioning or doubting, simply affirming.

'Nah, which one, lass?'

'Please, Father, do let Miss Atkinson explain the dogs' points. They both look strong but you and I don't really know what we're looking for.'

Miss Atkinson agreed silently and put the potential buyers on their mettle.

'Which do you think has the most distinguished pedigree of the two?' She would confirm their ignorance with her question.

Felicity chose the bigger one, as any amateur might.

'No, it's the smaller one... *Down, Chumley! Sit!*'

His obedience was instant.

'They've both got impressive coats and bright eyes – intelligent – sense of fun – firm muscles. *Up! Stand!*' The dogs stood as proud as guardsmen. 'Look how gaily they both wag their tails! Notice the long flat skull – especially Leo's – and the neck sliding away towards the shoulder. Now let's look at their teeth – well shaped and set. Look at both of them! But if I were judging I'd have to knock off points for Chumley's bite. Uppers meet the lowers. Now look at Leo's – upper teeth overlapping lower jaw. That's just one of his better points. It shows there!'

Hargreaves grew impatient. He could sell a thousand yards of worsted a lot quicker!

'Well, we're not going to be gawping at teeth all day. Is Chumley, as you call him, cheapest?'

Miss Atkinson was used to Yorkshire tykes: dogs and men.

'Weren't you brought up to be told "Quality remains long after the price is forgotten", Mr Hargreaves? Now you'll need a few days to get everything ready for Leo and I shall need time to settle the insurance transfer and registration of inoculations. Come into the house and we'll have a good talk over a cup of tea. I'm surprised you've not asked the price, Mr Hargreaves...'

'Eeh, Miss Atkinson, ah'm not stingy. Yorkshire folk play up to the tales th'ar told about 'em. Weer are *you* from then? Seemingly yer not from these parts.'

'Well actually I'm a Salopian; Shropshire, you know...'

Hargreaves caught the name of the foreign county and hastened to save her face.

'Well, yer can't help that, can yer? Not your fault,' he exclaimed. 'I'll pay yer now, if yer like, in sovereigns.'

The sun was level with their eyes as they drove home across the moors and a sharp breeze whistled through the gaps in the stone wall. Hargreaves, who knew the fickle way of Yorkshire weather, had relied on Gertrude to put a wrap in the trap for Felicity and he had picked up his country ulster from the back hall. Felicity pulled the wrap round her, set to enjoy the remains of the memorable day.

Although it would seem that she and her father had much to talk about, only a few sentences passed between them, thinned by the wind. She left him to talk.

'Did yer take in that theer Airedale puppy is only eight weeks old? Mak up yer mind now whether yer think yer can 'andle it. It's not too late ter change yer mind.'

'Of course I can handle it!' Her secure tone was disguising uncertainty. 'I shall take it out every morning early for training. You've not seen me, Father, coaching the junior hockey team!'

'Girls is different to dogs.'

This closed the conversation and the bright day closed behind the moor.

Felicity went off to her bedroom and her letters. Father was met in the hall by Jessie.

'There's a gentleman to see you, Sir. I've put him in the smoking room. It's Mr Overton from the mill. I told him you were out in the trap but he said he'd wait.'

The visit seemed serious enough for Jessie's best English.

'Wot the devil can 'e be doing 'ere? Nowt wrong, I 'ope.'

Thoughts came thick and fast in the brief time he took to take off his tweed country hat and coat and throw them on a chair in the hall.

The overall manager of the design and sample rooms, Edmund

Overton, a trusted senior employee of Hargreaves for fifteen years, remained standing and silent until Hargreaves had looked him in the face and received the signal that this mission was serious.

Men of Yorkshire birth and experience do not blurt out. Overton let Hargreaves break the silence.

'What's up, Edmund?' he asked, subdued.

'It's that Entwistle...'

'Well, out with it, Edmund.' There was a kindliness and sympathy for this trustworthy man.

'When he was here the other day he was let loose in the sample and design rooms, wasn't he?'

'Yes, I gave 'im a reet talking to. A telled 'im that London office 'as to grow or 'e was out! I made sure 'e got all the samples and designs 'e needed...'

'Did he mention Forth and Royd of Huddersfield?'

'Why yes! Said they'd offered 'im their agency. It were a threat, like, to me...'

'Well, Sir, he'd already signed and sealed a contract with them two days before. He's got every one of our new season's designs!'

Suddenly Hargreaves stamped his foot on the tiles. 'To hell with Entwistle and bloody Forth and Royd. Listen, lad, I want managers, foremen and finishers in my office at eight o'clock tomorrow morning. We'll get these designs on every machine in t'mill and out before that damn lot in 'Uddersfield can get Bradford Dyers to sell 'em our dyes... Sit thiself down, Edmund, an' 'ave a fill.'

The large tobacco jar had not been touched the whole evening. The meerschaum and the churchwarden were slowly filled while the two men, in this tranquil setting, silently wrought hell.

So ended the bright day. Felicity had no idea that it had brought forth an adder. She was elated that it had brought forth a gallant Airedale with a pedigree name of Chevin, after Otley Chevin where his ancestors were bred, but to Felicity he would simply be called *Leo*.

6

Aireley Methodist Church, situated as it was in the centre of the
closely bonded little town, had built up its own tradition of
procedure, not unlike the local parish church, to which it had no
ecumenical leanings.

In both churches, Sunday morning attracted all those who had
servants to cook the Sunday midday dinner, which in turn determined the seating order in church. The only local peer of the
realm in this Wesleyan chapel, whose ancestors had been on nodding terms with John and Charles Wesley, occupied the front pew
on the right of the aisle; the recently knighted chairman of the
Liberal Party bowed to him from the left-hand front pew. In rank-
ing order, behind, were various degrees of mill-owners and the
bankers, solicitors and accountants who knew all the intimate
secrets of Aireley's vital businesses.

The rest of the chapel filled up with those who preferred the
morning to the evening service, or who valiantly came to both; or
those cheerful folk who liked to get it over with or set an example to the children.

The morning service demanded the full-blown efforts of the
organist, Jack Quirk, and the adult and youthful members of the
choir. By dint of conferring the honour on to some flattered
volunteer, he managed to escape from playing the organ at most
of the evening services.

'I hear your daughter has now left school, Mrs Hargreaves, and
that she is making good progress with the piano and the *organ*.'
His stress on the word *organ* implied that the piano was a poor
relation. 'I am sure she would be delighted to play for the evening
service and it would certainly give her valuable experience.'

Gertrude's pink face grew pinker at the honour he was paying
her. Without reference to Felicity – even by name – she accepted
unctuously.

'That is very kind and thoughtful of you, Mr Quirk, and thank
you, thank you very much!'

So it was that Felicity came to be at the organ and not the

Bennetts' Sunday party. Comforted by the conglomerate smell of Michaelmas daisies, dahlias, chrysanthemums and the total contents of a greengrocer's shop, she had accepted without protest.

Long before the event Mrs Hargreaves and her eager team might have been organising the London Flower Show. Even her monthly At Home days stretched into the evening, when the women promised, on behalf of their husbands, the sheaves of barley, wheat and oats, which they could collect from friendly farmers in Wharfedale, Swaledale or Nidderdale. For although none of the men in Airedale had ever ploughed the fields and scattered the good seed on the land, all of their families, for two or three centuries back, had lived on the land where sheep were shorn and the wool was woven on hand looms. But the mass of produce for the chapel was home-grown as intensively as if for exhibition at the Yorkshire Show. Size and colour of the gifts were shrewdly assessed as if measuring the donor's devotion to Methodism:

'Don't say owt but go an' 'ave a look at Miss Whittaker's lilies. They look as if they've 'ad a week on t'gravestone!'

'Six tomatoes an' they've got a glass-'ouse full! Ee, ther that mean they wouldn't give yer t'skin off ther rice pudding, them Greenwoods wouldn't.'

But it was not all spite. Many times the gift was so thoughtful that all the helpers were called to view, very often to give tribute to one who deserved it. Not least Bessie Wheatcroft, who sewed for the whole community with love and care.

'Thank you, luv. By Gow, yer've spent some time on that! 'Ave yer been up all neet? Look, ladies, every little flower with its root in peat and moss. 'Ow ever did yer carry that tray, Bessie? Eee, yer a good-un!'

The donors themselves, not usually assertive, felt that on this day God had given them dispensation from meekness:

'There's mi mop-heads, Gertrude. Chryssies need a big pot. So I've brought mi own this time. Last year they were put in a common stone jam-jar and nobbut lived 'til t'Chewsdi.'

There was a whispered jibe going on between the two Misses Arkwrights, who had social aspirations.

Patience asked: 'Don't you think, Ursula, that it's time someone else did the pulpit? Lady Barwick's silver vases and hot-house carnations have had this pride of place for years. She says the minister *adores the perfume.*'

Ursula, the bitchier of the two, twisted her mouth to say: 'Nonsense, my dear, it's *she* adores *him*!'

104

Most of the working men in Aireley had an allotment, usually grace and favour gifts from the mill-owners. Miracles were performed, but as the weather and the sooty air were the same for everyone, all the outsize vegetables were at their peak at the same time. It never occurred to the growers that the larger the size the more insipid the taste. Produce was measured by girth. Higgins, the local butcher, needed two strong arms to lift his marrow.

'Feel t'weight of it, lad! Ther can't be a bigger marrer than that 'ere abouts! Sithee, 'ere's our Elsie's go-cart she lent mi ter tak it ter t'chapel.'

At the other end of Aireley, Ted Tomkins, a foreman at Armstrong's mill, was chatting to a rival grower in the next allotment:

'We're both cluttered wi' stuff any road, an 'ere ah've got best rhubub ah've ivver 'ad. Look over t'edge, Sam! Sithee, nearly a yard long and blood red, all t'length on it. Pudsey couldn't do better!'

To say that there was a surfeit in the chapel is an understatement. Even the porch had a tub of turnips and giant-size dahlias obliterating the noticeboard. Gertrude and her team sweated away finding pots and places but there came a point when she, as chairman, called a halt. Through the clatter, which she was trying to calm, Higgins arrived trundling his go-cart into the back of the chapel. From her key place at the altar, the produce officer, Mrs Field, bellowed the length of the centre aisle:

'No, Mr 'Iggins! We don't want no more marrers! Uz is overfaced wi' them!'

Sunday morning came and went with its usual decorum and unusual excess of decoration. The congregation was in its best clothes; the optimists in their summer suitings, the pessimists in their winter worsteds, not trusting Yorkshire weather in the 'back end'.

The Hargreaves were in their fourth row with a very good back view of the fashionable sleeves, high necklines and poised tip-tilted hats of the gentry. Gertrude had insisted that she and Felicity had new autumn mantles and short capes of russet velvet with gold braid, emphasising the fashionable neck and shoulder line: a worthy setting for Gertrude's gold earrings and necklace. Felicity ensured that she got an outfit completely different from Gertrude's by contriving to visit Brown Muffs in Bradford with Belinda, in the dinner hour, the week before Gertrude's visit. They had persuaded the head of the mantles department to show her mother the garment that they had already chosen.

After the morning service, Gertrude almost shared with the minister the handshakes at the porch door, congratulated by even the dourest folk on the spectacular harvest show.

Only Mrs Shawcross, positively wallowing in the miseries of widowhood, cast a gloomy note: 'It's all very well for those who've nowt wrong with 'em, but them flowers are murder for me with mi 'ay-fever and arthritis. I were stoppin misen sneezing all through t'service.'

Mr Quirk had enjoyed himself hugely, rolling out fortissimo the ploughing, sowing and reaping. Finally he sent them all home in a triumphant blaze of glory with a piece from Brahms which he had transposed from piano to organ.

Above the heads and ears of most of the congregation, certainly of those at the evening service. Miss Hargreaves would no doubt fill the bill. Such were his unchristian thoughts as he went through the now deserted churchyard to his Yorkshire pudding and gravy, sirloin followed by apple pie.

Felicity, seated at the organ, had a sideways view of the more sociable evening congregation. The *Moonlight Sonata*, not difficult for her on the piano, sounded too moonless in her organ improvisation, but she could see nods and becks and wreathed smiles in her direction and all looked to be in allegroish mood. She played on, endlessly it seemed, repeating parts of the sonata which were comfortably familiar.

The blaze of fruit and flowers had a releasing effect on voices and faces. Jaws usually held characteristically tight for Yorkshire speech dropped open into paeans of praise with music in the air. The three Robinson girls, mousey at home in their male-dominated family, burgeoned into unlimited joy in singing. Timothy Sparrow, a demon at school, a choirboy on Sunday, usually enjoyed letting his soprano voice rip, but today he seemed to be having trouble with his nose. The bank manager's frowns at Timothy were the only jarring notes in the lusty unison.

Felicity had no difficulty with *Come ye thankful people, come*! for no one could resist the invitation. But the second hymn, which the organist had transposed into a lower key to encourage the men to plough the fields and scatter, never quite got off the ground. That is, until the children, and all the warm-hearted adults who obey Christ's injunction to become as them, positively raised the roof with the chorus:

All good gifts around us
　Are sent from Heaven above

106

Then thank the Lord, O thank the Lord
  For aw-aw-all his love!

The final hymn was somewhat of a strain, new to Felicity until a week ago. The organist and his wife had been back to their native Isle of Man for the Bank Holiday and as a cultural addition to the usual kippers had brought back the Manx Fisherman's hymn: *Hear us, O Lord from Heaven.*

They certainly needed God's ears, for the music was struggling and the words were inaudible. The third verse added inadequacy to insecurity from the male singers, who had never earned their living on the land or on the sea. Their heads were almost hidden in the song-sheets, avoiding the possibility of catching the eye of any of their family as they tried to make the best of the trite and inept words:

Our wives and children we commend to Thee
  For them we plough the land and plough the sea
  For them, by day, the golden corn we reap
By night the silver harvest of the sea.

All Felicity could wish after labouring through six verses was that next year, the Quirks would only go as far as Morecambe and not the Isle of Man.

To send them all home in a more equable frame of mind she played them out with: *Sheep may safely graze...*

It was between the porch and the gate that Harold and Ida Armstrong invited Felicity and her parents to share their light Sunday supper.

As they set off, so Harold Armstrong added, in a voice which was meant to be heard by others: 'Company for you at our place, my lass. Archie's asked two of his cricketing friends.'

Ida muttered to Gertrude: 'Not wot we wanted. I wanted just our two to be together.'

Walking to and from church or chapel was the accepted custom in Aireley, as keeping the Sabbath holy meant using neither horse nor groom.

The group, without discussion, arranged itself in the British fashion: the two husbands together, followed by the two wives, with Felicity preferring her own company, rather than tagging on as a third female.

At last, Felicity thought, it will give me a little peace before I have to listen to Archie's boring cricket reports.

The Armstrongs' house, slightly smaller and more compact than the Hargreaves', had the same solid stone exterior with every window geometrically draped. Ida's pride was that her pull-down linen blinds on twelve windows were visible for exactly twenty-four inches until drawn for the evening. Although the important-looking front door was not locked, Ida rang the bell to show that she always kept one maid on duty with whom she was on homely but demanding terms:

'Norah, be a luv and set three more places. Have the boys arrived?'

The two Armstrong daughters were away at a small boarding school in Filey but the table could still have seated them and any friends they liked to bring home. Ida and Harold epitomised simple spontaneous hospitality. Ida earned the accolade to which all Yorkshire housewives aspired: to be a good provider and know the way to a man's heart.

Conversation was not of the same rich fare, but it was plentiful. Gertrude and Ida discussed where you could buy the best hams; this led to fish, fruit, jamming and bottling. Ida oozed warmth and a simple contentment of life.

'Nothing Harold likes better than a trip to Brid. Best crabs in England he always says. That's why we sent Archie to school there ...'

The sentence remained unfinished, Gertrude being mentally too sluggish to explore the relationship between scholarship and shellfish.

Harold and Arthur ignored the rest of the table, involved as they were in a serious discussion on the recent problems in wool manufacturing. Their initial plans for the future included oblique reference to Archie and the New Zealand developments. They moved on to a much more urgent subject, which Arthur precipitated. Harold was rather hoping that it would be sidetracked. They talked in collusion as if there were no-one else at the table:

'Ah've been meaning to ask yer, 'Arold, 'ave yer 'ad that second-storey floor inspected for safety, before a' send t'carding machine ah'm letting yer 'ave fer next to nowt?'

Harold flinched. 'No, and I'd better tell yer for why...' he hesitated.

'Come on then, out with it! Wot's opp? Summat wrong?'

'Well, Arthur, it's no use beating about t'bush ... I 'aven't the brass to buy that machine of yours – t'floor's no problem... Well, it's not going to be a problem now, is it?'

Their talk went on while Archie boringly analysed every man in

108

the Yorkshire cricket team and his record for the season: Brown, Tunnicliffe, Hurst and Peele. He reeled them off as if he were reading a catalogue of wax dummies in Madame Tussauds. He had neither the passion nor the vocabulary to do justice to those memorable Yorkshire and Lancashire matches, nor the humour to re-create those indomitable characters.

'I got all the autographs from Lord Hawke down. I'll let you see them before you go.' As if such men could be assessed as cricketers through cold calligraphy!

'You missed a treat: three whole days: August 5th, 6th and 7th... No, I'm lying, it was 6th, 7th and 8th... And at Horton Park here in Bradford – didn't even have to go to Headingley...'

Felicity could stand it no longer. Not a single word had been addressed to her the whole hour they had sat round the table. Archie's cockiness and the patronage he had shown to his friends, who had attended the local grammar school, were nauseating. She liked his parents but the only word addressed to her from them was an hour ago when Mr Armstrong, at the head of the table, had asked: ''Ow much pork pie can you put away, Felicity? That all right?' He held a generous slice poised in mid-air on the end of the carving fork.

Conscious that no-one was even looking her way, she slipped from her chair to the upright piano at the far end of the dining room. The Armstrongs' grand piano held pride of place in the drawing room but was played only when both girls were home from school. Felicity thought a Chopin nocturne might help to calm her anger and frustration but the hard edge she put on the notes would have made the composer cringe.

'How sweetly Felicity plays! Thoughtful of her to give us a tune. I do love the piano... '

Ida's good will was limitless.

Gertrude ignored her enthusiasm. She was put out by Felicity's lack of manners in getting down from the table without permission, then vulgarly opening and using somebody else's piano without a by your leave.

Ida, too kind to sense Gertrude's ire, continued her monologue. 'I wish I'd kept it up.' She relaxed into her homely Yorkshire speech. 'Yer know, Gertrude, I can just about manage t'Queen and a few simple hymns – and that's that!'

Gertrude's reply, squeezed through a tense jaw, was withering. 'Well, as her father paid for lessons for four years, she should be able to play. But there's a time and place for everything and it's not now.'

There was no calm night for Felicity in the last bars of the nocturne. *To think I could have been at the Bennetts'. I wonder what they are doing now?*

The Hargreaves walked home in silence but they were still having words – if only to themselves: Arthur was troubled by Harold Armstrong's inability to co-operate; Gertrude was embarrassed by Felicity's behaviour and Felicity felt diminished by the waste of an evening and the aridity of conversation.

It was a relief to be going back to college and to see Belinda's broad smile almost filling the space above the let-down window of the now familiar third-class compartment. Felicity was drawn into the train with an arm round her shoulder and a cheek-to-cheek nearness, which she never experienced at home. Perhaps the closest she had ever got to this intimacy was when she spent the Easter holiday with aunt Grace in Edinburgh.

'Did you have a good weekend, dearest?' The words came easily to Belinda.

Felicity felt that telling the truth would reveal too much of the paucity of social life in her sterile home.

'Not really.'

'How did your organ playing go?'

'Not too badly.'

'I did slip into the chapel after the morning service when I was out for a bicycle ride; the decorations were most impressive!'

'Yes.'

'I like to go to church when no-one's there. I can believe in God better on my own.'

The one-sided conversation came to an embarrassing halt.

Felicity felt guilty at causing it and eventually burst out: 'If I am allowed to swear, Belinda, it was a damned awful disaster!'

The mild curse brought them together again in laughter.

'Oh, Belinda, you should have heard us all struggling with the last hymn imported from the Isle of Man! You know our organist is called Quirk – well, that was the *quirkiest* hymn I've ever heard!'

Nothing is more bonding than a shared jest at somebody else's expense. Both relaxed.

'Any letter this morning, Felicity?'

'Oh none worth retrieving. I left them for Bob to take – I can open those two publicly.'

110

'Well, at least you've not received one that can trouble you. I worried about you the other day. What I am going to say now is serious. Remember we are friends and true friendship means sharing worries as well as joys.'

They had only one more station before Bradford. Felicity again thought about the chaplain's letter. It would surely reveal far more than she would be able to explain. She must leave it hidden away, still in the pharmacopoeia reference book. However, she ventured to ask: 'Does your father sometimes act as visiting consultant at Barlockend asylum?'

'Yes, occasionally... And as locum when one of the doctors is away sick. But why ever do you want to know that?'

The train obligingly let out its steamy signals of arrival and came gradually to a standstill on platform four. The subject was dropped.

The day followed its usual Monday pattern but, by this stage of the term, the girls had decided that three weeks of Mr Forster's cottage pies or steak and kidney pies had more than run their course. It was apparent, too, that their intrusion was straining the hospitality of his small staff. In fact after the first week Mr Forster, as manager of the insurance office, hinted that the dinner hour spent at the Midland Hotel was a good meeting place for his customers. He did not explain to the girls that it was *potential* customers that he was after. In their turn, the pungent smell of roasting coffee beans attracted them to Collinson's café for a light, but indulgent, lunch. They chose a small table in an alcove near the window where the two fugitives from college and Swan Arcade could share further confidences.

Having finished their omelettes and been served with the kind of coffee Felicity, certainly, never got at home, they still had a precious half-hour to themselves.

'May we continue our train talk, Felicity? You asked whether my father visited the asylum. Why do you want to know?'

'Does he ever talk about the in ... patients.' She was going to say *inmates* but disliked the word.

'You must know, Felicity, that doctors never talk about their patients, nor even mention the treatment they give...'

Felicity broke in: 'Sorry, Belinda, of course not.'

'But you still haven't explained why you ask.'

'I don't suppose you could ask him if he has ever come across a Miss Amy Ackroyd?'

111

'But you still haven't said why you want to know.'

Felicity drained the few last drops of her coffee cup as if thinking it would give her strength. 'Because she is my aunt.'

It was to Belinda's everlasting credit that she neither looked surprised nor shocked. She simply accepted the fact without criticism or emotion.

'Tell me about her, Felicity.'

'She's my mother's sister ... a few years younger. She was a twin...'

'Why do you say *was*, not *is*?'

'Well, you see, her twin left England to emigrate to New Zealand. She's married to a sheep farmer – well, someone who became a sheep farmer.'

Felicity swallowed, unable to tell Belinda about the thirty years when the twins had been inseparable and how the marriage tore them apart. Then she added: 'Does the Reverend Anthony Thompson mean anything to you?'

'It doesn't really *mean* anything to me. But, yes, I have heard my father speak of him... Oh, I know, I remember my father came back from a medical conference full of enthusiasm for a clergyman who had addressed them. Wait a second – it had an intriguing title, about the mind... I know, the title was: *What had you in mind?* Yes, he was called Thompson – Anthony Thompson. My father said he made them all take stock, and feel very humble... Do you know him?'

'Yes, that letter I didn't let you see. It was from him, Belinda!'

Homecoming for Felicity had much more significance since the arrival of Leo. He had given her a shared subject for talk with her father.

Arthur Hargreaves never spared money for anything that was to be on show, and the best craftsmanship had gone into the making of a substantial kennel, large enough to accommodate Leo when he had grown to be a full-sized Airedale. In front of the kennel was a twelve-foot long run with a made-to-last netted fencing over six feet high. Leo already had the air of a guardsman, ready to take on the world. Felicity, lead in hand, walked into Leo's freehold to receive the loudest, craziest bodily attack any young woman has ever received from a young man. It took all her feminine persuasion and force to wrench him away from her body. But the word *Walk!* worked like magic. He stood firmly on four legs as if a sergeant had commanded: *Stand at ease.* Felicity,

112

now holding the lead, felt that Leo knew who was his master.

The submission to stillness was short-lived. As soon as Stonegarth was behind them he tugged at the lead so hard that Felicity was dragged along too. She was determined to get the better of him:

'Come to heel! Sit!' By the side of the stile, which she intended them both to climb over, was a short post over which, with marathon exertion, she managed to loop the lead. Trying his tugging tactics against an immovable object soon palled. He was getting nowhere. 'Sit!' she spat out again. He sat. 'Lie down,' she almost snarled. He did. She unlooped the lead: 'Stand!' He stood. 'Walk!' and they were off again.

She had gone through all this procedure for a fortnight now and was confident of progress. When they reached the stonewalled field near the canal and were through the five-barred gate, she decided to let him off the lead and let him run wild. He was a joy to watch. If he could have talked he would have explained to her that in that field, and everywhere else, there were smells unknown to mere man. He positively pitied man's noselessness and left his mistress to her own limited senses. While she walked, sedately it seemed to him, just a few hundred yards, in a straight line, he bounded here and there over a mile...

It was a mellow, late autumn day with a cool sun hovering as if reluctant to leave this northern dale. The sturdy little coppice of trees let the light through, having parted with most of their leaves. The ground nearing the canal had soggy patches of decaying gold and bronze where the wind had blown the spent leaves. Felicity breathed deep and picked her way towards the canal, now and again returning an odd stick, which Leo brought as a gift to his mistress. She went through the repetition of *throw* and *return* until her arm ached. Consulting her watch hanging on a gold chain on her waist-length cape, she thought: Just time to watch a barge lifted up in one of the locks.

Nearing the five-barred gate exit of the field, she was mildly surprised to see it open. It was urgent to get hold of Leo. As she called his name she noticed a girl with a Welsh terrier had gone through and left the gate open.

Felicity shouted Leo's name in vain. He was following the scent and sight of that Welsh terrier. She rushed to close the gate to keep Leo on this side. But he was through and speeding as if the only creature in the world was the black and brown dog ahead of him.

She ran as she had never done in her life before. She was now at the bridge at the head of the locks, with the two dogs ahead of her. The girl at the other end was shrieking out 'Ivor' to no avail. He was leading the chase and determined to go on doing so. He turned left from the bridge, thoroughly familiar with every stick and stone of the ground, and knew when to slow down and veer away from the edge of the lock. Leo, however, ran straight on in the direction that Ivor had headed. The next thing any of them knew was that Leo had slipped over the edge of the lock and fallen down on to a mere platform of water on the dark floor of the sixty-foot-deep lock. He was trapped in a dungeon of foul air, spread-eagled on his belly, desperately pawing the water, instinctively keeping afloat.

Felicity's heart pounded with fear but the adrenaline in her made her act quickly, instinct overcoming reason. She was long past being able to call 'Leo' or any other name. The walled ladder, the height and depth of the lock, was on her side. She had manoeuvred five of the steps when a voice from the other side of the lock called out.

'Get back up that ladder, you idiot! What the hell are you doing there?' From his position on the path the lock keeper could only see the top of the lock and the top steps of the ladder.

'It's my dog! He's fallen in! Please don't just stand there! Help me to get him out!'

'Get up off that ladder at once. Leave it ter me.'

Felicity obeyed.

While the lock keeper was making his way over the canal bridge, she was encouraging Leo, only too aware that her young puppy, straight from the kennels, had never experienced water before. Thank God, he has the instinct to keep afloat, she thought. But for how long?

The lock keeper spoke slowly and calmly. 'Now, Miss, we'll get him out but it's going to take time. Keep calm and do wot I tell yer, an' nowt else. Sithee, we've got to fill this lock and bring t'dog up thirty feet before we can do owt. You get 'old of that there sluice wheel and turn it 'ard to let t'water inter t'lock.'

The bargeman appeared, sucking his clay pipe and ready for a chat. He was also waiting on the open canal to have the first lock filled. The lock keeper waved his arm.

'I'll need thee wen we've filled t'lock! Tell thee missis to warm 'er stove up an' cum an' 'elp. There's a dog down there struggling to keep alive.'

As the water was working its way through the outlet in the gates, so Felicity kept calling out any familiar words to Leo. He was being swept along to the far end of the lock, unable to

114

understand that the tumbling water through the gates was bringing him higher and higher and nearer the light. Although he had fear in his eyes, his legs seemed to get stronger as the water helped him. His paddling changed to a longer, firmer stroke. But the force of the water drew him towards the lower gate.

Suddenly there was silence; the water was still. Leo, now almost on a level with his mistress, looked at her with desperate appeal in his eyes.

'Leo! Here Leo! It's all right. The water's still now. Its safe for you to swim.'

Felicity talked to him as if he were her son. Tiredly, but nobly, Leo made one last effort to reach the arm stretched out to him. He looked pleadingly up into her eyes. Felicity grabbed his collar and tried to pull him towards her. He seemed to have doubled in weight now that his wiry coat was soaked and his energy was spent.

The two men, so used to throwing ropes, got a loop over his head to heave Leo over the top of the wall. He yelled with pain but somehow sensed it was a pain to be borne.

'Put the rope through 'is collar, Miss, and when we've got 'old of 'im you pull that.'

The bargee, without a word, got over the lock's edge, down three steps of the ladder and put his huge arms round Leo's buttocks. Without a word being said all three heaved in unison and Leo was dragged on to dry land.

It was getting dark now. Felicity, dazed with sheer exhaustion and relief, sat down on the ground and hugged her wet, exhausted friend.

Aggie, the bargee's wife, broke the silent moments.

'Cum thi' ways on, lass, inter t'barge. Kettle's boiling; stove's roaring. We'll get thi both dry before we go through t'lock.'

The lock keeper explained his apparent lack of hospitality.

'I'd tak thee in my cottage, lady, but missus is away and ah've not been in t'house all t'day. Ah've been that busy. An' there's fower barges waiting now to get through t'five locks... We 'ave got a telephone. Are you on t'telephone, Miss?'

'Sorry, my father refuses to have one. Could you telephone the Bennetts? Dr Bennett? I don't know their number but the operator would put you straight through. Tell them I'm in the barge by the top of the lock, please. I know they will help.'

Felicity had never been in a working barge before. Neither, of course, had Leo. He seemed to smell the warmth and welcome and made a dive for them. She followed him into the dark little cabin, where small flashes of light from the brass and the redder light from the coal stove seemed to welcome them in. Leo almost filled the rag hearth rug and took it as his due, while Felicity was given a seat next to the bargee's wife on the black-painted settle with its high back bright with scarlet poppies.

The pint mug of strong sweet tea which was pushed into her hands was nectar from heaven. Leo, being the most in need, had been served first with a bowl of barrel beer into which the bargee had dipped a red-hot poker. The steam from Leo's coat and the steam from his bowl brought sweat down all their faces, making them shine in the firelight.

The Bennetts arrived and with the courtesy born of compassion were immediately at home in the barge.

'It looks to me as if you've done more than a hospital could do for Felicity and Leo. Right as rain, as they say, though I'm sure rain isn't always right for you and your barge!'

They laughed together companionably while Belinda gave Felicity a hug, and Leo a stroke which did not need words. Felicity turned to her two hosts.

'We've made you late with the barge. I am so very sorry. Thank you for all your kindness! Where can I write to thank you?'

It seemed to Felicity that her stiff little speech was inadequate repayment for that hot, strong, sweet tea and the glowing fire.

'Ee, don't write, luv. We never know where we'll be! An' ter tell yer t'truth we couldn't read it. Could we, Alfie?' They laughed together, each holding one of Felicity's hands.

The ride home in the Bennetts' trap was full of omissions in trying to describe what had happened. The Bennetts were wise enough to understand the exhaustion of both girl and dog and did not ask too many questions. Felicity's mind was not even on any of the occupants of the trap. She was now full of apprehension about the reception that she would get at home. She was soon to know.

Gertrude Hargreaves rushed out to them: 'Wherever have you been, child? We've been worried to death.'

Felicity remained silent. Dr Bennett could do the explaining. But it was Belinda who moved forward with an outstretched hand:

'I'm Belinda, Mrs Hargreaves, I think we have met but only at school functions. What a wonderful daughter you've got. She saved Leo's life.'

Gertrude remained tight-lipped: 'Wonderful my foot, never even sent a message of what she was doing!'

116

'But you are not on the telephone, Mrs Hargreaves, so all Felicity could do was to telephone the surgery.'

Felicity had now escaped from this conversation to put Leo back in his kennel and give him a very late feed. She deliberately took a long time to do it.

Dr Bennett was still out in the drive dealing with his pony and bumped into Hargreaves coming from the greenhouse.

'Wot's all this about, Bennett? Wot daft thing 'as the girl been up to now?'

The Doctor told him as briefly and undramatically as he could what had happened at the lock.

'Well, Bennett, ah've known all along that t'lass couldn't 'andle that dog. An' this caps all. Wen ah get to t'mill termorrer ter t'telephone, ah'm getting through ter kennels and tellin' them to take t'dog back!'

The doctor's reply could have cut ice: 'Mr Hargreaves, don't you realise if you do that you could give your daughter a nervous breakdown – quite a serious *mental* breakdown ... I speak as a doctor!' The emphasis he had given on the word *mental* was not without intention and he detected a slight flinch from Hargreaves which stilted any response.

'And now I will go in to the house, if I may, and collect my daughter. We are all so pleased that she and Felicity have become such friends.'

'Well, ah can't blame yer daughter for this daft carelessness, any road. My daughter's one to blame. I'll see she pay's for it!'

Was there no end to the man's lack of charity, Bennett thought as he led his daughter to the trap.

All Felicity wanted now was rest:

'I've put two stone bottles in yer bed,' said Hilda, clutching a cold hand. 'They don't by rights start 'ere until mistress says so. First of November she reckons it to be. You'll sleep better with a good warm-up!'

'Thank you, Hilda. Whatever would we do without you?'

Hilda often thought that herself. But hearing it said by Miss Felicity made up for the miserable ten shillings a week.

Hilda, whose uncle was a lock keeper, knew something of canal life, but not of its importance in industrial Lancashire and the West Riding. Felicity, until that day, only knew of the canal through a child's eyes.

When one is a child, scenery, home-life, parents and siblings are taken for granted. Those who lived within *spitting distance* of, say, York Minster and the thrilling city wall, may pass these sights day after day without giving a second glance. Just as we all fail to realise that we are tomorrow's history.

So it was with Felicity. The 'Wonder of the Waterways', the giant staircase of Five Locks on the Leeds and Liverpool Canal, were an almost everyday sight in her childhood. Had not her nursemaid, Becky, manoeuvred a pushchair down through Clements Field to let her run around freely, before strapping her up again for the wheeled walk to the open-sided locks?

To a child the world has no limits. *It is there, so it is mine.* Felicity expected to see, and saw, sturdy working barges ceaselessly carrying coal, stone, wood and iron. She watched mesmerised by the strong men and women from the barges wielding the cog-racks, cogwheels, woven gears, followed by the slow opening and closing of the great canyon-like gates. Everything that moved fascinated her. Safe in her pram she could not look down, down, down into the dark dungeons. Becky was wise.

Now that canals had been in use for over a hundred years they were no longer either a novelty to Felicity, or a lifeline for the Aireley mills as they had been in her great-grandfather's time. In Felicity's lifetime trains, the greatest wonder of Victoria's reign, intensified the growth of the woollen industry. Aireley mill could put a bale of its fine worsted on the train in Bradford in the morning and receive a telegram, or telephone message, from the wholesale tailor in London saying that it had been delivered that day. As with all waterways, the coming of the railway sapped the profits of the Leeds and Liverpool Canal. But its broad locks took the largest barges and, with the broad-shouldered bargees of Yorkshire and Lancashire, moved the heavy stuff needed for industry, the coal, wool, iron and bricks. They managed to pay their way.

Speed demolished a precious little fragment of simple philosophy: that if there is an unbroken chain of barges carrying similar heavy weights, time is of little consequence. The barges arrive one after another, maybe not *on* time but *in* time, whatever that may be. If God made Time, and He made plenty of it, it is not going to worry a bargee that it takes over an hour to get up or down the Five Rise Locks. Time is an ally not an enemy.

Felicity, lying between linen sheets edged with fine crochet, went through all the anguish and fears of that late afternoon and evening. The initial anger of the lock keeper, and later his skill; the instinctive goodness of Alfie and Aggie; the immediate loving response of the Bennetts.

She thought of the hot, strong, treacly tea in the enamel mug

118

and relished its comfort. Then in a flash, the contrast of her mother's At Home: the Rockingham china cups held by manicured and gloved fingers, and she laughed – her first real laugh for hours.

Thinking it all over, she realised what a lot she had to learn, not just in college, but in the world around her.

7

A comfortable routine had now established itself. The walk from the station, through Forster Square into Market Street past the Wool Exchange, the Alhambra Theatre uphill to the college, seemed shorter and quicker now. Belinda and Felicity, so engrossed in their own talk, were oblivious of the fact that this twelve-minute walk took them past buildings that encapsulated the astonishing evolution of Bradford. They, of course, were unaware that in two years' time city status was to be granted by Queen Victoria.

The three-day college routine now included a dinner hour spent at Collinson's café where the head waitress put a reserved card regularly on the table in the little alcove by the window.

'Have you read your college prospectus lately, Felicity?'

'No, why should I?'

'Well you take a look, my dear. It says that students are expected to have dinner at the college and that the town is out of bounds!'

'Oh, Belinda, supposing they find out?'

'I think they are very conveniently keeping a blind eye! Perhaps they think we could not possibly fit in with ravenous Yorkshire lads scoffing their meat and potato pies!'

Felicity's ready laugh took over. 'It's the first time our ladylike education has worked in our favour. What fun! ... More coffee?'

'Let's enjoy it!'

They had now got used to one another's change of subject through their mercurial thought-catching. Belinda put her cup down slowly and lowered her voice.

'My dear, you've still not told me about your aunt. No, not Grace. Amy... Can I help in any way?'

'Yes, I think you can. I am going to Barlockend next week. Could you come with me?'

Wednesday, and the organic chemistry class finished at three o'clock. With the quick downhill walk to the station they caught the three fifteen to Barlockend, engrossed in their own thoughts and with no reference to their mission. It was easy at that time of day to find an empty compartment; but they travelled in an uneasy silence. Felicity, at last sensing that this was the only opportunity to put Belinda in the picture, initiated the conversation:

'Mr Thompson and I got into quite a deep conversation last time about the value or futility of prayer. He seems to have a disheartening feeling of failure as a chaplain. My own feeling is that he is spiritually and emotionally a lonely man and that his taking on the job was to give him some sort of identity.'

'Is he married?' Belinda enquired, not with the social curiosity of a girl but with the sifting scrutiny of an experienced woman.

'No, he seems not to have anyone very near to him. Perhaps that was why he wanted to confide in me about his inadequacy as an asylum chaplain.'

'He can hardly be inadequate if he takes such trouble with your aunt.'

'No, but he feels guilty that he spends more time with talented and sensitive ones than with the raving luna—'

'Felicity, would you be able to be compassionate with maniacs out of control of their minds and their bodies?'

The question was never answered. The train pulled up at Barlockend.

'We're here, Belinda! You'll enjoy the walk. The grounds are quite beautiful and the building, from the outside, is a West Riding showpiece.'

They walked up the long orderly drive to the forbidding front door. The bell clanged and echoed through the building as if warning people to keep away rather than welcoming them as visitors. Felicity remembered her fear on the first visit but this time the door was opened by the chaplain himself. He had already moved some of the prison-like bolts and chains. His open-armed gesture of welcome was inclusive of them both but his eyes and speech were directed at Belinda:

'How good of you to come, Miss Bennett.'

The hand-shaking was more than a social ritual, it emanated appreciation and apprehension.

'No band to brighten things up today, Miss Hargreaves. That's only once a month. It's hair cutting, so they'll come in and out of the day-room. Your aunt will already be in there. She's quite proud of her long hair and refuses to have it cut.'

'I'm glad about that, Chaplain.' Turning to Belinda, she added:

121

'It's beautiful hair but screwed into plaits over her head. It's her face that has lost its sheen.'

The chaplain, assuming the role of official guide, pointed out to Belinda the craftsmanship of the building: its lofty domed ceiling, the Italian tiles and marquetry of the floors, the carvings on the doors, the stained glass in the light-stopping windows. The catalogue, made elegant by his voice, seemed learnt by heart, as if he were evading the reality of the meeting ahead.

Only about forty of the eight hundred were in the day-room. Some of them sat lifeless, quietened almost to non-existence; others jabbed away at simple finger occupations with maniacal tenacity rather than zeal; a few were wandering round the room like lost souls. The explosive laughter of the noisy ones was devoid of wit or humour.

All alone at the far end of the room a woman with a lean dignified profile was sitting erect, her sewing rejected in her lap. She was pushing back the cuticles of her nails without looking at them, as if her face did not belong to her body. It was Amy Ackroyd.

Felicity found it impossible to unlock her aunt's hands so she touched her shoulder affectionately.

'It's your niece Felicity back again. I've brought my friend Belinda Bennett with me to meet you.'

The concentration of the hand on the cuticles continued. Her eyes looked straight ahead into space. The chaplain bent his head to catch her eyes.

'Miss Ackroyd, here are two friends to see you...'

Their visit had silenced the rest of the room. Like animals the lost souls stared at what was strange to them. Away in the distance there was a cacophony of maniacal noise coming from the padded cells. Belinda had the sensitivity not to comment but light-heartedly took out of her reticule a small voile bag filled with pastel-coloured sugared almonds, tied seductively with blue ribbon.

'This is for you, Miss Ackroyd.'

The fingers loosened and the elegant little poke was taken into her hands as if it were a gift from heaven. She lifted her hands and eyes to Belinda and stared. A shaft of recognition transformed her:

'Thank you, Caroline, thank you.'

Turning to the other two, she smiled, unaware that the words baffled Belinda.

'I knew she would come. Some day. Twins never part, do they, Chaplain?'

122

She was exquisitely articulate. Anthony Thompson knew it was more than a month since she had spoken. Relief and perplexity stunned him.

'No, Miss Ackroyd, twins never part.'

Belinda wondered whether to contradict the crazy misconception. The question hung in the minds of all three. The chaplain put his benediction finger on his lips. Belinda caught the signal and risked a conniving approach:

'It's good to see you, Amy. How are you?'

The question was not answered. Amy's imagination was far away in the Board school where she and Caroline had taught:

'Where have all my pupils gone, Caroline? That poor little lad who had irons on his legs. What's happened to him?'

Probably for the first time in her life Belinda felt useless. She looked imploringly at the chaplain. His moving hands and face signalled negation and turning to Felicity and his patient he said, 'Another present for you, Miss Ackroyd. Your niece has brought the book Caroline gave you when you were both twenty-one.'

Amy dropped the sugared almonds into her lap and almost grabbed the book. She greedily read the inscription in the Elizabeth Browning collection:

To my dear sister, Amy: on the occasion of our mutual
twenty-first birthday,
December 28th 1877
'Our two souls stand up erect and strong' (E.B.B.)
Always your devoted twin, Caroline

It was as if her three visitors did not exist; she was frenziedly glancing from one poem to another. Soon her voice slowed into a muttered chanting of a whole sonnet, which ended:

...And when I sue
God for myself, He hears that name of thine,
And sees within my eyes the tears of two.

The chaplain signalled to the girls to withdraw.

Amy was unaware that the visitors had crept away. Soon her reading became more rational, more secure. A loose leaf in her sister's dignified handwriting slipped on to her knee. It was a poem not by Elizabeth Browning but by Christina Rossetti, which Caroline had recited for her final examination at college. Amy read it in quiet but audible tones:

123

Remember me when I am gone away,
Gone far away into the silent land;
  When you can no more hold me by the hand
Nor I half turn to go, yet turning stay.
Remember me when no more day by day
  You tell me of our future that you planned:
  Only remember me; you understand
It will be late to counsel then or pray.

Yet if you should forget me for a while
  And afterwards remember, do not grieve:
  For if the darkness and corruption leave
A vestige of thoughts that once I had,
Better by far you should forget and smile
  Than that you should remember and be sad.

The book dropped to the floor and with it the sugared almonds and the forlorn little bag. The sheet of paper remained in her hand.

'Caroline! Caroline! You've not gone away? You were here!' She whimpered like a small child and let her dwindled body crumple down on the wooden settle.

Her visitors had deserted her, united in their mixed thoughts of helplessness, guilt and compassion. They were out in the corridor avoiding one another's eyes.

The chaplain adjusted the situation to a more social procedure.

'Have you time to stay for a cup of tea?'

Of course Belinda could stay, but she left Felicity to make the decision:

'Oh yes, thank you; my parents are getting used to the idea now that my home time can vary. There's a train from here at five twenty. Is that all right for you, Belinda?'

'Of course, my dear.'

The chaplain led them to the reception room, passing the great rack of enamel mugs piled up on trolleys near the refectory. They walked on until the smell of an institution seemed to fade away.

It was a surprise to Belinda to see how West Riding money had been prodigally spent in the reception area to give the donors a worthy setting for their beneficence. She sensed that the chaplain wanted to unburden himself about his work in the asylum, and the Amy Ackroyd problem.

Belinda avoided small talk.

'Where were you before you came here, Mr Thompson?'

124

'I was curate on the Wetherby side of Harrogate – you know the sort of people, I am sure: afternoon tea with cucumber sandwiches and visits to their homes to be a sort of religious governess to their children. Teaching them a catechism which I found hard to believe myself.'

It seemed as if he were deliberately forcing himself into cynicism to evade facing stark truths.

'Why did you come here then?' Belinda's question struck Felicity as impertinent, but she longed to know the answer.

'Well, Miss Bennett – may I call you Belinda?' She smiled her assent. 'Well, Belinda, that was the reason. It was no way for an active man in his thirties to fragment his time away... I had a breakdown... I could not reach out my hand to Him. Nor He to me.' He stopped. Should he enlarge on his feelings about the Church?

Surprisingly it was Felicity who determined the next stage in the conversation.

'But, Mr Thompson, is it because I have had such a sheltered life that I have never questioned belief before? Although even when I was a small child singing *Away in a Manger* I wondered what on earth the baby Jesus would do with gold, frankincense and myrrh!' She laughed her way out of her question.

'Stories are important, Felicity – far more important than earthly truth. They have mystical power. Myths and legends – like music – keep your imagination going. And if that's kept going, so is some kind of belief.'

Belinda had been listening, as she had been bidden by Felicity, but not passively.

'Tell me, Mr Thompson, what is the difference between faith, belief and knowing?'

'Belinda, my dear, if I knew that I might know what to do with my life. I sometimes think that if I joined a religious community I might get to *know* and not just vaguely *believe*...'

Belinda, who, unlike Felicity and her friends, had been brought up to question, persisted.

'If one just sits back and *believes* and has not the intellect either to *doubt* or to *know*, is it not just accepting some ready-made creed? Does it not need more moral and mental energy to *doubt* rather than just passively *believe*?'

She could hear discussion of this kind from her devoted father and mother. Compassionate Christianity – not Churchianity – permeated their lives.

It was a vast question, which the chaplain pondered on before answering. Why go round and round yet again? He had wasted ten years of his life doing just that.

His thoughts were interrupted by Felicity wanting the answer to clarify her own simple beliefs. She turned to Anthony Thompson, whom she now thought of as her mentor:

'Do you remember when we were young children, we sang:

> And He leads his children on
> To the place where he has gone.

Do you think He really does? And if so, why doesn't He take all the people in this asylum to the place where He has gone? To what we call Heaven?'

The chaplain risked his own limited answer. 'If I could really believe that God, and our Lord, either or both, are doing that, I would treat life here as an ante-room and wait patiently with the poor folk here and hope to go with them. But as soon as these unfortunates are favoured with death, another lot comes in. This place is crammed, Felicity. The church where I was curate was only half-full. This asylum will always have a full and crazy congregation, never knowing whether they are in the hands of God or the Devil.'

Felicity and Belinda walked to the station, making their comments with great care. Myriad thoughts lodged between them, unspoken but imperceptibly communicated.

Belinda, a rather more humble Belinda than the one who had set out that morning, waited for Felicity to break the silence:

'I'm so sorry, Belinda, about the *Caroline* thing.'

It was, she felt, a limp way to introduce such a bizarre and frightening subject.

'Caroline was a lovely woman. I remember the stories she read to me. The poems she recited.'

'Why did you say *was*?' Belinda asked.

'Because, I told you, she married and left this country to live in New Zealand.'

'And you still think she's lovely? Pushing her twin sister into a paupers' asylum and then leaving her?'

Felicity could not answer. She swallowed hard and saw the oncoming train through tears of anguish and anger: anguish for her aunt, anger at Belinda's callousness, but gratitude for her fighting spirit.

Today Belinda held the door of the train for Felicity to go in and then followed her. Instead of sitting opposite to her, as they always did, she sat down comfortingly beside her and held her hand.

'I know it seems so hopeless, darling, and that we are helpless but, if you'll have me, I'll always come with you. Your aunt will be quite different next time. Your book was a huge success. Remember we left her in another world! What more can we do than that?'

Felicity had sniffed the still tears away and could face her closest friend.

'Say whatever you like, Belinda, because it's all true. Just remember that you are the only one in the world – well, you and Anthony Thompson – to whom I can talk about this.'

Four hands held together said what words failed to do.

The train's rhythm overrode the conversation for a whole minute. Belinda had been thinking of the chaplain and, as people so often do, assumed that the listening friend was in the same train of thought.

'He's not happy, is he?'

'Would you be, working in a place like that?'

'It's not the work he doesn't like, Felicity – it's himself...'

'I think you're right, my dear, he seems as if he can't fit in anywhere...'

'I wonder how many people there are in the world who never find either a true friend or a true God?'

'Lonely as a cloud, I suppose. Thousands of people. All jostling near to one another and yet very lonely.'

'What a very odd choice of words from Wordsworth. Clouds have never struck me as lonely. They merge, unite without hurting one another, change and part and glide together again as good friends do.'

'And when they've had enough of each other they just turn grey and have an indulgent weep.'

'I wonder why every schoolchild has to learn this daffodil poem. There must be thousands of children in the cities who'll never see a host of daffodils.'

'But as our dear Miss Butterworth – living in her realms of gold – would say: "Ah, but now they've heard the poem, they can see the daffodils!"'

'Bunkum!' replied Belinda. 'Sheer bunkum!'

Felicity was standing up to leave the train when Belinda shot out: 'When is our next visit to be then? You decide! See you tomorrow!'

* * *

Time at the college went swiftly for Belinda and Felicity; there had been many tomorrows since Robert Mackintosh's first demonstration. He now made up his canny mind that, as he had all the students under control and in his power, they could move from the lecture theatre to the chemistry laboratory. The so-called practical experiments had now been written down in rough and in fair copy; no wasted chemicals and no mistakes. There was no *slack* in Robert Mackintosh after five years' teaching at George Watson's School in Edinburgh.

The train journey for the girls seemed to be following its usual pattern of seclusion in the Ladies Only carriage when, just as the train started, two male students, whom they knew by sight, shot in and shut the door.

'Excuse me, young man.' Belinda held forth like a stage duchess. 'But, as you see clearly, this is a Ladies Only compartment.'

The two giggling males answered through splutters: 'We've only done it for a bet, Miss. Keep your gob shut and we'll move out at the next station.'

Belinda changed from stage duchess to the stage dame in pantomime and drew Felicity in.

'I think, my dear, you will agree with my plan.' She turned to the two embarrassed louts in the quickening train. 'How much is the bet?'

'Two bob, Miss.'

'That's a lot of money! My friend and I will not report you if you will promise to give the florin to our favourite charity, saving the mill children of Bradford. The simplest way is to hand it over to me now and I will see that it goes to the right quarter!'

'I ain't got that much cash, Miss.'

'Come on, now! Between you!'

Sheepishly hands went into pockets and between them they produced two sixpences and a shilling:

'Now you may leave at the next station and join your pals. See you *get* your bet!'

The girls watched the lads put fingers to forelocks in respectful goodbyes. The ribald laughter coming from further down the train hinted that Belinda was being taken off for the entertainment of the gang.

'Belinda, you are the limit! I've never contributed to Bradford mill children in my life and neither have you! What are you going to do with the money?'

'You are going to add something from your father. My mother and father will subscribe, I know. We're going to take it tomorrow night to Margaret McMillan's meeting and *meet her!*'

Belinda's quick thinking coincided with the clank of the buffers as they drew into Bradford station.

As Belinda and Felicity stepped on to the platform a woman with a small child of about three came up close to them.

'Excuse me, ladies, but would yer just keep an eye on my little girl time I go and pick up a heavy parcel from the left luggage office? Shan't be a tick!'

'Yes, of course!' Felicity and Belinda said almost in chorus.

The so-called ticks went by, leaving the girls standing. Five minutes; ten minutes; twelve minutes... The child was mute and stuffily dressed.

'You stay there, Felicity, in case she comes, and I'll go to the stationmaster's office and report.'

Belinda moved swiftly. Felicity stood stolidly, holding the child's hand, looking for any possible sight of the child's mother. Comforting words brought no response. It was the face of a child who had never played.

The superintendent arrived, talking to Belinda. 'Well, you've given us a description of the woman and your name and address. I think that's all you can do. You'd better get off to college. Thank you for your trouble.' He spoke as if it were an everyday occurrence.

The two girls, realising they would be late for this important day of experiments in the lab, rushed up Great Horton Road quite unlike Academy ladies. Pulling off their bonnets they tore through the entrance hall then breathlessly on to the flight of stairs leading to the class.

'Slow down, Felicity, they will have to wait for us. Look, you've dropped one of your hairpins. Here! Put it back!'

Felicity had wayward wavy hair which, ever since she was seventeen, had resented being captured into adult conformity. She jabbed the pin back carelessly and went ahead of Belinda who called out, 'Stand still! Here's another one!'

Felicity ran on.

'Stand *still* and put it in *properly!*'

Belinda had no fear of making a late entrance and wondered now why she had let Felicity set the pace from the station.

Felicity slowed to a quick walk, both hands engaged in a losing battle against the falling strands.

They were twenty minutes late when they arrived at the chemistry laboratory. Robert Mackintosh, with a lighter in his hand and a grin on his face, turned to say: 'And did we enjoy our lie-in this morning?'

This was Belinda's chance again. She drew herself to her impressive height. 'Mr Mackintosh! My friend and I would have you know that she and I have been looking after a lost child. Not only lost but abandoned!'

For once Mr Mackintosh's repartee dried up. He decided that it was not the time and place for persiflage.

'You, Watts, and you, Jackson, tak your materials to the back bench. You, Watts, work with Miss Hargreaves. You, Jackson, you're a strong man – tak Miss Bennett and work with her. Mind you don't do it all for them!'

The other students exchanged smirks. Males and females had been separated all term, as was customary in the college.

Mackintosh stood patiently waiting for complete stillness. 'We will start where we left off. You've all had a go at lighting your burrners. Turn them off. Now light!'

The soft screech of the long yellow flames seemed to fill the lab and the weird blue flames followed quietly:

'You have a go now, Miss!' Watts urged Felicity.

Felicity held the gas jet, lit the burner and, without thinking, let the yellow flame turn towards her. The next thing was a rush from both sides as Felicity's loose hair flared. Instantly Watts crushed her hair to her head with his arms against his body. Jackson turned the gas off whilst Belinda came rushing to the far side of Felicity and instinctively stroked her head and hair all over to make sure there was no more flame.

Watts, so alert, so aware, so kind, had not realised that by pressing the flaming hair against his body he had also pressed it against her face. He went white with fear as he saw the master gently pushing the other two away.

'Jackson, you go and get boric acid powder and vaseline from the medicine chest and ask the lab assistant to come quick. You, Watts, run as fast as you can to Dr Knight's surgery over the road. It's his day in the local surgery. You, Miss Bennett, help me to make your friend comfortable.'

He turned to the class.

'Pack up your things and go to the library and make a list of the chemicals you've used this term and how they are used. And not a word to anyone outside this room!'

After the first cry of fright Felicity had fainted and now, helped by Mackintosh and Belinda, she was lying on the floor. Watts returned:

'I've called the doctor, Sir. I've asked him to come here. She's not fit to move yet, Sir, is she?'

'Go and get some sal volatile from the chemist. Here's a bob! That should do it. Why isn't there any in this damned place?'

Jackson returned and handed over the boric acid and vaseline.

Mackintosh made even this operation an occasion for a lesson.

'With a burrn the thing is to keep the air out. If I wipe vaseline on I may hurt her and wake her up. Now I'm just going to sprinkle this powder on her as gently as I can...' The huge Scotsman wielded his great hands. The powder fell so lightly that it would not have disturbed a dandelion clock. Felicity's towel on a bar by the bench was clean. He laid it on her face. He had done all he could before the doctor came.

Catching sight of Watts' face stricken white with fear and concern, he put his hand on the lad's shoulder and said in a voice as gentle as a Scottish *haar*: 'Ye did well, my lad. Dinna ye fash yerrsel. She'll be fine!'

Belinda was kneeling at Felicity's side simply holding her hand and looking into the closed eyes as if willing to keep them asleep. The face, now covered with boric acid powder, had the weird look of a ghost. The burn was mercifully masked. Thoughts of the future crowded in on Belinda's mind: Would her bright and beautiful friend be disfigured?

Would she be able to continue the course? Whatever would her parents say? She looked down on the singed hair, grotesquely blunted, but only on one side. That would grow. The funny little fringe – never quite where Felicity wanted it to be – was stuck together in a defiant triangle.

She watched the eyelids flicker; the mouth twist in pain and heard a voice, totally unlike Felicity's.

'Where am I? ... Water! ... What happened?'

Watts, still white with strain, handed the sal volatile to Belinda, who raised Felicity in her arms to guide the mug to the twisted mouth.

Moving her lips to swallow obviously gave pain but brought her into sharper consciousness.

Only Watts and Belinda were with her now. Jackson was outside obeying Mackintosh's orders. The master was on the front steps of the college ushering the doctor in.

Felicity straightened her back, sat up independent of Belinda's arm and shoulder and held a hand out to Watts.

'Thank you, Simon, thank you very very much!'

How strange! She must have been conscious while all of this frightening affair was happening. And why *Simon*? Of course today they were sharing his notes and she would have seen his name on his books. But to say it? Then Belinda remembered, with a sharp pang of snobbish guilt, that he was the son of the local chemist who, as the errand boy, delivered things her father needed to the surgery door. How strange that recognition is tied to the context in which one sees a person. Somehow people don't exist elsewhere.

She looked at the quiet young man again and said: 'I'm so sorry, I never knew your name. I never thought of you as a student in college.'

What she did not say was that the slim scrap of a boy, with flat cap pulled down and scarf rolled twice round his neck, who delivered stuff from the surgery had been, until this very minute, an anonymous errand boy.

Mackintosh and the doctor interrupted Belinda's thoughts. She knew when to make herself small and moved away for the doctor to examine his patient.

He quite failed to recognise Belinda as the daughter of Dr Bennett and ignored her to concentrate his attention on the girl lying down on the floor. He looked closely at Felicity's powdered skin.

'You've done the best thing you could in the circumstances. I'm glad you didn't stick her up with vaseline.'

He gave Felicity a reassuring look and touched her hands.

'You're going to be all right, my dear, but I'd just like you in my own surgery for a few minutes before we take you home.'

'May I come with her, Doctor?'

He turned surprised at the clear strong voice and looked quizzingly. 'I've seen you before somewhere, haven't I?'

'Yes, Dr Knight. I am Dr Bennett's daughter.'

'Of course you are! I ought to have recognised you. You're so like him. But what in heaven's name are you doing here?'

'My friend Felicity and I are doing a preliminary year at the college before going up to study medicine in Edinburgh.' She threw the news out more as a challenge than social small talk.

'Well I never! Up where Jex-Blake and all that troublesome lot got their way. Well if this young lady's going, we've got to get her right, haven't we? You get the other side.'

Felicity tried to smile. She could feel that only one side of her face could move. The other stuck together in searing pain.

'I can walk quite well, thank you both, but it's comforting to have arms to lean on.'

The doctor's neat little landau and groom were waiting patiently outside and it was not long before they had driven to the doctor's house at the town end of Manningham Lane. He had summoned Watts to go to the day surgery and ask the nurse-assistant to take over. Belinda ached for Felicity. She had never before realised how jarring a vehicle could be on the busy cobbled streets.

They entered the large waiting room in the early Victorian residence:

'There's *Punch* and *London Illustrated News*, Miss Bennett. Probably a week or two out of date, but you know what doctors' waiting rooms are.'

No one knew what the doctor did to Felicity's skin in the half-hour she was in his surgery but she came out looking incongruously attractive. The right side of her head, completely covered in crepe bandage, was turbaned at an angle to show her left greenish-grey eye framed with long dark lashes. The left cheekbone, perhaps paler than usual, shone roundly beneath the dark lashes. The full lips, on the unharmed side of her face, turned up towards the cheek, gave the usual suggestion of a smile. He brought her to the waiting room sofa and suggested twenty minutes' rest before driving her further. When he returned later he was wiping crumbs away from his mouth with a large handkerchief.

The doctor and Belinda guided Felicity out into Manningham Lane and sat each side of her in the leather-lined carriage heading towards Aireley.

The clatter of horse's hooves and the crunch and clout of the wheels made conversation impossible. But with Belinda's right arm round Felicity and her left hand across to Felicity's right, speech was unnecessary. The only words which were exchanged in that ride to Stonegarth were the doctor's and Belinda's instructions to the driver.

They turned into the curved drive at Stonegarth, crunching the shale into a sound signal of their arrival.

There was no question of ringing the bell. Mackintosh had telephoned the mill and the mill had sent a runner to the house. Both parents were at the door. They watched their daughter alight from the carriage with stoical silence on all sides, until the doctor took over.

'Good morning, Mrs Hargreaves. I would like you to take your daughter to her room and see that she gets to bed. There's nothing for you to do except put a jug of barley water at her bedside and keep her on fluids for a few days. Have you any straws? Drinking and chewing are not easy for her. And don't, whatever you do, touch that bandage. Nothing I can do now. I'll have a word with Dr Bennett – she'll be in good hands until I get a second opinion.'

Mrs Hargreaves and Belinda led Felicity through the front door into the hall, her mother emitting the clucking and soothing noises which fond adults make to small children. Felicity, with the sideways slant to her mouth, made a brave attempt at conversation. She was far more in command of the situation than her mother.

'Thank you both. I shall be perfectly all right. Belinda dear, you've been an angel. It was all *my* silly fault. I do hope you will all forgive me. Oh, and Belinda, could you call in at Watts the chemist's and leave a message with his father to thank Simon for all he did?'

Her mother butted in: 'You surely don't mean the errand boy? What's he got to do with it?'

Belinda explained that Watts, the chemist's son, was a student at the college.

'Well, I wouldn't know him if I saw him. Hilda answers the back door!'

It was not three o'clock. Hilda brought up Felicity's belated dinner of beef tea and custard to her. Jessie was preparing the dining room table for the usual high tea. In the rare moments when the two were alone they quickly dropped the formal servant-mistress relationship.

'Ee luv, ah'm sorry. Don't try to talk. Just let me plump pillers oop for yer... That's better.'

'Oh, thank you, Hilda. You are so kind.' The words came out through the one-sided smile. Pain subtly disguised.

'Listen, luv, ah've got a confession to make. Watts' errand boy 'as just coom to t'front door with some Michaelmas daisies. I thought 'e was standing in for t'florist like, delivering fer someone else – an' ah sent 'im off to t'back door. He said, "Would you give these to Miss Hargreaves, please, and tell her they're from Simon Watts." Ah could 'av died – ee luv, ah'm sorry. Ah've got 'em in t'butler's pantry waiting to be put in t'vase. Wot shall I tell yer mother?'

Felicity was unable to answer, moved to tears as she was by

Simon Watts' quick exit from the college and the prompt and simple gift. She also had been struggling to get beef tea into her mouth during Hilda's confession.

The door opened and Mrs Hargreaves, mistress now of a situation where she was in authority, turned on Hilda.

'The doctor has ordered complete rest and quiet for Miss Felicity. What are you doing here taking all this time with Miss Felicity's tray? Go down at once!'

Hilda caught a glance of the one bright eye and its shared understanding.

'That's my own beef tea, Felicity, get as much down as you can. It's the best thing you can take when you're poorly.'

'I'm sorry I'm slow, Mother. It's quite delicious. But I can manage. Please don't think you need to stay. I heard Dr Knight say that all I need was rest and that there was a good chance of my face healing...'

In the awkward silence, which followed between them, her mother conveniently noticed a picture that needed straightening and said, with her back to her daughter, as she fussed with checking the alignment: 'When you feel better, Felicity, I want to know your version of what happened this morning...' She turned round quickly at the distant sound of a doorbell. 'There's the front door. I'm expecting Mrs Cruikshank about next week's Mothers' Union. I'd better go, love.'

With most of the beef tea gone and a few spoonfuls of the custard left untouched, Felicity leaned back on the pillows, alone for the first time that day.

Thoughts went round and round in her head, recalling the grotesque pattern of this eventful day. All the other days of this term had been routine and predictable. But today! Suddenly she remembered the pale little three-year-old girl on the station platform and the speed with which her brazenly dressed mother departed. *Whatever's happened to the child?*

There was a knock at the door and her father followed before she could call 'Come in' through her clamped mouth:

'Well, 'ow are yer, lass? Let's get that tray out 'v yer way. Ah've brought yer t'evening paper. Nah, don't try reading too long. Ah've 'ad a word with Dr Bennett (ah didn't like that other chap) an 'e's coming termorrow. Ah told 'im yer'd 'ad enough on terday.'

To do Hargreaves justice, he felt deeply concerned for his only daughter. Sharp pains of apprehension shot through him when he thought that her good looks might have gone. He just had not the words, nor the habit, to express compassion. He felt out of place.

135

'Well, ah'll leave yer, lass. Yer don't want folks milling around. Peace and quiet's wot you want.'

'Thank you, Father, for coming to see me. And thank you for the paper. Better see what's happening in Bradford.'

She signalled goodbye with her now opened paper to hasten his exit.

How odd, she thought, that one can read almost as well with one eye as one can with two. Life isn't really so bad. Underneath the bandage she felt sure her right eye was seeing.

She scanned the headlines, realising how little she knew of civic and West Riding affairs. As perfunctory readers do, she turned to *Stop Press*.

'CHILD ABANDONED ON MIDLAND STATION, POLICE HUNT.'

No more, just the latest cricket score and the evening's prices on the Stock Exchange. How she wished she were able to telephone Belinda. If only she would come!

And Simon? His hurt feelings? Probably worse pain than her own.

It was to be many days before Felicity knew that the police were at that very moment in the Bennetts' morning room interviewing Belinda. She and the constable were sitting opposite one another at a small table, his blue and silver helmet between them. He licked his copy-ink pencil and in so doing left a purple stain on his lips.

'Miss Bennett, anything you can remember about this woman will be a help to us. Could you describe her face? Her clothes?'

Belinda felt at a loss, for the woman had made her departure so quickly that details had not been noticed.

'Well, she didn't say *good-bye* to the little girl – nor even look at her – and the child didn't cry when she was left...'

The constable did not seem to regard that as important. 'Appearance, Miss Bennett?'

'I suppose the way I describe her may seem rather snobbish. She was what Yorkshire folk call *common*.'

The constable wanted more. 'Er 'at, Miss. Ladies always notice 'ats.'

'It was,' said Belinda, now getting into her stride, 'a vulgar contraption, a crimson toque with two black feathers standing up at the front. Oh, I remember now, her costume was another shade of red with black braid edging ... and, oh yes, her cheeks were painted a rather defiant pink.'

She blushed to find herself describing a somewhat stereotyped *scarlet woman*. She hoped her own enthusiasm for theatre had not got the better of her and felt guilty that she had not asked the policeman about the child's welfare:

'But tell me about the little girl? Is she all right?'

'We've done all we can do, Miss. She's in the orphanage...'

'Where is the orphanage? Would it be possible to see her some-time?'

'Steady on! Bairn's got enough folks round 'er.'

'Officer, may I ask you? Have you heard of Margaret McMillan?'

'Can't say I 'ave, Miss. Oh yes, isn't she one of that Labour lot? I'm Tory miself, like mi dad and mi grandad.'

Belinda thought it was no use trying to convert the constable to child welfare and simplified the subject.

'You will hear of her. She's going to make her mark in Bradford and perhaps all over the world saving children from ill-treatment and poor environment.'

The policeman rose to go. He had no time for do-gooding. 'Thank you, Miss Bennett. I'll get back to the police station and see wot's gone wrong since I left. Good day, Miss.'

'Good day, Officer.'

Belinda joined her mother in the drawing room; her father was still in his surgery. Mother and daughter sat down opposite to one another ready to share the bizarre events of the day. This evening Hazel Bennett was the listener, Belinda the main speaker. Her mother's sympathy and empathy made it easy for Belinda to go deep down beneath superficial reporting.

'Do you think that Father will be able to do anything for Felicity – the burn – the scar?'

'Darling, if anyone can, he can. He's already been in touch with both Leeds and Bradford infirmaries. Since the last mill fire every one's been alerted. Leeds medical faculty is researching madly... Money's gone into that department.'

They talked on until darkness made the drawing room fire a friendly focus and Hazel went over to draw the curtains. Her hus-band's entrance coincided with the need for lights.

'Well, you are in the dark, darlings!'

The Bennetts, with far less money than the Hargreaves, had

managed to install their own electricity generator long before the rest of their neighbours.

He walked round the room to switch on the three well-shaded lamps, knowing his wife's dislike of the central chandelier.

'Could you manage the morning surgery tomorrow, Hazel darling? I'm going over to see the professor in the burns unit in the Leeds infirmary. I'm leaving Knight's dressing on until I've got the very best information. May get Felicity there, if that's what they think.'

Belinda touched her father's arm. 'You know how very fond Felicity is of her aunt Grace in Edinburgh? It will never occur to her parents to tell her about her niece. Do you think I could write?'

The Bennetts did not give snap answers where the Hargreaves were concerned. Hazel's agreement came first. Her husband had been thinking far beyond the present.

'Yes, Belinda, perhaps Miss Hargreaves would follow up your letter with a visit. There are things we all need to discuss with her ... and certainly it's time Hargreaves was in agreement about Edinburgh.'

'Father, that's the most wonderful thing that has been said since the accident. You really do believe Felicity will be able to cope with Edinburgh? And that they will have her?'

He put his arm round his daughter. 'She'll be all the better a doctor for this experience, Belinda,' and then with a laugh, 'Don't take that remark too seriously! I don't want you thinking you have to go through the fire before you go through medical school.'

They laughed together, a laugh born of compassion and companionship. Belinda stood up.

'I'll go and write that letter at once to aunt Grace. I remember the address from Felicity's letters.'

Up in her room Belinda wrote far more slowly than she usually did. She read the letter through, hoping it struck the right note. Belinda knew that if she posted it early next morning it would arrive the same day.

Dear Miss Hargreaves,

May I introduce myself? I am Dr Bennett's daughter and Felicity's friend whom you have kindly supported in our efforts towards becoming medical students.

Your niece will have told you that, on your advice and the conditions of the university, we are pursuing a course in chemistry and biology at the Bradford College.

138

I regret to have to tell you that yesterday Felicity had an accident in the chemistry laboratory, which resulted in her hair catching fire. This affected her right cheek.

All of us are hoping and praying that healing has already started but we shall not know until the dressings are removed and the specialist pronounces the diagnosis and prognosis.

Forgive me if I may seem intrusive but I do know that Felicity would love to see you; on the other hand I do not know how Mr and Mrs Hargreaves will react to my having dispensed the family news.

It is such a pity they are not on the telephone. A casual social call from you would have automatically extracted the sad news.

May I leave it to your tact and wisdom, Miss Hargreaves, to find a way through this difficulty?

I remain

Yours most sincerely,

Belinda (Bennett)

Grace read the letter with deep concern about Felicity and warmth in her admiration for Belinda. She quickly thought out her plan. She would propose a visit and get the letter into the midnight mail.

Precisely as Grace was penning the letter to Arthur and Gertrude, so her sister-in-law was writing a bleak little letter to her son.

Dear Henry,

Your father and I have not had a letter from you for three weeks, we thought letter writing at school was compulsory every Sunday.

This is to let you know that your sister has been injured (burns on her hair and face) and the least you can do is to send her a note of sympathy.

By the time you break up in December we hope and pray that she will be as near normal as God wills.

Give a thought to the distress of your parents at such a time.

Your ever loving mother,

Gertrude Hargreaves

PS: Did you receive the tuck I sent on the train after the Harvest Festival? No word from you, or your house-master, of its arrival.

Saturday arrived: the day on which aunt Grace came down from Edinburgh and Dr Bennett removed the dressings. Arthur went down to the station with the carriage and groom while Gertrude waited nervously for Dr Bennett's report. He would have liked to be on his own with Felicity but medical etiquette meant that he must suffer the irritating presence of Gertrude Hargreaves.

'This removing of bandages, Felicity, is going to hurt. But I shall try to be as gentle as I can.'

He unrolled and peeled layer after layer of bandage, each time getting nearer and nearer to the crimson skin.

It was off. The air flared across her face.

'My head feels lighter without that weight.' Felicity almost laughed to hide the pain.

Gertrude Hargreaves put her hands to her eyes in shock and let out a gasp of horror.

'This dark skin is only temporary. Much healing has to go on. It will change every day.' He put powdered boracic lint lightly over the right side of her face, leaving Dr Knight's skin dressing intact.

'May I have my hand-mirror please, Doctor?'

'No, my dear, not just yet. I just want your face to calm down a bit. Take these two tablets. Water, Mrs Hargreaves! Sleep is very healing, you know.'

He laid her carefully on her left side, pulled down the blinds and signalled to Mrs Hargreaves to withdraw.

He heard a carriage crunch its way up the shale drive. Anxious to avoid questions, he slipped out of the side French windows of the morning room and hovered until Hargreaves and, he presumed, his sister had time to be in the hall.

Gertrude had come down to the front door not exactly to greet her sister-in-law but to make sure that her stay began with the bad news.

The Hargreaves spent the evening in small talk. Gertrude and Arthur were not deliberately rude, they just had no idea how to ask questions that would elicit answers from Grace, nor would they have been interested had they received them. The music, art, literary and medical world in Edinburgh was a closed book to them. Grace kept the conversation going with enquiries about the

140

worsted trade; the recent election; Henry and his school, the Mothers' Union and the Masonic Lodge. Felicity came later in the conversation.

'I am delighted Felicity is doing well in her technical course. So clever of them both after the feminine curriculum of the Academy.'

'Nowt wrong with that. It's wot they went for.'

'But now the college course is preparing them for far greater things: the medical faculty in Edinburgh.'

'Oo's said she's going? She's not got my agreement.'

'I understand from Dr Bennett that you did agree but that it depended on the girls' success this year.'

'Ow could you know what Bennett thought? Ee's not gabbed to you, 'as 'ee?'

'No, I think it must have been in one of Felicity's letters...'

Hargreaves butted in. 'There seems to be a sight o' things 'appening which are kept from me. Wot I want to know is: 'oo's going to want 'er if 'er face is scarred?'

'Whatever do you mean, Arthur?'

'Well, college, society – an' chaps. And, and ... getting wed...'

Grace was so appalled at the crudity she sat silent for minutes. Gertrude had left the room to see what was happening in the kitchen. She had to keep up with her grand sister-in-law with a couple of ducks for their evening meal. Arthur, too, sat silent, drawing on his pipe.

'If, Arthur, it is true what you say, though I am sure it is not, do you not think Felicity will need to have her own career? You wouldn't want her to become an idle spinster, like me, would you?'

'Well you've not done blooming badly out of it, any road. Look what you get out of grandma's investment in engineering shares. I've watched them Scottish bridge-builders' share prices rise every year. Not like me 'aving to battle with all the ups an' downs o' wool.'

Grace realised the conversation was getting out of hand and that it was not helping Felicity. She was not prepared to pull punches.

'Arthur, has it occurred to you, ever, that the woollen trade in the West Riding is being overtaken by all those countries that have learnt our skills?'

With no reply from her brother, Grace went deeper and quieter. 'What if you can't leave your daughter an adequate private income, and she *didn't* marry?'

Grace hated herself for such an ill-bred argument and such a diminishing of Felicity, but allowed the words she had said to sink in.

'Well, sister, if our Felicity is determined, there'll be no peace 'ere if she doesn't go. But ah'll tell yer this: Wotever cap and gown she gets, she's not going to work as long as ah'm alive. Ah'd be ashamed if ah couldn't keep mi own daughter!'

'Thank you, Arthur, for agreeing to letting her go! You're a wise man to think ahead. She and Belinda will be accepted for next September. All you have to do is pay the fees.' She looked at him benignly. 'That's the easy part of a university education, isn't it?'

'Now, Grace, don't get soft. Brass is never easy! Well, wot will they be rushing me for? An' where's she going to live? With you?'

'No, Arthur. There are very pleasant houses in the Grange Road area, quite near the medical faculty. In fact I have been told of a very nice lady who is on the university billet list. She has a large room which Belinda and Felicity could share and a smaller one to let to another girl.'

'Come on, Grace, our Felicity as 'ad a room of 'er own all 'er life. I'm not *that* short of brass.'

'Well, shall we let Felicity and Belinda decide for themselves? It may be too late. I think Mrs McLeish has promised the spare room to a very nice girl who was at the Academy in Aberdeen...'

Aunt Grace knew when to throw in the appropriate snobberies.

'And just up the road there's a Church of Scotland which I go to...'

'An' wot's up wi' t'Methodists? Surely ther not that ignorant in Scotland.'

The conversation dwindled into trivia and gave Grace a hope of escape.

'Is it all right if I go up to see Felicity, Arthur?'

'You'd better ask t'missis. She'll know best.'

Grace went diffidently through the green baize door leading to the kitchen. The inner door was open and a remark she was not intended to hear rang through the back corridor:

'Get that quince jelly down from the store-cupboard, Jessie, for Cook. We'd better have two sauces for her ladyship.'

Grace tactfully slowed down her entrance.

'Sorry to interrupt you in the kitchen, Gertrude, but is it all right for me to see Felicity? Is she awake yet?'

Gertrude, startled by the intrusion, made it quite clear by her look that the green baize door was not to be opened by visitors.

'Yes, she's got a tray. I did the beef tea myself and cut the bread up into small pieces. If I know our Felicity, she won't want to be gawped at while she's eating. Don't tire her out!'

Grace had learnt through a much-travelled life to put the when-in-Rome advice into practice.

'What a splendid nurse you are, Gertrude. Of course I'll do as you say!'

She knocked gently on Felicity's door and waited until she heard a reply. It came through the door muted but welcoming.

Grace entered, not knowing what to expect.

She was relieved that the injured part of the face and head were skilfully hidden with neat but extensive bandages. The left eye still had a twinkle and the curve of the lips on that side of the face seemed so right for the name: Felicity.

'Aunt Grace, I can't believe it! How did you know? How did you get here?' The effort to speak must have hurt.

Grace's voice dropped to a whisper into Felicity's ear. 'Not a word, darling, but your friend Belinda got a letter to me by the next morning after your accident, and I put a letter into the afternoon mail and it arrived, evidently, yesterday evening! And here I am! It would all have been much easier if you had a telephone! The pretext is a share-holders' meeting in London, not that I ever go, but it seemed a reason which my brother would approve! Belinda thought that your parents had better not know that she had taken things into her own hands.'

'You schemers! Typical of Belinda. If anyone can get things done, *she* can.'

'Darling, I have wonderful news for you. Your father has quite come round to the idea of Edinburgh, but is adamant that you will never have to earn your living. Absolutely no need to think about that condition, my dear, and much water will flow under the Forth and Airedale bridges before that arises. Sorry, dearest, I haven't even asked how you are?'

'Talking's difficult, but that's mainly the bandage. I shan't really know until the specialist deals with me. You know Dr Bennett, don't you? Belinda's father? A friend of his is a specialist on burns. He has a research unit in the medical school in Leeds, so I couldn't be in better hands. Isn't that great?'

'My dear, everything in the world will be done that can be done, but nothing is as healing as your bright spirit. Your mother is a good nurse and your father will, I know, even though he sometimes sounds rough, not spare a penny if it can help you.'

'You are kind, Aunt Grace, I feel better already. Yes, my mother *is* a good nurse. Between you and me, we are both at our best, or so she thinks, when I am helpless.'

They both laughed, each with a different angle on the relationship.

It was the moment for Grace to remember Gertrude's instructions.

'You've managed most of your food. That's good. I was told not to stay long. Are you able to read, darling?'

'Yes. Isn't it strange? I can read almost as well with one eye as with two. And I think the bandaged one is hardly hurt at all. But my face...? Do you think...?'

Felicity struggled to find words which avoided self-pity and would not distress her aunt. She changed the subject with her one-sided smile.

'I'm longing to see what you've brought me to read!'

'I've brought you *Medicine as a Profession for Women* by Sophia Jex-Blake. She is a fighter still! Nearly thirty years ago she and women colleagues tackled Edinburgh with everything against them except their own pluck. I was twenty-two when she wrote this. Not exactly light reading, my dear, but it will spur you on. Pass it on to Belinda when you've finished it.'

Felicity's neat, well-shaped hands were unhurt and she took the book and opened it, talking into it as book-lovers do. 'You're the only person in the whole world who would think of such a present. Of course I can read and I shan't need my Nelsonian eye.'

Grace picked up the tray. 'I must leave you now. From my brief visit to the kitchen I know that we're having duck this evening – special treat for the guest – so I must change quickly before the gong goes! Make the most of your Yorkshire food, dear. You won't get your mother's cuisine in Edinburgh lodgings! I'll come up to say goodnight.'

'Please do! There's something I want to talk to you about and ask your advice.'

Grace had the good sense not to question now.

Felicity, as she so often did, finished the conversation on a flippant note: 'Enjoy the ducks! There won't be just one, you know! As your father used to say about duck: "There's ower much for one and nobbut enough for two!"'

The meal, instead of the usual high-tea time of five thirty, was at six thirty: Gertrude was anxious to demonstrate that she could keep up with Grace and her kind. Every item, small or large, was in a silver dish and the orange and quince sauces were in silver sauceboats. All of these were only used on special occasions or

144

Sundays. They were polished every week and each wrapped separately in green baize cloth along with the smaller silver items which came out on At Home days and the methodist minister's visits.

The special guest supper with its perpetual succession of rich fare demolished conversation. Grace went through all the permutations of praise of her sister-in-law's table (though in high society it was *not done* to discuss food) but not a single enquiry was directed at her about her life in Edinburgh or her travels.

After the serious main course Arthur pressed the bell with his foot on the carpet and Jessie appeared carrying a banquet-sized queen's pudding with its traditional bowl of pouring custard.

This was served and eaten in complete silence. It seemed the right time for Grace to make her exit.

'Would you excuse my leaving the table? Felicity asked if I would go up and talk to her for a while.'

The two other Hargreaves spoke in unison.

'Wot about cheese, lass? We 'ave this Wensleydale sent down every week from Leyburn. Yer'll not get this in Scotland!'

'Well, if you do go up, Grace, see that the gaslight's out at nine. Hilda's put arrowroot biscuits and a treacle posset. There's a night-light and matches on the bedside table...'

Grace half listened to Gertrude's instructions and then went upstairs. Felicity's visible eye glowed with welcome.

'Sit near here, Aunt Grace, then I shan't have to turn my head.'

They chatted through the small talk of the college courses, the fun of Belinda's friendship, Felicity's lack of interest in courting young men like the impossible Archie, the comedy of her mother's At Homes, the wonderful visits she'd had in Edinburgh...

'Felicity dear, don't tire yourself out. What was it you really wanted to talk about?'

'Does it shock you that Belinda and I have been to see aunt Amy Ackroyd in Barlockend Asylum?'

'Not shock, but surprise ... tell me more.'

'It was seeing her portrait and books in the attic – and no-one ever going to see her...'

'How is she? I knew her so little. You see, although the twins were very near my age – just two years younger – I never saw them after I went to Edinburgh in '72. But they were a wonderful pair. Completely devoted to one another. Inseparable. They lived on in the same house, after their parents died, and shared everything. Even the same big four-poster.'

'Tell me about their teaching. However did they manage to get to college?'

145

'They were very different from your mother. She was a home girl, pretty, attractive to young men. Burley in Wharfedale and its social round filled her life... The twins, three years younger, were highly intelligent, bookish, and lived in almost a secret imaginative world of their own. The local vicar recognised their talents and tenacity and gave them the run of his library. He prepared them for college. They loved it and came out top of their year!'

'Yes, I saw their prizes – but do go on.'

'They got teaching jobs in the same school in Ilkley. I do know how gifted they were because I went to an open day in the school and saw a stage production where every single child from the age of five to twelve was in it!'

'Do tell me! I wonder if that's where I get my love of drama, from – of all people – the Ackroyds.'

'Perhaps a little from the Hargreaves and...'

'Yes, Father told me that you played Queen Elizabeth in a pageant of Mary Queen of Scots in Holyrood Palace. He was not very enthusiastic about theatricals, yours or anybody else's, was he?'

'Oh, I've remembered the play Caroline and Amy did with the children. It was *The Pied Piper of Hamelin*. The youngest children were the rats and the older ones the children who went into the mountain. The grown-up parts were played by the teachers. It was splendid. The children will never forget it. The rats squealed with joy not fear.'

'And now she is a withered old lady and only thirty-eight years old...'

'Do you hear from Caroline?'

'Her husband, uncle Jack, writes to father now that he is exporting merino wool from New Zealand. Caroline adds a footnote – with no reference to her twin. Mother never speaks of either of them.'

'Back to your aunt. Your mother wrote a brief note saying that Amy had been put into a *home* on doctor's orders.'

The conversation came to an abrupt end as Gertrude entered without a preliminary knock. She spoke to Felicity across her sister-in-law as if she did not exist:

'Did you enjoy your supper, love? I got it ready myself. Say goodnight to your aunt.' She turned to Grace: 'Bottle's in your bed. We don't stay up late here, you know. Not like you do in the city. Father will take you to the station tomorrow morning for the Leeds train.'

'Thank you, Gertrude. My London train is twelve thirty and there are always porters to deal with luggage.'

Felicity was now with her one night-light and her thoughts of her aunt. How utterly unalike she and her mother were – but then, of course, they were not blood relations.

When Grace went into the drawing room the stridency of Gertrude's voice and the last few words were all that Grace caught as she closed the door.

'You're surely not letting that college and that Watts boy get away with it? She might have been burnt to death. Damages, I say! At least!'

Arthur just looked daggers at his wife and despairingly at his sister, whose entrance calmed the atmosphere.

'I've just come in to say goodnight. Felicity has settled down, Gertrude. May I take the blue album up with me? There must be several new photographs I have not seen.'

The thought of the solitude of the green room and the luxury of her own company sped Grace on her way well before ten o'clock.

She sat on the green velvet boudoir chair and opened the album.

She slipped over the familiar photographs taken in the thriving thirties when her great-grandparents had visited Russia to advise the Czar and the crown court on army uniforms. On to '73, when Arthur and Gertrude were married, as the Yorkshire folk put it, in slap-up style. She turned over the delicately painted floral mounts to see if she could find any photographs of the Ackroyd twins. Not one. She noticed one of herself, aged twenty-one, with her left hand lying over her right displaying an engagement ring. All the latest photographs seemed to be of Felicity with the gilt-edged insignia of Bradford, Ilkley and Harrogate photographers. It was evidently an annual event. The latest one of her niece was with her father standing each side of a heavily carved lectern, Felicity looking rather embarrassed. Her father was exuding self-satisfaction.

A ripple of fear ran through Grace's body as she looked at the intelligence and humour in Felicity's face, which even the static camera could not miss. How might that face look in the next photograph to be taken?

Grace Hargreaves, an undogmatic but true Christian, always made prayer a very private affair. She remained in the little green chair sending out healing thoughts, positively willing full recovery. Almost exhausted, she appealed to a distant God and then to a more approachable Christ.

147

Her mind went back to her own bleakest days, nearly twenty years ago, when her only salvation had been prayer. Now in her middle age she felt it was rather presumptuous to put the onus on to God. He has no hands but ours, she reasoned, and remembered the letter and poem she had received from her American friend just before she left Edinburgh. She took the poem out of her handbag. It was by the American poet Emily Dickinson. She read it slowly and just audibly:

> If I can stop one heart from breaking
> I shall not live in vain:
> If I can ease one life the aching
> Or cool one pain,
> Or help one fainting robin
> Unto his nest again,
> I shall not live in vain.

Dr Leonora Plunkett, an outstanding doctor in Boston, Massachusetts, had been seconded to Edinburgh two years ago. She had become one of Grace's closest friends and one of her musical group who met on a Saturday evening every month in Grace's house. Leonora was an agnostic whom Grace thought was more Christian than all her Christian acquaintances. Leonora had limitless compassion cooled with dry-eyed judgement. Grace knew that healing thoughts and professional advice would be generously winged across the Atlantic. She would write to her as soon as she reached home.

Grace Hargreaves lived up to her name as she joined Gertrude and Arthur at the breakfast table on the morning of her departure.

'I always enjoy sleeping in that lovely tester bed, Gertrude. I find the green room so restful.'

'Well, there aren't many houses where you'll have feathers and down from local geese, like you do here. Our feather mattresses are turned and shaken every week. Down quilts are hung outside and given a good beating. As soon as you've gone today, Grace, sheets'll be in the set-pot. It's a good job you're going on washing day.'

Grace was made to feel that one more day of her presence and the whole routine of Stonegarth would be put out.

Arthur, uninterested in domestic small talk, had just read a letter which had been delivered by hand.

'Well, Bennett's not wasted much time! 'E's coming this morning at ten and bringing t'specialist with 'im. So we need to get a move on. See everything's ship-shape, Ma!'

'You'll not be going to the mill then, Father, will you?'

'Nay, lass, sickroom's no place for the likes of me. Yer've got Grace. It's women's work!' He turned to his sister. 'Ah'll be back to take yer to t'train at ten minutes past twelve, Grace. See yer ready. Ah'll be off now.'

Gertrude's scowl at her husband's back spoke her thoughts: time for his sister and not for his daughter.

Even with half a face, the bandaged girl was welcoming. There were felicitations from three of them, but Gertrude was standing like a nurse on duty. The two men donned masks. The consultant scrubbed his hands at the wash-stand while Dr Bennett gently removed and rolled lengths of bandaging:

'It's going to hurt a little now, Felicity,' he said as he came nearer and nearer to the skin.

'Hold her hand, Miss Hargreaves.'

This was an awkward moment; Grace had deliberately put herself at a tactful distance on the stool in front of the little French desk, ten feet away from Felicity.

Bennett had chosen *Miss* Hargreaves, rather than *Mrs*, as he thought it would be too upsetting for her mother and that Felicity's aunt was more stable. Gertrude had posted herself on the right-hand side as the obvious theatre assistant. She went scarlet in the face with silent anger at the doctor's insult. Grace, without a look Gertrude's way, quickly drew up to Felicity's left-hand side.

The two men seemed oblivious of the silent drama.

Only the French wall clock broke the silence. Its encouraging pendulum seemed to be a metronome for the consultant's skills and a bidding to the onlookers:

Keep	–	*Still*
Keep	–	*Still*
Soon	*be*	*Over*
Soon	*be*	*Over*
Well	–	*Done*
Well	–	*Done*

The consultant bared the skin. It had an angry look of raw red and livid white. He touched the outer edges of the scar with a gloved finger and peered at the injured flesh through a magnifying glass. Felicity had, imperceptibly, been given a whiff of chloroform, but her left eye opened.

'The stuff I'm going to put on your skin, my dear, is as old as the hills and as new as the moon. You'll know it, Bennett, just the old fashioned Carron Oil, goes back to Thomson in the eighteenth century. We've still not found anything better.'

He signalled to Grace and Bennett and whispered his orders, masking them both as he explained that they were to assist him in a slight operation.

As the small scalpel was removed from the case, Gertrude gasped and threw her arm forward in protest. As he squeezed a local anaesthetic on the upper cheek he muttered through his mask, 'Keep back, madam, keep back!'

The only sound was the clock pendulum gently asserting that life was normal.

In less than a minute Mr Berkeley-Millington had rearranged the skin of the cheek and eyelid so as to release the painful contractions of the scarred tissue. It was a miracle of 'flap surgery' which was to give Felicity, in all the years to come, one unusually deep laughter line.

They all met again in the drawing room, where, surprisingly, a decanter of Madeira and glasses were set out. Arthur had decided that such an occasion demanded a slight shift from the restrictions of Methodism and indeed had already helped himself to a glass on his return from the mill. He greeted the consultant with Yorkshire caution.

'Well, I 'ope yer've made a good job of her, Sir. Folks tell me if you can't, no-one can!' He looked at his watch and his sister. 'Ready, Grace? Time we were off! Shipley's best for Leeds.'

At twelve fifteen Arthur and Grace stood on the Shipley station platform waiting for the train to Leeds.

'Yer can manage at Leeds all right, I reckon?' Plenty of porters. It's nobbut any distance to t'London platform.'

Arthur, who had put up a blunt front about his daughter's accident, was really more concerned than he ever disclosed. He also felt a pang of regret, as he watched Grace glide away, that his sister had not been given a warmer welcome.

He drove the carriage to the Midland Hotel in Bradford, turning over in his mind Grace's marked affection for his daughter.

He began to wish he had made more effort to make up for Gertrude's jealousy. As he ordered his mutton chops it crossed his mind that neither he nor his wife had given a thought to Grace's midday dinner.

'Well, she's got both common-sense and brass,' he said, salving his conscience. 'She can get summat on t'train.'

On Leeds station Grace's leather suitcase and matching hatbox were immediately picked up from the carriage by a porter: His practised eye spotted the destination *London* on the labels.

'Just nice time. London train starts 'ere so I can put you on right away, Madam! Goes out twenty to one.'

Grace was quick to intervene: 'Not London, Porter, Edinburgh, please.'

'Then I'd best take yer old labels off, Madam. Yer don't want yer luggage sent off to London, now, do yer? Yer've got forty minutes before t'Edinburgh train, so I'll put yer in t'ladies first-class waiting room and come for yer in 'alf an hour. Would yer like a paper, Ma'am? Or owt to eat?'

'Well, I would like the *Yorkshire Post*. No thank you, nothing to eat. Tea on the train is such a pleasure! Here's half-a-crown. Keep the change!'

The porter went off beaming. 'Not many like her. Don't seem Yorkshire or Scottish to me. Threepenny bits yer mostly get from them – a proper lady, however.' He said all of this facing the newspaper vendor, who supposed he was a bit off his head talking to himself like that!

8

The hours had seemed leaden yesterday but Felicity had woken up this morning consciously aware that the scorching pain was not as vicious as before. The stabbing fear of disfigurement had stilled her into acceptance of whatever was to come.

For the hundredth time, since she was alone in her room, she counted her blessings. Today it was a longer list than usual. She could *see, eat, drink, write, speak* and *hear*! And although she found the picture was a little grotesque, she could *smile*.

She was practising the movement into her hand-mirror when there was a knock at the door and Hilda came in with the breakfast tray:

'Eee, luv, I'm glad yer've 'ad a sleep! I fetched yer breakfast up an hour ago but when yer didn't answer I left t'tray on t'landing an' took porridge and tea back ter t'kitchen. It's all fresh, luv. Let's sit yer oop, comfortable like.'

Felicity had, of course, included Hilda in her blessings but she doubled it now.

'Hilda, you've brought the post, too! How did you...?'

'Well, luv, I took them straight out o' Bob's 'ands an' sorted out the dining room ones for Jessie. Yer'd laff at Bob, 'e says, "Them's been sorted by Miss Elsie, an' she says: 'Sithee, Bob, give them to 'ilda. She'll get 'em to Miss Felicity choose 'ow!'"'

Felicity, like all people with sharp curiosity, peered at the postmarks and the handwriting before opening the letters. As a gesture to Hilda she held two of the envelopes for her to see.

'Not a word, Hilda, but that's from the chaplain at Barlockend.' She looked again at the envelope but kept the surprising insignia of Mirfield Community to herself.

'Easy to tell the blue one, Hilda. Look at the writing! One day I hope you will meet Miss Butterworth. She was my favourite teacher and, secretly, I think I was her favourite pupil!'

Felicity put the letters down unopened.

'Hilda, I mustn't keep you, or Mamma will wonder what you are up to. But when you take Leo out for his walk would you please deliver this note to Watts' shop? It's a little note thanking Simon for the flowers and all his kindness.'

'Of course, luv. None of my business but I 'ope yer apologised for t'front door shut on 'im. Eee, I were that sorry! But I'd best be off! Crikee!! We've let yer porridge get cold!'

She made a quick exit from the room with the letter, leaving the tray.

Felicity's anticipation of two of the letters warmed up the porridge, which she noticed she could swallow more quickly than the day before. She left the bread but used the knife for the envelopes.

The third one, on which she had made no comment, bore a rather immature handwriting. It was from the insufferable Archie. She left that until later.

The Roberta letter was opened first, neatly, as it deserved to be.

My dear Felicity,

Belinda, the dear soul, has sent me the grievous news of your accident and here am I, physically so far from you, and unable to help except with my thoughts.

As you know, my dear, I have always been able to find words but at this heart-breaking moment I can only take the easy way out and turn to our Lord to say it for me.

> For he shall give his angels charge over thee
> To keep thee in all thy ways.

I have just read that psalm through and it seems so right for your brave spirit.

I am diffident about suggesting to your mother that I come to see you, for Belinda did not say whether visitors would be welcome or not.

Only know this, my dear, I shall be thinking of you night and day.

Do you remember the lines in Keat's *Endymion* which (I think) you learnt by heart? I wish, most fervently, his words for you: '…and a sleep / Full of sweet dreams, and health, and quiet breathing.'

What should we do without our treasure trove of poetry? Stimulating and comforting through all the changing scenes of life.

> May I always remain,
> Your affectionate friend and help-mate,
> Roberta (Butterworth)

Felicity returned it to its envelope affectionately, adding Roberta to her list of blessings.

She opened the next letter, wondering what Roberta, so secure in her faith, and Anthony Thompson, so uncertain in his, would make of one another. The Mirfield Community envelope intrigued her. Was he seriously thinking of joining a Community?

Dear Felicity (if I may be permitted to put this lovely name into writing),

Belinda (I trust this is in order too) has written to tell me the distressing news of your accident. I can only hope and pray, as all those who know you will be doing too, that God and his guardian angels are keeping a watchful eye on you and sending out healing thoughts.

It was difficult to keep my mind wholly on my Latin class this evening when I had just read the bad news. At such times one helplessly prays. Therefore, ignore the doubts I expressed when you were here and say with me: '*Non nobis, Domine sed tibi sit gloria.*'

(You may know the translation but to save your tired eyes let me put it into our own wonderful language: 'Not unto us, O Lord, but unto Thee be the glory.' Does that sound egotistical on His part?)

Read between the lines, Felicity, and you will feel His power. Doctors do the outward treatments, but you, and God, (Nature?) will do the rest.

Do not worry about not being able to visit here. Belinda has promised to do so on her own but I hope that on such a day I shall be on duty to accompany her.

I remain,

Your servant and friend,

Anthony Thompson

The letter made no reference to the Mirfield envelope. Had he just been a guest there?

The day seemed endless. Belinda had not yet arrived as she'd written to say she would. Now a slow sun was hovering in the west, scattering pink petals of light on to the pictures and mirrors in her room.

This ridiculous staying in bed, which her mother insisted on, was now becoming irksome. Surely healing skin did not depend

154

on inertia? Felicity had now recovered quite a presentable chunk of her inherited Hargreaves determination: She would meet her next visitor downstairs.

But how private could her conversation be with her mother and father around – especially her mother? Perhaps solitude was a luxury she might never regain. She decided to be a supine invalid until after Belinda came to see her. She would make the most of it. '*Soon, please, soon!*'

She re-read a letter she had received from the Winkleys.

Dear Felicity,

We have heard through Miss Butterworth, who had heard from Belinda, that you have had the most frightful accident in the laboratory at the Technical College. Dearest girl, we are all most terribly concerned about you and asked our dear old vicar to say a special prayer for you from the pulpit last Sunday, which he did in his own dotty way. (He called you Forget-me-not, which made us giggle, but God should be able to translate it to Felicity as he did get the Hargreaves right.)

Mamma will be telephoning your mother to ask how you are and to suggest that as soon as you are well enough we drive over to bring you here to spend the day.

Meanwhile, dearest Felicity, get better soon.

Tomkins, our head gardener, is delivering this letter and with it the very best of the Alicante grapes he is so proud of. His face lit up when we said they were for you and he very sweetly said (in that Yorkshire voice of his) 'Ee, ah really took to that Miss Hargreaves, not stuck up like some as come 'ere.' (I cannot write as he speaks but you are clever with Yorkshire dialect and will be able to read his voice.)

Everyone here (including Lassie, our Goldie, and Cato, the cat) send love and every possible good wish for complete recovery.

We remain,

Always your loving friends,

Olivia and Kate

P.S. Mamma and Papa send sympathy and good wishes and they hope that you will be fully recovered for Charlotte's Coming Out Ball on Friday, December 21st. Expect an invitation next week.

P.P.S. Charlotte was thrown from her horse last week but apart from a few bruises and a bad temper she seems all right.

She relaxed into thinking of the closeness of her friendship with Belinda. It really was a marriage of true minds. Where would she ever meet a man of such strength and magnetism? Certainly not in Aireley! That reminded her of the letter, in an immature hand, which she had tossed on one side:

Dear Felicity,

Ma tells me that you have burnt your face and that I should write to you. I suppose it's all you can expect working in a tech. Excuse me for saying but we all thought you were daft for going there. No place for pretty girls. You will not want to go to the Masonic Ball and the Rugby Dance now so scrap my invitations. No need to ~~right~~ write.

You will be pleased to know that I've joined the Territorials as a sideline. Nice work as going from a public school you go into the officer class right away. So look out for my pips!

Letter writing is not my line, as you know, so I will stop and just say: Keep your pecker up!

I remain

Your friend,

Archie

P.S. My serving time at your dad's mill finishes at Christmas so I hope to leave Aireley. Now that my aprentise is finished I am on the look-out for something bigger. Aireley's not much of a place when your ambishous.

Her reading – or misreading – was interrupted by a knock on the door, quickly followed by a breathless Hilda.

'Guess 'oos in the 'all, Miss? 'Tis Miss Belinda!'

'Bring her up at once, Hilda! Take all this debris away!'

Hilda removed the tea and supper things over to the mahogany stand fixed to the wall of the landing and with a speed which would have drawn wrath from her mistress, she ran down the stairs as far as the lower landing:

'Coom oop right away, Miss Belinda. Yer'll be a real tonic for 'er. Can I get yer a coop o' tea?'

156

'No thank you very much! You're Hilda, aren't you? I've heard such a lot about you – from ... Felicity.' Belinda quickly worked out that this relationship broke through all the servant/mistress barriers.

Hilda disappeared with a beaming smile, looking as if she had been made a member of a very exclusive club.

'Darling!' Belinda's voice used the endearment – so rarely heard in Yorkshire – as a benison.

'Belinda!' Felicity could say no more. Tears of joy drowned speech. It was whispered as if in answer to a prayer.

Belinda took the nearest chair, which was on Felicity's right side, and looked at the face lightly masked in gauze. Then standing up with her usual decisive movement she said: 'May I go to the other side and then I can see the twinkle in your eye!'

She pulled Felicity's buttoned velvet nursery chair to the left side of the bed and held the outstretched hand while still standing. It was Felicity who calmed the emotion of their meeting.

'Belinda, darling, you're wearing *bloomers*!'

'Yes, I've come on my bicycle. Actually the bloomers are Mamma's. At least ten years old, but not the least out of fashion! Don't you think they are rather fetching?'

Felicity found it painful to giggle but could not suppress it. She pulled her left eye into a grotesque wink.

'But who do you want to fetch?'

Belinda did not even ask how Felicity felt; she plunged into the future to give her friend the heart to face it.

'Just as soon as you are better you and I are going to ride over Baildon Moor and on to Ilkley Moor!'

'But my parents won't allow me to have a bicycle. Mother thinks they are common and Father would think it *infra dig* for a Hargreaves to be seen on one!'

'Oh! But *you* don't need to buy a bicycle, my sweet, I've got the loan of my parents' tandem!'

Felicity laughed and thought of *Daisy, Daisy* but knew that opening her mouth to sing would be agony.

'Belinda, that does make me want to get out and about. What absolutely glorious fun! Reserve the back seat for me, won't you?'

They were exhausted with laughter and love and fell silent. The next few moments were filled with both of them contentedly sharing the Winkley grapes. Belinda lifted up the envelope, an intimacy that would have been an intrusion from anybody else:

'Had they any news?'

'Not really. Just the usual Winkley good spirits. Oh yes, Charlotte had been thrown by her horse.'

'Hurt?'

'No, I don't think so. Charlotte is a survivor. You've not met her. You and she would make a formidable pair.'

'If you think I am formidable, you should meet Margaret McMillan! Oh, Felicity! What a woman! I went to her meeting and I am now forever her devoted disciple.'

'I'm going to lie back now and not try to talk any more. I'm just going to listen to your telling me all about Margaret McMillan. Lucky you!'

'Oh, my dear, there's so much to tell! As soon as Miss McMillan got on that bleak platform it was as if a beacon had been lighted. You know – but of course you *don't* know – she was trained as an actress. She has a superb voice and a magnetic presence.'

Felicity, captivated by Belinda's exuberance, longed to respond, in spite of the facial pain. 'Wonderful, dearest, but Yorkshire folk would write you off as *given to gush*. But do go on!'

'I just *have* to enthuse over this wonderful woman who absolutely riveted the attention of that odd crowd! Bradford has never heard anyone like her; she's an idealist, an educator ... almost a mystic and a passionate reformer.'

Belinda paused for breath. She looked to see if Felicity were still listening.

'I'm talking too much. May I have a drink of your lemon water?'

'Oh you're not, Belinda. There's a clean glass there. Do help yourself. What did she have to say?'

'I wish I could remember the exact words – but it was her eyes, Felicity, they were radiant with sheer conviction. She talked of the devilish half-time system where children went exhausted to school. She described how the knocker man had wakened them at half past five to do six hours' machine-minding – in all that thunderous and shrieking noise – and then to drag themselves to school. I don't suppose there were any mill owners in the audience to hear Margaret's voice ringing through that packed hall:

"How *can* you educate children who are dirty and ailing? How *can* children learn when they are exhausted?"'

Any blush would hardly have showed on Felicity's face but she felt ashamed that she was the daughter of a mill employer. Yet when her father had shown her round the mill, she did not remember seeing a single child at any machine. But she was not to know that her father, on that special day, had schemed with the foreman to change the shifts so that his child workers were at school that morning instead of in the afternoon.

Belinda saw Felicity's discomfort and changed the subject.

'You know, Felicity, we never appreciated our good fortune at the Academy in having our voices trained and our bodies looked after. Our Maggie – for that is what most of them call Margaret – said that she and Rachel had come from a world where the human body was almost worshipped and where every part of the vocal organ was understood and nurtured. Isn't it interesting that in their training for the stage they realised that education begins with getting the body in harmony? She wants children to be bathed, dressed charmingly, speak well, sing and dance.'

Felicity spread out her hands in despair. 'Oh, Belinda, we're light years away from that.'

Belinda, desperate not to kill hope, rushed in: 'The good news is that Margaret's been voted on to the School Board. At least Bradford is ahead in that! Dr Kerr, the medical officer, was there and got a wonderful reception – especially from the McMillans. Papa is on top of the world about it. No government or Ministry of Education has given any support before but, oh Felicity, he has support now! She is fearless where officials are concerned and somehow, without money, she has had pamphlets printed.' Belinda shuffled through her precious pack. 'Look at this one, while I revive my chattering tongue!'

She took a long drink of Felicity's lemonade.

'Darling, you will tell me when you are tired, won't you? But there's one marvellous thing I still have to report!'

Felicity, whose listening never wavered, responded at once: 'Please, please go on, Belinda, it's the first real conversation I've had since we were on the train together. Sorry, that's wrong! I'll tell you more later. You know your scheming worked wonders. Aunt Grace came! Let's talk about that when you've told me the highlight of the meeting.'

'Well, you know I said that Papa was there. Oh, Felicity, what a wonderful man he is! He took me up to the great McMillans and introduced us both. He finished by telling her he was a medical doctor. I caught sight of the glint in her eye! She has feminine allure, Felicity, and the strength of a Samson. There was absolutely no chance of Papa escaping. She dazzled him with her knowledge of the political and medical apathy and sheer brutal opposition, then picked out a leaflet for him to sign.

' "Don't sign it before you've read it," she said with a twinkle. "You don't know what you're letting yourself in for. We need medical inspectors in the schools who will demand that school baths are essential to start off with ... and finally we need the support of every doctor in the land on the need for nursery schools."

'Father asked her what enemies she had in Bradford. She's a wily one! She enthused about these vigorous honest Bradfordians and the great surge of middle class idealism at work caring for the urban poor. Then she raised her voice and head and proclaimed: "A very small population compared with middle-class greed and upper-class indifference."'

Belinda paused and quietened. 'Oh, Felicity, what blinkers we've all worn in our comfortable lives!'

Held hands said what words could not say, until Felicity whispered, 'It sounds to me that there is more real Christianity in her than in all the bishops added together!'

Belinda picked up the cue: 'Talking of bishops, one of her enemies, who poses as a supporter, is a highly intellectual and influential canon of the Catholic Church. He insists that she is doing things quite the wrong way round. According to him it's children's *souls* we should be caring for first!'

Belinda paused, aware that Felicity had used energy in her listening.

'Are you worn out, darling? I'm so sorry, I got carried away... Another day I want to talk about our plans for Edinburgh and the kind of doctors you and I are going to be. Perhaps we could link up with Margaret and Rachel McMillan and specialise on women and children. There's so much needing doing. Last week I felt committed to the mentally disturbed. Here am I talking again! And here we are still with our year to finish at the Technical College!'

Just then the plump body of Mrs Hargreaves came in without a preliminary knock. She startled both of them.

'Miss Bennett, my daughter has been ordered rest and quiet. I thought a doctor's daughter would know when to leave.'

Felicity's thoughts that night were not of her scarred face but the scarred lives of thousands of Bradford's children. But how could she possibly keep pace with Belinda? And had she the singleness of purpose and tenacity to be a reformer?

Belinda had left the Hargreaves' house feeling deflated by her dismissal but deeply thankful for her own loving, tolerant, broad-minded, happy parents. She had an ambivalent feeling of being stifled by a sickroom but elated by her conviction that she and Felicity had a great future before them.

As she pedalled away, comfortably free and warm in her bloomers, she got nearer and nearer to the wide-open space of suburban Wharfedale. Why had she not thought of the tandem before? Tomorrow she would get it out and ask her father or mother to ride with her. It never occurred to her to doubt that when she and Felicity were in tandem together that it would be she, Belinda, who would be at the helm determining the pace, pushing Felicity's pedals by the force of her own.

Felicity woke up the next morning, after a restless night, with a little more aggression in her system.

Belinda had opened her eyes and her mind. She caught sight of a tatty envelope; Archie seemed such a poor specimen of a man that she pondered, not for the first time, why women were called the weaker sex. She remembered playing Phoebe in *As You Like It* and recalled her feminine guile. *I'll write to him a very taunting letter...* And so would she now! Silvius did not deserve it. Archie did!

She was grateful for the invalid table, which her mother had unearthed from the attic, and the writing materials, which Hilda had picked up from aunt Grace's desk. Thank goodness my right hand is unharmed, she thought. Letters always had been important to her; now they were her lifeline. But not this one! She held the lined sheet with distaste. It was paper from a school essay pad, scrawled with writing that almost looked like a sneer.

Her reply, on an impeccable sheet of Stonegarth writing paper, was penned by a Felicity her friends would not have recognised:

Dear Archie,

Your withdrawal of the invitation to the Masonic Ball neither surprises nor inconveniences me. Thank you for such a prompt response to the unpleasant circumstances which have caused it.

Your ambitious intention of seeking employment away from Aireley is understandable after the excellent apprenticeship you have received in this small, but big-hearted, town.

I remain,

Yours truly,

Felicity (Hargreaves)

161

She licked the stamp with delicious malice. Getting the better of someone who is not worthy of respect was wonderfully restorative. She felt she had Belinda behind her when she addressed the envelope in a very firm hand.

'Please God, don't ever let *her* marry!' Felicity almost said aloud. 'We are a pair. Quite complete.' She pulled herself together and picked up the Margaret McMillan pamphlet, thinking that she must make an effort to keep pace with Belinda. But how could she possibly live the life she lived and yet work with the people who meant to destroy it.' Blood rose uncomfortably into her face as she read the facts listed by Margaret McMillan:

1890: 140,000 children under 12 were working in the mills and factories in Great Britain.

1894: There were still over 4,000 children in Bradford working half-time in the textile mills.

In the 1870s half the babies born in Bradford died before their first birthday. Things were better in the '80s and '90s. But when Margaret McMillan arrived in 1893 the infant death rate still stood at over a third of the births.

Felicity read on; the gist of the text was horrifying:

Bradford, although it had improved in the second half of the century, was still a killer: damp, low-lying, smoky, dirty, dark, insanitary. Children exploited, women slaving... Shortage of nurses and doctors.

She dropped the leaflet. Did her father know? Did he want to know?

While Felicity was meditating in her bedroom so was her father in his office. Turning over in his mind the contrast of the great surge of the industry in his father's and grandfather's day he tried to bolster his self-esteem by recollecting the steady growth of Airedale in the twenty years he had been in charge of Aireley.

He buoyed himself up reflecting on the new offices, new chimneys and the well-built sheds he had seen rise round him. That the pall of smoke had grown too never crossed his mind. 'Ter make brass, yer make muck.' They were companions never parted. He did not envy the Listers, the Salts and the Fosters. Three storeys and three hundred workers were enough for him:

162

'None of yer six-storey monsters fer me, he thought. We cutz uz coat according to uz cloth, and by Gow we turn out good cloth too. *And* at t'price folks can pay!'

Hargreaves' tight fist had paid dividends.

But he sat at his desk, desperately trying to get rid of the gloom that today's *Yorkshire Post* had cast on him. He thought of all the nous he had used in putting money back into the mill: fire alarms – to avoid having to buy replacements.

He preened himself that he had got the right man in the rail-way system to get him special rates... Yer need brains in this job, not just machine-minders, he thought, and smiled to himself at the deal he had made with the insurance inspector, having convinced him of the invincible state of the mill. He conveniently forgot to remember that only one of the three floors was heavily beamed and strutted to take the weight of the newest Lister machine he'd got his eyes on.

He stood up and looked at himself in the office mirror. Taking a comb out of his waistcoat pocket he slid it lightly over his oiled hair. Then with both hands he gave a twirl of satisfaction to his moustache and prepared for home.

No, Stonegarth is not one o' those great mansions, he mused as he walked up Spring Lane. Wot do I want with tennis courts, ballrooms and the like? It's good enough for me an' the missis. Hargreaveses are not show-offs...

The mental monologue went on while he approved of the sign leading up their lane: *No Hawkers – Licensed Tradesmen Only*. A new board installed since Leo's arrival: *Beware of the Dog*, seemed to add security to self-esteem.

Select, that's what Stonegarth was, select.

He had thrown his *Yorkshire Post* in his office waste-paper basket – an unusually prodigal gesture for him. In all thrifty homes, especially in Yorkshire, newspapers earned their keep in the pantry, the privy and the parlour.

The frown on his face tightened. Why had they, a Tory paper, given all that space to this new-fangled Labour Party and those two flighty women up from London? 'They know nowt about t'mills. Just ranters all t'lot ev 'em,' he said aloud.

In the walk up the drive he had worked himself up into a bad temper again.

'Daft arguments against child workers! 'Ow else do they think families can top up their wages? Wiv given 'em schools. Wot more do they want? It's all thin end o' t'wedge. Weer will it all finish up?'

163

It was not until he was at the front door that he gave a thought to his daughter – and, of course, the cost of her treatments. Well, ah don't mind 'anding over brass to that Mr What's-is-name but ah'm damned if ah'm going to pay that Bradford feller.

The thought of the doctor and specialist reminded him of his sister Grace and her antics in London. I bet she's 'ad some good news at that there share-'olders' meeting. Dividends soaring it said in t'paper.

The imposing Stonegarth door was never locked except at night so he let himself in to go straight to his smoking room. There were certain letters he kept at home, not trusting his office staff. He took one out from an inner pocket, unlocked the tall cabinet with its twelve slim drawers, slid the roll-top front up to its full height, pushed the letter into the drawer marked A and clattered the roll-top down again with an audible snort. *Good riddance!*

That was the end of the Armstrong contract and with it the daft idea of a marriage of convenience.

Now it was Saturday, so Simon Watts dropped his role of student and went back to his regular job of delivering. Amongst the pills and potions were two items for Stonegarth which Dr Bennett had ordered.

Simon, groomed for this special errand, went out into the garden behind the shop and took a penknife out of his pocket. It was a tiny but well cared for garden, his father's pride.

There was nothing rough about Simon Watts; he had affectionate, gentle parents who were too sensible to have spoiled their only son. The Watts family knew every plant in their small garden, for Charles Watts' green fingers, which had measured out pills and patent medicines all day, took on a different life in his leisure hours. Simon glanced at the outsize mop-head chrysanthemums and the glaring dahlias, netted over, carefully preserved for the late autumn flower show next week. There were six rose bushes waiting for deadheading, on which just one deep red rose was surviving. It held itself upright, decorously closed but ready to unfold. *Felicity*! He had never ever breathed her name before without the obligatory *Miss*. He cut the long stem diagonally across and lifted the rose up to the light. He was careful not to disturb the three raindrops catching the low western sunlight.

Alone in the quiet of the evening he knew there was no other young woman in the world who could hold a candle to Miss Felicity. Was it ever going to be possible? He would stick to his

164

studies; get a job with good money; educate himself through the library. His mother would help him with good manners because she had been a lady's maid to a baroness.

He let his dream keep him in the garden. Dare he say, even to himself, that he loved her? He had become bold enough to change her name in his mind from Miss Hargreaves to Miss Felicity. He must remember to keep his place when he delivered the rose and the package to the back door. He liked that maid, Hilda. It wasn't her fault about the front door. He knew his place – or did he?

A kindly voice called out from the back door: 'Get off, Simon. Some of those medicines are urgent and it's getting dark!'

'I'm just off, Dad.' The boyish reply and quick smile gave no hint of the lovelorn lad who carried an impossible dream in his heart – and a red rose in his hand. The iron carrier on his bicycle had space to spare but he would not risk that rose.

Arthur Hargreaves had arrived home well before Simon put his bicycle down near the back door of Stonegarth.

The door was opened by the maid he liked.

'I've brought these from Mr Watts. Dr Bennett ordered them. How's the young lady, Miss? I hope she's mending. Would you give her this, please, with my regards?'

'I'll take it to 'er right now, son, and thank you.'

As he turned to get on his bicycle, he heard footsteps on the gravel far behind him. He turned and saw a man, whom he assumed was Mr Hargreaves, the master of the house, walking from the walled garden carrying a trug of red roses. Arthur Hargreaves enjoyed giving to those less well off than himself, when the largesse cost him nothing. He took several perfect long-stemmed deep red roses from a full trug.

'Take a few of these to yer mother, lad, with the compliments of Mr Hargreaves of Stonegarth,' and went on through the back door.

Simon Watts, the lad who was going to conquer the world, shrivelled onto the saddle of his errand-boy bicycle and gulped back sobs of anger in the darkened air. *Blast the man and all his bloody money!*

Simon, hurt and angry, threw a curt goodnight to his parents, torn between devotion to Felicity and resentment of the Hargreaves' patronage.

Fury fired his ambition. Science would override class barriers.

165

By dawn he had imagined himself into the new century. He would work with men of science, not with men who exploited the poor.

That's what I'll be, he thought, a doctor of science: Dr Simon Watts.

The previous evening at Stonegarth it was the ritual of her mother's lights-out. Felicity always found this final fuss irritating.

'Flowers out first,' Mrs Hargreaves said, as if she were playing at hospitals with a small child. 'There's a bit of class about these gardenias. But them Winkleys know what's what.' She carried the Wedgwood bowl out of the room and came back to the bedside table.

'How come you've got this?' She held up the slim vase as if it were a tooth-glass needing cleaning. In it was one red rose.

'Oh, Hilda brought it up. Wasn't it thoughtful of her? Leave it there. I like the perfume.'

Felicity, alone in her room with a single night-light, got out of bed to where Hilda had left another letter. It was exciting getting one at this time of night. In fact, never in her life had she had so many letters in a week. Sad that one had to be ill for people to put pen to paper.

Bending over towards the grudging light she read:

Dear Miss Hargreaves,

Please do not judge the absence of a letter as indicating my lack of concern. On the contrary I delayed writing to give you the peace you need to get over a dreadful shock.

I am constantly in touch with Dr and Miss Bennett, who assure me that you are responding to treatment and, as I expected, literally putting a brave face on it.

That little blank on the back bench of the laboratory is a constant reminder (if any were needed) that you are missing classes. I can assure you the class is missing you. Miss Bennett and I are making quite sure that copies of the notes are being done for you, with extra explanations on the practical experiments.

If I know Miss Bennett aright she will not leave you in peace for long. She will no doubt, as a bonus, entertain you with a fair imitation of the writer of this letter.

A wee word in your ear. Your friend has more 'spunk' in her than most of the young men put together. Has she told you that she made an announcement to the whole class of a

166

meeting to be held next week on behalf of the neglected children of Bradford? She riveted their attention and urged them to attend, telling them of a meeting she had been to last week.

The speaker was that doughty Scotswoman McMillan. With a name like that she should cause a stir!

This letter needs no reply. Keep your energy (and the stamp!) for something more important.

I close with heart-felt wishes for your complete recovery.

I remain,

Yours sincerely,

Robert Mackintosh

Amused, and extremely touched, she decided she would not answer it until she had shared it with Belinda, who was the main subject in the letter. Could he...? Might she...? Such speculations must never be put into words.

She moved to a simpler subject. Or so it seemed to her. A brief letter to Simon would do. Yet what could she say to that gentle, vulnerable boy? She was several minutes before the short stilted letter was written.

Dear Simon,

How very kind of you to send me this beautiful rose with such a delightful perfume. Fortunately the silly accident has not affected my sense of smell.

Had it not been for you I am sure that the damage would have been much more serious. I now feel sure I shall join the classes again.

With gratitude, I remain,

Yours sincerely,

Felicity (Hargreaves)

She put the letter out of sight. Hilda would deliver it by hand tomorrow morning.

The night seemed endless and she was almost pleased when her mother came in punctually at her usual eight o'clock, as if she were a paid night-nurse.

They exchanged polite good mornings but Gertrude Hargreaves' weather was always worse than anybody else's.

167

'Well, yes, it's all right now, but we shall have rain before the day's out.'

Felicity was out of bed in her dressing gown. 'As you insist, Mamma, that I stay in my room I might as well try to do something useful. Some time ago you asked if I would inscribe the names in the blue album. Would you please ask Hilda to bring it up to me? I have my Academy italic script pen and ink here in my desk.'

Gertrude rang the bell and gave Hilda her orders, welcoming any reason for keeping Felicity in her room.

'Yes, that will keep you busy. But do you think you know them all? There are some Hargreaves and Ackroyd relatives we only see at funerals. Those Dewsbury ones – canary-mad, they are – and those Batley ones never even asked us to their Winifred's wedding, even though we did send them a cut-glass biscuit barrel with silver fittings. *And* in time for an invitation.'

Felicity cringed at her mother's suburban snobbery but avoided commenting on the elusive connections by simply explaining that she would make a list before finally inscribing the names on the gilt-edged mounts. Her mother took the album from Hilda at the bedroom door and glanced at it with no show of interest.

'It's ages since I had a good look at it, or put any photos in it, except yours and Henry's. Everyone's camera-mad these days. Who the heck's going to look at them in a hundred years' time? All those glum brown faces?'

Taking it from her, Felicity said: 'Who gave you the album, Mother? It is a beauty ... and I see your wedding photograph is on the first page.'

'Daft me, I was just going to say your auntie Grace gave it to us but, of course, she wasn't an auntie then because you came three years later. Right and proper we were... Not like some people I could mention...' She trailed off into her own thoughts and changed the subject for her exit from the bedroom: 'Dr Bennett says your face is back to normal – well, like, as near to normal as we can expect!'

Alone again, Felicity forced herself to go and sit at her dressing table where the triple mirror reflected three facets of truth about her face.

Courageously she looked first in the right-hand mirror to scrutinise the scar on the right-hand side of her face. To her complete surprise, the cheek showed the bloom of good health, high-lighted on the curve of the cheekbone. Ecstasy soon turned to despair when she realised, of course, that the image of the face's right-hand side was held in the *left* mirror. She turned her eyes to the slim-looking glass on the left. Here was the truth. Lifeless skin, like parchment, stretched from the high cheekbone to the hollow near her chin. She watched a tear slink down the shiny ivory surface then trickle down to become absorbed in the lace at her throat. She turned her gaze centrally to the wide mirror, which reflected her whole face. To her surprise her pulse stopped racing and without any conscious effort she found herself gathering strength in an almost unreal calm. She would and could live with that face as she hoped others would do. *Others?*

Although she had put love and marriage to the back of her mind in her desire to have a career, she had never doubted that one day she would love one man and together they would create a home like the Bennetts' – full of warmth and understanding.

Felicity would never know that when Dr Bennett had been inspecting her skin that morning he had merged his role as doctor into hairdresser and with loving fingers gently manoeuvred Felicity's wild hair to become his accomplice. Only a man who understood the art of being a woman could have achieved so much. No word was spoken. In the silent swings of the pendulum were measured the compassion of those skilled hands.

Later that evening when the Bennett trio were chattering through the happenings of their various days, the doctor explained, almost dismissively, his attempts at hairdressing and how Felicity could still be the magnetic girl she always had been for those who had loving eyes.

The three laughed together with the knowledge and huge relief that Felicity might almost be herself again. Compassion, affection and healing were mingled together with mirth, enhanced by the glow from that generous hearth. To say that the Bennetts were a close family would be too limiting. Their love stretched out to a wider world.

At that enchanted hour when the sun sank down in flames gilding Baildon Moor, the Bennetts' sitting-room fire suddenly shot into higher flames like the opening bars of the Ninth Symphony. The united love of all three was focussed on Felicity.

That evening, while the Bennetts conversed together, Felicity sat answering letters she had received by the first and second post, from aunt Grace, Belinda, their Methodist minister and the combined Winkley family. The third and last post of the day brought a stream of letters from the Academy staff and girls, who had evidently heard the news given out at the autumn term reunion, which was always the first Saturday in November.

The letters – put on one side to answer tomorrow – ranged from one-line notes, '*Get better soon, Felicity*', to long painstaking ones where the pen seemed to have been dipped in holy water and the flesh-and-blood writers – tough hockey players – had discarded their sticks and pads and acquired astral bodies.

The most intriguing one, as surprising as it was astringent, made it clear that the writer would no longer need to be jealous of Felicity's good looks.

I wish now I had been nicer to you. It will be easier to be friends now that you are perhaps no better looking than I am. As my mother says: *God moves in a mysterious way his wonders to perform*. She is a wise old owl, my mother, though she would hit me if I ever called her old!

Felicity put that one in the cover of her blotter. A gem to share with Belinda, who would be calling tomorrow.

She had just sealed the last letter she had written, which audaciously began: 'Dear Grace' when Hilda called in to remove her tray. She glanced at the album.

''Owever are yer goin' to get through all that lot? Wen yer told me ah could do so, I 'ad a reet good look at it – an' don't tell yer mother – I 'ad a reel gurt laff! That one of yer great-aunt Foster with a palm tree growing at 'er side an' a daft little Yorkshire terrier standing up begging in front of a marble pillar... Ee, am glad our lot 'adn't cash for such dadlededrums. Only picture ah've 'ad took was on Blackpool promenade on t'mill outing, an' ah'm clutching on to mi straw 'at as if mi life depended on it. Ee, but those paintings in t'book! Ah've never seen owt so luvley; roses an' t'lot! An't little scenes on t'bottom o' t'pages wi' t'sea looking wet-like an' churches looking as if yer could 'ear t'bells.'

Felicity had no need to reply. She had time in this strange interlude in her life to let Hilda rattle on and she revelled in the uninhibited chat, which was, strictly speaking, not allowed this side of the green baize door.

'Ah'd best be off, or yer mother will be after me.'

Felicity neatly ended the possibility of chat by handing her a pack of stamped letters.

'Be an angel, Hilda, and get these into the eight o'clock post. I'd like them there by tomorrow.'

Felicity spent the next two hours trying to decipher who was who in the album and to list them in number order. She gazed first of all at her parents' wedding photograph. Certainly her mother had a look of to have and to hold. The naively pretty face had complacency written all over it. Her father, sitting on an ornately carved chair, with the bride standing behind him, looked as if he took her vow to obey for granted. So profuse was the maidenhair fern, so obtrusive the golden roses, that little of the dress was visible. The wide leg-o'-mutton sleeves and the throat-throttling lace seemed to diminish the bride's face to the size of a porcelain doll. Felicity marvelled that these two statues could ever have conceived her. She turned over one by one the oval, square and oblong settings surrounded by delicate watercolours giving palatial splendour to plebeian figures.

She looked critically at the photograph of Henry and herself, taken when he was three and she was five. They looked to be children incapable of ever climbing on to a rocking horse, let alone cantering on a live pony. Why ever were they dressed up to smothering point?

She shuddered at the thought of the photographer's face and camera, under his black cloth, and having to keep still for a whole minute.

One of the pages had four photographs. She jotted the names down on her paper, in order, as she recognised them. They were: Uncle Percy Ackroyd, her mother's cousin, manager of the Yorkshire Dyers Association. Her mother disliked his loud laugh but approved of his large salary and diminutive wife. Gold lettering on the base of the photograph showed that it, and many others, had been taken by A.G. Taylor of Bradford.

The next one bore the words: *Wesleyan National Conference Bradford 1880*. There was no name but she gathered it was her grandfather Hargreaves.

The one with Uncle Alf and his wife, though static, caught a hint of pleasure as they gazed at the canary in the cage dangling at their side. The only name was *Illingworth of Bradford* in gold engraved lettering.

She was finding the job tiring and was just deciding to leave the rest until tomorrow when she turned over again and found two completely blank pages. On looking closer she noticed that in each space there was brown card protruding from the slit at the bottom of the mount. She slid the left-hand card gently out of its frame and turned it over. It was a young and beautiful woman of about twenty. It was aunt Grace. She was half-reclining against the

171

back of a chaise longue, her left hand folded over the right, drawing the light to the ring on her third finger.

How little one notices the jewels worn by people with whom one is familiar, she thought. They just become part of them.

She recognised the ring on this familiar hand. She had never looked closely before at the ruby and diamonds, set in a love knot of gold. The whole photograph was enchanting. It was the face of a young, intelligent woman: serene; secure yet with a zest for life: a strange contradiction of strength, vulnerability and charm. The strong line of the jaw was softened by rounded youthful cheeks, which seemed poised for merriment. There was no suggestion of the fashionable rosebud pout in the lips, nor the classical sculptured shapeliness. The lips were parted, ready to respond generously to language, laughter or love. So closely did Felicity explore the face that she imagined she was seeing it in colour instead of the pale sepia monochrome image.

Full of grace and truth. Yes. That summed her up.

'Grace.' Felicity said it aloud as if practising for the future. Yes. She could say it more easily now.

But she made a mental note never to be so familiar in the hearing of her parents. Yet Grace was, after all, her godmother and, as such, need not have been an aunt.

With the same care as before, she manoeuvred the hidden photograph on the opposite page out of its frame and turned it over. The figure was impressive: a light-haired upright man, in the uniform of the Royal Scots, filled the picture. No aspidistras, palms or Grecian statues competed for attention. Here was a man of virile stature but with a sensitive mouth and discerning eyes; one quick to make thoughtful decisions and dare to be his own man.

Where had she seen this face before? There was something so familiar in that glance: the tilt of the head; the humorous but kindly eyes; the short but not insignificant nose; the neat, not too intrusive moustache. It was a tidy, but not prim face which one knew, once away from the inhibiting camera, would wrinkle into laughter.

Tantalised with curiosity, she kept the two photographs of the alluring young woman and the intriguing young soldier in her hand. Whoever had framed the two lovers, so closely parallel, must have held them in high regard. But who could have extracted them so viciously and turned blank card towards enquiring eyes? She would make them her own personal property.

Having delved so deeply into the album, Felicity lost all interest in the remaining photographs. She brought the velvet covers towards one another, hinged them firmly into the brass lock and put the album on one side.

Her eyes were drawn again to the man's face. Who did he remind her of? Where had she seen that face before?

The question was still in her mind long after she was lying on her left side physically wanting sleep but mentally reluctant to leave the company of the two, who obviously had been sent to Coventry years ago. Perhaps, now that she had been invited to drop the word aunt and call her just Grace, and, in less than a year's time, would be on more intimate terms with her in Edinburgh, she could be told something of their troubled story. Until then not a word to anyone. Not even Belinda.

The next day, Simon was already in the chemistry laboratory when Belinda arrived:

'Begging your pardon, Miss. May I have a word with you?'

'Of course, Simon, is it about Felicity?' Belinda thought she was breaking the class barrier by using Christian names.

He blushed and stumbled: 'I thought perhaps if you were seeing Miss Hargreaves you could give her my kind regards. Excuse me if I am speaking out of turn, but is anyone sending her notes of the lessons – while she is off sick?'

'Well, I said I'd take the set notes and the text books which Mr Mackintosh has already offered.'

'But is anyone doing the diagrams and setting out of the experiments with the processes? Excuse me for saying it, but if she is going to be a scientist she'll have to learn to ask the right questions and prove her answers.'

Simon Watts had never spoken so forcefully in his life before; he blushed and wrung his hands together.

Belinda, unable to shake hands, touched his shoulder. 'That will be the biggest kindness anyone can do for her, Simon. I will be your messenger.'

9

The rain splashing belated autumn leaves on the windowpanes woke Felicity at six o'clock. Like her Hargreaves grandfather, she enjoyed both early rising and rain. Now she would have a whole two hours to herself before her mother appeared at eight o'clock. Today, dressing was a liberating experience, making her choose each garment with sensuous discrimination, as she had never done before. Had the night's dreams made her more conscious of her body? Or was it that her damaged face made her value her body more?

Felicity still could not get Grace and her lover out of her mind. Why had she taken her aunt for granted? Was this the fate of all spinster aunts? Yet she loved her in quite a different way from any of her other relatives – even her parents. There seemed to be an unwritten code, voiced very often by her mother, that all relatives were a cut above those who were not. 'Blood is thicker than water' was proved by paying last respects at funerals and complete disrespect when they became vultures over wills. Aunt Grace was quite outside this category, consequently she was the happy receiver of generous letters of thanks, not the painful duty ones which Felicity sent to the remote uncles and aunts. Yet her parents' attitude to Grace was distinctly guarded.

As Felicity dressed, her mind went back over the years, recalling letters, cards and gifts from her favourite aunt. In the big wardrobe drawer was a large chocolate box – the lid held on with blue ribbon – bulging with the written symbols of her aunt's affection. Felicity remembered vividly her tenth birthday when she had received, by post from Edinburgh, an excitingly illustrated edition of *The Water Babies*, followed by her aunt arriving at Stonegarth a week later. Though Gertrude and Arthur could not see the sense of such an expedition they had been persuaded by Grace that she should be allowed to take their daughter by train and then by coach to the village of Arncliffe, way beyond Kettlewell.

The truth was that although Arthur showed only the bleakest of brotherly love for his sister and Gertrude often seemed to try to

174

denigrate her, they were both in awe of this untypical branch of the family tree.

All those years ago Felicity remembered her father tossing the letter over to her mother and saying dismissively: 'Well, let 'er go, though 'ow she can find owt worth seeing in Arncliffe beats me.'

Felicity, taking time to wash and dress, relived vividly that day-of-all-days when she and aunt Grace had set off very early in the morning – so early that they walked part of the way, as far as the mill, with the clogged labourers. But she and her aunt went on beyond the mill to the station to catch the train for Skipton. A huge treat in itself. And then the local wagonette, packed with people, took them to Kettlewell and on to the hidden-away village. It was sheer magic for a sheltered ten-year-old.

Her aunt had told her, in her own words, about Tom, the chimney sweep, and how he arrived exhausted at a little old lady's house. All Felicity could remember of Arncliffe was being lifted by her aunt to look over the old stone bridge and see the bubbling river and the green lawn of the long low cottage. She remembered every word her aunt said.

'When Mr Kingsley – who wrote the book – was staying here, he looked over this bridge, to the cottage, just as you and I are doing now. He saw a lovely old lady coming out of the door in her red petticoat, short dimity bed-gown and clean white cap with a black silk handkerchief over it, tied under her chin, and he made her into Mrs Do-as-you-would-be-done-by in his story *The Water Babies*.'

Felicity remembered that she had questioned her aunt with childish curiosity: 'But how could the man make a little old lady – only God can do that.'

'Well, you see, my darling, when people with imagination write, they can make anything in the world be true.'

Felicity remembered that she was not convinced until she had become a disciple of Roberta Butterworth's and wallowed in history, fiction, poetry and drama, all bristling with exciting words and characters whom she knew more intimately than those living around her.

Her thoughts ran ahead to the worlds which were going to open out for her – and Belinda – when she was in Edinburgh and near her aunt.

Contrary to her usual practice, she had just completed the careful manipulating of her fringe and the strands of hair falling between her ear and right cheek when her mother walked in without knocking:

'I see you're up then. Now stay where you are for a day or two. I'll tell you when I want you down.'

Felicity ignored the remark and did not argue; she much preferred to see Belinda here on her own.

She spent the day usefully, albeit impatiently, reading, sewing, sorting out drawers and occasionally looking out on the trees where odd leaves clung to stark bare branches. The melancholy of autumn droned on – day after day. It seemed to be a lifetime since she had walked down Spring Lane to the station and she thought enviously of Belinda, who took everything in her long stride.

It was now getting on for four o'clock and she remained by the window, her eyes fixed on the gate. And there was Belinda looking as purposeful as always, her long coffee-coloured cloak blowing out behind as if unable to keep up with her. Felicity waved frantically but Belinda's eyes were fixed on the front door, her mind on how she might have to deal with Mrs Hargreaves.

Hilda's excitement made her knock a mere formality.

'Yer friend Miss Belinda is 'ere, Miss. Shall I bring 'er up? She's got some 'ot-'ouse chryssies with 'er. Shall I tek 'em an' put 'em in watter or would yer like to 'ave a look at 'em fost?'

'Bring her up with her flowers, Hilda! Don't waste a minute! Does my mother know she is here?'

'Yes, she's down there in the 'all fixing the new lace 'macassars on the sofa, so I'd best be off and give 'er an 'and.'

Hilda arrived at the foot of the stairs to hear the final words of the brief conversation. Belinda was speaking.

'Father should be here in an hour and a half and hopes that he will be able to take Felicity back home with us for supper.' She lifted the gold watch on its chain and flicked it open. 'It is four minutes to four now. My father has a surgery at six. I know he would be much obliged if Felicity could be ready to leave at five-thirty.'

Belinda's confidence went through to her fingertips; she tapped the watch closed and faced Mrs Hargreaves' podgy but pulled-in face and listened to her pinched reply.

'Nights are drawing in, I'll have you know. It's no time for an invalid to be out. She'll get her death...'

'May I suggest, Mrs Hargreaves, that if we want Felicity to be out and about, full of life as she always was, we must stop calling her an invalid.'

'Don't you argue with me, my girl. She is my daughter and

176

she's...' She paused to find a suitable word. 'Disfigured. And don't you forget it!'

Belinda reduced her voice to an icy pianissimo: 'Then the kindest thing to do, in that case, Mrs Hargreaves, is to leave all decisions to her doctor, wouldn't you say?'

The next hour was crammed with Belinda's news – starting, of course, with the reason for her father's visit. Her shrewd summing up of lessons, tutors and fellow students included impersonations of Robert Mackintosh with his bell jars, test-tubes and deadly acids. His movements were all brilliantly mimed.

Belinda entertained Felicity before drawing out from her satchel the daunting notes of every chemistry lesson. It was a composite file of neat calligraphy from the pens of Mackintosh, Watts and Belinda. Felicity could not believe her eyes. She flicked through the papers.

'Oh, Belinda, you are all so kind! One thing this wretched accident has done for me is to show what wonderful friends I have. But do you think I have the brains to understand from print how to produce hydrochloric acid, carbon, sulphur, phosphorous and the rest..?' She scanned the file, impressed but alarmed, closed it and faced Belinda. Her mind made up.

'Will you tell them all that I am coming back in January! I never thought I would long for all those ghastly smells!'

They laughed together.

Felicity's laugh stopped abruptly. 'Belinda, I didn't like to ask you ... but I must... Have you managed to visit aunt Amy? I know it's difficult...'

'Yes, darling, I went last Thursday. I arranged it with Mr Thompson – although he was not going to be there. No, I didn't see her... You remember one of the duties allotted to her in her laundry work is ironing sheets? They all have jobs, you know, and she had dropped a red-hot iron on her foot... She was in the sanatorium, the warden said. I'm so sorry, dearest.'

Neither could speak. Another burn. And on such a helpless, unhelped woman. Felicity lived again the excruciating pain... But she had been cosseted and cared for and given the best medical treatment in the land. How could her aunt survive? How could flesh heal without healing words and touch...?

Thoughts were left unsaid. The pendulum of the clock swung like a bell – fifteen slow seconds before Felicity spoke.

'And Anthony Thompson? What is he doing for her?'

'He's on retreat for still another week – praying for her, I suppose...'

177

Belinda hated herself for allowing bad news, grief and bitterness to spoil this precious visit.

'Come on, darling, Father will be here soon. Which cloak are you wearing?'

Felicity drew out a dove-grey cashmere silk-lined cloak, which Belinda wrapped lovingly round her friend. They stood between the open doors of the massive wardrobe in intimate darkness.

Belinda lowered her voice for her final words, almost speaking into the wardrobe.

'Felicity, I wonder if you realise how often Simon Watts tries to find an opportunity to speak to me – to ask after you? It's not easy for him. You know yourself no boy on the chemistry course wants to be seen talking to a girl, in case tongues wag... It's agony for him, he's so shy.'

Belinda looked closely for Felicity's response, which came falteringly.

'Tell me... *How* does he question you?'

'Oh, the usual enquiries about your health – when you are coming back to college – but yesterday he asked if he would ever be allowed to see you...'

Belinda held Felicity's shoulders and spoke into her shadowed eyes.

'Those flowers, my dear, are not from me. Simon hid them in his locker and waited until everyone had gone before he gave them to me. Listen, Felicity, that boy is devoted to you – helplessly and hopelessly in love...'

The knock on the door heralding her father and Felicity's mother gave time only for the snatch of a phrase:

'More, much more, later, when we are alone ... at home...'

'I see you are ready, my dear. How splendid you look!' Dr Bennett, unlike most medical practitioners, knew that this was the best tonic for any patient provided it was resonant with truth. 'No need for hat and gloves, Felicity, the landau is all closed up for this special night.'

This was the point where Mrs Hargreaves was not going to take doctor's orders. 'No daughter of mine, doctor, is leaving this house without hat and gloves. What would the neighbours say?'

The doctor knew he was beaten. Gertrude Hargreaves with her minimal intelligence had a genius for making a minor matter into a major concern. The doctor turned towards the door.

'Belinda, my dear, you and I will wait in the hall until Mrs Hargreaves' sartorial strictures are resolved. It is now twelve minutes to six. My surgery opens at six o'clock and I have reserved

178

the first fifteen minutes for very important treatment of this important patient whom I do *not* wish to see cluttered with hat and gloves.'

Felicity had the unique experience of feeling the wind taken from her mother's sails.

Within two minutes the three were through the front door and away.

Gertrude sat down to high tea, alone with Arthur, not knowing whether to report the doctor's high-handedness or to be the conveyor of the good news that their daughter was to receive still more treatment. She did both.

Arthur's brief answer was spluttered through a mouthful of roast ham: 'Surgery? Wot's wrong with Stonegarth?'

The Bennetts intended that the supper should be simple and *en famille*. It was the parlourmaid's afternoon off and Edna, the cook-general, was away for a family funeral. Hazel and Belinda indulged themselves together in the kitchen creating dishes which Edna would have thought too foreign and fanciful for Yorkshire taste.

Meanwhile this first appointment in the surgery was quite different from any other that Jeremy Bennett had ever given. He was away from his desk sitting directly opposite his young patient. After he had smoothed a thin layer of precious balm over her cheek, he leaned forward.

'It has healed well, my dear, but I must warn you that this is as far as the normal healing process may go. I brought you here to discuss something which may give you hope for the future, but not false hope, I trust.'

He took from his desk a medical journal, which he said he had received from Frankfurt a week ago.

'Wonderful things are happening in the medical world. By the turn of the century, when you will still be young, my dear, some of this research may have proven results. The Germans are ahead of us in this field and I, with my limited German, cannot vouch that I am reading the detail accurately. But Bradford teems with well-educated Germans – one or two are close friends of mine – so I shall be able to explain it all better when I have checked my rough translation with my friend Dr Steinberg.'

'But, Dr Bennett – if I may presume to question – you said that the healing was complete...?'

'Yes, my dear Felicity, Nature, you and, shall we say God, have done all they can, but men – and of course I must say women –

179

in this new scientific world are making history every day, fighting incessant battles against diseases and ignorance. They work quietly; they have neither guns, nor flags... I brought you to my surgery today, not just to see things at face value, if that is what we may call it, but to give you hope and a stake in the future. You are on the threshold of a medical career. Never lose your lodestar, Felicity. Look beyond this muddled little mill town and this very ordinary GP... It is your generation who will create the next chapter of history. At the college now, my dear, you are doing the five-finger exercises of science. In a few years' time, you and Belinda will not be dealing with theories and abstracts but human beings...'

He paused and took her hand.

'Sorry, my dear, I have talked too much and done too little. In my blunt and limited way I wanted you to know that your recent experience will be a contribution to your life and to all the fortunate people who come your way. You will have what many doctors lack, compassion, but, Felicity, it must be a correct compassion with dry eyes, skilled hands, sound judgement and practical empathy.'

Felicity spoke at last. It was the response of an uncertain child and a very certain woman.

'Will you please talk to me when you've got your German sorted out?' She laughed and then said firmly: 'Thank you, doctor. I hope you are not just flattering me. You see, you've given me a reason to face the future...'

Belinda came bounding from the kitchen into the hall to sound the gong. She had just put her surprise savoury – angels on horse-back – into the warming oven of the large black kitchen range.

Jeremy Bennett, not wanting to end on a serious note, responded to the noise with a laughing whisper: 'And, Felicity, don't let my bounding daughter dominate you. Stick up for *yourself*. Don't let her do it all for you.'

Belinda greeted the two who were coming through the door from the surgery with her broad grin and her blunt speech.

'Whatever can you two have been doing all this time? While you've been chatting away Mamma and I have prepared a celebration party.'

It was a meal as unlike the Hargreaves' good but monotonous meat and veg. as could be imagined. After leaving her Malvern boarding school, Hazel had had a year in Avignon living with a medical family, friends of her parents, while she did the first year of a nursing training in a French hospital. In that year she learnt more about positive good health from Madame Lejeune's kitchen than any hospital could teach. Belinda added her mother's recipes and style to the Academy's predictable Cordon Bleu course: She had her own way of getting fresh herbs and vegetables by making the gardener her scheming ally.

Conversation bubbled. Hazel and Belinda gave Felicity witty and shrewd descriptions of the people who were longing to meet her.

'You'll love the Wintertons. Our ages: Rosalie, your age, has the brains. Nicholas, my age, has the brawn. He beats everyone at tennis and was captain of cricket at Rugby. She's the star turn in charades … and plays the flute like an angel.'

That people of this lively world were longing to meet her seemed hard to believe. False or true, the statement unnerved her – as did Dr Bennett's next remark.

'Felicity, we know from Belinda that you are a pianist – and a talented one. Do play for us!'

This was a challenge she had not expected to meet tonight. Her sole self seemed dejected and inadequate. All the same, it was a huge compliment. It would be churlish not to accept. But in this mood, whatever could she give?

She replied in a toneless voice: 'You must excuse me tonight, Doctor; there are only a few hackneyed pieces I can play from memory. I really do need music in front of me to keep me in order…'

He moved over to her and put out a hand to raise her from her chair. 'Just one piece by ear, Felicity, even if it's only: *God save our glum old Queen.*'

Although she laughed with the rest, she was slightly shocked to hear any disrespect of the Queen whose Diamond Jubilee – her mother kept reminding her – was in two years' time.

She was back in the warmth of the family and seated at the piano. In truth ever since she was imprisoned in her bedroom, her uninjured fingers had been itching to play. She had not been close to this high-backed, candle-lit piano until this moment. Looking up, she saw that a narrow strip of looking glass linked the two brass candlesticks. The reflected candlelight flickered on the withered skin of her right cheek. Embittered by the reflection, she lowered her head towards the keyboard and only saw fingers blotched out of shape with tears. She closed her eyes. In a sightless world of her own she touched the keys softly and slowly as if soothing the sorrows of the whole world. Suddenly as she came to the closing bars of the Brahms lullaby, so the right-hand candle guttered out and the left one, nearing its end, broke into a spasm of soaring flame fed by its bed of waxen tears. She opened her eyes in shock. They were transfixed on the left side of the mirror. The magic light and music fused through her fingertips to a finale of glory.

With hands resting on the still keys Felicity's eyes met Belinda's reflection in this transforming light. It was as if they were both pledging never to look on the right side ever again.

Gertrude and Arthur sat each side of the fire in the morning room occupying their usual wordless world. She was knitting. He was pulling at his pipe.

'Why isn't she home?' Arthur muttered. 'What could a doctor be doing keeping 'er out until this hour?'

At least the grumbled enquiry broke the silence and gave Gertrude a chance to air a grievance which she had kept locked up for months. She used her syrupy-little-girl voice, which she adopted when she wanted to get her own way.

'Father, if we had a telephone, you wouldn't be having to worry. You would have had her home by now and told her off.'

'Well, if that's t'case there's one 'ooll be glad we ain't got one. Any road yer can stop fretting – she's 'ere!'

Felicity, accompanied by the doctor, arrived at that very moment. Had there been neighbours near enough to peep behind their blinds they would have thought ill of a doctor who brought a patient – a young girl at that – home on his arm at this late hour.

He raised his hat to the agitated father and disarmed him in one sentence.

'I see signs of improvement, Hargreaves. I was able to do a more thorough examination in the surgery. And we had the extra bonus of your daughter's delightful company for supper and music. When you go to chapel next Sunday, old chap, go down on your knees and thank God that Felicity's eyes are unhurt and as bright as they ever were...'

Hargreaves, behind his blunt facade, had moments when he had hopes of getting nearer to his God and a reserved seat in Heaven. He turned a fatherly face on his daughter.

'Go straight upstairs, my lass. Yer mother's put some 'ot milk in yer room and t'bottle in t'bed. She's gone up to see yer safely landed.'

'Thank you, Father, but as you heard from Dr Bennett, I can see for myself.'

Felicity left the two men standing in the hall. Hargreaves had good reasons not to get on the wrong side of the doctor.

'There's summat ah wanted to 'ave a word about, Doctor. Yer'll let me know wen yer want brass for t'laboratory, won't yer? 'Ave yer 'ad a letter from secretary of t'Woolsorters Disease? It's time you doctors got a move on. Masons 'ave done their bit. But, think on, infections moving faster than any on yer.'

Having gone through all the necessary responses, Jeremy Bennett drove back home, working out in his mind the next day's patients: those to be called on and those who might be in his surgery. He felt both disturbed and amused that three of Hargreaves' woolsorters stricken with anthrax were being sent by their wives to see what could be done for them. Those were the patients who would never receive a bill. A new, untypical, thought came to him. He would send one this time. He *would* send it to Hargreaves!

His mind turned to the future of Airedale and especially Aireley. If the trade unions grew at the rate they were doing, workers would, one day, be claiming damages for sickness created by the mills. And when they did, Hargreaves would look back on this little bill as a very small price to pay for the rotten conditions in which these men, women and children scraped a living.

The autumn of 1894 was passing quickly, darkening days shortening activity. Belinda seized on the occasional bonus of golden hours in late November for brief bicycle rides. Miss Elsie was still a good meeting point for her and Felicity.

'Good! I'm glad you're here and sensibly wrapped up. Father has asked me if I'll call and see two old folk who are losing their cottage in the demolition of the extension of Valley Mill.'

Neighbours, who said the old couple were sick and going to be homeless and were too proud to ask for help, had called in the doctor.

'Of course, Belinda, let's go now, though. It gets dark by five o'clock.'

'Ah, but we've not got lights on the tandem as some people have who are up with the times.' Both laughed.

They soon were pedalling hard towards the Bingley Road and found the little huddle of cottages that were destined for demolition.

A woman hanging washing out in the back yard next door called out: 'It's no use knocking, luv, ther can't 'ear. Deaf as t'door post. The're used ter me. Ah'll tell 'em. Wot's thi business, like?'

Belinda explained that she was Dr Bennett's daughter and had come, pending the time when he could come himself.

'Cum thi' ways in lass! It's not 'ow it used ter be. She wer proper proud, was Beattie before t'arthuritus got 'old on 'er. As fer 'im, 'ee wer toughest quarryman yer could meet and 'ere 'ee is bent over double like, coughing 'is 'art away.'

The neighbour had not exaggerated the scene. Various miscellaneous garments had been layered on top of one another in an effort to keep warm. A neighbour had banked up the fire with slack, with instructions to leave it be so that it burned slowly and kept on through the night. The large iron kettle on the hob never quite boiled but was lifted by the man to the enamel teapot to wet the tealeaves again and again.

The two benches by the sides of the table, on which their children had sat and fed and grown up, had been deserted for years. Three of the five had died before their parents, the other two had emigrated to Canada in a desperate move to make good.

Both Belinda and Felicity could have kicked themselves for not having brought food. Hazel would have prepared a big basket of tuck as she did regularly for her perpetually hungry sons. Perhaps the last generation was more mindful.

Belinda did not cover her omissions but plunged straight into the old folks' needs. She adjusted her speech to accommodate their hearing loss.

'We came to see if there is anything you need. We did not want to bring anything you already had.' The *already had* was a pathetic overstatement of the state of their bare little scullery cupboard.

'Thank you kindly but we've gotten good neighbours. They won't see us starve,' the woman said proudly.

'Trouble's not food, miss. 'Ave they tell't yer?' put in the old man.

'This cottage wot we've lived in all uz lives is being pulled down.' The woman chorused in with her husband on the last two words, and went on in tears:

'An' ther takking uz ter t'workhouse.'

He put out his hand to clasp her arthritic one. 'That's not worst of it, is it luv...?'

He was now too overcome to talk and she carried on: 'Worst is, ther putting uz in separate buildings, 'im in t'men's and me in t'women's.'

Belinda and Felicity could only touch gnarled hands and be silent. The pause held all the crass insensibility of a heartless official world.

184

Out of the impotent pause the woman whimpered a strange cry of love and hate: 'An' we've never bin parted, 'ave we, luv – never a day in fifty-two years.'

Belinda and Felicity found little joy in their ride along Bleach Mill Lane to Crag Top. They had learnt a lot since the Academy days but this meeting made them both realise how helpless they were. After surgery Belinda talked it over with her father, who told her how long the battle was going to be before a political party would dare to raise income tax to make a better life for the poor.

Felicity had no-one, except Hilda, with whom to talk it over; her parents would have had a simple answer. She could almost hear her mother saying: 'Well, the poor will always be poor. They never save, like we do, for old age.'

After the usual high tea of venison pie, home-grown cucumber and tomatoes and a trifle, Felicity slipped away to the sitting-kitchen and told Hilda where she and Belinda had been.

'There's a lot o' dark things goes on in this valley, Miss Felicity. I sometimes wonder – excuse me for saying – but I do sometimes wonder if there's summat wrong wi' God's eyesight.'

In spite of the deep misery and frustration Felicity felt, she started to giggle and could not stop.

'Have ah said summat ah shouldn't? When ah say mi prayers tonight ah'll ask 'Im ter fergive me fer bein' cheeky.'

Hilda's way of slipping out of an awkward situation was to get up and put the kettle on; Felicity's way of escape was to go up to her room and write to Grace, which she did.

The autumn, though shrouded with much melancholy for Felicity, was relieved by Belinda, who had a genius for lifting Felicity out of herself, taking her into the wide open moorland of Wharfedale and into the deep recesses of her mind and heart.

'Felicity, it is three weeks since I went to the asylum and I think it is high time you and I visited your aunt. I had a note from Mr Thompson that she is now out of the sanatorium but not able to stand for washing and ironing.'

'But, Belinda, is the sight of me going to disturb her...?'

Belinda interrupted impatiently: 'What an egotist you are! Is the sight of her going to disturb you? It's my half-day tomorrow. I shall call at two o'clock and bring this week's lecture notes for you. Get ready for the shock! We are going to *bicycle* to Barlockend. So be sensibly dressed and ready to leave!'

It was a typical West Riding moorland day when clouds moved so quickly that one was no sooner revelling in cool sunlight than the sky frowned regretting its sudden warmth. It was wet in Burley-in-Wharfedale, dry in Burley Woodhead, windy in Guiseley but now still and cool as they pedalled away up the long drive of Barlockend.

The warden told them aunt Amy had been put in a dark little anteroom adjacent to the sanatorium to practise walking. The three stood close in cold light and stuffy air. Felicity thought her aunt had aged, hunched as she was with a man's crutches so tall that her shoulders were forced up to the level of her chin. Her hair, which had been her pride, hung lank, as if it had no more reason for living. The one-time fastidious body gave out an odour which would have shocked Amy Ackroyd had she been aware of it. She hunched her weight on to her armpits to keep the crutches stable while she wrung her hands round and round like an un-attended Lady Macbeth desperate to blot out the plot of guilt. She talked to the floor and her bandaged foot. There was no sign of recognition when eventually she gazed at the two visitors and muttered on a level note: 'Have you brought me a clean handker-chief? They only give me rags here.'

Felicity habitually had an unused one in her bag and a bottle of lavender water. She sprinkled some onto the handkerchief and held it to her aunt's nose. It was snatched from her and hidden in the patch pocket of her twill overall.

'Don't let them see it! They'll take it. They took my book.' She pushed frenzied fingers into alien hair. 'They've taken my hair-slide.'

So far no words had been spoken by the girls until Belinda said: 'How is your foot? What happened?'

A grotesque mass of dirty bandage was lifted a few inches from the stone flags.

'It was the iron. Too hot to hold. There were four on the rack in front of the fire. Some days they're red hot... It was God pun-ishing me with hell-fire.'

At last she sat down on the bench and tears streamed down her face.

'It's God's punishment. Why can't he listen? If only he would let me explain! That man was in my bed – my bed...' She trailed off.

186

Felicity handed her the bottle of lavender water. Whether the hands were too numb, or whether the futility of owning anything caused rejection, was not clear, but the bottle crashed on to the stone floor. A demented shriek mingled with the lavender. Belinda and Felicity closed up each side of her on the hard wooden bench. Each took a hand and hoped in their despair that something of their good health could be passed into this tortured body.

It was at this moment that Anthony Thompson breezed in, treading on the fragments of glass. Belinda's hackles rose as his first banal phrase filled the small space.

'Hello! Are you ladies having a perfume party?'

Belinda rose, not as Felicity had done out of respect for one she considered to be her superior, but appalled that suffering could be accepted.

'Would you take me to the laundry room where the ironing is done? I want to see the conditions in which Miss Ackroyd was working.'

'I am afraid that area is not in my commission and is out of bounds.'

'Stop being afraid, Mr Thompson, and use your spiritual authority to do some good. There must be other women in danger!'

Anthony Thompson, fortified by the unquestioned authority of the Church of England and the traditional deference all women showed to his ecclesiastical gait, was appalled by Belinda's outburst.

'Miss Bennett, you came here as a visitor, not an inspector. I must ask you and Miss Hargreaves to see yourselves to the entrance hall, while I get an orderly to clean up this mess. The warden will see you out of the door.'

He swept out, taking fragments of glass with him on the hem of his cassock. He had never met opposition in this asylum except from a raving lunatic.

Felicity found she was kissing tears as she said goodbye to her aunt. Belinda, though angry that the chaplain had slighted her, felt that some good might come of her interference. She remembered the bar of Fry's bitter chocolate she had bought for aunt Amy. Bitter indeed.

'This is for you, Miss Ackroyd. I'll take the foil off for you and you can eat it now.'

It was as if the little anteroom was a nursery and the one-time schoolmistress was one of her own smallest pupils.

'Take this piece to my twin,' she pleaded, putting the precious foil back on the half-bar. 'Fry's was her favourite.'

They left her dazed with the half-bar of chocolate and the air drenched with lavender. She did not see the splinters of glass in the bandage on her foot, nor acknowledge the visitors' departure. In this unfamiliar quickening of taste and smell only Caroline was there. And no-one else. The crutches had fallen to the floor in the shape of a cross.

Belinda and Felicity mounted their tandem in silence. Felicity was appalled that Belinda could be so insolent to this saint of a chaplain. The wind was too strong and cold for talk; the light so weak that concentration was imperative. They had to pedal hard to make progress. They sat in tandem, but apart in spirit. Silence was an ally.

They drew up at Stonegarth.

'Get to bed, my dearest, as soon as you've had some food. You are worn out.'

'Good night, Belinda. You must be regretting that you ever became involved in this tragic mess.'

'Felicity, don't be an idiot. What are friends for?

Throughout November and December of this strange year, Felicity's visits to the Bennetts' became frequent occasions and Dr Bennett with his usual tact made the invitation arise from a brief, but apparently necessary, check-up in his surgery.

Little had been said about Felicity's progress apart from Belinda's insistence that the scar was gradually, almost imperceptibly showing signs of fading. The edges where blood had clotted into scabby encrustations started to fine down and a fraction of healthy skin seemed to be asserting itself. Dr Bennett's magnifying glass showed that the central patch of parchment-like skin was faintly swollen as if underneath good forces were at work.

Felicity appreciated that the impregnated lint, which she held to her face each night, was an inspiration of the doctor's and she was faithful in carrying out his orders. The salve, which she spread on in the morning, though giving her an unfashionable shine, was a small price to pay for the calming protection it gave her throughout the day. Weeks ago now the German letter had been translated into action and Dr Bennett showed her the samples he had received and the instructions of how the balm could be made up. It was not an orthodox prescription but an amalgam of herbs from Switzerland, blended into a lotion with flavin, which the doctor already had in his surgery.

When Felicity talked to Miss Elsie about it, since she knew that an unfamiliar parcel had arrived in her post office with a German postmark, she said in her quiet country voice:

'I shouldn't be a bit surprised, Miss Felicity, if one of those herbs ain't briony, arnica or maybe comfrey. There's a power of healing in those simple plants. Whenever we burnt, scalded or just bruised ourselves our mother slapped a comfrey leaf on. These must be wonderful plants this German doctor knows of that we don't. Sorry, Miss Felicity, I spoke out of turn. I'm not suggesting that yours is just a job for comfrey. That was daft of me.'

'Elsie, you could never be daft. You've more sense in your green fingers and more healing hanging on your kitchen rack than you might find in many clinics. But you are right, this prescription is not simple. According to Dr Bennett it is a very precise balance of several unusual herbs. The oils and powder he blends them with are just agents for the concentrated essences. Father pooh-poohs the idea.'

'If I may say so, Miss Felicity,' she had reinstated the *Miss* now her young friend was at college, 'if I may say so, you are looking better. When are you going back to college?'

'In six weeks' time, Miss Elsie! Isn't that splendid? And I shall be calling at the post office every day on the way to the station.'

'That reminds me, the stationmaster, Mr Dawson, was asking after you, wondering if he might call. You know he's the chairman of the Dramatic Society... I think he's got a suggestion to make... Has Miss Belinda said anything? From what he hinted I think he was going to see her too.'

Felicity walked back home, her steps hardly keeping pace with the speed of her thoughts. He couldn't be...? But it was not possible... She saw in her mind bitterly the faces of Viola, Rosalind, Celia and Beatrice. All sparkling and flawless! Oh yes, Belinda, she'd be all right! What a Beatrice! What a Katharina!

A mean thought jagged at her. Was she always going to be lagging behind Belinda? She pulled herself together and walked into Stonegarth determined to hold her own. A stray letter, evidently delivered by hand, was addressed to her. The writing was unfamiliar. She took it up to her room, and was glad the curtains had already been drawn and her bed turned down, as she settled herself into her armchair.

189

Dear Miss Hargreaves,

I hope you will forgive my boldness in sending a letter to you without asking permission of your parents. It is now nearly two months since I had the pleasure of seeing you aboard and alight from the Bradford train. May I say how sorely you have been missed by all those who work in the station. My feelings of distress about your accident were never written down as I felt it would be an intrusion on my part to assume that I could send a letter to your home. Having been assured by Miss Ellis that you would not be offended, I am taking the liberty of writing to you. Young Watts was going your way and he said he would deliver it for me. (What a polite lad he is – a cut above others round these parts.)

It has, for many years, been my privilege to present to Airedale and district a performance of a Shakespearean play or other worthy classical production. As you may know, this annual event takes place in the grounds of Aireley Hall. This next year, in fact the last week in June '95, I am planning to present that most delightful of all Shakespearean master-pieces: *Twelfth Night*. It is my custom to hold auditions for the major parts early in December of the previous year. I must tell you, in confidence, that although there will be several young ladies presenting themselves for auditions I cannot visualise any of them in the parts of Olivia and Viola.

Might I be so bold as to ask if you and Miss Bennett would care to present yourselves for audition on Saturday, December 7th at two o'clock in the Sunday School hall? This should give you time to read the play and select your own scene for a well-studied reading.

It is perhaps presumptuous of me to assume your interest in dramatics and indiscreet of me to hint at my casting dilemma, so I trust you will treat this letter as highly confidential until something is resolved.

The same request has been made in my letter to Miss Bennett, whom I feel sure will be in touch with you.

I remain, in honour to be at your service,

Herbert G. Dawson

Belinda, bursting with excitement, was round at Stonegarth the next day waving an almost identical letter. Hilda showed her into the morning room.

'Ah'll fetch 'er, Miss Bennett, yon's a reet dab 'and wi' flowers but she'll come sharp-like wen ah tell 'er 'oos 'ere!'

Felicity rushed from the butler's pantry, abandoning the hothouse fuchsias which a moment ago had enthralled her.

Belinda pulled her through the door. 'Here's mine! Let me see yours!'

Belinda never wasted time, always cutting through the social introductions which had been part of the Academy's deportment training.

'Calm down, Belinda! I shall never be allowed to join. In my father and mother's eyes *the stage* is the road to hell.'

'But if you tell them it's *Shakespeare* and *literature* spoken on the hallowed grounds of Aireley Hall, and that the vicar always introduces the first performance... Oh, Felicity, you are eighteen! You could be married and not living at home. They couldn't stop you then, even if you wanted to play Medea!'

'But I *am* dependent on them, and I am at home and not likely to marry a rich man... Or any man come to that!'

'Well, there's no harm in doing an audition... At least we shall know whether we've been considered for the parts. Mr Dawson gives the date for it in my letter. Look! It's Saturday at two o'clock on December 7th, next week. I'll call for you after lunch. We can walk to the hall.'

'You are incorrigible, Belinda, you force me into things. *You* go on your *own*! I am *not* going!'

'I despair of you, Felicity! *New woman* indeed! My father always says when I am weak: are you a man or a mouse?'

'Stop talking, Belinda, for once and listen to me! Why should you force me to let courage make me into a fool? Can't you see that there is courage in facing truths? And I mean *facing*. Can you find one heroine in Shakespeare's plays who isn't wildly attractive? Or poetically appealing? Or gently seductive? Mr Dawson saw me last when you and I got on the train the day of the lost child – the day we were late. He hasn't seen me since...'

'But he *knows* – he says so in his letter to you...'

'But he hasn't *seen*...'

'Felicity, sit down and listen. All right. We'll *both* listen. You have – we both have – a long and exciting life ahead. Are you going to let three inches of skin stop you doing everything that's adventurous, romantic and risky? Come home with me and let's discuss it with my mother. She has more sense than both of us put together, she'll...'

The sound of the door handle stopped the sentence and Mrs

Hargreaves came in carrying the fuchsias which Felicity had abandoned.

'Good morning, Miss Belinda. I might have guessed that you were the distraction. Felicity loves doing the flowers, don't you, love?'

Her daughter's eyes rolled upwards and her shoulders shrugged to go with them, but she was trained and conditioned not to utter a word of retort. Belinda felt suffocated and quickly thought up a lie, which could hardly be described as pure white.

'Subject to your agreement, of course, Mrs Hargreaves, Father requested that Felicity should come back home with me. We have a professor from Scotland coming to lunch. He's a specialist in dermal studies at Glasgow medical school. Papa thinks he would be interested in Felicity.'

As Gertrude had no idea what dermal studies were she took the word *interested* the wrong way.

'Don't tell me an old professor is going to be interested in a young girl. If he is I'd want to know more of his intentions.'

It was Felicity who was now desperate to escape from the banal chatter.

'If you will excuse me, Mother, I think Belinda and I should be going. The doctor will be waiting.'

'Days are drawing in. Wrap up well. I'll get your father to send the carriage.' She turned to Belinda: 'Think on, Miss, it's time that tandem was locked up for the winter.'

The contrast of the Bennetts' home never ceased to produce diametrically opposed emotions in Felicity: on the one hand sheer delight in the affection and fun which they all generated, on the other desperate depression that her own home had so little. Hazel Bennett seemed much more like an elder sister to Belinda than a mother, she enjoyed her daughter, and Belinda's brothers.

Belinda had shown her mother Mr Dawson's letter before she left to call on Felicity and had arrived at Stonegarth buoyed up with her mother's enthusiasm. Hazel was ready to pick up the cues of excitement long before the girls returned.

'Isn't it exciting, Felicity? Let's talk it over round the fire and make some toast.'

Toast at Stonegarth was made by a servant in the kitchen and fussily kept warm in a domed silver muffin dish. Here, at the Bennetts' house, toast went, well buttered, from hand to mouth. The young aspirants let Hazel lead the conversation. It was, of course, Belinda who wielded the long toasting fork, often in her wild gestures forgetting that she had a slice of toast on the end of it. Felicity had the more feminine job of spreading the butter, not unlike her role in real life.

They discussed Mr Dawson's proposals, including the doubt Felicity cast on the possibility of a stationmaster having the knowledge and talent to produce Shakespeare. It was quickly dispelled by Hazel.

'Forgive my saying so, my dear Felicity, but many of these men and women who left school early were intent on educating themselves. And they did. Mr Dawson is a leading light in the Workers' Educational Association as well as in the Dramatic Society and took on a three years' tutorial course where the professor expected an essay every week. Let me warn you both there will not be superficial understanding of the text in his production... Our little library here, built with Carnegie money, has kept him and his kind going now for years. Lots of the money-makers in this valley read little beyond the stock-market figures in the *Yorkshire Post*.'

Felicity looked round the book-lined library and thought of Stonegarth, where the only books visible were presentable sets, luxury editions. Gertrude judged a book by its binding, preferring leather, or sham leather, and gold.

'After that long speech, Mamma, you must be parched! What about another cup of tea?'

'Yes, I did rise to Mr Dawson's defence, didn't I? But I remember with such joy the talks about plays and the theatre I had with my father and mother. My father could be very funny! I remember the whole of one holiday when we'd gone up to Arbroath, he had a bee in his bonnet that Shakespeare's plots all depended on the absence of mothers. Just think, he used to say, if there had been a Mrs Prospero! What chance would Miranda have had to be loved by Ferdinand! And poor Prospero's scheming magic with Ariel would all have fizzled out ...' Then my father would say in pontifical tones as if talking from a lectern to students, but in fact paddling in the sea: "All art depends on knowing what to leave out and Shakespeare chose to leave out mothers in all the comedies."'

'Do go on, tell us some more. There are so few plays Belinda and I know. But I have just thought about *Twelfth Night*! Was their mother on the boat with Viola and Sebastian when they were shipwrecked? Was she drowned?'

'Oh no, my dear, they went off on their own. But do you remember that when the twins meet at last, at the end of the play, they check with one another that they did share the same father (remember the mole?) and that their mother died when they were thirteen years old! She was well out of the way when Viola arrived at the Duke's Palace in Illyria.'

'Oh yes, also in *Twelfth Night*, Olivia mourns her brother but hasn't a word to say about her mother!'

Felicity piped up offering a little controversy to the discussion: 'You've forgotten Romeo and Juliet. They both had mothers...'

Felicity was cut short by Belinda.

'And Hamlet. Gertrude ruined his life. And look what a miserable life and death Romeo and Juliet had with their mothers' interference.'

In a bizarre way it turned out to be a refreshing reminder to the girls of the Shakespeare comedies which could become their own possession well away from school textbooks.

Belinda heard the Hargreaves' carriage drawing up at the door.

'Heavens above! Your driver's here! I'll go and keep him waiting. Mother, please explain to Felicity that she is coming to the audition; that she is going to play Viola and that it is all going to be a huge success!'

Mrs Bennett's loving arm, generous words and encouraging eyes were more than Felicity could resist. She kissed her goodbye, thanked her for the toast and only in the carriage did she remember that she was supposed to have seen the doctor.

She also reflected that all the way through our formal lives we thank our hostesses for food but never know how to thank them for friendship and fun.

The barometer fell as she went through Stonegarth's door.

'You've had your tea, I suppose,' her mother said, checking the Bennetts rather than considering her daughter. The Bennetts, of course, had dinner, or less grandly, supper, after the doctor had completed his surgery and relaxed with his two womenfolk over a glass of Madeira or sherry.

It was only when he carried the decanter and sat down that Belinda burst out:

'How dreadfully inhospitable we've been! We've sent that poor girl home, or rather they came and took her, on nothing but toast. The Hargreaves' high tea will have been cleared hours ago. And, Poppy,' a name she often gave her father, 'you will remember, won't you, that you have seen Felicity this evening?'

Jeremy Bennett loved his two womenfolk dearly but at this

194

moment after a day coping with a serious accident at the Aireley Mill he could have wished them both far out of the room. He returned the Madeira and changed it for the whisky decanter.

'Keep the supper back a bit, Hazel. I'd like a few minutes before I eat.'

'You're late, darling. Anything wrong?'

'Yes, an accident at Aireley's. I don't know the mechanical details but two child workers – a boy and a girl – got their hands in one of the spinning machines – brother and sister – twelve and ten...'

'Oh, my dear, are they badly hurt? Who are they? Where do they live? Can I help?

'Their mother's a weaver at Aireley's, father works for Fosters. I've seen her – not him... The girl's in Bradford Infirmary, the boy's at home with his grannie.'

'Let's not talk about it until you've had your supper. I shall go and see them both tomorrow.'

Over at Stonegarth Felicity and her mother were continuing their halting conversation in the morning room, which was mostly used in the evening.

'Don't worry your father about anything tonight, love. He's had a bad day at the mill.'

'What's wrong, Mother?'

'An accident with one of the machines.'

'Anyone hurt?'

'He won't say – you know your father, he keeps things to himself. He behaves as he should – like a gentleman... Leave him be in the smoking room.'

'Excuse me, Mam,' said Hilda as she entered without knocking, 'but there's a man at the back door 'oo wants to see the master. Ah've tellt 'im that Mr Hargreaves is not well, and can't see no-one but 'ee's put 'is foot in t'door and refuses to go!'

'Shut the door in his face and lock it, Hilda. The master must not be disturbed.'

She stood with her back to the fire, the knitting abandoned, every nerve taut, straining to listen.

Within a minute there was a scuffle, anguished swearing and the door was bolted and barred.

And so it remained for the rest of the night.

* * *

195

The trade unions had, at this stage, too little power to make strikes advantageous.

The next morning, Arthur Hargreaves put on his frock coat, a white carnation in his buttonhole, donned his top hat, and then drove down to Aireley station in his carriage and greys. He walked into the Wool Exchange as if all was right with the world. He had called at the mill and taken his production manager into his office.

'There was nowt wrong with that machine, was there? Who's supervisor there now? Give 'im a good talking-to for we'll surely 'ave safety chap 'ere before long. And sithee! Get little-uns together this morning and this afternoon and bring those two bales of serge, returned from Leeds factory last week, down to t'clocking in. Let 'em choose which cloth they like. We'll give 'em each a winter coat. I 'appen to know that 'Iggins clothing factory is running on short time in Leeds. They'll be glad of an order, and kids will be chuff to 'ave new coats. Ah've asked my missus to send a side o' bacon to t'family and telephoned Bennetts' to keep us informed. Well, ah must be off. 'Change'll be busy today.'

Fortunately for Arthur Hargreaves, young Rosie Harker's fingers were set into place at the hospital and seemed set fair to heal, all except the forefinger which had been crushed in the spinner down to the second knuckle.

Her twelve-year-old brother Luke, doing an adult job all day now, had tried to pull Rosie's hand away but in doing so had battered his own. He was in agony with cuts and bruises but wore his bandages bravely. Three days later it was more fear of reprisal than genuine compassion that made Arthur Hargreaves ask Felicity to take a purse of four half-sovereigns to the Harkers' well-scrubbed house in Mill Street.

It was an errand which filled Felicity with guilt, shame and remorse but she was helpless to do more than comfort. It was Grannie who opened the door, taken aback at the sight of such a fashionable lady. Felicity's smile in enquiry helped.

'Are you Rosie's grandmother?'

'I'm all she's got. Her mother can't stay away from t'mill – we need t'money. Even more so now. They've sent 'er back from t'hospital. She's to go back in a week and they'll see if t'rest has to come off. Ee, but that Dr Bennett's a proper gentleman, our Rosie'll do anything for 'im. 'Ee'll get 'er better.'

Felicity took her hand and gave it a friendly stroke.

196

'I've brought you a gift from my father. I hope it will help a little.'

'Nowt'll put her finger back, will it? But it's good'v yer to come, Miss. Folks like you don't often come down this street. Ah'd ask yer in but we've used last o' t'coal until pay-day. Little lass needs to keep warm. 'Er fingers friz up in this weather; we're keeping 'er in t'chair by the fire, night and day. Luke's out doing a bit o' wooding – with 'is one hand.'

Felicity put the purse into Grannie's hand. She had reasons for not delaying her departure.

'Don't go, Miss, yet, ther's summat I want to tell yer. I were real frit when I saw yer at t'door – I thought yer'd cum ter complain like, about t'other neet. Yer must 'ave thought it were my son come to your 'ouse. It weren't 'im, Miss, it weren't 'im. It were one of 'is mates!'

Felicity could now put a name to her. 'Mrs Harker, you are a fine family and do not deserve such a dreadful thing to happen. I must go now but I'll be back. Shall I be able to see Rosie next time I come? And Luke? What if I come on Sunday after the morning service. Would Mr and Mrs Harker mind?'

Grannie looked on Felicity's damaged face in wordless under-standing.

'Well now, as I've met yer, Miss Hargreaves, I think I know yer would tak uz as yer find uz. Any road it's all right by me.'

Felicity remembered seeing the coal-dealer delivering to the houses at the mill end of Spring Lane. She would find him. Then she had a better idea. Outside the mill at the end of the delivery yard were tons of coals for the furnace, enough to keep all the houses in Mill Street warm for the winter. It was the very first time she had come to the mill on her own. Her father was in Bradford at the Wool Exchange. She would tell him when he returned tonight. She approached the boiler man.

'You do not know me but I am Miss Hargreaves. I want you to pack five bags of coal and get the wagon to take them down to the Harkers', number fourteen, Mill Street. It was their little girl Rosie and her brother Luke who have damaged their hands. They've no coal and they need to keep warm.'

'Well, if you'll make it reet wi' t'gaffer, Miss, ah'll tak mi orders from you! There's Ted coming in now.'

Three days later, after her visit to the Harkers' and no reference made about the coal from her father, Felicity broached the subject of the play. Gertrude left the judgement to her husband. The response was predictable.

''Ow does Dawson know yer, or 'ow yer can act? 'Ee's only seen yer both making fools of yerselves over that first-class argy-bargy.'

Felicity had really no answer to this so Gertrude put in her spoke.

'I thought it was just to educate the working class that Dawson did dramatics...'

Felicity could not resist picking up this cue. 'Surely, Mamma, it is our class, the mill-owners and their families, who are so ignorant about Shakespeare.'

Arthur bridled. 'All Shakespeare needs is reading at school – no need for all this dressing up. Ah could, if ah were daft enough, still recite: *Wen icicles 'ang by the wall* ... and it must be twenty years since ah 'ad to learn it.'

Felicity cringed at the thought of it.

'All I am asking is for your agreement that I go with Belinda for an audition.'

'An' wot's an audition, in 'eaven's name?'

'I think, Father, the explanation was obvious at the beginning of this conversation. Mr Dawson is trying me out for Viola in *Twelfth Night*.'

Rather than show his ignorance of the play and indeed any play of Shakespeare, Arthur said lamely to his wife: 'Well, Mother, if that's wot she wants to do, ther's no stopping 'er.'

'You know best, Father.'

Felicity and Belinda both went to the audition, the former with her parents' grudge; the latter with her parents' delight.

It was a strange afternoon. The would-be Olivias and Violas had put on their Sunday frocks and a secret blush of Bourgeois rouge from their little blue boxes. The Orsinos and Sebastians swaggered nonchalantly wearing best suits, clean shirts and cravats; Maria had had her hair wound in rags all night to make tight ringlets; Sir Toby was the local comedian who never had difficulty in getting a part. The one aspiring to be Andrew Aguecheek was no other than Archie Armitage, who made a bolt for the door as soon as he saw Felicity. Dawson was wondering if he would have to play Malvolio himself when, to his relief and delight, the local curate came and offered his talents.

There were a flock of miscellaneous also-rans who were quite happy as long as they got on a stage. This included the vicar's two daughters, who took on all the various odd jobs for which there were no auditions.

In spite of the amateurish-looking assembly there was no doubt that the stationmaster's background reading went far beyond timetables. He gathered them all into a circle, excluding from possible casting any of them who planned to have holidays in June or were getting married or doing anything else which interfered with rehearsals or the performance. He then began.

'You may be wondering why we, unlike Shakespeare's company, are doing this play in midsummer instead of midwinter – Twelfth Night in fact. Well, due to the generosity of our Honourable Patroness we have the grounds and the out-houses of Aireley Hall and Castle at our disposal and our production will be in the natural amphitheatre between the Castle and the Hall. May I ask if there is anyone who has not read the play?'

Four hands went up.

'The library had run out of copies,' said a hopeful Sir Toby.

'I've been doing exams,' said a promising Maria.

'Sir, I've been looking after my sister's baby,' said one who wanted only to be a lady in court, and had dressed for the part.

'Too difficult, Sir. We have a Shakespeare at home but nobody seems to read it: I couldn't get into it.'

'Well, I won't waste time on the first three, I'll talk to you, Geoffrey. You tried to read it, didn't you? You are nodding. Well, if you only do that you'll never get anywhere. You've to see it, hear it, speak it, feel it... Let's try a Viola on the ring scene and see if she can make you see the ring and be fascinated that Olivia has fallen in love with her.'

He called on a willing volunteer, the daughter of a Bradford headmaster who paid for his daughter to have elocution lessons with the wrong teacher. Her ambitious pupil gave every word its full value. Every pronoun, every preposition, every definite and indefinite article was given painful precision.

Mr Dawson gave her a benign smile of encouragement as he said: 'Thank you, Priscilla, you tried hard. Perhaps too much. Not a trace of Yorkshire accent, but then Viola would not have to worry about that, would she? Certainly every word carried – but *where*, Priscilla, *where*? We don't want to see the print, do we, my dear? Let it all come from your heart... Shall we see if we can put some blood into Viola? Let's help her by giving her someone with whom to fall in love. Miss Bennett, what about you having a go at Duke Orsino? And you, Miss Hargreaves, play Viola, disguised as the pageboy Cesario. Act one, scene four.'

'But, Mr Dawson!' Belinda exploded. 'I came to –'

Her interruption was ignored.

'Orsino, begin at: "Who saw Cesario…"'

It was a strange coming together in a scene they had not rehearsed. They certainly never envisaged Belinda in the role of a man. She had played the part in a local festival and failed dismally in trying to look and sound lovesick opposite to a Cesario with a dripping cold. Felicity knew the scene, having played it at school, paired with the hockey captain as a bullying-off Orsino.

They both felt cheated, having revelled in the wonderful scene where Olivia falls in love with Cesario, thinking Viola is a boy.

There were mumblings of dissent as the two girls rose to Dawson's command. Two in the group with their hopes on Viola whispered bitchy comments about that Miss Hargreaves' scar. Yet in spite of themselves, the group found that they were galvanised into attention.

Some magic alchemy transported the performers into another world. They were not just reading, they were catching and winging real thoughts to and from one another: Cesario in love with her master; Orsino sending fervent messages to Olivia but sexually stirred by his page-boy.

It was a disturbing but exciting experience to have Belinda, as a man, lording it over her. Felicity found that there was something quite genuine in her own role, not as Cesario but Viola falling in love with her master. She could feel Viola's pain, commissioned as she was to take Orsino's love to Olivia. She longed to disclose her sexual identity when Orsino praised her feminine charms.

At this point Belinda was not just seeing Cesario as her page but her own vulnerable Felicity, and almost stroking her skin, she said:

> Diana's lip is not more smooth and rubious
> And all is semblative a woman's part

Every eye and ear was on this single figure: the trinity of Felicity – Viola – Cesario as she took leave of Orsino to carry vows of love to the remote Olivia:

> I'll do my best
> To woo your lady: Yet, a barful strife!
> Whoe'er I woo, myself would be his wife.

She returned to Belinda's side only to find that all thoughts of

Orsino were being banished. Belinda was standing looking down her superior nose on Mr Dawson's seated figure:

'Mr Dawson, I came to be auditioned for *Olivia*. There are men here able and willing to play the part of Duke Orsino.'

There was a ripple of support through the hall. Several edged nearer to hear how the chief dealt with this forceful woman.

He remembered with a hint of satisfaction how he had got the better of her in his railway station; here he had a more important role.

'Miss Bennett, you evidently are ignorant of the complexity of Shakespeare's love relationships; the man-with-man; woman-with-woman; and the intriguing sex reversals. Shakespeare understood every single nuance of womanhood and manhood. Every man and boy in his all-male company could bring out the feminine side of his personality. If you use your strengths, as I think you can, you will help Miss Hargreaves to create the masculine side of her dual role. I hope, when you rehearse together privately, that you will play both Orsino and Olivia.'

Belinda could always take a fair defeat in good faith. She admired the erudition and the panache of the man. She turned an irresistible smile first on Felicity and then on the chief; and spoke Viola's line: '*I'll do my best to woo your lady*' and left it at that!

By the end of the afternoon, rather late for the high teas that were awaiting them, the cast was complete. The thwarted Violas, Olivias and Marias were made important by Dawson increasing the numbers and the grandeur of the ladies in court.

Dawson, used to timetables, had given everyone a rehearsal schedule and privately had his eye on using bible class time to do extra work on the limited talent of the curate as Malvolio. Tomorrow, after church, he was seeing Lady Aireley at the Hall to discuss the arrangements which could be made if June proved not to be the optimistic *golden* it was reputed to be.

On Monday he would be setting wheels in motion to arrange local transport times for the two important performances.

He walked home singing quietly to himself:

> Something attempted, something done
> Has earned a night's repose.

In spite of the short days and the long nights, December passed rapidly for Belinda and Felicity. Gertrude recognising, at last, that it was through Belinda's patient copying of notes and careful teaching of Felicity that her daughter was progressing, raised the temperature a little in welcoming Belinda to Stonegarth.

That Belinda was able to make chemical experiments and dry scientific facts memorable was largely through her brilliant mimicry of Robert Mackintosh, who was monitoring Felicity's progress with equal delight.

Although he had to conjure up a chaperone in the shape of the laboratory assistant to have private sessions with Miss Bennett, he looked forward to these meetings with glee. Her flashing eye and ready tongue made her a splendid sparring partner.

I've not met her like before and never shall, he thought as he handed over her friend's examination paper, which concluded: 'Well done! A-. Now Miss Hargreaves has proved that she will always tak the high road.'

Charlotte Winkley's coming-out-ball on December 21st had caused dissension when the invitation arrived at Stonegarth in late November; in the end it was a triumph all round.

'I am not going, Belinda. Who ever would want to dance with me?'

'Felicity Hargreaves, the Winkleys will know young men who expect more than a pretty face and they are far too aristocratic to think at that level! Pull yourself together! You have enormous personality and charm, why do you want to hide it? Your mother...' (Belinda stopped herself saying 'for once') '...Your mother has been wise and kind in choosing the perfect ball-gown as an early Christmas present. That deep ivory romaine silk and ecru lace are perfect for your chestnut hair and you are so fortunate in having small neat bones and a perfect throat. As for conversation and wit, the Winkleys think of you as the lass unparalleled – well, they would if they could quote Shakespeare!'

Belinda could always bring a smile, or a laugh, to her listener's face and so she did to Felicity's with that final remark.

'Very well, Belinda. I will go on condition that if I am a wall-flower you will concoct an urgent message to give me and we shall both curtsey to Lady Winkley, give a brief explanation of my mother's fall and order the footman to arrange our drive home.'

'Oh, Felicity, it is so easy for me to agree to the crazy scheme because the situation will never arise!'

In the event it was Belinda who might have been the wallflower – 'growing up so high' – as she could give several of the young men an inch or two, but she had the confidence, if not booked for a dance, to find the most amusing dowager in the room, and so ripple the air with laughter that the young looked to see what they were missing.

As for Felicity, the whole Winkley family treated her as very special in making sure she was introduced to the most entertaining of the young eligibles in the ballroom. So her white and silver dance card with its minute white pencil on a silver cord was almost filled up by the time the string quartet played the opening bars of *The Blue Danube* for the first waltz. It was the Winkleys' eldest son, Justin, home from Cambridge, who literally swept her off her feet into a world of flowers, candlelight and music. He led her back to her chair as if he were reluctant to part with her, lifting her wrist to look at the dance card hanging from it.

'But the only blanks are the Lancers and the Paul Jones and no-one books for those! May I stay and talk before the next lucky man claims you for the quadrille?'

They had only the briefest time together but he had heard from Olivia and Kate that Felicity was going to Edinburgh.

'Why are you not coming to Girton or Newnham? We have far too many bluestockings! I'm St John's – in my final year – law.' And then on an impulse: 'What about the May Ball?'

Her next partner was bowing and holding out a white-gloved hand. It was not often Felicity felt deep gratitude to the Academy but in the delicious hours which followed she kept remembering the Major's expert teaching of ballroom dancing and the lessons of etiquette which they all had to write down in their silk-bound, gilt-edged common-place books.

How they had laughed at the corseted comments which the Major made them repeat until known by heart:

> True grace in motion comes from art, not chance
> As those move easiest who have learnt to dance.

As she moved into the quadrille the Major's advice came back to her: '*It is desirable in the quadrille to dance with vigour but not rudely; easy and graceful without being languid...*'

She chuckled to herself. Her partner thought it was approval of his exquisite style, which she gathered had been painfully acquired at the Assembly Rooms.

Taken back to her chair and having been thanked with almost excessive zeal, she glanced at her fully initialled programme; the

203

variety of partners would have satisfied the Major: '*Change partners as often as possible – for the purpose of aiding social enjoyment.*'

There was just one dance, the polka, where her partner seemed unaware that the rhythm of the music should synchronise with the movement of the feet. She longed for the dance to end but remembered the Major's dictum: '*It is very improper to leave the dance before it is finished; the lady, upright and charming in demeanour, must allow the gentleman to draw her hand through his raised arm and to escort her back to the chaperone from whom she came.*'

Chaperones, of course, had little idea of the nuances of flirtation which could be travelling through the pressure of a hand; the tightening hold on the waist; the nearness of cheeks and the coy drooping and lifting of eyelids before a tantalising gaze.

Belinda's vigorous dancing would not have won the Major's approval but even she managed to keep track on Felicity's smooth liaison with the ballroom floor. When it came to the last waltz, Charlotte and her suitor, the Lord Lieutenant's eldest son, in honour of her coming-out, took the floor alone until they summoned the rest to follow.

But it was not until Felicity and Jeremy Bennett had swirled in complete harmony once round the floor – she with feminine fluency, he with protective virility – that the rest of the company let the final Schubert waltz encompass them.

Jeremy Bennett, accompanying his three splendid women to the ball, had asked Felicity, as soon as the ladies' cards had been presented, for the 'privilege and pleasure' of the last waltz. He reflected with joy as they drove back home that this protective gesture on his part – in case – had been wholly misplaced. There were a dozen *young* men who would have been honoured to put their initials in that very special place.

The Dawson rehearsal proved to be an inspiration. Here the word *amateur* held its true meaning: *one who loves*; it could never be used in a slighting way in the ambience which Dawson created.

Belinda and Felicity had just completed the wonderful scene where Cesario's histrionics convey, vicariously, Orsino's love for Olivia, causing her to fall in love with him, the messenger.

Dawson drew his little troupe towards him.

'Come and sit down, my dears, and all of you come and hear what promise we have in this encounter.'

Belinda and Felicity both knew that the scene had not been mercurial enough and had lacked radiance. They were surprised, since it would be months before a dress rehearsal, that he began on how to wear costumes.

'That elegant black which you are wearing, Olivia, may be in mourning for your brother but you must wear it as a coquette, a courtesan, a flirt, a woman of property and a very haughty lady...'

'You, Cesario, must wear your costume in such a manly way that the audience can believe in Olivia falling in love with you. So do not walk like a debutante – except perhaps to entice Orsino! Make it impossible, too, for Olivia to belittle you. Remember it is you, in the end, who marries the Duke! Throw that purse of money down with magnificent contempt...'

When they all met again in January he started the evening with a vivid picture of Shakespeare directing the players in the wooden O, the Globe Theatre.

'Shakespeare,' he said, 'made the building lose its scenic poverty with his *words*, and this is what you are going to do in the Working Men's Institute. And then in May and June we shall have the glory of the grounds of Aireley Hall. Then I want you to look as if you have lived there all your lives!'

It was heady stuff and they all thrived on it.

'Read the *plays* of Elizabeth's reign. There have been great *novels* in our Queen's century but the plays are second and third rate. I wonder why?'

Christmas was a solemn affair at Stonegarth, heavily weighed down with corpulent near-relations and an outsize goose which had sent Gertrude into tight-jawed action. Her idea of festivity was to recruit Felicity into folding heavily starched napkins, which Gertrude called serviettes, into water lilies and to put a funereal wreath of holly round the central candelabra of the dining table. Felicity decided that the simple branch of mistletoe – intended by her mother for the hall – should hang from the central gas lamp holder over the table, to make avuncular kissing with scratchy beards impossible.

It was the folk living down in the valley with modest incomes, or little money at all, who made Christmas cheer. Church, chapel and Salvation Army choirs started their rounds on Christmas Eve, their faces shining with the reflections of their oil or turnip-candle lamps.

Hands thickened with home-knitted gloves fumbled with hymn sheets and damp handkerchiefs and chased elusive humbugs in overcoat pockets. Most of the singers had borrowed, from someone in the family with bigger feet, extra socks which were pulled over boots to guard against slipping on the ice and snow, God having obligingly provided a white Christmas.

The Salvation Army band, resplendent with its red-braided navy-blue uniform and flashing brass instruments, outshone the church and chapel choirs. Their down-to-earth and easy-access-to-heaven conviction took away all inhibitions so that into their programme of carols they happily inserted any of the dotty ditties requested by the crowd round them. After the band and choir had heralded the angels it was an easy matter to get men, women and children spelling out their personal happiness:

> I'm H – A – P – P – Y
> I'm H – A – P – P – Y
> I know I am
> I'm sure I am
> I'm H – A – P – P – Y

The genius of the Salvation Army was in getting these Yorkshire folk of few words to revel in confessing their sins:

> My sins were as high as a mountain
> But he washed them away in a fountain
> He wrote my name down
> For a palace and crown
> Bless the dear Lord I am free (tee hee)
> He wrote my name down
> For a palace and crown
> Bless the dear Lord I am free

It was the Sally-Ally band and choir with its lusty singing of *Christians Awake*, which tempted the folk of Airedale to rise and salute the happy morn, not at five o'clock when on all other week days the knocker-up man rapped a command on bedroom windows, but at any time between seven and nine o'clock, when the labourers had their once-a-year lie-in. Sheer good spirits warmed the atmosphere. Even fractionally at Stonegarth.

Arthur, who usually only enjoyed shopping for himself, liked his women to do him credit. Two luxurious sable muffs, a slightly bigger darker one for Gertrude, and a smaller lighter one for Felicity, arrived from Brown Muffs in boxes which could have been presents in themselves. The larder shelves were groaning with the pick of the poulterer's, the butcher's and the fishmonger's. The elaborately iced Christmas cake and pork stand-pie must have been the biggest in Aireley. Gertrude, for all her inhospitable manner, was described by other housewives as a good provider, though they only saw, never ate, what she took pride in providing.

It was all quite different at the Bennetts'. Hazel and Belinda, though fairly economical in their church-going, were joyously prodigal in conjuring up the symbols of peace on earth, goodwill towards men. Simple white candles lighted the whole house, and branches of spruce and yew silhouetted against the skirting board behind cut-out tubs made a series of Christmas trees in the hall.

Although Prince Albert had introduced Christmas trees soon after his marriage, they remained a rarity in England and even after another half-century they were still a treat for lucky children.

Bradford probably had more Christmas trees twinkling than any other city in England for had not the Bradford businessmen travelled to Germany for twenty years or more and was not Bradford enriched by the German manufacturers who had settled in Worstedopolis and helped make the place so prosperous, so cosmopolitan? Even the German Jews seemed to like looking at the trees, a reminder, not of their religious customs, but of those great dark forests in their homeland.

So the Bennetts had, in the centre of their welcoming hall, a six-foot-high Christmas tree topped with its perennial white angel, which Grandma Bennett had made with wings of Nottingham lace and a gown of white Lister velvet. Year after year the silver candle-holders which clipped to the tree were refilled with plain white candles. Hazel, Belinda and the maids, with the German maid, Gretchen, from next door, started in Advent making the brilliantly coloured *Duten* which she had learned to make from her grand-mother. The two Bennett boys, when they came home from school, had neither the patience nor the aptitude for making *Duten* but joined in the gilding of Brazil nuts and walnuts and fix-ing them with gold wire to the tree.

Christmas at the Bennetts' started on Christmas Eve because lights need darkness. The Church of England choir made it their major call, preferring food and drink to hours outside in the cold. They had rehearsed, especially for the Bennetts, the carols which conjure up the dark beauty of the night: *While Shepherds Watch, Good King Wenceslas* and *Silent Night*.

They were ushered into the hall bright with candles and a blaz-ing log-fire. Belinda and the boys were rescuing roast chestnuts, peeling them and putting them in blue paper sugar bags to pro-tect fingers. The doctor had left the outsize punchbowl of mulled ale to draw the singers round the tree. He then picked up his old German accordion and in league with the organist tried out the notes of *While Shepherds Watch*. 'Let's all sing for our suppers first!' And on they went through the three carols until Hazel said: 'Don't let my husband tire you out! Jeremy, let us have a break. Serve out the ale!

The leader of the choir, church warden Bill Brampton, with a bass voice which matched his bulging belly, nodded approval at Mrs Bennett's suggestion, saying, 'Well I think I've earned my supper!'

It was a feast to remember: hot bacon pasties, egg custards, Yorkshire cheesecakes, hot mince pies well-laced with rum and a great cut-and-come-again fruitcake.

Belinda pulled the gas lamp pilot chain and the white mantels shone bright gold.

Bill Brampton, filling both his belly and the largest armchair, sampled everything twice and repeated his former remark, 'Well I think I've *earned* my supper,' to which the church warden Timothy Tindale, a lean man with a shrewd tongue chipped in:

'Well I thought you 'ad when yer started.'

All the mulled ale having been drunk and the room quietened with repletion, the doctor gathered the singers together round the tree for the final carol: *Silent Night*.

Belinda quickly pulled the ringed chain of the gaslight, thus leaving just the white candles on the Christmas tree to illuminate the singers' faces. Only the crackling of the fire broke the silence until the accordion, reduced to a haunting pianissimo, brought the singers into *Silent Night*. One could never have believed that Bill Brampton's voice could be so slim, nor Timothy Tindale's so caressing. Jeremy turned to the five Germans in the choir and then to Gretchen, the maid from next door.

'Now shall we sing it in German?' he asked. There was no hesitation, just a true bonding of friendly German and British voices. It was as if the singing between the two peoples would never be severed...

Stille Nacht, heilige Nacht.

Every singer went off with a little lace poke of sugared almonds presented by Hazel and Belinda. The boys brought from the kitchen a basket of hot jacket potatoes as hand-warmers for the walk to the next destination.

A well-fed member of the choir, who had eaten as if his life depended upon it, picked out a large potato with the remark: 'I'll be ready for that when we've done.'

Earlier in the day the Bennetts had brought presents out of secret places and put them on the floor round the tree. They were made even more intriguing by elaborate wrappings and cryptic messages. Belinda's presents to her brothers of Wisden's cricket records earned this inscription:

This present is a bore
I'd like to know more
Of a maiden bowled o'er

Their joint present to her, a parasol difficult to disguise, had the message:

If you think it's for rain – think again!

Now that the singers had gone, the Bennetts gathered together for presents. The maids and gardener received theirs first: blue and silver tins of Farrah's Harrogate toffee, each with a silver crown coin lightly stuck on the centre of the lid, and a card in Hazel's writing: '*All the Bennetts have benefited so much from your devoted service,*' with the five signatures beneath and five versions of Thank You.

Hazel's sister, aunt Jessie, was always a houseguest enlivening Christmas with her sense of fun. She was an adorable go-between in scheming secret presents, especially for her sister and brother-in-law to give to one another.

'This year,' she told each one separately, 'I will pack your present, as it is so large. Leave it to me.'

The family was bidden away from the tree to the drawing room. A gasp of amazement came from every member of the family as their eyes were drawn to lighted candles standing in exquisite Limoges triple candlesticks at each end of the mantelpiece.

'But, Jessie, the man in the shop led me to believe it was the only one!' Hazel exclaimed. 'And so did you! And how did you get Jeremy to know that this was what he wanted too?'

'Jessie, you schemer! You never told either of us that we were a pair!' Jeremy roared with laughter at her funny cunning.

'Well you are a pair, are you not?'

By this time Jeremy and Hazel were facing one another, within the light of the candles, each holding the other's hands: Slowly they drew near to one another and kissed on hands and lips. It was a picture never seen by any other sons and daughters in the Aire Valley, or perhaps any other valley. It was simply not done to expose one's emotions in public. The Hargreaves knew that and respected the convention without effort.

But the four onlookers were not *public*; they were all beneficiaries of Hazel and Jeremy Bennett's overflowing love. Their tears had no sadness, just sheer joy and gratitude: the three young Bennetts for their luck in having such wonderful parents and Jessie for the bonus life had given her sister and herself: an outstanding husband and brother-in-law.

Just before midnight Hazel went to the piano and played the simple little song they often sang as a family benediction last thing at night, to the tune of: *Begone dull care.*

> The day is done, we've danced and sung
> Our eyes have seen delight
> The day is past. We part at last
> To each and all: goodnight!

Christmas Day followed the usual tradition: morning service, Christmas dinner at lunchtime and charades and crazy games in the evening with the family next door.

On Boxing Day the *boxes* were given out to all those who had served them. The mobile tradespeople called and collected, the retainers were visited.

Belinda, taking a hamper with her, went round to see their old cook.

'Eliza, you look wonderful,' she said to the eighty-year-old. 'Not a day over sixty!'

'I'll look more miself when I get mi teeth, Miss Belinda. Crunching fair kills me!'

As Belinda undressed on Boxing Day night, she relived the two days to keep in her remembering.

It was everything a Christmas should be, she sighed with satisfaction, and then with regret.

Not quite.

If only Felicity had been there!

Charlotte's coming-out ball had been an unexpected boost to Felicity's morale. There could be whole days when she never gave a thought to her face. The return to college on January 13th was now a welcoming challenge, more difficult, she thought, for the gauche and shy students, perhaps, than herself.

To be back in the train with Belinda meant that the drought in life was over. 'Every river was full again'. Conversation flowed, encouraged by Mr Dawson's resumption as stationmaster. He had raised his hat, opened the door of Belinda's carriage and ushered Felicity in to Belinda with the Clown's final words in *Twelfth Night*:

'We'll strive to please you, every day,' he sang, swinging his top hat across his body in an Elizabethan bow.

As the two girls walked steadily up the stairs to the chemistry laboratory they both recalled the day they had hurried so much that Felicity's hairpins had fallen out. But today Felicity had done her hair with infinite care, painstakingly disguising as much of her right cheek as she could.

With cloaks and hats discarded they braced themselves to make an entrance. They were not prepared for the welcome.

Robert Mackintosh, wearing the tartan of his clan, was blocking the door. He held out his hands, took hold of Felicity's and kissed each one and whispered: 'Bide ye there a wee while.' He slipped away into the anteroom where the chemicals and special apparatus were stored.

He returned proudly holding his bagpipes.

'We are in the lecture theatre this morning. When I get the signal that everyone is present I want you to follow me.' He addressed his words to Felicity, but seeing Belinda move forward he called her back. 'Here, Miss Bennett, there's a wee drum my daughter lent me. Get it round your neck and join me! You, Miss Hargreaves, when we get in to the lecture theatre stand in front of the demonstration bench. The boys want to welcome you!'

The noise was horrible yet haunting. It was difficult to tell whether the tune was *Will ye no' come back again?* or *Bring back my bonnie to me*, but it brought cheers from the class and glued Felicity to the floor in embarrassment and then with wonder and delight. As the cheers increased, Simon Watts called out: 'Speech' and an uncanny silence gave her no escape.

She let her eyes travel across and down the benches, including each face with her smile.

'I want just to tell you how much I have missed you all and how glad I am to be back. But all these weeks, while you have been working, I have been having all my work done for me by Mr Mackintosh, my friend Miss Belinda Bennett and Mr Simon Watts. My notes will never be as perfect, my experiments never so well

211

proved and now my clapping will never be enough to express my gratitude. So will you all join me in thanking them with your hands!'

The lecture room resounded with a noise which Belinda later described as *clapture*.

The three silent ones could hardly believe that *they* were being applauded for a task that any of the others might have done. Yorkshire folk are usually slow to praise. It was Felicity's speech which spurred them into action. And a girl at that!

At four o'clock Simon Watts went home to the chemist's shop in a cloud of glory. Robert Mackintosh walked down Market Street with renewed pride in his tartan and his pipes.

And Belinda walked out of the college with Felicity on her arm as if the whole wide world were theirs.

PART TWO
EDINBURGH, SPRING 1895 TO AUTUMN 1896

1

Grace Hargreaves was now so much part of her beloved Edinburgh that her voice and speech had the charm, precision and lilt associated with those whom she frequently met in the New Town. Yet, to all those whose roots were in Scotland, Grace Hargreaves' speech and surname were those of a Sassenach. But when she had first returned to her native Yorkshire, the church warden wagged a critical finger and said: 'Yer've gone Scotch! Miss Hargreaves, when did yer stop speaking English? Well, Yorkshire 'owever!'

It needed a phoneticist to spot the slight variants in the vowel sounds which lingered from the mill-stone grit of the West Riding and the heather and sea of the North Riding where Grace had spent six years at school.

Grace's parents, Alderman Josiah Hargreaves and his wife, followed the fashion of the time and sent their daughter to a boarding school in Scarborough and then to a small establishment near Paris to be finished. Her brothers, after a few years at a public school in Cumberland, had followed the local tradition of coming home to add to the family prosperity by going through the mill.

Grace and her friends quickly adopted the modes and manners of new acquaintants, hoping to escape from the sooty valleys. The boys, however, quickly discarded the school's imposed pronunciation and comfortably reverted to speech the mill hands understood, and their overseers accepted, as being genuine. Arthur, Grace's eldest brother, whose only serious subject at school had been football, dismissed the whole curriculum as kids' stuff and happily joined a man's world.

Grace, contrary to custom, had insisted that she would not stay at home when she left school. It was a battle with her parents. How this spirited girl ever subjected herself to even more demanding strictures of a nursing training is hard to understand but her strong will and generous heart had joined forces to make her want to be a nurse long before she faced the reality of the training.

Perhaps the allure of the Royal Infirmary of Edinburgh, at the very helm of medical science, was challenge enough. She had read avidly about Joseph Lister's skill in operating; his experiments with anaesthetics and his initiative in the use of antiseptics. She was galvanised, as were his students, by his sense of theatre. She imagined herself watching an operation when Lister threw scalpels on the fire one after the other, dramatising his exacting standards of precision and hygiene in the tools that could determine life or death.

All that happened in her lifetime. It was his name besides those of Florence Nightingale and, more recently, Sophia Jex-Blake that had spurred her into action.

In her last year of school, now a quarter of a century ago, her friend Agnes Buccleugh invited her to spend Hogmanay week in her home in George Square in Edinburgh. On one never-to-be-forgotten day Agnes' father, Professor Hugh Buccleugh, FRCS, showed them round the Royal Infirmary.

Flakes of snow were falling but he kept his two charges outside the door until he made sure they had read every syllable of the inscription on the mighty door.

> *I was a stranger and ye took me in.*
> *I was sick and ye visited me.*

Patet Omnibus

'Open for all,' he had said. 'Everything for the patient. That must be your motto if you are to be nurses.'

Memories now came flooding back as Grace walked past the Royal Infirmary to the Meadows under the jawbone arch, which led her to Marchmont Road.

That holiday in Agnes' home had changed Grace's whole life. Not only did she become a sought after partner for the Gay Gordons, the Eightsome Reel and Strip the Willow, but saw the New Year brought in by a dashing young medical doctor, Felix Stewart, in his royal tartan.

There had been memorable talks with Agnes' professor father, who was determined that his daughter and her friend should not only become familiar with the great events in the medical world which they were inheriting, but also the part which Edinburgh had played in the miraculous growth of medical science.

She could hardly believe her ears that she was sitting at table with someone who had actually heard Pasteur speak in Lille in France about micro-organisms which fermented grape juice into

216

wine – but which also turned milk sour and caused infection in wounds.

Perhaps his most memorable story was about the midwifery professor, James Young Simpson. Grace and Agnes found it difficult to understand that for the first half of the century, anyone having an operation, however severe, endured all the excruciating pain and caught sight of the vicious tools which were being used. Patients, too often, died from the pain and subsequent infection, even though the operation was reported successful.

Agnes' father told the tale, in vivid language, of earlier experiments with laughing gas – ether – and its horrific after-effects like being drunk on bad whisky.

'But Simpson,' he said, 'was not going to be defeated. He went on trying out drops on himself and two of his friends. He was thrilled after they had now tried chloroform to discover that the two remained unconscious for some time after he himself had come round.

'He'd finally got the answer he wanted, only some seven years before you two were born. Simpson gave chloroform as an anaesthetic on a Highland boy who was having part of his diseased arm amputated by Professor Miller. The lad never felt a thing for the whole of the operation. And that, my dears, that is how the science of anaesthetics was born!

'Now if either of you ever become theatre nurses, just say a little prayer of thanks to Miller and Lister and even before that, to Pasteur!'

All these past events whirled through Grace's mind as she walked over the Meadows to Marchmont Road on this bright April day. She opened her bag and took out a card, which guided her to the house.

The card stated: *Lodgings for university students.*

The house had a frugal elegance about it as though its owner was determined not to let anyone know that she was scraping a living. The brass letterbox had been polished until the raised letters had withdrawn into the background; the doormat had been neatly repaired with fine string. Grace, kept waiting for less than a minute, noticed that the front door had been given a coat of paint by an uncertain hand. The long sash bay windows had a cautious look with blinds and curtains allowing only a quarter of Edinburgh's cold light to filter through.

The tidy little woman who opened the door looked as if she had done a quick removal of her hessian apron so that her frilled muslin one – which she wore underneath – could assure the caller

217

that the proprietor of the apartments was ready to receive visitors. She synchronised her good morning with a discreet movement of her eyes. With her head held poised she managed to give Grace a hat-to-gloves appraisal. Then, having assured herself that the stranger was a lady, she ushered her into the front sitting room and to a wooden armchair which had lost count of the number of times the cushion covers had been washed and repaired.

While Mrs McLeish moved to the chair opposite, Grace took a swift look round the lofty room. There seemed to be infinite space above – bounded by an ornate plastered cornice – but below there was no space unoccupied. The room was filled with three occasional tables, one of brass, one of bamboo and another of ebonised papiermaché, all too low for the odd high-backed chairs which stood adjacent to them.

A candelabra of gas mantles hung poised over a large dining table to give light for students either eating or at work. Over the dark grey marble fireplace was a grim oil painting of Glencoe, which made Grace wonder why the Campbells and the MacDonalds bothered to fight for it.

Mrs McLeish had repeated her rules many times: 'You will convey to your nieces that the front door is locked at nine o'clock and that the cocoa and baps are put on the table at quarter to nine.'

Grace nodded agreement and asked: 'And in September, when they come, who else will be in residence?'

'All being well – and they get their degrees – my two young gentlemen will be doctors, and be returning home to Glasgow. Och, I shall be sorry to lose them.'

In the whispered closeness, Mrs McLeish was about to play her ace card.

'I am proud to tell you, Miss Hargreaves, that this house has a water closet and a bathroom with tapped water. Come this way and I will show you.' After the prize pieces had been shown they walked on down the corridor. 'This is the room my young doctors share, until they get their caps and gowns. Apart from the two guinea pigs they've got for observation there's nothing objectionable there. It is the room your young ladies will have. You may take a wee peep in, they never arrive home before five.'

In Grace's fleeting glance she saw that at least there were two of everything – which had not been the case in the other houses she had called on. Mrs McLeish assured her that she had white quilts for the ladies, to cover the tartan blankets, which suited the men. It was the third house Grace had visited. This was certainly the accommodation that Grace preferred.

Subject to the approval of the two young ladies, it was agreed that they would take up residence in late September. So for the sum of one pound a week they would receive a substantial start to the day with porridge, followed by bacon, or smokies, finnan haddock or whatever was in keeping for the season. The main meal of the day would be a knife and fork high tea with ham or potted hough and an assortment of tea-breads. After studies were finished, there would be cocoa and baps on which to have a good night's sleep. Grace was also relieved to find that the canny landlady who opened the door had a surprisingly warm heart.

She walked back enjoying every second of the grandeur of her adopted city. There was no need to hurry home. She let the stringent air tingle her cheeks and quicken her mind. Not for the first time in the last twenty years did she thank whatever gods there were that fate (or was it her own contriving?) had brought her to this unparalleled city.

She reached Princes Street and walked almost the length of it and once again tried to find words powerful enough to explain the impact of that great rocky fortress. Today it looked as if some underworld giant had thrust his fist upwards and forced a mass of stone to coagulate into a castle which could never be ravaged by man.

Some days, in a wintry light, the castle stood aloof like a monstrous schoolmaster invigilating all the seats of learning in this scholarly city. On other days, when the clouds were racing across the sky to Arthur's Seat, the castle seemed to be moving in the other direction like a great Viking ship heading towards the west.

Grace crossed Princes Street to the shopping side to join the leisurely well-heeled folk whose studies were no longer urgent. She was not a compulsive shopper; her elegant appearance was a result of buying clothes which would last, but wearing them as if she did not care whether they did or not. Her independence, though fortified with a private income, stemmed from forebears who knew the sound of the knocker-up man and who became men-to-be-reckoned-with on the Bradford Exchange. She knew only too well, from the patients she saw in the infirmary, that round the Royal Mile were tenements stinking with human and animal excreta, less than a mile away from the stylish emporia of Princes Street. The wide open spaces on the castle side of the street had a perfumed ambience of daffodils, tulips and hyacinths; today the Walter Scott memorial seemed like a tree carved out in stone, towering above the flower beds, reaching its branches heavenwards as if to declare a holiday.

219

As Grace walked her way back to Moray Place, the warm breeze changed to a sharp east wind from the North Sea. She was glad to shut the door on it and enter the comfort of her own home. The houses in this distinguished looking circus were of a distinctive architecture with Corinthian pillars and entrances adorned with wrought-iron lamp stands and elegant gas globes. In spite of being a spinster of the parish Grace was an owner of such a house and therefore was accepted as a woman of property. The title *Miss* was normally looked down upon, even cooks were given the courtesy title of *Mrs*, but a spinster with a substantial private income had no difficulty in gaining public acclamation. Many houses had a full complement of servants ruled by an impressive butler. Grace's staff was modest by Moray Place standards: Maggie, the cook-general; Esther, the daily who came on the steam-bus from the Old Town; and Bob, the jobbing gardener, were all Grace needed to keep her house and garden immaculate. She had not the least desire to be grand.

Maggie, her one devoted resident maid, had most of the top floor to herself and stout independence to match. In the twelve years they had been together they had built up a companionable relationship, utterly reliable because respect came from both sides. Maggie summed it up: 'I know my place, and it's a place I never would think of leaving.'

Today was Maggie's baking day and the smell of pancakes and oatcakes made on the griddle and shortbread and gingerbread baked in the oven made Grace wonder why she ever stopped at Crawfords. Maggie gave her a résumé of all that had happened during the three hours her mistress had been away:

'The post's here.' She lifted the silver salver. 'He came early and Sammycat missed him. He's having a nice bit of a sulk on the kitchen rug.'

'Poor Sam! The postman is all he lives for!'

'Don't think I'm an inquisitive old besom, mam, but did ye find anything suitable for Miss Felicity?'

'Yes I did, Maggie. I think you and Mrs McLeish would approve of one another. Canny but kind! My niece and her friend are going to have very comfortable digs.'

Maggie looked puzzled. 'For Pete's sake, they're no' going to be digging, I hope!'

Grace laughed and explained the slang of the day.

Sam lay at her feet. After waiting for Maggie to place all letters on the silver salver he, like a major domo, led her in state to his mistress's side. Letters delivered, he hissed the dismissal of

220

Maggie, ordering her to leave the room with her empty tray.

There was an envelope with a Paris postmark and writing which Grace could only assume to be from Louise Wilson, the girl who had recently surfaced after twenty-four years' silence. Louise had sent shock waves far and wide when she eloped with the chef from their finishing school and was banished by her parents: *never to darken their doors*. The other girls were dazzled with her sheer bravado and courage but little knew that Louise had spent years of drudgery slaving away in a little café at the shabby end of Rue Mouffetard where students from the Sorbonne spent a great deal of time but very little money.

Bitterness against her parents made her excessively loyal to her Pierre and together they worked and saved until they were able to buy a *pension* and now had a small hotel with a prosperous restaurant in Rue Scribe.

It was then that Louise felt she could make an effort to get in touch with the only schoolfriend who would understand. She had tracked down Grace Hargreaves' address from the Aireley post-mistress.

April 20th 1895

> Hotel Nadar
> Rue Scribe
> Paris

Dear Grace,

I was sorry you did not come to Paris last year when I invited you. What about this summer? Pierre and I have now acquired a small hotel with a large restaurant attached and enough staff to make life comfortable and food presentable.

We are crazy about the theatre and opera and meet lots of theatre people and artists in our restaurant. I am trying to write this letter without using a word of French, which is quite difficult because for years now I have given in to Pierre's refusal to speak a word of English.

Any week in July would suit us! Just say when you are able to come and give pleasure to your old friend,

> Louise

Grace put the letter in her diary and was quite sure her friend Joyce would do her voluntary sessions at the Women's Hospital and Maggie would try to look after Sammycat.

221

The chosen week would depend on their good will but she was determined to see poor, dear, loveable and lovely Louise again, just as she looked forward to writing to Felicity, her god-daughter, regarding the digs she had visited.

Visitors and clocks were Sam's pet hate. He could read footsteps. He slunk away at the sound of any visitors and stayed away for the precise time of their visit. If the visitors were houseguests he could be away for days on end until the moment their footsteps or carriage took them out of Moray Place. Then, as if shot from a bow, he was back home again.

Sounds were highly particularised in Sam's world. He loved the sound of running and dancing water. But it had to be clean. He had no interest whatsoever in Monday washing day water or the wastewater in the bathroom's lavatory that conveniently ran out of his sight. His pleasure was in flicking the water as it came from the bath tap, making it dance in the air. Best of all were the days when the gardener came and used the watering can and flung the water high in the air for Sam to chase.

It was a miracle of iridescence: his own creation. It was on such a day that Sam, a dour cat if ever there was one, seemed as if he were flirting with a water goddess quite beyond the ken of mere human beings.

Grace had been aware from the first day she met him that there were things in Sam's heaven and earth that could not be explained in her, or anybody else's, philosophy.

Correspondence between Grace Hargreaves and her brother Arthur was short and rare but having fixed accommodation for the two girls, Grace felt that she had better make doubly sure that all was well for their enrolment at the medical school in the autumn. She recalled with irritation and amusement that Arthur had jibbed at the fees, an amount that would only make a small hole in his personal petty account. She decided to relieve him of such a financial burden!

Dear Arthur,

You will be pleased, I feel sure, that I have been able to find accommodation for Felicity and her friend, Belinda, in Marchmont Road, a very respectable area within walking distance of the college.

The landlady is both kindly and rigorous in social decorum so you can rest assured of the high standards she maintains.

May I, with your agreement, broach a subject that has been much on my mind since I visited you in September?

From your remarks (when the subject of Edinburgh was discussed) I gathered that you considered the fees for medical tuition to be excessive and I am sure that nothing has transpired since to make you change your opinion. That being so, I wonder if you would allow me the privilege of paying Felicity's university fees and thus give a rather absent godmother great pleasure.

Please give my affectionate regards to Gertrude and assure her that Felicity will have wholesome fare ('haelsome fairin' they say in Scotland) and healthy surroundings.

I remain,

Your affectionate sister,

Grace

One week later Sam was heard scratching away at the morning's letters and pushing a paw and hissing against one he seemed not to like. The brown foolscap envelope bore an overprint: *Aireley Mill, Airedale, Nr. Bradford.*

Had Sam some psychic sense far more subtle than reading? Or was it just chance?

Maggie hurried from behind the baize door. 'Maircy on me, that cat's up to no good.' She then bent down to settle the feline fuss. She pushed Sam away. 'Yer an interfering critter, and no' fit to bide in Moray Place!'

Sam slunk away to be at the breakfast table with his mistress, a woman he much preferred. He sat, an alien adjudicator, while his mistress read:

Dear Grace,

Your letter received the 14th inst.

As we had not heard from you since New Year your letter was a welcome surprise.

The proposal, as you call it, was certainly NOT welcome. I would have thought that you, a Hargreaves, would know that no Hargreaves accepts charity, least of all the one who remains,

Yours faithful brother,

Arthur Hargreaves

223

P.S. Mother and me are gratified for you finding accommodation for our daughter. That also will be paid for by her father.

Grace was not surprised at the reply. But there was something barbed in the predominance of family words: mother, father and daughter. Sam never stirred all the time his mistress's tea and boiled egg went cold.

Her thoughts had drifted back nearly twenty years – chilling recollections – and then further back still to the time when the Hargreaves grandparents had a great influence on the Hargreaves siblings. Grandfather, whose tenacity and skill created and built up the Aireley Mill, was at pains to make sure that his eldest grandson, Arthur, was more ambitious and responsible than the elder son bearing the title Deputy Director.

Gerald, with everything made for him and an astute father overshadowing him, preferred to identify with scions of the great families who lived it up in their great houses. In his twenty-first year he, like other privileged young men, did the Grand European Tour.

Grandfather Hargreaves chatted to little Arthur in broad Yorkshire, taking a pride in the idiosyncratic virtues by which true Yorkshiremen were known. Grace remembered hearing him entertain Arthur with:

> Do all, hear all, say nowt.
> Eat all, drink all, pay nowt
> An' if tha ever does owt for nowt
> Do it fer thi sen.

Of course these prosperous mill-owners did do *summat for t'rest o' t'folk* but charity on a large scale had to earn its keep and show results. The town halls, libraries, swimming baths, cathedrals and churches were outward and visible signs that manufacturers were also philanthropists who knew what was what.

Grandmother Hargreaves was different: a great power behind the throne. Grace adored her. She had borne ten children (two of whom had died in infancy) on that great four-poster bed in the master bedroom. Each babe, even after the shortest possible interval, had a joyous welcome as a gift from God.

Grace, still sitting at the uncleared breakfast table, remembered an extraordinary talk she'd had with her grandmother just a week before she died. She was lying propped up against linen and lace pillows; her pink and white – almost childlike – face topped with a fine white lace cap. They were alone for a precious half-hour in which the talk had reverted back to courtship and marriage.

'Now you are grown up, luv,' the endearing old lady said in clearly enunciated speech and warm Yorkshire tones, 'now I can tell you what I've not told no-one. I liked your grandfather mastering me. Ee, we had fun – him and me. He knew how to lead me on, he did. But it were only in God's sight. You know. No-one else could see what we were up to. Only Him!'

Grace felt words or laughter would be an intrusion so she just came nearer and stroked frail hands.

Grandma continued in close eye-focus: 'I'm sorry you're not married, luv. That one man of yours was a proper gentleman. Not many of his kind. It's not for us to argue with God's will. I reckon this world wasn't good enough for him – or so God must have worked out. But don't wait forever, Grace. Marriage isn't a bed of roses, we know that, but who'd want to lie on roses, any road, when you can have a bed like this and a great manly bed-warmer!'

The talk amazed Grace since the letters she had stored away were much more circumspect and God-fearing.

Grace moved over to her desk near the open window of her drawing room looking out over the circular garden of Moray Place. The sharp sunlight on the glass panes of the carriages and the entrance gate lamps formed a ring of silver and gold against the circular stone. It was a noble picture of transience and permanence which delighted Grace. But today something caught her eye that did not belong to this tranquillity. It was a garish little Hokey Pokey cart such as one only saw in the streets of the Old Town. Now, ringing through the cloistered air was the street call:

Hokey Pokey, a penny a lump
The more you eat, the more you jump!

She watched with amused curiosity as a maid came out with a copy of *The Scotsman* to hide three fluffy pink ices which were carried through the door of number twelve. Then a nursemaid, immaculately turned out in her blue and white striped uniform, slipped out of number eight, with a gleeful little boy gripping her hand. When he called out Hokey Pokey in chorus with the street cry the nurse put a hand over his mouth and quickened pace. They returned smartly, unable to hide their triumph: one Hokey Pokey in each of four hands. Suddenly, the social drawbridge came down again. The janitor of Moray Place, whom Grace had

225

always admired and praised, stood stiffly above the ice-cream man and his cart and ordered him away, pointing to the board at the entrance: *No Hawkers*. A cloud moved slowly across the sun whilst the chill of the ices themselves also remained as the little cart was trundled away.

But now, Grace was to spend a wonderful weekend in Aboyne on Deeside staying with a schoolfriend, long since married to a gentleman farmer who spent most of his time hunting, shooting and fishing. Travelling over the Tay Bridge, still looking shiningly new, was a thrilling experience not unconnected with thoughts of her great-uncle Samuel and other brilliant engineers whose names had now become household words all over the world.

One morning towards the end of June, Sam's sniffing and purring at the morning's post seemed excessive. There were three letters picked up by Maggie, who put them on the silver salver with a quick assessment of each postmark and handwriting. It was too hot for porridge so Grace had time for letter reading with her oat-cakes and Dundee marmalade.

Two of the envelopes were slim and were opened first. Louise's letter from Paris confirmed the time of the visit in July, the ferries, the trains and their meeting. Grace felt a frisson of excitement at the thought of this unexpected visit. Might she break her journey in Aireley? She would ponder that later. The second letter was an invitation from the Lord Provost to a garden party in the grounds of the castle, complete with the band of the Royal Scots Hussars. If Grace had Sam's purring ability she certainly would have purred now. There could not be anywhere in the whole world as exciting as Edinburgh in which to live!

The third letter, already recognised by Sam, Maggie and Grace, was the letter with the Bradford postmark that deserved time. She rang the bell for Maggie to clear the table and moved to the window of the dining room, which, like the drawing room, looked out onto Moray Place gardens. In this spot she could savour Felicity's letter.

The first thing she noticed was that the salutation had no apology or explanation but carried a ring of authority.

My dear Grace,

Thank you for your last letter in which you explained much more about Mrs McLeish.

June has been the most exciting month in my life and you

226

will gather from the earlier news I gave you of our having been invited to take part in the Airedale Dramatic Society's production of *Twelfth Night*.

Knowing how wise and discerning you are, you may perhaps have questioned Mr Dawson's judgement in giving two newcomers leading parts. Truth to tell there were some rumblings of dissension at the beginning from the old hands but when the play got under way and Belinda and I showed appreciation of Mr Dawson's astringent criticism, the company seemed to respect us as semi-professionals who were out to learn.

Would you ever have thought, Grace, that our local stationmaster could be such an informed task-master, so well-read and so cognisant of all the imaginative *vibration* of a Shakespeare play?

May I say, *to you only*, that even Belinda, who is the dominant one in most circumstances, took every point he made and built on it.

We were infinitely fortunate in the weather! It had rained for two dress rehearsals and suddenly, the morning of the first performance, the sun came out confidently, dried up all the wet ground, shone steadily for the performance and sank into a wonderful sunset for Feste's song.

On the second, and last night (you would never have believed it!) just as the plaintive notes of 'Heigh ho, the wind and the rain' drifted through the air, a few gentle drops fell and there, over a darkened Baildon Moor, was an evening rainbow, low down in the sky. It stayed intact through 'the rain it raineth every day' and melted away on 'our play is done'. No-one put an umbrella up. Their hands were engrossed in clapping!

Oh, my dear Grace, if only you had been there!

This letter is, I am afraid, a very self-centred one. I have omitted to enquire about your projected visit to Paris. I do think you are very adventurous to contemplate this on your own. The Bohemian life which you will be living is all a far cry from our 'Worstedopolis' and your decorous 'Auld Reekie'.

It is a long and exhausting journey. Would it not be helpful for you (and a special bonus for us) if you came away two or three days early? Edinburgh to Leeds is such a swift and pleasant journey, especially first-class, and Father would arrange for the carriage to meet you, if you would rather not change trains at Leeds.

You will have worked out how to send most of your luggage in advance to Paris, so you need not feel encumbered when breaking your journey.

When you come in July, Belinda and I will have much more to tell you about the play – especially the quite surprising male performers. Also to tell you about our tandem ride to Bolton Abbey and the terrifying accident we saw at the Strid, this danger point in the River Wharfe.

But I must not end on a sad episode, when most of life is truly joyous. There is so much to which we can all look forward!

Come as soon as you can to see,

Your ever loving god-daughter,

Felicity

P.S. I suppose I need not tell you that my parents did not attend the play. In fact I was in disfavour for most of the summer when my father learnt from the curate that I was to be dressed up in boy's clothes. Dr and Mrs Bennett came each night and before that helped in all sorts of ways.

What I must tell you, and in absolute confidence, is that Mrs Bennett applied a gentle theatrical make-up to my face (and to other players) but in my case it was a miracle of disguise. If my parents ever hear that, I think I should have the door shut on me.

2

Dr Jeremy Bennett had been summoned by Gertrude Hargreaves to call at his convenience since she had something she wanted to discuss.

On this warm June morning Aireley seemed to be in a healthy state and, therefore, he completed his rounds earlier than usual. It was convenient for him to call at Stonegarth although it was evident it could not be to see Felicity since he knew from Belinda's breakfast chat that today the two girls were bicycling to Saltaire to have a good look at the model village. Could his visit be for a personal malaise of Gertrude's? She was a remarkably healthy woman though she never would admit it. Her occasional headaches were a result of her Martha preoccupation of being 'mindful of many things'. In Gertrude's case the *things* tended to have no more urgency than the laundry being late or the milk having turned sour. He drove the carriage into the circular drive and was soon directed into the morning-room by Hilda, whose admiration of the doctor was this side idolatry.

'Good morning, Doctor, you've brought t'sunshine with yer. Come thi' ways in, Madam was hoping yer'd come before dinner.'

Gertrude was standing to greet him. There was a long association with the doctor but familiarity had not diminished professional respect. She remained standing for her opening remark.

'Doctor, there has been something on my mind which has been troubling me. It's about my daughter. No, not her face. I don't like to talk about my fretting – certainly not to Father. It's this cycling, Doctor. Isn't it wearing away on her, well on her...?'

He interrupted to relieve her of her embarrassment.

'Let me put you at ease about the cycling: If you will excuse me for a moment I have in the carriage a recent journal which includes a medical report which goes deeply into the subject. If you will excuse me!'

He brought back into the house a journal with the recent date of May 1895.

'Here it is: "A Medical View of Cycling for Ladies" by W.H.

229

Fenton. Sit down, my dear, I am not going to shock you. In fact this article makes very agreeable reading.' He pulled a chair up for her and turned another for himself so that they were both in direct eye-focus.

'If I may I will read part of it to you: "With cycles as now perfected there is nothing in the anatomy or the physiology of a woman to prevent their being fully and freely enjoyed within the limits of common-sense." '

'Yes, Doctor, that's all very well. But Felicity's a headstrong daughter. Common-sense may just belong to common people. With all her faults you can't call her *that*.'

The doctor waved the journal a little impatiently in the air. 'Shall I go on? I would like you to hear the advantages of cycling!'

As she raised no objection but raised eyebrows of scepticism he continued, half-reading, half-paraphrasing.

'It goes on to say that ninety per cent of women's diseases stem from boredom and lack of opportunity to do a useful job. Cycling helps to work off their superfluous muscular, nervous and organic energy. All those petty miseries called nerves disappear in the most extraordinary way with the fresh air inhaled and the stimulus to the tissues brought about by exercise and exhilaration.'

He stopped there, conscious that *exhilaration* was hardly an experience Gertrude expected, or gained, from life. Certainly she gave no sign that it had any place in the marital bed. He waited patiently for her response:

'As for our Felicity and your Belinda, it's not seemly, like, pushing away at pedals, lifting their skirts up, displaying their legs!'

Conversation had become, as was usual with Gertrude, empty chatter, time-wasting and boring:

'I tell you what I will do, Gertrude.' He lapsed into familiarity. 'I will leave this serious medical journal for you and Arthur to study. There are very modern articles on man-woman relationships.'

He opened the journal at random to disclose the titles 'Corsetmania' which had eluded him in his initial reading whilst the article on the opposite page proclaimed 'A Mother's Task in Sex Education for Daughters'.

Gertrude stood up, flaring disgust in her eyes and hands:

'Take that vulgar rubbish out of this house, Doctor. My husband is a Christian gentleman who has never allowed sex to rear its ugly head.' She lowered her voice to an unusual level of intimacy. 'I'll have you know, Doctor, that my husband has never seen me naked, nor I him. Respect, that's what we have. Respect and modesty!'

230

As far as Jeremy Bennett was concerned he wanted to get away. He looked forward to meeting a few *common* people in his surgery that afternoon and later to sharing Gertrude gossip with Hazel.

'My horse has been kept waiting too long. I must go. Please do not bother to see me out.' He picked up his journal, *The Nineteenth Century*, and bowed himself away.

He swallowed a quick lunch, attended to just four patients in the surgery and found Hazel in the garden. She was sitting relaxed in a deck chair with two other chairs waiting for occupation:

'Hello, my darling, how did you get on with Gertrude? Sit down and tell me all!'

Jeremy, who had a huge curiosity about people over and above their medical condition, always hoped that Hippocrates would forgive him for breaking his oath of confidence. His affectionate indiscretions were a spontaneous antidote to a compassion which bordered on obsession. Hazel, and quite often Belinda, were the two people in the whole world with whom he could share all the idiosyncratic sidelights which he experienced peering into the depths of other people's lives.

He recounted the midday meeting, gave an exaggerated summing-up of the journal and ended finally with Gertrude's declaration of decency.

Hazel pulled herself up out of the deck chair and went over to his side.

'Darling.' She kissed him lightly on his right ear and whispered into it: 'You would never pass Gertrude's test of a Christian gentleman, would you?'

They laughed together as if anticipating the sheer comforting bliss of lying in bed together, in a few hours' time, revelling in the joy of being one.

But now they settled down into a shared silence, comfortable and intimate, as only those know who never doubt the permanence of their love. Jeremy had drifted into that blissful state when he was conscious enough to know that he was neither asleep nor awake.

'Jeremy, I forgot to give it to you. There is a letter here that came by the midday post!'

'You horror, I was nearly asleep – oh the plague of living with a talkative woman!'

Someone eavesdropping on that bit of the conversation might have thought they were bickering, but it was the kind of genial

231

banter which saved their day-to-day relationship from being cloying. He got up from his chair, lightly rapped her knuckles and opened an envelope which conveyed half its message on its exterior. It was from the Royal College of Physicians, Edinburgh, and bore its resplendent insignia. It was, as he expected, an invitation to the August Convocation to which he, as a graduate of Edinburgh University, made a yearly pilgrimage.

It was always held when the city was emptied of university undergraduates and was warm enough for the colleges to be spared the trouble and expense of coal fires. The subjects on which they were to confer, he read in the leaflet accompanying the gilded invitation card, were:

Presence of Husbands during Parturition
Anaesthesia in Midwifery
Plain Facts about Sexual Life

He laughed aloud at the thought of Gertrude seeing the contents of this letter, which he handed over to Hazel.

'What would Gertrude think of that?'

Hazel chuckled as she handed it back. 'You said she quoted Queen Victoria as the model to follow! Somewhere in the house I must find my mother's press-cuttings and read out to you the Court Circular from *The Times* – 1857 I think it was – "The Birth of a Princess..." It lists the names of all those present, I think there were about twenty in the room including, of course, Prince Albert... How about that for feminine modesty?'

Hazel immediately reflected on the visit to Edinburgh.

'Jeremy, why not call and see Grace Hargreaves while you are there? You know she has a very special regard for you, and with good reason. Felicity was saying that she is spending two nights at Stonegarth in a few days' time. It is difficult to invite her here. We know, for certain, we shall not be invited there.'

'Yes, I'll write to her after supper suggesting possible times in August. But I only wish you were going to be with me, Hazel.'

Grace meanwhile, was engaged in the preparations for her journey south. The moment came when, for a fleeting moment, she and Felicity were left alone in the Hargreaves' garden shortly after her arrival en route to Paris.

Now they plunged into the subject which Felicity was longing to tell and Grace was waiting to hear.

232

'When do you get your college results, my dear?'

'Oh, Grace...' Felicity stopped short. She must remember never to use this familiarity here. 'Aunt ... you have arrived for the nerve-racking bit! They are going to be announced *tomorrow!*'

'Would you like me to come with you? Not that I think you need moral support, but it might be good to have someone with you to share your triumph...'

'Or disaster! Yes, do come, but might I suggest that you have some other errand in Bradford? Otherwise, would it not seem to be making me appear too important?'

Her aunt caught the message and was quick to find an excuse.

'Yes, my dear, I do quite *urgently* need to see my solicitor about a change in my will. In fact it might not be a bad idea if you came in with me, since the codicil does affect you.'

'*Aunt* Grace!' (She emphasised the aunt with a nod and a twinkle.) 'Please do not talk of wills, and death. You will outlive us all! But are you sure your solicitor will be in his office on a Saturday morning? I thought they had all caught the London habit!'

'His firm, Felicity, Wainwright, Wainwright and Parkinson, have been in business for over a hundred years and what their grandfather said ten years ago and their great-grandfather said fifty years ago are still the ten commandments and always will be.'

'Good! Then you will meet Belinda! We shall get on her train, *third class*, Grace, and be able to look at the results together.'

The evening went reasonably well because Arthur was able to dominate the conversation with Leo's conversion to Orderly Behaviour.

'If I'd not insisted on that dog going to the police-station for proper training' we'd never 'ave 'ad no peace, I can tell yer. Now even Felicity can make 'im come to 'eel, can't yer, lass?'

'Yes. And far more than that! He sits, stands and fetches and carries to order!' She turned to Grace. 'Father takes him to watch cricket. Leo sits quite still and even keeps his eye on the ball!'

'And how is the woollen trade, Arthur?'

'First of all, *you* ought to know that in Aireley yer don't talk of *wool*. It's *worsted* in these parts!'

Somewhat deflated, Grace corrected herself. 'Worsted, then, how is the worsted trade?'

The rest of the meal was completely covered with the state of trade; the foreign market; exports, imports, strikes at the dye-works; his brother-in-law's progress in New Zealand, the quality of Australian fleeces and how Aireley mill was holding its own. One had to admire Arthur's knowledge but it was hardly helpful to

233

digestion. Gertrude's requests, made in the rare pauses, damned up any mouth-watering one might have had at the approach to the laden table.

'Have some more tongue, Grace, it will only be left.'

Felicity tried once to steer the conversation away from the worsted world. 'Is it not exciting that aunt Grace is on her way to Paris?'

'If I didn't get orders from those *aut couters* I wouldn't 'ever 'ave truck with the place. Wot would I want with all that nightlife? Watch yer step, Grace, in Paris. I 'ope yer've got a nice 'omely woman to go with yer!'

The dreaded Saturday came, ending all the beautiful weather which had brought an early harvest. Felicity's bedroom seemed dark at eight o'clock in the morning. She put her weatherproof cloak over her weekday clothes, picked out an umbrella instead of a parasol and joined Grace in the hall. The small trap was at the door with its depressing black oilcloth cover and even the groom seemed to be aproned in tarpaulin. It was a relief to get to the station.

Its master, Herbert Dawson, cheered the morning. Keeping himself and his top hat under the station roof he responded to the introduction to Miss Grace Hargreaves with: 'You should have seen your niece playing Viola, Miss Hargreaves: grace was in every step ... as the Bard said.'

Herbert Dawson was aware how apt his compliment was and he overtopped it as he held the door of the Ladies Only third-class compartment, which Belinda had already half opened:

'And here is Olivia, Miss Hargreaves! You would agree that her face would *endure wind and weather* would you not? It will have to today, Miss Bennett.'

Even Grace Hargreaves, extremely liberal by the standards of her day, was amazed at the familiarity of a stationmaster with his rather distinguished passengers. Had she been on her return journey from Paris her reaction might have been slightly less puzzled.

The train went through the rain with its usual speed and time passed quickly with snippets of quotations from the producer of the play and the final exchange on Belinda's father's projected visit to Edinburgh in August.

They spoke very little as they climbed up the hill to the college, intent as they were in keeping their umbrellas under control. The atmosphere in the college was very different from the usual working days. The Principal was in evidence; students were chatting with members of staff; students, in varying degrees of nervous strain, were peering at the lists. Felicity introduced her aunt to the registrar and asked permission for her presence.

'Have they brought you for moral support, Miss Hargreaves? I don't think these two need their hands holding!'

They edged near the board. 'Thank goodness they are not in graded order.' Felicity thought imagining herself well down the list.

Physics: Theory and Practical
Chemistry: Theory and Practical
Biology: Theory and Practical
Pharmacy: Theory and Practical
Botany: Theory and Practical

Pass mark: 60. Honours: 80 and over

They looked intently, picking out their results. Belinda, whose surname began with B, was quick to spot her own results well up the alphabetical list.

Physics 78, Chemistry 81, Biology 77, Pharmacy 74, Botany 75

Felicity further down the lists made a note of hers:

Physics 69, Chemistry 80, Biology 78, Pharmacy 80, Botany 76

They could not believe their eyes. Felicity was the more amazed. They could both understand why they had done best in chemistry with the close monitoring and tutoring which her accident had engendered. But however had Felicity beaten Belinda in pharmacy? And then she remembered the clarity of Simon Watts' notes, the meticulous diagrams, the bonus of his explanations. This had given her a head start. She looked further down the list at his results: Honours in five out of the five subjects. An overall Honours!

Her weak mark in physics stemmed from the bleakest information she had received from the physics master: simply a list of numbered pages in a textbook. The last two terms were crippled by the first. She never had caught up. How would this affect entry to Edinburgh?

Meanwhile, Grace in the background was doing a quick bit of mental arithmetic. Belinda's total marks added up to 385: Felicity's to 383. It seemed too good to be true. Belinda so confident; Felicity so held back by her accident.

Had Grace known the full circumstances she would have realised that Belinda had given a great deal of her time in order to tutor her own mind.

Grace felt proud of her god-daughter when she saw her throw her arms round Belinda and say: 'I would never have done it without *you*.'

Belinda's response brought tears to Grace's and Felicity's eyes as Belinda swept Felicity into the air as if for all to see: 'I would never have done it without *you*.'

Grace was glad she'd asked Gertrude's permission to take the girls out for luncheon. She had telephoned the Bennetts to ask their permission, which, of course, was joyously given.

Relief is a good appetiser so the three settled down in high spirits in the alcove in Collinson's, where Felicity and Belinda were regular customers. It was here that Belinda and Robert Mackintosh had plotted their plans for Felicity and fed one another's appetites for laughter.

Belinda, the skilled raconteur, brought that first term to life for Grace: the accident, the quick action of Simon Watts, the wit and kindness of Robert Mackintosh, the vicarious studies which Felicity had done so well, the joyous welcome she was given on her return in the New Year.

To each of these episodes Felicity added a paean of praise and then, thinking that all this was perhaps becoming a little cloying she said: 'But you know, Grace, Belinda often bullied me into action. Every time I weakened she had a metaphorical stick, first to whack me with, and then for me to lean on. I can see her, in a few years' time, not only taking medicine but *teaching* it!'

They had the luxury of dawdling over Collinson's excellent coffee to talk about the play.

Grace, well versed in Shakespeare asked: 'And how was your Malvolio? The last production I saw, quite recently in Edinburgh, the actor made him totally ludicrous, whereas it is only through atrocious treatment that he becomes so. He should have a whole superstructure of pride and nobility...'

'I think our curate played it rather too much like Uriah Heep. But it got laughs from the audience. They revelled in seeing their curate yellow-stockinged and cross-gartered!'

There was much more talk about the play and then Grace excused herself to go to see her solicitor on her own. This was not the time to separate the two friends. She would confide in Felicity later.

'Can we meet at the station for the three thirty?'

236

They watched Grace pay the bill, order fresh coffee for them, then sweep her elegant braided silk skirt through the door.

Belinda broke the silence. 'I think Grace is the most wonderful aunt I've ever met. Why did she never marry?'

That intriguing question filled the next twenty-five minutes. Felicity closed this very probing discussion with a description of Grace and her fiancé in the album.

'He was more than an officer and a gentleman, Belinda. He looked to have wit, charm, intelligence and style. His face reminded me of someone I know – but for the life of me I cannot remember whom.'

The three returned to Stonegarth with the news of the examination results. It was the first time Belinda had been invited for a meal – a farinaceous feast on which she heaped excessive praise.

'What delicious scones, Mrs Hargreaves. I think your cook must have a lighter hand than ours!'

'There are certain things, Miss Belinda, which I insist on doing myself, these and Yorkshire cheese curd tarts. Cook comes from the south, you know, and they don't seem to know about these things.'

Gertrude was at a loss, however, to know how to reply to the examination results, so gambled on criticism since it was important that the child did not become vain:

'What happened to your physics then? How did you come to lose thirty-one marks in one examination?' She tried to cover her paucity of physics with a display of mental arithmetic.

Grace butted in. 'Physics, my dear Gertrude, is a very difficult subject and sixty-nine is only eleven marks from Honours.'

Fortunately Mrs Hargreaves missed Belinda's jubilant smile. She picked up her prestigious silver teapot to assert her position of hostess.

'Ask Hilda to make another brew, Felicity, and give everyone another cup. Physics is enough to make everyone parched.'

Arthur Hargreaves arrived conveniently for the renewed teapot. He had been at an afternoon meeting of the Lodge, where a theologian had done an erudite survey of the historic roots of Masonry and its complex symbols. It was not that side of Masonry that attracted Arthur to join the Airedale Lodge.

'Thank you, Mother, I'm fair parched! We've bin fair ear-stopped listening to a feller too clever by half. Well, let's be knowing 'ow you girls 'ave gone on.'

Grace took over, determined that her brother should appreciate both girls' achievements:

'Arthur, your daughter has gained three hundred and eighty three marks for her total examinations. Is it not a wonderful achievement?'

'Well, I don't go in for gush like some I could mention. No true Yorkshireman does.' He turned to Felicity. 'Yer've not done badly – considering! ... And you, Miss, 'ow have you done?' He turned to Belinda and gave her handsome face a sensual look of approval.

'Felicity beat me in three subjects, Mr Hargreaves. Are you not proud of her?'

The question was never answered as Arthur was sticking the remnants of fruitcake on to well-licked fingers and pushing them into his mouth. The nod of approval coincided with a lip-cleaning exercise involving his tongue rather than a serviette.

Simon Watts had arrived at the college on his errand-boy bicycle half an hour before Felicity; in fact he was being blown rapidly down the hill returning from the college while they were holding their umbrellas against the wind and struggling to walk uphill to their goal. With his head down and theirs hidden behind umbrellas they failed to see one another.

Felicity and Belinda had yet to retrieve their results when Simon's were being shown to his parents behind the chemist's shop. Saturday was a day the Watts had help and so Charles Watts and his wife settled round the kitchen fire with Simon and gave their son their undivided attention.

Mrs Watts made a middle-of-the-morning pot of tea and as an unusual treat opened a packet of ginger nuts, which they enjoyed dunking.

Learning was sacred to Charles Watts. Everything he knew of pharmacy, and the world which made pharmacy a necessity, was learnt through the Bradford night school, the public library and his own fervour for self-learning.

He examined each of Simon's examination subjects separately, valuing the opportunities for his son which he, who had left school at twelve, never had.

'Physics has come a long way, Simon, since my day and has a long way to go yet! It's part of everything.'

'It's hard work, Dad. I've had to struggle. I only just made it: Eighty. You need mathematics to make a proper job of it.'

'But Simon,' his mother chipped in, 'you've *made it* into Honours. Don't underrate yourself. Yer a clever lad!'

'You helped me with botany, Dad, all that propagating, grafting, growing from seed and cuttings. You made me *look* at everything, honestly you did! I'd never have got eighty-five without you.'

'What about your biology, Simon lad? Erranding medicines tells you quite a lot about folk's ailments, doesn't it? My! Eighty-seven for that! That's champion!'

Mrs Watts, quietly refilling the cups, was more interested in people in action than ill in bed.

'Ee, Mr Mackintosh must be pleased with you, eighty-nine for chemistry. I always say: next to Yorkshire folk I like the Scots best. They're a hard-working lot who find time to laugh!'

'Yes, he made me remember everything twice over! You know Miss Bennett and I did all the notes between us all over again for Miss Hargreaves when she was off sick. Miss Bennett did the instructions and I did the explanations and drawings. I'll tell you this, Mam, I did hers more carefully than mine!'

'All I say,' said his mother, with the wisdom of an educator, 'all I say, it's the teacher that counts. Well, I only went to the local Board school but there's one teacher I'll never forget. It was a Mr Simms, he taught geography. By Gow, he was a storyteller. He made us feel as if we'd sailed the Amazon, driven combine harvesters in Canada and excavated the Pyramids. I can see him now...'

'That's enough, Mother, it's today we're talking about. What else have you got there, lad?'

'Pharmacy! I kept this till last! I think half these marks are yours, Dad...'

'Ninety! Well I'm blessed! Aren't you glad now that you watched me and helped in the dispensary?'

Simon omitted telling his father that, nowadays, pharmacy, with its range of new chemicals, had outgrown his shop. What his father had taught him was Pasteur's and Lister's hygiene, precise prescriptions and accurate dispensing. That would never be out of date.

'I'll tell you this, Sonny.' (When his father was feeling proudly parental he often used this diminutive from childhood.) 'You're going to be a first-class chemist to follow on my job.'

His son, no longer *Sonny* shattered his father with his reply:

'A chemist, yes Dad, but not in a shop! I want to do a research job working with someone like Dr Bell or Eurich inventing new drugs, new treatments.'

His father covered his deep disappointment. 'Aye, and no reason why you shouldn't, lad. You've got everything before you. And I've got the shop, which I'd better get back to!'

Once Belinda had left for home, Felicity slipped up to her room to write a short note of congratulations to Simon – a Christian name she felt she could use now that college days were over.

Dear Simon,

I was delighted to see your outstanding examination results. This must be a college record – Honours in every subject! Your parents must be very proud of you especially as you have been able to help them too.

May I express my personal thanks for the meticulous and kindly way you sent notes of the chemistry and pharmacy lessons, especially the latter as you did this entirely on your own. I do not suppose, in the excitement of your results, that you happened to look at mine. I have pleasure in boasting to you that I got an Honours mark for this subject. This was entirely due to your correspondence course. I now realise with your teaching ability I should have sent my homework back to you to be marked! That would have rattled Dr Gaston, would it not?

The year in the college has been a wonderful experience for Belinda and me, not least for the friendship we have had, especially from you and Mr Mackintosh. Chemistry is essential for entry into the Edinburgh Medical School and the highs mark for pharmacy will be an immeasurable bonus since that is an essential subject in the first year.

I shall be happy to hear of your progress as you proceed through your course to be a pharmacist.

With kindest regards and thanks,

Yours sincerely,

Felicity (Hargreaves)

It was a letter she must keep well out of sight of her mother. Writing to an errand-boy! This would shatter her mother's idea of all that was right and proper in a well-structured society. Felicity put the letter in her bag to post on Monday. In their house it was forbidden to post anything on Sunday. Then she had second

240

thoughts. Why post it? Watts kept a very charming brand of attar of roses; she would visit the chemist and the post office on Monday morning and tell Miss Elsie all the exciting news!

Sunday came and went with its usual routine of morning service, roast beef and Yorkshire pudding dinner and her father's brief summing up of the sermon. Today's minister was an up and coming young man from Leeds. Felicity had found him bracing as he had based his sermon on quotations from Ruskin:

'Let the law of human life be, Effort; and the law of human judgement, Mercy.'

It was the Hargreaves custom to invite any visiting Methodist minister to Sunday dinner but this time Gertrude, hearing that the young man was of little consequence in the Leeds ministry, carefully omitted the invitation. She was the first to demolish him:

'Well, I'm glad I didn't ask him to dinner. Not a single mention of the Bible in his whole sermon.'

'Well, yer would go, wouldn't yer? Nowt wrong with that bit about effort, was ther? It's wot ah think, misen.'

Grace addressed her remark to Felicity. 'I was so impressed with his ideas of the obligation of the State that its first duty is to see that every child is well housed, clothed, fed and educated. What do you think, Felicity?'

'Oh yes indeed! I went one evening with Belinda to hear Margaret McMillan. This is what she is fighting for in Bradford and in London...'

'Good, I am so glad you have heard her. Next term she is coming to speak in Edinburgh, so perhaps we could go together.'

On Monday morning Felicity accompanied her godmother to Aireley station for the train to Leeds. On this occasion, Grace having been too dominant in her conversation, the carriage to Leeds was not offered. She left Aireley behind with no regrets but with a mixture of apprehension and delight at the thought of the journey ahead.

3

Miss Grace Hargreaves, well turned out in dove-grey summer alpaca, created the impression that her holiday started when she tipped the first porter at Waverley Station.

Confidence and curiosity are the two best ingredients for travel and Grace had them both in good measure. She even enjoyed the smelly cab drive through London's crowded streets from King's Cross to Victoria Station, especially driving down the Mall past Buckingham Palace.

Only two years to go before the Queen will be driving here in state for the Diamond Jubilee, she thought, and it seemed to add a special glow to her own journey. There were porters in profusion to take her small dressing case into the carriage, where tea was served in comfort. She was fascinated with the patchwork pattern of the fields and the rise and fall of the Sussex Downs. Her spirits rose to the heights of the steam funnels in Newhaven harbour, thrusting from the boat that was to take her, through the night, to Dieppe. She enjoyed the challenge of settling into a cabin the size of the butler's pantry in Moray Place. On deck she let the cobalt blue of the July night and the deep indigo of the sea widen her horizons of hope. An endless train of stars lighted the way to France. She had no ill feeling lying awake listening to the grinding, slapping and steaming sounds of the boat. She was old enough to be confident and young enough not to need all the tiresome trappings of habit. The strange bed feared by her elders was to Grace an adventure as it would be to a child.

Louise was there to meet her at Gare St Lazare; there was no mistaking her even though the years had left their mark. She was standing in a commanding position flanked by two porters and a handcart. *Chic* would have been too diminutive a word for this imposing young matron but the white feathers and lace in her stylish aquamarine outfit ensured that she could not be ignored.

The kiss on both cheeks, the cloud of Worth perfume, the

signalling to the two porters, all drew Grace into Louise's distinctive ambience.

Twenty-four years slipped away as the two embraced.

'Grace, *chère amie. Comme tu as l'air prospère!* Sorry! – I must use my English...! Are you in good health?

The fine lines round the eyes and mouth told their own tale of hard work and humour. The wild curls of carefree school days had been swept into a suave chignon, which behaved impeccably beneath the tip-tilted Parisian hat. She seemed taller but in fact she was the same height of five feet five, which brought her shoulder to shoulder with Grace.

As she led the way to the jaunty little pedal carriole with *Hotel Nadar* printed in shell pink on its cream sides; she explained:

'*Cette petite carriole, c'est Pierre qui l'a fait construire* – he designed it himself!'

As they joggled through Place de L'Opera Louise warned Grace not to try to speak French to Pierre.

'He will sweep you aside ... Pierre likes an audience. He will take the words out of your mouth and say it all for you with his eyes, his hands and his ... *je ne sais quoi* ... devilish charm.'

They turned into Rue Scribe and there was the small, but elegant hotel with wrought-iron balconies giving an impressive welcome. They went to a side-door marked PRIVÉ, which had the same brass-lacquered importance as the visitors' entrance.

Pierre's welcome took Grace back to the soufflés and crepe suzettes of the Cordon Bleu days. Since then he had acquired a small pot belly and a large balding patch. He had not lost, but broadened, his panache.

He showered compliments on Grace.

'*Chère Madame Grace, je suis enchanté de vous revoir! Ah! Vous êtes même plus élégante qu'aux jours du Cordon Bleu!*' Then so fast that she could not keep pace, he painted the Parisian scene, identifying himself – as if he were a close friend – with Toulouse Lautrec. He pointed to a poster advertising Le Moulin Rouge and then, kicking a leg to the level of his pot belly, he announced the name of the famous cabaret artiste La Goulue.

'*Quelle danseuse!*' He flicked a kiss from his lips with his finger and thumb and followed it through with rolling eyes.

Louise sensed that Grace, after all her travel, could do with an hour alone in peace. This understated English lady would need the whole week to acclimatise herself to the overacting of Pierre. Grace was enchanted with the private apartment, which was lightly furnished but luxuriantly draped and cushioned. In contrast her small, white bedroom with its crucifix hanging over the bed would have suited a Mother Superior had it not been for the profusion of crimson roses in a white china bowl and the vermilion poppies decorating the toilet set on the white wash stand. But the bed, with its four big square satin pillows, its white muslin draperies and deep quilted duvet seemed prepared for a courtesan – not a nun!

A neat uniformed maid immediately followed the knock on the door. '*Bonjour, Madame, je suis la femme de chambre!*'

She walked over to a panel of white moiré silk and turned a small brass handle to reveal a dressing room almost the size of the room. '*Voilà, votre malle. Puis-je vous aider à la défaire?*'

Hanging from dressmaker's rails were rows and rows of padded hangers, each with a small bag of pot pourri or perfume. Built-in drawers and cupboards covered in the same white moiré silk of the walls could have held the lingerie and millinery of a much travelled princess.

Grace did not want to dismiss the maid, though she did not need her help. It would be an opportunity to try out homely French. '*Oui, merci. Comment vous appelez-vous?*'

When Jeanette had gone, carrying the tartan tin of Crawford shortbread, Grace looked at the small pile of books on her bedside table and laughed at their incongruity. Evidently salvaged, by Louise, from their Scarborough Academy were Blake's *Songs of Innocence*, Palgrave's *Golden Treasury* and *Jane Eyre*, Zola's *Thérèse Raquin*, Flaubert's *Madame Bovary* and Victor Hugo's *Les Miserables*; all well-thumbed, they suggested that lively personalities had made them their bedside reading. Grace had read the last two in translation. Tonight she intended to brush up her French with Émile Zola.

Detached from the pile was a current theatre programme of Molière's *Le Malade imaginaire*. The week obviously held out delights far removed from Edinburgh, not least the food.

She joined her host and hostess for a *dinner* in their private room and marvelled at the multi-coloured hors d'oeuvres glistening with freshness. There followed crayfish and a fine Chablis taking the centre stage. Fresh peaches, apricots and nectarines were piled up on an epergne but before dessert Pierre held the cheese board and explained its delights.

Louise had made up her mind that the Hotel Nadar was going to do without her company this week. She would devote herself entirely to Grace. It would be a pleasure, for once, to be able to be a guide and to see her beloved Paris, as if for the first time, the city that had experienced the whole gamut of her emotions.

After a jaunty little drive in an open cab Louise and Grace were soon walking in the Jardins de Luxembourg, where parasols and canopied bassinettes seemed to heighten, not subdue, the summer sun. Paris was already *en fête*. Louise pointed out en route the hidden little pension St Marcel where she and Pierre had worked all the hours there were, desperately trying to salvage romance from their wild escape into a tough world.

As they walked along, Grace spotted the Pasteur Institute and exclaimed with almost possessive delight. 'My hero! Pasteur.'

It seemed of little consequence to Louise.

'But Louise, Pasteur has saved the world from rotting! Shall I be able to go *in* the Institute?

'Yes, but... Another day, *oui?*'

She summoned a cab with her white-gloved hand.

To Grace every building was a joy whether standing behind its own courtyard in the tree-lined boulevards or within the almost hidden passages.

Louise was at pains to point out *her* Paris which led the world in fashion and its great department stores. Her sights were set on the Galeries Lafayette, Bon Marché and Samaritaine. She dismissed the Louvre as too dull and touristy, preferring the flashing eyes of the habitués of haute couture to *les yeux un peu rusés* of the Mona Lisa.

Every window of every store was a work of art, highlighted by the new wonder of electricity. Grace had always admired the well-covered models in the windows of Jenners, Moules and Cranston and Elliotts in Princes Street, on which, at sunset, the blinds came discreetly down. Here she was transported into a magic world. She dawdled, entranced, window gazing, but Louise was impatient to get inside. *'Il te faut voir la Vente de Blanc.'*

Grace blinked unable to believe the dazzle of the White Sale. Everything seemed to be made of snow, ice and frost, yet was sunny and warm with electric light. She did not mention to Louise that her house in Moray Place was on a long waiting list for the installation of electricity!

The chandeliers in the store were hung with white streamers of ribbon almost touching the customers' fashionable heads. In the perfumery department exotic cut-glass bottles were displayed in a framework of ivory ruched velvet. At the far end of the emporium a pianist in a white linen suit lingered nonchalantly on the ivory keys of a white baby grand. Louise and Grace joined the tea and coffee drinkers. They were shown to a small table by a waiter who, when they were seated, handed to each of them a perfect gardenia and bowed saying, '*Pour la Fête, Mesdames.*'

By this time Grace almost longed for sunset to fall on this wonderful day and prayed that she would stop perspiring in the overheated store. Louise, cool as a Scottish burn, spread her smile of satisfaction round the tables of the café and silently congratulated herself that she had opened her friend's eyes.

Time drifted away unnoticed as they relaxed to the undemanding notes of the pianist, which seemed to slip down the sleeves of his white linen jacket.

'To know Paris you must get to know our new electric trains, so let us take one which goes near the river.'

Grace had never dawdled by the River Forth. To her it was a sea-going work place busily heading for Leith and its port. The famous Forth Bridge was far away inland, its great swoops and arches supporting the steam trains heading north and south. Here, in Paris, the many beautiful bridges beckoned people to sail under, ride over, or just gaze on their beauty. Louise and Grace sat down on a bench on the embankment near Le Pont Neuf – and talked.

When two people have been apart for nearly a quarter of a century – and life has given them both blows and caresses – getting to the heart of the matter takes time. Louise was less inhibited than Grace and had spilled out all the incredible details of the elopement: the trunk she had filled up with hockey and lacrosse sticks and school clothes and sent home, ahead of her, to disarm her parents. She had described the appalling sea voyage – the cheapest form of travel – from Hull to Dieppe; and the shock of the dingy little *pension*.

Bravely she dismissed in a few sentences the first five years of married life when the two of them were the only staff to serve hungry students, penniless artists, struggling writers. A time when sleep was more urgent than sexual desire in the double bed which practically filled the little garrety room.

'Did you ever want children?' Grace ventured.

Louise's hands flicked negation with the single word: '*Non*. But that is enough about me. Tell me, Grace, why has a beautiful woman like you not married? I have noticed that engagement ring on your wedding finger. Forgive me … but I have a feeling that you want me to know, don't you?'

Louise pulled a long lace glove from her right hand and held Grace's left hand, not just in affection but with the quizzical look of a connoisseur.

246

'*C'est d'une beauté exceptionelle* ... exquisite and so unusual.'

Grace quickly ran over how she met her Lieutenant-Colonel Stewart at the Medical Ball following the Hogmanay celebrations and how she kept him at bay for two years.

'Then, Louise, he was brought into the Royal having broken his shoulder in a hunting accident. It was sheer good luck that I was assigned by the Sister for what was really nothing but orderly duties. But it did mean that, as an officer and a gentleman, he had special meals and attention in a private ward. He had a charming way of delaying all the attention I gave him. Later, when he was out of hospital, I let him monopolise my very precious free time – especially that Christmas and New Year holiday. It was during that week he told me he was under orders to leave for India as a medical officer on a troop ship setting out from Leith. It was, forgive the cliché, a whirlwind affair. He never even consulted my parents.

'The proposal, its acceptance, betrothal, giving of the ring, vows of everlasting love – it was a whole life in fourteen days!'

Louise, showing a hint of green eye mumbled, 'Lucky you...'

'Louise,' Grace bit her lip, 'there was no luck anywhere. He was not returning to England for two years and we had just two weeks together.'

'But, darling, what happened?'

'The very worst that could. He died out there of cholera. It is the most deadly disease...'

Louise gripped Grace's hand. '*Oh chérie, qu'est-ce que je peux dire?*'

The river flowed on. A red rubber ball bounced past Grace's feet followed by a small boy with his nurse. There were raucous shouts from a barge and red white and blue banners flying from the bridges. Nearby an artist was packing up his easel.

Grace let the water under the bridge float the rest of her story away.

Grace's thoughts, too deep for words, and too *spirituelle* for Louise, ran like some bizarre electric current through Grace's mind.

She stood in front of her bedroom mirror, reviewing the strange pattern of her life since she had detached herself from her Yorkshire roots.

Was it death which had protected and preserved her idealistic love? What price had been paid? By whom? To whom? Was it still being paid? Was it a God of revenge who had taken her one and only lover? Was she preserving the playroom for any real purpose? Or was it to escape from reality and keep the haunting flame alive?

A tangle of questions went on while she pulled out long pins from the large leghorn straw hat and unfastened the wrist to elbow buttons of her silk lace gloves. The disturbing question of God and his debt to be paid coincided with the ritual fingering of slightly disturbed hair. The reflection in the mirror failed to reveal the deeper reflections of a disturbed mind.

These questions were never discussed with Louise – not through lack of sensibility but rather because Louise's major mission was to be the engaging hostess and Grace's to be the responsive, appreciative guest.

On the final night at the Comédie Française, Louise's laughter was quicker and louder than Grace's. The finesse and timing of words and movement delighted Grace but she was conscious she was missing nuances of *Le Malade imaginaire* which titillated the Parisian audience.

Earlier in the week she had sent the expected picture postcards: a rather dull sepia photograph of the ten-year-old Eiffel Tower to Arthur and Gertrude. For Felicity she chose an exquisite colourprint of Monet's *Femmes du Jardin*.

A souvenir for herself was already packed flat in the base of her trunk: It was an imperial-size print of Monet's *On the Seine at Berricomt*. Although this girl was sitting in the country, dressed more simply than ever she and Louise had been, it reminded her of the day when the flow of the Seine eased thoughts into the open and then floated them away again – unspoken.

Jeanette's entrance and her look of disappointment at the trunk followed the knock at the door. '*Vous avez fini, Madame!*'

'*Pas encore, Jeanette, j'ai quelque chose à vous offrir.*'

Grace opened Jeanette's hand and put into it as many francs as a month's wages.

Gratitude prompted Jeanette to use the courtesy of formal English: 'Thank you very much, Madame.'

And then a week's admiration glowed into her natural speech. '*Vous êtes trop gentille.*'

The glittering holiday was over and Grace did not know whether to be glad or sorry that it was so.

She looked at the tiny bronze model of the Eiffel Tower, bought as a present for Maggie, and smiled to herself at the irony of giving something so miniscule to convey the Tower's heaven-soaring height.

It seemed a very fragile monster compared with the earth-clutching castle, which gripped so much of Edinburgh... But that was her *home*. And, when the emotional farewells were over, that was where she most wanted to be.

Meanwhile at Stonegarth July was taken up with visits to Busby's and Brown Muffs in Bradford and Madame Nanette in Leeds for important clothes. In between times there were fussy little intimate sessions with the Miss Musgraves in the sewing room for garments they referred to as *private wear* and her mother described, in her newly found word, as *lingerie*.

August came in with a heavy heat. The trees stood solidly covered with dusty leaves and Arthur Hargreaves' roses, once big and brash, had lost their virgin freshness.

Felicity, like the trees and bushes, longed for September. But there was still the visit to the photographers in Leeds, which Felicity dreaded and Gertrude considered to be her personal triumph.

'I have made an appointment with the hairdresser, three doors away. Of course we shall go there first. The appointment with him is ten o'clock and Mr Thawley at eleven.'

Felicity felt as if all her own individuality had been taken out of her hands but, remembering Grace's advice, she conditioned herself into being the lamb to the slaughter.

The face she hardened into Hargreaves stubbornness was not one to appeal to a photographer. The cubicle where her hair was dressed, far removed from the only other customer, was thick with the steamy heat of the August day and the artificial heat from the curling tongs. She loathed the experience and recalled how deftly Hazel Bennett had persuaded the hair to suggest the pageboy Cesario and then loosened it into a feminine frame for Viola. That was something her mother would never understand.

They walked into Mr Thawley's in silence.

He rubbed his hands together, looked at the right side of her face with prepared sympathy, nodded to her mother and then said, as if Felicity were not in the room, 'Do not worry, Mrs Hargreaves, I think I can deal with the problem.'

An over-carved chair had been placed in front of a red velour curtain, swathed back to give a curve of gold bobbles behind the right side of Felicity's face.

'Kindly sit facing that exquisite landscape, Miss Hargreaves, so that your left profile is right for the camera. Are you happy with that arrangement?'

He retreated to his camera without waiting for an answer and put his head under the black cloth.

'Smile at the picture, Miss Hargreaves, or at least try to look pleasant.' He spoke as if she were a small child. 'Ignore me and the camera... Head a little higher, my dear. Quite still now!'

She could hear the plates sliding in and out. Surely three were enough. Then another. She prayed for finality.

'All over, Miss Hargreaves. You have been very good.' He was like a dentist addressing a difficult child. Now the head had emerged from its black tent Gertrude was able to speak.

'When will they be ready, Mr Thawley? I would like them to be on show for her birthday in September and my At Home day.'

Mrs Hargreaves was acting the solicitous mother. Felicity was putting on her bonnet and picking up her parasol as if that were the decisive movement of the day.

The words longing to escape from her stubborn mouth were: 'Oh, the falsity of it all!'

They sat in the train from Leeds to Shipley and on to Aireley as if they were total strangers both sharing the same rhythm of the train. The nice side of Felicity felt sorry for her mother that she had such an unappreciative daughter. But for nine-tenths of the journey she wondered why on earth her parents could not be more like herself.

The nice side of Gertrude glanced at her daughter and thought: you went through that quite well. But for nine-tenths of the journey she wondered why her daughter was not more like the parents who had brought her up.

What strange compositions of kindliness and cruelty we all are! Why should such a trivial episode as the photographer's bring out her claws and flaws?

Mother and daughter went into Stonegarth in silence.

Leo ran out to greet them as if conscious that his young mistress needed consolation. He leapt up to caress her. Felicity's bad-tempered tears, which had been suppressed all the morning, found affectionate release. She bent down and let them flow over Leo, indulging in his understanding.

It was well into August before Belinda and Felicity made another visit to Barlockend. By now the chaplain, Anthony Thompson, had cut out the formal ritual of reception and departure reserved for the elegant part of the asylum, and took them straight through to the women's day-room. Felicity was almost ashamed that she now took the background noise of wailing and shouting, threatening and weeping for granted and concentrated her attention solely on the comparatively normal folk with their afternoon occupations.

At the far end of the room, deep in the corner, a large sheet had been torn in half in order to be re-joined sides to middle to give the sheet a new lease of life. From the far end of the room it seemed like a shroud almost covering her aunt from toe to chin. Above the grey-white sheet her face had new hollows: the eye sockets casting shadows over lightless eyes. Felicity paused near the door, shocked at this travesty of human life.

'But, Mr Thompson, she's wasting away! There's nothing of her!'

Belinda put a supportive arm round Felicity and the three walked slowly to the corner where Amy had tried to hide herself.

She had no strength to greet her visitors. With the shock of their presence she let the sheet fall to her side to reveal a makeshift outsize shoe on the burnt foot.

'How is your foot, Auntie?' Felicity tried conversation. The only reply was a negative nod of the head. 'Can you walk now? I see you are free from your crutches.'

Anthony Thompson whispered to Belinda: 'Give her the block of chocolate you always bring. And you, the handkerchief, Miss Hargreaves. She is starved of luxuries...'

Bony hands clutched the handkerchief then ran fingers round the lace hem as if to give her assurance that it was there. She dabbed eyes, which were not weeping, just wet and sore with misery. She tried to say thank you but no sound came, just dribble through withered lips.

The block of bitter chocolate so stylishly wrapped in brown and gold defeated her. There was no way her bitten nails and arthritic fingers could tear the paper. She dropped it in her lap.

Belinda came to the rescue, tore the wrapping apart and broke off a few squares.

None of the three could decipher the garbled words struggling to escape. They were said with a thrust of half the bar towards Belinda.

251

'For my sister, my twin...'

A futile ten minutes of duty and despair dragged out endlessly. Belinda, longing to bring the visit to an end, was relieved to hear the chaplain's quiet words: 'I think it's time to go now.'

Felicity was ashamed at her desperate desire to get away from her aunt. She kissed an unresponsive hand. The burden of not being able to forget the picture of a face withered with hopelessness, she knew would haunt her all her life.

The chaplain lifted the sheet, retrieved the needle and cotton and put them into her hand. He picked up the chocolate and handkerchief and dropped them into the institutional sewing bag at her side. His spirit seemed to be far away, drained at the futility of the visit.

'Come into my office,' he said. 'I have this week's medical report.'

He opened the report on the large foolscap piece of paper filled with closely packed Indian ink calligraphy. ' "Refuses all food, which she says has a horrible taste. Refuses to go to bed. Suspicious in manner. Frequently grinds her teeth. Bites her nails. Does little to occupy herself." That is this week's report. All the other weeks on this page are similar. One says: "Likes to get in a corner by herself. Does not speak to anyone." '

Belinda was conscious that this was not the day to be cynical of Anthony Thompson's doubts, self-pity and philosophic analysing. He looked shattered. She drew the visit to a conclusion.

'Felicity, we shall just catch the five past four if we go straight away. Thank you, Chaplain. I am so sorry there is so little we can do.'

In the train the two could not bear to discuss Aunt Amy's present and future. But both were going through internal turmoil.

It was Felicity who broke the uncomfortable silence. 'I am so worried, Belinda, about the future. By the end of September you and I will be in Edinburgh. Who is going to visit her then?'

'Does it matter? Sorry, I didn't mean that! What I am trying to say is: Do we do her any good? The medical reports say that she wants to be alone!'

'Yes, but we will be tortured with conscience.'

'The awful thing, my dear, is that we shall be so frantically busy that our consciences will be totally occupied.'

'Belinda, how can you be so callous? She may not be your aunt, but she is mine!'

A few minutes of their silence emphasised the relentless, rhythmic cacophony of the train.

'Belinda, I have been thinking. Don't put me off my suggestion, please!'

'Carry on, my dear, I haven't a positive thought in my head! And I need yours.'

Felicity picked up the cue. 'Do you remember the time Roberta Butterworth came to Aireley last New Year and we were up in your bedroom trying to put the world to rights?'

'Yes, I do. I remember she said that teaching Academy girls, who only thought of their "coming out" and successful marriages, was not making use of her knowledge, nor her social and moral obligations. But, my dear, you are not thinking, surely, of asking *her* to go all the way from Harrogate to Barlockend?'

'The train and tram journeys are quite reasonable. It is remarkable how well Barlockend is served. Remember it is almost a little town in its own right.'

'But the visit, Felicity. We have become used to the horrors. Roberta is such a gentle, vulnerable little soul. I don't think she could bear it!'

'Belinda, haven't you had further thoughts about Anthony Thompson's blighted loneliness? So many of his years were spent with a doting mother. Do you remember, again in your bedroom, Roberta bemoaning how her classical education was cut short through her not being able to go to the university after her father died...'

'Felicity Hargreaves! I think you are trying to do a bit of matchmaking! You witch! Roberta's religious faith is as sound as a rock; Anthony Thompson's seems to me rather crumbly!'

'Well, his classics teaching isn't crumbly. Perhaps we could get her to sample him through his *amo, amas, amat*!'

'Felicity, you are not like the girl I first knew at all! Where have you learnt the cunning art of managing people?'

'From you, my dear Belinda, from you!'

They parted not with tears, but laughter.

Felicity, walking back to Stonegarth, reverted to the serious plan she had in mind.

Roberta Butterworth had a finely honed intellect; a well-reasoned faith and proverbial wisdom. They were wrong in the facetious reference to the *amo, amas, amat* estimate of Roberta's Latin, for did she not teach classics up to Oxford Senior level? And could she not explain the classical content behind Milton?

She would be a wonderful asset to Anthony Thompson's advanced class, where they read Latin for pleasure and did not have to labour through the network of translation.

She owed Roberta a letter. She would write tonight.

Father's high tea concluded with a lecture to Mother that surely Hilda could be found a bit of time to deadhead roses. The gardener had enough to do looking after tomatoes and grapes. Felicity excused herself and went up to the haven of her own room. She sat facing the outline of distant mills and hills.

Dearest Roberta (she now felt able to address her by her Christian name and paused to wonder if her parents had been disappointed that their third child was not Robert),

Belinda and I have been together today and were thinking about you, and, as usual singing your praises.

We both agreed that we should so much like to see you before we leave for Edinburgh and before you start term.

Looking at the map – especially the physical one with all its hills and dales – it does seem rather too difficult and time-taking to come to Knaresborough on our tandem but quite possible by train and station wagonette. Perhaps you could advise us on the most appropriate transport.

There is an important matter on which I need your advice and help but, knowing your altruistic nature, I feel sure that such help will be both readily given and, on my part, gratefully received.

Perhaps it would be more considerate if I warned you of the request before we meet, since that would give you time to think it over and facilitate your sending a refusal if it should be so.

You will be shocked to hear that I have an aunt who is in the infamous Barlockend Asylum, a result of her having been abandoned by her twin sister when the latter married and brought her bridegroom to the family home to become master of the house in permanent residence. I leave it to your imagination to piece together the plight of the unmarried sister, my aunt Amy.

No-one in the family admits her existence since (as you in your charity know) it is considered to be a matter of shame. Belinda and I have taken it upon ourselves to be aunt Amy's only visitors (every three weeks or so) and we are both concerned that when we go to Edinburgh she will have no connection whatsoever with the outside world.

We have been much helped by the Reverend Anthony Thompson, the chaplain, a sensitive scholar who felt that life

254

as a Fellow of Magdalen was too sybaritic for someone committed to Christ's pastoral compassion. You and he would have much in common as he, in addition to theology, has a classics degree from Balliol. To keep his mental works from rusting he runs an advanced course in Latin literature in his home. What an escape from the Academy that would be for you!

Having gone far beyond what I intended to write it would now seem (if you are interested in the suggestion at all) to be better if we all converged at Barlockend. We could meet you at the Barlockend station from Leeds or Bradford and escort you through the beautiful grounds and into the presence of the chaplain.

Forgive me if I have trespassed on your time and loving heart.

Yours affectionately,

Felicity (Hargreaves)

P.S. The first Thursday in September would seem to be a suitable time for all three of us and I feel sure the chaplain would be there not only by duty, but by choice.

4

Jeremy Bennett walked away from the Royal College of Physicians Medical School exhilarated by the nobility of the buildings etched golden in a sharp eastern light. Some of the papers which had been given at the Convocation were so painfully print-bound that even reading them in the *Lancet* promised more blood in the veins. At least in private reading one could stop and question assumptions and assimilate important findings and perhaps detect a beacon which might illuminate medical progress.

He chuckled to himself that after the seminar on Medical Consequences of Alcohol the leading members of the discussion were gathered together in one of the elegant reception rooms drinking the finest malt whisky that Scotland could produce.

It was a pleasant cab drive to Moray Place on this clear late August day.

Maggie, in her best afternoon apron, was at the door almost before Sam. He held back his hissing but scrutinised the stranger with his inscrutable stare. He then walked off to deliver the message to his mistress well ahead of Maggie. It was months since he had taken up his eavesdropping site underneath the piano stool in the drawing room, but this was where he made a comfortable furry circle of himself today.

'Come this way, Doctor! Madam is expecting you.' She did not realise she was slightly anglicising her speech for the important visitor.

Grace was amused at Maggie's bobbed curtsey as she announced: 'Dr Bennett, Madam,' and glided out of the room, taking the gentleman's stick and top hat en route.

The formality of the letters they had written melted away. Here standing close together were two friends who had first met twenty-four years ago. Their stillness spelt trust.

'Grace!'

'Jeremy!'

He took her hands in his and kissed each one. They smiled, not just into one another's eyes but into the laughter lines around.

'Last time we met you were chasing off for the London train!'

'And you were looking after Felicity.'

'What a lot has happened since that day!'

He dropped her hands. 'Do sit down, Grace, and then I can!' He laughed as if they lived in the same house.

If they had lived in the same house he would have been filling his pipe by now but somehow it seemed *de trop* in this elegant, but not austere, drawing room. Grace, knowing how much they had to talk about, thought she would first skim over all that she knew from Felicity's letters. But before that there were certain social formalities which Grace eased into informality.

'How is your dear Hazel? I could almost say our dear Hazel. I always felt she was a Nightingale in spirit even though she was training as a doctor, not a nurse. Although she threw herself into the cause she never took sides in the Sophia Jex-Blake troubles.'

'No, my Hazel is one of the rare women – and you are another – who can always see both sides. But you asked after her health. She really *enjoys* good health and makes good use of it. I never asked after *your* health – I just looked at you!'

'Vulgarly healthy, I suppose Gertrude would describe it. I am not adept at languishing with the vapours! Talking of Gertrude – that reminds me to say I am so sorry I did not see Hazel in that brief weekend in July but we were all absorbed in examination results. How proud you must be of Belinda!'

'And you of Felicity. Indeed they have both done so well that I have been putting out a few feelers. Keep this to yourself. Entry, apart from the basic chemistry, into the medical faculty is very pragmatic. Some of the ladies slink in with school sciences; others with apothecary qualifications. Our two girls have added biology, physics and pharmacy at quite a high level. I think it *might* be possible to by-pass the *inter* year and reduce their training from five to four years. Remember, Grace, I only *think*, I do not know.'

'Jeremy, you are a wonderful father and friend. My lips are sealed! But not today. You have excited me so much, I need tea. And so do you. Do you realise – if your idea is successful – that they would be qualified by the turn of the century – the twentieth. I cannot believe that in four years we shall be putting *nineteen* instead of *eighteen* on our cheques and letters.'

This was Jeremy's cue: 'Going back rather than forward in time....' He reached for a small bag by his chair. 'I have some-

257

thing which I have brought to show you. I am sorry it is not a present but I borrowed it from the dining hall wall.'

'You've made me very curious.'

Jeremy looked at her intently before unwrapping the package. 'It may make you feel very sad...'

He took out a framed photograph, the kind that could be seen in scores of colleges and universities now that photography was almost a mania. It was a group of medical students – all male – in their caps and gowns, taken in the courtyard of the faculty with the engraved motto and insignia above them.

'For some reason or another, we none of us seemed to get prints that year, in fact it was not the official photograph at all. Can you see anyone you know?'

Grace took the picture, sat down and examined it, looking at one face only in the three rows.

'Yes, it does hurt. Here I am, in Moray Place, nearly a quarter of a century later, and he is still a void which can never be filled. And look, there are you, next to him – as you were, and I hope always will be.'

'Grace, my dear, was it wrong of me to bring it? We have never spoken of him since. I wanted to bring him back into our lives...'

'Tell me, Jeremy, when he sailed away on the naval ship to India and you saw him off, what was the last thing he said?'

'He put his arms round my shoulder, which was not done in uniform, and said: "I shan't be at your wedding, Jeremy, but in eighteen months' time you will be at mine, as our best man... Keep an eye on her for me won't you?" I remember those words exactly. He looked strikingly optimistic in his officer's uniform, embellished with the insignia of a medico.'

Grace now relaxed into reverie, glowing with pride and the relief of, at last, being able to talk closely about her dead lover.

'He left me in Edinburgh on February the thirteenth and you in Southampton on the fourteenth. I remember the date exactly because it was St Valentine's Day and he had ordered crimson roses to be sent to me at the Nurses' Home. What with that and the ring I was *not* popular with Matron. Of course I didn't wear the ring. *No jewellery* was one of the unbreakable commandments!'

'How was it Hazel and I never saw your ring until after...'

'I wore it on the finest of silver chains, round my neck but hanging out of sight...'

'I hope you will not think my next question is impertinent – but why were you so insistent on staying in Edinburgh?'

'No, it is not impertinent, just a very long delayed question. I thought you knew, or rather I took for granted you knew. Letters to and from India, the army and the solicitors took weeks. No telegrams were sent to me because, of course, I was not *kith and kin*. The *blood is thicker than water* precept can be very cruel. I was only his fiancée. I think in their formal way, the Stewart parents – who were living in London – did what they should but it was weeks before I got a letter from the solicitor informing me of the contents of the will. It is all rather complicated to explain. I am still confused about some of the legal detail – but long before we were engaged his parents had entailed the Moray Place house to their son when his father became a senior consultant at St Thomas's in London. They moved there – then they changed *entail* to *transfer* and left the house and all its contents to him.'

Jeremy's mind was now back over twenty years. 'Yes, he did once say in a rather cryptic way that it would be difficult for him to leave Edinburgh.'

Grace followed his thoughts and her own. 'So I went to see the solicitor – fortunately in Edinburgh, so I could go in my half-day. He told me – though it took him an hour – that everything had been left to me...'

Jeremy stretched his hand across to hers. 'That was so like him. He was the most thoughtful, generous man I ever knew – and an outstanding doctor. Though I confess I never understood why he wanted to be an *army* medical officer. I don't think he'd bargained though on being sent overseas so soon. Troops galore were being shipped out to India that year. Well, perhaps the Queen wanted to show the world that she had been proclaimed Empress of India and to make the India Army a force to be reckoned with.'

Grace had something more personal on her mind.

'The Stewarts' solicitor eventually sent me a copy of his death certificate. Just the bare words: *Died of cholera* and the date *April 30th 1876*. Only twelve weeks after he left home! But I did not receive it until late on in May.'

'It is a lethal disease, my dear Grace, and attacks the healthy and fit just as brutally as it kills the poor and ill nourished.'

Grace wanted to avoid any more talk on how he died. It was too awful to think of. She changed the subject. 'He used to say to me: *Never be frightened of life, my darling, meet it head on*. He never mentioned death.'

There was a pause in which both of them were picturing the man in his prime.

'He did meet life head on, didn't he?' was all Jeremy could find

259

to say. He took her hand. 'Grace, my dear, I can't think of another man good enough for you, but have you never thought of anyone else for you?'

'Jeremy, forgive me if this seems materialistic; I can assure you it is not meant to be. This house holds all his childhood. On the top floor there are still his model railway; his scarlet tin soldiers and the family rocking horse. I offered them to his sisters – sweet girls – but they said the toys should be set out in the way he left them, ready to go into action. I was pleased they took their dolls' house, though, because in it were a set of chairs their brother had made out of horse chestnuts – *mahogany* chairs with silk webbing threaded in and out of pins for their backs. I have not seen them, or any of his family, since.' She paused. 'Perhaps I should explain how I have been able to stay here ... on my own.

'Living in this house would not have been possible if I did not have a private income. Grandmother Hargreaves invested her money, as you must know living in Aireley, in the engineering side of the family, and left it to...'

'Yes, of course, everyone in Airedale knows that she was sending her good fortune down the female line. Grace, my dear, do you mind if I make a very personal suggestion? You must get your solicitor to set down your wishes. Otherwise, your grandmother's – now your – inheritance will be legally trapped for the nearest males, your brother and his son...'

'Rest assured, Jeremy, my solicitor and I have already thought of that. But thank you for caring in such a practical way. I do not need to remind you that Felicity is the nearest female as far as I am concerned...'

'Hello, Father! How was Edinburgh? How was the conference? Most important of all, how was Grace?' Belinda couldn't wait to be told.

'She was fine and sent her love... But how was your tennis?'

'Oh, I rarely win at the Winkleys' in singles, but Justin and I together are quite a pair! But you know I think he preferred talking to Felicity and he waited on her hand and foot at tea. Oh, it was gorgeous on the terrace near the lake – and it was such fun because Justin dived in to collect the tennis balls that we'd sloshed in... He's at Cambridge, you know, studying international law. I suppose he will get a cushy job with the diplomatic service!'

As usual Belinda's conversation positively bulged with quick flashes of news, which often drew a caustic comment from her father.

'Darling daughter, while you have been using up your excessive physical energy, your mother and I have been having serious conversations on Edinburgh, the medical training and women's training. And here are you sounding as if you are a mere debutante ready to queue up on the Mall to curtsey to our very old Queen...'

'Never, never, never, Father! I refuse to wear a fleur-de-lys and to fill the season with dinners and balls in the hope of finding a rich young man.'

Hazel sat enjoying both of them and ran her eye down Belinda's athletic height. Was she seeing aright? There were Belinda's white stockinged ankles blatantly uncovered below her Macclesfield silk tennis dress:

'You minx! You've shortened your skirt!'

There was no criticism in Hazel's exclamation, rather a mischievous sense of conspiracy.

Belinda picked up her cue from her mother's smile. 'Yes, I have. Isn't that better for tennis? If I could wear flannels like Justin I'd beat him at his own game! When will women realise that they'll never have freedom while they are trailing skirts and wearing corsets? Between you and me, Mamma, I must tell you I have not worn my corsets all the holidays!'

'And Felicity? Has she...?'

Belinda chipped in quickly: 'No, darling. Remember, in many ways she is *still* attached to the umbilical cord...'

'Belinda you are incorrigible! Whatever would Gertrude say?'

Her father added: 'And don't you pick up medical language from me, my girl, *ladies* think it's rude!'

'You haven't forgotten that Felicity is coming here tomorrow, Belinda? Your father thinks it will be a short surgery and he should be with you both at six thirty. He has something important to talk about – a pleasant surprise, I think!'

'I think I have a surprise for him too!'

Felicity arrived at the Bennetts' house just as the doctor was returning from his rounds in their modest little gig. With him was their groom, Fred, who did duty as gardener, and with the change of role he put on well-worn livery, far below the standard approved by the Hargreaves.

'Good-day, Felicity, you've brought the sun with you again! Go

261

right in; the door is open and the ladies are looking forward to your coming! I shall see you after surgery.' He returned a slightly moth-eaten black topper to his head and alighted with spirits raised after the brief talk with the charming girl whom he now thought of as a daughter.

Belinda was at the door holding a letter in her hand.

'Come in quickly, my dear. Just throw your bonnet and gloves off in the hall. I want Mamma to share in this. She's in the sitting room!'

Belinda, Felicity thought, attracts incidents as blue serge attracts lint. What *is* she up to now?

Mrs Bennett embraced her with a kiss on each cheek. She had the wonderful gift of making the person she was talking to feel the most important person in the world.

'Felicity, I haven't seen you since the results. How splendidly you have done! Are you all set for Edinburgh? Belinda can't wait to get away from us, can you, darling?'

Belinda put the tip of her tongue out, in fun, but it was Felicity who held Hazel's attention:

'Thank you, Mrs Bennett! You are so kind! It depends what you mean by *all set*! You should see the mass of clothes spread out in the spare bedroom and two big cabin trunks waiting to be filled and then to go "luggage in advance". Mother has had the Musgrave sisters concocting garments she calls *combinations* in thick flannel to wear against the Edinburgh cold. She thinks I am going to Greenland!'

'How thoughtful of her!' Hazel said in her nice-to-everybody voice. Could there be a hint that her tongue was in her cheek?

'Do sit down, both of you! You must listen to this letter.' Belinda held out the envelope. 'Do you recognise the writing, Felicity?'

'Yes, of course, and the college insignia, but why be so tantalising? Don't keep us in suspense any longer! Read it please!'

Belinda enjoyed having important news. She straightened her skirt and the folds of the paper, signalling she needed concentrated attention. Then, as if addressing the Academy, she slowly delivered each word:

Dear Miss Bennett (and then she threw out an aside: 'You notice he's reverted to a formal address'),

At the recent Board of Studies meeting the results of the final examinations were given careful scrutiny so that we could guide students for the oncoming academic year.

262

After considerable discussion it was agreed that as you are following a diploma, and not a degree course in your medical studies it could be possible to make a recommendation. Your five subjects (on which you have gained highly satisfactory marks) should facilitate entry into the second year of the course.

You will remember that your provisional acceptance was, of course, dependent on your final examination results and a further form was enclosed with the initial reply.

Will you, therefore, complete that form and forward it to the registrar as directed. Meanwhile, the recommendation from the college will be sent forthwith.

May I take this opportunity of wishing you every success in your future career and assure you that I have not the slightest prejudice against women in their fight for their rights. I could wish that statesmen and politicians shared the same liberal views as.

Yours sincerely,

Robert Mackintosh

All three started to speak at once:
'Wonderful, darling!'
'Belinda, I've thought of something – listen'
'Father will be surprised and delighted...'
But it was Felicity's response which took more explaining. 'What an idiot I am! I thought it was a bill or a circular. I had a letter with me to read in the train! But I'm jumping to conclusions. He doesn't mention me in your letter. Oh, Belinda, I hardly dare open it!'

Felicity fished in her bag, and the letter was pulled out of her hand.

'I dare, if you don't.' Belinda tore it open and held it so they all could read.

It was the same letter – word for word, except it began: 'Dear Miss Hargreaves'.

Surgery time had few patients but one serious one. It was a rather feckless but pitiable woman in her late twenties with a thin pale child at her side, the youngest of eight:
'I'm sick of 'earing 'er coughing, Doctor, night and day, so I've brought 'er fer a bottle...'

Jeremy Bennett looked at the wasted body and drew it towards his stethoscope.

'Any phlegm brought up with it, Mrs Turnbull?'

'Yes, nasty green and yeller and spots of slimy blood.'

'I'm sorry to have to give you bad news but the bottle is not quite enough. This isn't just a cough, you know. Bring a specimen of the sputum in this.' He took some lint in a package and handed it to her. 'And a specimen of urine in this.' Handing her a small glass jar, he added, 'Tomorrow if you can. Slip her dress off for me, Mrs Turnbull. I just want to take a blood specimen. It's only a prick. It won't hurt!'

There were yells too big for her lungs at the undressing and squeals at the prick of the needle. The doctor was tired and on edge. Frustration rose at his own impotence and the evils of poor sanitation, foul air, malnutrition – all fostering TB.

What an idiot he was to let his own daughter become a doctor, and the more vulnerable Hargreaves girl. Was the news he was about to give them good? He questioned his own judgement and went into the house, failing to pull himself together.

He found he was resorting to the post-surgery glass of malt whisky much more frequently. He gulped it down to bolster himself before meeting his womenfolk.

Jeremy Bennett had reckoned without the energy and enthusiasm of youth. Belinda almost bounded towards him, flaunting the Mackintosh letter at arm's length. Felicity stood quiet and smiling behind his daughter, painfully conscious of the different ways they approached their respective fathers.

'Read this, Father, it's from our chemistry tutor, Robert Mackintosh.' She leaned over his shoulder rereading it too, as if to make sure he didn't miss a word.

It seemed to fall flat. She expected whoops of joy like her own. Her father looked up from the letter and forced a smile.

'Well, that was the surprise I was going to give you, but you've beaten me to it.'

He hated himself. Why should such good news add to his personal depression? Yesterday or tomorrow he would have behaved differently.

'Let's go and tell your mother!'

'Oh she knows. She's read the letter.'

Hazel came in and, as usual, changed the whole atmosphere.

'Jerry, *your* letter – from the Professor – where is it? It actually says – oh, Jerry *read* it!' She sensed his mood. 'No give it to me, I will read it! I'll run over the beginning about your meeting again: Ah! Here's the important bit: "The Convocation gave me an opportunity to discuss, with the powers-that-be, all that you told me about your daughter and her friend. This would not have been possible in the normal vacation but they are all in agreement that the qualifications of the two entrants satisfy the requirements for the exemption of the induction year…"'

Hazel stopped and flung her arms round Jeremy:

'That puts everything right. Oh my darling, if I weren't married to you I would fall in love with you all over again.'

The Bennetts had no inhibitions about hugging. They, and Felicity, ended in a close circle of affection with the three significant letters on the floor at their feet.

Jeremy began to doubt the effect of the malt whisky. It had not moved his depression in the least. This was a more potent spirit. The depression cleared away like a Bradford fog chased over Otley Chevin.

He walked into supper with his three graces in front of him, as if on air. The day was transformed. Hope seemed not just an excuse for inertia but a positive light on the horizon, something to hold on to, to grapple with. Perhaps, in their time, his girls would see wrongs righted. He thought back to his childhood in the manse, to his father at the piano and his mother leading the singing with her six children, mostly out of tune, but in tune with her. He remembered the Sunday teas when the table, the food, the family were all extended to the limit and the first rumblings of socialism were sublimated into song:

> These things shall be. A loftier race
> Than e'er the world hath known shall rise
> With flame of freedom in their souls
> And light of science in their eyes.

September seemed disinclined to drift into a season of mists and mellow fruitfulness but shone blue and gold in a prolonged summer. Roberta Butterworth was bored with Knaresborough, her scenic home town, and out of tune with the day trippers watching with curiosity the stalagmites grow up and the stalactites drip down in the limestone caves. She was glad to mount the horse-bus for Harrogate and walk down James Street to the station. The first two weeks of the holiday she loved the crags and caves of Knaresborough and the restless River Nidd but now the mental inertia of the beauty spot irritated her. Mother

Shipston's prophecies of doom petrified people as the limestone water petrified the articles hanging in her cave.

It was luxury to visit Harrogate out-of-term and to wander slowly down James Street revelling in all the luxurious gowns and jewels she did not want nor could she afford to buy. Roberta, who gained great pleasure from routine orderliness, found changing stations and picking up connections exhilarating. She arrived at Barlockend glowing with her adventure and delighted to meet her former students, whose small difference in age did not exist now they had left school.

'Felicity, you look wonderful!' She beamed first at Felicity and then at Belinda, who did not need those words.

Belinda took her hand. 'Was the journey too frightful, Roberta? Changing at Leeds can never be pleasant! The air here is so different, we always enjoy the walk to Barlockend, do we not Felicity?'

Belinda, conscious that the way must be prepared for the asylum, had the idea that one could always condition people into making them enjoy the things one enjoyed oneself. However, it was easier to be enthusiastic about the fresh air than the asylum and the chaplain, so she threw the ball into Felicity's court.

'Felicity knows the chaplain better than I, do you not, dearest? We have just ten minutes' walk before we meet him, so you put Roberta in the picture!'

Felicity did not seem to find the request difficult. She talked almost with awe about his commitment to his vocation; his impressive scholarship; his enthusiasm for the classics. She glossed over his religious doubts and his obvious need for a woman's (or man's) loving understanding. That must be allowed to emerge.

The Reverend Anthony Thompson had received good notice of this threesome visit and, hearing that Miss Butterworth was in charge of the English Department at the Academy, he expected a settled spinster with controlled grey hair, pince-nez and an intellect to match.

He concentrated his whole attention on this wide-eyed innocent-looking young woman over whom the Bennett girl towered. He took both her hands but in the manner of one giving communion:

'I think God has sent you here, Miss Butterworth. How else could you have found your way?'

Felicity cringed when she heard Belinda butting in: 'Well, actually, Chaplain, she's caught three trains all by herself and loved it!'

'I think, Miss Bennett, Miss Butterworth understands the deeper meaning of that remark!'

And to Roberta Butterworth's everlasting credit, she did. And showed it.

The chaplain repeated his guidebook tour through the reception room, entrance hall and corridors as he did the first time Belinda went there with Felicity. But it was Roberta to whom he pointed out details of craftsmanship, which gave them all a delaying interval before meeting aunt Amy.

The warden and day superintendent hovered near the office ready to be introduced to the 'lady high up in education', which seemed to be how Anthony Thompson enhanced the occasion.

Today, Amy Ackroyd was not hiding in a corner. It was obvious she had been cleaned up and placed in one of the more important chairs. The crocheting in her hands was fine white lace edging, quite unlike the rough sewing which was her usual recreation. There was a small helpful table at her side, which the regular visitors had not seen before.

Felicity was amazed at the introduction.

'Here is another teacher of English come to see you, Miss Ackroyd. She has heard you know a lot of poetry.'

Roberta Butterworth produced from the silk bag hanging from her waist an illuminated card with a silk cord and opened it for Amy to see. All four watched Amy looking at it blankly in silence. They marvelled at her calm.

Had they given her laudanum? Belinda wondered. This stillness and almost sweetness was uncanny. They knew that very often restless patients were sedated.

Felicity thought: I wonder if it is because they have treated her as a lady and that for one brief moment she has become one again.

The Reverend Anthony Thompson positively oozed satisfaction. His preparation had gone well so far. He addressed Amy as if she had all her senses.

'You and Miss Butterworth have one very important thing in common – you are both great readers!'

At the words *great readers* Amy Ackroyd's lips twitched forward as if she were trying to say something. Roberta knelt down and held the card nearer to the lifeless eyes.

'It's the print. I can't see it,' came out in spurts. 'You read it.' This was said more by pointing than speaking.

Fury rose up through Belinda's tall body.

'That's it! Has no-one ever found out that her sight is failing? How could she possibly do that fine crocheting? It's a pretence!'

It was Roberta Butterworth who saved the situation. The girls at the Academy had always admired the elegant gold lorgnettes she wore folded and hanging on a long exquisitely wrought gold chain. She never seemed to need them for reading but they had a magic which kept the children in the Junior House enthralled.

'Let's all say a magic word and see if it opens the glasses! One, two three – abracadabra!' And without the slightest movement from Miss Butterworth the single glass swung open to make two.

'Who knows another magic word? Yes, right. One two three! Open Sesame!' and the lens parted into two without a finger being moved, just a pinpoint tip of one chamois polished nail. The magic never failed. It dried homesick tears; silenced squabbles; delayed greedy snatches of cake; gathered children together for story-telling.

Here and now at Barlockend, Roberta mesmerised her audience of four. She raised the chain over her own small poke bonnet and carefully lowered the chain over Amy Ackroyd's head. There were no magic words in this grim building. Roberta simply put Amy's thumbnail in place and gave it the minutest pull. The glasses sprang apart in Amy's unbelieving hand.

For the first time in a whole decade, Amy Ackroyd laughed.

She laughed and indicated that she wanted the lorgnettes closed again.

Roberta called 'Abracadabra!' And the magic worked. But there was another magic which only Amy was seeing – it was a little class of eight-year olds in her primary school in the slums of Holbeck. It was years since she had gathered them round her for *The Pied Piper*; years since she heard them sing their multiplication tables to the lively tune she had made up for them... Fortunately her vivid recall kept the singing in her ears.

Roberta took the gilt and cream card she had given her and held it in front of the glasses. It was difficult to help her to hold them still and at the right distance but gradually the print became clear.

Amy groped her way into the words: 'Shepherd ... green pasture s... still waters.' She was picking out the words of the twenty-third psalm. She was looking at it almost greedily. And then she laughed. Not the abracadabra laugh but a soft gurgle of triumph.

She passed the card back to Roberta and moved her hand in a gesture as if to say: 'Not needed.'

'I remember it. I can say it.' She stumbled into speech and, in her own private trance, whispered the whole psalm.

Never in her life had Belinda Bennett been so silenced.

Never had Felicity Hargreaves been so overwhelmed and humble.

Never, in the academic shelter in which she lived, had Roberta Butterworth experienced such divine concentration.

Never in his scholarly and clerical life had Anthony Thompson been so speechless.

Without disturbing her new world, he put the pretentious crochet back into the bag and then signalled to the three bewildered observers to withdraw.

No-one spoke a word until they were in the reception room, where the small table was set with a tea tray.

'Roberta!' Belinda whispered. 'Roberta! You've left your lorgnettes!'

Roberta replied very calmly: 'Yes, indeed. With your co-operation, Mr Thompson, I'll leave them and come again tomorrow. Those were my mother's lorgnettes and the gold chain her mother's. I am not so altruistic that I would part with them. But I have a pair of spectacles which my mother used for the last years of her life. Nothing complicated, they simply magnify. I will bring them tomorrow and I will see if Miss Ackroyd will take to them. I also have a large-print edition of Tennyson's poems – illustrated. It was published to celebrate our Queen's golden jubilee. I think Miss Ackroyd would be able to read that without glasses. Shall we try?'

Felicity could hardly find words to thank her. 'I am having to pinch myself to make sure that what happened this afternoon is true.'

She then turned to the chaplain who was quietly scheming moves for the future: not just for Miss Ackroyd but for himself.

'Mr Thompson, how little all three of us have done compared with Miss Butterworth. You won't, please, let my aunt slip back into...' She could not find the right word and left the sentence hanging in mid-air.

'It does pay to trust in God sometimes, does it not?' He was twisting the ring his mother had given him on the day he was ordained.

Felicity was wholly satisfied with the chaplain's question; Roberta less so. Belinda doubted someone who found God so handy.

Roberta, although impressed with the man, thought the word *sometimes* was hardly a modification one would expect from a don of divinity who had experienced the sequestered life of Magdalen. She looked forward to returning to Barlockend the next day, little knowing the usual order of the institution's day.

Felicity remembered her last visit to Barlockend: the sedated inmates and the restless ones crammed together in sweaty constriction. In contrast, today all, except her aunt, were out of doors in the far paddock almost out of hearing. She thought again of her last visit: the grey-white sheet, a shroud in a dark corner. Today her aunt was cleaned up, sitting up, looking up in a chair with a high back and a deep cushion.

The September sun was fooling the Dales that summer would never be done... And the asylum, from the outside, looked almost magnificent.

She shrank from thinking of the future and Roberta Butterworth's part in it.

On the way to the station the three made facile little plans as if life were both malleable and logical.

Belinda faced the facts with her father when she got home:

'It was a miracle, all that happened today, Father, but I felt angry and showed it – angry that no-one realised that aunt Amy needed spectacles. Listen, Papa, she can *read*, but how can she read without a book or spectacles? She can *talk*, but how *can* she, if no-one talks to her? She can *laugh* – but for years there has been nothing to laugh at and no-one to laugh *with*!'

Dr Bennett went very quiet and still. 'If I were you, Belinda, I should leave it to Roberta Butterworth. If I am right in my judgement, behind that fragile appearance is a tough little pilgrim who may be finding the way she wants to go.'

5

The girls' arrival in Edinburgh was not heralded by the sun. In fact it was very much the same welcome as John Knox received: 'mist sae thick the sun was not seen to shine two days before and two days after'. The Yorkshire girls had left a golden late September day in the Dales, where stooks of wheat and barley perked up with proud independence not far from the shadow of the mills. Today all the noble buildings in Edinburgh, on which Belinda and Felicity had expected to gasp with delight, were shrouded by the haar, that miserable, dulling dampening mist slinking its way across the German Ocean.

Groping in the mist they hailed a reluctant cab. The driver, a damp and canny Scot, only consented to take them to Marchmont Road when he sized up the value of their purses. They saw little but his back and that of the steaming, streaming unloved horse. On their arrival, Felicity, seeing the driver's critical scrutiny of the money Belinda had put in his hand, moved with the speed of a pickpocket and added a threepenny bit. She followed her friend and their hand luggage to the door. It all looked very grim. A damp dismal grey.

Mrs McLeish had been peeping round her curtains for half an hour, praying to her accommodating God to blow the haar away. She lost her piety and decorum on seeing the driver: *God in heaven, the poor lassies have got the only cabby who's a bad lot. The others will have gone home.*

She heaped apologies on the girls.

'Dinna ye fash the man. He's a rogue! And we'll shut that haar oot!'

She pulled down the blinds, rattled the curtains closed, and took the fine hats and cloaks from them.

'Your luggage is all here, safe and sound. It's a hot cup of tea ye'll be wanting. Just go into the front room and make yerselves at home.'

The kindly monologue was interspersed with a variety of thank-yous from the two grateful lodgers, who sensed that living with

271

Mrs McLeish was going to make their four long years seem shorter.

She returned with the tray and an apology. 'The shortbread is just to put ye on. Real tea is at quarter to six when Miss Nell comes home. She's on days this week, so you're lucky! Och, and there's a letter from your aunt to welcome ye both. She left it two days ago.'

Mrs McLeish handed it over to Felicity.

'What a fine handsome woman. You must be proud to carry the same name.'

Both the girls enthused in chorus but were anxious to open the letter. They waited for their landlady to leave the room before opening the envelope. Felicity read it aloud, noticing the courtesy of putting Belinda, the elder, in first place.

My dear Belinda and Felicity,

Welcome to our beautiful city. I hope the sun goes on shining as it is doing today. (They laughed at the reality.)

Lectures will not be starting for a few days so could we meet on Saturday morning at Moray Place. It is quite a pleasant walk for you.

Perhaps before we meet you might like to have a look at the enclosed. It will make you feel less like freshers when you make your first entrance into the daunting medical school. Take heart! When you have been there a month you will walk in as if you own the place!

I close with the sincere wish that the four years in Edinburgh will be shiningly memorable and a lodestar for life.

Remember my home in Moray Place is always there whether you want to relax, report, rage, revolt or restore.

I shall always remain for you both, your loving godmother,

Grace

Felicity clutched Belinda's hand. The letter was such a comforting way to walk into a frightening new life. She held the pamphlet for them both to read: '*Edinburgh Medical School Calendar and Guide to Students 1895–1896.*'

'Can you think of any other aunt in the world who would have thought of that?'

'How does she know so much about medical affairs in Edinburgh?'

'Surely your father told you about the Nightingale nurses. They

272

were held in just as high esteem as the young doctors and male students. In fact all the medical males, whether practising, or in training, treated them with more respect than they treated women medical students.'

Mrs McLeish returned with two letters in her hand. 'I didna want to face you with these. Now put them down and attend to yer tea first.'

Their new life was beginning to crowd in on them and they were quite glad to escape to the long refectory table with its wholesome but frugal tea. The two envelopes had impressive insignia: *Edinburgh Hospital and Dispensary for Women & Children, Bruntsfield Lodge, College of Physicians, Edinburgh.*

Belinda pushed them out of the way when she heard voices in the hall.

'They've arrived, Nell,' they heard Mrs McLeish say with excitement. 'Come thi ways in – just a wee wash of your hands, nothing more, no changing...'

'I'm a wee bit scared... Are they very grand?'

'Not grand at all. Just two nice wee lassies ... not small, mind ye... Miss Bennett is head and shoulders over me.'

Nell, who'd lodged with Mrs McLeish for quite some time, walked into the room with her head shyly lowered but with a complexion and hair that any London lady of St James's would have envied. In spite of the day's work, her nurse's uniform looked immaculate and she, as bidden by Mrs McLeish, was still wearing a becoming starched linen cap which would have graced any face.

The conversation was predictable. Confident Yorkshire warmth and the soft Highland correctness melded in harmony. Nell's head began to lift in laughter as Belinda described their cabby and the drive through the damp mist. There was no song from the canary, but Mrs McLeish had warned them he took a few days to size up strangers.

Belinda, always in the advance guard when it came to planning her own comforts, decided that friendship with Mrs McLeish would not only be a pleasure but a distinct advantage. The thought of four years of the austere study-cum-dining room was a little chilling.

The four settled down in the haven of the hearth like fire-worshippers. They were so at ease that they let conversation take its inconsequential path. It sparked up, dropped down, kindled, glowed and burnt bright like the fire on which they focussed.

'I have had such a funny thought.' Belinda paused to collect her audience's attention. 'Have you noticed anything odd about our Christian names?'

She gave them little time to think, wanting to top the question with her own answer.

'Well, the funny thing is we three all have a rhyming syllable at the beginning of our names:

'Nell, Fel and Bel! What about *that* for a trio?'

It was a perfect end to an uncertain day and Mrs McLeish had the instinct to know when the curtain should be brought down. She put the fireguard in its place.

'Time to say goodnight, ladies! Your first night in strange beds and the church clock chiming every quarter may disturb ye. But ye'll soon get used to it. Goodnight! Sleep as best ye may.'

Although the girls' friendship had woven a network of affectionate intimacies, Belinda and Felicity had never shared a bedroom. A formality born of social sensibility made them excessively polite to one another: They looked at the beds, the chests and the wardrobe:

'No my dear, *you* choose.'

'Dearest, I don't *need* four drawers!'

'No, you have the coat hangers! Mother thought of everything. Look! All, of course, padded...'

It was as if they were newly acquainted children playing doll's house rather than two exhausted young ladies with two, still unopened, official letters.

The next morning was filled with checking the instructions in the two official letters and studying the long book list that was enclosed. On the third day the ghostly haar had vanished, leaving a scintillating city tempting them to explore. They planned to find every single building that would be important in their new life. Nowhere could have been more uplifting. The late September air braced and soothed; the sky-line exhilarated; the way ahead challenged. The whole world was theirs!

As they walked into the Meadows, Felicity, whose first love was literature, felt the same sense of discovery as Keats:

> Then felt I like some watcher of the skies
>   When a new planet swims into his ken;
> Or like a stout Cortez, when with eagle eyes

274

He stared at the Pacific – and all his men
Look'd at each other with a mild surmise
Silent, upon a peak in Darien.

There was far too much to see to let talk distract them, but they did stop to read the inscription on the whale's jawbone arch. Belinda always thought that printed words gained power by being spoken – especially if she were the one who was speaking them. She read aloud, in the hearing of unheeding pedestrians who walked under the arch so frequently that they never noticed it.

From Zetland and Fair Isle Knitters' stand.

Edinburgh Exhibition 1886.

'Just nine years ago,' said Felicity. 'Grace was at the Exhibition. She said there was a forceful group rallying fighters for Home Rule for Scotland. If they're at the university I don't suppose they'll welcome students from England.'

'They'll welcome our sovereigns,' said Belinda, 'and I think they'll welcome our Sovereign!'

They walked on to the medical school and viewed the impressive entrance. Dare they go in?

Belinda quickly checked the name of the registrar from their official letter and drew Felicity forward. Striding up to the desk, Belinda announced both their names.

In dignified but devastating tones they were told that women students registered through the other door in the quadrangle clearly labelled: *Women Students.*

It dawned on them, Belinda with arrogance, Felicity with fear, that in this august medical empire they were going to be the least of the lesser lights.

Calling at the students' bookshop raised their spirits since their well-fed Yorkshire wallets and fine clothes won the approval of the various assistants ready to serve.

'Yes, madam, may I show you where you will find first and second year medical books? Of course you will not want the second-hand department. Would you two ladies like to open a quarterly account?'

After the books had been selected by an assistant, the manager took over.

'May I ask to which address you would like the books to be sent?'

Marchmont Road seemed to signify respectability,

'Your statements will be sent at the end of the quarter. To whom should those be sent? A parent? A guardian?'

'To us,' the two said in chorus.

'To the same Edinburgh address as the books,' added Felicity. They were bowed out and the door held as if conferring the freedom of the city. A little of the early elation was restored.

Later that afternoon, Grace arrived unexpectedly, bringing with her a letter for Felicity which had been addressed to Moray Place. They reported vividly their morning's experiences, including the disagreeable incident of being shown away from the main door.

'Oh yes, I know. Those who oppose feminine progress in the professions have a certain intonation for the word *women* as if they were a lesser breed. You will get used to that. Remember, though, there are some splendid doctors, and several male students, who champion women's rights. I shall introduce you to a few.'

Grace always added warmth to any atmosphere. Felicity glowed in her aura.

'Thank you for the letter! Would you excuse me if I open it? There may be messages for both of you. Belinda, I see you have recognised Roberta's blue writing paper, and her elegant calligraphy.'

Felicity, sensitive of the courtesy of including one's friends, read the personal messages aloud and then went on: 'There could never be a letter from Roberta that isn't laden with literature. Here we are: "How I miss you, Felicity, especially in the advanced English classes and my Sunday afternoon seminars. Have you heard of the poet W.E. Henley? I enclose a copy of one of his poems."' She handed the copy of the poem to Grace. 'Shall we read that later?

'"What a saintly man he must be! Such a suitable poet I thought for Sunday afternoons and what a noble philosophy for Academy girls to take with them when they leave school: 'I am the master of my fate/I am the captain of my soul.'"'

'Why does it make you laugh, Grace? He sounds like a saint to me.' Felicity held the letter away from her and appealed to Belinda with her eyes. She hated to think that Roberta might be criticised.

'I knew him, my dears. I nursed him in the Lister Ward. He was neither a Sunday poet nor a saint. He was the most rampant Bohemian you could ever meet! But it is a long story, which I would like to tell you in more detail.

276

'What about coming to Moray Place, before our Saturday arrangement for coffee? What about tea tomorrow? We'll spend the evening together. Roberta has brought extraordinary memories back, which I'd love to share with you.

'Goodbye my dears! Come early! Shall we say four o'clock? Don't be alarmed if Sam spits on you!'

The walk to Moray Place was enchanting and quite a new experience for Belinda. She looked at the great grey circus with its ring of wrought-iron beacon holders and thought with what rectitude the occupants must keep an eye on one another.

Maggie welcomed them in at the door with one voice for the visitors, and quite another for Sam, who walked the circumference of Belinda's skirt, not quite making up his mind.

'An ye can behave yerself, ye besom. Be off wi' ye!'

Grace was not far behind, glowing in a gown of soft apricot cashmere and ecru lace. She concentrated on Belinda, who had not crossed this threshold before. They exchanged pleasantries on the walk, the sights, the numerous churches and the happy disappearance of the haar.

'It steals up on us when we're not looking. It's almost as if the countries the other side of the German Ocean have a grudge against us!'

Chat in the drawing room included Belinda's interest in the house.

'Felicity, while it is still light, do you mind if I show Belinda round? You know it well! There's *The Scotsman* if you want something to read, or perhaps you would prefer the Paris fashion magazine which Louise sent.'

When the two arrived at the playroom on the top floor Grace explained each of the toys, confiding more in Belinda than she had ever done in Felicity.

'I sometimes think *he* is keeping an eye on them, my dear.' And then almost in a whisper: 'I don't think he has ever left this house.'

'Shall we start the Henley story before we have tea? It is not just *his* story, it is mine too! I think I told you that I went up to Edinburgh to join the Nightingales in December '72. Oh my dears, you must tell me if I bore you about nursing at the Royal, but it was a new epoch – a huge new challenge, for everyone.'

Felicity's eyes opened wide. 'But how did you escape from the West Riding?'

'Yes, I should explain. The Infirmary was now to be run on Florence Nightingale lines and my grandmother worshipped her. Work really started in earnest when Miss Barclay, Miss Bothwell and Miss Pringle were sent up from St Thomas's in London. I think I had come from too sheltered a background. You know all about the minions. We had to do the scrubbing and polishing. The wards were neat enough but the beds were too close, the windows too small and most of the nurses low-class and untrained. But I'll show you a photograph, taken by Miss Pringle, of all of us looking very neat and starched up.'

Looking at the photograph, Belinda asked: 'Did you *live* in the hospital?'

'Yes, you'll never believe that I had to share a bed with another nurse. She couldn't go to sleep without crunching an oatcake. Things you won't have to put up with, my dears! I had to remember to shake the crumbs out in the morning!'

Felicity gasped. 'Whatever would my mother say to that?'

Sunday morning in Edinburgh had its own holy ambience: silent, serene and slightly melancholy. It was not a haar but rather as if a spiteful spider had decided to weave a web of sanctity over the whole city and bring its residents to their knees.

'It's no' raining the noo but the weather has no respect for the Sabbath. I've taken the liberty of bringing yer mackintoshes from the back hall.'

'But, Mrs McLeish, there's not a sign of rain and remember we are used to some ungodly weather in Yorkshire. And,' Belinda added 'we've ordered a cab. You see, we're taking my cello!'

'Ye *thought* ye were, Miss Bennett, but not from my hoose. Do ye' no' ken it's the Sabbath? No music-playing – except hymns on the organ.'

Felicity was amazed to see Belinda so docile. It seemed as if this pious city had numbed her: 'Sorry, Mrs McLeish, I should have learnt by now, when in Rome...'

'Don't mention Rome in these parts, my dear. All that play-acting wi' bells and candles and incense...'

'But, Mrs McLeish,' Felicity felt compelled to defend Roberta, 'my favourite teacher at school is a Roman Catholic and she is the most Christian woman anyone could ever know!'

'Well all I can tell ye, Miss Hargreaves, she must have come under some dark influence when she was a wee lassie. That's what they do, catch them when they are too innocent to argue.'

The girls made for the door but were held back by Mrs McLeish with a voice that could shatter the Presbyterians' peace: 'How did yer git a cab to come on the Sabbath? 'Tis double price for a cab on a Sunday!'

The two would have laughed all the way to Moray Place but there were so many churches, so many silent family processions, so much black and grey, and now the clanging bells, that laughter – even smiles – were curbed. They sat upright as if to convince those who frowned at the cab that their errand was urgent and holy.

'Come, my dears,' Grace was there to greet them. There was no sign of Maggie or Sam. She looked at the departing cab with surprise.

'My dears, you look as if you have been to a funeral! Oh it is depressing weather – so grey. Come to the fire, and just leave your mackintoshes there on the chair in the hall.'

'Grace,' Belinda explained. 'It's not the weather, it's the Sabbath. Do you know I was forbidden to bring my cello?'

'Never mind, my dear, I have one here that is crying out to be played!'

'But evidently it daren't cry out on a Sunday, Grace, or all the Wee Frees and the Presbyterians would break its strings!' They laughed together.

Felicity was in earnest. 'Seriously though, Grace, does that mean no music at all on a Sunday? I was so hoping that you and I might do duets together!'

Grace quietened her voice as if Sam were there and might tell the neighbours. 'Early in the day, with the curtains open – and sometimes the windows – I play favourite Scottish hymns, and of course, the favourite psalm *Crimond*, so that he who hath ears can hear. Later in the day after I've been to church, and I hope forgiven, I draw the blinds and the heavy curtains and play Chopin and Schubert very quietly...'

Belinda was appalled. 'But, Grace, you don't really mean to tell me that your neighbours can think that God objects to Chopin and Schubert!'

'No, my dear, they don't just think – they *know*! Ah, there's Maggie! She goes to the early service so that she can help the children find the hymns, then she comes home to finish off the Sunday dinner. In a few minutes her Yorkshire puddings will be sizzling in the oven!'

279

Part of Maggie's pattern on Sunday was to use the *front* door, subtly indicating that in those hallowed hours she was not a servant but a lady.

Grace relished the gentle assertion for she respected Maggie all of God's seven days. Maggie was not just a cook but a companion who helped to make Grace's house a home.

'That sounds like a Christian after Roberta's heart: church in the morning, confessions all over by noon and literature seminar in the afternoon!' Felicity's voice warmed in praise as if even just saying Roberta's name gave her joy.

The neighbours would have been surprised, even shocked, to see Sunday dinner, that great celebration of Yorkshire midday, steaming away jubilantly on Grace's sideboard and round table.

The knightly sirloin was brought in under its huge silver cover, which was lifted off by Maggie in triumph. In some odd way the gesture reminded Grace of Pierre, who would have synchronised the flourish with *Voilà!*

Maggie had her own special baking tin for the traditional Yorkshire pudding: large and square. It filled a whole meat dish.

She had long outgrown a traditional parlourmaid's decorum. 'None o' they wee bun tins! Scots Yorkshire pudding needs four crispy corners and plenty of room for the air in the middle!'

Next door, the neighbours, who prided themselves on the *lowness* of their particular Church, so low indeed that humour had been interred, were sitting trying to make their crunching of water biscuits less audible by sipping from their tumblers of cold water. The grace before and after was as dry as the biscuits, the length of the grace a little over-generous for the frugal meal.

The three, having finished Maggie's blaeberry tart and cream, withdrew to the drawing room. Had it been a weekday, it would have been the time Grace usually relaxed with her tapestry, but even the liberated Grace had been conditioned in childhood not to pick up a needle.

Felicity was longing to sit at her aunt's black ebony Bechstein Grand. She tried to make it permissible with her opening remark:

'But there are some wonderful hymn tunes and words – even you will agree, Belinda. May I try myself with those I know? One glorious thing about hymn tunes, they are easy to play!'

'Of course, my dear. You'll be familiar with the Methodist hymnal at home. It really does have all the best tunes. Here it is!

280

Belinda, you and I must sing! We can't have hymns without words!'

Belinda, who had been looking enviously at the cello, turned to respond to Grace's idea of singing. Whether in talk or song Belinda loved the sound of her own voice.

'What fun, Grace! Yes, of course!'

Grace smiled to imagine her neighbours ever thinking that hymns could be fun.

As if on cue, the front door bell clanged and Sam shot out, desperate to be the one who adjudicated whether it be friend or foe. Grace, on Sundays, relieved Maggie of various duties but Sam was there first.

His fur softened, for he knew this visitor well and respected him. But why had he come on the wrong day?

'Alistair, what a surprise! Beautifully timed. A day when I have guests who are longing to meet you!'

'I think I can guess who they are! Am I right in thinking your niece and her friend have already arrived? I thought it was tomorrow that they were coming. Perhaps I have timed it better than I planned.'

'Come in and meet them first, Alistair, and then we shall hear why we are so honoured.'

Grace slipped into the formalities of introduction presenting him to Miss Bennett first and Miss Hargreaves second.

'Dr Fraser is not only professor of psychology but the one who holds our little music group together.'

Alistair ignored the compliments and said to Felicity: 'I notice that your aunt introduced you in alphabetical order. Would it be impertinent of me if I suggested it be in order of age too? Welcome to Edinburgh! The medical school will be a brighter place for having you two in it.'

Grace interrupted. 'But, Alistair, to what do we owe this honour? You said that the timing of your visit was especially fortuitous.'

'Grace, my dear, the young ladies will not be surprised to know that you have talked about their coming for weeks – and of course of their talents.'

He turned to Belinda.

'I hear, Miss Bennett, that you play the cello and you, Miss Hargreaves, the piano. What a delightful combination that is! And how splendid that it was Beethoven's delight too, and that is why I am here. One of my favourite pieces of music is his sonata in G Minor for piano and cello – particularly the first movement.

281

I am hoping you will do me a great favour and, one day – given time – one day you will play it at one of our soirées. I have brought the music as a little present to welcome you to Edinburgh.'

Belinda was bursting to protest. 'But, Dr Fraser, you overrate my ability with the cello. I am hopelessly out of practice. Felicity would be able to tackle the piano part. She is a gifted pianist but I dabble inconsequentially with any odd stringed instrument that is around. I haven't even a good enough ear for tuning the strings.'

Felicity was feeling impatient that he had not been thanked.

'First, Dr Fraser, thank you so much for the most thoughtful present, so wonderful for both of us. I heard that sonata earlier this year at the Leeds Town Hall. My music mistress took me. It haunts me still – especially the piano melody in the first movement.'

To her surprise, he quietly hummed the opening bars looking straight into her eyes.

She knew those magic seconds of sound would live with her forever!

She was brought back to earth by the doctor's sudden response to the chiming clock.

'Goodness! It's half past five and I have promised to sing in the university choir this evening at a memorial service! I'll let myself out, Grace, and fly! Goodbye, everyone! So sorry for this impolite exit – how good that we shall meet again very soon.'

6

Belinda was impatient for the term to start. Felicity wanted time to stand still, not only to halt the daunting prospect ahead but also to give her time to act.

It was now the first Sunday in October. Edinburgh and all its surrounding hills looked like old Sheffield plate, silver sunlight on copper trees. The girls walked eastwards, where, against the horizon beyond, Arthur's Seat crouched like a lion as if protecting the whole city.

Belinda was on top of the world, elated by her first introduction to the university; the noble building, the caps, gowns and hoods of the professors, suited her lofty ambitions. Felicity, although acting during the morning as an ardent sightseer, was in fact rigid with fear of what the future held. The slang word *pluck* for *courage* lodged in her throat in its real meaning: the bloody offal of goose and fowl drawn by the cook in the kitchen at Stonegarth. She visualised entrails in the hands of a surgeon in an operating theatre and felt sick. Belinda's voice brought her back to the Royal Mile.

'We mustn't be late for Maggie's Sunday lunch!'

Felicity waited until they were well into the New Town and, steering Belinda into Queen's Street, she chose a deserted spot and suddenly pulled Belinda to a halt.

'Belinda, before we see Grace, there is something I must tell you...'

'Is it about Grace?'

'No, Belinda, it's about me.'

'I didn't think you and I had anything we hadn't told...' She smiled down warmly.

'I am afraid you are not going to like what you hear.'

'Carry on, my sweet, you know whatever you want or suggest I shall agree!'

'Belinda, don't promise until you have heard. It's serious. Stand still and listen!' Anguish twisted her hands. 'I've decided ... that ... it's quite *wrong* of me ... to take a medical degree... I'm not cut ... out for ... a doctor.'

283

If they had not been in public view Belinda would have grabbed her by the shoulders, but this was far too undignified for Queen Street. She spoke frigidly, almost through her teeth.

'We shall not argue on the way to Moray Place. And we shall not talk. I simply ask you to go through every reason for this thoughtless remark and set it against this: for over twenty years women have suffered rejection and given their all so that women like you and me can become doctors. And here you are, in this great medical city, cringing at the thought of it.' Belinda tossed her contemptuous head and set off again.

The chilling condemnation stung Felicity more than a fiery blast. She walked the length of Queen Street ignoring its eighteenth-century elegance.

As they neared Grace's house Belinda broke the silence. 'Then what *do* you want to become? Why did you waste a year of your life and other people's in Bradford?'

Felicity flinched at the sting in the last question but gathered strength to answer.

'Think back, Belinda, did I ever *say* I wanted to be a doctor? This week in Edinburgh has confirmed that what I want to be is a historian.'

It was too late for recrimination, they were facing the front door.

They went through the formality of ritual social behaviour, forcing smiles on Grace and not on one another. They praised Maggie's Scotch beef but ate little of it.

Grace could not believe that these two, usually so stimulated by one another, could cross swords.

'Is something wrong, my dears? If so, can I help?' she asked gently.

Felicity thought hard. Only she could tell her aunt. And now she dragged the words out of an abyss of despair.

'I have just told Belinda I can't be a doctor. Please, both of you listen. I am not fitted for a medical career. It's better to *say* so now, than to *prove* so in the years to come.'

Maggie, coming in to clear the table, found three women, usually bonnie chatterers, locked in their own silences.

Sammycat, who had crept in with Maggie, sensed the disturbed atmosphere, hissed and shot out. Grace, aware that Belinda knew Felicity better than she did, left the first move to her.

Belinda, knowing that Grace would be more diplomatic and kind than she would, left the first move to her.

The hall clock struck three.

Grace had one hope: Alistair. She was used to him calling on a Sunday afternoon after exercising his horse, which he stabled a mile or so west. It was a fine dry day for cycling and riding.

Belinda could bear the silence no longer. She stood up from the table.

'If you'll excuse me, I shall go for a short walk.'

'Wear your overcoat, my dear, there is an east wind.'

Felicity watched Belinda go, then stood up. 'If you'll excuse me, Aunt, I'll do some piano practice.'

'Before you do, is there any way I can help?'

'Only if you can help me about my whole future.'

She let Felicity go. They both needed help.

Grace sat quite alone in the drawing room. The silence was so strong that if there had been any piano playing she would have heard it. The hall clock chimed four hours, and then the quarter hour. There were sounds outside, the familiar bicycle, but more than one person. It was Belinda, of course. She and Alistair had converged at the gate, having come from opposite directions.

Grace answered the door and recognised by their faces that he knew. She whispered and mimed where Felicity had hidden herself, explaining that so far not a note had filtered through the door. As if in answer, three Rachmaninoff chords crashed their opposition to any further attempt to persuade her.

'Alistair,' Grace whispered, 'she needs help and guidance. We two were useless.'

'Is it not intruding?'

'Of course it is, and needed. Now.'

It was nearly five thirty before Alistair emerged, alone, with a brief request for tea for Felicity.

No-one would ever know what barriers had been put up or taken down. It was neither in his nature nor his profession to break confidences, but he did explain later to Grace that he had sensed that it was a *cri de coeur* from her feeling of inadequacy, not a desire to quit. He recalled two of his women patients who had threatened suicide but who really were crying out for belief in themselves and to be given strength to lay hold on life.

As for Felicity, she was to take many of his wise, stern, encouraging and practical words with her through life, constantly reinforcing belief in herself.

He did not oppose her attraction for history, but went with it.

'It's a many-faceted treasure trove, which begins and never ends with curiosity, discovery, more and more knowledge. It's far too exciting to button up in a timetable. Leave that to academics, Miss Hargreaves, leave it free. Leave it free to lay hold on in those precious leisure hours.'

The first week was heavy with new experiences, each day projecting the girls into situations where even Belinda was not always at ease. When they arrived at the lecture theatre there were about sixty male students already seated and only six women. The professor was concerned with his papers and apparatus but on hearing a sudden scraping of feet looked up. Standing rather self-consciously were about twenty male freshers who had risen on seeing the ladies enter. The lecturer was quick to recognise English public school formality, which had no place in a male-dominated university.

'Gentlemen, please be seated! You are not in an English drawing room now, nor at an Etonian reception. You are here to work not to bow or scrape to anyone. The ladies are here on sufferance. Ladies, be seated – on the back benches please. Remember there will be no fraternising with the male students during your studies in this medical school. Remember you are here to work. It is a concessionary privilege that you are able to attend certain lectures with male students. Please do not take advantage of this, nor expect this concession from all lecturers.'

Once the zoology lecturer got into his stride, Belinda and Felicity were aware that there was to be nothing more sexually revealing than the subdividing Amoeba, Paramecium; Hydra; Hirudo and Arenicola all to be viewed under a microscope. In fact, in this course of studies, the Darwinian sequence stopped short at the mammal when physiology and anatomy would take over. Human male and female bodies would be explained; therefore, male and female students would then be segregated.

Chemistry, physics and pharmacy had the bloodlessness which satisfied the academic mind that they were *safe* subjects for the sexes to be together and would cause neither embarrassment of the ladies nor bawdy references from the young men.

Anatomy, they were soon to realise, was a different matter, which demanded total segregation from the men. It also meant paying extra fees to a professor willing to teach the women on their own.

286

Belinda and Felicity read the outline of the first year's course:

THE MEDICAL SCHOOL, EDINBURGH

It is intended in this course of lectures to bring before the students, in a systematic manner, the structure of the human body.

The different systems and organs will be described fully in the more obvious arrangements and relations of parts, which can be examined by the naked eye and in their more minute or microscopic nature.

After more detail on the kind of specimens and the use of the microscope the syllabus continued:

To assist the junior members of the Lecture Class to acquire knowledge of osteology, tutorial demonstrations on the bones will be given during the earlier months of the session without additional fee.

ANATOMICAL DEMONSTRATIONS: 4p.m. in the Theatre.

The structure of the human body is displayed and demonstrated topographically from the surface inwards. The Professor and the demonstrator, David Hepburn, MD, will jointly conduct the course.

PRACTICAL ANATOMY: under the superintendence of Professor David Hepburn, MD, and J.B. Yeoman and several other assistants.

Dissecting Rooms are open from 9a.m. to 5p.m. and Saturdays 9a.m. to noon.

TUTORIAL DEMONSTRATIONS: will also be given to Senior Students on the joints, brains, sense organs and other viscera.

WOMEN STUDENTS

Please see special notices on the notice board of Sir William Turner and Professor David Hepburn, which refers to application for these courses. Fees to be paid direct to the relevant professor.

It was the end of the first week; every day had presented Belinda and Felicity with some problem or negotiation where women were at a disadvantage. Felicity gritted her teeth and accepted Belinda's militancy.

'It was as if,' Belinda said, 'man had never been born of woman.'

'Yes, I can't see a man putting up with labour pains!'

On the Sunday morning at the end of the week Mrs McLeish's lady lodgers were quietly going through and writing up their week's notes on which Mrs Mac cast a blind eye on this breaking of the Sabbath. She was thrifty about use of time and had argued with herself over the years that God surely understood that if he had landed us with all these illnesses, then someone had to deal with them, and who better than Edinburgh-trained doctors?

Belinda lifted her head out of: *Elements of Modern Chemistry* and looked across at Felicity.

'Are you keeping a journal of this odd life we are leading? I've bought one especially for here – I'll show it to you.'

'Belinda, there is going to be so much writing to do with both our academic and social life. May I make a suggestion?'

'Of course, my dear.'

'I wondered if with your memory and orderly way of recording – I wondered – if you would keep the day-to-day record of our lectures? It seems rather unnecessary to duplicate it all. I could then concentrate on the extra-mural hours, here and at Grace's and our fun times together in Edinburgh. We can write quite independently in the vacations.'

Belinda was not to be had so easily. 'I think, my dear, you are harking back to those difficult days in Bradford when I wrote up the notes for you. Well I certainly shall not do that now...'

Felicity rushed in. 'But you won't need to do that. We shall *both* be doing detailed class notes for the profs.'

'What I shall write about is our experiences as women medical students. Do you realise that women of the future – medical or not – are going to be intrigued by it all? They surely will have a more open life than we have, just as we are having more support and freedom than Garrett Anderson, Jex-Blake and Elsie Inglis had twenty years ago.'

'All right, my dear,' Felicity agreed, 'we'll talk over each day with our late night cocoa and between us we'll write something we can pass down to the next generation.'

* * *

288

The weeks quickened as the two became familiar with the curriculum. Perhaps the fact that chemistry, physics, pharmacy and biology were scarcely more demanding than the Bradford courses gave them confidence. The men in the class were surprised and piqued that two of the women knew more of the answers than they did and were already so familiar with the apparatus and chemicals they were handling.

At the end of the fourth session the pharmacy extra-mural lecturer called out:

'Will Miss Hargreaves and Miss Bennett please stay behind. I would like a word with these two ladies.'

Both of them went through the usual apprehension – what had they done wrong?

Professor Stevenson never wasted words. His speech was as concentrated as the chemicals he explained and dispensed. He smiled patronisingly as if talking to two schoolgirls.

'Ladies, you have surprised me with your efficiency and informative responses in the classes. Tell me, pray, have you had any preliminary teaching in this subject?'

Here was their opportunity to put Bradford on the map, a chance they had not had before, nor the confidence to be proud of their home background.

As usual Belinda started first. 'Yes, we had excellent teaching at Bradford Technical College!'

He lifted his nose in the air and looked down it. 'A Technical College? In Pharmacy?'

'Yes, and other scientific subjects,' Felicity added.

'Did women do the courses?'

'Yes, in all subjects.'

'With the men? I suppose there is a lack of delicacy in Yorkshire which we do not condone in Edinburgh.'

Felicity mounted her war-horse. 'Professor, my highest marks were in pharmacy, not only because we had a competent teacher, but also because I received extra coaching from the chemist's son.'

The Professor, irritated that the whole conversation had become distastefully provincial and now quaintly parochial, drew the conversation, which he had intended to be brief and suitably patronising, to a close.

'Good day, ladies. I feel sure you will, by the end of the course here, become quite accomplished in pharmacy.'

On the way back to Marchmont Road the conversation naturally included Simon Watts.

'Do you think, Felicity, it would be a pleasant gesture to send

289

Simon Watts a card from Edinburgh? I feel sure he is beavering away to make his way in the world – to be worthy of you.'

Felicity hesitated. 'Of course, it would be a kindly thing to do, but would it be wise? I should not like to give him the wrong ideas...'

'Felicity, you sound like your mother! Wrong ideas? The man is as pure as a mountain stream and you are his lodestar, shining overhead!'

As usual Belinda had the last word and left Felicity following a new train of thought.

There always seemed to be more post on a Tuesday, possibly because letter writing on a Sunday in Yorkshire was an allowable occupation.

Felicity picked up a tuppence-coloured postcard with a foreign stamp. It was a garish version of the Colosseum in Rome written in her brother's puerile handwriting:

Am here with Tom Dickson on the Grand Tour. This build-ing is monstrous, but all these so-called sights are old and boring. We return next Saturday through Paris. More my line. Regards from your brother, Henry.

'My brother is a philistine. What a waste of money giving him the Grand Tour.'

Felicity knew Belinda's opinion of her brother so she was not surprised that there was no comment.

'Look, this is to both of us. It's from Roberta. Shall I open it? You read it aloud – she is really your friend.'

They waited until hats and coats had been removed, college satchels dumped and Mrs Mac had brought in the welcome put-you-on cup of tea, then Felicity read the letter aloud:

My dear Felicity and Belinda,

Not a day goes by but I think of you. I hear such contra-dictory versions of life as a student in Edinburgh: my nephew is studying history and is enamoured with the whole city and the lectures; my god-daughter is studying domestic science at Atholl Crescent and finds life to be very restricted and (her words) genteel and starchy.

You are in a different and more exciting world and I feel sure that you are both thriving on the challenge.

My news is very small and must seem rather provincial.

290

Strangely enough it is from your part of the world – not Harrogate. I am becoming very much attached to Airedale. It is through your introduction, Felicity, that I felt encouraged to invite Herbert Dawson to address the senior girls on 'Shakespeare on the Stage'. Mr Dawson was a great success and received the Principal's approbation as he did make a point of including the set play for the Oxford Senior Examination. Of course, as she is such a *snob* I did not tell her that he is the local stationmaster!

I have, as you wished, been to see Miss Ackroyd, twice. I wish I had good news to report. Mr Thompson takes me into his confidence now and shows me the monthly reports. They are disappointingly repetitive but the spectacles and the books which I take her have at least encouraged her to read a little. Of course I read aloud to her when I visit. That she can find comfort in George Borrow's *Lavengro* surprises me. It is surely impossible for her to feel 'a wind on the heath' in Barlockend.

I have now become a member of Mr Thompson's advanced Latin class, which conveniently falls on my Wednesday half-day. He gave me a piece of Virgil to translate for reading aloud to the class. His praise was far too flattering to repeat. He asked me to stay after the others had gone, to find another extract. A man living alone seems rather sad and I was touched that he allowed me to make the tea. His kitchen is far too large for the modest food that is prepared in it. I think he misses his mother quite dreadfully.

It will soon be the end of term when I hope we shall meet to share, perhaps, a small part of the season's festivities.

> I remain,
>> Your constant friend,
>>> Roberta (Butterworth)

'Felicity, do you think he might ever propose to her and, if so, do you think she would accept him?'

'Oh, Belinda, she is his willing slave. I am absolutely sure she would never think he had the slightest intention of moving out of his academic solitude.'

'And he,' Belinda put in, 'if he has any sensibility would never think of imprisoning any woman in Barlockend.'

They turned to Belinda's letter from her mother, who always brightened the day.

Darling Belinda,

Oh how I wish that Edinburgh were just a bicycle ride away! Your long newsy letter told me so much but I have hosts of questions still to ask.

You do not mention how you and Felicity *are*. I suppose that is a sign that you are both bubbling over with good health.

I have a plan buzzing around in my head which I hope will get your approval. Of course you will both want to be home for Christmas and of course we want you here. But we thought that Hogmanay in Edinburgh should not be missed. Have you met father's friend Dr Ramsey Donaldson yet? He is a darling man with a charming Scots wife and three delightful children. He has suggested an exchange of houses for the New Year. He would act as locum for father and then we could celebrate Hogmanay together: you, Felicity, Grace, father and I. Talk it over, the three of you, and tell me your reaction. I am not unaware that this might be difficult for Felicity but as New Year is of little consequence in Yorkshire, perhaps her parents could be persuaded to let her return to Edinburgh with us on December 30th.

Excuse the short letter, but it is surgery time and it is my turn to help. I am thinking of you many times a day and frequently picture you standing up to all those men, which reminds me to tell you that Margaret McMillan is back again, making good things happen in Bradford.

From your very loving Mamma,

Hazel Bennett

P.S. Of course Papa sends his love and says he would like to hear news of your classes. Next week he is attending a conference at the BMA in London, where the new discovery, X-Rays, are to be demonstrated. On his return he intends to send you some of the latest news of Marie Curie. Another great woman.

It was Grace's December soirée, a charming diversion, light years away from the smell of nauseous gases, antiseptics and anaesthetics in the medical school and the Sunlight soap-scrubbed linoleum of Marchmont Road.

The permanent little group were Grace, Alistair Fraser with

292

sister Mary Rose and her friend Mary-Ann and a long lean tenor called Bruce Heriot. He had a curious height, which made him look rather like a Tenniel figure in *Alice in Wonderland*. Measured from shoulder to feet he would not have seemed excessively tall, but his long neck with its mobile Adam's apple and his long thin pointed head, with a perpendicular tuft of hair at the front, added a good eighteen inches to his body. His voice came out exactly as one would have expected: a sopranoish tenor with latent strains of a choirboy, suggesting an innocence which his erudite vocabulary belied. He had a Fellowship in Philosophy and was currently engaged on a D.Phil. thesis, which would eventually be leatherbound and kept remarkably unthumbed on the shelves of remote academics.

The title of the thesis was: *David Hume's Influence on Morals and Religion in the Eighteenth Century and his subsequent Influence in the Nineteenth Century with Particular reference to the City of Edinburgh.* It was a relief to know that the spine of the publication was to read: *The Natural Religion of David Hume.*

His tastes outside his life of scholarship were engagingly simple: fresh herrings; salty porridge; oatcakes and kippers; singing in the local musical society; and tossing the caber in his Heriot tartan kilt.

Belinda sparked off his rather puerile humour, but Felicity's scarred beauty slightly embarrassed him. He was more at ease in his dusty academic gown in the senior common room than ever he was in a ladies' drawing room. But his mother, reluctant to let go of apron strings, made sure that he was invited to her friend Grace's house when he came three years ago to take up the Fellowship.

At the second soirée two of Grace's friends returned, and by so doing increased the size, shape and sound of the music-making group. The girls already had heard of the eminence of the Emeritus Professor Sir Angus Mackenzie and that he had recently retired to marshal all his researches for a scientific tome: *Compatible Bacteria in the Human Body.* His holistic attitude to healing had, in recent years, turned him away from many of the precepts of orthodox medical treatment to study homeopathy, which he described as *happy healing.* He certainly was a robust example of his beliefs.

So, even before he and his wife arrived at Moray Place, the girls were already in awe of him but when they heard his voice in the hall they were almost alarmed. The tiled floor and the coruscated ceiling were reverberating with the good wishes he was loading on

293

to Grace. He drew his wife forward, then thrust his huge body through the drawing room door and, as if he were a human double bass, roared out: 'And, Lucinda, these are the two beautiful ladies we have been missing while we have been away.'

His leonine eyebrows, a sandy grey, protruded beyond his humorous eyes. Heavy cheeks lopped down over his half open jaw. Laughter tossed truant strands of hair backwards and forwards on a brain-packed brow. He was engagingly larger than life – magnetically unhandsome.

His wife, equally impressive, certainly not in his shadow, but in his laughter and light, was as narrow as he was wide; as pale as he was ruddy; as tight-skinned as he was furrowed. She had the transparency of complexion that is the mark of many Highland women whose skins have never been exposed to hot sun. Her eyelids, pale and prominent, held fair eyelashes which made an almost invisible fringe. Her lips, through forty years of flute playing, were turned over and inward, subtly conveying her infinite discretion.

The programme was generously informal, allowing both spontaneity and order to have their place.

On this occasion Sir Angus assumed the role of Master of Ceremonies, gathering the group together with easy grace, leading the three men into simple folk songs ending with the deep boom of *Clementine* and its convenient final line: 'But I kissed her little sister and forgot my Clementine.'

'Now, Bruce, let's have something more in your line, old boy. A Scots song for these two English ladies. And you Scots lassies, join together with the men in *Over the sea to Skye*.'

It became an evening of pure delight with Alistair, Angus and Bruce singing student songs, including a suggestion of Belinda's which her father had sung from his medical days in Edinburgh. Bruce sang this verse with a mimed stethoscope and an imaginary bare-chested lady:

> Now as I am by rote all British pharmacology
> I'll try again to diagnose, my lady's cardiology
> I feel that surely now, this medical pathology
> Has diagnosed correctly too, my lady's cardiology.

Then on to more serious stuff: Felicity and Belinda played a Beethoven sonata duet for piano and cello.

They were followed by the two Maries, with a gentle singing of *Ye Banks and Braes*. Grace, accompanying them at the piano, remembered her own '*depairted joys, depairted never to return*'.

294

Then it was the turn of Sir Angus and his wife. He filled the curve of the grand piano, his wife standing forward on his right with her silver flute poised near her lips. It was an astonishing performance of *Lauriger Horatius*, a song sung by the wandering students in the Middle Ages. He sang in Latin, but so expressive were his eyes, so sensuous his lips and so silvery her flute, that one caught the mischief of:

'If we may not kiss the girls, drink while time is flying!'

Lucinda's flute, a whole octave above his bass voice, gave her an elfin quality of captured youth, proving that music was not only the food of love but also the wine of youth.

When the song was finished this great bulk of a man kissed her hand, escorted her to her chair and turned to Grace and said: 'Isn't she just the bonniest flautist you've ever heard? Now what about you two playing that song – the one we heard in Eriskay, you remember, the tune the bonnie lassie sang as she cleaned the herring. I heard you were trying it out on the harp and flute.'

It was a magic moment of the evening when Grace with her harp and Lucinda with her flute spirited the notes of a Hebridean love song into the air, a song that had never been set down on a printed sheet.

When they were putting their instruments away Lucinda put her arm round Grace and said: 'You're in love with your harp, aren't you, Grace? Just as I am with my wee flute.'

Angus got up to carry the harp away. 'You took me back to Eriskay tonight, my dears, I could hear those waves and the wild sea. Now let's have a song from you, Alistair. Grace tells me you've managed to entice a charming accompanist. Come along, Miss Hargreaves, and don't let him drown you.'

Shortly before the others arrived Alistair had presented Felicity with a devilishly difficult accompaniment of a love song in Latin, *Per Secale*. Felicity, unconscious of how beautifully her deep turquoise velvet gown draped over the piano stool, had recognised under the daunting score the simple Scots melody of *Comin' thro' the rye*.

Alistair, moving close to her shoulder, said disarmingly: 'If I'm singing in Latin I'd better make sure of the words.'

The effortless baritone voice resonating through her body was both a shock and a delight. He sang in Latin. She thought in the Scots words:

Gin a body, kiss a body, need a body cry
Ilka lassie has her laddie, naen they say ha'e I

295

The song ended. It was spellbinding. For several seconds no-one clapped. But through a bonding which neither could be explained nor expressed, Alistair knew that at the piano that night there had been a consummation of the spirit (almost of the body) which surpassed all imaginable earthly joys. To bid her goodnight, with all the rest saying it to her and to one another, would destroy his dreams. If he could not be alone with her, he craved to be alone with himself.

He walked away knowing that the fading scar on Felicity's face was more than skin deep and that the girl who had, such a short time ago, taken charge of his singing with social poise was as vulnerable as a bird with a broken wing. Deeper still, he sensed there was a hidden scar on her life, which all the fine clothes and physical cosseting could not hide.

The party broke up. Alistair, determined to be alone, refused the ride home which the two Maries had already accepted from the Mackenzies. Bruce Heriot changed into brogues and walked to his bachelor apartment, humming the little tune.

Felicity and Belinda were, as usual after a soirée, staying the night with Grace in her spacious home. Belinda looked forward to being able to unwind and talk things over with Grace. Felicity was thankful for the luxury of solitude, in a separate bedroom, on this night of all nights.

Alistair hailed a vacant cab and let the dark night and the city lights etch out the shadows on his troubled face ... She was the only woman he would ever want to have and to hold and it would be four years before he could declare it. He knew it was as much as his professional life was worth – and hers – ever to be seen alone together. From his former casual acceptance of women he had become a suppliant at her door, shaken in body and spirit. And he was now shattered at the impossibility of it all.

It was the first time since their arrival in Edinburgh that Felicity was relieved that at Grace's she was not sharing a bedroom with Belinda. Her senses, sharpened through a fitful night, were still exhilarated and hurt by Alistair's nearness. She was lost in a wilderness where love must never be shown; a love without speech or a written word. Her gift to him must be her absence, allowing him to get on with his career as she must get on with hers.

The clock in the hall struck three. Would she accompany Alistair Fraser at the Christmas soirée? In a heavy daze of emotion and fatigue she crumbled into oblivion.

* * *

The end of the year arrived all too quickly and Belinda's journal was packed with the day-to-day mental stimulants – and often boredom – which make up an intensive university course. She found that her main objective was to be neither repetitive nor merely to record a demanding timetable. The six professors – Bayley Balfour for botany; Ewart for zoology; Cum-Brown and Dobleu for chemistry; Dr Tait for physics and Turner for anatomy – would have been surprised to read observations on their beards, moustaches, the cut of their coats, and their oddities of voice and speech. Some of the thoughts and highlights were in light verse. One of them showed her eagerness to get beyond theory into practical medical procedures:

> *The boredom of botany*
> *Is its monotony*
> *I ask: Do we need?*
> *To examine each seed?*
> *And duly take heed on*
> *Each dicotyledon.*
> *Oh God, the monotony*
> *Dissecting in botany!*
> *Can't we work in a ward?*
> *And soon! Dearest Lord!*

Days of hard work, in college and at home, ended with relaxation over cocoa.

'What silly rhyme have you got for your journal today, Belinda?' Felicity had just written up their brief practice on the Beethoven sonata.

'Oh, I don't think I shall put it in. It's unfinished but it amused me.'

Belinda was sharpening a pencil with a penknife. She put them down and picked up her journal and said:

'Did you notice how noisy we all were this morning when Prof Tait – was late? If your mother had heard some of the ribald remarks made by some of the men you would be back in Aireley tomorrow! Well, I've only done the first four lines:

> *The thing about Tait*
> *He's often late*
> *You should hear what they say*
> *When he's away!*

297

'Why don't you do one on Professor Cum-Brown? I enjoy his chemistry lectures enormously but he's terrifying if one handles things carelessly in the lab and *you* know I am quite pathological in case I ever do *that* again!'

'Oh, I wrote a silly limerick on him – last week, I think.' Belinda turned back the pages. 'Here it is with a pen and ink sketch of him:

> '*A chemistry Prof. called Cum-Brown*
> *Had a terribly frightening frown*
> *When I put hydrochloride*
> *Instead of fluoride*
> *He shouted and roared: Put it down!'*

But Felicity dearest, it's not all nonsense, those are the bits I read to you. I suggest that in the vacation we exchange journals and read our summing-up of the term.'

'Mine is terribly patchy. Last week when you and I were battling away with Beethoven I only wrote the titles of the songs and music.'

'Well, you will get a surprise when you read the lofty bits of mine. You know: the logic of evolution, the miracle of the behaviour of atoms and how they combine in extraordinary patterns, I've even enthused over the wonders of pollination! Aren't we lucky, dearest? New worlds opening every day? And let's admit it, wouldn't it be dull without the men?'

Felicity had never seen Belinda so bursting with excitement. She inspired response.

'Oh Belinda, I'm glad you persuaded me to go on with...'

Belinda's disbelief was registerd with a huge gasp. '*I* persuaded you? Dearest Felicity, there was only *one* person who persuaded you, and one day, he may persuade you –'

'Belinda! Don't you ever dare to think such things, let alone *say* them!' And then, secretly wanting Belinda to go on being indiscreet she said, 'And we owe everything to Grace, don't we? Just think of the people we've met in Moray Place – especially through music.'

'Especially one, Felicity, especially one...!'

Belinda tactfully returned to her journal, conscious that she had gone far enough.

'Remember Dr Mann explaining the effect of alcohol on the bloodstream – quite out of context of his physics lecture? Well here we are!

'A doctor of physics called Mann
Gave a temperance talk which began
Drinking beer, rum or gin
Is a cardinal sin
On which I declare total ban!'

The end of term came and with it the examination results. There was Scottish reserve in the marking. Percentages, even for the brilliant, were kept well within the lower eighties, and the Pass or Fail, without any grades in between, were gloomy for those who were outstanding, and a let-out for those who had scraped through. It was, of course, disastrous for those who failed, as it meant a whole year's work to be repeated.

Belinda and Felicity were walking into the medical school porch when male students were coming out with various expressions on their faces, having seen their results.

Felicity observed: 'You know, Belinda, we do get to know those who approve of us by the number who raise their hats. I've counted four this morning. A record!'

'Two more approaching now.' Belinda giggled. 'It's a pity there isn't a suitable gesture women can make. Smiling excessively does make one look rather forward and bowing makes one sink to the level of obsequiousness from which any woman of spirit is trying to escape.'

'That reminds me, there's a suffragette rally tonight in the Usher Hall, no less. Christabel Pankhurst is to be there. Shall we go?'

'I think in the rules for women it says that women undergraduates are not permitted to go to any public meeting or social event in term time. We'd better not risk it!'

'How prudent you sound, Belinda! Don't let Edinburgh tame you. I rely on you to encourage me to take a few risks.'

They moved up to the fatal notice board without Belinda voicing her curiosity on what exactly Felicity meant.

'Here they are – in alphabetical order.'

Belinda ran her finger through the Bs and Hs. 'Goodness, my dear, we're not even on the list! Do you think we've failed?'

Felicity had moved on to a notice board headed: *Women Students.*

Belinda, in a voice which carried – not always where she wanted it to go – remarked: 'Of course! As usual we're divided into sheep and goats.'

Dr Balfour was standing behind, courteously waiting to pin up his own results. He was known for his championing of women's rights. With a twinkle of eye and a resonance, not only of voice but also of personality, he picked up Belinda's cue.

'Remember, Miss Bennett, it is because of your male supporters that sheep may safely graze here at all! And looking at your results, nothing from either of you below seventy percent, I should say this pasture has fed you well! And look, Miss Hargreaves, at your pharmacy mark, eighty-three! Higher than any of the men!'

Dr Balfour, unlike his colleagues, had a charming way of flirting with indiscretion.

It was a delightful note on which to end the term and they returned to Marchmont Road satisfied that they had done a good job and had earned their Christmas holiday.

There were two letters on the salver in the hall, which Felicity picked up.

'Good heavens, you'd never believe it, but there's a letter from my father. I don't think I've seen his careful writing for months.'

'Not bad news I hope?' For that was Belinda's immediate suspicion. 'Open it, Felicity! I hope I'm wrong. I know! It must be money for Christmas shopping!'

All speculation ended with both heads facing a letter on mill writing paper.

Dear daughter,

You will be surprised to hear from me as I leave family letter writing to your mother, at any rate, to you and your brother. She is the one who has time on her hands.

There is news to report which I want you to hear from me and not from the Bradford papers, which your aunt Grace gets sent to her.

Newspaper chaps always make things worse than they are and they've been hanging round the mill with their cameras ever since last Thursday. Looking for bad news.

If that fellow Armstrong had done what he promised and bought that carding machine, which I offered him cheap three years ago, none of this would have happened. Trouble is it's the heaviest machine in the mill and with it not being in use, and all that floor out of commission, no one had been near it and wet and dry rot had set in and the floor gave way. No one killed – thank God.

My worry is will the insurance pay up? If they don't then we may have to lay off some of the hands.

300

Christmas will not be up to much but you will get a Yorkshire welcome from your affectionate father, and Leo, who, you will be pleased to hear, has become your father's best pal.

Yours truly,

Arthur Hargreaves.

P.S. Your mother joins me in sending regards but she's not writing as she's upset about the mill and all those relations turning up. Nothing they like better than a bit of bad news.

The second letter was addressed in unfamiliar writing: assertive but amiable. The Harrogate postmark signalled 'Winkley' but it was not one of the sisters. Felicity correctly assumed Justin. It must be an invitation to their Christmas Ball, she thought.

She regretted starting to read it aloud to Belinda, but it was too late to stop:

Dear Miss Hargreaves, (I wait to be told if I am permitted to use 'Felicity' in letters. It has become customary on the tennis court and dance floor.)

You will be surprised to receive a letter from yours truly but it was important to put you in the picture before meeting you during the Christmas festivities.

To come bluntly to the point: my parents, who have for years been liberal-minded about my random sowing of wild oats, are now insisting that I settle down and learn how to run the estate. Not only that but the pater hints darkly about an heir.

The mater and a couple of maiden aunts are working on a short list of debutantes. Quite frankly (may I now say, Felicity?) they bore me. Before they activate their 'cupid bows' I know what they are going to say. They have neither the high spirits of my sisters, nor the wit and grace of the inimitable Miss Hargreaves.

Please let me know the date on which you will be coming down from Varsity and we can arrange a meeting. I shall then attempt to put into words what I cannot say in a letter.

I shall always remain your admirer and friend.

Justin (Winkley)

P.S. I got a 2-1 with notoriously little effort and a half-blue for tennis. Please pass this information on to your friend Miss Bennett and my kind regards.

Belinda's face reddened with fury as she heard the content. She snatched the letter from Felicity's hand.

'The arrogance of the man! The insulting patronage! That he could think you would ever consider marrying him! I'll never play tennis with him again, or if I do he'll get love for every game! Who does he think he is?'

Felicity, who had been slightly flattered and intrigued by the proposal, changed course to synchronise with Belinda's outburst and laughed and laughed and laughed.

'Belinda, you gorgeous virago, you shall compose the reply! Come on, let's do it now! But remember we do enjoy all the Winkleys, even Justin, and Winkley Hall is so welcoming.'

'Well then, give me time to calm down. Put ice in the inkwell, replace the ink with a poisoned arrow.'

Belinda created a stinging reply, which Felicity copied on stiff card.

Dear Mr Winkley,

Your insensitive letter conveys the impression that you are quite ignorant of my position.

You ignore the important fact that I am well on the way to graduating as a Doctor in the demanding School of Medicine in Edinburgh. I have no ambitions whatsoever to become the lady of a notable Yorkshire household, nor to be the means whereby an heir is produced.

I think, from the tone of your letter, that the advice of your maiden aunts would be most appropriate in this uncertain period of your life.

However, I see no reason why we should not acknowledge acquaintanceship when we cross paths, no doubt on the invitation of your sisters, for whom I have a great deal of affection.

Yours most truly,

Felicity Hargreaves

Belinda read it aloud with pompous panache and looked to Felicity for expected applause.

'It's not the least like me, Belinda. He'll guess you had a hand in it.' She paused. 'In fact I rather hope he will!'

302

'Felicity Hargreaves, be fair! You know I'm not against *all* men. I've proved it, haven't I?'

Felicity's eyes softened and the laughter line deepened: 'You have, Belinda, my dear. You have.'

Felicity tore Justin's letter into fragments and hand in hand they watched them flare to their death in the fire.

Grace arranged for her monthly soirée to be the Saturday before Christmas. The academic term was over and the girls would be returning to Yorkshire on Monday the 23rd.

They would say goodbye to Mrs McLeish on Saturday morning and take a cab to Waverley Station to send their trunks ahead of them. An extra bonus would be to arrive at Moray Place mid-morning just with the clothes they would need for a splendid weekend.

Grace was one of those delightful women who organised things to the last affectionate detail and made it seem that it was not the slightest effort. She decided that Christmas decorations should be early this year. Nature, subscribing to her plan, brought a chorus of snowflakes on to Bob and Maggie's branches of holly and ivy just as Belinda and Felicity alighted from their cab.

From the joyous response of the girls to the whole scene, no-one would have guessed that Felicity carried in her bag the disturbing letter from her father. She and Belinda between them had decided that they would wait until Sunday before they showed it to Grace.

Had the two bright ones known, Grace was also putting on an act to make a success of the weekend. The truth was that yesterday she had received her usual Bradford weekly paper, which was devastatingly critical of Arthur Hargreaves' neglect of the health and safety of the workers. The long feature article was an opportunity for the socialist reporter to let off steam. It was just the ammunition the Independent Labour Party needed to support its manifesto.

The cause of all the trouble was simple. Some time ago a bird had built its nest in the soak-away pipe from the roof gutter and months of debris had built up around it, causing water to soak into the ceiling and wall of the top floor. On this floor was the carding machine which Armstrong had refused to buy and Hargreaves was unable to sell. The maintenance men, who so carefully inspected other machines and the floors supporting them, had not gone near the top floor for months. November and

December storms had been the last straw in sweeping through a broken window and accelerating the wet rot. The king beam, thought to be as strong as the king's army, had fractured to half-breaking point, moving iron and wooden struts, which crashed on to the machine. The great carder, almost as if it resented the way it had been neglected, shattered the floor beneath it. Five spinners, at work below, were injured; three seriously so, one with a fractured skull.

The paper, which Grace had read, used strong language: *gross neglect; irresponsibility; catastrophic outrage; evil employers; malevolent practice*...

The truth was that Arthur Hargreaves' only sin was pride. He could not bear to look at the machine which had thwarted his ambitions and now rankled him as a non-seller. Mentally and physically that top floor, and the white elephant that filled it, had been out of bounds. Because of the shame he felt for his 'gormless plan', his pride was hurt that he'd let idiots get the better of him.

Before the girls arrived, Grace had decided that her gentle-hearted niece must never read that Bradford newspaper. Her ingenuity made sure of its disappearance.

Once they were in the hall, their eyes were fixed on the branches of holly and Grace was on top of the steps. Secateurs in hand, she said: 'Oh, Felicity, that packet on the tray is for you. It's two Schubert songs from the *Winterreise* cycle. Alistair hopes you will accompany him tonight on the *Courage* and *Goodnight* songs.'

Felicity made no move. 'Please, Grace, would *you* accompany Dr Fraser tonight? The end of term has tired me and I don't want to let him down,' she said pleadingly.

Grace looked down through a long pause. Belinda and Maggie were engrossed in exchanging small talk and arranging branches at the other side of the hall, quite unaware of a very different exchange of opinions.

'Think again, Felicity. May I suggest to you that such a refusal would be very cruel? He has run through the songs himself but – if I read between the lines of his message – he is singing them especially for you.'

'That is what unnerves me. The Schubert music is not difficult – but I do know ... some of the words...' She stopped short as Belinda approached.

Belinda's eyes went from one to the other. 'You two don't look a bit Christmassy! Can I help?'

Grace and Felicity shared questioning looks.

'Well, yes... Perhaps you and Grace are the only ones who could understand why I feel I can't accompany...'

Belinda always picked up cues before they were ready for picking. She looked across to make sure Maggie had gone.

'Can we please, all three of us, be more open with one another? Felicity, please get off your high horse!'

Grace beckoned them to withdraw.

Belinda, usually not the quietest of speakers, opened the discussion with a whisper: 'Felicity, admit it. You are in love with the man and he with you. If you accompany him at the piano you needn't even look at him, nor he at you. Moreover, the audience will not see your face. Grace and I will understand if the words upset you. Grace, what do you think?'

'Alistair is a complex man. I've known him for many years. He is in great torment. He has something on his mind – not just you Felicity. I think he needs all our support.' She moved closer. 'Be gentle with him, my dear, as he is being with you.'

Felicity was still subdued and confused. 'Why did he persuade me not to give up the idea of being a doctor – of staying in Edinburgh? You don't know how he touched each finger of my hand and looked into my eyes, ignoring my scar? He knows that we can never meet in close friendship. Nothing but pain can ever come of it!' Turning to Grace she said: 'You know Edinburgh, Grace, and academic strictures. He is a professor and I am only a second-year student...' Then turning to Belinda she softened her tone:

'In any case, you and I, Belinda, need one another...'

She didn't know how to finish the sentence but Belinda did.

'Inseparable! For three and a half years more, my dear. A woman's love is very different from any man's. Listen, Felicity, I will forgive and understand anything and everything you ever do, my dear, except *one* thing. I ask you not to commit yourself to *any* man until we have both finished at the medical school.'

Grace indicated support with a gesture and a nod of approval and took up where Belinda had not quite left off.

'But that doesn't mean hurting a man who is not able to tell you of his...' The word *love* was used sparingly in the northern parts where she had been born and bred. She modified it: 'fondness for you. Concentrate tonight on his singing. But lock some of those words away in your heart. I know that this is Alistair's winter as well as Schubert's. This isn't a time for weeping, Felicity, it is a time for strength – and even joy!'

* * *

305

The evening came and with it not only the music group but a few invited guests. Some of their carriages were driven away but three remained with their patient drivers. One was a stylish landau with its hood adjusted to keep out the cold and the hesitant snowflakes. Another was a neat little dogcart heavily tarpaulined. The third, a glass-windowed brougham, reflected the grandeur of Moray Place with a coachman whose livery outshone the rest.

Maggie, keeping the peace, locked Sammycat in the woodshed with a saucer of milk and the remains of the fish pie. She then brought the three drivers into the front kitchen and put them before a roaring fire.

The massive copper kettle and the outsize brown teapot gave the impression that here lived a prolific family instead of the two small women who just managed to lift the vessels from the hob. When the mugs of tea were in hand the highly liveried coachman drew a leather flask from inside his coat and laced his drink:

'Here's to ye all!' he said. 'But maistly misel'!'

Maggie, 'black affronted' at such manners, brought, from her own cupboard, her secret bottle and topped up the mugs of the other two.

'This'll warm the cockles of your hearts. There's some ye ken with no hearts to have cockled!'

Meanwhile behaviour in the drawing room, though equally warm-hearted, was in a different style.

The group had opened, with Grace at the piano, singing a four-part arrangement of *Green grow the rushes, O*. It was obvious that Sir Angus got more fun out of it than the rest, and he took Belinda in his roving glance.

> *The sweetest hours that e'er I spent*
> *And spent among the lasses, O!*

Tonight, Bruce Heriot, who usually sang rather ribald student songs, chose to give a mournful rendering of *Barbara Allen*, which Grace regretted long before it got to the line 'Young man I think you're dying'. He made up for it later with a duet with Mary-Ann of *Oh no, John, no John, no*, though one could almost tell at the beginning with her fan flirtation that she was more than ready to say *Yes!*

There were delicious items on Lucinda's flute, Grace's harp and Sir Angus' *Ae fond kiss and then we sever*. Had he Alistair in mind when he chose it?

Felicity and Belinda's inspired playing of the opening part of the first movement of the Beethoven sonata surprised and delighted everyone.

Good, thought Alistair, at last Felicity is the dominant one. But Belinda has had to work hard to hold her own and she's done it!

Alistair indulged himself with: *Will ye no come back again?* Was he hoping that one day very soon someone would say that about him?

Grace had deliberately chosen *Over the sea to Skye* as it was by Robert Louis Stevenson and also it gave an opportunity for solo and chorus singing, with the male voices accentuating the melody.

She had put Alistair's songs from Schubert's *Winterreise* at the end of the programme, as this might be the last soirée he would be attending for a long time. He announced that he was singing the song in German, but gave it the English title *Courage*, a word which Felicity, although concentrating on the piano, sensed as a challenge.

The message of the lyric was Alistair's philosophy: If there is no God on earth, we ourselves must be gods.

Angus was the only one in the audience who got the full meaning, as he was the one with almost fluent German. But Grace sensed that Alistair's strong voice and upright stance were disguising a troubled mind.

His last song: *Gute nacht*, he decided to sing in English, a translation that he and his German friend had worked on together. Felicity noticed that on the music sheet it was written in Alistair's hand, the English words freely escaping the rigidity of bar line translation.

The song held no benison of *goodnight* for the listeners but rather projected his feelings when he would be thousands of miles away in America. He would arrive there in May time. But now he must find his way through a personal dark winter. The song ended:

> Love seeks to wander
> God shines the light
> We leave one another
> My dearest, goodnight

Angus and Grace exchanged quick glances as Alistair put out a hand and brought Felicity to share the applause. There was no disguising her tears. There had been times in those poignant verses when tears had blurred the printed music and the piano keys.

When the listeners' emotions and applause had died down,

Angus and Grace drew the whole company into a circle for their usual goodnight ending. No accompaniment needed for the simple song:

> Friendship makes us all more happy
> Friendship gives us all delight
> Friendship consecrates the droppie
> Friendship brings us here tonight

As Alistair gripped Felicity's hand in the circle, she knew now that nothing in the world could ever separate them. And he knew that separation of their bodies must only strengthen and prove their love.

In the haven of her room she hoped that God would not mind being usurped by the man made in His own image. The lines quoted by the Scottish clergyman remained in her memory. Almost in defiance she said aloud: 'For I am persuaded, that neither death nor life, nor things present, nor things to come, can ever separate me from ... Alistair.'

Tears had gone. A great glow of hope and mounting courage heralded the New Year. She was so exhilarated that she smiled at the thought of her mother's disapproval of her taking the Lord's name in vain.

She undressed and sobered down, wondering how on earth she could ever live up to a man of Alistair's intellect and erudition. Was it all a stupid dream? Would three more years' medical training do anything for her mind? She did not want to be a little wife at home. She wanted to be a true companion, a soul mate – a genuine colleague. The relationship of her parents with one another, the unbreakable habit of marriage, was anathema to her.

And Alistair? Knowing his obsession with his career, why should he ever want to marry?

With her father's letter about the mill on her mind, Felicity was more saddened at leaving Edinburgh than she was gladdened by the thought of the predictable Stonegarth Christmas.

As the train steamed through Berwick, Darlington, Newcastle and York to Leeds, Belinda's spirits rose and Felicity's sank. If only the emergency chain could reverse the train's direction.

Belinda, as usual, knew how to get the best out of everything,

308

including the dining car attendant. He had already assured her that the table, the food and the drink would be perfect for madam and her companion, at twelve thirty, their arrival time at Newcastle.

'Felicity, my dear, why so sad? It's our holiday and time to take lunch. Our table is all ready for us!'

Normally Felicity would have enjoyed the experience of excellent service, with both speeding and eating so beautifully synchronised. It was not like her to be a wet blanket, so she made polite and approving conversation the rest of the way to Leeds. She was grateful that Belinda had arranged that it was the Bennetts' gig and groom which met them at Bingley station and that she was delivered to Stonegarth first.

'So you've got here,' Gertrude said with relief rather than joy. She had no faith that trains, going at the speed they did, would stay on the lines, or if they did, that they would be able to stop!

'Take Miss Felicity's case up, Hilda. I don't want her carrying anything! You'll have a surprise when you see your room. I told Hilda and Jessie we wouldn't wait for spring-cleaning.'

Felicity kissed her mother and piled up her thanks before ever she saw the highly polished and laundered room. It certainly outshone Mrs McLeish's standards but then the contents of this room were hardly in need of the elbow grease Mrs McLeish used on her well-worn but homely lodging house.

For the three days before Christmas, Felicity was enlisted as a helper with the decorations, setting out the conventional Christmas cards in a conventional way; folding glassily starched napkins into waterlilies and bishops' mitres. Gertrude, who glowed in showing her specialist knowledge of household trivia, supervised all these operations.

'Look, Hilda, I'd like more elbow grease instead of polish on those brass handles. And look at these silver cruets! They won't do for the Christmas table.'

She turned to Felicity. 'Well, I'm surprised they didn't teach you how to do waterlilies at the Academy. Father and I often think you'd have done better at a domestic science college instead of that medical one.' And so it went on!

There was no mention of the mill accident but Felicity felt sorry for her father. There were days when he looked ashen. She wished she knew how to sympathise with him. She felt he was as lonely as she was, in a very different way. But there was no demonstration of affection in her family.

They *got through* Christmas with the usual overloaded table and the short measure of cheer. The Ackroyd and Hargreaves uncles, aunts and cousins treated the visits as duties rather than celebrations and returned hospitality on a chop-for-chop basis: 'Well, we had them last Christmas. It is their turn...'

Felicity was assigned to take children to the old nursery after they had stood piously under Uncle Arthur's eagle eye to thank God (and Gertrude, of course) for what they had received.

Once away from the Victorian *children should be seen and not heard* ritual, all hell was let loose, mainly by the Ackroyd children, who were closely related. Too close for Felicity's comfort, she thought, and she could have done without the Robinson cousins, twice removed – if only they could have been farther removed, on this day of all days.

In desperation she slipped downstairs to bring Henry up to stop the Turner boys wrecking his precious Hornby train and rails, but he had made a quick exit to join his pals, who were listening to the brass bands playing carols and community songs on the Leeds United football ground.

She tried to organise the little party into a game of musical chairs but as soon as the prim ones made for the chairs, so the Turner boys slipped in under them and threw the party-dressed girls on to the floor. The Methodist minister and his wife, who, by tradition, were always at Stonegarth for Christmas dinner, gladly handed over their two nine-year-old girls to Felicity. They had been painfully brought up by their parents always to have a book with them to read in order that they did not speak. So with the Turner boys thundering round them they settled down to *Jessica's First Prayer* in painful piety. They took out spotless handkerchiefs for the inevitable tears.

Felicity's New Year resolution was born that Christmas Day: 'I resolve here and now never to become a children's doctor!'

Boxing Day was the ritual Arthur Hargreaves enjoyed most, for it was on that day that he dispensed his well-thought-out beneficence. In the pay packet, brought from the mill, he put a sixpence for the errand-boys, a shilling for the deliverymen. The florins were reserved for those who sold from their vans the milk, the yeast, the coal, the meat and fish: owners of their own businesses.

Arthur enjoyed their Boxing Day calls: the raised hats, the slight bows and the expansive thank-yous. He returned to the house with a feeling of satisfaction and missed hearing the coalman's rough mutter: 'Miserly bugger! 'as 'e ever carried an 'undred bags of coal, day after bloody day?'

The old year was nearly worn out and so were many who had lived through it. The *New* Year, this year, had a special significance for Felicity and Belinda. They were to have the joy of being in Edinburgh for Hogmanay with the friendly exchange of houses, which Jeremy Bennett had arranged.

During the whole of Felicity's life, though she had only recently been aware of it, Dr Bennett got his way with her parents. So Felicity, beautifully equipped, joined the Bennetts at Leeds station on December 30th and travelled by train to Edinburgh in a first-class compartment totally reserved for the four of them.

Food, with silver covers, was brought into the carriage; hot-water bottles were put under their feet and rugs round their legs. Porters were waiting at Waverley station to put their luggage into the landau to be driven to their elegant, but comfortable, house in George Street.

Felicity felt as if the whole city of Edinburgh was hosting them. The Donaldsons' house was a joy. The wide stone steps, the dignified front door spoke *welcome*. This generous promise of hospitality blinked in the brass letterbox, the central doorknob, the brass knocker and the long gleaming threshold plate.

A lingering smell of cigars and a log fire in the hall created a setting for the cook, the parlourmaid and housemaid to give them a welcome. Log fires and copper cans of hot water in their bedrooms made them forget the northern chill.

The girls were offered either separate rooms or to share a huge end bedroom dominated by a draped four-poster and a three-quarter tester bed. They chose to share the palatial one. Belinda, Felicity decided, would not be lost in the four-poster and the smaller, tester bed was just right for her.

It was a spacious setting, the next day, for two young ladies to dress for Hogmanay. Standing in her white ball gown, looking into the cheval mirror, Belinda said: 'I wish I were a Scot. I'd have a scarlet tartan sash right across my bosom instead of this feeble blue. What are you wearing on your gown, Felicity? You look lovely as you are without a sash.'

'It's here! Would you help me to fix it? Mamma has put hooks and eyes on it. She didn't ask me what colour, so of course it's her favourite, pink. But she does think of everything, doesn't she? And don't you think it was kind of them to let me come away?'

Felicity longed for Belinda to find something pleasant to say about her parents but nothing much ever came.

'There's the gong, darling. Are you ready?'

'Yes, nearly. Be an angel and fasten my necklace, please!'

It was a pearl and amethyst necklace with earrings to match, which her parents had bought at Ogdens in Harrogate for her seventeenth birthday. Fleetingly she remembered her father's comments as she opened the case and was overwhelmed by its magnificence: 'I'll tell yer this, lass. Yer'll see nowt as good as that at t'Masonic Ball next week. Ah've seen to that!'

New Year's Eve day buzzed with preparations until the twelve guests arrived all ready and willing to fling themselves into dancing with the right partners in the right place. Jeremy Bennett, as host, looked as if he had lived in the house for years. It was a huge surprise to Felicity to know that Alistair had been invited, and she was even more surprised when she heard Belinda's father call out: 'Dr Fraser, will you partner Miss Hargreaves? And Murdoch, you're the tallest man here, could you take on my daughter...?' And so on until the sixteen had become eight pairs. For with the reels it was no use leaving things to chance. Jeremy thought secretly: we English have got to get it right!

Alistair and Felicity's hands were linked through all Jeremy's procedures, invisibly sending messages of love without even looking into one another's eyes.

The drawing room with its huge central chandelier had been transformed for dancing, with a tightly drawn, heavily glazed cloth stretched and pinned down to be as smooth and firm as a professional ice-rink. On a raised podium, the fiddler, who normally functioned as groom, stood waiting, fiddle in hand, to start the reel. His kilt declared his ancestry, for had it not been handed down from father to son for three generations of a humble branch of the Black Watch?

A chord stilled the dancers. Then the yell, which starts all reels, shook the cut-glass drops of the chandelier. The air was alive. Every foot in that charming drawing room seemed as if on springs. As the yells grew louder the feet went higher. During the close partnership of the *Reel of Tulloch* she felt that she and Alistair belonged to one another in dance. There seemed in this partnership to be more time for him to catch and hold her eye. Never had she felt so exhilarated and transported into another world. It was as if their feet had known one another in another life and, for years, had been on dancing terms.

There was a long last satisfied chord and the frenzy dissolved into decorum. Alistair bowed, kissed her hand, put it through his arm and gently led her into supper. The dining room was set out with four round tables with four guests at each. They joined Sir Angus and his lovely Lucinda.

Exotic food and drink abounded: pheasants, oysters and champagne. Exotic fruits: apricots, peaches, grapes and pineapples were piled high on the silver epergnes. Two hired waiters supported the Donaldson staff, and all of them seemed to read the minds of the guests.

Before sitting down, Felicity excused herself to fix wayward hairpins and to retrieve the diamond-studded hair comb which had flung itself away in the reel. There seemed to be no embarrassment in tidying-up, for in the delirious discipline of the last half-hour there was now no-one in the room who was not in need of a little grooming! And it was in the two inter-connecting bedrooms that the ladies exchanged their delicious gossip. Grace and Lucinda were enjoying a quiet exchange about Jeremy's bringing Alistair and Felicity together. They stopped short on Felicity's arrival and almost in chorus said:

'Felicity, my dear, how enchanting you look!'

'My dear, you danced brilliantly!'

Having discussed their table places, Lucinda and Felicity returned together to join their two men, just in time to hear Angus say: 'She's worth waiting for, my boy.'

What could all that mean? Was this something to do with the rumour which everybody else seemed to know about?

Supper over, there was another hour of dance when everyone changed partners for the *Gay Gordons* and *Strip the Willow*. This time Felicity was more conscious of the other men with whom she danced and somehow she felt that the glances she exchanged with Alistair were freer and the rapport more deeply understood than at the beginning of the evening.

A pause between the dances brought them together again for a rest and a glass of champagne. Felicity noticed Mary-Ann, on the other side of him, flirting outrageously with her fan without much response from the kilted young man on her right. Now it was nearing midnight.

Jeremy Bennett was standing near the fiddler, with his hunter watch open in his hand. Alistair, from his gilt chair next to Felicity, had his eye on Jeremy and caught the cue that now was the time to move. The hands of the watch were at five to midnight; the French clock on the white marble mantelpiece had a habit of haste and already said two minutes to midnight. At one minute to midnight Sir Angus and the fiddler opened two of the four sash windows to make sure the old year could get out.

Suddenly the entire city's clocks chimed in syncopated unison and the guns in the castle grounds fired a salute. The dark man in his Fraser tartan kilt knocked on the drawing room door. The first-footer came in to cries of delight, bearing on a tray:

> A piece of coal – to warm the house
> A bottle of best Scotch whisky – to warm the heart
> And a bottle of salt – to save and savour the food

Jeremy and Angus saw that all glasses were charged before Alistair recited:

> A guid New Year to yon and a'
> And mony may ye see
> An' sae through a' the days to come
> Full happy may ye be!

As first-footer it was Alistair's duty and privilege to kiss all the ladies and shake hands with the men.

There was kissing all round and sixteen different ways of giving the greeting. Angus finished with:

> Oot with the Old
> In with the New
> May ye never be cold
> An' naught may ye rue

There were more wee drams and more and more dances, a hilarious singing and dancing of *Do ye ken John Peel* though he had lived a hundred miles away from Edinburgh.

Alistair's first-footer kiss with Felicity lasted fractionally longer than the kisses with the other ladies. As he sprinkled salt over her shoulders, so he whispered into her right ear: 'The first of many New Years to come.'

When the clock struck two the fiddler finished the dance with a resounding chord and a high flourish of his bow. Jeremy called out: 'A circle now for *Auld lang syne*.'

The ritual was so familiar to them all that without choosing or finding a partner they alternated man, woman, in a circle of friendly hands. The vigorous singing of *John Peel* had faded away. Almost with tears of joy and affection they sang the well-worn words to one another. The peak moment of this ancient song brought hands and arms across bodies, changing the right part-ner to the left and vice-versa.

> So here's a hand, my trusty friend
> And gie's a hand o' thine
> An' we'll tak a richt good willie waught
> For auld lang syne

When the ladies were up in the bedrooms donning their cloaks, Alistair found an opportunity, in the hall, to have a word with Angus on his own.

'Would you allow me to come to see you, Sir? I would like your advice, if I may, before term starts.'

'What about next Thursday afternoon? My wife's flute group meets then and we'd have the place to ourselves.'

7

The Bennetts and Felicity returned to Airedale for the rest of the holiday laden with goodies, which they hoped would give pleasure at Stonegarth. Felicity was only too conscious that any enthusiasm for Edinburgh was a sore point with her parents, so the New Year celebrations had already become a touchy subject.

Among the presents was a large tin of McVities petticoat shortbread, always a winner with other folk. Gertrude's response was predictable: 'Thank you, love. Not bad considering they're shop. But there's nothing like your own, is there?'

Her father received the splendid walking stick with the bone and silver handle more enthusiastically: 'Well, that's a bit of all right, that is, but I bet you paid through the nose for it with them Scots.' Arthur's travelling, which was quite considerable on European trains, had never taken him north of Newcastle. He thought that Hadrian was on the right lines but hadn't gone far enough.

Felicity was glad to get back to college and the demanding curriculum, which would perhaps quieten her heart and motivate her mind.

Belinda was delighted that the winter term brought new courses with an introduction to some clinical instruction. The practical lessons at this stage were not too critically medical but at least study involved human bodies and not just inanimate specimens.

Among Felicity's and Belinda's presents from Aunt Grace was a copy of *The Story of Leith Hospital,* just published. Belinda was shocked to read that people seriously ill or injured were being refused because of shortage of beds:

'How can they choose who they take in if there are so many needing treatment?'

'I wonder,' said Felicity 'if they are refused because of their dirty condition?'

'No, Felicity. You and I have seen folk carried into the outpatients department quite filthy and coming out looking very different from when they went in.'

'I think we have to admit that if cleanliness really *is* next to god-liness, then nurses and doctors will be nearer to God than other folk!'

'I don't think anyone could remain dirty for long if the Lady Superintendent were anywhere near! I'm so glad we saw her at the Royal.'

'What a glorious creature she is! That beautiful lace-edged cap with the flowing ribbons down the back, and look, Felicity, at those long starched cuffs and apron-bib meeting that high starched collar.' Belinda, with her usual expansive gestures, was *wearing* the things as she spoke.

'Yes,' Felicity added, 'lady doctors don't look nearly so impres-sive.'

The women students now had selected occasions then they could visit women's wards. Usually they were received with wel-coming chat. One patient shook her fist at any woman from the medical school who came to her bedside.

'Ye'll no' put your hands on me, Miss. If God intended women to be doctors he wouldnae ha'e given 'em busts!'

Now that new doors were opening to them they realised the unique quality of the Edinburgh Medical School, which was an example to the world. Here theory was put into practice quite early in a doctor's training. Skilled practitioners wearing a medi-cal gown, not with the caps and hood of academia, proved the title Professor in the ward or theatre.

Felicity was both humbled and heartened on seeing patients in the wards. Ironically, the sight of other people's suffering had a stimulating effect on her.

'Does it sound heartless, Belinda, that seeing other people's scars and wounds makes me grateful for my painless one?'

'No, my dear, and it almost makes me go down on my knees and thank God for my vulgar health.'

'But what hope is there for some of these folks stricken here!'

'We need to start *before* they are ill, Felicity. I can't help think-ing that, in the end, my place is in the slums of Bradford working with Margaret McMillan and the Medical Board.'

'Yes, but Alistair said we should enjoy Edinburgh and its music and that we need an antidote to the medical school.'

'Of course, dearest! Didn't I tell you that part of my Christmas present from my dear Papa was the score for the *Archduke* piano trio by Beethoven? Now we are back, Fel, Nel and Bel are really going to get into action. Only the first movement, of course. Quite enough!'

317

Rehearsals depended on Nell's duty times, but Belinda and Felicity could work on their piano and cello duet. Belinda found that, for the first time in their life together, she was only just able to hold her own.

The following Sunday, when they happily returned to Moray Place, Grace enquired: 'How are you getting on with your trio? I hope Nell is happy with you. Please bring her to the next soirée. Remember it is in three weeks' time. Even if you don't feel ready to play together, I should love to have her here.'

'We have suggested her coming but Nell is *very very shy* and seemed rather frightened that it would all be too grand,' said Belinda.

Felicity added: 'She's the salt of the earth, Grace. You would love her and, of course, she would love you!'

'Leave it to me. I'll write to her.' Grace always acted without any fuss.

Spurred on by this, the three found that practice had a purpose. Every evening after high tea they spent an hour in Mrs McLeish's front kitchen. The cat, the canary and her well-worn upright piano seemed at home with the *Archduke*'s magic. The three players proved how friendship thrives on shared music, rising above all differences of class, education, money and occupation. Fel, Nel and Bel were more than a trio – they became a trinity.

While all this was going on at Marchmont Road, Alistair was keeping the appointment he had made with Sir Angus. He was acutely aware that this visit could affect his whole career, indeed his life.

There was no-one in the medical field in Edinburgh with such kindly wisdom or one in whom one could so easily confide.

'Come in, Alistair. It's not as warm as it looks. January gives promises it doesn't always keep.'

A flaming coal fire almost burst the bars of the study's narrow little fireplace. Sir Angus liked comfort and never hurried his guests into conversation until they were well settled. The deep-seated high-backed leather armchairs had the accommodating comfort of old shoes.

'Try one of these, Alistair.' He had opened a cedar wood box of cigars. 'We brought them back from Tripoli – half the price they are here.' Angus was canny but generous. His thoughts were not on the cigars, nor their cost, rather on the reason for this special visit. Neither was wasting words. Alistair had a letter in his hand, which was obviously waiting for discussion.

'This came a week ago. I haven't answered it. I wanted to talk it over with you first.'

Sir Angus settled down in his armchair filling the whole wide seat. His unique blend of sybarite and scholar made even the scientific tomes on the book-lined walls seem homely and approachable.

He looked at the address on the outside of the envelope; scrutinised the name and address on the writing paper and, before reading the content, said: 'Ah! William James' pioneering lot in Harvard! Splendid!'

He read it slowly, between puffs, evidently reading, not just the lines, but what was implicit between them. Then he handed it back, folded, as if the matter were settled.

'Tell me, Alistair, my boy, why do you need my advice? And why do you need anyone to make up your mind?'

'It's a long time to be away, Sir. Nearly three years. And what about my job? Would it be here when I returned?'

Angus' reply sounded as if he were stroking a long woollen scarf.

'When you look back on a career of fifty years, as I do, three years is just a phase – like a paragraph in a piece of writing with helpful punctuation and a satisfactory full stop. What is holding you back, Alistair? Tell me more! But I warn you, I shan't change my mind.'

Alistair took another envelope out of an inner pocket.

'They included a resumé of the research and what would be my contribution to it. There are three of them working in James' psychology unit researching on the causes and treatment of insanity and various degrees of mental derangement – especially in women. Apparently the lecture I gave in Boston last year on "Mental changes in women through the menopause" triggered off response. In fact I did receive...'

'In that case, Alistair you're more than halfway there. You'll be as valuable to them as they will be to you!'

Alistair still hesitated. 'But what about all that I'm doing here? The post-graduates who are researching with *me*?'

'New doors will open here, Alistair. Psychology and psychiatry are new sciences and we need men like you to halt all the pseudo stuff. And challenge the charlatans who exploit the subject and their patients. And – between you and me, my boy – those obsessed with Freud, sex and blaming one's parents for everything.'

319

Alistair answered as a professional. 'Yes, personally I have much more faith in William James' philosophical psychology and his human understanding of other people's religious beliefs.'

Angus' mind switched to practical issues. He looked slightly apologetic as he asked a logical question of a Scot.

'Now it's not my business, Alistair, and Edinburgh's hardly known for squandering its money, so I may be asking an unnecessary question, but are they making it financially worth while?'

'Oh much more than that: a spacious apartment, near Harvard, adequate staff, first-class passage, there and back on the *Turbinia* steamship and, of course, a salary nearly twice as much as here!'

'Then what are you waiting for, my man? It's a chance in a million!'

'But, Angus, it's not just what I may, or may not, come back to professionally ... it's leaving friends and...'

Angus drew himself forward from the depth of his chair and instinctively lowered his voice.

'Alistair, I may know more than you think. I'm not blind, you know, and Lucinda has a woman's intuition. Don't think we are two nosy old people, well perhaps we are – folk who've had a loving marriage revel in romances! But there *is* a lady sweet and kind, isn't there? And I'll tell you this, my lad, if she is the woman we all think she is, she will be here, qualified, strong, unclaimed and free when you return.'

Alistair walked away from Charlotte Street composing the letter he would write to the Psychology Unit in Harvard. It was easier to do that than to decide how he would tell Grace and Felicity. More difficult still, how could he expect a young girl of twenty to tie herself down for three years when any discerning man would fall in love with her?

The formal research programme, heavily sponsored, did not start until the fall. They had offered full pay from the end of the Easter vacation to give him time to acquaint himself with all that Harvard and Boston had to offer, not only in the university but also in the famous hospital in Boston.

He would risk calling on Grace, here and now.

Later that Thursday afternoon, Grace sat down and wrote:

My dear Felicity,

There is something I need to discuss with you, which is all tied up with Hargreaves family fortunes. I feel sure that

320

Belinda will understand that you and I must sort this out on our own.

Am I right in thinking that Nel and Bel sometimes practise cello and violin together? I seem to remember that you and she alternate on Wednesday evenings. If next Wednesday is convenient, could you have supper with me at seven o'clock instead of your usual high tea at Marchmont?

I have asked Maggie to wait for an answer. This will please her as she enjoys chatting to Mrs McLeish.

I look forward to Wednesday evening and our private meeting.

Ever your loving confidante!

Grace

As she sealed the envelope, guilt shot through her at the falsity of the message. She wondered, as she often did, whether it was possible to go through life telling the truth.

'Wait for an answer from Miss Felicity and give my very kind regards to Mrs McLeish. And, more than that, to the two young ladies.'

Felicity read the brief note with surprise. But as Grace had used the word *fortunes* she could only think it was linked with a Hargreaves will – a subject on which her parents often speculated. Surely she didn't need to be consulted? Great-aunt Emmeline, who had died, aged ninety-three, two months ago couldn't have left *her* anything. In truth, family relief and hopeful speculation had made for a very large and satisfactory funeral, the like of which had not been seen in Guisely for years.

Felicity responded immediately to the request.

My dear Grace,

I cannot think what family fortunes require my discussion, but I will, of course, be able to join you for supper, at seven, on Wednesday at Moray Place.

Your loving confider!

Felicity

Maggie, handing the letter to Grace on her return, said: 'She's a fine lady, that niece of yours. She called a cab for me as if I were the Provost's Lady! I dinna bring the cabbie to ye. The lass had paid him already out of her own pocket!'

Wednesday evening came and Belinda, sensing there was more to this than Hargreaves' money, had Nell all lined up with her fiddle.

Felicity, now familiar with Edinburgh's cab force, had ordered one to be at Marchmont Road for six forty. For although she had found nothing to fear in the New Town, there were occasional drunks whom she would prefer not to encounter. Grace had arranged that the simple supper for two should be at the little table near the drawing room fire. The central gas candelabra were unlit and tonight she herself had lighted the kinder oil-lamps with the rose-coloured globs. She felt that Felicity needed protection and loving care.

After the usual greeting it was Felicity who opened the conversation almost bubbling with laughter.

'Grace, my dear, you're not going to tell me you've had a legacy from great-aunt Emmeline! From the gossip I've heard over the years, everything was being left to her grandsons. She never had much time for her daughters, still less for her granddaughters.'

'No, my dear, it's more important than that. Something that affects *you*. And I must confess now it has nothing to do with the Hargreaves.'

'Then why not Belinda?'

'Although Belinda does *not* know, I think she understands. But let us eat first, my dear, all on our own. By the fire.'

After the meal and trivial gossip, they moved back from the table to the Chesterfield set at right angles to the fire.

'Tell me, Felicity, how much do you know about Alistair's work?'

'Well, when he was bringing me round to the idea of becoming a doctor, he did explain that he worked on people's minds, not their bodies ... that he was a psychologist...'

Grace paused and looked at the *youngness* and trust in those wide-open eyes and the beauty, which the now-faint scar only slightly marred.

'Do you, my dear, know anything of his eminence? Of his reputation? Not just in this country but overseas?'

'Well, he did, just in passing, mention Harvard.'

'Did he refer to William James, the *founder* of psychology in America?'

'No, I don't think he did, but honestly Grace I was in such a daze. The way he talked to me and the way he looked at me. At one point he even held my hand ... and touched my fingers ... as if I were a child needing help... I could have missed some of what he said.'

'Felicity, did all that nearness – and at our musical evening – make you feel you would do *anything* for him? Things that might hurt you but further his career?'

'Dear, dear, Grace! How could I, a humble woman medical student, help a man like Alistair? You are romanticising!'

'My dear Felicity, *you* can help him more than anyone in the world! He has just been offered the most wonderful opportunity...'

Felicity interrupted. 'But, *of course*, I'd be pleased! Why do you doubt me?'

'An offer from America.'

Felicity covered her incredulity. 'Yes, I understand! He went to America before – to lecture.'

'This is different. It's an assignment for nearly three years, my dear. To work with William James' team at Harvard. It is the most wonderful chance Alistair could ever have – and he's hesitating, actually hesitating, my dear, I think, because of you.'

Through her tears Felicity said: 'But aren't we apart now? In some ways thousands of miles apart. There will be three years before I am free of the university, anyway.'

'Yes, that's true. In many ways he may be more free away from his own university... Felicity, do you remember how you used Miss Elsie as a go-between?'

There was no need for Felicity to speak a reply. A smile of understanding struggled through tears.

'Well, will you let me be your Miss Elsie, here? Letters can even be addressed to me. Your name need never appear. You can keep the secret from Belinda, if you so wish. But I think there's too big a bond between you for that!'

'Grace, you're an angel! But you haven't told me *when* it is to be!'

'They want him there this summer term, to find his feet before work starts in earnest in the autumn term – or the fall semester, I think that's what they call it there.'

The brutal truth was dawning on Felicity: a few weeks more with him here, then two and a half years without ever seeing him at all. She forced tears back.

'Well, it is only four months since we met and in some ways we hardly know one another. In America he will surely make new friends; meet attractive women, have honours poured on him. He will return quite a different man from the one who sails away.'

'Yes, he will be different, and so will you, my dear.'

Felicity flashed out: 'Grace, face the truth! I shall still be nothing much more than a student – not beautiful – not clever or witty – an absolute nonentity!'

'My dear Felicity, if you go on calling yourself a nonentity that is what you will become. What about the new, independent women you and Belinda are supposed to be? You don't want him to come back to a woman needing psychiatric treatment surely? What Alistair *will* need is a happy understanding friend. Don't forget that!'

The shock to Felicity's pride forced her to pull herself together.

'You are right, Grace. Oh dear, you always are! It will be hard work, and I'll need a lot of luck, to make myself into something worth coming back for. But why do we assume that by then I shall have the least hold on him? We have only made music, never made –'

'Darling girl, true love does not have to be *made*. It flies into the heart and mind and nestles there, but it has to be nurtured.' She stopped short, conscious that she was looking back on her own life.

'Grace, I am too young to have hindsight. But, if I were true to my roots, I'd use my gumption and say: "Working like that without any distraction did her a power of good. She sticks at it!"'

They both laughed at the blunt Yorkshire accent which she used. But Grace was looking at the firm lips, the strong jaw and the distant but penetrating eyes, all of which made her look both younger and older than her years.

There was an eloquent silence between them, resonant with resolution and then Grace said quietly: 'Felicity, your man will come back. Mine, as you know, never did. Make the most of him while he's here. Even if it's only knowing that he is.'

'Yes, Grace, I will! It's next Saturday we meet now, isn't it? Those piano keys are going to *zing*!'

Then it was work as usual, with a broken leg to observe being put in plaster, a clear and not intimate job that allowed men and women to be in the theatre together.

'At least,' said Belinda, 'it's a real leg and not a rubber one, and a part of the anatomy we're allowed to see!'

That evening, back at Marchmont Road there was a letter from Roberta and another, not at first recognised, with it on the tray. After the usual salutations and enquiries of health the letter went on:

Your aunt, who might seem to be a helpless, useless person in the world, has brought about a most wonderful happening, which of course she will never be able to understand, though I have tried to explain it to her.

It was my eighth visit to her, since you left, and I found dear Anthony already at her side trying to stop her crying out for her twin sister, Caroline. I must explain that she is quite convinced that *I* am her sister so I have accepted the role and gently respond as if I were.

Anthony (for that is what I can now call him) has arranged that after my visits I go back to his house for tea and talk. On this particular day – a day I shall never forget – he went down on his knees to ask me to marry him, pleading with me that he could not live without me.

He must have anticipated my response for he had a most beautiful ring of his mother's which he put on my finger most tenderly and then kissed my hand. So it is you and your aunt, dear Felicity, whom I have to thank. How else could I have met such a dear creature as Anthony if you had not given me the privilege of meeting and looking after her?

The rest of the letter conveyed the news that the wedding was to be in September; that she had given in her notice, to the surprise of everybody in the school; that the school chaplain had agreed to marry them and would Felicity and Belinda please be bridesmaids.

The last bit of news brought Belinda's first comment.

'God, Felicity! Do I look like a bridesmaid? If I have to be in the wedding party, wouldn't maid of honour be a more appropriate title?'

'But aren't you thrilled for *both* of them? Isn't it absolutely wonderful?'

'Yes, I suppose I should be. He's got a slave and she's got some one who needs one. Is that your idea of marriage?'

The next letter made brevity into a fine art.

Dear Miss Hargreaves and Miss Bennett,

Please excuse my sending one letter but your dual response is inevitable under the circumstances.

I trust you will be pleased to hear that I have asked for Roberta's hand in marriage and that she has kindly consented to be my wife.

You will be receiving formal invitations both to the wedding and to participate in the ceremony.

I trust that your studies in Edinburgh are proving to be congenial.

I remain,

Yours most sincerely,

Anthony Thompson

P.S. In confidence I should like you to know that dear Roberta has completely restored my faith.

The next weeks had an air of unreality. Felicity and Alistair both found it hard to believe that nearly three years must be lived through before they saw one another again.

Grace contrived a meeting where they could be entirely on their own for a whole precious hour and took Belinda into her confidence.

'Tomorrow, as it's Sunday, I've invited Alistair to spend the rest of the evening with Felicity in the drawing room. You and I have a lot of plans to make, Belinda, for the vacation and Alistair's departure. They do need time together.'

Sunday morning ended at the church with their own brands of silent worship: Grace praying for Alistair and Felicity's long life together. Belinda praying that Felicity should establish herself as a doctor well before Alistair came back. Felicity praying that there would be no peril on the sea nor on the distant land which was to be Alistair's home.

Alistair's talk with Felicity cannot all be told for there were many times when thoughts were too deep for words. Sometimes they touched one another with the gentleness of healing hands. There were fleeting butterfly kisses on tired eyes, and on ears which needed a rest from listening to anxious questions.

The doubts and difficulties were all Felicity's.

'Alistair, my dearest, can you trust what I'll become or may not become in three years? You are at the peak of your career, I haven't even started mine.'

'You, my darling, have not made the mistakes I have made, nor met the jealousies I have encountered and the poor souls I have never cured. Nor have you ever become cynical or disillusioned.' He drew her gently towards him with his arm around her

326

naturally slim waist and whispered: 'There is no woman in the world so unmarred.'

'Alistair, don't say that – it's not true... I have something that you must hear. It may alter our whole relationship.'

Alistair could not believe what he had heard. 'Remember, "*Till a' the seas gang dry, my dear*".'

'Sit down, Alistair, and don't interrupt until you have really thought about what I am going to say.'

She sat down, gathering her thoughts together.

'Alistair, you don't know my family at all, except Grace. She's different. I hope you will like my father, blunt as he is. He is true to himself. My mother has never quite known how to keep money out of the conversation. But, as they say in Yorkshire, she means well. They both certainly want the best for their only daughter – but not for other people's daughters! Relations have told me that all my mother wanted of my father, from the day she was married, was a baby girl; and she did not rest, or give him any peace, until she got one. And I was it – three years after their marriage.'

'It's probably the best joint effort they've ever made, my dear. And weren't they lucky?'

'But, Alistair, what I have to confess is something very serious. My mother's sister – you cannot believe it of a rich and healthy family – is in an asylum – a paupers' asylum. Totally ignored by the family except for my occasional visits.'

Alistair caught Felicity's hand. 'She'll have another visitor, my dear, as soon as I return and we are married...'

Felicity almost stopped him saying the word *married*.

'Please, Alistair. There's insanity in the family. It is never admitted and never discussed.'

'Felicity have you forgotten my vow, already...?'

She cut him short again. 'But children? Supposing we have children?'

'They will be like you and me, my dear. And I hope they are more like you!'

He stopped her talking with a kiss and took out of his pocket a small notebook and pencil.

'Her name, my dear?'

'Amy Ackroyd.'

'Name of the asylum?'

'Barlockend – in Airedale.'

'Don't bother with the address. I have it in my register. But it would help if you know the name of the doctor who looks after her.'

'No, I've never seen him. But I can tell you the chaplain's name.'

Alistair wrote every detail down.

'Felicity, when I come back, the first important thing I do is visit her. Remember it is my job, as well as my interest. Why ever didn't you let me know sooner, you silly, silly, girl?'

It was not the usual way to end an evening of love but their understanding of one another had deepened. It made parting all the harder to bear.

Inexorably the time for departure came. Angus had risen early on this day of drenching rain, the day he and Alistair travelled by train from Edinburgh to Liverpool. They were both experienced travellers but Alistair had a way of checking tickets, trains, times and boats which Angus smoothed out. Angus' bulky body disliked all the business of cabin finding and climbing stairs to the first-class deck. He had, therefore, arranged that an old friend, who was the director of the imposing Liver building on the waterfront, should entertain Alistair and himself to lunch. The grandeur of the main city buildings confirmed the common tag of *Liverpool gentlemen, Manchester men*. The Liver building, with its great gold Liver Birds reaching towards the sky on the two green-stained copper domes, was opulent.

'If this skyline is the memory of England which I take away, America should bow to me when I land in New York!'

Angus, who enjoyed being larger-than-life, introduced Alistair to his august friend with the professional grandeur to match the dining-room. The three had that urbane way with them that they could establish their eminence simply by not trying to. Each led the other into conversation that would have entranced any erudite or curious eavesdropper. But the butler, who took eminence for granted, was more concerned that his guests were introduced to his master's choice in vintage claret.

It was time to board the great and proud *Turbinia*. A chief steward from the first-class deck was shown into the dining-room and saluting Dr Fraser, addressed him by name.

'Port side, Dr Fraser. All your luggage needed on voyage is in your cabin. My name is Jackson, Sir. My cabin crew and I will look after anything you need on the voyage.'

Alistair and Angus said goodbye the way English gentlemen do: hats highly raised, hands coolly shaken with the briefest of farewells from stiff upper lips:

'*Bon voyage*, old chap.'

'Thank you, Sir.'

'Don't worry, old boy, we'll look after her.'

Angus stayed the night at the Athenaeum Club then took the train back to Edinburgh the next morning. He had arranged with Lucinda that he would have lunch on the train and would she please invite Felicity for early afternoon tea. He emphasised that she was to be on her own. Felicity loved the Mackenzies' house, which seemed to have grown round them, but today she arrived with bloodshot eyes and signs of no sleep.

Lucinda and Angus were with the maid at the door.

'Leave us, Olive. We'll look after Miss Hargreaves.'

Touch seemed to be more tactful than talk. Each held a hand.

'You talk to Felicity, Angus, while I go and infuse the tea.'

Angus drew Felicity forward.

'Sit here, my dear, and I'll tell you all about it.'

Lucinda deliberately lingered in mixing two blends of tea in the glass bowl in the centre of the mahogany box. She decided with Olive that perhaps the scones should go back in the oven for a warming up again.

He took time to be slow and sweet.

'He got the right kind of send-off, Felicity. Dignified ... made to feel important. But he doesn't need to be *made*, does he? Splendid ship too. We kept our eye on it during lunch in the Liver dining-room.'

Felicity was finding it hard to do anything more than nod.

At last she said: 'You did say *goodbye* for me, really and truly – I mean: *God be with you.*'

'Felicity, I said it for you and the whole world. Alistair gave me a note he had written, for you. It's here.'

'Would you excuse me if I read it, Angus?' She read silently: G has a letter for you. Look up SS XVIII.

She handed it over for Angus to read, and explained. 'Before he left he gave me a splendid edition of *Shakespeare sonnets*, numbered in the same order as his own copy.'

'You'll treasure those words, my dear.'

Felicity had left it until she was back in bed at Moray Place to read the eighteenth sonnet. It was: 'Shall I compare thee to a summer's day?' She held the book close to her, in order to see by the candlelight. Her tears fell on the book as trembling fingers extinguished the candle.

329

But would Alistair's own eternal words ever reach her from overseas?

She tossed about wondering. A hideous dream took her into a world of endless ocean waves where floating sheets of paper cried out to be saved by the men and women who should be receiving them. No-one could breathe. No-one could see.

Long before the postman arrived, long before Sammycat swept downstairs to attack, Grace crept up to Felicity's bedroom with a tray of tea and a letter.

'How have you slept, darling?'

Felicity kept her nightmare to herself. 'I love this bed, Grace.'

'Alistair left this letter for you, my dear. He is very sorry it will be months before you get another from him!'

PART THREE
1899

1

Felicity and Belinda were now very different young women from the two who drank cocoa that first night at Mrs Mac's. Belinda had written major issues on their clinical and hospital experience of the last four years to her parents, using the stark medical facts of life and death. The battles and brilliance of the physicians and surgeons were of keen interest to Jeremy, who responded with a ready pen, often on scribbled notes in the surgery, to the key figures and events in the medical world. Hazel, who raised letter writing to a fine art, had kept the girls amused and enriched by her wise and witty choice of words. All that Felicity could write to her parents were the banalities of weather, food and answers to Gertrude's repeated questions on her daughter's health. Grace, with whom Felicity shared the horrors, small triumphs and sheer hard work, followed every move in the girls' uphill struggle. She too had learnt anatomy from a dead body unclaimed by relatives. Grace knew before they did that the Edinburgh School of Medicine for Women was to close in 1898. She had noticed the change in their chatter now that they had proved they were as good as – often better than – men. Belinda's summing up of the Medical School of Edinburgh University was: 'we've to be twice as good as the men to get the same mark.'

Felicity butted in 'But don't forget we got better reports at Leith Hospital, they've supported women for years.' Felicity, once scared of blood, often had discussed with Grace her own grim sights: a suicide's cut throat, bodies covered with blood from a factory accident, TB patients coughing up blood... But in her weekly letters to Alistair she had to use words of cool, correct compassion for such incidents and leave space for her own loving heart. Now, as they faced a new life and a new century, they wondered how they would live without all that Edinburgh had and could still give them.

'You can't have it all ways, Belinda,' Felicity argued. 'You want to jump over the moon and mine for gold all at the same time.We've had good years here and...'

'But think of all the things we haven't done – the campaigns we haven't joined; the meetings we've not attended; the invitations we have refused!'

'Belinda, what sweeping statements you make! Just think of how you've held your own at *both* debating societies; the WDS and the MWDS. Even when you didn't believe a word of what you were saying you carried the motion! I'll never forget your holding forth that the higher education of women tends to unfit them for domestic duties. Your burlesque of the helpless academic in the kitchen was hilarious...'

They laughed, recalling the memory. They were now going through the endless tasks of sorting out books, papers, letters, reports and sheets of notes which had accumulated over the years. In so doing they were also auditing the pros and cons of what the years had done for them.

Belinda, tidying the sheets of music, picked out the score of Hadyn's piano trio in E Major and hugged it under crossed arms.

'Oh, Felicity, do you remember how Alistair took us through and through the opening bars – just two minutes to play but hours and hours of practice...'

'How could I forget the way he persuaded my fingers to do staccato bass notes with my left hand and long legato notes with my right...' She stopped in mid-sentence, thinking that what she was going to say would sound too pompous: *'harmony: not just of the music but of kindred spirits.'*

Belinda picked up the cue on 'staccato'. 'Oh yes, I'd never realised that one could get such impudent staccato notes out of a cello. But it was the power of that incredible calm harmony he got from the three of us that still haunts me. Heavens, how I miss the man!'

'Belinda, you're gorgeous! I thought that was my line of dialogue not yours!'

'Don't be possessive of him, dearest starry-eyed one. Alistair shares himself willingly with folk he likes – not just with the one he loves.'

'Thank you for the reminder. Yes, we're *all* counting the days. But I think my days are longer than anybody else's! You do realise, Belinda, that he'll go straight from Liverpool to Edinburgh. I'll be in Aireley...'

'*And*, there too, when he comes to see your father! I've been thinking, dearest, that when he's in the lion's den you should be coyly hiding at the Bennetts' as the maid-in-waiting!'

Felicity closed the box of *Medical Papers to Keep* and moved over

334

to Belinda and the music, which prompted her to say: 'Just think what we've had through knowing Grace. I suppose we did miss the social life of Crudelius House and Masson Hall by not being in residence, but I wouldn't have missed Mrs Mac and her canary – and Nell – for all the *new women* in the world.'

'Felicity, have you ever considered all that you've done, since that hair-raising week when you were going to quit?'

'You were very patient, my love. I was so feeble – scared of a drop of blood or the thought of a dead body. How can I think back – it's not been one life, my dear, I've had several lives since then.'

They had left until the last the pile of press photographs and reports sent with well-meaning but boring regularity by Gertrude.

'Do you want to keep any of these, Felicity?'

'Not really.'

'Right! Out they go!'

'I'd better not destroy the real photographs. Mamma will expect them to be put in the album.'

Belinda picked out one of Henry wearing his blue velvet tasselled captain of rugger cap.

'You know, I've never met your brother. Should I?'

'Well if you want to meet the answer to a mother's prayer, he's there! A boy, an heir, three years after me. I'm told I bit him!'

'Oh good for you, my dear.'

She picked out another photograph.

'I like this one of you, even though you are dressed up for your twenty-first birthday. Why not send it to Alistair?'

'Belinda, I've never sent a photograph and never shall. Nor has he. We never discussed it. Just assumed it was part of the pact.'

'But he has written now and again to you, what's the difference?'

'Letters aren't shown to other people as photographs are...'

Belinda picked up the cue rather too sharply for friendship. 'Yes, I've noticed that.'

'Belinda, it's not that I want to hide anything from you, it's just respecting his confidence. They're *his* letters, remember.'

'Careful, my dear, you're in danger of becoming a little wife who thinks her husband should own her and everything she possesses. Dear Felicity, do watch out! Don't please let this oh-so-eminent man take possession of you!'

'Quiet, Belinda! If you'd read every word of all the letters, you'd know he hasn't even proposed to me.'

'Well, I haven't read a word of even one letter nor even seen one –'

'But I've told you the gist of them.'

335

'Giving me the gist is like taking the filling out of a Scotch black bun and giving me the outside crust.'

Felicity thought hard. Love between two women who live and work together has an intuitive rapport and she understood Belinda's feeling of exclusion.

'Well, if you promise not to breathe a word, not even to Grace or Angus...'

'Felicity Hargreaves! Were you there when I called that awful Agatha at the Academy: "You're a sneak-pig-ass-rat-cat-cow-pig-dog-worm!"'

Belinda and Felicity were quick to laughter.

All Alistair's letters, except the last one, were locked away in the secret drawer of the desk in Grace's study. This had been delivered ten days ago by a courier from a cargo and mail ship docked in Liverpool. It had been ten weeks in the company of bales of raw cotton and leaf tobacco.

Felicity took his letter out of a deep patch pocket, an action which, on her own, she had done many times. The envelope showed signs of loving wear and tear.

'Would you like to read it yourself, or shall I read it to you?'

There were times when Belinda was remarkably perceptive and tender. She sensed that no-one's hands but Felicity's should ever touch Alistair's letters.

'You read it to me.' And then with a giggle, 'So that I shan't know what you're leaving out.'

Felicity was blushing, not with nervousness, but with the anticipation of reading the letter again, which she knew almost by heart. She curled her legs onto the little sofa, breathed in and out luxuriously, and began.

My dearest Felicity,

That is the name, my darling, you must always be, I simply could not strip away the valuable syllables which spell *happiness* and reduce you to *Fel.* If I were in Edinburgh, I would sing over your shoulder that lovely Schubert song *I want to carve your name on every tree.* Instead I can only write '*Felicity*' and hope you hear my voice.

The middle of my letter always has to be news of what is going on in my working hours in this wonderful old city (don't think that everything in America is new). So forgive me if I become a minor Solomon spilling over with words of wisdom.

336

As you must have gathered from my last letters, working with William James (or even with his team) is a huge privilege. Some day I hope to get him to Edinburgh to give a series of lectures, but that wish is only at the *hoping* stage and, of course, a secret between you and me.

Felicity stopped short.

'Oh, Belinda, you see I've already betrayed his confidence! Forget I ever said it.'

'My dear, even if I were the crudest of gossips, not one person I know would ever have heard of – what's his name? – William? – What? You see I've safely forgotten already!'

They giggled together before Felicity went on.

Today I had him on his own and basked in the luxury of telling him about you. He is, as you know, a brilliant scientist, philosopher and psychologist, yet he approves of each individual having his own idea of faith, hope and charity. He is a deeply perceptive listener and positively helped me to be able to re-create you. I have never been able to do this to another living soul.

Does it sound too fulsome to say that there was love in his listening? I quote his exact words: 'Alistair.' he said, 'a true harmonious relationship gives a zest for life, an assurance of safety, a temper of peace. You lucky man, to have found a Felicity. And she, of course, to have found you! Do you think, not too far in the future, I might meet her?'

Oh, my dearest, he puts heart into everybody. Many psychologists and psychiatrists are so analytical and uncharitable that they can paralyse simple feelings and bring out completely warped ones. James's central core of philosophy is that truth is curative. He explains brilliantly in his lectures that we should make our nervous systems our allies instead of our enemies.

This is what you did, my dearest Felicity, when you conquered your nervous doubts and decided you would become a doctor.

I can hardly believe that your four years are nearly over. What a wonderful life lies ahead of you, my dear, with all your knowledge, compassion and charm. I cannot express in a letter, at this stage, my hopes for a life where concord of body, mind and spirit unites us.

It would be churlish to ask you to destroy my letters, but

they are, I trust, locked away where not a living soul can even see the envelopes. (It has just reminded me, of course, they are not even addressed to you but to our very dear Grace!)

It may be over a month before you receive this letter. Oh, if only you and I could use this miracle cable and make our voices meet!

I remain, always, your devoted,

Alistair

P.S. Sonnet XLIV

P.P.S I cannot even ask you to give my warmest regards to Belinda since, of course, you cannot convey them – I must leave it to Angus to do that.

'It's a wonderful letter, my dear. Of course you must never destroy one of them. But how odd, the way he writes, as if you spend your life in the medical school.'

'But, Belinda, that's how it is. These photographs we have here of Roberta's wedding, my twenty-first birthday party, the mill celebration and last New Year's ball at the Winkleys' would not mean *anything* to him. The only social life he mentions in letters is nothing to do with the Boston Tea Party. It's the lavish, but informal, Boston lunch and dinner parties in Harvard, Cambridge and Boston where brilliantly talkative women seem to hold sway. I get depressed when he quotes one of them. Is that mean?'

'Darling, I'm sure that America goes to most people's heads after England. Our stiff upper lip and all that. Don't you think that people's speech here, in the upper classes, tends to be arrogantly short or pontifically long?'

They laughed together again. Felicity picked up a press cutting. The three or four hundred people on it had to be small, including Arthur Hargreaves, because the mill chimney shot up to the edge of the photograph, where the bold caption stretched across the page:

AIRELEY MILL SCORES 100 – FOUNDED 1797 –
STILL GOING STRONG 1897

'I can't believe it's nearly two years since that celebration! Look at my hat in the photograph then you'll know. My mother's choice! It's hideously over-decorated and out of date already!'

338

*   *   *

Whilst Belinda and Felicity were sorting out the years' accumulation of papers and books, Alistair was doing his sorting out in Harvard. He was making scholarly synopses of the lectures he had given, the seminars he had conducted and, above all, transcripts of the lectures and discussions inspired by William James. Not only had James sharpened Alistair's perceptions but he had also softened his criticisms. He was returning to Scotland a more tolerant and forgiving man than the one who set sail on the *Turbinia*.

Perhaps he had also been surprised to find that most of the Americans he had met – of whatever social or professional class – had simpler faith and more spontaneous ways of expressing their beliefs than the restrained, well-trained Christians he met in his native land.

He pondered over Felicity. Her letters had shown a maturing which he must respect. His falling in love over three years ago – he saw with well-honed hindsight – had been compounded of anxiety to comfort, protect and support a lost child. It was important to reassure her, before he reached British shores, that his love had grown through her letters and that there was no question of having to get to know one another again. America had, in many ways, eased his Scottish reticence and given his innate, but controlled, buoyancy rather more freedom of expression.

Was it an omen of progress in life ahead that he was now sailing back to England on the *Oceanic*, the well-known steamship that had been ahead of its time ten years ago? He began to pull himself out of his regrets at leaving Harvard and to anticipate the long and thrilling journey home. Just one more visit to make.

It was his last private meeting with William James. They discussed where psychology and psychiatry were going.

'Fraser, psychologists think that they own a separate subject. Get your students to realise that all experience is interrelated and that every mental process needs sensory nerves, blood vessels and glands. Try, if you can, Fraser, also to get your general practitioners to understand that every thought *affects* the nerves, blood vessels and glands. Shakespeare, three hundred years ago, was ahead of us when he said simply: "There's nothing either good or bad but thinking makes it so." We have no idea what jealousy, resentment and greed do to the human physical condition.'

They talked round the subject for an hour or more.

'May I change our discussion, Sir, to a more personal subject? I

339

have only mentioned it to you before. What do you think I should do about Felicity's aunt in Barlockend Asylum? You and I have lectured on insanity, and theorised many times, but never discussed what I should do.'

'We are too late for your Miss Ackroyd, I'm afraid. I have a feeling from what you told me that she became insane because she was expected to be so. People grow to fit the label which others have stuck on them. Living in an asylum, she had no alternative except to be a lunatic. Shakespeare's tag applies there too. You say two doctors have to certify insanity? May I ask what qualifications they must have to do so? Go back, Alistair.' He used the Christian name when conversation had become more intimate. 'Go back and *probe*. You as a doctor can get hold of her medical record. Analyse the initial entry. Find out who was pushing the certification. You told me she came from a well-to-do family. Why was she in a *paupers'* asylum? Who wanted her out of the way?'

Arthur and Gertrude Hargreaves returned from Edinburgh somewhat chastened by the pomp and ceremony of the medical school graduation day.

They were relieved to be home, where everything belonged. Arthur had been ill at ease in a place where others dominated. Gertrude felt all the effort she had made to be stylish for the occasion counted for nothing in the company of caps, gowns and hoods, traditionally well-worn or triumphantly new. It was lost on her that many of the shabbiest, but more elaborate, academic garb carried the most glory.

Sadly she felt awkward meeting people with whom her sister-in-law had an easy camaraderie. Though Grace behaved impeccably, drawing her brother and his wife quietly into the circle which she and Felicity enjoyed, Grace knew that her effort gave no pleasure. The Yorkshire Hargreaves were quick to sense patronage. They had left their own importance two hundred miles away. Folk here, in Edinburgh, they thought bitterly, were too stuck-up even to enquire about it.

Grace had not been insensitive to their social nervousness. She had arranged for them to have two quiet days, as her guest, in the Waverley Hotel so they could enjoy Edinburgh on their own. But Gertrude had no zest for sightseeing and Arthur none for shopping.

On the last afternoon he went off alone to the castle having armed himself with the most expensive guidebooks to show as evidence to Aireley folk.

Gertrude, exhausted by Princes Street, had an afternoon sleep and then, on her own, boldly rang the bell to order tea to be brought up to her room. She stored up the experience for her next At Home proving her role as a woman-of-the-world.

Now that the two were safely back in Aireley their routine gave pleasure. The silver letter tray restored their identity; one letter already from Grace surprised them with its speed. They read it without comment, in the hall.

My dear Gertrude and Arthur,

I was so glad you were present for Felicity's great day; it is an awesome sight made even more so now that there are many women graduates who outclass the men.

The excitement of it all is tiring, and, meeting so many strangers, as you were, can be exhausting. I trust the train journey was comfortable and that you arrived home in good spirits.

Now I am introducing a subject which I was too cowardly to discuss with you face to face.

There was, in the event, too little time when the three of us were on our own. I do not have to tell you what we must talk about.

There have been several times in Felicity's life when it seemed only fair for the truth to be known, and yet unfair for those most deeply concerned. I was tortured during her twenty-first birthday celebrations, two years ago, cognisant that coming of age (legally) should be treated seriously. But I could not bear to think of shattering the carefree world in which she radiated happiness.

It is to your credit, and I hope pride, that she is now a mature young woman, highly qualified and socially poised. Unlike most young women of her age she has witnessed extreme physical suffering and watched, at close quarters, critical operations. She has dealt with deplorable conditions which demanded serious judgements. She may not have told you that she had to overcome fear and repulsion at the thought of a medical training. This last year she and Belinda carried out tedious hours of duty in the women's wards of Leith Hospital and the Royal Infirmary. In the presence of

341

other people, she and Belinda tend to make light of the gruelling demands made on medical students and junior doctors, especially women. One reason for their reticence is, I think, that all their experiences are, in a sense, confidential and the terminology too technical for a layman's comprehension.

But I must return to the issue which concerns us so deeply.

In order to explain why I feel a new urgency for the truth to be told is because it means breaking a confidence, which is closely personal to Felicity.

During the time of study, here in Edinburgh, a senior member of the medical staff (one of my musical circle) has become deeply fond of her. May I say at once that your daughter and the eminent doctor have behaved with the utmost decorum and no breath of their friendship has filtered through the academic walls. It was, I think, as well for both their sakes that they should be parted until Felicity's studies were complete. Fortunately, a prestigious offer for his services came from America and he has spent nearly three years away across the Atlantic. He will be returning to Britain in a month's time. The pattern of friendship will take a more open course, now that Felicity is no longer a student and he is, as it were, a freelance member of the academic staff at the university.

No-one can predict the future. I only ask that, in your wisdom, you consider the possibility that things may have to be revealed – and in the near future.

Please trust me to support you in all your decisions.

I remain your devoted sister,

Grace

Gertrude went straight up to their bedroom, got rid of her finery, loosened her corsets and waited for Arthur. For the first time in his married life he took his pipe to the bedroom, and after filling it, wrenched the stiff white collar from its gold studs.

Both of them were sorely in need of an early night, comforted by familiar possessions. They made no comment on Grace's letter but their actions betrayed their concern for what was in it. It was the first time in their married life they had undressed in one another's company – in comforting, but shaken, silence.

Arthur put an arm round Gertrude drawing her to an easy

342

chair. 'Sit down 'ere luv. There's summat in Grace's letter you and me 'ave got to talk about.'

'Well, it was all her doing. If anyone should do the telling it should be her.'

'But you're 'er mother. What else after twenty-three years?'

'Oh, Arthur, can't you see I'm tired out? Can't we talk in bed – for a change?'

'No, yer can't think lying down. Not summat as important as this.'

There was a silence, which made Gertrude's opposition harder.

'Well, *I'm* not telling, so there! It's not right.'

'Quiet, lass, and listen. It's got to be done some day...'

'Why has it? Come to your senses, Arthur!'

'Nay lass, yer codding yersen. From wot ah picked up in Edinburgh – an' don't ask me 'ow, but Grace 'as let on in 'er letter – there's a man takken a fancy to 'er. If she ever marries, 'e'll 'ave to know!'

'All right then. Man to man. *You* tell her.'

'Nay, Gertrude, it's a woman's job – 'er *mother*.'

It was the first time the word *mother* had unnerved her. It brought back much that even Arthur did not know.

There was another uncomfortable silence. Her mind was back in the Station Hotel in York a lifetime away.

'If it's got to be done – and I see no sense in it, what about asking Jeremy Bennett? He went up to Edinburgh and brought her into the world. He knows more than anyone.'

'Leave the man alone. He's kept 'is gob shut. He's 'ad enough of two daft women: one wanting a kid, and the other wanting to get rid.'

Gertrude was not attempting to stop her tears and now wailed through them: 'Three years married. And all I'd 'ad at the end of it were two miscarriages. I was beside myself wanting a baby. You *knows* that!'

The words choked out until all she could produce was a strangled whisper.

'You know you agreed with Dr Bennett. To save the scandal...'

He took hold of her shoulder, shook her and spoke softly. 'Shut up, Gertrude, and give me a straight answer: Any regrets?'

The cold douche halted the tears and brought out a truth, which surprised them both.

'She's the best thing that ever happened to me, Arthur lad. I've always been proper set up with our Felicity.'

'Funny that when th'd stopped maitherin', our 'Enry came along.'

343

They relaxed a little but with nervous smiles.

She wagged a playful finger. 'Well, as your father would have said: you must have *framed* better that time!'

Gertrude was on form now, thinking that Arthur had dropped the idea of her being the one to tell.

He was recalling the first three years of marriage when every night she pecked at him like a goose wanting a golden egg. Then the whole remembered horror of his sister's plight and the threat of family disgrace shot through him.

Gertrude's silence was filled with recalling how swiftly she had fallen in with Jeremy Bennett's suggestion, which would give her a child. Here was the chance to shift the blame.

'I did it to help you, Arthur, and your sister. We couldn't have the Hargreaves name smirched, could we?'

'Think on, Gertrude, none of that. You're a Hargreaves too. And proud of it.'

There was another silence while Arthur filled his pipe again and Gertrude twisted a strand of hair round a curling pin.

'Arthur, can't I get you to see sense? If she has to be told – and you've never suggested it before – why not ask the doctor who brought her into the world?'

'Sithee 'ere, Gertrude, Jeremy Bennett's kept 'is word all these years and ah reckon 'es allus going to. I don't know if 'is wife knows but if she does she's different from most women. She's never gabbed, or 'er daughter would 'ave. What I'd like to know is 'ow 'e came to know mi sister. There's a lot been kept from me. P'raps mi own fault. I didn't want to know owt about it.'

'No, you didn't. But you did know that the father was a doctor – an army doctor – and that he was at college with Bennett. That's how Grace knows him. They were all close friends in Edinburgh when she was at the Royal.'

On hearing Grace's name, it struck a note of resentment in Arthur's mind.

'I tell you this, lass, our Grace, only twenty-two she was, couldn't 'ave done all that scheming and planning without the money she 'ad from our grandmother. And she couldn't 'ave set herself up in all that swank in Edinburgh – high-class maternity home and that big house – without a pile of Hargreaves brass!'

'Only part of it. The Edinburgh house and contents were willed to her, Arthur, from her fancy man. Right and proper too. Men always get away with a good time and go off. It's the woman who pays.'

'Stop ranting on, Mother...' He lapsed back into his usual way of addressing her and then stopped short. He looked at the bedroom clock.

'It's after ten and yer've not answered mi question. And like it or not, we're not going to bed until yer do.'

'All this talk and not one thought for our Felicity. How's she going to feel, a qualified doctor, being told,' Gertrude hesitated, 'that she's a bastard.' It needed all Gertrude's strength to say the word. In the whole of Felicity's life the word had never been used in relation to her.

Like many other babes, the love child had been conveniently passed on to a near relative. Felicity had not been legally adopted, nor had her birth ever been registered. Had it been so, the stigma of *illegitimate* would have been on the birth certificate under the column headed: FATHER.

Gertrude went into attack again, red with fear, on behalf of Felicity.

'If that medical association finds out, she'll be struck off the register. And what man is going to marry a girl who hasn't even got a birth certificate, I should like to know?'

She broke down in tears again and gave up the appeal, feeling sure that her husband's Wesleyan and Yorkshire pride would make him unable to face such a public disgrace.

The bedroom clock ticked on to ten thirty. It was checkmate. They sat silent until the clock struck eleven.

It was the first time he had been defeated by his wife. He weakened.

'Ah'll tell yer wot luv. If she doesn't get wed, an' thuz no question of 'er 'aving to show t'registration form, we'll keep uz mouths shut. Ows that? Yer'll only 'ave to tell 'er if a wedding's fixed.'

Gertrude was too tired to go on arguing.

They got into bed, leaving between them a blank corridor of stiff linen sheet.

Arthur's irritation kept him awake for an hour; Gertrude tossed and turned, reliving that day in September '76 when she met their doctor in a private room of the Station Hotel, York.

Sleep did not come to her until the mill-hooter sounded at five and the cold autumn light fell on a tear-ravaged face. She looked every day of her forty-six years, for Gertrude Hargreaves had lived in fear through the night.

Way back in the early seventies, Jeremy Bennett had been drawn into her grumbles against her husband, as if he were responsible for the miscarriages. However much the doctor tried to explain that it might be *her* body that was not fully functioning, she thought it was a doctor's job to do something about it. Her ignorance of human reproduction was such that she still had a childish faith in the doctor's little black bag.

The Hargreaves' friendship with the doctor had been established on their setting up home at Stonegarth. He introduced himself as a close friend of Miss Grace Hargreaves and her fiancé Lieutenant-Colonel Felix Stewart.

Dr Jeremy Bennett, MD (Edinburgh), had been warmly welcomed to Stonegarth by Arthur, who liked to talk of his wealthy sister, even though privately he resented the route by which she had acquired the wealth. It was the doctor who first told them the tragic news of the death of Grace's fiancé out in India.

Gertrude wept childish tears.

'Dreadful things happen in foreign parts,' she whimpered. 'Why did he have to go?'

'Queen and country. Army orders.' Jeremy used the soldiers' formula for hiding grief.

Three months later a dignified letter of confession came from Grace. The *birth* was received very differently from the *death*.

Arthur summed up his response in three words: 'The brazen hussy.'

Gertrude's reply was spoken in a voice and speech she had copied from the vicar's wife.

'What is the world coming to? A year younger than me! What a disgrace for the Hargreaves family!' She was relieved it was not an Ackroyd.

Underneath this facade of righteous condemnation she was jealous. *To think that someone not fit to have a baby should have one when I can't.*

She had wanted to talk to someone about God's lack of judgement: Dr Bennett, perhaps, but he was away in Edinburgh.

On his return, he had gone straight to Stonegarth to talk to Gertrude at a time he knew that Arthur would be at the Exchange in Bradford. He also knew the house well and, taking control, guided the young mistress into the morning room. He dismissed the maid by giving her an errand to the post office.

Gertrude had nothing to say, childishly weeping with shame and envy. Jeremy was relieved she was not talking; he found her childish prattle irritating at the best of times:

'There, there, don't bother to talk. I want to talk to you. Listen carefully to what I have to say. Felix Stewart was my best friend, an officer, a doctor and a gentleman. We were at the medical school together and served in the army medical corps. He stayed on as a professional army doctor.

'Now, Gertrude, I want you to sit quite quiet and listen to me carefully. Get all those pious thoughts against your sister-in-law out of your little head. If you had searched the whole world you could not have found a finer man than Felix. He and Grace were deeply and tenderly in love. Remember he was going to be away for two whole years. She desperately wanted to give him something of herself and to possess part of him. Of course they were foolish. People in love are. But it was a noble carelessness, Gertrude, a nobility few folk experience.'

Gertrude was out of her depth and had had no strength to moralise.

Bennett used her silence for useful flattery. 'You are being very brave, and very generous, my dear. I am going to ask you to add wisdom to your bravery.'

He was not unaware that her simplistic reaction had changed to a disturbing jealousy. Suddenly her pretty face looked shrewd.

'It's a girl, isn't it?' There was more than enquiry in her voice.

'Yes, I brought her into the world. She's perfect. Grace has called her *Felicity*. It means happiness, my dear. Your sister-in-law is being very brave and completely selfless. Her one thought is for the child. She does not want her to have the stigma of being born out of wedlock. Yet she wants, if she can, to give her the name *Hargreaves*.'

Gertrude was not stupid when she could see her own wishes coming true. 'I think I know what you are thinking.' And then her mouth puckered into protest. 'On one condition, doctor, that she's *mine*. Mine and Arthur's. The natural daughter of Mr and Mrs Arthur Hargreaves!'

Jeremy was amazed that the suggestion had been so quickly and easily accepted, but alarmed at her toughness. Did this innocent and ignorant young woman know what she was taking on? It was the first time he had heard her speak with authority on any serious subject.

'My dear, we have only an hour before your husband gets home. You and I will have to be very close accomplices. I have talked it over with Grace and the matron of the nursing home. Grace is known by the way as *Mrs* Hargreaves, they think it was her *husband* who died of cholera. Everything has to be highly respectable on the west side of Edinburgh. I have offered to return there to make arrangements for the baby to come back with me. Of course depending on your agreement.'

There was a sudden outburst from Gertrude. 'Doctor, stop! Supposing Arthur doesn't agree?'

'Dear Gertrude, Arthur is going to gain more than anyone from this scheme. First, he is going to become a young and happy father, second, you are going to stop nagging him, and third, his sister's shame need never be made public. Best of all, you are going to be happy and fulfil your dreams. But no time must be lost. Will you listen, without interruption, and allow me to explain the plan?

'The baby is already nearly two weeks old and only six pounds in weight. If *you* are to give birth to the child we don't want her overweight, do we? Forgive these blunt words, but I am having to be crude. You must be silent and discreet. I know that from time to time you do go to York to visit your great-aunt Sarah and do some shopping. Well, you are going next week. On Monday, September 18th. If I may be personal, you have often led people to believe you were *expecting*, as they say, in order to prove your fertility. This time, amply plump as you are, you have teased them all with your secrecy. Remember, if any nosey-parker comments on your rash visit to York when you were well on in pregnancy, remember that you were only at the seventh month – and fighting fit!'

When she had been assured of Arthur's connivance, Gertrude's thoughts had turned to her then young housemaid, Hilda. She had had none of the airs and graces that Gertrude resented in servants.

Brought up on an East Riding farm, Hilda had lived near enough to Hull to know the grim side of fishing and farming. Stonegarth with a cook, a kitchen daily, a parlourmaid and herself as 'tweeny' was, to use her own words, *a fair cop*.

She was just two years older than her young mistress, but scrubbing, washing, churning, lambing, haymaking, harvesting, albeit with laughter running through, had weathered her skin into lively middle age. Gertrude's young face had always had the bland surface of one who has never given tough life a thought.

Birth was no mystery to Hilda, she had struggled with foals, calves, lambs and babies even when still a schoolgirl. She took it for granted that if you were married you were pregnant, breast-feeding or going through the change but she hadn't been able to make out what was going on with her mistress. She was plump enough to look as if she was in the family way but Hilda had been

348

there a fortnight and nothing had been said. Not until the doctor had been for the second time that week.

'You'll keep a secret, Hilda, won't you? Your mistress doesn't want people to know in case she has the same experience as last time. But in two months' time there should be a little occupant in that nursery.'

Hilda, weighing it all up to herself, thought, seven months gone and looking like a blooming rose.

Thus it was in 1876 that the twenty-three-year-old Gertrude Hargreaves took the train from Leeds to York very early on a golden September day. Her great-aunt Sarah, of course, knew nothing of her coming and was, in fact, paying her annual visit to her brother's farm on the Wolds.

Dr Bennett had told Gertrude to go straight in to the Royal Station Hotel, where a room had been booked for her to spend a week. Lunch had been arranged in a private room, reserved by the resident doctor of the Queensgate Maternity Home, Edinburgh. Her travelling outfit for that day showed a cunning that suggested she was not the innocent she looked. Her dress of soft blue alpaca had had a surcoat of the same material, loosely covering any real or feigned pregnancy, thus making sure that 'seven months gone' was possible, should she encounter some acquaintance on the train.

The hotel had its own corridor from the station, from which the hotel porter conducted Gertrude to her own room. On the arrival of the Edinburgh train, an important little group, with an excessive amount of portered luggage, was welcomed by the manager and taken by the hotel porter to Gertrude. Introductions were made as if this were a social occasion quite usual in the precinct of this grand hotel.

Dr Bennett turned to Gertrude and then to the holder of the baby. 'May I introduce Nurse Wigmore to you, Mrs Hargreaves? Nurse will introduce the precious little bundle herself.'

Immediately the introductions were over, the doctor with infinite tact and charm excused himself . He knew that the most intimate things had to be explained to *Nurse* Wigmore who was, in fact, an ex-member of the staff of Queensgate. She had been hired as a wet nurse, having recently had a baby who had died.

Gertrude grew up considerably in the hour they were alone together. She certainly heard more about childbirth and care of a baby from Winnie Wigmore than she had ever heard before.

There was no question of interviewing for a job. Winnie had been engaged in Edinburgh with excessive enthusiasm. Gertrude accepted her and the baby, cooing over the baby in a voice no-one had ever heard before.

Cooing now came easily to Gertrude from her pretty, childish face, but when Winnie opened up her bodice to feed the baby, Gertrude showed embarrassment and distaste. As she confided later to Arthur: 'Oh I didn't know where to put myself!'

The truth was that her youthful prettiness gave a glow of innocence which disguised stupidity. It could more properly have been described as ignorance.

However, for a person of such limited intelligence, she had a remarkably high level of low cunning. She wanted, as quickly as possible, to sever any close bond Winnie had with Grace by asserting herself as the perfect mother.

'How anyone could part with her own baby girl I just can't understand. She must have a heart of steel.'

'On the contrary, Madam, Mrs Hargreaves was, and is, a mother in a million. The child's welfare comes first.'

'Well, you're right in this. The baby's welfare has come first, she's got a real mother and father now and a perfect home.'

Jeremy Bennett had planned this strange alliance with sensitive care, giving time for all the necessary attention to the babe and for Winnie and Gertrude to get to know one another. He was to return to Arthur and report.

Gertrude and Winnie Wigmore had been booked to stay at the hotel for a week, the wet nurse to occupy the large dressing room. Most women would have suffered acute claustrophobia and loneliness. Not Gertrude. The wish of her life had come true, and before the week ended she had almost convinced herself that the child, though suckled by a stranger, had in fact come from her own womb.

All the delights of having a baby were hers: the bathing, cuddling, rocking and cooing. The unpleasant jobs were smoothly kept out of her sight, leaving her hands free to build herself up with Terry's fruit drops and Rowntree's walnut creams, all made within smelling distance of the hotel, and Bassett's liquorice allsorts made a few miles away. Gertrude had thoroughly enjoyed the indulgence of feeding for two and the unhealthy indulgence of never stirring outside the hotel.

Jeremy Bennett returned to the hotel a week later, having hired a closed, well-sprung brougham, with a driver both deft and decorous, for the eighteen-mile drive to Aireley.

350

Close as the four were in the brougham, there was little conversation, partly because the baby was asleep, and must be kept so, but mainly because the silences of the adults were worlds apart.

Jeremy's silence was filled with the agony that Grace must be enduring. He had brought many women through labour but never had he taken a child away from its mother. So swift and strong had been the social pressure that he had not stopped to consider whether he was committing a criminal act. He had carried out Grace's wishes, conscious that if Felix had been alive, this inhuman separation would not have been tolerated. The torture grew all through the journey from York to the hills and dales of the West Riding.

Gertrude's silence was smug. She was congratulating herself on having had the foresight to make a nursery when they built Stonegarth. Like a small girl with a doll's house she had been totally engrossed planning all the pink trivia she would add, now that she was bringing her baby girl home.

Winnie's silence was gashed with thoughts that cut deep. First, and overwhelming everything else, was the picture of her own baby struggling to live for barely three weeks on earth, pathetically fragile. God was away and somewhere else, she thought bitterly. And now this man-made separation of mother and child! A love-baby: the casualty of an intolerant society. She thought of Grace Hargreaves – a noble woman, with great courage. Was her baby-bereavement harder to bear than mortal death? Winnie thought it was. She had pulled herself together to take on a role caused by two untimely deaths and a cherished life.

The brougham drew up, in the dark, at Stonegarth.

It was thus that Felicity Hargreaves started life with her new birthday, Monday September 18th, 1876.

Only Grace and Jeremy Bennett knew that it was on September 4th that the love-child had fought her way through the agony of her mother's labour pains.

2

Alistair gloried in the size, speed and grandeur of the *Oceanic*. But it was now nearly the end of the second week. The endless succession of meals, not always welcome, the autocracy of many of the first-class passengers, the indulgence of the gourmets and gourmands and the novelty of dining at the Captain's table began to pall. He walked away from the music, the dancers and the massive candlelit chandeliers and went out on deck.

It was sundown. The four massive funnels thrust their white smoke westwards and, catching the gold-vermilion light, hurled it back into the dying sun. His scientific mind marvelled at the collective genius which had created this ship. He felt the vibrations of the distant engines, powering and controlling all this energy.

Why had it slipped his memory that telephone cable across the Atlantic was now a reality? Curiosity made him stop a passing steward.

'Is it possible to see the cable transmitting office? Is it in operation?'

'Yes, sir. It's quite a walk. So follow me!'

Five minutes later Alistair was standing next to the chief officer of communications. He enjoyed talking to anyone doing a skilled job and the officer was happy to have a listener.

'Yes, it's over fifty years since they set about the cable laying, fighting every disaster known to God or man. Many broken cables lie fathoms deep below us. Take a look at that, sir.'

Alistair looked up at the framed certificate, which proudly stated:

August 18th 1858
Europe and America are united in telegraphic communication. Glory to God in the highest, on earth, peace, and goodwill towards men.

'What about sending a cable yourself, sir? It means a lot to folks at home.'

'I wonder. Most people associate a cablegram with disaster...'

He took the cap off his fountain pen and picked up paper bearing the insignia *SS Oceanic*. The words he had in mind were far too private for that chap's inquisitive eyes. How could he by-pass this engaging intruder? All his boyhood and since, Alistair was fascinated with puzzles; he also needed a break in the monotony of luxury sailing.

Had any woman ever received a proposal by cable, he wondered. Well, Felicity must be the first. But for privacy it must be in code.

He scribbled and then tore up the efforts. At last he left one sheet unspoilt. Slowly he copied it out, much more slowly than he had written the original, for he was thinking one letter at a time. He read it over. It appeared to be utterly devoid of romance. He made a copy to keep for himself.

He waited until it was another officer on duty.

'I want this sent to Aireley Post Office in the north of England. This is the postmistress's name and address and this is an accepted PO code.' He handed over the message and its destination, with Felicity's name as the recipient postmistress.

'OK. That will be in order, sir. The cost is more than a telegram, you know.'

'Oh, never mind that. The postal service in Britain is booming!'

'Thank you, sir. The charge will be put on your cabin account. The cable will be sent at once.'

It all seemed quite simple now. He sent another brief cable to the same name and address. It was just four words in plain English: *Move the letters back.*

The term was over, not only the term, but also graduation and the whole medical course. Belinda and Felicity wept at the thought of leaving Edinburgh and all that it now meant to them. However, it was a relief that they would no longer have to cope with the slings and arrows levelled by some of the male students and, less obviously, by a few of the formally polite professors.

They had a weeping session with Nell after their final playing of the *Archduke* piano trio. Mrs Mac, their only audience, wept and smiled her applause. She would miss these two more than any students she had ever had. The walls of the parlour had vibrated with such rapport that the canary was inspired to add its own little pizzicato.

The anguish of parting, heightened by Grace introducing a

353

summer soirée, wounded less when they thought of the great world, which lay ahead of them. The *unknown*, such an optimistic challenge for the young was, though she never showed it, an underlying fear for Mrs Mac. The three flights of stairs grew more difficult every day and the coal scuttles got heavier.

Going home meant quite different things to Belinda and Felicity. Stonegarth shone with polish, but little else. It was Leo's welcoming bark and Hilda's Yorkshire warmth which filled the silences. The doctor's house glowed with bowls of haphazard flowers from the garden and books and music, well in use. Hazel had put the latest *Strand* magazines on Belinda's bedside table so that she could keep up with Sherlock Holmes, her hero made alive by Conan Doyle.

Meanwhile, Felicity found Hilda relieved the monotony of Stonegarth's household perfection with kitchen trivia. She introduced the new kitchen maid.

'Riley and me are giving t'black-leading a miss this week. But don't let on, will yer? That kitchen grate 'as to be as black as t'family bible. It's as 'oly te yer mam, any ways on!'

Felicity renewed her friendship with Miss Elsie. Quite apart from her affection for her, she was to need her even more now.

But Alistair was on the sea and no letter came.

A long but pettily busy week passed with Felicity being shown off to the most important neighbours. Those who asked what Felicity was going to do with her *doctoring* were quickly put in their place by her mother.

'One thing she'll never have to do, or be allowed to do, is earn her living. There are plenty of nice ways of helping sick neighbours without taking money.'

Fortunately, Belinda made sure she and Felicity met frequently and that there were opportunities of talking medical matters and other things with Belinda's father. He had always treated Felicity like another daughter.

Carefree holiday time was running out. Next week Belinda was to start work as an assistant medical officer for women in the Health Department of Bradford City Council. She was to analyse and re-file all the medical records to give her a background of what this city had achieved. There was much more Belinda discovered off the record, which she rooted out.

* * *

354

It was the last day of July. Felicity was to remember July 31st 1899 to the end of her days.

Bob delivered the post at his usual eight o'clock but waylaid Hilda.

'Give this note quick to Miss Hargreaves. Miss Ellis says it's urgent, like.'

Hilda nipped up the stairs to Felicity's room and pushed it into her hands, then ran back to the hall to sound the breakfast gong.

The note was brief: *Come as soon as you can. Urgent. Elsie.*

Felicity could hardly wait for breakfast to be over. Leo was impatient too. She repeated the set piece she had used through girlhood: 'May I leave the table? I'm just taking Leo for his walk.'

It was past paper and post time before Elsie and she had the shop to themselves. The village knew that Miss Ellis quite often had an hour to herself, having been up since five. She turned the key on the inside.

'Come into the back parlour, Felicity. There's something come that's fair flummoxed me!'

She took time to introduce her prize object, re-opening the envelope as if it were from Her Majesty.

'Have you ever seen a cablegram before? Well, you're seeing one now. But I can't make head or tail of it. It's just a list of letters! It's fret me, I can tell you. It came in the middle of the night and I've not slept since.'

Elsie spread the two papers out on the table. One was a jumble of letters in her own writing. The second was a formal list of the same letters officially confirmed in type.

OPX ZPV BSF GSFF (Stop) J BN B TVQQMJDBOU BU
ZPVS GFFU (Stop) DBO XF OPU QVU PVU UIF GMBHT
(query) XJMM ZPV NBSSZ NF (query) (End)

She had to leave Felicity trying to decipher it while she answered the telephone again. It was another cable with just four words: *Move the letters back.* Felicity was still pouring over the first cable.

'It's not sense, Elsie, not sense at all.'

'Come on, sit down at the table. Now say *no* if you don't want me to help you. But in a post office we get used to some rum messages on telegrams. Folk leave any word out to save a penny!'

'*Letters back*,' they were muttering quickly now. 'Back? Where?'

Although Felicity longed to keep it to herself, it was Elsie who had spotted the simple code.

355

'No, Elsie, sit with me. I'm sure your alphabet is better than mine. My mind now only works on chemical formulas!'

'N to M – O to N.' Elsie got smartly into action, slightly ahead of Felicity.

'You go on, Elsie, at the beginning and I'll start at the end. We'll be quicker that way!'

She hadn't realised that her letters were going to make less sense the wrong way round, but she persevered: F to E – N to M – Z to Y

It was a tedious business but written down it began to look at least like words.

'Sorry love, I can't keep the shop shut any longer. There's that Mrs Bassett banging on the door. I'll leave it to you! I've got the eighth word and it's a rum'n. Never heard it before!'

Felicity worked on, crossed out her mistakes, grouped the letters into words, put the three stops in their place and then she read, between gasps,

NOW YOU ARE FREE (stop) I AM A SUPPLIANT AT YOUR FEET (stop) CAN WE NOT PUT OUT THE FLAGS (query) WILL YOU MARRY ME (query) (end)

Felicity was still sitting there, a mixture of shock, incredulity, wonder, gratitude and adoration, when Elsie came back to the parlour at eleven o'clock for her usual cup of tea.

'Well, I can see from your face that those are tears of joy. Am I allowed to know?'

'With all my heart, dear Elsie. With all my heart.'

Elsie, used to telegrams, read: *'NOW YOU ARE FREE. I AM A SUP-PLICANT AT YOUR FEET. CAN WE NOT PUT OUT THE FLAGS? WILL YOU MARRY ME?'*

At last the long journey home for Alistair was nearly over. A message came to him on board that Sir Angus Mackenzie would be waiting at the Customs House in the Director's reception room.

The three years telescoped in Angus' warm handshake. Over the roast beef lunch, and the finest claret in any Liverpool cellar, Alistair felt at home again.

For the first half-hour they talked of everything *but* Felicity: the ship, the sea, the weather, Harvard, Boston, William James and Alistair's lectures, Grace, Moray Place and Lucinda. Now Angus felt the temperature was right for more intimate talk:

'And Felicity? I'm sure you know more about her than we do

here. Belinda and she have stuck it out valiantly these last three years. But Felicity's a good correspondent – and you too – so I believe. Thank goodness you've done more than write lectures and learned papers.'

'Well, Angus, there *is* something that even Grace doesn't know. I've proposed to her!'

'And not before time, if I may say so! And how long did she have to wait for that to travel across the ocean? Weeks?'

'Angus, you'll be surprised. I sent it by cable!'

'So all the Merchant Navy knows something we don't!'

'Not at all. I made up a simple code.'

'Well I'm damned! Alistair you sound like a reader of *Boys' Own Paper*! Has she said *Yes*?

'Well, she replied, not turning me down, by cable. I hope she's more excited than she sounded on the cablegram. I've been told, in no uncertain terms, that I've to see her father.'

'Good for her. She wouldn't have spent money on a cable if she were *un*certain, now would she? So when are you going?'

'As soon as I've said hello to Scotland. Next week, in fact.'

'Well, I met her father and mother on graduation day. You'll be surprised. You'd never think Arthur Hargreaves was Grace's brother, or that Gertrude was Felicity's mother, come to that.'

Angus wondered just what Alistair would make of them:

'There's a peculiar Yorkshire saying. I think it applies to you: *He'll charm the skin off a rice pudding.* And that's what you will do! Your *Doctor* title will help, especially with her mother. She looked a bit bewildered on degree-day. I don't think she'd seen doctors in caps, gowns and hoods before.'

'Angus, there's something more to my visit to Yorkshire. We Scots make railway fares earn their keep, don't we?'

They laughed easily together as if they were of the same clan, but Alistair's laugh betrayed nervousness.

'You're not thinking of buying a Yorkshire mill, old chap, to manufacture Fraser tartan?'

'It's serious, Angus, and here I really need your help.'

Alistair told Angus the story of Felicity's aunt and Barlockend, as he knew it. But he made it clear how little he knew.

'James's advice was to get hold of the medical record and, as he put it, *probe*.'

'He's right too. Who put her in?'

'The *loving* family,' Alistair said bitterly.

'Are they any better about treating and – and avoiding – insanity in America, Alistair? Did you have access to any asylums?'

357

'I only went into rather luxurious *mental* homes where fees were high. And of course both James and I lectured – God help us – on mental breakdown. But it's different when it's a relation of someone you know...'

'From my experience, and get this firmly in that head of yours, most cases of insanity are induced, not inherited!'

'Yes, that's James' view too. Angus, do you know anyone in Leeds who could give me some background on the place?'

'Go to the Leeds Infirmary and find out. Well, write to an ex-student of mine, Moynihan, first. I'll give you his address and an introduction.'

While he was doing so, the waiter entered and stood at his side.

'Excuse me, Sir Angus, the carriage is here to take you to your Edinburgh train.'

'Yes, Alistair, time we were off. You'll be glad to be in Scotland again.'

'Good-day, Sir! Thank you, Sir.' The waiter pocketed a generous tip; it was a good deal more than he expected from the gent with the Scottish accent.

Home seemed small and rather darker than Alistair remembered it, but Simpson had stayed on as servant to the visiting don and his wife who had rented the apartment. All was in perfect order but the August day suggested that 'auld reekie' had tired of the summer and would welcome an autumn breeze. The whole city was still, grey, smoky and unchanged, as if it did not know that he had been away.

He needed someone to talk to – and it was not Simpson. Grace was the nearest he could get to Felicity. He set off westwards and watched the filtered sun making a giant silhouette of the castle. It all signified *home* and he must try to make it so.

He was now at Moray Place, once more debating whether to clang the door-knocker or pull the bell. Either would trigger Sammycat into action. He lifted the brass dolphin knocker and let it fall. Sam's waterfall descent of the half-staircase was too quiet to sound through the imposing door, but the resultant scratching was familiar and friendly. Both Grace and Maggie were at the door, speaking in unison:

'Dr Fraser! Yer home!'

'Alistair! Welcome back!'

He was most truly *home*. And it seemed as if, in this house, he were a hundred miles nearer to Felicity.

Maggie rushed off to get tea. Grace ushered him into the drawing room then drew out a letter from her little boudoir desk. He tried not to show his eagerness to get it into his own hands:

'What a marvellous go-between you've been, Grace. Oh, it's good to be home!'

After a few words of welcome and enquiry, and a decent interval, Alistair said: 'Grace, has she told you? I proposed to her by cablegram from the ship.'

She showed no surprise at the news. 'And has she accepted you?'

'I wasn't exactly rejected. But in a few words, on a reply cable, she managed to rap me on the knuckles!'

'This is the *new woman*, Alistair; beware! But tell me, why?'

'I was commanded to see her father and, I suppose, in the social jargon, "ask for her hand".'

'Not the *new woman* at all,' Grace laughed. 'How long will it take, I wonder, for women to be independent? But, tell me, why do you want advice?'

He laughed. 'Well, it's a long time since I've been interviewed for a job. What will he want to know?'

'Briefly and bluntly, he'll want to know if you can keep her in the station to which she has been accustomed! I don't know, really. You'll have to be very pro-Yorkshire if you want him to consider his daughter marrying a *foreigner*!'

They laughed but there was nervousness edging through the laughter.

'When are you going, Alistair? May I make a suggestion?'

'Of course!'

'Why not stay with the Bennetts?'

'Do I know them well enough?'

'Of course you do. And, if I may say so, you need to get to know them better.'

Alistair did not understand why, but he liked both the doctor and his daughter.

Grace continued her role as go-between. 'Would you like me to make the approach? I have known them for years, and we tend to like the same people. If you want to see Felicity on her own, I suggest you avoid staying at Stonegarth. Her mother is corseted in convention. Felicity will be chaperoned every minute of the day.'

Alistair had never heard Grace utter a word of criticism of Felicity's parents before. He was slightly shocked. For some reason she was not as relaxed as when he'd arrived.

Grace knew that, if she did not use this evening, there would not be an opportunity before Alistair went to Stonegarth.

'Alistair, I have told you quite a lot of the Hargreaves/Ackroyd history, but there is an important part which I did not tell...'

Alistair picked up the cue quickly to cover her embarrassment. 'You mean Mrs Hargreaves' sister? The one certified for lunacy? Yes, Felicity told me. I think she thought I might want to sever our relationship.'

'Yes, Felicity is an extraordinary mixture of social confidence, self-doubt and fear. It was impossible to assure her that she need not have any fear of – inheritance – although that is perfectly true! But what I am going to say will need all your understanding. Felicity is not my niece, Alistair. She is my *daughter*!'

He was stunned into silence. Then, as he tried to understand, there gradually came over him a thrilling revelation. But of course, of course – they were so near, so right.

Many different emotions raced through his mind. How could one be appalled and exhilarated, at the same time? If only William James were at his side.

He pulled himself together, rose from his chair, went over to Grace, and held both her hands:

'Does she know?'

'No, Alistair! You see, all her life she has been their daughter. There was no question of adoption. They *are* her parents.'

'Grace, may I ask a very personal question? Why did you...'

'I know what you are going to say – part with her. It is a judgement that needs Solomon. Can you be very patient and very understanding? *Society* can be very cruel ... the stigma of being illegitimate would have scarred her for life.'

'I know, I know – people worship a God of all-embracing love but are miserly and selective in placing their own.'

'Oh, Alistair, forgive them. They inherit their prejudices and their morals, as we all do. We are all casualties, or benefactors, of our forebears and we inherit their codes.'

'But surely, Grace, the wonderful thing is that Felix's life is not over; it is *here*, in Felicity! And *your* life will go on now, through her and, I hope' – he hesitated – 'through our children.'

Grace was so overwhelmed that she could only look at him through tears of gratitude.

There was so much to say that they both fell silent until facing the future became insistent.

'Is she to be told, Grace?'

'Yes, her mother has agreed to do so, depending on marriage.

They decided that if she remains a spinster there would be no cause for her to be told. But the only one who could stop the marriage is her father. You'll not find that difficult; though, knowing my brother, he will appear to make it difficult out of pride. But, Alistair, you must realise that the *only* reason anyone is being told is because of your union with Felicity. Please understand that Arthur and Gertrude will always be her *parents*, addressed by us all as Felicity's father and mother. I shall always remain just *Grace*, her aunt and her godmother.'

It seemed as if the habit of twenty-three years had defined her role, which must remain unchanged. She was determined not to break down in front of Alistair.

'Get it firmly in your mind that the only people in the whole world who will ever know, my dear, are: Felicity, her parents, Jeremy Bennett, you and me. Henry has always had an elder sister. She will be his natural sister for life.'

'I understand. But part of me would like to proclaim her parentage from the housetops! When Felicity has been told, and she has recovered from the shock, she will be silently *proud*. Can just we three, you, Felicity and I, have a very private celebration of gratitude?'

Grace took his hand. 'Alistair, there have been times when I've thought of you as a genius but never, until now, as a *saint*! But may I say again that it all must end there? Felicity's parents are Arthur and Gertrude Hargreaves. Forgive my labouring the point. My brother and sister-in-law will want an elaborate wedding for their daughter. Please fall in with their wishes however irksome they may seem to you. Remember, in the church vestry her parents will sign the register. I shall be in the second pew on the opposite side to your parents. Either before or after the ceremony, you will introduce me as Felicity's *aunt*. Your parents must never be told anything that you and I have discussed today.'

He was amazed how calm and logical Grace had become once the truth had been revealed. Even with his training in psychology he failed to realise that she had been steeling herself for this kind of confrontation most of Felicity's life.

'And Alistair, you do not know anything of all this until Felicity herself tells you. It is her secret and only hers. I do not know whether we have been kind or cruel in keeping it from her all these years!'

3

Alistair Fraser left Edinburgh on the six thirty morning train on this memorable Sunday. After being shown to his first-class carriage, Alistair made for the Pullman dining car. Pristine starched linen tablecloths caught the sheen of the silver cutlery and the sparkle of a cut-glass vase holding white heather and white roses. Showers in the night, and now an early morning sun, turned Edinburgh's grey stone into silver. Alistair's apprehension had changed to exhilaration. Whatever might happen, he thought that the next few hours' journey to Leeds could be an agnostic's idea of heaven.

The white and gilded menu card included all the things that would be offered for breakfast in a gracious country house.

He alighted at Leeds feeling that he had had a brief holiday. The little train labelled *Ilkley* was standing ready for him. The vast steam engine was to pull just three coaches of corridor compartments past factories, mills and mean and mighty houses. Soon the train was flanked by banks of trees and bushes leading to the signboard *Barlockend*. He had never quite believed there was such a place until now.

The highlight of Barlockend was the unexpected glory of the grounds, and meeting Roberta. Alistair had not known what to expect of a woman who had chosen a paupers' asylum as her bridal home.

In the event he met a woman of such good breeding that she made no apology for the frugality of living space in the gatehouse which was a partner to the porter's lodge. She was neatly and perfectly dressed in quiet clothes made to last, rather as if she were an extremely articulate Quaker.

'My husband and I usually have Sunday dinner with the inmates, which means I give my whole attention to the women and Anthony to the men. I hope that joining us for this main meal of the week you will get an overall view of our life here.'

'I consider that a privilege, Mrs Thompson. Thank you very much.'

'I don't know whether you have heard but we have here a belief in music as cathartic for the insane. When we interview folk for jobs we always ask about musical talents. Sorry you will miss our Sunday afternoon concert, as that is the time you are meeting Mr Hargreaves.' Alistair felt he should have consulted the Thompsons before making his plans.

As Alistair contributed the expected small talk, he was thinking. Who does she look like? There was a portrait he had seen quite recently... Ah, I remember now, in a *Strand* magazine. It was Christina Rossetti.

He continued to answer her questions: on the journey: his arrangements for visiting Stonegarth later that day when he was going to see Felicity once again.

'Before we discuss Miss Ackroyd, may I talk about Felicity? Some time ago she wrote an extraordinary letter thinking I should want to throw her over, as there was lunacy in the family.'

'You haven't met her parents, have you? She is completely unlike them in her attitude to life and the way that she conducts herself. Facially she has a slight resemblance to her father, although I only see it when she is being either arrogant or stubborn.'

'Now, Mrs Thompson, you sound like her schoolmistress. But yes, I have seen her look defiant – but to me, attractively so!'

'Dr Fraser, may I suggest – though I know that this is our first meeting – that you call me Roberta. Then perhaps I shan't sound like a schoolmistress.'

'And you, Roberta, must call me Alistair and then I shan't sound like a doctor.'

They laughed gently into relaxed understanding. Her quiet voice confirmed their mutual trust.

'You are seeing Mr Hargreaves shortly. May I, if you agree, help to put you in the picture?'

'Of course – especially as I have to get his approval.'

'This county, Alistair,' she hesitated using his Christian name, 'although mainly agricultural, has the biggest woollen industry in the world. When Arthur Hargreaves inherited the mill it had dropped from five hundred workers to a hundred and fifty.'

'What caused the decline?' Alistair asked.

'Fierce competition and ageing machinery. Now he has three hundred worsted hands and some of the finest machines in the West Riding. His father and grandfather went to public schools and his sister, Grace, to a boarding school in Scarborough, but he left his local school at fourteen and went into the mill. His broad Yorkshire speech is compounded of defiance and pride. But he can, when he wishes, use his platform voice, which doesn't sound the least affected. It is just Arthur Hargreaves in his Sunday suit and still thoroughly Yorkshire.'

Alistair was fascinated by her shrewd description and said so: 'I suppose you mean cream on the apple tart instead of custard?'

'Pie, Alistair! A tart hasn't a top in Yorkshire!'

Alistair introduced the subject they had shelved.

'When I meet Miss Ackroyd is there anything I can give her as a present?'

'Strangely enough, for all her mental derangement and abysmal quality of life she is obsessively clean and wanders for hours round and round the wards as if washing her hands like Lady Macbeth. The other day when I visited her, she went stamping round the day room killing imaginary cockroaches. The only thing she ever asks for is a clean linen handkerchief. Felicity used to bring one every time she visited her and I followed the practice. I keep a small store here.'

She got up and opened a mahogany tea box.

'Please give that to her. Watch her fingers. She'll run them round the lace edging as if to test its quality.'

He looked at his hunter watch; time was going far too quickly for what he had to do.

'Would it be possible to see Miss Ackroyd now?'

'They're in the chapel. The service will be finishing soon. Let's go quickly before they come out. You'll be able to see her from the west door.'

As they reached the chapel door, Alistair whispered to Roberta: 'Where is Miss Ackroyd?'

'She's up there, in the gallery, on her own.'

Alistair looked up and saw a ghost of a woman on her knees bent over what looked like a Book of Common Prayer. Her whole sorry story seemed to be summed up in that desolate figure.

Roberta had arranged that Amy should be put next to Dr Fraser for Sunday dinner.

He joined the eight hundred or so in the refectory. Alistair was not to know that at least fifty inmates were manacled in solitary confinement or in padded cells, eating alone.

Alistair smiled at Amy and handed her the lace handkerchief. After rubbing her hand round the hem she looked into his face and recoiled, whilst the others at the table peered at this strange man's action. All conversation stopped. For ten minutes, after grace was said, Amy Ackroyd never answered one of Alistair's questions, but edged away from the man she had wrongly assumed to be Jack Fieldhead, who had stolen her sister away. Unlike the others at the table, she sat upright, held her knife and fork as she had done as a well brought up child, put finicky pieces of food in her mouth until she had eaten about half. She then replaced her knife and fork and wiped her mouth with the handkerchief that Alistair had given her and stared with anger into her enemy's eyes.

There was a sudden shout from the warden at the end of the long table: 'Amy Ackroyd! Eat up!'

The whole dining room was silenced. Those at the table watched her response. She glowered at her plate, then taking her fork, she violently shot the remains of the food into the large napkin on Alistair's lap, shrieking as she did it. 'Take it to Caroline. You're starving her.'

Two wardens rushed forward, grabbed the distraught woman and thrust her out of the room.

Roberta came to the rescue. Swiftly she folded the napkin over the remnants of the food, dropped it into the waste can before ushering the doctor through the visitor's door.

Alistair's best suit was only slightly soiled but Roberta, with more practical good sense than feminine decorum, was gently wiping this most intimate part of the man's body when her husband interposed.

'Roberta! Stand up! What do you think you are doing? I will take Dr Fraser to the staff washroom myself!'

Roberta, apologetic, but not the least ashamed, was thinking only of Dr Fraser's welfare: 'Why not go back to the Lodge? You have more than an hour before you need set off for Stonegarth. We always leave the doors open, the porter looks after the gates...'

'How kind of you! Please don't worry, Roberta. All I need is just a little quiet time. I shall be quite dry by the time I've walked down the drive! Please, never tell Felicity or Belinda! Felicity would be awfully embarrassed and Belinda would be wickedly amused!'

Alistair could hardly believe that he had only known Roberta for such a short time. Damp but clean, he followed the chaplain's flowing cassock out of the room, wondering whether he would be respectable enough to appear before Mr Hargreaves at three.

It was now two fifteen. Alistair had taken a brief leave of the

Thompsons, and of Roberta in particular, before he returned to stay the night as invited. He gave his hair a careful stroke, his shoes a rub on his calves, adjusted his tie, stroked his bowler hat, put on his gloves, and set off down the drive to the station, where he caught a train to take him to the next station: Aireley.

He paused by the closed village post office and silently saluted Miss Elsie. In a few minutes a *Beware of the dog* sign hinted that the five-barred gate was never left open. A large Airedale bounded up to the gate, proving the sign.

The maid who answered the door seemed rather more excited and welcoming than he had expected. She used his name with unexpected confidence.

'Come this way, Dr Fraser. The master's waiting for you. Can I get you a cup of tea?'

Arthur Hargreaves was wearing his newest and best worsted suit and a white carnation in his buttonhole.

'Yer surprised me, Doctor! I never 'eard t'station wagon or t'cab.'

'No Sir, the train was early, so I walked.'

'Sit thiself down, tha must be fair done up. 'Ow about a fill-up. Are yer a pipe smoker?'

'No, I'm afraid I'm not; though most of my doctor friends are.'

'Well sit thee down and mak yerself comfortable an let's 'ear wot our Felicity's been up to.'

'Your daughter, Mr Hargreaves, has done four years' gruelling work as a medical student. I have been away for three years working hard in America.'

'Ow come then tha knows 'er well enough ter think o' marriage?'

'Your charming sister, Sir, introduced me to her, when your daughter first arrived in Edinburgh. She joined Miss Hargreaves' musical circle, which I had known well for several years.'

'Well, ah'll grant yer our lass can play. But so she should, with all the teaching she's 'ad. And two pianos in the house! But let's come ter' t'point, young man. Tell uz wot yer offering. The missis and me know yer a doctor, an' that's about all! Wot sort of doctor?'

Alistair felt that he would have to show off to impress the man, otherwise he might lose his Felicity.

'I am a specialist, a consultant in psychology and psychiatry and have recently been researching in Harvard.'

'We speak blunt in Yorkshire! Dusta mean folk who'er off ther 'eads?'

366

'Well, yes, I suppose I do. Some of them! Others are just mentally exhausted.'

'An 'oo pays fer 'em? We've spent a lot o' good money in Bradford on such like and can't see we get aught owt of it.'

'If I may say so, Sir, it is a difficult subject, but if it reassures you, I am paid by the university at Professor level. So – I think – I could keep your daughter.'

'It's not just a matter o' keep, young man! 'Tis keeping 'er in t'style as we've brought 'er up in! She's 'ad everything she's wanted and more. Nowt's been spared for our Felicity!'

Alistair looked him straight in the face: 'In that case, Mr Hargreaves, you may want to give your only daughter a dowry. I should not be insulted, and I would make sure that she had a personal bank account.'

A sudden flash of appreciation of this young doctor came into Arthur's head. T'lad's got 'is 'ead screwed on, he thought to himself.

'Ah'll tell yer wot, ah'll give 'er three 'undred a year fer t'start and a 'undred more a year fer each bairn.'

'Mr Hargreaves, Sir, you've promised that before you've said I can marry her, but I appreciate that a Yorkshireman doesn't waste words!'

'An' ah'll tell yer this, yer don't want a father-in-law ter call yer *Doctor* now do yer?'

'No Sir, absolutely not, Sir! I'm Alistair.'

'And I don't want anyone else calling uz *father* and *mother*. Just *Arthur* and *Gertrude*. Well, it's all settled and we can go and tell missis in t'dining room. Cum and meet 'er. Tell 'er t'news thisen!'

Alistair followed Arthur into the dining room but was left to introduce himself.

'Mrs Hargreaves...' It was far too soon to say *Gertrude* and, looking at her, he could not imagine there ever would be such a time. 'I do hope you are happy to hear our good news!'

Gertrude, fiddling with her own engagement ring, blushed.

'Well, you know what they say, doctor, we'll be losing a daughter and gaining a son.'

Alistair cringed inside but outwardly charmed her with his smile without picking up the *son* cue. He had not quite recovered from meeting his in-laws.

Gertrude had set out the table for an elaborate knife and fork tea. He thought of another platitude *The way to a man's heart...* The sight reminded him of Sunday in Edinburgh where the

Sabbath was not a killer. He looked at the spread and commented: 'What a delightful welcome to your home.'

'Missus is known as t'best provider in Aireley,' Arthur replied. He looked down and saw the table was set for three, then turned to Gertrude. 'So where's our Felicity? I thought she'd want to know it's settled.'

'She's at the Bennetts'. Seems to live there. They're all right. I'm not complaining.'

Arthur dealt with a large pork pie and a roast ham, while Gertrude served the salad still fresh from the garden. There was trifle and a large treacle tart to follow. Yorkshire folk either talked for hours over Sunday tea, like the Bennetts, or, like the Hargreaves, treated it as a serious business where conversation grew only out of the food.

They *withdrew* at half past five, Gertrude back to her reading of the *Methodist Recorder*, while Arthur took Alistair to the drawing room and hall to show his future son-in-law the two pianos.

'An' wen's t'wedding ter be? But that's missis' job not mine...'

'I thought the last day of the year, Sir, with a brief honeymoon in York for one night and just a weekend in Edinburgh. Our real honeymoon will be in America later in the New Year.'

'Ee lad, yer must be daft! Wot about them icebergs in t'winter?'

Alistair laughed it off. 'These liners know their ocean, Sir. They sail well south.'

'Ah'll believe yer, thousands wouldn't.'

Alistair picked up his hat and gloves.

'Goodbye, Sir, and thank you very much for giving me Felicity. She's a wonderful woman. You must be proud to have a daughter like her.'

Suddenly all the bombast seemed to have deserted him and Arthur mumbled: 'Well by rights, she's not mine to give...' And then very softly with a sad smile: 'Yer can't own yer children, can yer now?'

Alistair left Stonegarth, intrigued by Arthur Hargreaves whose bluntness obscured the hurts and doubts of a sensitive man. The brief journey back to the Thompsons' Lodge by-passed the mill but Alistair could see its huge chimney, the massive letters spelling out AIRELEY MILL.

He did not accompany the Thompsons to evening service, excusing himself in order to prepare questions he wished to ask the medical officer the next morning. The chaplain held an envelope in his hand, which was obviously intended for Alistair.

'This was delivered while you were out – by the Bennetts' gardener. I know they are expecting you.'

'Would you excuse my opening it?'

It was a brief note:

Welcome to Airedale. As arranged by Grace we are expecting you Monday evening for dinner at seven o'clock or thereabouts and to stay overnight before you return to Edinburgh on Tuesday.

Jeremy is sorry he cannot drive you to Leeds for the train, but we will see that the family governess cart, and our groom, are at your disposal.

At breakfast the next morning, which Roberta had prepared herself, as the daily general did not arrive until eight thirty, conversation seemed limited by Anthony Thompson's sense of duty.

'Sorry I'm so late. There's been a suicide.'

Roberta frowned. 'Not Lawrence Singleton?'

'Yes. Yesterday they put him to work in the butchery and he smuggled a knife into his bed.'

Roberta turned to Alistair. 'Sorry – so sorry – we shouldn't have mentioned it, but he was our violinist...'

Her husband turned to her as cool and collected as an undertaker. 'Roberta, I have told you before. This house is too small for secrets. Dr Fraser is used to death, as all doctors are.'

And then looking at her weeping eyes, he said: 'And it's no time for tears. You will have to report on his customary behaviour when they come to do the post-mortem tomorrow!'

Turning to Alistair: 'Dr Mabbott will see you at nine thirty in his surgery. I shall absent myself since I feel that you will both be more free if I carry on my usual duties, which, this morning, include arrangements for a funeral service. Most of the people who die here are buried in our own graveyard, since few have relatives to claim their bodies.'

Roberta put in a word: 'Yes, there are hundreds of graves here; it's a sad sight.'

'Roberta, my dear, try to be more accurate. There are precisely one hundred and ninety-eight people buried here and twenty-seven in the parish grave.'

A whole relationship, Alistair thought, was summed up in that cold correction. The spirit will go out of her, just one inch at a

369

time, until it is all drained away. He had already noted how much more confident her speech was when her husband was not there!

'Please come back for tea,' she said after her husband had departed. It was more the appeal of a child needing comfort than a confident hostess. He took her hand.

'Of course I will, and perhaps we can talk about Felicity. She has a huge regard for your intellect and sensibility.'

They were words Roberta desperately needed to hear. At the Academy, at least she had been respected as a faithful teacher; here she was treated as a novice who had the good fortune to have an intellectual priest for a husband.

Alistair walked down the drive thinking that here was another woman like others in his casebook. Poor Roberta, whose hero was Robert Browning. Alistair wondered if she had ever read *Christmas Eve* and even now recalled 'the preaching man's immense stupidity'. But Anthony Thompson was not stupid. He used his erudition as a scalpel to remove any trace of confidence there might be in those less academic than himself.

Alistair was shown into the medical officer's waiting room, where *Punch*, going back to 1895, failed to give the room humour. He looked up as Dr Mabbott entered.

'Dr Fraser, good morning, I understand you are interested in the case of Amy Ackroyd.'

'Yes, doctor, she is related to my fiancée.'

'Are you – assuming the insanity may be passed on?'

'No, Sir, I think that is your assumption, not mine, She is not a blood relation.'

'I have looked out Miss Ackroyd's medical record. It is here in my surgery. Come through and I will give you all the help I can.'

They sat down opposite to one another so that Alistair was dependent on the doctor's interpretation of the small black spidery writing.

'How old is she, Doctor? I have seen her but I am sure she looks much older than her years.'

Mabbott turned to the relevant sheet. 'Er ... born in 1856. That makes her now forty-three and according to this record she was put in the asylum in 1887, aged thirty-one!'

'I am told by my fiancée that early the next year, the twin sister and her husband emigrated to New Zealand. Does anyone know the reason?'

370

'Dr Fraser, I speak now, not as a doctor, but as a friend of the Ackroyds' next-door neighbour. But I would rather you heard what is officially reported before you accept anecdotal evidence. Here are the remarks of the doctors who certified her. The second report, my own, adds little to these facts:

'"I was summoned to Mayfield House because her sister and brother-in-law said they could not cope with her. Miss Ackroyd was wildly excited and kept saying that her body was rotten from the waist down. She avowed that they had taken her soul away and rotted it. According to her the whole world knew that her body was rotten from the photographs which she imagined had been distributed. Her twin, Caroline, Mrs Jack Fieldhead, informed us that Amy had tried to kill her husband –" And now here's the strange phrase – "because of his purity".'

He looked up at Alistair:

'You're a psychologist, Fraser; whatever can she mean by *purity?*'

Alistair thought hard. 'Anything I say, Mabbott, is only supposition. Perhaps we can link the former remarks about her body being *rotten from the waist down* with this one about *purity?* Do you think she perhaps wanted a sexual relationship with him and he resisted her?'

'That must wait until you hear the anecdotal gossip. You are hearing *facts* now, Dr Fraser, not Freudian fancies.'

Alistair took the snub philosophically and wished that William James could be a listener to this strange story.

Mabbott was fingering the first two sheets of the official document. 'Shall we keep to the record, Sir, before we create answers?'

'Yes, of course,' said Alistair, 'but I must remind you, Doctor, it was you who asked the question!'

'So I did, Fraser, so I did! But we simple doctors think that psychologists ask questions to complicate the issue when a bottle of physic could move the trouble in days.'

Alistair cut in: 'And doctors never ask open-ended questions because they have their answers neatly bottled up!'

They fenced without malice. Mabbott returned to the reading:

'This is the *reason for certification* section. "She wanders round continually and refuses to sleep in the bed her sister had prepared for her in the spare room. Night after night she banged on the married couple's bedroom door which was locked."'

Mabbott raised his eyes from the script:

'I'll turn on to comments after her arrival here. Many of the remarks – sixteen pages of weekly reports – are repetitive. "Clean in her habits; cries a good deal; refuses food; refuses to answer

371

questions; wanders round calling out 'Caroline'. A remark she makes often is: 'Tell Nellie I'll be home for tea.'"'

Mabbott explained that Nellie was their living-in general maid. 'Another remark she says, after crying to our Lord Jesus is: "What's the use of a God who can't hear?"'

Alistair cut in on this. 'Well, Mabbott she'd every reason for saying that, hadn't she?'

Mabbott and Fraser eyed one another quizzically. Mabbott sat back, doubting Fraser's faith. He moved on through the record.

'Every week or so there are medical comments on the occupations that she is asked to do: "Too frail to lift wet sheets and blankets in the laundry" ... "This week she has attempted simple sewing but soon tires."'

Mabbott glanced up at Alistair. 'Only twice in the next few weeks are there any encouraging signs and they are contradicted. "Slight improvement" is followed the next day with "Demented behaviour". Pages more of it, Fraser, but this is tedious for both of us. It is time for my visits to bed-patients. If you will excuse me I will hand over the report for your own observation. Please keep it until you have extracted all you need.'

He lowered his voice to a whisper although there was no sign of anyone who could possibly hear.

'I'm giving you an important contact, which is in total confidence. Please destroy it when you have noted the name and address.'

After a formal exchange and thanks from Alistair, Mabbott left the room as if all of any consequence had been exhausted from the report. He had lost interest. After all, she was only one of more than eight hundred cases. *These psychiatrists get them one at a time, on a couch.*

Alistair opened the envelope and read:

There is an old servant: Nellie Beswick, in her eighties, who was a living-in maid to the Ackroyds before and after the marriage of Caroline and Jack Fieldhead – she can a tale unfold. I have told her that a doctor is coming to check on her rheumatism. Her address is 6 Leeds Road, Burley Woodhead. She expects you early this afternoon. Her daughter will come in to make a cup of tea.

The note was devoid of salutation or signature. Alistair memorised the name and address and destroyed the note. He enquired at the porter's desk for directions, and enjoyed the short journey through charming country and the good lunch at the local inn.

He knocked on the cottage door and was given a called-out welcome which was as warm as the small room from which Nellie Beswick rarely moved.

'Come thi' ways in, Doctor. Ee, I'm reet glad to see thi. I've nob-but few callers these days.'

Behind those words – which were her life story – there was a hint of the girl she had been. Her head, bent over her chest, made a letter C of her body. She creaked her head up slowly, to give her important visitor a smile.

Alistair went through friendly questions about her health and especially her rheumatism. The reply was ready-made, repeated as it had been now for over twenty years.

'Well, doctor, it's no use maithering about summat yer've got to live with, is it? Mi daughter's a good 'un, she'll be in with a pie or summat before t'day's out. Ah sez mi prayers each day an' tell 'Im a'm ready to go.'

Alistair felt humble in this little room. He wondered how to steer the conversation to the Ackroyds but decided to plunge in.

'Well, you've done your whack, haven't you, Nellie? I believe you were a wonderful servant to the Ackroyd family in Mayfield House. Do you remember the twins when they were young?'

'Ee, I don't half! Dressed alike they were reet up ter goin' to college. Just different sashes and ribbons, Caroline pink; Amy blue. Eee they were a pitcher!'

'And how long were you there, Nellie?'

'Reet up ter t'ouse bein' sold. Saddest day o' mi life, that was. Clearing up that empty 'ouse. But mi mind was on Amy. They tried not to let on that she was in t'paupers', but then I'd seen t'Black Maria take 'er off.'

'But the wedding, Nellie. Did you like Miss Caroline's bride-groom?'

'Like 'im or not, doctor, I never got over t'shock. Them twins 'ad never bin out o' one another's sight, even shared a double cradle they did. Their mother used to say: "Like two rosebuds on one stalk." An' their father used to put one under each arm an' kiss 'em in turn.'

'Sorry, Nellie, I'm making you talk too much. Have a little rest. There's lots for me to look at in this room.'

He got up to look at the framed photographs. There was one of the twins, aged about twenty, in their identical Sunday frocks. The next was of a wedding. Here the twins were separated: Caroline on her bridegroom's arm and Amy flanked by Arthur and Gertrude with two fussily dressed five-year-olds as brides-maids, nearer the bride. Alistair returned to Nellie, who pulled herself out of a snooze with a crackling snore. He gave her time to return to the Ackroyd world and to bring the tale forward.

'Tell me, Nellie, what went wrong?'

'Ow could it go right, luv? 'Er bringing a man not one 'ev uz 'ad ever set eyes on, into t'family 'ome. She wouldna 'ev done that if 'er pa and ma 'ad bin alive, would she now?'

'I suppose not, Nellie, but folk do some strange things when they're in love.'

'Listen, doctor, try to use your gumption! She brought 'im inter t'place those twins 'ad never left. Bedroom they'd played in. Bed they'd slept in all their lives ... together ... never parted! Just think of Amy, seeing a big man in the 'ollow yer've made with yer own body in yer own bed...'

'I do understand, Nellie, tell me what happened that they took her away?'

'They gave me t'job of taking 'er up each night to t'room we always called spare bedroom. I 'ad ter drag 'er screaming. Some nights I couldn't 'old 'er. She'd bang on bedroom door – locked like – and then she'd kick it and rattle t'knob. Ee, I'll never forget that last night! Miss Caroline and me was bottlin' t'marmalade we'd just made and Miss Amy crept up on 'er own. Ther wer a great row goin' on, with Miss Amy pushing 'im out of 'er place in t'bed and 'im trying to push 'er out. Ee what a job we had, Miss Caroline and me, carrying 'er to t'spare room!'

'Nellie, did you ever think that Miss Amy was jealous of her sister? That she ... envied her having a lov...'

Nellie picked up the cue with a speed which belied her age.

'Think on, doctor! When a lass gets over thirty she's on t'shelf and she'll git desp'rate. Miss Amy allus thote she'd niver be separated from 'er twin. Neither of 'em 'ad ever 'ad a man before. An' wot her sister 'ad, she 'ad to have, too.'

Alistair saw the old eyes drooping and rose to go. 'One thing I must tell you, Nellie! Miss Ackroyd calls out for you, telling you that she'll be home for tea. You must have meant much to her.'

Nellie gave a long sigh. 'Well, yer see, doctor, I was with 'er longer than 'er mother. There weren't owt about Amy Ackroyd I didn't know. Ee! Wot I could 'ave told 'em, but they niver asked me – niver asked owt. An' 'oo wuz I te tell 'em, any road?'

Was this why two doctors had been summoned the next day? To certify *Miss Amy Ackroyd, School teacher, Spinster of the Burley-in-Wharfedale Parish (March 15th 1887).* And condemn her to a life

374

sentence in the pauper asylum, Barlockend. And why Jack Fieldhead gave his notice in to the *Leeds Mercury*, and then spent the following day in the emigration office in Liverpool?

Alistair returned to the Lodge, thinking that he had got more from Nellie Beswick than he would ever discover from the medical report. Too late for tea with Roberta, he quietly washed and changed, then prepared himself for dinner with the Bennetts.

4

'That's the doctor's house, Sir, that white'en. Do you want surgery? That's at far end. Yer all right. Ee's never in a rush. Should be there. It's just comin' up seven. Time to close, but he never does.'

Alistair didn't interrupt the woman, whose friendly curiosity about a stranger made her garrulous. He smiled but gave nothing away.

'Thank you! Good-day!'

He went towards the front door, aware that his guide had turned round and was standing still to check which door he was using.

Belinda was there before the hanging bell had finished its clanging.

'Alistair! I can't believe it! You're here! You've not met my mother, have you? Darling, this is Dr Fraser.'

'*Alistair*, please, Mrs Bennett.'

'That won't be difficult, I've been hearing that name for years.'

There was no ice to break; no awkwardness in adjusting to one another; just so much to ask and to hear.

'My husband is still in the surgery, but he asked me to give his apologies.'

'Thank you! Please don't hurry him. I know what happens to generous doctors. Hours aren't counted.'

But how could he get Dr Bennett on his own? he wondered.

Belinda took over. 'You walked from the station? Are you exhausted? Come upstairs to the drawing room and have some of Mamma's lemonade. Papa will give you something stronger when he's finished.'

It was vital that he saw Jeremy Bennett on his own.

'Would you mind if I just slipped down to the surgery? We doctors are always interested to see where the work is done.'

'Of course not!' Hazel led the way and left the two together. Alistair was pleased to see that Jeremy was locking the surgery door. After cordial greetings, during which they both recalled

376

their brief meetings in Edinburgh, Alistair came quickly to the point.

'Dr Bennett, could you tell me if Felicity is here? Neither your wife nor Belinda mentioned her name.'

Jeremy lowered his voice in conspiracy. 'Just be hugely surprised. It's a secret!'

'Could you spare a few minutes before we return to the house – before I meet Felicity?'

'Of course. My family is used to my unpunctuality.'

' I want you to know that Grace has told me the whole story.'

'And my part in it?'

'Of course.' The answer encapsulated his depth of friendship with Grace.

'You do know I brought Felicity into the world? Well, two worlds really.'

Alistair nodded then spoke into Jeremy's eyes with deep feeling: 'I want you to know that I am grateful – just inexpressibly grateful and, I can only say it to you and Grace, overjoyed.'

Tears of relief came into Jeremy's eyes. 'It's what I hoped to hear, but never really believed it could happen. You and I both know Grace well. Felix and I were undergraduates together, I was to be their best man...'

'I think you have been that for a quarter of a century. I met Grace ten years ago when I was an immature undergraduate. I worshipped her. She gave me the confidence in myself I most desperately needed. She also, without realising it, showed me what genuine love, not just falling in love, should be.'

'Yes, she listens with her heart, doesn't she?'

'And responds with it, too,' said Alistair.

Jeremy put the final question: 'You've seen her more recently than I. Has she told Felicity?'

'No, and I don't think she should. But you know more about what goes on at Stonegarth than I do. Have her parents told her?'

'No-one has. It has to be Gertrude, her mother for all these years. But tonight, Alistair, all that you disclose is that her father has agreed to your marrying her. The rest, for all of us, is silence.'

They returned to the house, Hazel greeted them.

'He's not had you dispensing medicines I hope?' She made light of their lateness, knowing that both had much to discuss. Belinda came towards Alistair looking radiant.

'We've kept dinner late, and given Cook an evening off – so it's not quite ready. Would you like to sit in the conservatory, Alistair? There's a letter there for you. I hope you don't think I'm prying but I couldn't help recognising Grace's handwriting and the Edinburgh postmark. There – through the dining room.'

As Alistair moved through into the conservatory he saw a haze of blue and lavender. And there she was with her back to him, half-hidden by an orange tree.

'Felicity!'

She turned and did not move towards him, but simply lifted her arms in a curve of welcome.

'Alistair!'

He drew into her soft silk warmth. 'Don't try to talk, darling.' He put his fingers gently on her lips. 'Just don't try to talk;' he whispered.

He took his fingers away from her lips and put them tenderly on her cheeks to trace the tears away.

Felicity smiled into his eyes. 'What funny creatures we are. You are crying too.'

It was a long-delayed meeting of lips. Time did not exist. The rest of the world was far away. He took her in his arms and led her to the old wicker sofa with its deep cushions.

'Darling, I've seen your father. I thought we got on well. All is settled.'

She still questioned him with her eyes. 'He's not an easy man to know, but oh, Alistair, I do hope you liked him.'

'He's not at all the thick-skinned man I'd expected to meet. In fact he seemed rather nervous. And finally very humble.'

He wondered whether to repeat her father's last remark but decided *not* to do so, since it would not mean anything to her – yet.

Alistair pulled a small silk sachet out of his brocade velvet waistcoat pocket, opened it, and held out a ring:

'I've carried this next to my heart for a fortnight, my sweet. May I put it where it belongs?'

He slipped it on the third finger of her left hand:

'I love you and plight thee my troth.'

Felicity looked at the ring in amazement. 'You are an absolute marvel, Alistair! Where on earth did you find a ring exactly like Grace's? I've coveted that for years! Not seriously, of course, because it was where it belonged.'

'My dearest, it *is* Grace's ring. She insisted that we should have it and that you should wear it, not just as an engagement ring, but...'

Felicity almost shouted protest: 'But it is Grace's! Her link with her lover who died. I cannot accept it, Alistair. It is part of her.'

378

'Listen, my darling. Grace said, "When Felicity comes to Edinburgh I will explain why I have given it to her." Try to understand and...'

The dinner gong interrupted the argument. Alistair kissed the ring, then, with his arm round her shoulder, they went through the conservatory door to the dining room. The three Bennetts, a few seconds ahead of them, were taking up glasses of elderflower wine. They raised them in unison.

'To Felicity and Alistair!'

Jeremy handed glasses to the two who had been toasted and in so doing looked at Felicity's hand. He turned to Alistair.

'Ah, I see you've given her the ring. Felicity, do show it to Hazel and Belinda. There never has been an engagement ring in all the world encircling so much love. I knew the man who chose it, and now I know the man who has been entrusted with it. Best of all, the four of us know you, Felicity: the woman whom both men have honoured.'

It was a long speech for Jeremy. Hazel sensed his emotion and brought them all back to earth.

'Come and eat, my dears. You must all be famished.'

It was a lively dinner. Conversation passed, as it should, from one to another, in turn and together, but it was Alistair, of course, who was the one they turned to most.

Hazel and Belinda bombarded him with questions about his voyage.

'And the food, Alistair? Was it the most *haute* of all *cuisines* you've ever eaten?'

'Oh yes, very grand. But rather too much of it.'

Alistair, holding his glass, praised the wine, which was accompanying local duckling with sauce made from their own black cherries.

'May we three, Hazel, Jeremy and I, with this excellent claret, praise Felicity and Belinda for their hard work and final success.' He turned to Jeremy and Hazel. 'We know what a backbreaking course it is, don't we? To Felicity and Belinda and the Edinburgh Medical School.'

As they sat down again, Hazel sparked off conversation with further enquiries about Alistair's ocean journeys. Felicity, because she already knew more than the others, concentrated on listening. Jeremy wanted to talk about knots per mile, weather conditions and the calibre of the captain and his crew. Belinda had some searching questions about American women: their status, intellect, independence and their exclusive social register. By the end of

379

Belinda's brainstorming, Hazel felt that it was time for a little light relief.

'So many of our top men in politics and society have married dazzling American women. What have they got that we over here seem to lack?'

Alistair felt that it was time for thanks to the Bennetts and a compliment to Hazel.

It was easy to reply to Hazel's question. He turned to her daughter.

'Belinda, if, in twenty-five years' time, you are as handsome and charming as your mother, I hope you will be matron of honour at our silver wedding. As for American women, Hazel, you could hold your own at the White House with any First Lady of America!'

Alistair waited for the laughter to die down, then took Felicity's hand and raised her to stand next to him.

'There is one person, not with us tonight, who, one way or another, is closely related to us all. Jeremy and Hazel, you have known her longer than any of us and comforted her in her sorrows. Belinda, you have gloried in her friendship and inspiration. Felicity, you have had her love and guidance all your life. I, as a gauche but ambitious undergraduate, owe any success I've had to her. She took me into her world of music as I think I took her into mine. I ask you to rise and drink a toast to a very special lady. *Grace.*'

Each of the five had different memories. Jeremy could not help but look at the sacrificial ring. Hazel looked at the tears in Felicity's eyes. Belinda looked at Alistair and thought he was the only man she had met to whom she would entrust her Felicity. They sat down again to the table which Sarah had cleared ready for the bilberry mousse and Wensleydale cheese. Conversation picked up where it had left off. Jeremy had kept his important question to the last.

'And when is William James coming over here, Alistair? I hear it is being discussed in high places.'

'He has a lot of commitments. But he definitely is coming. He and I have discussed lectures that would be well received. Don't pin me down on this, but it should be in a couple of years' time.'

It was a cue for Felicity to say something quite important. So far her role had been the guest who listens and draws other people out.

'Has Alistair told you yet – no of course, how could he? But we

380

are hoping to have our real honeymoon in America, later in the New Year.'

There was an outburst of interest and surprise. Belinda's was the strongest voice.

'But when did you arrange all this? We don't even know the date of your wedding.'

Felicity spoke quietly. 'Well really, neither do we – exactly. But we do write to one another, you know. Alistair had a letter waiting for him in Edinburgh from me and I had a letter from him, which I only opened yesterday. Alistair, can we assure our dear Bennetts that they will be the first to know our plans?'

'Yes, my love, if you and I are ever to meet long enough to *make* plans.'

This gave Hazel her cue. 'While you've all been talking, I've been thinking.' She turned to Alistair. 'Do you *have* to go back to Edinburgh tomorrow?'

'I suppose not really. All the welcome-back rituals are over. I've no lectures for four more weeks and I think Simpson would rather like to have the house to himself, especially since its owner has been endlessly unpacking!'

'Well, I propose that you stay here for as many days as you wish.'

Belinda broke in. 'What a marvellous idea, Mamma. We'll see that Felicity and Alistair have time to talk, won't we?'

It was typical of Hazel, Jeremy thought. 'Trust your mother to come up with practical good sense.'

He turned to Alistair.

'It will not only be a great pleasure for us, but I think you will be needed.' He thought of what lay ahead.

Felicity piped up in more conventional language than was reeling in her head: 'Thank you, Mrs Bennett, how kind of you. But I must be going. My parents expect me home before nine o'clock and it's turned half past eight already.'

Jeremy put an arm round Felicity and tossed the question to his daughter: 'Do you hear that, Belinda? *Before* nine o'clock.'

'Dear, dear Papa, you know that if I am late it is only when I am out with you and Mamma at a concert, or a theatre or a political meeting.'

He grinned and turned to Felicity. 'My dear, I'm taking you home; it's Tom's evening off, which I insisted he took. I hope you don't mind the trap and Belinda's headstrong Peggy.'

He turned to Alistair.

'I think we need your company, old chap. It's not done for a young lady to be out with a groom, on her own, at this time of the night! We do need a chaperone, don't we Felicity?'

This ingenious move in the Bennett plan was just the right note on which to end a memorable evening.

The farewells and thanks could have gone on all night, but Jeremy was sensitive to the Hargreaves' family rules.

'Just give me a few minutes to harness Peggy. Hazel, could you get the thick rugs for the trap and bring our special passengers to the back door.'

'It's a beautiful evening, but just a bit chilly,' she said to the two starry-eyed lovers standing next to her, sharing the night. Jeremy brought the trap up to the door and when the two were seated he wrapped one rug over their four knees.

'There, there,' he said, as if they were a couple of his married patients. 'Keep each other warm.'

It was the longest, closest time together that Felicity and Alistair had ever had, but both were too well brought up to embarrass Jeremy with their togetherness. Clasped hands closed the physical gap of the last years. As he caressed the ring encircled round her finger, a frisson of sheer rapture ran through their bodies from the four hands. It was a night which would return in their remembering for many years to come.

The occasional words they spoke were courteously inclusive of Jeremy. Felicity, relishing the drive, said: 'I love this pony and trap. It reminds me of the wonderful times Belinda and I had exploring the Dales.'

'Yes, Peggy is a match for Belinda. Headstrong, like her mistress!' It was said with admiration not pride.

Alistair, seeing the starlight in Felicity's eyes glanced heavenwards. 'Look, darling, have you ever seen Venus look so bright? It's your star, radiant with love.'

Jeremy did not hear the words, just the caressing whisper and sensed that the parting at Stonegarth would hurt.

'Before we arrive, my dears, can you settle when you are to meet again? Felicity, what about Belinda coming over for you tomorrow and bringing you back for lunch?'

'Oh that would be heaven, but, Dr Bennett, it is the week before harvest festival and Mother really counts on my help.'

'My dear girl, when you are living in Edinburgh, or honeymooning in America, your mother will have to do without you, won't she?'

'Yes, but that makes her feel that I should be with them as much as possible now. Doctor, will you do me a big favour? You know that my mother always accepts your word as gospel, so will *you* ask her?'

It seemed incredible to Alistair that four years' independence of her mother had given Felicity so little autonomy. He kept quiet but noticed that Jeremy's agreement to talk to Gertrude was taken for granted.

Jeremy halted the trap at the front gate. 'Alistair, you stay where you are. Best not to be seen.'

As Alistair gently kissed Felicity goodnight, neither of them saw the dark cloud passing over Venus but they felt the star disappear. Jeremy took Felicity's arm and led her up the drive to the front door.

'Don't bother to ring,' she said. 'Father doesn't lock up until half past nine.'

Gertrude's welcome had more relief than warmth in it. 'So here you are. Not before time either. You've no idea, Doctor, how worried Father and I get when she's out late.'

Jeremy sighed. 'Well, I suppose worry is a sign of affection, Gertrude, but your daughter is going to be twenty-three next week. Can you just try to let her grow up?'

Gertrude had mixed feelings, touched that he remembered September 18th, but put out that he still dominated her.

'Tomorrow, Gertrude, Dr Fraser will still be with us. Now that Arthur has consented, and the two are formally engaged, it is important that they get to know one another and make plans.' He turned to Felicity. 'Belinda will be here with the trap to collect you at eleven thirty and bring you to lunch.'

Gertrude was still put out but was reduced to a feeble complaint: 'We've only got a few days before the harvest festival. I need her help.'

When Gertrude bored him, Jeremy could change the subject in a flash.

'You've given me an idea! What about Dr Fraser staying over next weekend? I am sure your future son-in-law would like to see your lavish harvest display and enjoy the singing. What a splendid way to feed the village gossip!'

Felicity claimed an early night. She had wondered whether she would try to have a friendly chat with her mother and show her the ring, but decided it was not the right time. She would wait until tomorrow.

Gertrude had intended, if Felicity had come home earlier, to have the dreaded talk with her daughter. She decided it was not the right time. She would wait until tomorrow.

Arthur was going through his usual routine. Gertrude was in bed.

'So did yer tell 'er?'

'How could I, Father? Jeremy Bennett did all the talking. There wasn't much of the evening left and Felicity went straight to bed. It wasn't the right time.'

'It never is, I reckon. It's fourth time tha'z said it wuzn't right time.'

He was tired – not in the sense of needing sleep, but rather of being too tired to make the effort to keep awake. He would drop the subject. He pecked his wife goodnight and they both turned back to back as if they were two strangers.

Felicity missed the morning dressing sessions in Mrs Mac's house, which she and Belinda had shared as a lively prologue to the day ahead. Now, in Stonegarth, she made it her business to be up early and down to breakfast as bidden by the gong. Today, whilst giving herself a final check, the cheval glass reflected the ring. She hesitated whether she should wear it or not. Breakfast was not the time for display so she put the ring in her pocket.

Meanwhile Gertrude, having sewn new lace on her favourite morning dress, sized herself up longer than usual in her mirror, then remembered with a start that this had to be the day she talked to Felicity. Yes. It must be today.

Breakfast followed the usual pattern, three well-primed silver chafing dishes, two large racks of toast and enough butter pats and home-made marmalade for a cricket team. For Arthur, the food, the *Leeds Mercury* and the morning post precluded conversation, except for one remark to Felicity.

'I might go to Headingley tomorrow. It's last match of t'season. Are you interested, lass?'

'Sorry, Father, I've arranged to go to the Bennetts'. My fiancé is to be there. It's a chance to see him.'

'And what's wrong with meeting at Stonegarth, your own 'ome, I'd like to know? Your young man seemed to like it from what he said.'

'Of course he did, Father. Did you like him?'

'Well, he seemed to have his head screwed on, like. He saw nowt wrong with me giving you a dowry.' Felicity flushed. It didn't sound a bit like the Alistair she knew. There was a silence whilst her father read the paper and her mother put the leftovers from the three silver dishes on to a plate for Leo.

No wonder, thought Felicity, he's got so fat.

Gertrude turned round from the sideboard and addressed her daughter.

'I've got a new autumn outfit for the harvest festival, luv. Would you like to see it? Leave the things, I don't believe in making the servants idle. It's what my mother always said. No use keeping a dog and barking yourself.'

Felicity followed her mother to the master bedroom. Hilda was stroking the white counterpane into the ship-shape demanded by her mistress.

'Do the dusting later, Hilda. I've something I want to show Miss Felicity.'

The expensive garment was hanging outside the wardrobe.

'Don't bother to put it on, Mother, I can see that it is just your taste and very feminine.'

Gertrude had no intention of undressing in front of her daughter. That remark was ignored.

'I suppose you mean ladylike. Well, I always go to the model gowns floor in Brown Muffs, not the common frocks department. You can't go wrong then – can you?'

Gertrude pursed her lips into critical approval of her own good taste. Then remembering the real reason for summoning her daughter, her face sagged in and flushed with fright.

'Stay a few minutes, Felicity. I've got to have a talk with you.'

'Of course, Mother.'

They sat together on the velvet sofa, not making eye contact. Felicity, assuming that her mother wanted to talk about the wedding, asked: 'Would you like to see my ring, Mother?'

'Of course I would. That's the best part of getting engaged, surely.'

Felicity took it out of her pocket and held it in front of her mother, who exploded.

'But that's your auntie's ring! I'd know it anywhere! How come you've got it?'

'Aunt Grace gave it to – Dr Fraser – to give to me.'

'Well I'm blowed. Couldn't he afford one himself?'

Felicity had never thought that anyone could misinterpret this gift. How ever could she explain the deep love? The tragedy of the one who died? The ring with all its memories which Grace had treasured all these years?

She felt crushed at the insult to Alistair.

'I think Grace wanted Alistair and me to take the sadness out of it.'

The words floated unheeded into space. The sight of the ring brought Gertrude's blood pressure to danger point but also gave her courage.

'Will you promise never to wear it?'

Felicity thought hard before she replied.

'No, Mother. That would be hurting three other people apart from myself.'

Gertrude was fiddling with her own wedding ring, conscious that she had alienated her own daughter into the wrong mood for receiving the news. She softened her voice to get round her daughter's stubbornness, as she had done many times over the years.

'Couldn't you just wait until you know *why* you mustn't ever wear it? We're taking about your auntie Grace – and me.'

Felicity was confused. 'Mother, I just do not understand. You're not even her sister. She's *Father's* sister. You never knew aunt Grace's fiancé, did you? According to everyone, he was a splendid man and she was heartbroken when he died. You and Father surely remember the tragedy. It happened just a few months before he and Grace were to be married.'

'Well, she seems to have told you a lot. What else has she told you?'

'Oh, that he died of cholera in India and that it was weeks before she knew.'

'Well, she didn't do badly out of his will, I can tell you; that big house and everything that was in it.'

'Yes, I knew that. Did aunt Grace show you his study when you were there? It is full of his memories.'

'No, we were shown what she wanted us to see, I suppose. Nothing private.'

The dialogue lapsed into dual discomfort. Each was wondering what to say next, or if, in Felicity's case, anything more should be said at all. It was Gertrude who changed the subject, so abruptly that Felicity was taken off her guard.

'Listen, Felicity, to your mother. I've never told you about the struggle I had to get you. All I wanted was a baby. And it wouldn't come. My mother said to me, and I'd no idea what she was talking about, "Always oblige your husband in the bedroom", and I did. I gave myself to him night after night. It wasn't natural, not natural at all. God never intended us to have a child – well not then.'

Felicity thought that she could help out by using medical terms and medical discipline.

'Did you have to have a caesarean operation? Or instruments? Or was I induced in some way?' She could hardly believe that it was her own voice she was using, and to her mother.

'No. I told you I didn't have a baby... Well not until our Henry came three years later! Don't you see?'

Felicity could see there was only one alternative. 'So I was adopted then, was I?'

'Not really. Not by law you weren't.'

'Oh, Mother, why can't you tell me the truth instead of all this secrecy?'

'Father and I were never going to let on, but now you are going to be married I've got to tell you. Listen, luv, I never carried you.'

Felicity kept calm. 'I've gathered that.'

'But I've been your mother for all your life and intend to be for the rest.'

'Of course, nothing can change that. But Dr Bennett said *he* brought me into the world. So this person, whoever she may be, lived round here?'

'No, but far enough away for no scandal.'

'Do you mean by that, I am illegitimate?'

'Don't *ever* use that word! You came of a very good family with a good name...'

'What name?'

'Well, if you must know, *Hargreaves.*'

While Gertrude lapsed into weeping silence, questions and answers were going through Felicity's mind. She remained sitting, her eyes travelling round and round a patch of carpet pattern.

'Leave me by myself, Mother. I don't want to talk about it any more.' Then, glancing up, she saw her mother's distress and got up, kissed the pink swollen face, and, in her role as doctor, not daughter, she said: 'You've been very brave. Go and lie on your bed for an hour or two. I'll leave you and go to my room. There are things I must think about on my own.'

She didn't have to be told the truth; her own intuition and logic pieced it together. It could only be Grace. The shock of illegitimacy dominated her thinking but gradually her love of Grace eased the pain. Anguish returned when she realised that Alistair would have to be told. One thing she could never expect him to do was to marry an illegitimate woman. Whatever he felt, there would be fierce objections from his family. She would put it all in a letter and give it to Belinda when she came tomorrow. Would she ever have the courage to visit the Bennetts again? She would confide in Belinda. But, deep in her heart, she knew that what she most needed was to get back to Edinburgh and talk to Grace.

And the ring? That must be returned to Alistair at once. Belinda could take that too.

Belinda arrived promptly at eleven-thirty driving the trap like a triumphant Boadicea. She had purposely not invited Alistair to accompany her. A time alone with Felicity was almost a hunger. The return journey tonight would be different. She planned to be the accomplice driver giving the two lovers their precious time together.

Hilda was at the door before the bell stopped clanging. 'Miss Felicity's up in 'er room, Miss Bennett. Can't understand 'er. Not speaking. Not like 'er at all. Go up, you know the way. See what *you* can make of 'er.'

Belinda knocked and entered in one movement. Felicity was sitting at her desk in her morning frock. There was no sign of hat, coat or gloves. She half turned.

'Sit down, Belinda, there is something I must tell you and you must know.'

'All right, but remember we are due for lunch.'

'I'm not coming for lunch – you will soon understand why.'

Felicity started the story at her mother's outburst on seeing the ring and in a few sentences came to the word *Hargreaves*. She paused, and for the first time, looked Belinda in the eye.

Belinda, holding Felicity's hand, had listened to her news in sympathetic silence but without comment for ten minutes. She showed no sign of shock or surprise but could not help a sigh of relief spreading over her face. Felicity interpreted it as Belinda's usual outdoor glow.

'So, Belinda, to put it in one crude word: I'm *illegitimate*. Here is a letter for Alistair, freeing him from our engagement. I am not coming to lunch. Please go.'

Belinda was thinking quickly; she understood Felicity well enough to know that no argument would alter her decision; Belinda realised too that, without Alistair, nothing could be resolved.

Felicity expected sympathy, not Belinda's rebuke.

'All right, my dear, stay here. How little you know of your man. And how little you understand of Grace. You should be down on your knees thanking God for what you have inherited.'

388

It was cruel, she knew, but Felicity must be brought to her senses, and quickly.

Without a farewell word she swept out of the room. Never had the pony and trap been driven away with such speed.

She found Alistair reading in the little conservatory, chewing a few black grapes he had picked from the Bennetts' rather wild vine.

'Alistair, Felicity is not coming. She's had bad news. She sent this letter!'

As he opened it, the ring fell out of the envelope to the floor. Belinda picked it up and, without a word, put it on the stool at his side.

'Excuse me, I'll just explain to Mamma about lunch. The trap is at the door ready for you, if that is what you want.'

She went off, leaving Alistair reading the note. He was almost behind her back as she went through the kitchen. She was addressing her mother.

'You and Papa have your lunch. We're going back for Felicity. Don't worry. Everything will be all right.' She had predicted Alistair's response.

He and Belinda had never been alone together before but they both had an intuitive way of thought-catching.

'Would it help if I drove?' he asked.

'No thank you, Alistair. Peggy can read every breath of mine and sometimes she's too impulsive for her own good.'

Time was short and there was far too much to say, but they exchanged a few thoughts when they were well on their way.

'Are you shocked, Alistair?'

'Oh no, not at all for myself. But I am worried for Felicity. Grace told me everything. Am I being callous?'

'Papa told me a week ago. Oh, Alistair, isn't it the most incredible news?'

'Belinda, whatever is the matter with Felicity? How could she doubt me? But I must be careful not to show too much delight in the news. My affection for Grace must not seem to be a criticism of her Arthur and Gertrude.'

Belinda slowed the trap down. 'Alistair, you and I are being quite egotistical in our reaction. We're making it into a fairy story. Felicity will *need* time to get over just the stark fact that she is illegitimate. It may take years for her to have the inner vision to appreciate how much she has *gained* by being Grace's daughter.'

'But why this obsession about the reaction of my people? She's not even met them! My mother's Fabian lot has little truck with the conventions of this Victorian age.'

Belinda was quick to defend her friend. '*Do* realise, Alistair, that it is not easy for a girl brought up in a Methodist stronghold of the West Riding to flout conventions. The God they worship has set out a list of taboos.'

'Quieter, Belinda! Do you realise you're shouting out these things over the noise of the hooves and wheels!'

It was odd that they were both smiling when they turned into the gates at Stonegarth but their expressions quickly changed as they stopped at the front door.

'You wait in the trap. I'll get her from her room. I'll only come for you if I need force.'

She found Felicity busy writing to Grace.

'Belinda! What *are* you doing here?'

'Come quickly, Felicity! Alistair's destroyed your letter! He's in the trap waiting. Don't argue. Here's your bag. You don't need hat or gloves. Just take this wrap for the drive back.'

'I must tell Mother.'

'No, you needn't. They know you are supposed to be at lunch with us, anyhow.'

Alistair was standing in the trap ready to pull her in. There was nothing sentimental about the gesture; it was just a job to be done.

Gertrude was at the dining room window, Arthur at the rose garden gate and Hilda, disturbed by the noise, had rushed to the front door and all were watching the trap disappear.

Too much had happened for talk. Alistair waited until they were well clear of Stonegarth before he even took Felicity's hand. He noticed Belinda was slowing down the trap.

'Do you mind if I call at the post office? Elsie has something that needs my signature.' She edged the trap through the open gate on to the little lawn outside the cottage back door. Only Belinda could have devised such an oasis of quiet for two lovers. She headed for the back door.

'Shan't be long!'

Alistair put his hand in his pocket and drew out the ring and smiled down into Felicity's face.

'Do you remember the singing game we acted when we were children?

390

'Now put your left hand out, my doubting darling, and see for yourself where this ring belongs.'

Her tears, held back for hours, now had their chance to flow.

'Never, never take it off, Felicity. It is not just an engagement ring – that would be easy to buy any time. This is a symbol of supreme love. It is from Grace to you.'

He held both her hands in both of his, then took one away.

'Here's a clean handkerchief. I'll leave you to dry your eyes while I tell Belinda and Miss Elsie that they can stop writing signatures!'

The rest of the journey was bathed in reconciliation and understanding. Belinda's talk was tactfully directed to Peggy with a few mild curses thrown in. Alistair did most of the whispered talking.

'The cruel letter you wrote to me is in shreds in the Bennetts' waste-paper basket. But it has alerted me to the need for you to meet my mother. You'll understand her if you know that she is a kindred spirit of Olive Shreiner's. Have you read her book, *An African Farm?*'

Felicity felt it was important to draw Belinda into the conversation for it was she who had made this miracle happen.

'No, I haven't. Have you read it, Belinda?'

'No, I haven't either. Reading medical tomes for years makes one positively illiterate.'

The remark brought the three down to earth and into a very late lunch with all emotions civilly controlled.

Hazel came in apologising for the cold meal, which needed no apology. It was an attractive cold collation.

'Belinda, my dear, I'm taking some magazines and journals to the women's wards in the infirmary this afternoon. If you can spare the time, it would be such a help if you came with me.'

Hazel and her daughter knew one another so well that Belinda caught the intention behind this remark. Immediately, she turned to Felicity.

'I'm sure you two have lots to talk about which doesn't need me. Would you excuse me if I go?'

There was agreement all round. Alistair and Felicity both disguised their pleasure.

Hazel was amused at her daughter's mental agility. Belinda was admiring her mother's ingenuity.

The two lovers were on their own at last, both determined to avoid the vital subject.

'Alistair, do you mind if we have a walk first? We have many years to re-trace. What about the Five Rise Locks? I'll show you where Leo had to be rescued.'

'Dearest, Felicity, I'll just follow you wherever you go! It's all new to me.'

'Don't make rash promises, Alistair, I might lead you astray! What a pity Leo isn't here!'

An easy companionship had grown between them in the Bennett's house and it seemed symbolic that the Five Rise part of the canal was mid-way between the Hargreaves and the Bennett houses. All Felicity's talent as a raconteur came to life as she described Leo's imprisonment in the bottom of the lock and the efforts made to rescue him. So vivid was her recall that Alistair felt that he was inside the barge, smelling the bargee's tobacco, Leo's steaming coat and the strong tea. Felicity explained the effect it had on her:

'You can imagine, now you've been there, how Stonegarth seemed too bland, too clean and polished after the weather-beaten affection of the barge. Alf and Aggie tossed swear words into their talk as terms of endearment, but one knew their bond of love would never be broken.'

Alistair listened entranced. He sensed she was comparing the bargees with the master and mistress of Stonegarth.

'Now you have mentioned your Stonegarth, Felicity, may we talk about the parents who brought you up? Remember they will soon be my parents-in-law.'

Felicity butted in. 'Alistair, there is no *law* in it at all. My birth is illegitimate.'

'Remember that you are that genuine lovechild. Please concentrate on that. If the angels in heaven had contrived to find the most perfect pair to beget you, from the most perfect love, they could not have found two more loving people in the whole world than Grace Hargreaves and Felix Stewart.'

'You seem to know more about me than I know about myself. I have only heard part of it from my mother. I guessed the rest.'

392

'Yes, Grace told me everything – well, everything that concerned her. Try to imagine, my dearest, the intimate situation they were in. Suppose we had known one another as Grace and Felix did; that we were in my house on our own without a chaperone...'

'Stop, Alistair! It could never happen to us... And I wouldn't want it to.'

'Felicity, I want you to understand Grace...'

'But why didn't they marry, before they...?'

'Dearest, he was called away. Queen's orders – literally Queen's orders – two weeks' notice.

He took her ringed hand.

'I think we both agree that a true love of two people has a strange sort of arithmetic; it's one and one making two; but more important it's two making one. Even more it's *each* one making two. I feel to be twice the man I am when you are with me – even when writing to you ... or you have written to me...'

'Oh, Alistair, you've taken one of my lines. I wanted to say that with you I feel I can do twice as much as I can by myself: sing, play the piano, dance, talk, think, ride... and touch...'

He stroked her hand. 'Perhaps one day – not too far away, I hope – you will be able to say *connect* in all the many meanings of that word, my love...'

'When shall we make it happen, Alistair? Do you realise that we haven't, as they say, fixed a date? Our talk, quite rightly, has all been on marriage, not a wedding. That's something different.'

Alistair raised a quizzical eyebrow.

'How long does a woman need to prepare for her wedding? I hope not too long.'

'I am ready now! It's the mother of the bride who needs the time! Mamma will supervise the making of every garment in a large trousseau: outerwear; underwear ... nightwear. She'll want to make sure that every bit of me is modestly and decoratively covered!'

'Felicity, we keep going off at a tangent and never finish what we start to say. I want to start a new life, with a *new woman*, in a new age. What about the last day of this century and then on the first night of our honeymoon seeing in the New Year, 1900? To welcome in the new century – in a city where bells jostle with one another, just a short train journey after the wedding for our first night. What about York?'

Would she ever know, Alistair thought, that York was the city where she first met her 'mother' and her birthdate was given her for life?

393

'It's all going to be in the depth of winter so let's keep journeys short and nights most exquisitely long. What about that? December 31st 1899?'

Felicity agreed. The whole idea was charged with romance and hope. 'It sounds perfect! What day is that?'

He took a slim diary from his pocket and flicked through. 'No good, dearest, it's a Sunday. The church has odd rules. Babies are pure enough and innocent enough to be christened on a Sunday but weddings would break the Sabbath!'

'Saturday! Then we could invite people from the mill!'

'Good. Let's both sign it in my diary. Now that's settled, may I finish my guideline? All the time I was in America I had to imagine you, my love. And I *did* imagine you, every single inch of you night after night, and caressed you from head to toe. My dear sweet innocent, I do plead with you not to be ashamed of your bodily passion. It is through our bodies, as well as our minds, that we show every vestige of our tenderness, generosity and unselfishness. It is through our eyes that the whole world reads the splendour of our love, just as you and I are reading one another now.'

Felicity kept her eyes on his. 'You are making me much more understanding about Grace and Felix. I begin to see that it was through their love that you and I are together, here, today.

Alistair looked closely into her trusting eyes. 'Now, dearest, think of her, twenty-four years ago, her whole world centred on her lover, and his world centred on her. I'm not talking of lust, my magnetic Felicity, I am talking of the ultimate fulfilment when two people unite, body and soul.'

'Yes, Alistair, but we are lucky: we can look forward to marriage; they could not. Does it sound trite to say until then ours must be a marriage of true minds?'

'Of course, my darling, but truth can never be trite. And, my dear, our marriage must never become either trite or taken for granted. Trust me, my dearest, I shall be very, very tender with you, and love you *till all the seas gang dry.*'

He looked round the lock path. There was no-one anywhere in sight, not even the lock keeper. It was rapturously quiet. He gave her the gentlest of kisses. All they could hear was the water trying to push its way through the locked gates and the reeds near the banks swaying to and fro sensuously in concord with their love.

'Alistair,' Felicity whispered, 'when you see Grace, will you tell her how proud I am to be her child?' Holding hands, they walked through sunshine to find Hazel had returned home from the infirmary.

'Just the man I want! There are specially good roses out of my reach.' She indicated with the secateurs and the overgrown rose bush and then turned to Felicity. 'My dear, my husband's finished surgery. I think he'd like a word. Be an angel and go and talk to him.'

Hazel had the gift of a stage director, so neatly were the moves devised. She turned her attention to Alistair.

'Jeremy wants to explain a few things to Felicity. I hope you don't mind my parting you.'

'If a rose had another name it should be Hazel. I see the ones you want, they are perfect – and for you, quite obtainable.'

Felicity, opening the surgery door, noticed that the doctor was taking off his white linen gown.

'Am I too late to help?

'Come in, my dear, and sit down. There must be questions you want to ask which only I can answer. But first of all, congratulations on being a wise virgin. You were somewhat cruel, Felicity, sending that ring back. Your real father was one of the finest men I've ever met. Remember when you wear that ring three people have given it to you: Felix, Grace and Alistair.'

'Yes, I do see now. But please do realise that when you say the word *father* – I only see one familiar face.'

'Your *mother* took you,' he said (Felicity noticed the emphasis on the ambiguous word), 'on condition that you were accepted as the natural daughter of Gertrude and Arthur Hargreaves. And that, my dear, you will always be to the whole world – except for ... Grace, Hazel, Belinda, Alistair and myself.'

'Dr Bennett, was I a – co-operative – baby, or did I give Grace much trouble?'

'I don't have to tell you, who have seen so many births, that there was excruciating pain, but you fought your way into the world with huge determination – and you've never lost it. By the way, with a little more determination I hope you will stop calling me doctor. It's Jeremy.'

'May I ask you, Jeremy, to tell me more about my m— about *Gertrude*, since we all seem to be on Christian name terms. You must have known of her obsession to have a child.'

He then told her the whole story, with such tenderness and caring for the new-born child that he could have been describing an immaculate conception and a wise man following a star.

'Thank you, oh thank you, Jeremy. You've made me feel very special. You've also given me a new insight into ... both my mothers. Let's face it, I must have been a horror to bring up: headstrong; argumentative; unappreciative...'

'Forget all that, my dear, they are very proud of you. Let them go on being so. After all, Stonegarth will always be your childhood home.'

Felicity went on probing. 'One thing I should like to ask you. When was I really born? You said that the journey from Edinburgh was on my birthday, September 18th and that I was two weeks old.'

'Yes, my dear, I don't know what stars we are contradicting but Grace and I brought you into the world on September 4th.'

'Does Belinda know that?'

'No, she hasn't asked. Need she?'

'Well, no. But she's planning a birthday tea for me next week, on the eighteenth.'

'And September 4th has come and gone without any celebration.'

'Would it be best if I forgot it?'

'I think it would, my dear. Only the stars need know.'

'And Grace and you.'

'Shall I tell you a secret? Well, I must, because I think Grace might feel it was my secret.'

'Please, Jeremy, there must be no secrets between you and me now – about me, I mean.'

'No, except this one.' He took her hand.

'Every year, every September, I go up to Edinburgh and I always plan to visit Grace on September 4th. You and Belinda were on vacation here in Yorkshire these last four years but you all three knew that I was at a conference, which was true, and that I called on Grace. What you didn't know was that the date was carefully chosen.'

'Oh, Jeremy, that is wonderful – the strangest of birthday parties...'

'Now I am going to make a suggestion, and then we must go back into the house. When you and Alistair are married and settled in Edinburgh, what about the four of us celebrating your day of birth, and not even Maggie or Sammycat knowing what we are celebrating!'

He had his arm round her waist as they went into the house. Alistair looked straight into her eyes, which he was surprised to see were glowing with wonder and delight. He glanced with gratitude at Jeremy and thought: This man's genius for healing goes far beyond medicine bottles. What a day it will be when I introduce him to William James.

Wisely the Bennetts ended the day with music. Alistair chose the Schubert songs followed by the Burns love lyrics, all of which Felicity enjoyed accompanying. Years ago Alistair had fallen in love with Felicity's hands, which were capable of playing the lightest arpeggios and the solemn chords in a Bach fugue. Tonight he pressed for Belinda and Felicity to play their Beethoven sonata for piano and cello in D major. Before he went to America, he had chosen the last movement of the allegro fugue for them to work on, but with examination pressure and clinical work in the wards they had had little time for practice. He understood their close relationship and was anxious that their bond of love should not be broken.

'You two are a wonderful partnership. Don't deprive Belinda's cello of the piano, Felicity, and you, Belinda, are so right for the witty links in this last movement. Do make the most of this time you and Felicity are together.'

It was a generous speech, which had the right effect. They took time in the tuning, looking at one another as if this were something they would have to do in real life. Perhaps it was the affectionate audience whose listening contributed to their modest success.

'Bravo!' beamed Jeremy.

'Well done, darlings,' choked Hazel, in tears.

And Alistair: 'Oh, thank you both for the huge effort.' He walked forward and stood between them, putting an arm round each:

'You know, when Beethoven wrote this movement he was determined not to let the cello be pushed into the background by the piano. But he didn't know our Belinda, did he, Felicity?'

They all five laughed together. It was Hazel who played the introductory bars to the goodnight song to bring them round the piano. The song of the soirée had become part of the Bennett repertoire.

The day is done; we've danced and sung.
Our eyes have seen delight.
The day is past; we part at last,
To each and all: goodnight.

One day, Felicity thought, as the glow in her eyes fell upon Alistair, we shall not be parting!

Sleep eluded Felicity. Thoughts went round: foul and fair; catching up on one another, contradicting; reasoning until she hardly knew where she was or what she was. The dawn chorus reminded her of Alistair, as everything did. A haunting melody – a snatch of a tune – went round and round in her head, chasing personal problems away. Grace and she had played it as a piano duet. She saw the four still hands on the keys. Why couldn't she remember the title or the first line? Alistair had sung it.

The very next day she felt she *must* talk to her father – but that had to wait until he returned from the mill. He was in his little smoking den, which she rarely entered.

'May we talk for a few minutes, Father, before tea?'

'You do t'talking! Ah've got my pipe, Ah'll listen.'

She pulled the Windsor chair nearer to him and lowered her voice.

'Mother's already told me. Well, half told me. I've guessed the rest.'

It was quite obvious, from his flushed face, that this was painfully embarrassing to him. His pipe was no comfort. It was shaking. Felicity realised that somehow she had to be the one to help. *The child is father to the man* came into her mind. He had become her patient. She spoke in gentle terms, one to another.

'Father, it's all over now – the telling, I mean. After all, you've lived with the situation for years and years. I haven't. The shock is mine, not yours. I shall get over it!'

They were silent.

She's a real Hargreaves, he thought, not weeping like most women would. She's faced up to it.

'Let's get this straight, luv, you're a Hargreaves, and always will be. An' don't forget this: I'll always be your father, an' called it. Yer mother is yer mother, nothing different. If it 'adn't been for yer wanting to be engaged and wed, nowt need 'ave been said!'

So Alistair was the reason. It had been thought out by her parents; it was not Gertrude's outburst on seeing the ring. She had prepared a speech – one she never gave.

'Why didn't you tell my fiancé that I was not your child? Surely that would have been the honourable thing to do?'

'Listen, lass, honour's nowt to do with it. 'E came for my permission an' 'e got it.'

'But Father, surely you understand. No family like the Frasers could ever let their son marry a girl who...'

Arthur cut into her sentence: 'And why's Fraser a better name than 'Argreaves, tell me that!'

She knew she had offended him and she felt sorry. Getting up, she gave him a light kiss on his forehead.

'I'm proud of the name, Father, but I'm also proud of Grace. But you and mother have done everything you could as parents and I'm – grateful.' She hoped she had found the right word.

The *as parents* carried logic but not much filial love. She was trying to work out the real relationship of them to her. All four of us carry the name *Hargreaves*, she thought. She tried a diversion; perhaps it would take a little weight from the father/ daughter relationship and make her father realise he was not talking to a child.

'Father, have you ever thought that, although you adopted me, I am in fact a close relative. As Grace is your sister, I am your niece!'

'Rubbish. I never want to 'ear such daft talk. I've got two nieces, one on yer mother's side and one on mine. Aye! An' one's as daft as Dick's 'at-band, and t'other's thick as a brush.'

Felicity laughed with joy and relief. He'd changed in the last few minutes from a nervous, embarrassed man to the one she admired – trenchant and tough.

The gong saved her from further discussion, but he pulled her back from the door:

'Remember, there's no change in our Grace, she's mi *sister* and nowt else. It were a pact we made when she 'anded you over. No-one in t'world knows except yer ma and pa, mi sister, Dr Bennett, an' now you.'

They went into high tea.

Gertrude worked hard at being pleasant. 'It's your birthday next week,' she said. 'What would you like, luv? You've only got to say!'

'How kind of you, Mother, but I've really got everything. Just one of your delicious cakes would be quite enough.'

But it was *not* her birthday. And her mother knew it.

Was Jeremy Bennett the only one who told her the whole truth?

5

In the sleeper on the midnight train, the wheels beat out a rhythm to Alistair's thoughts:

> *When shall we meet? When shall we meet?*
> *When shall we meet? When shall we meet?*

He shut his eyes and tried to sleep but his mind then travelled to Barlockend and the hapless Amy Ackroyd.

> *How can I help? How can I help?*
> *How can I help? How can I help?*

He worried that he had the revealing medical record in his hand luggage. The cryptic phrase overrode the wheels. 'What did she mean about *purity?*'

Through the arches of the Newcastle bridge the sound changed to a higher pitch. He looked out of the window and marvelled at the engineering genius that had created it all. A frisson of ecstasy and hope ran through him as the train rushed past the ancient stone of Alnwick and Bamburgh.

Soon she'll be mine. Soon she'll be mine, the clattering wheels seemed to be saying.

Sleep would not come. The rhythm changed to calm monotony on the level stretch out of Berwick. He told himself that any sane person would have let the train's soporific pulse ensure sleep for the whole journey. But too much had happened in the long weekend in Aireley to make it possible to pull a blind down on his mind.

His training in psychology gave him reasoned academic answers, but his heart was too big to accept them as definitive.

The attendant slid the door and entered with the morning tray of tea. 'Had a good night, Sir?'

Alistair answered with his usual polite optimism. 'Yes, thank you... I always enjoy travelling by sleeper, such an escape from the outside world.'

Felicity, now back in her room, was wondering how on earth a reason could be found to make a visit to Edinburgh imperative. She reread the letter she had written to Grace, conscious that she was trying to put into words thoughts that no pen could encompass. Self-doubt made the paper tremble.

My dearest Grace,

I can only hope that Alistair fills in the gaps, which I find impossible to express in a letter.

Briefly the truth about you and me has been told: awkwardly by my mother; passionately by Alistair; and, oh so comfortingly by Jeremy Bennett.

Now I have had time to think about what has been hidden from me, I am absolutely amazed that the truth was never revealed for all these years.

Women are supposed to have intuitive sensibility. Have I been stupid in failing to realise that your support, concern and magnificent love surpassed anything one could expect of a *god*mother?

Dear, dear, Grace, I must admit to you that my *first* reaction was anger, shock and shame. To be illegitimate seemed to exclude me from the society on which my life had depended and to whose rules I was committed.

It was Alistair who showed me that I was a *privileged* child: the outward and visible manifestation of a supreme love.

Grace, please understand, that although I must go on being the daughter of A and G, I shall always treasure, in my heart, that God gave me the most wonderful mother any child could have. When we talk together, as we must do soon, Grace, soon, you, I know, will tell me about the man you overwhelmed with love, and who, through his love for you, created me.

I cannot write any more. Too many tears are blinding me.

Please send your reply – as I am doing with my letter – via Miss Elsie, who will never know that she is the angel bearing tidings of great joy.

My love and gratitude always,

Your own Felicity

The next three days Leo had the excessive exercise he needed to reduce his weight. Back and forth, three times a day, he led his mistress to the post office. On the third day Miss Elsie, on seeing Felicity, stopped putting sugar into the blue bags and came out to take Leo's lead. He remained tied to the boot scraper while the letter with the Edinburgh postmark was put in Felicity's hand.

'Oh thank you, Elsie. I won't open it here; Mother has taken to her bed for a few days and I'm supervising the kitchen – not in her way of course!'

Returning home, she let Leo go at full speed off the lead and then gave him the freedom of the paddock behind the sign warning folk to beware.

She went straight upstairs and stopped Hilda from going into her bedroom.

'I'll do my bed, Hilda. Isn't it a gorgeous morning?'

She was alone at last, sitting at her desk in the window bay. In the field on the horizon were minute bent figures gleaning the wheat that reapers had left behind. She opened the envelope carefully with her paperknife. Even the envelope must be preserved. The writing suggested that the letter had been penned very slowly.

My dearest girl,

How can I ever thank you for your brave and loving letter? I am torn between rejoicing and regretting that you now know the truth, which cannot help but bewilder you in accepting your past and confronting your present and future life.

I am comforted by knowing that without Alistair, my dearest, your closeness to me, and I to you, would have remained locked in my heart. The ring is our eternal testimony.

When can we talk together, Felicity? There is so much we both need to explain and understand which cannot be put in letters, but I am anxious that you do not rush away from Stonegarth. Your parents (the only word we must ever use) have done everything for you within their powers, coping with the everyday tasks and worries which are all part of bringing up a child. I have had the joy and the anguish of loving you from afar, but have been repaid a thousandfold watching you grow into a loveable and intelligent woman whose understanding and spirit have enriched many people's lives.

May I suggest that now Alistair is back here in Edinburgh you take comfort and guidance from Jeremy Bennett? He will understand your need to be here in Edinburgh and he is the only one who could find reasons acceptable to Arthur and Gertrude.

Forgive me, dearest, if this all sounds devious, but twenty-three years of playing a part have made me tread softly in these sensitive relationships.

Does it sound selfish when I say that having Alistair back in Edinburgh is my greatest solace? Now he is here I feel that 'my Persephone' is not as far away from 'her Demeter'.

I shall always remain,

> Your loving godmother,
>
> Grace

The first reading of the letter was swift with relief; the second slower and infinitely revealing; the third highlighted Grace's wisdom and her uncanny way of sensing other people's feelings.

Felicity sank into her velvet armchair feeling cushioned with love. She marvelled at the way Grace eased the troubles of the past into a radiant future. All doubts were swept away. She stroked the ring. She felt as if a guardian angel had been at her birth and guided her whole life. She had always been a cheerful little girl who counted her blessings; now she had grown beyond counting.

Three days later Alistair's letter came by registered post, care of Miss Elsie, who handed it over in the parlour. Felicity glowed as she read the messages of love and then read a more serious paragraph.

> Angus called on me yesterday bringing the latest news and gossip of the medical faculty. According to his grapevine, the powers-that-be are questioning the number of clinical cases completed by recent graduating students. I must warn you that it may affect you and Belinda. This may prove to be an irksome time for you but I must confess a time of rejoicing for me. Please do not breathe a word of this until it is confirmed.

It had become an unspoken assumption between Belinda and Felicity that confidentiality was shared; in almost every facet of life they needed one another.

'Elsie, may I use your telephone, please? I have an urgent message for Belinda.'

'Well, of course you could, but why waste money on a telephone call? Never, I say, disturb a doctor with telephone messages unless it's a matter of life and death. Bob's taking a telegram to Dr Bennett, so if you write a message here he'll take it along. She'll get it in half an hour.'

The message which Bob delivered asked Belinda to get off the train at Aireley when she came home from work the next day. Felicity suggested that she had her bicycle on the train to ride up to Miss Elsie's.

Leo was surprised and delighted the next day to have a walk at an unexpected time, leaving the house when the family was usually at tea. One could not claim that Leo could *tell* the time but he instinctively knew it. At five forty-five Leo and his mistress were standing on the station platform chatting to Herbert Dawson, whose affection for, and knowledge of, Airedales, almost equalled his understanding of Shakespeare.

'They're a fine breed, Miss Hargreaves, stout of heart and lithe of limb; I've never understood why those fussy little toy dogs were called *Yorkshire* terriers...'

The puffing smoke and steam of the Bradford train ended the speculation. Dawson and Felicity watched Belinda bounce into action, commandeering a porter to go to the guard's van. Leo recognised her and pulled his mistress towards her.

'Belinda, you've not brought the tandem? I've got the dog with me.'

Herbert Dawson was at Belinda's side.

Belinda always asked questions for help in the positive; it gave no opportunity for refusing.

'We can fix that can't we, Mr Dawson? I'm sure you could tie the lead to the tandem.'

And so it was that Leo had his first aptitude and initiative test speeding along with his pedalling mistress. The three arrived at Miss Elsie's back door – not through the shop, which now had its butter, bacon, hams and cheeses shrouded in clean mutton cloth for the night.

'I'm just doing the post office daybook so you two go into the parlour. I'll fasten Leo up.'

They sat on the small window seat, their heads framed by potted geraniums.

'How's the job, Belinda? Do they appreciate that they've got a fully-fledged doctor doing the work of a clerk – and *unpaid*!'

'Yes, they've funny ways of rewarding me. Today they actually gave me a clean sheet of blotting paper, three pen nibs and a

404

clean ink pot, and the young lad who delivered them said: "That'll set you up, Miss, won't it?" And you, Felicity? How is life with you?'

'Well, this is why I am here. I've had a letter from Alistair with a secret message which may affect both of us.'

Felicity opened the letter then folded it so that the proclamations of love were out of sight but with the important paragraph in evidence. Belinda read it quite aware that the rest of the letter was obscured.

'Well, I did wonder about all the varieties of clinical experience. Is that all he says? It seems to me to be enough to disturb and not enough to elucidate, but we have kept a good enough account of our clinical practice. Surely, in any case, they will have it down in their records. I am sure that I could do mine here at the infirmary in Bradford. Papa could arrange all that.'

Belinda had a genius for knowing answers before the questions had been asked and was quick to make plans for Felicity.

'Obviously, in your case, our deficiencies could be your delight.'

There was a tinge of regret in Belinda's remark as if their separation would be coming sooner than she had thought.

Felicity answered briskly. 'How foolish we are to jump to conclusions. Trying to cross bridges before they are even in view. Remember, Belinda, Alistair wrote this in confidence – so not a word.'

'If you trust me, why do you warn me? After all *tandem* is our telegraphic address, isn't it? Let's get on it now. I'll drop you and Leo off at your home. Meanwhile we *share* all our troubles and are generous with our joys.'

Their pedalling was in perfect unison and Leo's four legs found a way of moving to the rhythm of the wheels.

Felicity's longing was to get to Edinburgh to talk to Grace and Alistair, not to become involved in wards and operating theatres. Grace had suggested, with good reason, that Belinda's father could help, but she was talking of Stonegarth not the medical course. As Felicity now took for granted the Saturday visit to the Bennetts', she found a way she could talk to the doctor on her own. His Saturday surgery finished at midday. She would telephone from Miss Elsie's tomorrow and ask the doctor, if she could, as a training exercise, do the dispensing on Saturday morning.

He instantly agreed adding wryly: 'I can't get Belinda interested in medicine at all. She always says that a placebo delivered by my hand would cure half of my patients.'

'That shows her faith in you, Dr Bennett, Jeremy, not her disbelief in *materia medica*.'

She arrived at ten thirty braced for action.

'Come in, my dear. There are only twelve prescriptions to be made up. I think you would do better with my case book than try to read my shorthand. Hazel's got so used to it that she only needs to glance at the daybook. I think if the truth were known she would welcome a few more new and more expensive drugs. But people are very strange, they like repeats of the medicine they believe in, they don't realise that it is their belief not the potion which is the cure.'

Felicity knew that he was underrating his own instinct in guiding his patients to what he called 'good kitchen medicine', which usually included wholesome food. Often he was in despair, knowing that it was poverty and housing conditions which were the killers and he worked behind the scenes to get the health authority to step in with help. Felicity was quite unaware that eight of the bottles which she made up and packed neatly in white paper would never be paid for. She labelled them by name only and stood the twelve bottles in the porch for collection. The outer door was always left unlocked. She approached Dr Bennett:

'Might I have a word with you before we go in? I need your help.'

'Anything I can do for you, my dear, is always a privilege and a pleasure.'

Felicity hesitated. 'After all that I have been told, by you and Mother, I feel I must talk to Grace. You are the only one who understands how desperately I need to do so; I simply daren't suggest to my parents that I go to see her. It could be wrongly interpreted...'

'Felicity, my dear, you and I must try to get your priorities and self-esteem in order. You are twenty-three, highly educated and with a mind of your own; you must learn to state your intentions and not ask permission. I shall speak to Gertrude!'

Things moved quickly in that first week in October '99. Letters and telegrams were exchanged fixing Felicity's arrival. There was much rejoicing in Moray Place that Felicity would have a time with Alistair in Edinburgh before the December wedding. An official letter, heavy with implication, was delivered by Bob direct to

Stonegarth from the Senate of Edinburgh Medical Faculty. It requested that Miss Felicity Laura Hargreaves should present herself between October 12th and 20th at the Registrar's office.

Precisely the same letter was delivered to Miss Belinda Geraldine Bennett. Felicity's railway ticket was already booked for October 3rd and Grace's hospitality duly acknowledged. Hazel juggled with all the news in collusion with her husband and daughter:

'Belinda, wouldn't it be tactful if you travelled to Edinburgh on October 11th, and that you and Felicity got the university visit over on October 12th?'

A letter came from Alistair direct to Belinda enclosing a letter from Lucinda Mackenzie inviting her to be their guest. It was in Lady Mackenzie's minute, immaculate calligraphy and ran:

My dear Belinda,

The news that you are summoned to present yourself at the university must be distressing to you, but Angus and I have to confess that we are rejoicing.

We value, very much indeed, the close friendship, which developed between us in your undergraduate years. Obviously we were saddened when graduation ended a period of great joy.

This uncovenanted bonus of Felicity's and your visit to Edinburgh encourages us to hope that we can share the pleasure of your company. We shall be delighted and grateful if you would agree to spend your few days here, as our guest, and make both our home and Moray Place meeting places for our reunion. May we expect you on October 11th and leave it to you to say how long you can absent yourself from the important position we hear you have acquired in Bradford?

Both Angus and I look forward, very much, to meeting you again and, we hope, making music both here and at Moray Place.

Yours in friendship

I am most sincerely,

Lucinda Mackenzie

Fate seemed to be working in a neatly convenient way for the lovers to meet, a new relationship to be honoured, friendships to burgeon and officialdom to be appeased.

Included in the brief note from the Senate was a reprint from

407

the prospectus containing a list of studies and clinical requirements to be completed in the final year.

Belinda and Felicity pored over the details, fully satisfied that every examination had been taken and satisfactorily passed. But they both had doubts about the range of clinical cases which they had observed and treated.

Felicity thought that at least the letter could reinforce the importance of her visit to Edinburgh in the minds of her parents. She brought the subject up the next day over high tea.

'I am grateful that you understand that it is a good idea to visit my aunt. It will entirely close a chapter in all our lives which is firmly in the past. Here is the letter you gave me from the tray this morning. Perhaps you and Father would like to read it yourselves.'

Gertrude took it, but showed little interest in its content, and handed it to Arthur. Felicity saw that her parents were quite out of their depth. But it was Gertrude who gasped her protest.

'But you're getting married in less than three months' time and we've got the invitations to get out in November and all the arrangements to make for the ceremony and reception. So you must get back as quickly as you can!'

Alistair was at Waverley station to welcome Felicity. The significance of this meeting was not lost on either of them, for this was the first time they had been alone together in Edinburgh, outside Moray Place. He shook her hand circumspectly, as far as the outside world could see, but the throb of contact and the meeting of eyes made an exclusive globe where no-one else existed.

He helped her protectively into the waiting cab while the porter and driver strapped her suitcase on to the luggage frame.

'I'm taking you on a small mystery tour, my dear, before we go to Moray Place, somewhere you've never been before!'

The way the two girls had walked unceasingly to discover Edinburgh in their first weeks was unknown to Alistair. Felicity happily responded to each of the beautiful streets and squares, as if seeing them for the first time.

The cab drew up in Drummond Place and without any signal of their arrival, except the clatter of hooves and wheels, Simpson was at the door. Felicity was aware that his discriminating eye was viewing her in the way he looked at the label on a bottle of port which he was keeping for Christmas. But her greeting immediately dispelled any misgivings that Simpson might have had about the future lady of the house.

'How kind of you to be looking out for Dr Fraser and me. I am so glad the train was on time and that you were not window-bound for too long.'

Simpson was a good judge of women (not having narrowed his life down to one) and very soon approved of his master's choice.

'It will be a guid cup of tea you'll be wanting ma'am. It's all ready for ye, except for the infusing.'

He went off to the kitchen, leaving his master to make the lady feel at home.

Alistair led her through the hall and pointed out a horizontal photograph of Harvard.

'That's the psychology faculty group, and there's William James, but I've lots more to show you of Harvard whenever we have time. Come into the sitting room, my dear, it's the only one I keep tidy, all the others are cluttered with books. Splendid! Simpson's got a good fire going. He thinks you are from *the South*, which all your people call *the North*. He's anxious to protect you from Edinburgh's chill.'

Felicity relaxed into the corner seat of a long leather sofa. Alistair came next to her so that they were both facing a piecrust round table with a crocheted cloth set out for afternoon tea. It looked like a feminine oasis in a man's world.

In a few minutes Simpson entered with a Georgian silver teapot on a silver salver and placed it on the table as near as he could to his master's lady.

'Excuse me, Sir, but I think it is a lady's privilege to pour out the tea. May I move the table nearer to Miss Hargreaves?' He made Felicity feel blessed as if by a bishop, so noble his bearing, so impeccable his speech. The thanks between his servant and his betrothed assured Alistair that the only hurdle there might have been in abandoning bachelorhood was cleared in this brief meeting. He knew now that Simpson would be with them, wherever they might choose to be. He was even more heartened by the way Felicity accepted his home as a place where she would happily belong. She held the teapot in a style it had earned for over a hundred years and then, after pouring the tea into the fine Royal Worcester cups, she put the teapot down and giggled.

'Oh, Alistair, isn't it quite absurd. I know you so well that I don't even know whether you take sugar or not.' They laughed comfortably, realising that the question would never have to be asked again.

'Can you face it, my dear, helping me to sugar thousands and thousands of times in years to come? Is it too, too monotonous to face?'

She laughed teasingly. 'Yes, I think I can, if you promise not to use your teaspoon as if you were making a Christmas pudding. I do sometimes think it is the little things that make marriage intolerable. How my fussy mother puts up with my father clutching his knife like a poker, I simply do not understand. But I suppose she was brought up to think that men are always right.'

Alistair enjoyed this perfect moment of insight and honesty; it was so different from the usual feminine afternoon tea. It was another proof that Felicity was a very special girl – and soon would be his. He put his cup down and held her hand.

'Dearest, I have made wrong judgements and decisions many times in my life, but I know I am right in the most important decision in any man's life.'

He kissed her hand and turned the ring round and round her finger.

'I wasn't wrong about this was I? You're the turning point in my whole life.'

When they discussed the impending interview, Alistair explained: 'Don't get worried about it, my sweet, it is a feather in Edinburgh's cap that the medical school insists on so much practical clinical experience. What a great team they are. I think they are checking up on a possible houseman year. Belinda's got herself in the right place for doing a year with the health authority. You, my dear, must blame our betrothal and your mother's short-sighted domestic horizon that you have not committed yourself to a year's practice.'

'Oh, Alistair, you have made me more nervous than ever. Shall I tell, whoever interviews me, that I am engaged to you?'

'My dearest Felicity, the grapevine in the faculty of medicine is more lively than a telegraph wire; Angus, in his retirement, treats it and the Royal College of Physicians like clubs. Don't tell me that they don't know.'

'But will they approve?'

'Yes, my dear, most of them. But there are many others giving lip service to the cause of women doctors who still feel that the be-all and end-all is marriage.' He closed both her hands into his. 'Seriously, my sweet, do you think that you and I, in harness, but not in handcuffs, can prove that women can have both a marriage and a career?'

Felicity was quick with her answer. 'Of course, Alistair, and I can tell you this: that if we don't, I shall go down with a bang in Belinda's eyes – and that would grieve me, more than anyone, even you, could ever know.'

He looked at her and the clock. 'Felicity, this time we have together is very, very precious. It is nearly six o'clock and I promised Grace that I would have you there by six thirty. May I, before we leave, add a little rider to our marriage vow? I leave it to you to ask the minister to omit the word *obey* in yours. Mine is a personal vow to you.'

He kept a steady eye on her. 'You, my dearest, will be my wife, my life. But let us not stand so close that we live in one another's shadow. I will be your guardian but not your guardsman; your lover but not your possessor. Felicity, my love, always remember that you have a mind and a soul of your own. You must nurture them and I will protect your independence to my dying day.'

Alistair and Grace had planned these precious October days with infinite precision and perception. There was no question of being asked into Moray Place; he took Felicity up to the front door and handed her over to a waiting trio: Grace, Maggie and Sammycat, while the driver carried Felicity's cases into the hall. Sam sniffed that it was an occasion for decorum and knew that in gesture, greetings and social exchange he must be circumspect, but it was the warmest welcome any mother could give a daughter.

Maggie's welcome was very practical. 'The sun's bin out until the noo, and if the auld softie isn't off behind the clouds! But I've put a wee fire in your room to cheer ye, Miss Felicity. So just ring the bell if you'd like it bigger!'

One of the joys of thrift is being able to be generous. Maggie should have been thrift's patron saint.

It was not until after their light supper that Grace and Felicity sank into the velvet cushions of the chaise longue.

It was Felicity who introduced the main theme for the evening, slowly and solemnly, like the opening bars of a Chopin prelude – but she was not playing the piano, she was now stroking the ring on her left hand:

'Dear Grace, you've not regretted giving it to me, I hope? It is the most wonderful thing I have ever possessed.' Her eyes travelled to her aunt's left hand. 'Look, there is a white ring mark around your finger where the sun has never shone.'

'The sun can get to it now, my dear, can it not? You know, Felicity, all my life I have had the feeling that beautifully crafted, or even well-made useful things, absorb something of the wearer's or user's spirit. Have you noticed that the clock in Felix's study is stopped? I am told by Jeremy that that was the time Felix died, but earthly time is at the mercy of the sun. Time in India would be quite different from ours.'

Felicity picked up a different cue. 'That reminds me, have you ever noticed that Lucinda never lets anyone touch her flute? It's not that she's possessive, I'm sure; it's because she feels that in her flute – in every particle of silver in it – there is something of herself. This is how I feel about you and Felix and the ring.'

'You know, over the last weeks I have felt almost as if he were in the room, approving of the ring being on your finger, and somehow guarding it. His presence here seems to be telling me that he approves of Alistair.'

Felicity mind had become a network of tangled thoughts. She selected one with both a frown and a smile on her face.

'How very strange it is, Grace, to think – but only you and I can ever say it – Felix is really Alistair's father-in-law. And you...'

Grace could hardly believe that she was laughing on this strange night.

'Please, my dearest girl, please don't say it. The thought of being Alistair's mother-in-law is too, too bizarre for words.'

She could see Alistair now, in former times, so close to her in his undergraduate days, seeking love and understanding from a mature woman. She remembered meeting him later, graduated and mature, a bachelor who had rejected the idea of finding a woman he could love. Now here he was, a true lover of her own daughter. It seemed as if fate had patterned their lives.

Felicity was thinking that she and Grace had travelled far in their letters. It was a relief that they could take one another for granted a little and need not try to explain all that Alistair had made so clear. But for the first time, she looked at Grace, marvelling that she was her true mother.

'Grace, staying here with you, knowing all that I never knew before – oh, does it sound too pious to say – *I feel I have been born again*? That all my past life has been a preparation for this...?'

'I do understand. Don't try to put it into words, unless you want to. I think music will help – well, it's always helped me.'

'And helped me. You'll never know the number of times I've played Stonegarth out of my system, and even at school, when life was as dry as the chalk on the board, I've shut myself in one of those dingy cubicles and dreamt myself into Handel...'

'Do you feel like playing the piano tonight? A duet for four hands?'

'Delighted! Oh Grace, it is where we belong.'

As they moved on to the double stool, Felicity said: 'However

412

did female duettists manage to play the piano when they wore crinolines? They wouldn't be able to sit down!'

'No, I remember your grandmother saying that composers stopped writing piano duets in the earlier part of this century, because of the crinolines. Odd that one rarely sees gentlemen playing together.'

'How appalling that such a stupid fashion killed a charming form of music!'

In the next few days, Felicity was caught in a magic haze of walks and talks with Alistair. She could hardly believe it could be true. From being one of a crowd of students with moderate intellect and experience, she had become Alistair's consort whom he was proud to present to erudite friends. In his urbane, confident manner he made her feel that she was a social asset.

The grand and noble buildings of the Royal College of Physicians, the Royal College of Surgeons, the Royal Institution and the National Gallery all seemed to open their doors to Alistair. Felicity now, without a guidebook, had her guide at her side. She realised that Belinda and she had missed so much when first walking in the New Town.

Now she followed Alistair's finger, which was pointing out the Doric, Ionic and Corinthian architecture in this splendid city with its everlasting joys.

They moved further along Princes Street to the University Club. How glad she was that Yorkshire had given her sturdy leg muscles.

'I'm ashamed to tell you, dearest, that I can't take you in here. Men only. But one day I'll take you to my *new* club, where one is allowed to entertain a lady to lunch, provided she is escorted into the building through a side door.'

'Oh, Alistair, will there ever be a time when men and women meet on equal terms?'

He grinned down at her. 'Why not, my sweet, enjoy being unequal and superior? I am sure that men don't like having women in their clubs because it means minding their p's and q's.'

A steam tram was drawing up level to them.

'Would you like to go on this?' Alistair asked.

She quickened her step towards it. 'Oh yes, of course, they're such friendly things and so convenient.'

He held her back. 'Let's have lunch here first. It's a splendid hotel next to the Caledonian station. The wonderful thing about the railway companies is that they didn't just build lines and engines, they realised that passengers needed to eat and sleep in luxury.'

As they walked towards the hotel he said: 'Look over to the left. That's St Thomas's: it's Church of England. The Scottish Episcopal bishops are very piqued because it is outside their jurisdiction. It must be the only bit of Scotland that England really owns.'

They needed a rest after lunch so were both glad to get into the tram, although the seats were hard and the wind quite cold. They talked of Belinda's arrival when she came to stay with Sir Angus and Lucinda, of the musical evening they would all enjoy together. But first, Felicity and Belinda were to face their interviews.

The quadrangle in front of the medical school had only a scattering of men and women, most of whom Belinda and Felicity recognised as being from their year.

'Have you been in yet?' Belinda asked three women who were only third class, academically, but who were fun and would, no doubt, turn into human and helpful doctors.

The liveliest one of the group summed up for all of them: 'Oh, we've all three decided to come back, in any case, to improve our results and probably to do our Masters. At the moment, I must admit, I can't feel very pleased about doing morbid anatomy again – I don't think I could raise a flag even if it were *amusing* anatomy!'

After wishing them well and calling out good luck to the rest of the group, Belinda found that her name, alphabetically ahead of Hargreaves, was called first.

Belinda always believed in making appeals sound like agreements, which tended to disarm the challenger. During the first preliminary questions and explanations, Belinda pleased the Registrar by agreeing with everything he said.

'Yes, I agree. I think we female students all needed much more time and practice on women's diseases and gynaecology. The men seem more fortunate than the women in this respect, but, of course, they would need more time for teaching and practice in subjects where their own experience is so slight, would they not?'

The Registrar was thinking that these modern women were getting too big for their boots. Well, if they were, he hoped the boots pinched.

'And what do you propose to do about it, Miss Bennett?'

'Well, as you must know from our earlier conversation, I am of the opinion that the Edinburgh Royal Infirmary is the best in the world; but – if you will permit a Yorkshirewoman saying so – the Leeds and Bradford infirmaries run a very good second. My father, Sir, is a doctor who chooses to be a general practitioner, although he did qualify here in Edinburgh as a gynaecologist. He works in close co-operation with the Bradford Infirmary and the Women's Hospital, and I am sure, subject to your permission, he will arrange for me to do a year's ward and theatre practice. Currently, I am working with the health authority studying every aspect of public health. Mostly sitting at a desk!'

At last the Registrar smiled, but cannily. 'Well, Miss Bennett, in that case you won't need to trouble *us* any more, will you? We do know Dr Jeremy Bennett. May I assume that your father's address is the same as yours, though with you *new women* one never knows!'

She did not dislike the man. She could use his sardonic humour as a foil for her own repartee. He had the kind of calculating face that enjoyed getting the sum right. They parted with cautious geniality.

Evidently there were only two to be interviewed before H. Felicity was called not long after Belinda had come out beaming. On hearing her name, Felicity rose to move in, encouraged by Belinda's 'Good luck, my dear, you'll charm him.'

The Registrar recognised this girl from Yorkshire and then remembered that the Dean, no less, had handed him a note, which he had not yet read. He recalled that underneath his name, on the envelope, was inscribed: Ref.: Miss Felicity Laura Hargreaves. He glanced at it quickly and read: *Before interviewing Miss Hargreaves I think you should know that she is engaged to be married to Dr Fraser of our Faculty in December of this year.*

He returned the note to the envelope, and put it carefully in his waistcoat pocket, but he was thrown off course. This girl, just recently a student, how could she be within three months of marrying one of the most promising men in the Faculty? Where and how had they met? Hadn't Fraser been in America for three years?

The silence was lengthening. No, he would not change his dialogue. He would put her through his usual inquisition.

'And what do you propose to do, Miss Hargreaves? Depending, of course, on what we agree you should do.'

Felicity tried to sort out the explanatory words about her intention to marry but could only produce a blunt statement.

'Before we begin, Sir, I think I must tell you that I am engaged to be married.'

'And when, if I may ask, is the wedding?'

'This term, Sir, December 30th.'

'And who, if I may presume to ask, is the lucky man?'

Felicity blushed. Her interviewer smiled with satisfaction. He had thought these *new women* had forgotten how to blush.

'Surely it is not a secret, Miss Hargreaves?'

Felicity hesitated. 'I thought perhaps ... you already knew...'

'Oh no, dear lady, we in the university have to read more important announcements than births, marriages, deaths and engagements.'

Felicity drew herself up to her small height.

'My fiancé is Dr Alistair Fraser, who is, I am sure, well known to you.'

'I have known him as a bachelor, of course, for several years. A very talented and erudite man, if I may say so. May I congratulate you, Miss Hargreaves? Dr Fraser is a distinguished member of the Faculty. When there is a Chair for such a thing as a Psychiatry Department, I think it could very well be his.'

Felicity was only too conscious that his laudatory remarks about Alistair were only designed in order to diminish her.

'Thank you for your congratulations. I shall do my best to deserve them.'

'Do you regret that you have gone through the toil of qualifying for a career that is already ended before it has begun? A married woman's place, as you know, is in the home by her husband's side. In this case, of course, you will not only have a career as a wife but as an escort to a very important man.'

Felicity could not stop herself blushing. He had succeeded in making her feel inferior. There was no end to his chauvinism.

'In this case, Miss Hargreaves, it would neither be possible, nor appropriate, nor even necessary for you to fill in the gaps of your clinical cases. You have chosen the highest position a woman can attain: that of a good wife and, I trust, the mother of his future children. Good-day, my very best wishes. You are a very fortunate woman.'

Belinda was waiting for her:

'My interview was a walkover – how was yours?'

'Don't speak to me until we are out of here! I know I shouldn't feel as I do, but his attitude...'

'You look shattered. Let's go to Crawfords and have coffee, then you can tell me all about it.'

The conversation, which Felicity tried to repeat to Belinda, was rather like a broken bar of chocolate; there was nothing wrong with the ingredients or even what she had been asked to swallow.

416

It was simply that everything Alistair had made logical and whole to her had been broken apart.

Grace had sent out the invitations to her musical group bearing the words: *Come with a song or a poem from your own repertoire.*

Nell, Bel and Fel had been requested to play their movement from the *Archduke* trio and Grace and Felicity had spent magic hours on the Schubert rondo. This special Saturday, the last soirée when they would all be together, was to be exclusively for the performing group. Grace had made two exceptions: Maggie and Mrs Mac, a gesture that would not have occurred to any other hostess in the west of Edinburgh.

The evening following the interview, Felicity had put her grievance to Alistair about being 'only a woman' in the eyes of the Registrar. It was quite obvious to Alistair that the man had shattered her confidence. He tried to comfort her.

'My dearest, people who know you love you and believe in you; the rest do not matter. Tomorrow you are going to sing and play as you have never done before. Shall we look at the song you thought of singing?'

Felicity picked up the libretto and piano accompaniment of the *Mikado*.

'It's here. The Moon song. What do you think about that?'

Grace, who had come in to tell them that she was going to spend the rest of the evening practising her harp in the study, heard the question and said:

'Yes, that would be wonderful. What about Alistair accompanying you? That will give you more freedom to enact the part. You can make much more of this song if your hands are free.'

'Grace, you must have been reading my thoughts. Alistair doesn't know, but I have an idea which I think we can work on tonight.'

Grace turned to Alistair, quick to sense that every minute counted.

'You two stay here. I've moved my harp into the study – I need to practise.' She left them alone with the piano, the music and their healing love.

Felicity turned to Alistair. 'I'm thinking of it as a two-part song, with you as the Sun and me as the Moon.

He thought for a moment and laughed. 'It's a glorification of a woman, not a man's song at all. So, if you insist, you must be a full Moon... And I will be your setting Sun!'

There was more in this allegorical casting of parts than they first realised. It was important to Felicity, so soon after the Registrar's snub, that she should establish herself as Alistair's eternal, but not inferior, partner. He was her Sun. She did not mind receiving his reflected light but that did not mean being his shadow.

Apart from the occasional kiss for praise and encouragement there was no pause in their singing and playing, as they rehearsed together for Saturday's evening of friends making the best of music.

> Ah pray, make no mistake we are not shy
> We're very wide awake the Moon and I
> Ah pray, make no mistake we are not shy
> We're very wide awake the Moon and I

As the memorable soirée ended, so the full moon, shining over Moray Place and the haunting music of *The Moon and I*, accompanied the guests all the way home. Alistair dismissed the cab he had booked for himself for eleven o'clock, but made sure the cabby went off smiling his 'Goodnight, Sir' by making the unused fare a generous one.

He then rejoined Grace and Felicity, who were reliving the joys of the evening.

'Alistair, I thought you'd gone...'

'Grace knew the night was not over, didn't you, Grace?' To Felicity's surprise he led her back to the piano. There he opened the lid of the stool and beneath her eyes was an elegant jewellery box.

'Goodness, Alistair, to think I've been sitting on that gorgeous thing all evening!'

He lifted it out and put it in her hands. 'I knew tonight would give us years of remembering and I wanted you to have a memento – a keepsake. I know you are going to wear this very near to your heart.'

Delight, wonder and love delayed the opening as she showed it to Grace. She stroked the blue velvet box, then turned and kissed the hand that had given it to her. Inside the box was a slim gold locket which at her touch opened, revealing oval frames enclosing two miniatures of exquisite clarity; one could not tell whether they were finely painted photographs or portraits on ivory, but they were of her parents: Grace and Felix.

A stab of recognition made her eyes remain on the miniature

418

of Felix. The earlier photographs she had seen of him were full-faced, taken in uniform with his regiment. This was an intimate profile. She could see without doubt the same bone structure as her own. So that was the elusive person she had seen in her own face.

Alistair took the opened locket, closed it gently, then walked behind her to clasp the chain round her neck. Talking into her hair he said: 'Grace and I chose this portrait of Felix because it was so like you.'

She could not speak. Thoughts had travelled back in time. The two lovers portrayed in the locket must have been together almost for the last time in the New Year of 1876. Just nine months before she, Felicity, was born.

All she could do was to thank both Alistair and Grace through her tears.

Grace read Felicity's thoughts and feelings and putting an arm round her she whispered: 'We sat for those portraits the day before he left for Southampton and that is how I remember him. India was a whole world away – a whole cruel, silent world away – but Felix is here, my dear, in this very house.'

419

6

Back in Stonegarth, Felicity had the uncomfortable feeling that she was a visitor in her own home, making conversation in an effort to be more than just agreeable. It was all so different from Moray Place; there, reading a book in the morning one was not regarded as idle; here, a book in one's hand was a signal for Gertrude's interference.

Felicity was in her room unpacking – a negative occupation, for the clothes were being put away, whereas in Edinburgh, one was unpacking for joys ahead. The floor was strewn with tissue paper, taken from the folds of her dove-grey velvet dress, which was now hanging, dark and dull in the vast wardrobe. She tried to hum the Moon song, but it choked in her throat.

There was a knock on her door. It was Hilda.

'Ee luv, why didn't yer ask me to side yer things? I can't stop now, yer Mam sent me to fetch yer down. She wants 'elp with t'last of the tomatoes. Now leave all paper and stuff. I'll clear it up later.'

'You go down, Hilda, and tell Mother I'm coming.'

She could pick up an apron downstairs, but the greenhouse, in this bedraggled late autumn would shed dust and dried pollen on to her hair. She found a cotton scarf, wound it into a turban around her head, pouted at herself in the mirror and joined her mother.

Gertrude had a genius for finding work for idle hands to do. The servants, by never allowing themselves to be caught sitting down, rarely needed work to be found for them, but Felicity, at home with nothing useful to do, needed – or so Gertrude thought – jobs to be found which fell outside the servants' routine. From her reading of *Home Chat*, Gertrude had gathered that many society ladies considered a little gentle gardening to be an agreeable and appropriate occupation.

The greenhouse was dripping with tired tomatoes which had given up the struggle of trying to ripen. They were hanging on bent and broken stalks, bleak with shrivelled leaves. The pungent

420

smell of green tomatoes, quite different from the red, would be changed to carbolic when the greenhouse was stripped clean.

Gertrude was in her element. 'There's no need for any waste, here's the box of brown paper bags for the best ones. Hilda's picking the small ones for chutney. They're going in this bowl. I've chosen the best ones and put them in sawdust. They should be ripe well before Christmas.'

Gertrude had no sense of curiosity, except into other people's lives; it was Felicity with her inquiring mind who paused as she put the first green tomato into a brown bag.

'Who thought of the idea of ripening tomatoes in brown paper bags, Mother? They do have to be brown, haven't they?'

'Ee, I don't know, I learnt it from my grandma as she did from hers, I suppose. It doesn't matter *who* as long as we get the place cleared ready for the scrubbing out.'

But Felicity's probing mind had been sharpened in the study of sciences. 'Both sawdust and brown paper come from trees. I wonder what chemical it is in wood that preserves and ripens fruit?'

Gertrude was getting impatient; conversation was holding up action.

'There's no need to stop work to ask questions. You've not changed much, have you? I remember how you nearly drove me mad when you were little with your *hows* and *whys* and *whats*.'

Felicity and Hilda were glad that they soon had the greenhouse to themselves. Hilda had been waiting for a chance to ask a question:

'I've not 'eard yer mention Barlockend lately. How's yer auntie?'

'Well, I don't worry so much about her now, with Mrs Thompson there, but I'm going next week with Miss Bennett. She helps me to face it.'

'She'd face anything, Miss Bennett would. Oh I never told you. My cousin, Bess – 'er who lives back end of Bradford – cleans at public 'ealth place. She says Miss Bennett is the only one of the whole lot who steps over the bit of floor she's just washed and says: "Good morning, Bess" and "Excuse me".'

'Yes, Hilda, she's my best friend; a fine woman and she will be an outstanding doctor.'

'Well I never! A woman doctor! That's summat to look forward to. It don't seem right for a man to be 'andling a woman's private parts!'

Felicity made no comment, until the last green tomato had been cleared; her mother must not find them talking. She looked at her hands; they were covered with a film of smoky grime, dried pollen dust and sticky green from the dead leaves and tomatoes.

'What a good thing I took my ring off,' she said, half to herself and half to Hilda.

'Leave the rest to me, luv. I'll take the boxes down to the cellar! Can't think why yer mother gave yer this clarty job to do. You should keep yer hands in good fettle for the piano. 'Ee, I luv 'earing yer play. Do yer get it from yer auntie? You two are the only ones I have ever heard playing in this house. Did yer mother never play?'

The question was never answered. They could hear Gertrude coming down the gravel path.

'Didn't you hear the gong, Felicity? Leave Hilda to do the rest.'

'Sorry, Mother. Just give me time to wash my hands.' She slipped into the butler's pantry to do this, pulling the turban off to shake her hair free. The mottled mirror made her grimace at what she saw.

It was Exchange Day and she and her mother were on their own, eating a lighter midday meal than Father would be having. They were in the breakfast room with the second best cutlery. Felicity, searching in her mind for something to say, resorted to the banal.

'Well, Mother, there should be some lovely red tomatoes for Christmas, shouldn't there?'

Gertrude replied with her well-worn platitude. 'It's what I always say, and some folk don't seem to practise: *Waste not want not.*'

Felicity made her exit as soon as she decently could. She had an unopened letter in her pocket from Alistair and this afternoon Miss Davison, bidden by Gertrude, was coming to discuss wedding outfits: an occasion which had little appeal to Felicity. Her mother always treated a visit from this high-class modiste as demanding her Sunday best apparel and had brought up her daughter to follow the same ritual. Felicity, conscious that the bridal dress would be the dominant subject of discussion, and that she would be closely examined, measured and appraised, took more time than usual on her toilette. The last hairpin had been put in place, when a draught through the open window blew a few strands of hair over her face. She moved to the window and pulled the sash down to shut out the November breeze. A patting here and there, and one or two re-pinnings, made her presentable. The mirror reflected her ringless finger; her mother would want to show the ring to Miss Davison. She looked down to the crystal tray.

The ring was not there. But that was where she had put it.

It must be there – somewhere... *Where?*

In a frenzied search she moved everything, piece by piece, from

422

the dressing table and ran her eye and hand over the linen and lace mats. She poked distractedly into the open lacework – there was no ring...

Perhaps it had been blown on to the floor by the wind... She grovelled over every inch of the carpet. Then she knelt on the polished floorboards in the window bay and slid her hands over the surface even though she could see there was no ring. Two hairpins had dropped out, loosening strands to fall over her tear-stained face.

She felt sick. Her whole world had crumbled.

In despair she prayed, not to her God, but to St Anthony.

At the other end of Aireley the humble little shops clung together in one straight line.

One window and one door separated the butcher from the baker, the draper from the grocer, and the haberdasher from the ironmonger. Each tradesman minded his own business but jealously watched that there was fair dealing all round.

Watts the chemist was a different matter: the double-fronted site fitted across the corner of the street with a door that opened out flush to The Square. The Dog and Gun, diagonally opposite, had a slight connection with Watts through customers who suffered from overindulgence. The members of the Working Men's Institute, on the other corner, had only to cross the road to get their favourite Tadcaster ale.

Poised above the door, the chemist's red bottle signalled an attractive red light, telling the world that here was no ordinary tradesman but a genuine chemist with a ruby red carboy to prove it.

All the minor and major ailments and small vanities of the folk in Aireley had made it financially possible for Watts to send his only son, Simon, to Leeds University for a three year degree course in biological chemistry. Every day in rain, snow, sun or fog young Watts cycled to Shipley, put his bicycle on the train, travelled to Leeds and bicycled uphill to college.

Every night for three years he had swotted away in his little back bedroom, cramming into a tired head facts and formulas which left little room for fantasy. But his dreams of Felicity never quite went away. She was still his lodestar, almost his *raison-d'être*, but with the years of separation, the real woman, whom he had actually touched, had almost become a myth, a symbol of a stratum of society on which he had set his sights.

An incongruous figure he made on the way to fulfilling his ambition, for he was too short to be distinguished; too frugally dressed to look urbane and too serious to be socially at ease. Perhaps his being the only child of quite old parents made him old before his time, and his intention to go 'beyond the shop' caused both pride and sorrow in his parents.

'He'll go far,' admiring aunts and uncles gushed, but his mother's unspoken prayer was: 'Not too far, please God.'

Now a BSc graduate, Simon had a good position with Bright and Moston, the distinguished printers in Leeds, where, in a small laboratory, he conjured up unique coloured inks and new techniques in marbling and gilding. His modest salary was brightened with promised prospects which, they only hinted at his interview, would depend entirely on his own achievements. He more than earned his keep at home, paying his mother a guinea a week for food and doing odd dispensing jobs for his father.

On this November night he put his bicycle away, picked out an apple from the bowl on the sideboard, pulled the *Bradford Evening Argus* from the letterbox and settled himself down by the kitchen fire for a rest before tea.

It was too good to last. His father came in to the sitting room from the back of the shop.

'Simon, my lad, will you give me a hand? Leonard Stocks called today for the carbolic he needs for the Hargreaves' greenhouse. I'd only got half a gallon, but the delivery came this afternoon. Would you take this other half on your bicycle? It is paid for. Just put it by the greenhouse door. No need to disturb them in the house.'

'That's all right. As long as I'm not seen errand-boying. Wouldn't it be better if I took the stuff straight to Len? He could take it himself.'

'Nay, lad, Len's a mile out of your way. You could be there and back to Stonegarth in ten minutes.'

His father would never understand why he, Simon Watts, BSc, did not want to be seen as an errand-boy by the woman he most admired, but he did not want to hurt his father's feelings. He lit his bicycle lamp and set off.

November skies, especially when the moon is dappling moving clouds, have a magic all their own. Simon had been brought up to look at skies with his father's scientific curiosity and his mother's sense of wonder. It was a moon drenched in sunlight. In the garden of Stonegarth the moon picked out a light in a dark patch on a branch of a holly tree. It was an outsize nest, dome-shaped, spiky with thorny twigs jutting out like ramrods to keep intruders away. It was from one of these that the light pierced the surrounding dark. The tree was in the garden but well away from the house and a good place to leave his bicycle. He removed his lamp and swivelled it from side to side of the nest. The light changed colour: at first piercingly red, then green with a dazzle of white between.

He remembered Gregson, a lively teacher at his grammar school, who took the boys who were interested, bird watching. He told them exactly how and why each individual bird made its nest, the colour and size of the eggs, the feeding and caring until the day of independence and finally when and why the nest was deserted. There was no doubt about this one: it was a magpie's triumph.

He gasped at the very thought of what this light might be.

Could it be? ... Was it possible? ... Could it be a jewel?

7

Sooner or later – and now it was later – one would meet every inhabitant of Aireley in the village shop. Elsie Ellis, had she been both opinionated and indiscreet, could have written a chronicle of Aireley which would have shocked and fascinated all those who liked to peer through other people's windows.

It was now December and Watts the chemist was busy with cough medicines and linseed, liquorice and chlorodyne lozenges.

'I'll take Miss Elsie's, it needn't wait for Bob.' Mrs Ivy Watts was posting a parcel of samples from the pharmacy which her husband thought were beyond most purses in Aireley. All this was explained to Miss Elsie, a courtesy she had come to expect, when chatting over Post Office despatches.

'And how's Simon getting on?' Miss Elsie's eager smile proved her genuine interest.

'Oh, we can't keep up with him, even Dad doesn't know half the chemicals Simon uses. He's worked out a new marbling process for all those big leather ledgers they make. They've already had orders from America!'

'You must be right set up with him. A son you can be proud of. Oh, by the way, did you see Miss Felicity when you came here? She left just a few minutes ago. Isn't it good they've found her ring? She was wearing it today! Pleased as Punch she was! Daft expression isn't it? Punch always looks narky to me!'

'Don't rush on so, Elsie. I didn't know she'd lost it. When? And where?'

'Haven't you heard? Constable Giles found it, on a magpie's nest, one night when he was on his beat.'

'So *that* was what our Simon saw in the tree – Miss Hargreaves' ring!' She could have bitten her tongue out. Simon wouldn't thank her for letting on he had been delivering errands to Stonegarth, but he'd alerted constable Giles to what he'd appeared to have seen by the light of his cycle lamp!

Elsie's eyes opened wide. 'No-one's mentioned Simon!'

Ivy Watts subdued her voice. 'Well, we've not told anyone, Elsie,

426

because we didn't know how to tell it without letting our Simon down. Do you think we should?'

'Now look here, Ivy! Just think on how Simon helped Miss Felicity in the college days. Not only the day she burnt her hair, but doing all those notes for her with Miss Belinda. Now out with it, Ivy. Let's be hearing.'

There was an interruption in the shop, so Elsie was kept in suspense while she served a half-crown postal order to one customer and a packet of Jacobs's crackers to another.

Soon they had the shop to themselves again, but even so, Ivy Watts thought the information should be whispered. She had already settled herself on a chair and was leaning over the counter in conspiracy.

'Well, that night, Dad had asked our Simon to deliver some carbolic to Stonegarth. Not very nice for Simon, going there as an errand-boy – after all, Elsie, he went to a university too, and like her he's *got on* and has a degree. Between you and me, I think he's rather sweet on Miss Felicity.'

'I agree with all that, Ivy. But get on with your story.'

Ivy, a gentle and imaginative soul, retold Simon's version with a whisper but with a sense of wonder and mystery worthy of a theatre.

She warmed up as good storytellers do. 'Fantastic jewels, those lights were – diamonds, rubies, emeralds and sapphires, I said to Simon. But he put me in my place with his "sciencey" voice and told me that they couldn't be jewels until proved so. Well, now you know the truth, Elsie! It was indeed Miss Felicity's ring with three grand stones. More than that, I think the ring's got a history...'

Ivy was suddenly on her guard:

'Please don't tell Miss Hargreaves it was Simon, Elsie. How could he account for being outside Stonegarth at that time of night?' But Elsie knew Felicity better than that. She would explain the truth to her and get her to write to Simon at once.

Dear Simon, (Felicity's letter began)

It has, at last, come to my ears that it was you, not Giles the constable, who discovered the magpie's nest and the jewels lying on the rim. How very ungrateful you must have thought I was, for you must have expected that your name would have been in the constable's official report. Please accept my profound apologies.

I do not know whether it has been explained to you that it

was, in fact, my engagement ring, which the impudent – but clever – magpie picked up from my dressing table. As you can imagine, I was distraught by the loss.

It is, perhaps, therefore an appropriate opportunity to invite you to the wedding service at 12 noon on Saturday, December 30th at the Eastbrook Methodist Hall, Bradford. Only close relatives, and certain family friends, are being invited to the service and the reception, which will take place at 1 o'clock in the French Room at the Midland Hotel.

You will be receiving a note about the service, on which I am adding in my own hand: *please no presents*, as I am anxious that people who can ill afford it are not spending their hard-earned money. You have given me so much kindness whilst at college.

May I say, once more, how truly grateful I am for your wonderful discovery. Would it be a possibility, if I arranged to make a purchase in your shop on a Saturday afternoon, that I could show you what you only saw at a distance? Please do not feel it necessary to pen a reply. I shall call next Saturday and trust that I might have the good fortune to see you in the shop.

I remain,

Your former fellow student,

Felicity Hargreaves

His parents were infinitely curious about the letter, but too polite to be intrusive. Simon never mentioned it, or made any reference to *Miss Hargreaves*. Yet for him *Felicity* had not just been a name to conjure with. Over the years it had become his everyday generic noun: *felicity* – encapsulating all that dreams were made of: happiness, love, spiritual joy, the divine centre of being. For him it meant a harmony of minds.

Reading this letter the word dwindled into the cold murky air of Aireley. Tearing the letter to pieces, he wished to God he had never met her.

Felicity had only on one rare occasion been inside the Watts' shop and for the first time saw the different colours in the three interior carboys and the rows of small mahogany drawers with cut-glass knobs. On the counter were the apothecary's brass scales

428

and on the floor at the end of the counter the weighing machine. There was a professional mystique about it all, which had meant nothing to her, when as a young child her nurse had taken her there to have her knee bandaged after a fall in the road. Charles Watts came into the shop from the back of the house and apologised for keeping her waiting.

'What can I do for you, Miss Hargreaves?'

'Would you be so kind as to tell Simon that I have called hoping to see him.'

'I'm sorry, ma'am, but Simon is not here.'

'Oh, I am so sorry. I wanted to thank him, in person, for being the one who spotted the jewels and to show him what was eventually revealed. It was this: my engagement ring.' Her ungloved hand came forward and she registered the astonishment on Watts' face which she had hoped to see on Simon.

'It is beautiful, ma'am! May I bring my wife in to look at it? Ladies are always interested in good jewellery, but even more so in a betrothal.'

Ivy Watts came into the shop busily tying her afternoon lace-edged pinny. There was a hint of a bow in her approach.

'Good-day, Miss Hargreaves. My husband and I very much appreciate your visit.'

Felicity's gloved right hand, firmly clasping her own, gave Mrs Watts the courage to touch Felicity's left hand and look at the ring.

'I've never seen anything like that in all my life,' Ivy gushed. 'No wonder Simon couldn't find words to describe it.'

Felicity was beginning to be embarrassed by the obsequious manner they both presented. But Ivy was now glowing with pride.

'Charles may have told you that Simon is in Leeds seeing a gentleman from London who is interested in patenting Simon's latest chemical discovery.'

The Watts could not understand why their visitor was blushing, nor why she withdrew without suggesting a future appointment with their important son. Felicity had already drawn her glove over her left hand, showing her intention of departing.

'Please give my kindest regards to your son and convey my sincere good wishes that his meeting in Leeds was successful.'

She walked back home humbled, ashamed and only too conscious that she never could withdraw such an insensitive letter. She tried to excuse herself that the class structure was built into her very being. It determined the ceremonies and formalities which patterned her life.

It was a salutary thought that Belinda would have behaved differently; but then, her parents had given her an attitude to life that broke through rigid social barriers.

She went home to her room and criticised herself that in these few short weeks in Aireley she had become a cog in the wheel of outdated tradition. Bigoted class attitude; acceptance of the domestic role of an intending bride; religious formalities and duties had taken over. She had let all the petty conventions from which she and Belinda had escaped engulf her.

Her own thoughts were now centred on New Year's Eve and a new century: the year 1900 was signalling a new life, when all the paraphernalia of getting married would be over.

Meanwhile, she had to put up with the endless sessions with the modiste and her team of three seamstresses and the trivia of Maud Musgrave's plain sewing. The ever-mounting trousseau, her mother's pride, was an outward and visible sign, as far as Gertrude was concerned, that her daughter was 'marrying well'.

Another irritant in the marriage preparations was more corrosive as it was not openly discussed.

Early in the year word had come from Caroline and Jack Fieldhead that now they had a team of twenty men working on their sheep farm in Canterbury in New Zealand, and they had the time and freedom to do the sea journey to England. They had set their hearts, they said, on being in the country to celebrate the arrival of the new century.

Felicity had written to Alistair warning him that Caroline and Jack Fieldhead were to be wedding guests and that they would be in residence in the Midland Hotel, where his parents, and other London guests were already booked in.

All through November and December Felicity's dread of the wedding had darkened the days, but the wheels of preparation were relentlessly turning. The printed invitation cards had been distributed to Gertrude's satisfaction.

She turned to Felicity. 'You can do the chapel notices. They only need putting in the envelopes. We can get Hilda to give them out to folk, or drop them in. I don't even think you need put names. I can give her the list.'

Some one hundred gold engraved cards had already been sent out to the honoured guests. Miss Davison arrived the next day in the station cab with her fitter and seamstress carrying large heavy dress boxes, a Gladstone bag and a Japanese basket holdall. A fire had been put in the master bedroom, a luxury that brought wreaths of smiles from the two underpaid helpers. Miss Davison had already underlined, before they came, the privilege of working for the gentry.

'Wash your hands in the bowl, here, before you handle the gown. I have brought a towel. Replace it if you please in my laundry bag.'

This ritual over, the layers of sateen, which were used by a superior modiste instead of tissue paper, were drawn out from the folds of the sacred garment and hung on the screen, where the combination undergarment was hanging ready for Felicity to define the bridal silhouette. She gasped with amazement and apprehension at the sheer grandeur of the gown. It was, she had to admit, a sculptural masterpiece. Most of it was completed, but sections of it were waiting for the appliquéing of the velvet motifs. The back of the skirt, elongated into a train, was temporarily only running-stitched, waiting for the bride-to-be to perambulate in front of the modiste. The fitter carefully ascertained the weight, length and movement of the train and visualised it making an impressive picture down the aisle.

The ivory brocade had been specially chosen in Lister's showroom, together with the café-au-lait pan-velvet edging the bodice and ruched and tiered skirt. Miss Davison explained that at the centre of each motif a pearl was to be sown. It was her *pièce de résistance*, suggesting royal connections transforming her, she felt, into the realm of court dressmaker.

'It is absolutely majestic, Miss Davison, but I am not a majestic person. It is far too princess-like for me.' There was nothing more she could say. The hard-working girls were looking triumphant. The fitter knelt on the floor to pinch and pin a fragment of fabric, to squeeze out a quarter of an inch to tighten the waist even further.

'Kitty, please take that pin out! Remember that after the ceremony I shall have to say how-do-you do and shake hands with a hundred people and I shall have to be able to breathe! I firmly refuse to be sacrificed just to follow fashion!'

Miss Davison, with a look of piety, said: 'If I may be allowed to say so, Miss Hargreaves, my ladies *lead* the fashion, others merely *follow* it!'

There had been a letter from Alistair by the evening post, as Miss Elsie predicted. It was full of loving messages, work problems and an amusing account of an evening of song at Moray Place. His letters made little reference to the wedding. This one ended with information which at least showed he was making some preparation for it:

I think it is usually expected that both bride and bridegroom have resided in the parish where the wedding is to take place. You, I know, will be pleased to hear that the Bennetts have invited me to stay with them from December 23rd. Shall I be allowed to see you? I am hopelessly ignorant about English weddings, so you must instruct me on every detail, otherwise my Scottish reticence and Scottish exuberance may 'gang agley'.

Dear Felicity, I thought you would like me to wear the Fraser dress kilt, with all its historic paraphernalia.

My best man is my brother Graham Fraser, QC, twice-engaged, never-married sterling man in Stirling city staying with his barrister friend in Ben Rhydding. He will be wearing a dress kilt too.

Is it not wonderful to think that in less than three weeks' time you will be a *Fraser* too? Does that sound arrogant and chauvinistic on my part? Please allow me to show you off as *Felicity Fraser*, for you will be honouring an ancient clan.

I send this imperfect letter with perfect love.

Yours forever

Alistair

Preparations by the Fieldheads for their return to England from New Zealand had been going on for months. Most of the discussion between Jack Fieldhead and his wife Caroline centred on the practical details of management of the sheep station; choosing the shipping line, with dates of departure and arrival. All of these matters caused little dissension. The difficult issue was how they changed roles from being discarded relatives, eleven years ago, to welcomed blood relations.

Caroline lapsed into Yorkshire bluntness. 'Well, I'm not staying at Stonegarth, so there.'

'I never suggested we did. Just somewhere near. We'll have to call on them.'

'No, Jack, we won't *call*! We'll *entertain* them. We are not going back as assisted-passengers, not on your life!'

432

The Hargreaves, however, as their nearest of kin, were to be given a valuable present, an original painting commissioned by Jack of the finest view in the sheep station. The artist, a leisurely young man with rich parents, had no interest in counting sheep; rather he preferred counting the red stickers on his paintings in the fashionable galleries in Wellington and Auckland.

Because he did not need the money, he could put a high price on each picture and in his prestigious catalogue. He knew that such lofty presentation opened the wallets of the well-to-do. There were several artists in New Zealand more talented and more original – many of them Maoris – whose works were sold for a pittance.

Sadly, these artists could only afford to remain poor.

The night before they were due to sail Jack suddenly confronted his wife. 'There's something we haven't faced, Carrie, and it's your problem, not mine – Amy. What are you going to do about *her*?'

Caroline's voice, usually light and pleasant, went flat and defensive.

'Listen, Jack, it's eleven years since we saw her – she was done for then. What's the good of trying to see her? She wouldn't know us. We wouldn't know her. She may have passed away for all we know.'

Jack was thinking deeper than she knew. He spoke slowly and quietly.

'Listen, Carrie, are there any folk in Airedale who remember you were her twin?'

'*Were*,' Caroline emphasised. 'Were! And that's the word for it. We are not twins *now*.'

'But what about Gertrude? She's her sister as well as you. She's never mentioned Amy once in her letters, has she?'

'She wouldn't, would she? She blames us; we blame her. And there's only one person to blame – that's Amy! Gertrude has discarded most of the Ackroyds, anyway.'

8

Tilbury was ugly, dark and grey. England's green and pleasant land was a myth – a dream. The train drive into Liverpool Street was grim and slummy, showing them a London they had not seen before. Caroline thought of her travel trousseau in the leather trunks and the months she had spent getting and spending to make it perfect. What had she come to?

The cabby they summoned looked at their luggage and refused their fare.

'Not bloody likely, Sir! No room for that lot, even without you two.'

The two porters with their flat-wheeled wagons were waiting for a tip.

'What about hiring a station wagon, Sir? That'll get you to Kings Cross.'

And so it was that Jack and Caroline Fieldhead, with all their baggage, climbed on to the rickety goods wagon and clattered their way on the cobbles of the East End of London. At Kings Cross Caroline departed with embarrassing haste and left Jack to summon porters. She entered the Great Northern Hotel, and making for the ladies boudoir, restored the angle of her hat and her self-possession. By the time Jack joined her, she had summoned the head waiter, chosen the table for luncheon and was examining the menu.

There's nothing like good food, she thought, to give you back your faith.

The hotel was built to keep out the cold and also the noise of the trains. The hot rolls, the carving trolley with its *baron de bœuf* and the high-hatted chef made her feel that she really was in England at last.

'Even the coffee's good: hot and strong.' She spoke as if she were a connoisseur.

'Yes,' added Jack, hoping to sound travelled. 'A rare treat in this tea-soaked country.'

A smartly uniformed head porter appeared to escort them to their first-class carriage.

The two hundred mile railway journey produced little conversation except disparaging remarks on the puny fields and sooty towns.

'Sheep farming!' Jack exploded contemptuously. 'They should see ours!'

The Midland Hotel, Bradford, was not going to be beaten by a New Zealand summer so there was a large fire in their bedroom and a four-poster bed to ensure that the Fieldheads had a warm roof over their heads. They quickly adjusted to these luxuries, determined that there would be no mention of their earlier tough life. They would let it be assumed that New Zealand led the world in its modern conveniences. Jack was used to shouting orders to the men on the sheep station but neither he nor Caroline were used to the bows and curtseys of the decorous hotel staff. Such deference justified her best clothes. As business bookings had slowed down with the darkened days of Advent, and Christmas visitors would not be arriving for nearly three weeks, the manager had time to make a fuss of his new visitors.

The hotel was almost boringly quiet for Caroline; she liked people who talked – even more, those who were good listeners to her stories from 'out there'.

It was the Fieldheads' fourth day when the manager came to their luncheon table.

'Would you do me the honour of being my guests on Saturday? I am giving a ball and banquet in the Prince's Room for our valued guests of past and present. You will find the printed invitation in your room.'

In their bedroom Caroline allowed her polished speech to drop into blunt truth.

'I told you so, didn't I, Jack? Aren't you glad you took heed of me? White tie and tails. Evening dress. Lucky for you that I made you bring your morning dress too. You'll be right for the wedding now.'

In front of the well-stoked fire Jack sweated, recalling his days of khaki shorts, open-necked shirts and endless open air. The lively picture in his mind produced a deadened reply to Caroline's sartorial stuffiness:

'I've not a bloody breath left in my body.'

'Language, Jack! Shame on you! In a high-class hotel too!'

* * *

Guests were now arriving from afar for the festive season. Yorkshire folk tended to spend Christmas at home with relatives they took for granted as annual visitors but business friends were 'treated' later in the week with grandeur in the Midland.

On arrival from the Edinburgh train, Sir Duncan and Lady Fraser had been presented with a letter in their son's handwriting, which they took up to their vast bedroom. They drew two small armchairs up to the fire. Deborah Fraser opened the letter; then giggled to herself before bringing in her husband:

'Duncan, *do* listen to this description of Alistair's future in-laws: "You will find them rather difficult to get to know for they do not indulge in conversation; rather they go in for time-saving assertions. They are affluent but thrifty, hard-working, straight-laced and strict Methodists. You may wonder, as I did, how all this equates with the French Room reception, but prosperous Yorkshire folk are thrifty in order to cut a dash on special occasions!

' "My bride-to-be, Felicity, is not exactly a cuckoo in the nest but, at least to your son, a bird-of-paradise! There is an explanation why she differs from her parents. I hope I shall have time to tell you when we meet at the Midland." '

Towards the end of Alistair's letter a single sentence conveyed little by way of an introduction to the Fieldheads:

' "Among the guests there will be Mrs Hargreaves' sister and her husband, who are over from New Zealand. Their detachment from Stonegarth may seem strange. I think I know the reason. But it is a long story." '

Deborah paused to laugh. 'Listen to the P.S., Duncan.

' "By the way, the Mackenzies, whom you remember from your Edinburgh days, have chosen to stay at the Swan Hydro in Harrogate, smaller, quieter and less showy than the Midland, but rather more *distingué*. But your choice of hotel, contiguous with the main line station, is surely the more convenient from all points of view." '

Soon after the Frasers arrived, during dinner, they were made aware of the couple who assumed superiority from having arrived well before Christmas, after a three-month steamship journey.

The saga was to continue through the week, describing life on board the *Shakespeare* and the long summer the Fieldheads had left behind for the grim Yorkshire winter. Lady Fraser could not identify their accents. Had she done so she would have caught the loud emphasis of industrial Leeds in Jack Fieldhead and the honed version from his wife which Leeds Girls High School demanded of its pupils.

The day after his parent's arrival, Alistair was in Bradford buying Christmas presents for the Hargreaves; a task he found both difficult and dutiful. The Bennetts were delightful hosts and recipients of gifts who would appreciate every detail in the books, music, cognac and family games which Alistair was to bestow on them. He had chosen blatantly expensive Scottish gifts for the Hargreaves: solid silver carving rests with Scottish thistles.

A display of Leeds pottery with its famous white interlacing caught his eye as perfect for Felicity. She would love that, and it would grace their home. He spent an extravagant half-hour and concluded by arranging for the whole set, except one piece, to be sent straight up to Edinburgh.

He had planned to meet his parents tomorrow, but as he had finished shopping earlier than he thought he would go into the Midland on the off chance of seeing them, and invite himself for lunch. The head porter greeted him:

'Sorry, Sir, it was such a fine day that Sir Duncan and Lady Fraser decided to take the train up to Ilkley.'

'Thank you. If you would kindly show me to a table for luncheon I should like to stay here.'

'Of course, Dr Fraser. I feel sure your parents would wish you to be their guest and to occupy their table.'

Alistair bowed a 'good-day' to the couple next to him, who looked delighted to be relieved of the boredom they found in one another.

The lady spoke first. 'Have you come far, Sir?'

'Well, yes, I suppose I have – from Edinburgh actually...'

'Oh, we've come all the way from New Zealand.' The two said in syncopated chorus.

'Took nearly ten weeks,' added Caroline on her own.

'Round the Cape, you know,' put in Jack.

'On the *Shakespeare*, you know.' Caroline said, as if he knew of its eminence.

'Well, Madam, you flatter me. I don't know that ship at all, nor the sea route, but that you can enlighten me will give me pleasure.'

The conversation went on, encouraged by Alistair's questions. He ventured at last with something more personal, which he deliberately addressed to her husband:

'May I ask, Sir, are you here to find your roots, or are they known to you already?'

'We were both born in Bradford – and proud of it. Fieldhead's the name.'

The medical record flicked into focus and there on the first sheet was the name Jack Fieldhead witnessing Amy Ackroyd's lunacy. In seconds Nellie's horrifying story was dominating Alistair's mind.

Fieldhead's face showed neither cowardice nor cruelty; it had the laughter lines of a man who looked out on far horizons. His wife? Yes, of course, she had a look of Gertrude Hargreaves but she was slimmer and more at ease with her husband. Alistair decided to take down the barriers there and then.

'You are here for the wedding, I presume? So are my parents. In fact this is their table. They have only been here a few days, but I think you will have met them.'

Caroline looked impressed. 'So you are a Fraser, too. Pleased to meet you. Shall we be seeing *you* at the wedding?'

Alistair grinned broadly. 'I'm afraid there will be no wedding if I am not there!'

'Listen to that, Jack. Mr Fraser must be the bridegroom!'

Jack tried to explain their ignorance of the bridegroom's name:

'We haven't seen our niece since she was a young girl. All I remember is she was called Felicity.' The conversation had met a dangerous corner, which Alistair sensed. They looked to be a little on edge, but he was determined to know more. The waiter approached and addressed the Fieldheads.

'Will you take your coffee in the lounge, Sir? And will Dr Fraser be joining you?'

There was no escape. The three had the small coffee lounge to themselves.

'So you are Mrs Hargreaves' sister, Mrs Fieldhead?'

'Well, yes, but we have been so many years apart she seems more like – well – a pen-friend.'

'Then, of course, you must be my fiancée's aunt.'

Jack was getting impatient. 'Yes, we told you that.'

Alistair did not choose to take the remark as a rebuke. 'I seem to remember her saying that the aunts on her mother's side were twins?'

'Yes, *were*. Sadly my twin died soon after we got to New Zealand, and there's no way we could have got back to the funeral...'

Alistair forgot he was in the Midland Hotel. It could have been his consulting room. His concentration was on Caroline Fieldhead's eyes, yet he was questioning her husband.

'Did *you* know your wife's twin, Mr Fieldhead?'

He watched the fear in her eyes as she waited for her husband to reply.

'Oh, less than a year! I don't think she took to me. Good thing she did pass away, I always thought. Not quite right in her head... You know what I mean.'

The head porter opened the door. 'Sir Duncan and her Ladyship have returned, Sir. They asked me to tell you that you will find them in their room.'

Alistair took time to rise from his chair, but he was determined to say something – even if it spoilt the Fieldheads' holiday. Whatever he said or heard they would all three be dabbling in half-truths.

'I must go now and join my parents. But before I meet them I must reassure you, Mrs Fieldhead. Your twin sister, Amy Ackroyd, is not dead. She is a permanent resident in Barlockend Asylum.'

He turned quite slowly and held Jack Fieldhead's gaze.

'Good-day to you both. This good news must make your long journey worthwhile. No doubt there will be an opportunity to exchange a word with you at the wedding.'

His talk was heavy with irony, which was not completely lost on the two. Carrie's handkerchief was screwed into a tight, damp ball. Jack drained his cold coffee and walked to the window, looking far away from his wife. He spoke as if he were seeing Amy's ghost spying on him through the windowpane.

'Why can't you go away, you bitch? For God's sake, go away.'

Alistair dragged his guilt up every step of the wide staircase leading to his parents' room.

Lord, what have I done? he thought. This was Felicity's secret, not mine. Why did I act so impulsively? Yet, I was right. They were lying. How could they say that Amy was dead and refer to her funeral?'

The porcelain knocker on the door put an end to his personal thoughts for within seconds his mother was welcoming him.

'Alistair, my darling, what a wonderful surprise. Do come in and see our palatial apartment. I don't know how we shall ever live up to it.'

His father shook his hand. 'Well, my boy, I hope you enjoyed your host's luncheon. Generous folk those Frasers, aren't they?'

From being a small boy Alistair had revelled in his father's teasing.

'And you made sure, with your hosting, I wasn't left without folk to talk to, either. I'd say thoughtful lot, those Frasers!'

His father joined in the joke. 'And did you get everything, sheep, ships...?'

'Well not sealing wax, anyhow. But I must tell you both, if you don't already know, that Mrs Fieldhead is my mother-in-law's sister. So I suppose she will be some sort of in-law to me.'

'Darling, don't take on more of the family than is absolutely necessary. It has always been my belief that families, especially in the plural, are far more tiresome than one's friends.'

As far as the Bennetts were concerned, they were 'open house' for Felicity for every day Alistair was staying with them. It was now December 23rd; Felicity would be seeing Alistair at the Bennetts' on Christmas Eve for an informal supper and an evening of music. He would be at Stonegarth for a formal tea on Christmas Day.

Early that morning Felicity had been up in the attic retrieving the red and green ribbons which, every year, tied the holly and the ivy in their accustomed places. Her eye was caught by the books that she and Hilda had left uncovered. Like all book-lovers she could be diverted from any task for a 'read'. The one she picked up at random was Amy's gift to Caroline, celebrating their mutual twenty-first birthdays. Felicity turned to the inscription, and there, with a shock of reminder, she saw the date: December 28th 1877.

She picked up the ribbons, ran downstairs, threw them on the hall table, returned to her room and wrote:

Dearest Alistair,

I have just discovered that Aunt Amy's birthday is on December 28th, two days before our wedding. I know we are both heavily engaged but I feel the least I can do is to go to Barlockend and hold her hand. One cannot, in truth, wish her Many Happy Returns of the Day; that would be cruel.

If you agree to accompany me, you will be able to explain to the Bennetts where you are going, and why. I must be silent and will need to be in collusion with the Bennetts to cover why I am away from home. Could you contrive that for me, Alistair dearest, please?

440

Would you be so kind as to ask Belinda (whom I trust has leave from her job for Christmas week) if she could possibly come over for me in the trap. (Not the tandem, I think, in this biting weather!) The trains go every twenty minutes from there to Barlockend, so I propose we catch the 2.19 and get the 3.37 back. I can drop off at Aireley on our return.

We shall meet, of course, before then but I did want to make sure you were free that afternoon and the Bennetts were happy to help us on our way.

This somewhat curt and commanding note is not in the least what is in my heart, my dearest. Read between the lines, Alistair, my loved one, and you will find our words. Isn't it wonderful to think that very soon now I shall be Felicity Fraser, so here I am getting a little practice in writing my new name?

I shall always remain

Ever your own,

Felicity

. P.S. Aunt Amy will be forty-three, on that day, having spent twelve years in Barlockend. How can we 'celebrate' such a painful anniversary?

Christmas worked its way out with duty and delight in uneven measures. December 28th brought a very different celebration. Plans were changed as Belinda lent her pony and trap to Alistair and Felicity for the journey to Barlockend.

'Good luck, my dears, give her my love...' Belinda, who had been bursting with energy and laughter while preparing her pony and trap, was now standing protectively still. It was as if she were trying to add her strength to theirs. She had pushed a ribbon-tied bag of sugared almonds into Felicity's hand. The card, linked into the bow, carried no wish, it simply bore the words: FOR AMY in print which could be read without glasses.

The two drove off, every part of them well wrapped, except their faces which quickly reddened and tightened in the relentless cold. Speech needs warmth and there was none about, except the warmth of silent love.

The Thompsons had been told of their visit and the special reason for their coming; so Alistair and Felicity called at the Lodge first.

'I knew you'd be on time. I've got cocoa ready for you first, though, and a good fire.'

Ten minutes of Roberta's warmth did wonders, releasing tongues in friendly exchange to fill the gap of recent months. She waited for the right moment.

'I must warn you both that Miss Ackroyd is not well. She has been confined to her bed for over a week and is in very low spirits, but she was one of our show patients for the official opening of the ward last week. I'll not come with you, I saw her this morning.'

Felicity did not comment on what seemed an unhelpful way for officialdom to treat a sick patient who needed quiet.

'Don't worry, Roberta, we shan't stay long. But we couldn't miss her birthday.'

An impressive Sister showed them to the new sanatorium, a large airy room with floral cubical curtains and bed covers. Unlike the other wards, the beds had a thirty-inch space between them facing a large bowl of flowers on the table in the middle of the room.

Alistair looked round with a doctor's eye, recognising the picture presented to the city fathers on a day when their benevolence was on show.

'Your aunt's waited a long time for this,' he whispered in Felicity's ear.

The Sister was ahead of them: 'Wake up, Miss Ackroyd, you have visitors!'

It was a firm, but not harsh, voice and at least her aunt was addressed by her name.

'Fifteen minutes,' the Sister ordered Felicity, while adjusting the sheet an inch so that the centre crease was in line with Amy's nose. The patient lay inert, shrivelled and grey, quite unable to disturb the sheets out of their hospital symmetry.

Felicity stroked her hand. 'Amy, my dear, it's your niece, Felicity, with her fiancé. We have brought something for your birthday. Here are winter bed-socks to keep your feet warm.'

Amy lifted hands that were all skin and bone except for rope-like blue veins. She drew the socks to her face. Then, as if the socks were too heavy to hold, she dropped them on to the sheet.

Alistair had brought her a single red carnation, which he held for her to smell. She breathed with an effort and her lifeless eyes filled up with tears. It seemed as if the tears were the only living friendly part of her body. Felicity hesitated about burdening her with Belinda's gift of sugared almonds, then decided as there was

442

still a vestige of sight she would show her the pretty ribbons and the pastel shades of the sweets. She took one out and held it to her aunt's dry grey lips. They parted, and almost greedily, she sucked the sweet into her mouth.

Alistair was watching every sign that life was still there and marvelled that four of the five senses could be brought to life with these simple gifts.

Felicity folded the gnarled hands into the warmth of her own. 'May love be all around you on your birthday.'

The words floated away into the disinfected air. There was no sign that they had been received. Felicity turned to share the negation with Alistair, in silence.

He whispered: 'Loss of hearing makes people very lonely and it is usually the first of our senses to go. But your words won't be lost. They are round her now – a spoken, but silent, blessing.'

The Sister returned, holding a feeding cup in her steady hand, secure in her starched uniform.

'You can see yourselves out by the staff door – nearer for you. Thank you for coming. There are hundreds in here who have never had a visitor, and never will. You should have been here last week at the opening. These were the chosen patients for the Mayor, Corporation and important guests. Miss Ackroyd was a fortunate one.'

The cruel irony of this belated care silenced Felicity and Alistair. They had driven a mile before Felicity said: 'Do you think, Alistair, they'll let her stay there until ... she leaves this world?'

'For God's sake, let it be short, my darling. This mocking of life owes her a peaceful death.'

This would be their last meeting before the wedding. Alistair drove Felicity to Stonegarth and was escorting her into the house when she said: 'Remember, we've come from the Bennetts', won't you? Will you stay for a cup of tea?'

'No, my love, I'm dining with my parents this evening and I have to change and get the train.'

They stood enclosed in the porch. Their cold hands clasped together.

'Goodbye, my darling. It will be a different world at Eastbrook on Saturday... Please, Alistair, do come in and just have a word with my mother. She's very proud of you, you know!'

They moved inside and Felicity went to fetch her mother into the hall.

'Well, are you all set for Saturday?' Gertrude gushed. 'You've got a surprise coming, hasn't he, Felicity?'

443

Her daughter was unwinding the long woollen scarf from her neck.

'Well, I shan't be wearing this, for sure, and you are also going to get a surprise, Mother, on seeing Alistair with bare knees!'

Alistair eased himself out of the social chat.

'Sorry I can't stay, Mrs Hargreaves. I'm dining with my parents. They sent their warmest regards to you and your husband and very much look forward to the day you have both planned so generously.'

He decided that a kiss on Felicity's hand would be the most decorous gesture to please her mother.

The two parted formally, hiding their silent secrets.

It was a short train drive to Forster Square and the covered way into the Midland Hotel sheltered Alistair from the evening gloom of Bradford's city centre. His long black cloak, lined with red silk, and his black top hat were taken from him in the foyer of the hotel. The chandeliers and deep crimson carpet and curtains were such a transformation from the sooty station that Alistair found himself blinking the dark and cold away in sparkling light as he was greeted by the head porter.

'Sir Duncan and Lady Fraser have gone into dinner and are at their table awaiting your company.'

Alistair bowed to the Fieldheads at the next table.

'Good evening to you both. I trust you have had a pleasant day.' He could see Mrs Fieldhead's mouth open to tell him, but he let his parents be an immediate magnet. It was always a pleasure for Alistair to be with his parents because they made few demands of him and he of them. Gentle disciplines having been got over in his early years, they were able to enjoy one another's company.

As a family the Frasers treated meals, however frugal or festive, as great talking times and Alistair was soon to hear all about his parents' train ride to Saltaire to see the great Titus mill and the village round it.

'It's Yorkshire's version of Toy Town,' Sir Duncan commented. 'Except for the smoke from that massive chimney.'

Talk on muck and mills incongruously went on as they studied the Yorkshire-Parisian menu and gave orders to the waiter.

'And what have you been doing today, Alistair? Do they let you see that fine bride-to-be of yours? I must say we took to her when we met at Miss Hargreaves' in Edinburgh.'

'Well, Papa, if you must know, Felicity and I have been to a

444

place you and Mamma will not be visiting: Barlockend Asylum.' Alistair's voice was usually strong and resonant but on this occasion he subdued the volume and sharpened the enunciation. He made quite sure that the words reached the alerted ears at the next table.

'A professional visit, son?' his father enquired.

'No, a very personal one – with Felicity. An aunt, on her mother's side, has been in there for twelve years and Felicity is the only one who goes to see her...'

His mother, about to ask questions, felt that it was not fair on Alistair to have the dinner spoilt.

'Alistair, there must be a long and sad story to hear. Shall we wait until we are in our room?'

She returned to her crêpes suzettes.

'Well, yes, it is a long story and a harrowing one so I'll just tell you the reason for our special visit today – it was Miss Ackroyd's birthday.'

Caroline Fieldhead was wearing the gold bracelet which Jack had bought for her forty-third birthday; they had spent an indulgent half-hour at Ogdens in Harrogate that morning. Almost unconsciously, on hearing the word birthday, she drew the silk cuff over her wrist.

The waiter came to the Fieldheads' table:

'Savoury, Madam? Devils on horseback?'

'No thank you. We have had an excellent sufficiency. Would you serve coffee in our private room?'

The Fieldheads swept out with polite, cold bows, leaving the elder Frasers wondering if they had offended them.

The Frasers went to one of the small drawing rooms, where their cognac and coffee followed them.

'Alistair, I'm curious to know more about our New Zealand pair? We have heard too much about their obvious success, but what about here?' his mother asked, managing not to make her enquiry sound gossipy.

Alistair drew nearer. 'Perhaps you had better know more, since you will be near neighbours also at the wedding. Mrs Fieldhead is sister to Felicity's mother and twin sister to Felicity's aunt.'

'Does the other twin sister live round here?' asked his father.

'That was the long story we decided to leave until we had finished dinner, Mamma. It is not a happy one...'

'There is never a right time, my dear, for unhappy or disagreeable stories. But as you two have your malt whiskies and I have my cognac, perhaps now...'

Alistair recounted the long life of the twins, never apart until Caroline Ackroyd – now Fieldhead – brought her husband into their family home; indeed into the bed the twins had shared for thirty years. He was just at the crisis of the story when there was a knock on the door and a page handed over a letter. It was addressed to Dr Alistair Fraser.

He read it with amazement:

Mr and Mrs Fieldhead would be obliged if you could call at their private sitting room (number 44, second floor) some time this evening as there is a subject of importance they would like to discuss with you.

Please send a reply by the page.

The Fieldheads greeted him with a good deal more warmth than they had shown on their exit from the dining room. Something must have happened between then and now.

They were in no hurry to begin and used their usual social anodyne to ease into conversation:

'We've a good Highland malt here we brought from the boat; would you like that or Napoleon brandy?'

'A very small whisky, please. My father and I have already antici-pated the New Year.'

There was just five minutes of small talk before Caroline Fieldhead moved in to the major issue.

'Dr Fraser, my husband and I have been having a quiet talk together about my sister, whom you have found to be alive. You, and my niece, have evidently much more knowledge of her than we have, hasn't he Jack? Nobody wrote about her ... her niece never did.'

Alistair interrupted. 'But you knew where she was?'

'Not really – it was only temporary – while she got over her tantrums.'

Jack joined in. 'We put her in the care of the doctors and seri-ously thought they would see her through a short life.'

There was an uncomfortable pause.

'I am here as your guest,' Alistair bowed, 'and I do not intend to cross-examine you, but I think, so that we keep things straight, you should be aware that I have a copy of the medical record and my own notes on the case. Time is short, for all of us. Could you explain why you have brought me here?'

Jack took over. 'Dr Fraser, we have come back to England in a

446

very different financial position from when we went out. Very different. I have put money over the years into Barings and they will do money orders for any transaction in this country or overseas...'

Caroline thought Jack needed prompting. 'What my husband and I were wondering was if you would help us to see that a monthly sum of money gets to the right place at the right time when we've gone back to New Zealand.'

'Surely Barings will do that for you, Mrs Fieldhead. They are used to overseas bank drafts and standing orders...'

'But this is something that will affect your future wife – my niece.' Caroline tried her most persuasive smile on Alistair.

'Perhaps you could explain how the money is to be allocated. I can assure you that my future wife is more than adequately provided for by her father and, I hope, by me. There would be no question. She would refuse it.'

'No it's not for her. It's this, Doctor.' Jack felt they knew where they were now. 'We've heard there's a good private place in York, well thought of, where folks go who can afford it, who are not quite right in the head. What I'm asking is that you give doctor's orders to where she is now and where we'd like her to go.'

'And you would just sign the banker's order.' The intonation suggested 'so that's your little game'.

Alistair finished his Scotch and stood up:

'I am sorry, but what you are offering is about twelve years too late. Miss Ackroyd is so conditioned to institution life: the asylum bell, the asylum food, the asylum clothes and the grey monotony of the asylum beds with their recognisable smell. She would be confused and embarrassed. It would be as cruel to move her into the Haven as it would be to move her into Buckingham Palace. I think I have said all I need to say except this: I am sure you had no intention of going to Barlockend, but if you had suggested it I would have pleaded that you did not go. The dream of her twin, which she kept alive for years, does not exist any more. Good night to you both.'

It was ten thirty. He went up to the next floor and into his parents' room. They were sitting by the fire in their dressing gowns, his mother brushing her fine long hair while his father read aloud snippets of the *Yorkshire Post*. Their apparent comfort was disturbed by apprehension about their son and they both showed relief on his entrance.

'It's late, my dears, I shall not stay. They were offering conscience money to set Amy up in an expensive retreat in York. I told them it was too late. And turned it down!'

447

9

Christmas and a wedding, all in one week, proved to be a social challenge which demanded exhausting cheerfulness. Gertrude's open 'At Home' on the day after Boxing Day kept Jessie and Hilda busy responding to both the back and the front doors of Stonegarth. The tradesmen came to the back door for their Christmas boxes; the hatted and gloved brought their visiting cards and their wedding presents to the front door. Their discreet parcels wrapped in white paper would later be opened by the bride, no doubt to reveal embarrassing duplicates of toast racks, sugar tongs, nutcrackers and fish knives and forks.

The week at the Bennetts' was open house for the Frasers and Felicity. When Graham arrived in high spirits from Ben Rhydding, the days usually ended with Highland dancing and singing. Alistair put his brother through the formalities of being a best man and quickly introduced him to Belinda, with whom he would be in league. They immediately found a meeting point with humour in their eyes and one could have guessed that the word *solemn* would soon be removed from *The Solemnisation of Marriage*. Belinda (for she at once gave him permission to drop the Miss Bennett) described the two attendants as: the wriggling Priscilla and Harry the Page who, the last time he was in church, spent the entire sermon pulling feathers out of his grandmother's boa.

'But believe me, Mr Fraser, they will both be angelic, for I shall bribe them so that they will behave exactly as I ask them to do.'

Graham turned to his brother. 'I hope you've got presents for the little brats. It's an awful long agony for the wee things.'

'Yes, I've got theirs but I hope to give my gift to the maid of honour very soon. Stay exactly where you are, Belinda, and I'll bring it down.'

It was an amber necklace, carefully chosen by Felicity and Alistair to enhance the deep gold velvet gown she would be wearing.

'Oh, Alistair, and Felicity, what a gorgeous choice for me! You know how I hate glittery jewellery. Look at the light of the amber:

448

it's sunshine; firelight; gold and autumn brown. Feel how warm it is! May I bring my gown to show you how perfectly they go together?'

It was the first time her mother had ever seen Belinda drool over a feminine garment. She and Jeremy exchanged amused smiles of sheer disbelief.

Among her northern friends, Grace Hargreaves had always been considered the most peripatetic. Her school and college friends were either tethered down with children and husbands, or the unmarried ones, all hope abandoned, were dutifully caring for aged parents. She had, therefore, several pressing invitations that she could choose for the wedding. Her old schoolfriend, Emerald Green, appealed most. As an infant she had rebelled against her parents' stupidity by changing her name to Emmie as soon as she could read a paint box.

Emmie's solid stone house, a hundred yards or so from the Grove in Ilkley, had been left to her, with all its clutter and priceless pieces, by her grandmother. The *objets d'art* and Emmie's books on women's rights might have seemed incongruous to others, but not to Emmie. The tapestry cushions and her latest Pankhurst tracts, Sherlock Holmes or Wilkie Collins lived together comfortably while Emmie walked up to the college to do her intelligent best to enliven teacher training. There was, Grace and Emmie had decided years ago, a lot to be said at times for being spinsters, especially if the shelf on which one was left was clean, quiet and comfortable and above all filled with books.

Grace suggested to Alistair and Felicity that, as they wanted to return to Edinburgh soon after their wedding, she would be honoured if they would stay at Moray Place for the first week of their honeymoon. She intended to go on from Ilkley to an old college friend, Hetty Illingworth, whose husband ran an hotel near the banks of Ullswater. Grace was delighted to see, on the brochure, that Mr and Mrs Grenville Illingworth were in partnership, which meant that she, Grace, had the freedom of being in an hotel with the fun of being a private guest of a carefree family.

During the preparations Grace had talked over the wedding with Jeremy and Hazel, who could sense the moments when the hurt would be most acute. The three had discussed the decision which Alistair and Felicity had made to stay in the Royal Station Hotel for the two nights of their honeymoon in York.

'I suppose Felicity's date of birth as September 18th 1876 will be on the marriage certificate?' Grace asked.

Jeremy replied: 'We know better, Grace, do we not? Do you think that Felicity wants to lay the ghost?'

Hazel, seeing Grace bereft of a reply, answered almost in a whisper: 'She was so definite about wanting their first days together to be in York and Edinburgh. Do you think perhaps she wanted to establish with Alistair that both birth dates are now one?'

In Stonegarth preparations were more solemn. Gertrude had laid out the honeymoon garments on the bed in her own room.

'We'd best get your packing done, Felicity. There will be plenty to do tomorrow without that.'

'Thank you for helping, Mother, but I shall need very few garments for the first few days when we are at Moray Place. I've labelled my trunks to go to Alistair's house – that will be our home until we leave for our honeymoon visit to America in February.'

'Well, you know what I think about that, don't you – so I won't mention it again.'

They were silent for the next few minutes, folding every garment with layers and layers of tissue paper. Gertrude held up a finely embroidered night-gown, turned the sleeves over centrally and then folded it to the exact size of a white satin night-dress case. The action must have alerted her thoughts to her daughter's marital bed.

'There's something I've wanted to say to you all the week, but we've hardly seen anything of you. But now I've got you on your own, Felicity, I want to give you some advice. It had to wait until you were ready for it...'

She paused and lowered her voice to match her solemn face.

'Always oblige your husband in the bedroom...' She paused to let the advice sink in. 'Don't ever let him see you undressed. Be properly covered when you are in bed. Any uncovering that's done must be left to your husband. Of course in the dark – under the bed covers.'

Felicity was so shocked at the crudity of the advice she simply said: 'I think, Mamma, we are talking about very different husbands.'

The conversation was brought to a halt with Hilda's knock.

'A letter for you, Miss Felicity, the only one in the second post.'

'Put it on my desk, Hilda, I'll read it later.'

The rest of the packing was done in silence and suppressed exasperation: *When shall I ever wear all these clothes?*

An hour later she sought her own room and read the letter: the address from a city office in Leeds was not familiar.

Simon had typed his reply to the wedding invitation, feeling a need to show his distant lady that, although she had snubbed him, she had been a spur to his ambition.

Dear Miss Hargreaves,

I thank you for the invitation to your wedding, which I shall be unable to attend.

Your special occasion coincides with a demonstration I have been asked to give to the senior chemists of the Bradford Dyers: new dyes for the twentieth century. Excuse my not sending this reply to your parents but I thought my reason for not accepting would have more meaning to you.

Please accept my good wishes for your future.

Simon Watts

The thought passed through her mind that she had underrated the man.

A knock on Felicity's bedroom door was followed by the expected arrival of Belinda, who came in clutching a dress box. She sensed that all was not well but tried to cheer Felicity by drawing attention to the attendants' outfits and running through their duties and hers.

'Felicity, it would help if I saw the guest list. I would like to know most of their names. Not easy with that crowd.'

Belinda accepted Felicity's explanation of sheep and goats (those only at the service; those at the reception) before she knew the details. This division was inevitable with the Hargreaves' attitude to those whom they dismissed as the common people. Felicity referred to the former en bloc, but read out the names of each favoured guest, with brief comments on social status and relationships. She reached M in the alphabet; *Robert Mackintosh* was one of several Macs.

'Oh good. I'm so glad you've asked Robert; he was, and is, a wonderful friend to both of us.'

Belinda then waited expectantly for *Watts*, but Felicity ran on to

451

the final name, *Young*, and added: 'You know – the Leeds tailoring company.'

'What about *Watts*? Surely you're inviting Simon? He did just as much for you as Robert Mackintosh.'

Felicity blushed and added lamely: 'Mamma agreed to Mr Mackintosh because she said he was a professional. It surprised me since I thought the only professionals she recognised were doctors. Not her daughter, of course – she only wants me to be a young lady.'

Belinda glared in anger.

'Isn't it time, Felicity, you cut the umbilical cord? Simon Watts worships you and proved it in the way, week after week, he taught you to be a scientist – not just a mother's daughter. I suppose you patronised him by including him in the tradesman lot. I hope he tore it up and did not reply!'

A stinging silence separated them. Felicity had hoped that Belinda's visit would wipe away the anger her mother's crude concept of marriage had caused.

'He did reply. Here's his letter. It's a genuine reason for not accepting.'

Belinda took it and read between the lines, sensing the heartbreak and revenge that prompted it. She did not spare Felicity's feelings.

'You deserve it, my girl. This is not just a formal reply to an invitation it is a response to an insult and a deep, deep hurt. It is also to show you that he's making a career for himself. Painful pride. Out of character. You ought to know how self-effacing the man really is.'

Felicity sat silent, numb with shock that her closest friend would be so cruel on the eve of her wedding.

Through suppressed tears she muttered: 'It's too late to do anything now. In any case he couldn't come.'

'Before the end of the day, I hope you're going to write a letter of congratulation on his success. Not with Hargreaves or Fraser patronage but from a fellow science student, whose burnt face he helped to heal and whose brain he kept alert.'

Thoughts were too strangled for words. Belinda walked away to the window and remained silent. Felicity sat stunned. Her hand moved to her face for comfort but tension tightened the scar under her fingertips. It had not completely gone – but Simon had.

Belinda thought of the evening she had planned and knew that she had to make the first move. She walked slowly back, held out her arms and drew Felicity to her.

452

'It's our last time together, my dear, come with me.'

She took her stricken friend back to her home, where she picked up her cello en route for the drawing room and the grand piano. Lowering Felicity on to the stool, she said: 'Do you remember how Franck's Sonata in A brought release after the stress of clinical lectures?'

Felicity made no move to open the score, which Belinda had put into her hand. She had been accused of ingratitude and contempt for a man she had underrated. Music offered no comfort. It was being left to her to break the silence.

'Yes, Belinda, I suppose you're right. I'm still trapped in the Hargreaves' social net, even after those years of so-called liberation. It's easy for you, with your background, to get to know Simon. But Belinda, he surely couldn't think that...?' She could not finish the sentence.

Belinda could have done, but resisted. She came to the point, gripping Felicity's shoulder.

'All you can do now is to write a letter of congratulation and *mean it.*'

The move of the score to the music stand and a nod to Belinda of agreement cleared the air for the intense concentration they needed for a small part of the first movement of the sonata. Soon they became enveloped in Franck's serene and luminous music. Friendship did not fail them now, it was strengthened with truth.

The wedding day dawned crisp and clear with a whisper of snow over Baildon and Ilkley Moors. The wind had the tact to be blowing from Wharfedale, rather than from the sooty skies of the industrial smudge round and below Bradford.

Eastbrook Chapel, grandly Gothic in style, had no wedding bells. Was it not built when Bradford was becoming prosperous and the followers of Methodism could look at their own watches and clocks and know the time, without being summoned by bells?

The guests, in all their finest feathers, tended to arrive early, giving them time to look at the white and gold narcissi and daffodils decorating the chapel. They also liked to be in their places, well before the bride entered, to see what every arrival was wearing.

Madame Davison, sitting in front of Watts and his wife, eagerly awaited the appearance of the bridal gown.

Those in the back rows, including the Musgrave sisters, unconsciously humbled themselves to support the class hierarchy and watch the performers, the titled, the dignitaries and the close members of the family, take their places in the front rows. Herbert Dawson, whom Felicity had insisted should be present, looked upon the cast with an experienced eye, as if he were selecting characters for his next production. Robert Mackintosh, wearing his Highland dress tartan, looked as if he had come down with the Scottish guests, rather than the short journey from Burley-in-Wharfedale. His fine bearing swung the kilt into a rhythm which teased every feminine eye.

Amongst the lesser fry was the bank manager's wife who, noticing the Winkley girls wearing tiffany and taffeta, leaned close to her eldest daughter to whisper: 'I hope they are wearing combinations and comforters underneath or they will be frozen.' Unfortunately the remark coincided with a lull in the organ introit and the word *combination* travelled to Hilda, Jessie and Elsie, who needed just that to relax them into smiles.

The famous organ swelled out a diapason of sound as the Winkleys took their seats. They had sauntered down the aisle, stopping to give amiable greetings to those they knew. They gave a sense of high church theatre to the chapel and joining the Mackenzies, affably introduced themselves with an assumption of being *en rapport*. Sir Angus and his wife had been fussily ushered to their seats by Henry, who, concentrating on the hierarchy, had quite forgotten that earlier on he should have given three nervous spinsters his support.

Felicity had insisted that there was no question of guests being asked whether they were a friend of the bride or bridegroom, otherwise there would have only been twenty-five on the bridegroom's side. The Fieldheads, feeling relieved not to be too near to the Hargreaves, were affronted that they were well behind the titled on the other side.

The great moment of silence and rustle had come and there were the bridegroom and best man in splendid Fraser tartan looking down the aisle for the approach of the bride. Felicity, in a glory of ivory brocade and velvet, clouded with an ivory veil, brought mystery to her beauty, and a composure which no-one who had seen her the night before would have thought possible. She walked, arm in arm with her father, as if it were quite a usual occurrence.

When she came to the front row, she paused to give Gertrude a kiss on her cheek then turned to the row behind to acknowledge Grace. She was conscious of a hint of a tug from her father and a stilling of the train from Belinda. Most of the congregation glowed at Felicity's spontaneous charm. She had confided her intention to Belinda and so it was that the two little attendants were as still as a Dutch painting.

The organ strains of the *Archduke* trio – such a change from the usual Mendelssohn – touched Belinda deeply. It was a signal of friendship, which only the two of them would fully understand. Her tight squeeze on the hands of the train-bearers was a way of pushing back tears to tell herself that this was to be a day of rejoicing. Now that they were all in their places Parry's music of Felicity's favourite hymn rang out:

> Dear Lord and Father of mankind
> Forgive our foolish ways!
> Re-clothe us in our rightful mind
> In purer lives thy service find
> In deeper reverence praise.

Although she was on her father's arm she felt the presence of Alistair intensely, for this was a hymn they had shared, in their discussion of marital love and physical passion. The quiet power of John Greenleaf Whittier's words in the last verse gripped them. They both knew that in their future intimacy there would be times of ecstatic stillness.

> Breathe through the heats of our desire
> Thy coolness and thy balm;
> Let sense be dumb, let flesh retire;
> Speak through the earthquake, wind and fire
> O still small voice of calm!

The minister gave the opening proclamation of the marriage service, but paused before the vows. Felicity had arranged with him and the organist that there should be unison singing of the Welsh hymn *Guide me, O thy great Jehovah.*

What the Methodists lack in bells, chalices, croziers, candles and mitres they make up in music and song. The words 'Bread of Heaven' with the bass voices of the men and the descant of the girls and boys in the choir rang through to the rooftops.

The minister, unlike many others, did not say the words of the service as if he had repeated them a hundred times, but rather as if the two in front of him were in his protective care. Even so, the words were awesome.

'Therefore if any man can show any just cause, or impediment, why they may not be joined together, let him now speak, or else hereafter forever hold his peace.'

A sharp chill went through Felicity, remembering Jane Eyre and Rochester.

Alistair almost winced at the words: 'as ye will answer at the dreadful day of judgement' and wondered if he really would like to meet such a threatening God. He felt more secure as the minister asked: 'Wilt thou have this woman to thy wedded wife, to live together after God's ordinance in the holy estate of matrimony.'

Although both she and Alistair had read the service in the quiet of their own rooms, it was different hearing it travelling through the chapel in front of so many witnesses. The minister was now concentrating his whole attention on Alistair.

'Wilt thou love her, comfort her, honour and keep her in sickness and in health and forsaking all other, keep thee only unto her, so long as ye both shall live!'

Alistair's 'I will' carried conviction to the back of the chapel.

A similar question was put to Felicity, but the words 'obey him' were omitted. There was a distinct rustle amongst those who were following the service in their books of prayer. Gertrude and other 'long-marrieds' thought it must be the minister's oversight. They would never know that he, Felicity and Alistair had been in collusion to omit the three-hundred-year-old promise. It came to the question put to the bride's father: 'Who giveth this woman to be married to this man?'

Arthur, making the most of his small part, let the whole chapel know that he did, but resented the way the minister took his daughter without a by-your-leave or thank-you. Memories of his own marriage were vague and unemotional; he returned to Gertrude without even touching her hand.

It was soon time for the retreat to the minister's vestry for the signing. This was the part of the ceremony that Felicity dreaded, knowing that incorrect information of her parentage was to be signed on a legal document. Her parents were behind her, but where was Grace? The weight of the train increased; Priscilla and Harry were there trying to cope, but where was Belinda?

Those in the front of the chapel watched a distinguished-looking lady, near the front row, being drawn from her chair and led into the minister's room by the maid of honour.

'All is well, darling. Belinda is bringing Grace,' Alistair whispered to Felicity.

The Registrar was there, waiting with the marriage certificate laid out in front of him. He called each signatory in turn to fill in the narrow spaces which would complete the contract.

Marriage solemnised in Eastbrook Chapel in the County of the West Riding of Yorkshire on December 30th, 1899 between Alistair Iain Fraser, bachelor of Edinburgh, Occupation, Doctor and Felicity Laura Hargreaves, spinster of Aireley, Yorkshire.

The male parents' signatures were also followed by their occupations:

Arthur Hargreaves: Mill owner

Sir Duncan Fraser: Medical consultant (retired)

There was a pause when the Registrar asked for witnesses. Alistair took over.

'My wife and I would like our marriage to be witnessed by Miss Belinda Bennett and Miss Grace Hargreaves.' Alistair brought the two forward. Belinda looking delighted and Grace slightly embarrassed. Belinda added to her full signature, *Maid of honour.* Grace Laura Hargreaves' signature was followed by the single word: *Godmother* next to the printed word: *witnesses.*

The legal ceremony ended with: *by licence by me Alfred S. Harvey: Registrar in the Registration District of Bradford.*

Congratulations ended with a shuffling into processional order. The opening of the door was the signal for the organist to peal out the opening bars of the Schubert rondo. It was not at all the music which Gertrude and Arthur expected for their important walk to the west door, nor could they feel at home with the New World symphony of Dvorak, which followed. They would have been even more confused had they known that Alistair had chosen it because of the composer's life in America and his empathy with Negro music.

The regression was in fact pure joy for Felicity. With veil thrown back she felt free, not only to smile at Alistair but to every one of the guests, including the humble folk at the very back of the chapel.

Instead of processing on the arm of the best man, Belinda did her own tactful rearranging:

'You look after Grace and I'll have Priscilla and Harry with me. We mustn't let the little angels fall from grace. Remember the poor things have to go on standing still for the photographs.'

Graham grinned. 'Do you think I should give them a humbug?'

457

'No, Graham, certainly not. Botticelli angels do have blown-out cheeks, but that's from playing their trumpets, not sucking humbugs!'

Robert Mackintosh's thoughts quickly spun from the bridal pair, his eyes mesmerised, seeing Belinda Bennett in a completely new role as a dazzling woman rather than a challenging student.

He chuckled inwardly. In her usual clothes what a companion she would be! He must make plans to meet her again. What about inviting her to the Caledonian Ball?

The chosen guests had only a short walk from Eastbrook Chapel to the Midland Hotel; even so, there was a procession of carriages and cabs, garlanded with white ribbons, to drive the guests through the holly and ivy archway. Inside the hotel at the top of the stairs a pergola of white gardenias and camellias framed the bridal pair. Next to them the attendants and best man were lined up with the Fraser and Hargreaves parents to shake hands with, and consistently smile at, over fifty guests. Felicity felt like an actress without a script. It was so difficult to remember who gave the toast racks and who the sugar tongs, and sound highly delighted with them all.

Velvet was the chosen fabric for this winter wedding, with ermine, chinchilla, and sable positively spelling out the 'brass' which created it all. As the ladies lifted their gowns up the crimson carpeted staircase, the chandeliers shone on their jewels and reflected their light on the brass railing of the wrought-iron balustrades.

The E-shaped sprigged arrangement of the four tables, each with a name on every setting, was a miracle of social and psychological manoeuvring.

As the principle of 'blood is thicker than water' had to prevail on such an occasion, the Fieldheads were on the high table but at the extreme end, quite the worst place for seeing and hearing the speakers in the centre.

The scarlet uniformed toastmaster sounded his horn. Arthur said his usual grace, not only to signal to the guests that the feast had begun but to show that a Worshipful Master, a mill-owner and a lay preacher could add style to any occasion.

The wedding breakfast was, of course, a sumptuous affair: game pottage or beef consommé, oysters, whitebait and guinea fowl. A

458

huge *baron de bœuf* on a heated and lighted trolley was carved with generous precision by a high-hatted chef. Nearby was a table of silver epergnes piled high with exotic fruits, and coloured jelly moulds shone like jewels. Savorin trifles and charlotte russe were flanked with Yorkshire custard pies, cheesecakes, spice cakes and deep apple pies.

Although quite intemperate as far as food was concerned, most of the guests had been brought up with Band of Hope temperance. The Midland Hotel tactfully substituted the forbidden champagne with elderflower wine, which, in spite of its homely name, was in fact frivolously heady. In the hotel kitchen the chefs had a row of liqueurs which they shook generously into the trifles and jelly moulds to loosen the tongues of the teetotallers.

When 'replete' was an understatement, the toastmaster sounded his horn and Arthur rose to give his tribute to the bride. His basic speech had been re-trimmed for the occasion to include 'Mrs Hargreaves and myself' and to thank the guests for their generous presents.

'I yield to no one in admiration of our daughter, Felicity, who has, all credit to her, bravely faced being away from her own Yorkshire home for four years in another country.'

On which the Scottish guests picked up their discarded napkins to hide smiles and stifle guffaws.

Arthur was quite unconscious of his chauvinism and total misrepresentation of his daughter's joyous enterprise, and concluded:

'Mrs Hargreaves and myself will watch her grow into an obedient wife and a model mother with her husband. Pray rise to the toast to Dr and Mrs Fraser.'

The Scots and a few others needed something rather stronger than elderflower wine, but the presence of the next speaker, Alistair, brought a hint of sun, sea, heather and fresh air to the centre of the high table. He was completely relaxed and confident, giving himself time to smile on the people he thanked and paying particular attention to his parents-in-law.

'As I look round at this splendid gathering I remember lines I learnt by heart at my preparatory school. They are from Hiawatha's wedding feast: "*And the wedding guests assembled/Clad in all their richest raiment.*"

'My wife Felicity and I wish to thank you all for being present with us today. Many of you have travelled far, not easy in this darkest month of the year, and we ask for your forgiveness and tolerance in our choice of December 30th for this most important day in our lives. Felicity and I chose this date because we wanted to

459

take one another into the new century. We had hoped that the wedding would be on New Year's Eve, but as that was a Sunday it could not be.'

Turning to the minister he said: 'Perhaps our minister, who made our service so memorable, could explain why babies can be christened on a Sunday but people may not marry. I should have thought, Sir, that we adult sinners need more of a holy day than innocent babes but, of course, weddings are very time-consuming.'

Arthur did not appreciate *that* remark at all. It was not minister's time that cost owt, it was the wedding paraphernalia that consumed the brass.

'It is my duty and pleasure today to thank the bride's attendants. First our impressive maid of honour, Belinda. It has been a joy to me to witness, over the years, an incomparable friendship. Without Belinda's support and encouragement I doubt if Felicity could have so successfully completed the last years. Today, as her chief attendant, she has guided Priscilla and Harry through very demanding roles.'

He turned to the pageboy.

'First we owe you an apology, Harry, that the *train* you looked forward to taking up the aisle turned out to be made of velvet and not of steel. But over there, near the cake, is a large box for you to open when you get home and this is the key you can have now, which may give you a hint of what is inside! And you, Priscilla, have a big box over there; it also has wheels and you, too, will be the driver.'

He turned back to the guests.

'I was talking to Priscilla and Harry earlier in the week and asking them what they thought would happen in the new century. Harry said he thought it would be boring as everything has been invented. I can understand your thinking that, Harry; the nineteenth century has been bristling with inventions: trains, telephones, steam engines, tram cars, and now even motor cars on the roads! Both you and Priscilla are seven, Harry, or rather you will be in January. I wonder what will be happening when you both come of age and are twenty-one. Seven now, fourteen years more isn't it? Can you add fourteen to 1900?'

Priscilla, blushing at hearing her own voice, gave the answer: 'Nineteen fourteen.'

'What exciting things you will see invented, and who knows where we all shall be.'

He paused and glanced round at the adults, catching Gertrude's impatient eye.

'As I said, Felicity is taking me into a new age and I shall walk beside her with enormous pride. Let us in our toast to the bridal attendants wish them, and all of us, a wonderful new century with our Poet Laureate's vision ringing in our ears.'

He picked up a sheet of paper in front of him.

'Take these words from Tennyson's *Locksley Hall* home with you:

' "For I dipt into the future, far as human eye could see,
Saw the Vision of the world and all the wonder that would be . . .
Heard the heavens fill with shouting, and there rained a ghastly dew
From the nations' airy navies grappling in the central blue;
Far along the world-wide whisper of the south wind rushing warm,
With the standards of the peoples plunging through the thunderstorm;
Till the war-drum throbbed no longer, and the battle flags were furled
In the Parliament of Man, the Federation of the World!"

'Will there ever be, I wonder, a Parliament, a Federation of the World? And now I have a gift for my wife, which I know will be a total surprise to her: Priscilla and Harry are patiently standing here with a heavy weight hidden from sight. Hand it over, my dears, to the bride.'

Felicity removed the blue velvet cover and there – she could not believe her eyes – was a shining brass plate engraved with the words:

FELICITY FRASER MBChB

She took the nameplate, set in its mahogany base, and lifted it to face the wedding guests. There was a roar of applause and clapping from the Frasers and their friends; the Mackenzies; aunt Grace and other guests from Edinburgh. The chosen staff of Bradford College clapped with tears in their eyes. Hilda, Jessie and Elsie stared with amazement and admiration.

The Yorkshire blood-is-thicker-than-water relatives sat, in clotted silence, thinking, in their different ways: How could a newly married woman defy a sacred tradition? What vulgarity for a lady to advertise herself with a plate on her gate!

Dumbstruck at first, Gertrude and Arthur glared into one

another's shock, then Arthur rose to his feet and shook his fist towards the bride and the brass plate.

'Put that down and never let me clap eyes on it again! No daughter of mine's goin' to earn 'er own living. 'Ave yer no pride? Both of yer.'

Alistair's speech dwindled in the chilling response of the Hargreaves parents. He relieved Felicity of the brass plate, covered it with the cloth, put it down on the floor and held her hand all through his brother's speech.

Graham, stunned as he felt inside, was determined to restore good feeling and give Felicity and Alistair all the praise and love they deserved. He cut out much of his light-hearted speech and concentrated on the bride and bridegroom. First he paid compliments to all who had participated, then he had fun referring to the Scots invasion through Hadrian's Wall and the warmth of hospitality in Yorkshire.

'It is my duty and pleasure to reply on behalf of the bridesmaids – well, that was the instruction given to me by my big brother. But first I should like to do what I have never done in my life before – that is, stand up in front of a grand assembly and praise him! It had never dawned on me before this week what good taste my brother had until I met his charming and gifted bride. Some of you will have noticed the necklace she is wearing with the ruby pendant; he has shown his good taste in that too. Do you remember the lines from the Old Testament? "Who can find a virtuous woman for her price is far above rubies?" Well, her delightful face and lively head are above the rubies too! And as for virtues, she has them all!

'And what vision he has shown in his last gift to her: the brass plate bearing her new name and her professional status. I should like to convey my personal congratulations to them both for the trust they have in one another!'

Standing again under the garlanded pergola to say their goodbyes and thank-yous to each of the guests demanded renewed stamina. Alistair had the gift of making each person he addressed feel very special. The only time the glow fell rather low was when Caroline and Jack Fieldhead gushed their congratulations. Felicity, slightly conscious of this cooling in Alistair's response, added for good measure: 'And a Happy New Year.'

Alistair sensed that Priscilla and Harry had stretched their good manners for long enough, so he had prevailed on one of the

462

waiters to find a box of games. The two were now in a quiet corner working off their young aggression in the ups and downs of snakes and ladders.

Belinda waited for the last handshake and then took Felicity upstairs to the bedroom reserved for her to change.

'You were perfect, Felicity, just perfect. But if only those philistines could understand true values they would know that it was the brass plate which made a unique bride.'

As Felicity's gown dropped to the floor she looked down at it:

'Just think, Belinda, all that glory and I shall never wear it again!'

Belinda smiled. 'What about your father having it on show in the Exchange? It could be a showpiece, you know. Remember all the fabrics were made in Airedale, except the French lace.'

'Oh, Belinda, don't mention Father! No! I think it should be kept in my true father's wardrobe in Moray Place.'

'Of course, of course! That's a great idea.'

Belinda realised that she could not delay the delivering of a letter any longer. Felicity immediately recognised unmistakable writing:

'But Roberta and Anthony have already sent their good wishes. Whatever can it be?'

'It must be important, Felicity. They left it for you with the hotel porter.'

Felicity read the letter silently.

Dear Felicity,

I feel sorry, my dear, to send this sad message on such a joyous day but I must inform you that your aunt Amy died at nine thirty this morning. God rest her soul. She will be buried, with three others, in the Barlockend graveyard on Tuesday, January 2nd at eleven o'clock.

Roberta and I will act in your absence but I am saddened that other members of the family will not be there. Of course the Registrar of Deaths will be informing them, legally, as nearest of kin, but I cannot think it will bring any response.

Roberta joins me in sympathy and support.

I am,

Yours in God's service

Anthony (Thompson)

The bridal glow of the day drained from her face:

'Belinda, please fetch Alistair. I must talk to him. But first read the note yourself.'

'I already know, Felicity. Graham opened it and told me the news.' She put a protective arm round Felicity. 'Do not grieve, dearest Felicity. We must thank God she is at peace. Sit down and I'll go and fetch Alistair.'

It was early days for a bride to be weeping; the grief was not for her aunt's death, for that was a kindness that was owing to her; it was for a lack of love and understanding round the deal coffin with its cheap plate. Not a single member of the family would be at the funeral if she herself were not there.

Alistair stopped in the doorway. His bride's face was completely drained of colour, except for the red blotch of tear-stained eyes.

'Alistair, I can't go away. Aunt Amy has died. I must be with her!'

Alistair held her hands and looked into her stricken eyes. 'She has *died*, my darling; she is not here. Just be thankful that she will no longer be living at Barlockend. If your God is the God of love, Amy will now be in caring hands, won't she?'

'But Alistair – not a single mourner...'

He took a large handkerchief from his pocket and gently dried her eyes and held her hands again.

Belinda put her hands on both of theirs. 'Don't spoil your honeymoon, my dear ones. Roberta, Anthony and I will see that everything is dignified and – as beautiful as we can make it.'

'Oh thank you, Belinda, but what can I do?' She looked round the room in despair and her eyes rested on her bridal bouquet. She went over to the dressing table and picked it up.

'Belinda, could you possibly take this to Barlockend tomorrow and ask that it should be put on her coffin? Alistair, could you find me one of the marriage service cards, please? I must write a message for her.'

Belinda, holding the bouquet, said: 'Of course I'll go to Barlockend tomorrow morning and stay for the Sunday service. They may even make an announcement of her death.'

Alistair returned with the card and put his fountain pen into Felicity's hand. Quickly she wrote: *For my beloved aunt Amy from her niece Felicity*. She then turned the card over to the blank side and rested the pen in thought, before she printed very carefully:

AND ALL THE TRUMPETS SOUNDED FOR HER ON THE OTHER SIDE.

464

The three sat in silence turning over thoughts that the quotation had evoked.

A sudden knock on the door broke their silence. Alistair opened it and, on seeing a porter, signalled him not to enter and to be quiet. The porter, baffled, lowered his voice.

'The bride's mother asked me to say, sir, that many of the guests are waiting to accompany you and your wife to the station in order to give you a good send-off on the train.'

Felicity picked up the word 'train':

'Belinda, would you be an angel? Instead of coming with the crowd to platform four, would you go to platform two – I think it is – where the train will be leaving shortly for Carlisle. Grace should be on the train by now. You'll find her quite easily as your parents will be there seeing her off. Please tell Grace of aunt Amy's death and explain, as best as you can, that I shall not be at the funeral. Grace will understand. Oh, Belinda, it does seem so hard-hearted... But go now, my dear, the train leaves in five minutes!'

Alistair had reserved a whole first-class compartment to take them to York. It was not a long distance but he felt that after all the excitement and talking to so many people, absolute solitude was imperative.

Being *seen off* – a courtesy which the sender thinks is a kindness – can in fact be a long-drawn-out discomfort on both sides. It was particularly so today, when the nearest, and not necessarily the dearest, followed them with rice and rose petals and waited on the platform with fixed smiles. Only a few could be near enough to the carriage window to talk, and that was very small talk indeed. The bride's parents had already gone home.

Arthur and Gertrude drove home in a silence they found impossible to break. Although Gertrude agreed with him about the role of a wife, especially their daughter, she was humiliated by his vulgar behaviour.

It was long after their usual tea-time when Gertrude tried to make conversation:

'There's one thing, Father. When our Henry gets married it won't be you who'll be paying.'

* * *

465

Alistair watched the green flag being waved and listened to the whistle with gratitude and relief. And then immediately wished he could have stopped the train, for there was Belinda rushing up to say goodbye.

'I found her – she will be writing to you,' she called out.

Felicity waved from the window and then sat down, exhausted. 'Isn't she the most wonderful friend?'

'Yes, my dear, I don't know any other girl like her. I'm so glad she caught us. Sit back, my dearest, you must be worn out. Not that you showed it, you were wonderful. It was an impressive, lovely wedding, Felicity – forget the wicked bit. It's your father's way of showing his care of you! I don't know how you managed to look as fresh as morning dew all through!'

'Alistair, I can't help but think of aunt Amy. It seems so callous to go off like this.'

'Sweetheart, no one can put the past right. If Amy had not lost her reason she would have been here, on the platform, wishing us God's speed on our honeymoon. Who knows, she may, now she's free, have been doing just that.'

He took off her hat, pulled each glove, finger by finger, kissed her hands, stroked her hair and lifted her legs on to the seat.

'Lean back into my arms. Why not try to sleep? Close your eyes, my sweet. It is all over and you were wonderful!'

The sigh that eased her whole body was an outward and audible sign that she could relax unreservedly in his presence. He kissed her closed eyes and her slightly open lips and did not speak a word until York Minster was in sight.

10

He did not stir until he saw her eyes blinking and felt the train slowing down: 'Look out there. The Minster's greeting us! Can you hear the bells?'

Just as the Midland in Bradford almost had a red carpet from the train to the hotel, so had the Royal Station Hotel in York. A retinue of porters in immaculate uniform transported Felicity and Alistair to their suite. The windows looked out on to the awe-inspiring towers of the Minster and the Roman wall enclosing it.

Alistair took a deep breath as if he were trying to take it all in.

'I see why you wanted me to get to know York. I've often passed it on the train, on my way to London and back, and wanted to get out and walk those walls.'

'Yes, that's what so many Southerners do. They chase up to Edinburgh and miss out York and Durham, my favourite cities.' She blushed. 'But then I haven't seen many others.' She turned away from the window. 'But look at our room, Alistair. Isn't it a dream? And a fire and champagne!' She undid the card tied to the bottle. 'It's a welcoming note from the manager. How kind! Smell these hyacinths! Did you tell them we were on our honeymoon?'

'Of course I did. Look at the four poster bed and its velvet hangings.'

He walked to the other side of the room.

'Come over here and see my dressing room. It's certainly not for you. Look at the trouser press and shaving strop.' They were like two children wide-eyed with wonder. Felicity almost ran from one side of the bedroom to another.

'Alistair, come and look at my dressing room and the outsize bathroom.' She turned a brass tap on and let the water gush into the bath.

'Absolutely boiling hot water! And a positive glut of bath sheets!'

To hear Felicity one would have thought she lived in one of the back-to-back terrace houses in Aireley. Of course they had

467

running water at Stonegarth, but only one smallish bathroom. She was amazed that an hotel could surpass even the most affluent of mill-owners' homes.

In the ecstasy of being in love and loving, Alistair and Felicity would have found a crofter's cottage to be paradise, but they were both willing sybarites for these few honeymoon days.

Felicity had been brought up by home, school and social habit that one wrote thank-you letters immediately after any hospitality; it blighted birthdays and Boxing Day. After an early dinner, she said: 'Alistair, I think we should start on the thank-you letters tonight, or we shall never get through them.'

He tipped her chin and laughed. 'Dear, dear Felicity. Forget duty, forget other people. Tonight – oh tonight – I am going to put you to bed and gently stroke you to sleep.' He drew her down on to his knee. 'Letters can wait. We've a whole world of ecstasy ahead of us. We need all the time in the world to make hidden mysteries our own. Let's not rush! Just sleep away stress and strain tonight. Winter is such a lovely time for a honeymoon with its long, long nights.'

Felicity closed her writing case and put it on the floor. 'Of course, Alistair, all our days will have nights. All our own...'

He held her close. 'And every particle of you will be treasured...'

'Alistair, you and I are wearing honeymoon blinkers and just living in the present. Can we talk about the future?'

'Of course. I've been wanting to for hours, but I kept the brass plate out of sight. I knew you couldn't face it.'

'Bring it out, Alistair. I must face it and all that goes with it.'

It was hidden underneath clothes, flat at the bottom of a suitcase, and still in its blue velvet cover, which Alistair removed. He held the plate in front of her eyes.

'Look right into it, my darling, as if it were a mirror. See yourself as a professional, not just the wife of Alistair Fraser. Tell me, Felicity, what you most want to do?'

She put her arms forward and held the plate with him, looking first at her own image and then into Alistair's eyes.

'Dearest, to complete my training, as you know, I should do three years' probationary clinical practice...' She hesitated, not quite knowing how to express her hopes.

Alistair filled the pause. 'I do understand.' He took her hand: 'Listen, Felicity, in a few weeks' time we go to America. What about getting into one of William James' courses at Harvard? I have a little influence... And then when we come home...?' He waited for her reply.

Felicity's thoughts were tearing ahead. 'And then, after I've done a probationary year on the wards, do you think they'd let me do the next two years observing and learning in your faculty? If that were possible ... then some day... *I* could be treating women who are mentally ill and those suffering mental anguish.' She quietened to a whisper. 'Alistair, I owe it to aunt Amy. If I can be helpful and compassionate with women whose minds are tormented, she won't have suffered and died in vain...'

He withheld the reminder that it would entail a post-graduate degree.

'My dear, dear Felicity, I will be your Protestant to the end of my days. Remember the song?' He spoke the first lines with a new and wiser voice: "Bid me to live and I will live/Thy Protestant to be..." And you know what I'll be protesting about? All the rotten prejudices against women in social and professional life.'

'But not now, dearest, Let's finish the poem. Can you remember the last verse? I can!' Together they spoke the words:

> Thou art my life, my love, my heart
> The very eyes of me:
> And hast command of every part
> To live and die for thee.

Words drifted away, needed no more. Through the magnetism of skin next to skin, and sensitive fingertips in perceptive exploration, the day's delights and difficulties were forgotten. In that mystic glow of perfect union the indigo night, brightened with moonlight, guarded their secrets.

The next evening dinner was deliberately late for New Year's Eve, to make midnight come sooner.

'Don't you usually go to the watch night service, holy one?' Alistair asked. 'I'll fit in with anything you want to do.'

'We ought to go, I know. It will be quite, quite memorable, but it's the only night you and I will see a new century dawn – at least I hope so. I can see no joy in being a hundred and twenty-four, can you? So I would much rather, if you agree, that we spend tonight in our own room, with a view of it all.'

'Good! That was what I hoped you'd say.'

To Alistair this New Year's Eve was more than Hogmanay. It was what he had dreamed about all the way from the New World.

They dressed for dinner but warmly so. The guests danced sedately as if they were putting in time. Alistair and Felicity slipped away to their room at eleven o'clock and he undressed her slowly in front of the fire, as if that were part of the celebrations ahead.

'But, darling,' Felicity asked, 'who will be our first-footer?'

Alistair grinned. 'Won't I do?'

'Well, you can't very well let yourself in, can you? And neither can your dark woman.'

'I hope I never see one carrying coal, my dear...'

'No, but I'd like to be the salt of the earth for you.'

It was getting near to midnight. Alistair picked up her fur cloak and put it over her dressing gown and stoked up the fire.

On the first stroke of twelve, he threw open the window just as Great Peter pealed out from the Minster. They stood together, warm with love and excitement as every clock and every church bell in York seemed to be saluting them.

Great Peter made no apology for upstaging all the other church bells in the city; his loud arrogance gave assurance of York's immortality.

Alistair closed the window, pulled down the blind and drew the curtains. He gently removed the fur cloak and her dressing gown, lifted her up into his arms and carried her to their bed.

Sleep evaded them, but generously so. With their two heads on one pillow they whispered their shared joys of the day and night, until their tenderness became a mounting passion and, as night turned to day, passion resolved itself into a tranquillity as if the new century were to be a hundred years of peace.

The first day of the twentieth century was crisp and clear, with cool sunshine promising hope. The hotel dining room was sparsely filled and no-one seemed concerned that the honeymooners were not down for breakfast. At ten o'clock, a gentle knock on their bedroom door and a decorous voice announced that there was a tray on the butler's table outside the door. Alistair carried it to the fire and they sat, comfortably together, over tea and toast as if they had lived together for years.

They decided to walk the Wall from the opposite end and have a good look at the Mansion House. It was important to them that they should have completed what was almost a circle of iridescent limestone wall. They arrived at the castle and climbed up the mound to Clifford Tower and turned themselves round and round trying to take in the whole panoramic view of the old enclosed city with elegant bridges spanning the two rivers. From this viewpoint they could see the original shape of the Roman city and the great plain of York beyond and around it. They were both looking far into the horizon when Alistair suddenly changed his sighting to Felicity.

'Dearest, we need hours to take all this in but we must be back in the hotel by twelve.' Strange that Felicity did not ask why, he thought.

She immediately agreed. 'Yes, I think we'd better get back the quickest way over Skeldergate to Rougier Street.'

They had only been back half an hour at the hotel when the head porter announced: 'Dr and Mrs Bennett and Miss Bennett have arrived, sir.'

Neither looked surprised at the news, but both looked surprised that the other did not. The truth was that Belinda had let Felicity into the secret – as was their wont – and Jeremy had let Alistair into the secret to make sure the two were in the hotel when they arrived.

Belinda had to confess that there were no secrets between her and Felicity. It was a pact they had made, not with a schoolgirl's oath with mingled blood but coolly when they were at college.

Conversation bubbled along from one to another; catching up on the latest after-the-wedding news: Grace's offer to come back for Amy's funeral; and Belinda's taking the bouquet to Barlockend. This was the moment for Belinda to explain the gesture she had made, which concerned Felicity.

'My dear, I do hope you'll forgive my taking a liberty. As you know, I took your wedding gown and cloak home with me to take care of until you wanted them sent to Edinburgh. Well, when I got to Barlockend, Roberta took me to the mortuary to see poor, dear Amy. She was lying in a cheap deal coffin. There were no brass handles, no velvet lining as there were for my great-aunt. I had a sudden impulse to ask Roberta if she would allow me to cover the coffin with your wedding cloak – just until the interment, of course, from the mortuary to the grave and then remove it before the coffin was lowered.'

Felicity interrupted. 'Belinda, please don't bring it back! Let it go with her.' She turned to Alistair. 'Please support me in this. It's a mere token compared with what..'

The others were all silent, none of the four wanting to interfere in such a personal altruistic gesture. Alistair was out of his depth:

Jeremy realised Felicity's need: Belinda knew now that she had acted just as Felicity might have done. Only Hazel was able to see that the gesture would perhaps be a symbol of Felicity's detachment from her expensive cushioned life: the Yorkshire brass which bought the velvet cloak.

'May I just put in a word for Felicity?' The others relaxed with relief on hearing Hazel's voice.

It was Alistair who expressed agreement in words. He looked at his determined young wife.

'Dearest, you're sure you won't regret an impulsive gesture? What about your mother?'

'Grace would be the first to support me – remember, Belinda, I told you that the bridal outfit was going to rest in peace at Moray Place, but can we please hear what Hazel was going to say.'

'I was going to say, my dear, that you are starting a completely new life and, knowing a doctor's income, you know you won't be living on velvet. Though I never met Miss Ackroyd, I do know, from what you've both told me, that she never had a luxury in her life. So why not give her just a little glory. She, too, we hope is starting a new life.'

Felicity went over to Hazel and, without a word, kissed her. The men, conscious that this was a woman's world, remained silent until the gong went for luncheon.

Alistair turned to Jeremy. 'You must be famished. What time did you leave home? Did you have long to wait in Leeds?'

Felicity sparkled through luncheon. Somehow, although it was only a materialistic gesture, it helped to make the words *And all the trumpets sounded for her on the other side* have more substance.

Jeremy was thinking how, when asked about her mother's reaction, Felicity, without hesitation, had assumed that Alistair was referring to *Grace*. Hazel and Belinda, astounded and overjoyed, steered the conversation to Felicity so that over lunch she became the eloquent rapporteur of the York celebrations.

Time was short. Jeremy needed to talk to Alistair and Felicity on their own, before the 3.13 train left for Edinburgh. Belinda came in with what seemed the craziest of non sequiturs.

'Papa, do you still want Mamma and me to buy the hankies? I've got the newspaper advertisement here.' She took out from her bag a cutting from the December 27th edition of the *Yorkshire Evening Press*. It was a flamboyant advertisement filling a whole column, declaring: HARDING'S LINEN WAREHOUSE, 20 AND 21 OUSEGATE, YORK. It shouted out in bold capital letters:

This advertisement had relevance to Dr Bennett's custom to start the New Year with a note to his patients. The only reply needed was if they no longer wished to be on his register. In all the years of practice he had never had one negative reply. Years ago it had been Hazel's idea to enclose a calendar with New Year good wishes for health and happiness. On seeing the advertisement she had the idea of adding, to the 1900 calendar, a gift of a handkerchief to every patient to whom the letter was addressed.

'Yes please, Belinda, a hundred and twenty ladies' handkerchiefs and a hundred for the gentlemen. That should cover it. I think I have two hundred and nineteen patients altogether.'

Hazel got up and put on her coat. 'Will you excuse us then if we leave you. It's not very far from here, and we could do with the walk.'

It was, of course, skilful planning on Jeremy and Hazel's part; he could easily have ordered the handkerchiefs by post, but Hazel insisted on seeing the quality before buying them.

Alistair saw them out, apologising for their having missed coffee. He returned to find Jeremy and Felicity deep in conversation. Her voice was lowered.

'You did say, Jeremy, that one day you would satisfy my curiosity as to where I was on September 18th 1876.'

'And so I shall.'

Felicity included Alistair in her glance. 'I'm sure Alistair would like to see my second birthplace. It's been difficult explaining it to him.'

Jeremy got up. 'Come with me now. The manager has given me the key of the room where you were *delivered*. The word was incongruously apt.'

There was nothing exceptional about the room, although Jeremy did notice that the carpets and curtains were now of a fashionable Morris design. He recalled briefly how the delivery of Felicity had been arranged with Grace, the maternity home, the nurse and Gertrude. He put in an unexpected remark.

'You know, Felicity, it needed a great deal of courage and

473

ingenuity for a woman to do what Gertrude did. I know, of course, that she was at her wits' end to have a child, but this needed exceptional determination on her part, and, if I may say so, the talent of an actress.'

Felicity thought before answering. 'Yes, I never realised, until we were here in this room, what an ordeal and a risk it must have been for her.'

Alistair remained a silent witness to it all.

Jeremy took a large envelope out of his pocket and handed it to Felicity. 'And now, here is my New Year wedding present for you both.'

Like a child still believing in magic, she opened it with wide-eyed curiosity. When she unfolded the long paper she could not believe her eyes. It was a birth certificate.

She read it avidly, nurturing every written detail under the printed columns across the form unaware that this was a master-piece of law-breaking.

DATE AND PLACE OF BIRTH: *18th September 1876 The Gables Maternity Home, Edinburgh.*

NAME: *Felicity Laura*

SEX: *Girl.*

NAME AND SURNAME OF FATHER: *Felix Nicholas Stewart deceased, India April 30th 1876*

NAME AND MAIDEN SURNAME OF MOTHER: *Grace Laura Stewart formerly Hargreaves.*

RANK AND PROFESSION OF FATHER: *Lieutenant Colonel, formerly Medical Army Officer.*

SIGNATURE, DESCRIPTION AND RESIDENCE OF INFORMANT: *Dr Jeremy Bennett, of Airedale, Graduate of Edinburgh University.*

DATE OF REGISTRATION: *Fifteenth October, 1876.*

SIGNED BY THE REGISTRAR: *William Albert Parkinson in the City of Edinburgh.*

There was really only one word which broke the law, *Stewart* following *Mother*, but it meant that the foul word *illegitimate* was never used. The certificate was clear, accurate and, unless examined scrupulously, appeared to be legal.

Felicity was aghast, but excited. 'But how did you get the certificate? I can't believe it. I did ask Father about my birth certificate as soon as I was engaged to Alistair. He said it had been burnt in a mill fire.'

'My dear, there are some advantages in being a doctor. I kept Grace confined to her bed and, of course, as your father was deceased, I was the only one able to explain to the registrar how your father died of cholera out in India. Mr Parkinson showed sympathy and interest, especially to hear that I was your father's closest friend and worked with him in Scotland.'

'But why didn't Mother, I mean Gertrude, ask you for the certificate when you handed me over?'

'Think, Felicity! That was information she never wanted to see in print.'

'But, if I may say so, Jeremy, why did you not give it to me before?'

'It would not have been fair to anyone, least of all Arthur and Gertrude. I told Grace briefly about it, when we saw her off on the train on your wedding day, but she has never seen the actual document. Now that you are Felicity Fraser and not a resident in Stonegarth, I am giving it to you and Alistair as your own private possession.'

The horse pulling the cab trudged up the slope out of the station and on to Princes Street as if it could have done so without a driver, so familiar was the route to Moray Place.

Felicity had to admit to herself that everything in Edinburgh looked higher, wider and grander than York, but the two great cities were so different that it was quite foolish to try and compare them.

'Lovely to be back, Alistair, isn't it? Odd though to be in Moray Place without Grace.'

'My dear, she has the same intuitive response to life that Jeremy has. It has often struck me that his friendship with Felix and Grace gives you a bonus in life.'

'Perhaps,' Felicity said, as the horse moved level with the brass dolphin on the door, 'perhaps I have gained something by having two families. If it had not been for Jeremy coming from Aireley to Edinburgh, I would never have met you, would I?'

Sammycat had been sitting on the half landing peering between the banisters and keeping his ears alert for the last hour. Alistair knew the door would be unlocked and that they could just walk in, but that would spoil things for both Maggie and Sam. He

475

clanged the knocker and Felicity pulled the iron handle of the bell so that all heaven was let loose for Sam as he skithered and skated down the stairs. He made a great purr as his paw went from the door handle to the floor, and then whined with feline fret at Maggie's slow steps.

At last Maggie opened the door and to her infinite surprise she was kissed by both Dr Fraser and Felicity. Such things did not happen in this dour country and for a time she was speechless. Felicity, quick to sense Sam's jealousy, picked him up and solaced him with long soft strokes. He made them do, but the long wait up the stairs and the plunge down were for his mistress.

'We're here, Sam. We really are here.' He accepted Felicity as the next best thing and purred under the sensuous strokes.

Alistair took Maggie's right hand and said with a slight bow: 'Maggie, may I introduce you to Mrs Fraser, known in the trade as *Doctor* Fraser.'

'Oh, Miss Fel— Mrs Fraser. I shall never remember to say it. Come in the noo. Tea's all ready except for the infusing. There's a fire in your room and I've put a jar in your bed every day since my lady left.'

'Oh thank you, Maggie, and thank you for the lovely present you sent with my aunt: the two beautiful whisky glasses! We shall sit, like Derby and Joan, with the pair of them and drink to your health every special night! So sorry not to have written a thank-you letter yet, but you must blame my husband for that.'

'That, if you'll pardon me for saying it, would have been an awfu' waste of a penny stamp, for it could have come on the same train as yoursels.'

'How right you are, Maggie.'

Alistair added, 'You and I will have to teach her Scottish canni-ness, won't we? That reminds me, are there any letters?'

'Yes, Doctor, you'll find them on the table in your room.'

It felt strange to be taking over Grace's bedroom, which, with its dressing room attached, stretched across the whole front of the house. Felicity was wide-eyed with excitement.

'Isn't it wonderful to be in a real home instead of an hotel, Alistair? All the lovely personal things: the silver dressing table set and scent bottles and the photographs and pictures.'

Alistair had his eye on a silver-framed photograph at the bed-side. He put it down quickly.

'It's tempting just to stay up here, but Maggie's infusing the tea. Let's take the letters down with us and open them there.'

'Alistair, don't breathe a word that we had tea on the train.'

476

They opened a motley collection of letters and cards, mostly of good wishes and welcome. Grace's letter said:

Welcome home, my dears. Remember wherever life takes you this is your second home and, in the far future, entirely yours.

It was a wedding to remember. You both looked so handsome and happy I had to keep stopping myself getting near to you to tell you so. If I looked and seemed aloof, it was because I was anxious not to intrude. It was not only your day, my dears, it was Arthur's and Gertrude's too and I did not want to encroach.

Downstairs in the drawing room I have put out a journal kept by Felix, during his brief time in India. Also there is a little addition, which I hope you will put in your own bedroom when you go home.

Please do not hesitate to ask Maggie for anything you want. The more you ask of her, the more she will feel she is doing what she has been looking forward to for many weeks.

My friend Emmie has persuaded me to stay a little longer, so the house is yours if you want it. When Simpson delivered his letter he did hint that he wanted to get various jobs finished before you took over.

My loving thoughts are with you now and forever

Grace

As Maggie came in to clear the tea, Felicity picked out a small packet from the table. She opened it when she and Alistair were alone again. It contained two photographs mounted in a double frame.

Underneath the left-hand one was inscribed: *Felix Nicholas Stewart, aged 21, 1870* and under the right-hand photograph – *Felicity Laura Hargreaves, aged 21, 1897*. Felicity and Alistair looked from one photograph to the other, amazed at the likeness.

'Only Grace could have thought of this.' Felicity was weeping with joy and a strange feeling of being so near to this stranger, her father, yet so very far apart.

It was Alistair who spoke:

'I never told you that when I returned from America I received this letter from Grace. I've kept it for this very occasion. Here is what she writes:'

Felicity is so like Felix that very often when I look at her I

477

want to rush out of the room and weep. But I don't. I've stopped thinking about her looks and remember, after all, half of her is Felix. She has the same tenacity; the talent for music; his honesty and the funny little way he had too, of putting his forefinger in his mouth when he was thinking. It hurts to see the way she tilts her head when she is sticking up for herself ... or explaining something ... exactly as Felix did.

Felicity turned on him in exasperation. 'But why didn't you both say this to *me*? Why have I been kept ignorant all these years?'

'Dear one, it would only have upset you when it was important that your loyalties had to be away from here. Sometimes truths are too disturbing to tell...'

'But didn't you know that for years I'd wondered who it was reminded me of myself? I had seen the photograph on Grace's bedside table and it must have remained in my subconscious. I was only thirteen and too shy to ask questions. In any case, young people tend to dismiss those who live in the past!'

Alistair looked at the photographs again. It made one realise that Felix, even after all these years, was never out of Grace's mind.

They were not long in the dining room after supper. Their bed-room was far too alluring to be left empty any longer.

'You're tired, beloved and so am I.' They walked up the stairs together, holding hands. Alistair was humming a little tune to the rhythm of their steps.

'Do you ever get a tune on your mind, which simply will not go away? I think it was the welcome-back note from Nell that started it off, and of course this house is soaked in the sounds of music.' He hummed a few more bars. Felicity recognised it as the Brahms *Wiegenlied*.

> Guten Abend, gut' Nacht.
> Mit Rosen bedacht.
> Mit Näg'lein besteckt
> Schlupf' unter die Deck';
> Morgen früh, wenn Gott will,
> Wirst du weider geweckt!

He stopped before the second verse. 'You know the English words,

478

I don't. I tried translating the German once, but I just couldn't get it right.'

She laughed. 'Alistair, I can't sing when I'm getting undressed. Let's sing it together in bed.'

A strange couple they made, with the carved mahogany tester bed framing their heads as they sang the lullaby simultaneously in two languages. Their faces, close to one another, were in perfect profile with eyes and ears in harmony.

Guten Abend, gut' Nacht.	Slumber sweetly, my dear,
Von Englein bewacht.	For angels are near.
Die zeigen im Traum	To watch over you
Dir Christkindleins Baum:	The silent night through;
Schlaf' nun selig und süss,	And to bear you above
Schau im Traum's Paradies!	To the dreamland of love!

They sang the last two lines pianissimo and slipped into the warm comfort of togetherness:

And to bear you above
To the dreamland of love...

Their caressing was silent until the long day closed, and their night began with Alistair's slow, quiet words:

'Do you realise, my darling, you were conceived in this bed?'